William Shakespeare

PERICLES, PRINCE OF TYRE

CYMBELINE

THE TWO NOBLE KINSMEN
(with John Fletcher)

The Signet Classic Shakespeare
GENERAL EDITOR: SYLVAN BARNET

REVISED AND UPDATED BIBLIOGRAPHY

A SIGNET CLASSIC

NEW AMERICAN LIBRARY

NEW YORK AND SCARBOROUGH, ONTARIO

These books previously appeared as single volumes in Signet Classic editions published by New American Library.

Library of Congress Catalog Card Number: 85-63518

 SIGNET CLASSIC TRADEMARK REG. U.S. PAT. OFF. AND FOREIGN COUNTRIES
REGISTERED TRADEMARK—MARCA REGISTRADA
HECHO EN CHICAGO, U.S.A.

SIGNET, SIGNET CLASSIC, MENTOR, PLUME, MERIDIAN AND NAL BOOKS are published *in the United States* by
New American Library,
1633 Broadway, New York, New York 10019,
in Canada by The New American Library of Canada Limited,
81 Mack Avenue, Scarborough, Ontario M1L 1M8

First Signet Classic Printing (Combined Edition), July, 1986

1 2 3 4 5 6 7 8 9

PRINTED IN THE UNITED STATES OF AMERICA

Shakespeare: Prefatory Remarks

Between the record of his baptism in Stratford on 26 April 1564 and the record of his burial in Stratford on 25 April 1616, some forty documents name Shakespeare, and many others name his parents, his children, and his grandchildren. More facts are known about William Shakespeare than about any other playwright of the period except Ben Jonson. The facts should, however, be distinguished from the legends. The latter, inevitably more engaging and better known, tell us that the Stratford boy killed a calf in high style, poached deer and rabbits, and was forced to flee to London, where he held horses outside a playhouse. These traditions are only traditions; they may be true, but no evidence supports them, and it is well to stick to the facts.

Mary Arden, the dramatist's mother, was the daughter of a substantial landowner; about 1557 she married John Shakespeare, who was a glove-maker and trader in various farm commodities. In 1557 John Shakespeare was a member of the Council (the governing body of Stratford), in 1558 a constable of the borough, in 1561 one of the two town chamberlains, in 1565 an alderman (entitling him to the appellation "Mr."), in 1568 high bailiff—the town's highest political office, equivalent to mayor. After 1577, for an unknown reason he drops out of local politics. The birthday of William Shakespeare, the eldest son of this locally prominent man, is unrecorded; but the Stratford parish register records that the infant was baptized on 26 April 1564. (It is quite possible that he was born on 23 April, but this date has probably been assigned by tradition because it is the date on which, fifty-two years later, he died.) The attendance records of the Stratford grammar school of the period are not extant, but it is reasonable to assume that the son of a local official attended the school and received substantial training in Latin. The masters of the school from Shakespeare's seventh to fifteenth years held Oxford degrees; the Elizabethan curriculum excluded mathematics and the natural sciences but taught a good deal of Latin rhetoric, logic, and literature. On 27 November 1582 a marriage license was issued to Shakespeare and Anne Hathaway, eight years his senior. The couple had a child in May, 1583. Perhaps the marriage was necessary, but perhaps the couple had earlier engaged in a formal "troth plight" which would render their children legitimate even if no further ceremony were performed. In 1585 Anne Hathaway bore Shakespeare twins.

That Shakespeare was born is excellent; that he married and had children is pleasant; but that we know nothing about his departure from Stratford to London, or about the beginning of his theatrical career, is lamentable and must be admitted. We would gladly sacrifice details about his children's baptism for details about his earliest days on the stage. Perhaps the poaching episode is true (but it is first reported almost a century after Shakespeare's death), or perhaps he first left Stratford to be a schoolteacher, as another tradition holds; perhaps he was moved by

> Such wind as scatters young men through the world,
> To seek their fortunes further than at home
> Where small experience grows.

In 1592, thanks to the cantankerousness of Robert Greene, a rival playwright and a pamphleteer, we have our first reference, a snarling one, to Shakespeare as an actor and playwright. Greene warns those of his own educated friends who wrote for the theater against an actor who has presumed to turn playwright:

> There is an upstart crow, beautified with our feathers, that with his *tiger's heart wrapped in a player's hide* supposes he is as well able to bombast out a blank verse as the best of you, and being an absolute Johannes-factotum is in his own conceit the only Shake-scene in a country.

The reference to the player, as well as the allusion to Aesop's crow (who strutted in borrowed plumage, as an actor struts in fine words not his own), makes it clear that by this date Shakespeare had both acted and written. That Shakespeare is meant is indicated not only by "Shake-scene" but by the parody of a line from one of Shakespeare's plays, *3 Henry VI:* "O, tiger's heart wrapped in a woman's hide." If Shakespeare in 1592 was prominent enough to be attacked by an envious dramatist, he probably had served an apprenticeship in the theater for at least a few years.

In any case, by 1592 Shakespeare had acted and written, and there are a number of subsequent references to him as an actor: documents indicate that in 1598 he is a "principal comedian," in 1603 a "principal tragedian," in 1608 he is one of the "men players." The profession of actor was not for a gentleman, and it occasionally drew the scorn of university men who resented writing speeches for persons less educated than themselves, but it was respectable enough: players, if prosperous, were in effect members of the bourgeoisie, and there is nothing to suggest that Stratford considered William Shakespeare less than a solid citizen. When, in 1596, the Shakespeares were granted a coat of arms, the grant was made to Shakespeare's father, but probably William Shakespeare (who the next year bought the second-largest house in town) had arranged the matter on his own behalf. In subsequent transactions he is occasionally styled a gentleman.

Although in 1593 and 1594 Shakespeare published two narrative poems dedicated to the Earl of Southampton, *Venus and Adonis* and *The Rape of Lucrece,* and may well have written most or all of his sonnets in the middle nineties, Shakespeare's literary activity seems to have been almost entirely devoted to the theater. (It may be significant that the two narrative poems were written in years when the plague closed the theaters for several months.) In 1594 he was a charter member of a theatrical company called the Chamberlain's Men (which in 1603 changed its name to the King's Men); until he retired to Stratford (about 1611, apparently), he was with this remarkably stable company. From 1599 the company acted primarily at the Globe

Theatre, in which Shakespeare held a one-tenth interest.
Other Elizabethan dramatists are known to have acted, but
no other is known also to have been entitled to a share in
the profits of the playhouse.

Shakespeare's first eight published plays did not have his
name on them, but this is not remarkable; the most popular
play of the sixteenth century, Thomas Kyd's *The Spanish
Tragedy,* went through many editions without naming Kyd,
and Kyd's authorship is known only because a book on the
profession of acting happens to quote (and attribute to Kyd)
some lines on the interest of Roman emperors in the drama.
What is remarkable is that after 1598 Shakespeare's name
commonly appears on printed plays—some of which are
not his. Another indication of his popularity comes from
Francis Meres, author of *Palladis Tamia: Wit's Treasury*
(1598): in this anthology of snippets accompanied by an
essay on literature, many playwrights are mentioned, but
Shakespeare's name occurs more often than any other, and
Shakespeare is the only playwright whose plays are listed.

From his acting, playwriting, and share in a theater,
Shakespeare seems to have made considerable money. He
put it to work, making substantial investments in Stratford
real estate. When he made his will (less than a month before
he died), he sought to leave his property intact to his
descendants. Of small bequests to relatives and to friends
(including three actors, Richard Burbage, John Heminges,
and Henry Condell), that to his wife of the second-best bed
has provoked the most comment; perhaps it was the bed
the couple had slept in, the best being reserved for visitors.
In any case, had Shakespeare not excepted it, the bed would
have gone (with the rest of his household possessions) to
his daughter and her husband. On 25 April 1616 he was
buried within the chancel of the church at Stratford. An
unattractive monument to his memory, placed on a wall
near the grave, says he died on 23 April. Over the grave
itself are the lines, perhaps by Shakespeare, that (more than
his literary fame) have kept his bones undisturbed in the
crowded burial ground where old bones were often dis-
lodged to make way for new:

Good friend, for Jesus' sake forbear

To dig the dust enclosèd here.
Blessed be the man that spares these stones
And cursed be he that moves my bones.

Thirty-seven plays, as well as some nondramatic poems, are held to constitute the Shakespeare canon. The dates of composition of most of the works are highly uncertain, but there is often evidence of a *terminus a quo* (starting point) and/or a *terminus ad quem* (terminal point) that provides a framework for intelligent guessing. For example, *Richard II* cannot be earlier than 1595, the publication date of some material to which it is indebted; *The Merchant of Venice* cannot be later than 1598, the year Francis Meres mentioned it. Sometimes arguments for a date hang on an alleged topical allusion, such as the lines about the unseasonable weather in *A Midsummer Night's Dream*, II.i.81–87, but such an allusion (if indeed it is an allusion) can be variously interpreted, and in any case there is always the possibility that a topical allusion was inserted during a revision, years after the composition of a play. Dates are often attributed on the basis of style, and although conjectures about style usually rest on other conjectures, sooner or later one must rely on one's literary sense. There is no real proof, for example, that *Othello* is not as early as *Romeo and Juliet*, but one feels *Othello* is later, and because the first record of its performance is 1604, one is glad enough to set its composition at that date and not push it back into Shakespeare's early years. The following chronology, then, is as much indebted to informed guesswork and sensitivity as it is to fact. The dates, necessarily imprecise, indicate something like a scholarly consensus.

PLAYS

1588–93	*The Comedy of Errors*
1588–94	*Love's Labor's Lost*
1590–91	*2 Henry VI*
1590–91	*3 Henry VI*
1591–92	*1 Henry VI*
1592–93	*Richard III*

1592–94	*Titus Andronicus*
1593–94	*The Taming of the Shrew*
1593–95	*The Two Gentlemen of Verona*
1594–96	*Romeo and Juliet*
1595	*Richard II*
1594–96	*A Midsummer Night's Dream*
1596–97	*King John*
1596–97	*The Merchant of Venice*
1597	*1 Henry IV*
1597–98	*2 Henry IV*
1598	*Much Ado About Nothing*
1598–99	*Henry V*
1599–1600	*Julius Caesar*
1599–1600	*As You Like It*
1599–1600	*Twelfth Night*
1600–01	*Hamlet*
1597–1601	*The Merry Wives of Windsor*
1601–02	*Troilus and Cressida*
1602–04	*All's Well That Ends Well*
1603–04	*Othello*
1604	*Measure for Measure*
1605–06	*King Lear*
1605–06	*Macbeth*
1606–07	*Antony and Cleopatra*
1605–08	*Timon of Athens*
1607–09	*Coriolanus*
1607–08	*Pericles*
1609–10	*Cymbeline*
1610–11	*The Winter's Tale*
1611	*The Tempest*
1612–13	*Henry VIII*

POEMS

1592	*Venus and Adonis*
1593–94	*The Rape of Lucrece*
1593–1600	*Sonnets*
1600–01	*The Phoenix and Turtle*

Shakespeare's Theater

In Shakespeare's infancy, Elizabethan actors performed wherever they could—in great halls, at court, in the court-yards of inns. The innyards must have made rather un-satisfactory theaters: on some days they were unavailable because carters bringing goods to London used them as depots; when available, they had to be rented from the inn-keeper; perhaps most important, London inns were subject to the Common Council of London, which was not well disposed toward theatricals. In 1574 the Common Coun-cil required that plays and playing places in London be licensed. It asserted that

> sundry great disorders and inconveniences have been found to ensue to this city by the inordinate haunting of great multitudes of people, specially youth, to plays, in-terludes, and shows, namely occasion of frays and quar-rels, evil practices of incontinency in great inns having chambers and secret places adjoining to their open stages and galleries,

and ordered that innkeepers who wished licenses to hold performances put up a bond and make contributions to the poor.

The requirement that plays and innyard theaters be licensed, along with the other drawbacks of playing at inns, probably drove James Burbage (a carpenter-turned-actor) to rent in 1576 a plot of land northeast of the city walls and to build here—on property outside the jurisdiction of the city—England's first permanent construction designed for plays. He called it simply the Theatre. About all that is known of its construction is that it was wood. It soon had imitators, the most famous being the Globe (1599), built across the Thames (again outside the city's jurisdiction), out of timbers of the Theatre, which had been dismantled when Burbage's lease ran out.

There are three important sources of information about the structure of Elizabethan playhouses—drawings, a con-tract, and stage directions in plays. Of drawings, only the so-called De Witt drawing (c. 1596) of the Swan—really a friend's copy of De Witt's drawing—is of much significance. It shows a building of three tiers, with a stage jutting from a wall into the yard or center of the building. The tiers are roofed, and part of the stage is covered by a roof that projects from the rear and is supported at its front on two posts, but the groundlings, who paid a penny to stand in front of the stage, were exposed to the sky. (Performances in such a playhouse were held only in the daytime; artificial illumination was not used.) At the rear of the stage are two doors; above the stage is a gallery. The second major source of information, the contract for the Fortune, specifies that although the Globe is to be the model, the Fortune is to be square, eighty feet outside and fifty-five inside. The stage is to be forty-three feet broad, and is to extend into the middle of the yard (i.e., it is twenty-seven and a half feet deep). For patrons willing to pay more than the general admission charged of the groundlings, there were to be three galleries provided with seats. From the third chief source, stage directions, one learns that entrance to the stage was by doors, presumably spaced widely apart at the rear ("Enter one citizen at one door, and another at the other"), and that in addition to the platform stage there was occasionally some sort of curtained booth or alcove allowing for "discovery" scenes, and some sort of playing space "aloft" or "above" to represent (for example) the top of a city's walls or a room above the street. Doubtless each theater had its own peculiarities, but perhaps we can talk about a "typical" Elizabethan theater if we realize that no theater need exactly have fit the description, just as no father is the typical father with 3.7 children. This hypothetical theater is wooden, round or polygonal (in *Henry V* Shakespeare calls it a "wooden *O*"), capable of holding some eight hundred spectators standing in the yard around the projecting elevated stage and some fifteen hundred additional spectators seated in the three roofed galleries. The stage, protected by a "shadow" or "heaven" or roof, is entered by two doors; behind the doors is the "tiring house" (attiring house, i.e., dressing room), and above the doors is some sort of gallery that may sometimes hold spectators but that can be used (for example) as the bedroom from which Romeo—according to a stage direction in one text—"goeth down." Some evidence suggests that a throne can be lowered onto the platform stage, perhaps from the "shadow"; certainly characters can descend from the stage through a trap or traps into the cellar or "hell." Sometimes this space beneath the platform accommodates a sound-effects man or musician (in *Antony and Cleopatra* "music of the hautboys is under the stage") or an actor (in *Hamlet* the "Ghost cries under the stage"). Most characters simply walk on and off, but because there is no curtain in front of the platform, corpses will have to be carried off (Hamlet must lug Polonius' guts into the neighbor room), or will have to fall at the rear, where the curtain on the alcove or booth can be drawn to conceal them.

Such may have been the so-called "public theater." Another kind of theater, called the "private theater" because its much greater admission charge limited its audience to the wealthy or the prodigal, must be briefly mentioned. The private theater was basically a large room, entirely roofed and therefore artificially illuminated, with a stage at one end. In 1576 one such theater was established in Blackfriars, a Dominican priory in London that had been suppressed in 1538 and confiscated by the Crown and thus was not under the city's jurisdiction. All the actors in the Blackfriars theater were boys about eight to thirteen years old (in the public theaters similar boys played female parts; a boy Lady Macbeth played to a man Macbeth). This private theater had a precarious existence, and ceased operations in 1584. In 1596 James Burbage, who had already made theatrical history by building the Theatre, began to construct a second Blackfriars theater. He died in 1597, and for several years this second Blackfriars theater was used by a troupe of boys, but in 1608 two of Burbage's sons and five other actors (including Shakespeare) became joint operators of the theater, using it in the winter when the open-air Globe was unsuitable. Perhaps such a smaller theater, roofed, artificially illuminated, and with a tradition of a courtly audience, exerted an influence on Shakespeare's late plays.

Performances in the private theaters may well have had

intermissions during which music was played, but in the public theaters the action was probably uninterrupted, flowing from scene to scene almost without a break. Actors would enter, speak, exit, and others would immediately enter and establish (if necessary) the new locale by a few properties and by words and gestures. Here are some samples of Shakespeare's scene painting:

> This is Illyria, lady.
>
> Well, this is the Forest of Arden.
>
> This castle hath a pleasant seat; the air
> Nimbly and sweetly recommends itself
> Unto our gentle senses.

On the other hand, it is a mistake to conceive of the Elizabethan stage as bare. Although Shakespeare's Chorus in *Henry V* calls the stage an "unworthy scaffold" and urges the spectators to "eke out our performance with your mind," there was considerable spectacle. The last act of *Macbeth*, for example, has five stage directions calling for "drum and colors," and another sort of appeal to the eye is indicated by the stage direction "Enter Macduff, with Macbeth's head." Some scenery and properties may have been substantial; doubtless a throne was used, and in one play of the period we encounter this direction: "Hector takes up a great piece of rock and casts at Ajax, who tears up a young tree by the roots and assails Hector." The matter is of some importance, and will be glanced at again in the next section.

The Texts of Shakespeare

Though eighteen of his plays were published during his lifetime, Shakespeare seems never to have supervised their publication. There is nothing unusual here; when a playwright sold a play to a theatrical company he surrendered his ownership of it. Normally a company would not publish the play, because to publish it meant to allow competitors to acquire the piece. Some plays, however, did get published:

apparently treacherous actors sometimes pieced together a play for a publisher, sometimes a company in need of money sold a play, and sometimes a company allowed a play to be published that no longer drew audiences. That Shakespeare did not concern himself with publication, then, is scarcely remarkable; of his contemporaries only Ben Jonson carefully supervised the publication of his own plays. In 1623, seven years after Shakespeare's death, John Heminges and Henry Condell (two senior members of Shakespeare's company, who had performed with him for about twenty years) collected his plays—published and unpublished—into a large volume, commonly called the First Folio. (A folio is a volume consisting of sheets that have been folded once, each sheet thus making two leaves, or four pages. The eighteen plays published during Shakespeare's lifetime had been issued one play per volume in small books called quartos. Each sheet in a quarto has been folded twice, making four leaves, or eight pages.) The First Folio contains thirty-six plays; a thirty-seventh, *Pericles,* though not in the Folio is regarded as canonical. Heminges and Condell suggest in an address "To the great variety of readers" that the republished plays are presented in better form than in the quartos: "Before you were abused with diverse stolen and surreptitious copies, maimed and deformed by the frauds and stealths of injurious impostors that exposed them; even those, are now offered to your view cured and perfect of their limbs, and all the rest absolute in their numbers, as he [i.e., Shakespeare] conceived them."

Whoever was assigned to prepare the texts for publication in the First Folio seems to have taken his job seriously and yet not to have performed it with uniform care. The sources of the texts seem to have been, in general, good unpublished copies or the best published copies. The first play in the collection, *The Tempest,* is divided into acts and scenes, has unusually full stage directions and descriptions of spectacle, and concludes with a list of the characters, but the editor was not able (or willing) to present all of the succeeding texts so fully dressed. Later texts occasionally show signs of carelessness: in one scene of *Much Ado About*

Nothing the names of actors, instead of characters, appear as speech prefixes, as they had in the quarto, which the Folio reprints; proofreading throughout the Folio is spotty and apparently was done without reference to the printer's copy; the pagination of *Hamlet* jumps from 156 to 257.

A modern editor of Shakespeare must first select his copy; no problem if the play exists only in the Folio, but a considerable problem if the relationship between a quarto and the Folio—or an early quarto and a later one—is unclear. When an editor has chosen what seems to him to be the most authoritative text or texts for his copy, he has not done with making decisions. First of all, he must reckon with Elizabethan spelling. If he is not producing a facsimile, he probably modernizes it, but ought he to preserve the old form of words that apparently were pronounced quite unlike their modern forms—"lanthorn," "alablaster"? If he preserves these forms, is he really preserving Shakespeare's forms or perhaps those of a compositor in the printing house? What is one to do when one finds "lanthorn" and "lantern" in adjacent lines? (The editors of this series in general but not invariably, assume that words should be spelled in their modern form.) Elizabethan punctuation, too, presents problems. For example in the First Folio, the only text for the play, Macbeth rejects his wife's idea that he can wash the blood from his hand:

> no: this my Hand will rather
> The multitudinous Seas incarnardine,
> Making the Greene one, Red.

Obviously an editor will remove the superfluous capitals, and he will probably alter the spelling to "incarnadine," but will he leave the comma before "red," letting Macbeth speak of the sea as "the green one," or will he (like most modern editors) remove the comma and thus have Macbeth say that his hand will make the ocean *uniformly* red?

An editor will sometimes have to change more than spelling or punctuation. Macbeth says to his wife:

> I dare do all that may become a man,
> Who dares no more, is none.

For two centuries editors have agreed that the second line is unsatisfactory, and have emended "no" to "do": "Who dares do more is none." But when in the same play Ross says that fearful persons

> floate vpon a wilde and violent Sea
> Each way, and moue,

need "move" be emended to "none," as it often is, on the hunch that the compositor misread the manuscript? The editors of the Signet Classic Shakespeare have restrained themselves from making abundant emendations. In their minds they hear Dr. Johnson on the dangers of emending: "I have adopted the Roman sentiment, that it is more honorable to save a citizen than to kill an enemy." Some departures (in addition to spelling, punctuation, and lineation) from the copy text have of course been made, but the original readings are listed in a note following the play, so that the reader can evaluate them for himself.

The editors of the Signet Classic Shakespeare, following tradition, have added line numbers and in many cases act and scene divisions as well as indications of locale at the beginning of scenes. The Folio divided most of the plays into acts and some into scenes. Early eighteenth-century editors increased the divisions. These divisions, which provide a convenient way of referring to passages in the plays, have been retained, but when not in the text chosen as the basis for the Signet Classic text they are enclosed in square brackets [ ] to indicate that they are editorial additions. Similarly, although no play of Shakespeare's published during his lifetime was equipped with indications of locale at the heads of scene divisions, locales have here been added in square brackets for the convenience of the reader, who lacks the information afforded to spectators by costumes, properties, and gestures. The spectator can tell at a glance he is in the throne room, but without an editorial indication the reader may be puzzled for a while. It should be mentioned, incidentally, that there are a few authentic stage directions—perhaps Shakespeare's, perhaps a prompter's—that suggest locales: for example, "Enter Brutus in his orchard," and "They go up into the Senate house." It is hoped that the bracketed additions provide the reader with the sort of help provided in these two authentic directions, but it is equally hoped that the reader will remember that the stage was not loaded with scenery.

No editor during the course of his work can fail to recollect some words Heminges and Condell prefixed to the Folio:

> It had been a thing, we confess, worthy to have been wished, that the author himself had lived to have set forth and overseen his own writings. But since it hath been ordained otherwise, and he by death departed from that right, we pray you do not envy his friends the office of their care and pain to have collected and published them.

Nor can an editor, after he has done his best, forget Heminges and Condell's final words: "And so we leave you to other of his friends, whom if you need can be your guides. If you need them not, you can lead yourselves, and others. And such readers we wish him."

SYLVAN BARNET
Tufts University

William Shakespeare

PERICLES, PRINCE OF TYRE

Edited by Ernest Schanzer

Contents

Introduction

Pericles presents several unique problems. Most critics are agreed that, while Acts III, IV, and V are substantially Shakespeare's, Acts I and II are not. The questions to be asked, therefore, are: Who is the author of Acts I and II? And, further, how did the non-Shakespearian first two acts come to be joined to the Shakespearian last three acts? As to this there are two main possibilities: 1) that Shakespeare collaborated with another playwright, as he did a few years later with John Fletcher in *Henry VIII, Two Noble Kinsmen,* and the lost *Cardenio;* 2) that Shakespeare came across a complete play on the subject of *Pericles* and began to rewrite it at the point where the subject matter caught his imagination, the point at which Pericles, during a storm at sea, is suddenly confronted with the death of his wife and the birth of his daughter. According to this hypothesis, Shakespeare, being an extremely busy man, did not bother to rewrite the first two acts, except, perhaps, to add a few touches here and there.

Of these two possibilities the latter seems to me by far the more likely. That Shakespeare should have collaborated with the author of the first two acts seems very improbable. To collaborate with John Fletcher is one thing; to collaborate with the exceedingly mediocre talent that could produce Acts I and II of *Pericles,* quite another. It is true that these first two acts must have been a good deal better than they are in the text in which they have come down to us. For the Quarto text—and this adds greatly to the intricate problems presented by the play—is very corrupt, not only in Acts I and II, but in the Shakespearian part as well. Whole lines are missing, others are garbled, verse is frequently set out as prose, and occasionally prose as verse. It is, most scholars are agreed, a text based on a report made from visits to the theater, and bears the usual marks of such a reported text—above all, a large number of auditory errors and mislineation of Shakespeare's blank verse.

The Quarto of *Pericles,* then, is, in many ways, very imperfect. But where for other Shakespeare plays with bad Quarto texts we also have a good text, for *Pericles* we have only the one text, published for the first time in 1609, in what was, no doubt, a pirated edition (i.e., it was printed without the permission of Shakespeare and his company). The problem of the authorship of the first two acts is therefore made much more difficult by the absence of any good text of the play, and scholars have not been able to agree on the probable identity of the author, though various candidates, such as Thomas Heywood, George Wilkins, and, most recently, John Day, have been put forward.

The whole matter is further complicated by the publication in 1608 of a prose narrative by George Wilkins, entitled *The Painfull Aduentures of Pericles Prince of Tyre,* "being," we are assured on the title page, "the true History of the Play of *Pericles,* as it was lately presented by the worthy and ancient Poet *Iohn Gower.*" And in *The Argument of the whole Historie* the reader is entreated "to receiue this Historie in the same maner as it was vnder the habite of ancient *Gower* the famous English Poet, by the Kings Maiesties Players [i.e., Shakespeare's company] excellently presented." There is every indication that Wilkins' claim is trustworthy: that he had witnessed one or more performances of Shakespeare's play and had based his novel on this, while also drawing freely (and without acknowledgment) on Laurence Twine's prose version of the same story, *The Patterne of Painefull Aduentures,* which had been reprinted in 1607, and is one of the two chief sources of *Pericles.* In publishing his novel in 1608 Wilkins, no doubt, attempted to exploit the great popularity which the play, according to all indications, enjoyed from the outset.

Wilkins' novel is of great interest and value since, next to the Quarto text, it provides the only clue about the nature of the play as performed by Shakespeare's company that we possess. Not only can editors of *Pericles* draw on it in devising their stage directions (as has been done in this edition, for instance, at II.ii.16, where the s.d. "As each Knight passes, his page, who goes before him, presents his shield to the Princess" is based on Wilkins' "their Pages before them bearing their Deuices on their shields . . . which being by the knights Page deliuered to the Lady"), but they can find support in it for emendations of corrupt readings in the Quarto text. For example, the change of the Quarto's certainly corrupt "untimely" to "uncomely" at I.i.129 is strongly supported by Wilkins' "hee was become both father, sonne, and husband by his vncomely and abhorred actions with his owne child." At one point in the text of this edition (III.ii.84–87) even a whole sentence, which in the Quarto is manifestly corrupt, Cerimon's

>   I heard of an Egyptian
> That had nine hours lien dead,
> Who was by good appliance recoverèd

has been replaced by the corresponding sentence in Wilkins' narrative, which, with the words in parentheses omitted, sounds very much like Shakespeare's verse and thus may well reproduce what he had written: "I haue read of some Egyptians, who after foure houres death (if man may call it so) haue raised impouerished bodies, like to this, vnto their former health."

Lastly, there is one scene where the Quarto text is undoubtedly deficient, and where Wilkins' novel, even if we cannot draw on it for emendations, affords us glimpses of what the main outline of the Shakespearian original appears to have been. It is the scene between Marina and Lysimachus in the brothel (IV.vi.70–122). In Wilkins' novel, as in the play, Lysimachus is depicted as an old client of the bawd, led to the brothel by lust. But in the novel, as the result of Marina's passionate pleas and reproaches, he undergoes a reformation, declaring: "I hither came with thoughtes intemperate, foule and deformed, the which your paines so well hath laued, that they are now white." It is here that the novel diverges most sharply from the play, where, at the corresponding point, Lysimachus is made to declare:

> For me, be you thoughten
> That I came with no ill intent; for to me
> The very doors and windows savor vilely.

This stands, of course, in complete contradiction to what we have been shown in the first part of the scene, where Lysimachus is presented as an old and favorite client. This contradiction has led some scholars to suggest that Lysimachus' later claims reflect a change of mind on Shakespeare's part, a belated attempt to make him a more acceptable husband for Marina. But it seems incredible that Shakespeare should not have bothered to bring the earlier part of the scene into line with this new conception. Furthermore, the writing, which is for the most part Shakespearian up to line 110, ceases to be so at precisely the point at which Lysimachus protests his innocence, and we get such wretched un-Shakespearian stuff as his "For me, be you thoughten. . . ." I believe, then, that lines 110–22 represent the reporter's attempt to reconstruct an only dimly remembered passage, which, for some reason, was missing in his report, and that in doing so he turned Lysimachus from a character somewhat like that of Bertram in *All's Well* into one closer to the Duke in *Measure for Measure*. The great value of Wilkins' account of this scene is not only that he preserved for us what I believe to be Shakespeare's version of it, which had been distorted by the reporter, but that he incidentally seems to have kept a good many of Shakespeare's lines which are missing in the Quarto text, as the following extract from the dialogue between Marina and Lysimachus will show. The lines which seem to me Shakespearian have been italicized and the blank verse line-division has been indicated.

If you take from mee mine honour, *you are like him,/ that makes a gappe into forbidden ground,* after whome too many enter, and you are guiltie of all their euilles:

my life is yet vnspotted, my chastitie vnstained in thought. *Then if your violence deface this building,/the workemanship of heauen, made vp for good,* and not to be the exercise of sinnes intemperaunce, you do kill your owne honour, abuse your owne iustice, and impouerish me. Why quoth *Lysimachus, this house wherein thou liuest,/ is euen the receptacle of all mens sinnes,/and nurse of wickednesse,* and how canst thou then be otherwise then naught, that liuest in it? It is not good, answered *Marina,* when you that are the Gouernour, who should liue well, *the better to be bolde to punish euill,* doe knowe that there is such a roofe, and yet come vnder it. Is there a necessitie (my yet good Lord) if there be fire before me, that I must strait then thither flie and burne my selfe? Or if suppose this house, (*which too too many feele such houses are*)/*should be the Doctors patrimony, and Surgeons feeding;* folowes it therefore, that I must needs infect my self to giue them maintenance? O my good Lord, kill me, but not deflower me, punish me how you please, so you spare my chastitie, and since it is all the dowry that both the Gods haue giuen, and men haue left to me, do not you take it from me; make me your seruant, I will willingly obey you; make mee your bondwoman, *I will accompt it freedome; let me be/the worst that is called vile, so I may still/liue honest, I am content:* or if you thinke it is too blessed a happinesse to haue me so, *let me euen now, now in this minute die,* and Ile accompt my death more happy than my birth. With which wordes (being spoken vpon her knees) while her eyes were the glasses that carried the water of her mishap, the good Gentlewoman being mooued, hee lift her vp with his hands, and euen then imbraced her in his hart, saying aside: *Now surely this is Virtues image,/or rather, Vertues selfe, sent downe, from heauen,/ a while to raigne on earth,* to teach vs what we should be. So in steede of willing her to drie her eyes, he wiped the wet himselfe off, and could haue found in his heart, with modest thoughts to haue kissed her, but that hee feared the offer would offend her. This onely hee sayde, Lady, for such your vertues are, *a farre more worthy stile your beuty challenges,* and no way lesse your beauty can promise me that you are, *I hither came/with thoughtes intemperate, foule and deformed,* the which your paines so well hath laued, that they are now white, continue still to all so, and for my parte, *who hither came but to haue payd the price,/a peece of golde for your virginitie,* now giue you twenty to releeue your honesty. *It shall become you still/ to be euen as you are, a peece of goodnesse,/the best wrought vppe, that euer Nature made,* and if that any shall inforce you ill, if you but send to me, I am your friend. With which promise, leauing her presence, she most humbly thanked the Gods for the preseruation of of her chastitie, and the reformation of his mind.

I should mention at this point a hypothesis which attempts to account for the stylistic differences between the first two and the last three acts of the play in a radically different way from those mentioned so far. In an important article *(Shakespeare Survey 5,* pp. 25–49) Professor Philip Edwards has suggested that Shakespeare may have been responsible for the entire play, and that the difference in style between the two parts may be due to the different methods adopted by two reporters: the one reporting Acts I and II, the other Acts III–V. The former "welds into mediocre verse the words, phrases and general sense of the original so far as he can remember them. He is at his best in prose, where remodeling is not attempted. The second reporter, perhaps giving the original very much more faithfully than his predecessor, makes no attempt at rewriting, and after the first scene does not make more than desultory attempts to write down the verse in lines." This hypothesis is in many ways attractive. For instance, it accounts better than any other for the intermittent occurrence in the first two acts of lines that are manifestly Shakespearian. But there are several grave objections to it, which make it in my view untenable: 1. It seems hard to believe that two men should be willing to adopt such utterly different methods of reporting in order to achieve a composite text. 2. If the first two acts were really by Shakespeare, then those lines in the Quarto text which are identical with passages in Wilkins' novel ought to be acceptable Shakespearian verse. But this is clearly not so. For example:

> A gentleman of Tyre; my name Pericles;
> My education been in arts and arms;
> Who, looking for adventures in the world,
> Was by the rough seas reft of ships and men,
> And after shipwreck driven upon this shore
>
> (II.iii.83–87)

agrees almost word for word with the corresponding passage in Wilkins' narrative, but is plainly not Shakespearian. 3. If the report of the last three acts of the play is so much more faithful than that of the first two acts, we ought to find more verbal echoes of the Quarto in the part of Wilkins' narrative corresponding to the last three acts than in that corresponding to the first two. In fact, rather the reverse is the case.

The likeliest hypothesis seems to me, then, that late in 1607 or early in 1608, at about the time he was writing *Antony and Cleopatra,* Shakespeare came across a manuscript play on the subject of *Pericles* (which may or may not have been performed on the stage), written by some very minor playwright; that he rewrote entirely the last three acts, and had it performed by his company at the Globe theater in the spring of 1608.[1] But it seems that Shakespeare rewrote not only the last three acts, but also occasional lines in the first two acts and, I believe, one whole scene, II.i.

As we read through the wooden, jog-trot, largely end-stopped verse of the first two acts, we come across lines which are late Shakespearian in diction and movement. The most notable example of this occurs in the play's opening scene, in Pericles' speech to King Antiochus after he has solved the riddle. It begins with the mediocre verse typical of the author of the first two acts:

> Great King,
> Few love to hear the sins they love to act;
> 'Twould braid yourself too near for me to tell it.

---

[1] The latest date of composition of the Shakespearian part of *Pericles,* May 1608, seems provided by the play's entry in the Stationers' Register in that month. Its earliest date seems determined chiefly by the style of the verse, which cannot be much earlier than 1607.

> Who has a book of all that monarchs do,
> He's more secure to keep it shut than shown;
> For vice repeated is like the wand'ring wind
> Blows dust in others' eyes to spread itself;
> And yet the end of all is bought thus dear:
> The breath is gone, and the sore eyes see clear
> To stop the air would hurt them.

Then come a few lines which are unmistakably Shakespearian:

> The blind mole casts
> Copped hills towards heaven, to tell the earth is thronged
> By man's oppression; and the poor worm doth die for't.
> (I.i.92–103)

And then the former verse continues on its jog-trot way.

As for the opening scene of Act II, consisting of a mixture of verse and prose, few commentators have been bold enough to assign it to Shakespeare. But if it is not his work, it is remarkably like it, both in its verse and prose; and it certainly cannot be by the author of the remainder of the first two acts, for it is utterly different in style and manner. If we make allowance for the corruption of the text, there is nothing in the scene which one needs deny to Shakespeare. Pericles' opening speech is quite Shakespearian, though it deteriorates towards the end:

> Yet cease your ire, you angry stars of heaven!
> Wind, rain, and thunder, remember, earthly man
> Is but a substance that must yield to you. . . .

There enter three fishermen, and the ways in which they are made instantly real and vivid with the greatest economy of means, and in which they dispense their worldly wisdom and witticisms, bear the mark of Shakespeare. The fishermen's prose is counterpointed by Pericles' verse, and some of this is undoubtedly Shakespearian, e.g.,

> What I have been I have forgot to know;
> But what I am want teaches me to think on:
> A man thronged up with cold.   (lines 75–77)

and two lines towards the end of the scene, which no one but Shakespeare could have written:

> And spite of all the rapture of the sea,
> This jewel holds his building on my arm.
>
> (lines 161–62)

There remains still the problem of the authorship of the choruses. This is made much more difficult by the fact that they are written in a purposely archaic idiom, to suit their speaker, the poet Gower, a contemporary of Chaucer, whose version of the story in his *Confessio Amantis* served as the play's main source (see pp. 156 ff.). Most of the choruses are clearly written in imitation of the octosyllabic couplets in which Gower had told his story. And their archaic idiom also suits the old tale which is the play's subject matter. Ben Jonson referred to *Pericles* contemptuously as a "moldy tale," but the appearance of the mold of antiquity is clearly just what its authors wished to achieve. This is vividly brought home to us by the opening lines of Gower's first chorus (lines 1–10). From the first, the story's antiquity is emphasized as one of its chief virtues.

Which of the choruses are by Shakespeare, and which by the author of Acts I and II? All the indications are that the Shakespearian choruses start precisely where we would expect—at the beginning of Act III. Shakespeare tries to maintain a certain continuity with the earlier choruses in the play by using archaic diction and octosyllabic couplets (though he abandons these for decasyllables after the opening chorus of Act IV). But though written purposely in a naive and simple idiom, the Shakespearian choruses are quite devoid of the clumsy, empty, elliptic diction and lame rhythm of the earlier choruses. The juxtaposition of a few lines from each will make the difference manifest. Here are the opening lines of the chorus at the beginning of Act II:

> Here have you seen a mighty king
> His child iwis to incest bring;
> A better prince and benign lord
> That will prove awful both in deed and word.

> Be quiet, then, as men should be,
> Till he hath passed necessity.
> I'll show you those in trouble's reign
> Losing a mite, a mountain gain.
> The good in conversation,
> To whom I give my benison,
> Is still at Tharsus, where each man
> Thinks all is writ he spoken can;
> And, to remember what he does,
> Build his statue to make him glorious.
> But tidings to the contrary
> Are brought your eyes; what need speak I?

And here, by contrast, are the opening lines of the chorus at the beginning of Act III:

> Now sleep y-slackèd hath the rout;
> No din but snores the house about,
> Made louder by the o'erfed breast
> Of this most pompous marriage feast.
> The cat, with eyne of burning coal,
> Now couches 'fore the mouse's hole;
> And crickets sing at the oven's mouth
> All the blither for their drouth.
> Hymen hath brought the bride to bed,
> Where by the loss of maidenhead
> A babe is molded. Be attent,
> And time that is so briefly spent
> With your fine fancies quaintly eche.
> What's dumb in show I'll plain with speech.

We still have archaisms (y-slackèd, eyne), but the verse is incomparably more vivid, vigorous, and accomplished. Moreover, into these Shakespearian choruses enters an element not found in those of Acts I and II, but familiar to us from the choruses in *Henry V*: the audience is repeatedly asked to use its imagination to eke out what is being presented on the stage (e.g., "And time that is so briefly spent/With your fine fancies quaintly eche"; "In your supposing once more put your sight:/Of heavy Pericles think this his bark").

The story of Pericles, or Apollonius of Tyre, as he was called previous to Shakespeare's play, had been one of the most popular tales in the Middle Ages and the Renaissance. Probably it goes back to Hellenistic times, having its origin in some lost Greek romance. Not only the story's names and settings point to this (Pentapolis is located in the play as somewhere in Greece, while Tyre, Ephesus, Tharsus, and Mytilene, where the rest of the action takes place, are all on or near the coast of Asia Minor), but the outline of the story is typical of the Greek romances. These are tales of marvelous adventures, marked by an abundance of shipwrecks; hairbreadth escapes from wild beasts, bandits, or pirates; innocent maidens, who preserve their virtue in spite of all assaults; and ending in miraculous reunions of parents and children, brothers and sisters, husbands and wives, long believed dead. The main emotion which the Greek romances set out to arouse in the reader is a sense of wonder at the strange incidents which they describe. And a sense of wonder is also one of the main emotions aroused by Shakespeare's Last Plays; "rare," "strange," "wonderful," "like an old tale," are expressions which characters in these plays use again and again to voice their response to the events they witness, and this response is also shared by the audience.

In the English drama written before Shakespeare there is one type of play which sets out to evoke this response, and which is linked with the Greek romances: the miracle play or dramatized saint's legend, a form of drama highly popular beginning with the twelfth century, and still performed in Shakespeare's youth. Unfortunately few of these plays have survived, but from these and extant French miracle plays one can infer their nature. Like the Greek romances, they are tales of strange adventures, separations, wanderings across seas and lands, rescues miraculously effected, dangers overcome and trials passed, until the final triumph of reunion with loved relatives or the triumph of martyrdom. It has been claimed—justly, I think—that these miracle plays had a much profounder influence on the development of English Renaissance drama than had the medieval mystery plays. And the editor of the New

Arden *Pericles* has suggested that it was from such miracle plays that the broad structural features of the play may be derived.

In its structure *Pericles* is unlike any of Shakespeare's earlier comedies. This can be seen most readily if we compare the handling of time. In the comedies before *Pericles* Shakespeare either observed the most rigorous unity of time, as in *The Comedy of Errors,* or he contained the action within a few days, as in *A Midsummer Night's Dream,* or at most within a few months, as in *All's Well.* But nowhere had he used a time scheme similar to that of *Pericles,* where between Acts III and IV there is a time gap of fourteen years. This time scheme is used once more in *The Winter's Tale,* where between Acts III and IV there is an interval of sixteen years. And in both plays, while in the first three acts our attention centers on the royal father (Pericles, Leontes), in the fourth act his place is taken by his daughter (Marina, Perdita), while the fifth act is given over to the reunion of father and daughter, followed by the reunion of husband and wife. In consequence we have in these two plays a kind of double focus, upon father and daughter, which is quite unlike anything found in Shakespeare's other plays.[2] In the earlier comedies our attention is sometimes divided between different pairs of lovers, as in *Two Gentlemen, Love's Labor's Lost,* or *The Taming of the Shrew;* or between different groups of characters, as in *A Midsummer Night's Dream, As You Like It,* and *Twelfth Night.* But nowhere else do we have this shift of focus from father to daughter, and the great gap of time in the middle of the play.

In *The Winter's Tale* this structure is all-important as a vehicle of the play's significances by contrasting the images of wintry barrenness and desolation centering on Leontes with images of spring and fertility centering on Perdita. In *Pericles* the function of the double focus is less immediately obvious. The parallels between the misfortunes that

---

[2] This double focus is well brought out by the Quarto's title page: "The late, And much admired Play, Called Pericles, Prince of Tyre. With the true Relation of the whole Historie, aduentures, and fortunes of the said Prince: As also, The no lesse strange, and worthy accidents, in the Birth and Life, of his Daughter Mariana."

befall father and daughter—in both cases their afflictions begin with a plot to murder them, which they escape, only to be overtaken by further calamities—have a similar effect to the parallels between main plot and subplot in *King Lear* and *Timon of Athens*. The sudden and violent blows of fortune which strike Marina, as they had struck her father, deepen and widen the play's image of the world as a lasting storm, whirring us from our friends (IV.i.19). But to this parallel Shakespeare adds a contrast, found in the way in which father and daughter respond to these afflictions.

A number of critics in recent years have claimed that Pericles, as Shakespeare depicts him, is an embodiment of patience in adversity, a kind of male Griselda-figure, and that the play presents an *exemplum* of this virtue of patience that leads to restoration and happiness. Now it is true that, compared to his prototypes in the sources, Pericles behaves under the earlier blows of fortune with much moderation and restraint. For instance, in his reception of the news of his wife's death, where in Gower and Twine he indulges in the most frantic display of grief, in Shakespeare's scene he expresses it much less vehemently. Yet nothing suggests to me here that he is meant to be seen as an embodiment of patience in adversity. The nurse, Lychorida, repeatedly calls upon him to be patient: "Patience, good sir; do not assist the storm" (assist, that is, by his loud cries of grief); "Patience, good sir,/Even for this charge." (III.i.19,26–27). It would be odd to be preaching patience to a figure embodying that virtue. His reception of the news of Marina's death, as described in dumb show and chorus, suggests even less that Shakespeare thought of Pericles as preeminently a patient man. "Cleon shows Pericles the tomb," we are told, "whereat Pericles makes lamentation, puts on sackcloth, and in a mighty passion departs." And Gower comments:

And Pericles, in sorrow all devoured,
With sighs shot through and biggest tears o'ershowered,
Leaves Tharsus and again embarks. He swears
Never to wash his face, nor cut his hairs.

He puts on sackcloth, and to sea. He bears
A tempest, which his mortal vessel tears,
And yet he rides it out.   (IV.iv.25–31)

The "tempest, which his mortal vessel tears" is, of course,
the storm of his "mighty passion" that ravages his mortal
body. He does not die ("And yet he rides it out"). But he
shuts himself away from all human society, and when
Marina visits him, he has not spoken to a living soul for
three months. Can Shakespeare really have thought that
this is the way in which exemplars of patience accept the
blows of fortune? Wilkins certainly thought otherwise, and
makes clear his view of Pericles' action of shutting himself
away from his fellowmen by making Lysimachus declare
that "though his misfortunes haue beene great, and by
which he hath great cause for this sorrow, it is great pitty
he should continue thus peruerse and obstinate, or so noble
a gentleman come to so dishonorable a death," and having
Marina tell her father that "hee was borne a Prince, whose
dignity being to gouerne others, it was most foule in him
to misgouerne himselfe."

Neither can I believe in the suggestion made by one of
the proponents of this view (J. M. S. Tompkins in *Review
of English Studies,* 1952, 315 ff.)—a suggestion which has
been widely accepted—that Shakespeare called his hero
"Pericles" after the Athenian statesman, whose life he
could have read in Plutarch, who stresses the patience of
his hero at the beginning and end of the "Life." I can
perceive no resemblance between the two, apart from the
fact that they are both excellent fellows. Previously it had
been held—and, I think, rightly—that the name has been
derived from the *Arcadia,* Sir Philip Sidney's great prose
romance, which is full of incidents like those described in
Pericles. One of its two heroes, called Pyrocles, is depicted
as a pattern of all princely virtues. That Shakespeare had
Sidney's hero in mind while writing his play seems proved
by the fact that Marina's description of her father's behavior during the storm at sea in which she was born
closely follows Sidney's account of Pyrocles' behavior during the storm at sea which precedes his shipwreck (see p.

155).[3] Like Sidney's hero, Pericles is depicted as an exemplar not of patience but of all princely excellences. The episodes in the first two acts—often claimed, I believe unjustly, to be insufficiently integrated with the rest of the play—serve not only to present instances of the many blows of fortune that strike Pericles, but also to exhibit his various excellences: his perspicacity in solving Antiochus' riddle (even if it does not seem to *us* a particularly hard one); his loving care of his subjects, which makes him grieve over the danger to which he has unwittingly exposed them; his surpassing excellence in the tournament; his accomplishment in ballroom dancing in full armor (in the *Arcadia* it is the other hero, Musidorus, who dances featly in armor); his supreme skill as a musician; and his modesty, courtesy, and graceful bearing throughout these scenes. Only in his response to the blows of fortune does he fall short of the princely ideal, most signally in his self-seclusion from all human society after being falsely persuaded of the death of Marina. In this he again resembles Pyrocles, whose only discernible fault is a lack of patience in adversity, which culminates in the episode in which he attempts to brain himself by running his head against the wall, after being falsely persuaded of the death of his beloved Philoclea. (The parallel is increased by the resemblance between Dionyza and Sidney's Cecropia, which has been noted by commentators.)

Just as Pericles is depicted as the pattern of all princely

---

[3] That the author of the first two acts also had Pyrocles in mind when writing of his hero's adventures seems indicated by II.i and II.ii. As J. C. Maxwell has pointed out, there is nothing in previous versions of the story about the fishing up of the rusty armor, or about the hero's participation and victory in a tournament. In Gower he takes part and excels in athletic games held in the presence of the King; in Twine he gains the King's favor by his expertise in playing tennis with him and washing him in his bath. The idea of Pericles entering the lists anonymously, in an old, rusty armor inherited from his father, with a pair of bases made from a fisherman's cloak, and proving victorious over all rivals, would seem to have been suggested by Sidney's description of how Pyrocles, in mean attire, entered the lists and defeated the champion at a tournament at the court of King Basilius: "For he had neither picture, nor device; his armor of as old a fashion (besides the rusty poorness) that it might better seem a monument of his grandfather's courage; about his middle he had, instead of bases, a long cloak of silk, which, as unhandsomely as it needs must, became the wearer. . . ." (*Arcadia*, I.17.5).

excellences, so Marina is shown to be the pattern of all
excellences becoming to a princess. This is made manifest
both in the action and in Gower's commentary upon it,
above all in his opening choruses in Acts IV and V. If
we are looking for a figure in the play exemplifying
patience in adversity, it is here that it is to be found. This
is emphasized in the great recognition scene, when Pericles
exclaims:

> Tell thy story.
> If thine, considered, prove the thousandth part
> Of my endurance, thou art a man, and I
> Have suffered like a girl; yet thou dost look
> Like Patience gazing on kings' graves, and smiling
> Extremity out of act.   (V.i.137–42)

Her endurance has, in fact, proved much greater than his.
Instead of shutting herself up in her grief, after suffering
a series of afflictions which more than equal his, this fourteen year old girl becomes the admired teacher of many
skills to pupils of noble race. She then endures Pericles'
initial rough reception of her, yet continues to look "Like
Patience gazing on kings' graves, and smiling/Extremity
out of act."

We have seen, then, that the play's double focus on
father and daughter serves to bring out a contrast as well
as a parallel between them, both of which are important
to the play's full effect. Elsewhere, too, in *Pericles* such
basic parallels and contrasts are to be found. In the non-
Shakespearian part there is above all the extended parallel
and contrast between the main action of Act I and Act II.
Having presented in Act I the wicked king with his wicked
daughter, whose hand Pericles tries to gain by solving a
riddle, the playwright presents in Act II the good king
with his good daughter, whose hand Pericles tries to gain
by winning a tournament. Just as he was successful in
solving the riddle, he is successful in winning the tournament. And where the wicked king, Antiochus, pretended
friendship towards him, while actually planning his death,

the good king, Simonides, pretends enmity towards him, while actually planning to make him his son-in-law.

In the Shakespearian part there is the extended parallel between Pericles' mistaken belief in the death of his wife and his mistaken belief in the death of his daughter, and his final reunion with each. Less obvious is the contrast between the monstrous incest of father and daughter in Act I, brought out in such lines of the riddle as

> He's father, son, and husband mild;
> I mother, wife, and yet his child   (I.i.69–70)

and the blessed "incest" of father and daughter in Act V, suggested by Pericles' words to Marina, "Thou that beget'st him that did thee beget" (V.i.198).

It is such parallels and contrasts—which are typical both of Sidney's *Arcadia* and of Shakespeare's previous plays—that help to give shape and coherence to the episodic and formless romance material on which *Pericles* is based.

I have taken issue with the view that Pericles is an exemplar of the virtue of patience in adversity. Even more misleading I find the common assertion that Shakespeare presents the main events of the play, both the misfortunes and the reunions, as the work of divine Providence. The whole pattern of Pericles' painful adventures, as these critics see it, is a pattern imposed by the gods. But the notion of a divine Providence that persecutes wholly virtuous characters so cruelly and for so long is repugnant, and so several of these critics are driven to discover some offense in the protagonists for which they are punished. Such an attempt to find a pattern of sin, punishment, expiation, and restoration in the play seems to me to violate and distort its whole spirit. It is to assimilate *Pericles* to *The Winter's Tale* and *The Tempest*, where sin and expiation do play an important part. In *Pericles,* as in the miracle plays, we are confronted with the *undeserved* sufferings of the wholly innocent and entirely virtuous— of Pericles, Thaisa, and Marina. And both their misfor-

tunes and their restoration are shown to be mainly due to
accident, to chance. The goddess who presides over the
play is not Diana but Fortuna. It is by accident that the
waves throw up the coffin containing Thaisa at Ephesus
near the house of Cerimon, just the person who possesses
the rare medical knowledge and skill needed to restore her
to life. It is accident that brings Pericles' ship to Mytilene
and Marina on board this ship, thus enabling father and
daughter to be reunited. To see in all this the hand of
Providence is indeed to take away from our sense of wonder. Only once in the play is there any clear evidence of
supernatural intervention: in V.i., where the Goddess
Diana appears to Pericles in a vision. Without this vision
the final reunion of Thaisa with her husband and daughter
would have been difficult to bring about. In both of Shakespeare's sources this vision is found, though only in Shakespeare is it the goddess Diana that appears to Pericles.
Gower speaks of a vision sent by "the high god," while in
Twine's version an angel appears to Pericles in his sleep.
But I can find no suggestion in the play that Diana had any
other part in its events.

It is true that, like all Shakespeare's virtuous and noble
characters, Pericles sees the hand of heaven behind all the
accidents that befall him. At the news of Thaisa's death
he cries out,

> O you gods!
> Why do you make us love your goodly gifts,
> And snatch them straight away?　　　(III.i.22–24)

And at the reunion with Thaisa he exclaims:

> You gods, your present kindness
> Makes my past miseries sports.　　(V.iii.39–40)

But, as with Shakespeare's great tragedies, this view is not
imposed by the play upon the audience. It is above all con-
tradicted by the choruses (except for the final moralistic
one, of doubtful authorship), for Gower insists repeatedly
upon Fortune's responsibility for the events. It is Fortune,

he tells us, at the beginning of Act II, that threw Pericles ashore near Pentapolis. It is "Fortune's mood," he remarks at the beginning of Act III, that conjures up the storm during which Marina is born.

> Let Pericles believe his daughter's dead,
> And bear his courses to be orderèd
> By Lady Fortune;   (IV.iv.46–48)

he comments in Act IV. But Lady Fortune is merely the personification of the power of accident in human affairs.

I have spoken of the sense of wonder and amazement which Shakespeare's Last Plays seek to evoke in both characters and audience. It vents itself in a language which is characteristic of these plays, and which has appeared only fitfully before, chiefly in Shakespeare's late tragedies. It is a simple, translucent language, melodious in sound, slow in pace, remote and dreamlike in its effect. Certain images tend to recur, above all images of precious objects: pearls, jewels, silver, and gold. Here are two examples of it from our play:

>   She is alive! Behold,
> Her eyelids, cases to those heavenly jewels
> Which Pericles hath lost, begin to part
> Their fringes of bright gold; the diamonds
> Of a most praisèd water doth appear
> To make the world twice rich. Live,
> And make us weep to hear your fate, fair creature,
> Rare as you seem to be.   (III.ii.99–106)

> I am great with woe, and shall deliver weeping.
> My dearest wife was like this maid, and such
> My daughter might have been: my queen's square brows;
> Her stature to an inch; as wandlike straight;
> As silver-voiced; her eyes as jewel-like
> And cased as richly; in pace another Juno;
> Who starves the ears she feeds, and makes them hungry
> The more she gives them speech.   (V.i.108–15)

Apart from the more powerful evocation of a sense of

wonder, and the style in which it expresses itself, what is it that chiefly marks off *Pericles* from Shakespeare's preceding comedies, and that points forward to the other Last Plays?

Closely related to this increased sense of wonder is a greater predominance of fairy-tale motifs and fairy-tale atmosphere. *Pericles* is full of such motifs, from the opening scene, in which the young Prince has to solve a riddle in order to gain the hand of the beautiful princess, to the play's epilogue, which announces, in the manner of fairy tales, the reward of the virtuous and the cruel punishment of the wicked. This fairy-tale atmosphere makes it easier to accept the improbabilities in the play's action: Pericles' failure to visit his daughter for fourteen years after leaving her with Cleon and Dionyza; Thaisa's decision to lead the life of a vestal because, unaccountably, she will never see her husband again. (This could easily have been motivated, as it is in Gower and Wilkins, by her mistaken belief that her husband was drowned during the storm at sea. Perhaps some lines to this effect have dropped out of the text.)

Allied to the increased predominance of the fairy-tale atmosphere is the intrusion of the supernatural, which does not enter into the earlier comedies, with the single exception of *A Midsummer Night's Dream*. In *Pericles* Diana appears to the hero in a vision; in *Cymbeline* Jupiter descends on his eagle and prophesies; in *The Winter's Tale* we have the oracle of Apollo; and in *The Tempest* Ariel and his fellow-spirits.

I have already spoken of the difference of structure which marks off *Pericles* and *The Winter's Tale* from all of Shakespeare's other plays. Next, there is the difference in the young heroine. It is partly a difference in age: Marina is fourteen years old, Miranda fifteen, Perdita sixteen, while the young heroines of the preceding comedies, such as Beatrice, Portia, Rosalind, and Viola, seem a good deal older. For a heroine in a previous play who is of Marina's age we have to turn not to a comedy but to an early tragedy. Juliet, too, is fourteen years old. In personality also Marina is more like Juliet, or like Cordelia, than she is like Portia, or Beatrice, or Rosalind, who dazzle us above all by their wit. And unlike all the heroines of the preceding comedies, Marina exists primarily not in relation to a lover but to her father. She is given a husband at the end, but in a most perfunctory way, and we are never even told whether she loves him. Shakespeare is clearly not at all interested in the Marina-Lysimachus relationship. In the other Last Plays there is no parallel to this. While the relation of father and daughter is also of some importance in them, it is the relation of the daughter to her lover, of Perdita to Florizel, of Miranda to Ferdinand, of Imogen to Posthumus, that mainly concerns us.

Finally, these Last Plays differ from the preceding comedies in the weight and scope given to the scenes depicting the reunion of loved relatives long separated and believed dead. This motif is dominant in *Pericles, Cymbeline,* and *The Winter's Tale*—much less so in *The Tempest.* It had also occurred in some of Shakespeare's earlier comedies. In *Twelfth Night* and *Measure for Measure* a loved brother, firmly believed dead, suddenly appears alive before his sister. In *Much Ado* and *All's Well* a bride believed dead appears alive before her bridegroom or husband. In the final scene of *The Comedy of Errors* Shakespeare staged the biggest reunion of them all: not only two pairs of twin brothers, who had been separated since babyhood, are reunited, but the parents of the one pair with each other as well as with their sons, all after some thirty-three years of separation. It is the perfunctory manner in which these reunions are dramatized, the absence of any expression of their emotional experience, which makes these scenes in the earlier comedies (with the exception of *Twelfth Night*) so different in impact from the reunion scenes especially of *Pericles* and *The Winter's Tale.*

Till the closing of the theaters in 1642 *Pericles* seems to have been one of Shakespeare's greatest stage successes. The fact that the Quarto text was reprinted five times between 1609 and 1635 alone bears witness to its popularity. At the Restoration it was the first of Shakespeare's plays to be revived, with Betterton in the title role. But in the two hundred and fifty years from then until the beginning of this century the play fell into disrepute, receiving only a handful of performances, and even these giving the play in a radically altered or mutilated form. Only in the last few decades has it begun again to receive the attention it deserves from producers and critics, who have come to see that, as well as being full of highly effective scenes for the stage, it contains some of Shakespeare's loveliest and most haunting verse.

ERNEST SCHANZER
University of Munich

Pericles, Prince of Tyre

Gower, as Chorus
Antiochus, King of Antioch
Pericles, Prince of Tyre
Helicanus } two lords of Tyre
Escanes
Simonides, King of Pentapolis
Cleon, Governor of Tharsus
Lysimachus, Governor of Mytilene
Cerimon, a lord of Ephesus
Thaliard, a lord of Antioch
Philemon, servant to Cerimon
Leonine, servant to Dionyza
Marshal
A Pander
Boult, his servant
The Daughter of Antiochus
Dionyza, wife to Cleon
Thaisa, daughter to Simonides
Marina, daughter to Pericles and Thaisa
Lychorida, nurse to Marina
A Bawd
Diana
Lords, Ladies, Knights, Gentlemen, Sailors, Pirates, Fishermen, and Messengers

Scene: dispersedly in various Mediterranean countries]

Pericles,
Prince of Tyre

[ACT I

*Before the king's palace at Antioch, with heads
displayed upon its walls.]*

Enter Gower.° [1]

Gower. To sing a song that old° was sung,
   From ashes ancient Gower is come,
   Assuming man's infirmities,°
   To glad your ear, and please your eyes.
   It hath been sung at festivals,
   On ember-eves° and holidays,   *5*
   And lords and ladies in their lives
   Have read it for restoratives.
   The purchase° is to make men glorious;
   Et bonum quo antiquius eo melius.°   *10*
   If you, born in those latter times,
   When wit's more ripe, accept my rhymes,
   And that to hear an old man sing
   May to your wishes pleasure bring,
   I life would wish, and that I might   *15*

1 The degree sign (°) indicates a footnote, which is keyed to the
text by the line number. Text references are printed in **boldface**
type; the annotation follows in roman type.
l.s.d. Gower John Gower, fourteenth-century poet **1 old** of old
3 Assuming man's infirmities putting on man's infirm body **6 ember-
eves** evenings before the fasts known as "ember days" **9 purchase**
gain **10 Et . . . melius** and the more ancient a good thing is the
better it is (Latin)

45

Waste it for you, like taper-light.
This Antioch,° then; Antiochus the great
Built up this city for his chiefest seat,
The fairest in all Syria—
20 I tell you what mine authors say.
This king unto him took a peer,°
Who died, and left a female heir,
So buxom,° blithe, and full of face,°
As heaven had lent her all his grace;
25 With whom the father liking took,
And her to incest did provoke.
Bad child, worse father, to entice his own
To evil should° be done by none.
But custom° what they did begin
30 Was with long use accounted no sin.
The beauty of this sinful dame
Made many princes thither frame,°
To seek her as a bedfellow,
In marriage pleasures playfellow;
35 Which to prevent he made a law,
To keep her still, and men in awe:°
That whoso asked her for his wife,
His riddle told° not, lost his life.
So for her many a wight did die,
40 As yon grim looks do testify. [*Points to the heads.*]
What now ensues, to the judgment of your eye
I give my cause, who best can justify.°   *Exit.*

---

17 **This Antioch** this is Antioch   21 **peer** companion, consort   23
buxom gay, lively   23 **full of face** beautiful (?) with a round face (?)
28 **should** which should   29 **custom** through custom   32 **frame**
direct their course   36 **To** ... awe to keep her always to himself,
and to keep others from demanding her in marriage   38 **told** expounded   41–42 **What** ... **justify** in what now ensues I submit my
case to the judgment of your eye, as you are best able to acquit me
(of the charge of having told an incredible tale)

[Scene I. *Before the palace of Antioch.*]

Enter Antiochus, Prince Pericles, and followers.

Antiochus. Young Prince of Tyre, you have at large
received°
The danger of the task you undertake.

Pericles. I have, Antiochus, and, with a soul
Embold'ned with the glory of her praise,
Think death no hazard in this enterprise.   5

Antiochus. Music!   [*Music sounds.*]
Bring in our daughter, clothèd like a bride,
For the embracements even of Jove himself;
At whose conception, till Lucina reigned,°
Nature this dowry° gave to glad her presence.°   10
The senate house of planets all did sit,
To knit in her their best perfections.

Enter Antiochus' daughter.

Pericles. See where she comes, appareled like the
spring,
Graces her subjects, and her thoughts the king
Of every virtue gives° renown to men!   15
Her face the book of praises, where is read
Nothing but curious° pleasures, as from thence
Sorrow were ever razed,° and testy wrath
Could never be her mild companion.°
You gods that made me man, and sway in love;°   20

I.i.1 **at large received** learned fully   9 **till Lucina reigned** i.e., before
her birth (Lucina is the goddess of childbirth)   10 **this dowry** i.e.,
her beauty   10 **to glad her presence** to make her presence delightful
(?)   15 **gives** which gives   17 **curious** exquisite   18 **razed** erased
19 **her mild companion**   the companion of her mildness   20 **and
sway in love** and who govern in love

That have enflamed desire in my breast
To taste the fruit of yon celestial tree
Or die in th' adventure, be my helps,
As° I am son and servant to your will,
25 To compass such a boundless happiness!

Antiochus. Prince Pericles—

Pericles. That would be son to great Antiochus.

Antiochus. Before thee stands this fair Hesperides,°
With golden fruit, but dangerous to be touched;
30 For deathlike dragons here affright thee hard.
Her face like heaven enticeth thee to view
Her countless glory, which desert must gain;
And which without desert, because thine eye
Presumes to reach, all the whole heap° must die.
35 Yon sometimes° famous princes, like thyself,
Drawn by report, advent'rous by desire,
Tell thee, with speechless tongues and semblance
    pale,
That without covering, save yon field of stars,
Here they stand martyrs slain in Cupid's wars;
40 And with dead cheeks advise thee to desist
For° going on death's net, whom none resist.

Pericles. Antiochus, I thank thee, who hath taught
My frail mortality to know itself,
And by those fearful objects to prepare
45 This body, like to them, to what I must;
For death remembered should be like a mirror,
Who tells us life's but breath, to trust it error.
I'll make my will, then; and, as sick men do,
Who know the world, see heaven, but, feeling woe,
50 Gripe° not at earthly joys as erst they did,
So I bequeath a happy peace to you
And all good men, as every prince should do;

24 As as surely as   28 Hesperides the daughters of Hesperus, the
evening star (but here, by confusion, the garden containing the
golden apples, which, with the aid of a dragon, they were appointed
to watch)   34 the whole heap the whole body   35 sometimes once
41 For for fear of   50 gripe grasp

My riches to the earth from whence they came;
[*To the Princess*] But my unspotted fire of love to
  you.
Thus, ready for the way of life or death,   55
I wait the sharpest blow, Antiochus.

Antiochus. Scorning advice, read the conclusion°
  then: [*He throws down the riddle.*]
Which read and not expounded, 'tis decreed,
As these before thee thou thyself shalt bleed.

Daughter. Of all 'sayed yet,° mayst thou prove prosperous!   60
Of all 'sayed yet, I wish thee happiness.

Pericles. Like a bold champion I assume the lists,°
Nor ask advice of any other thought
But faithfulness and courage.

           [*He reads*] *the riddle.*

    I am no viper,° yet I feed   65
    On mother's flesh, which did me breed.
    I sought a husband, in which labor
    I found that kindness° in a father.
    He's father, son, and husband mild;
    I mother, wife, and yet his child.   70
    How they may be, and yet in two,°
    As you will live, resolve it you.
[*Aside*] Sharp physic is the last.° But O, you
  powers,
That gives° heaven countless eyes to view men's
  acts:
Why cloud they not their sights perpetually,   75
If this be true which makes me pale to read it?

---

57 **conclusion** riddle   60 **'sayed yet** who have yet assayed   62 **assume the lists** undertake the contest   65 **I am no viper** (vipers were
believed to be born by eating their way out of the mother's body)
68 **kindness** (1) kinship (2) affection   71 **How . . . two** how these
things may be, and yet all be found in two persons   73 **Sharp physic
is the last** the last condition of the riddle is an unpleasant medicine
74 **gives** give (the third person plural in *s* is not unusual)

Fair glass of light,° I loved you, and could still,
Were not this glorious casket stored with ill.
But I must tell you, now my thoughts revolt;
80   For he's no man on whom perfections wait
That, knowing sin within, will touch the gate.
You are a fair viol, and your sense° the strings;
Who, fingered to make man his lawful music,
Would draw heaven down, and all the gods to
    hearken;
85   But being played upon before your time,
Hell only danceth at so harsh a chime.
Good sooth,° I care not for you.

                [*He turns towards the Princess.*]

Antiochus. Prince Pericles, touch not, upon thy life,
For that's an article within our law
90   As dangerous° as the rest. Your time's expired.
Either expound now, or receive your sentence.

Pericles. Great King,
Few love to hear the sins they love to act;
'Twould braid° yourself too near° for me to tell it.
95   Who has a book of all that monarchs do,
He's more secure to keep it shut than shown;
For vice repeated° is like the wand'ring wind
Blows° dust in others' eyes to spread° itself;
And yet the end of all is bought thus dear:
100   The breath is gone, and the sore eyes see clear
To stop the air would hurt them. The blind mole
    casts
Copped° hills towards heaven, to tell the earth is
    thronged°
By man's oppression; and the poor worm° doth die
    for't.
Kings are earth's gods; in vice their law's their will;
105   And if Jove stray, who dares say Jove doth ill?

77 glass of light i.e., one who reflects light, as does a mirror, but
does not contain it   **82 sense** senses (?)   **87 Good sooth** truly
90 dangerous rigorous   **94 braid** upbraid   **94 too near** touching you
too closely   **97 repeated** talked about   **98 Blows** which blows   **98**
to spread in spreading   **102 Copped** peaked   **102 thronged** crushed
103 worm creature

It is enough you know; and it is fit,
What being more known grows worse, to smother
    it.
All love the womb that their first being bred;
Then give my tongue like leave to love my head.

Antiochus. [*Aside*] Heaven, that I had thy head! He
    has found the meaning.   *110*
But I will gloze° with him. [*Aloud*] Young Prince
    of Tyre,
Though by the tenor of our strict edict,
Your exposition misinterpreting,
We might proceed to cancel of° your days,
Yet hope, succeeding° from so fair a tree   *115*
As your fair self, doth tune us otherwise.
Forty days longer we do respite you;
If by which time our secret be undone,°
This mercy shows we'll joy in such a son.
And until then your entertain° shall be   *120*
As doth befit our honor and your worth.
                         [*Exeunt all but Pericles.*]

Pericles. How courtesy would seem° to cover sin,
When what is done is like an hypocrite,
The which is good in nothing but in sight!°
If it be true that I interpret false,   *125*
Then were it certain you were not so bad
As with foul incest to abuse your soul;
Where now you're both a father and a son
By your uncomely° claspings with your child,
Which pleasures fits a husband, not a father;   *130*
And she an eater of her mother's flesh
By the defiling of her parents' bed;
And both like serpents are, who though they feed
On sweetest flowers, yet they poison breed.
Antioch, farewell, for wisdom sees, those men   *135*

111 **gloze** talk speciously   114 **cancel of** the canceling of   115 **succeeding** resulting   118 **secret be undone** riddle be solved   120 **entertain** entertainment, reception   122 **seem** make a specious appearance   124 **sight** outward appearance   129 **uncomely** improper (see
Introduction, p. xxiii)

Blush° not in actions blacker than the night,
Will 'schew° no course to keep them from the light.
One sin, I know, another doth provoke;
Murder's as near to lust as flame to smoke.
140 Poison and treason are the hands of sin,
Ay, and the targets,° to put off° the shame.
Then, lest my life be cropped to keep you clear,
By flight I'll shun the danger which I fear.   *Exit.*

Enter Antiochus.

Antiochus. He hath found the meaning,
145 For which we mean to have his head. He must
Not live to trumpet forth my infamy,
Nor tell the world Antiochus doth sin
In such a loathèd manner.
And therefore instantly this prince must die;
150 For by his fall my honor must keep high.
Who attends us there?

Enter Thaliard.

Thaliard.   Doth your Highness call?

Antiochus. Thaliard,
You are of our chamber,° Thaliard, and our mind partakes°
Her private actions to your secrecy;
155 And for your faithfulness we will advance you.
Thaliard, behold, here's poison, and here's gold!
We hate the Prince of Tyre, and thou must kill him.
It fits thee not to ask the reason why.
Because we bid it. Say, is it done?

Thaliard. My lord, 'tis done.

160 *Antiochus.*   Enough.

Enter a Messenger.

Let your breath cool yourself telling your haste.

---

136 **Blush** who blush   137 **'schew** eschew, avoid   141 **targets** shields
141 **put off** avert   153 **of our chamber** our chamberlain   153 **partakes** imparts

Messenger. My lord, Prince Pericles is fled.   [*Exit.*]

Antiochus. As thou wilt live, fly after; and like an
arrow shot from a well-experienced archer hits the
mark his eye doth level° at, so thou never return   165
unless thou say Prince Pericles is dead.

Thaliard. My lord, if I can get him within my pistol's
length, I'll make him sure° enough. So farewell to
your Highness.

Antiochus. Thaliard, adieu! [*Exit Thaliard.*] Till
Pericles be dead   170
My heart can lend no succor to my head.   [*Exit.*]

[Scene II. *Tyre. A room in the palace.*]

Enter Pericles.

Pericles. [*To Servants without*] Let none disturb us.
Why should this change of thoughts,
The sad companion, dull-eyed melancholy,
Be my so used° a guest as not an hour
In the day's glorious walk or peaceful night,   5
The tomb where grief should sleep, can breed me
quiet?
Here pleasures court mine eyes, and mine eyes shun
them,
And danger, which I feared, is at Antioch,
Whose arm seems far too short to hit me here;
Yet neither pleasure's art can joy° my spirits,   10
Nor yet the other's distance comfort me.
Then it is thus: the passions of the mind,

165 **level** aim   168 **sure** unable to do harm   I.ii.4 **used** customary
10 **joy** give joy to

That have their first conception by misdread,°
Have after-nourishment and life by care;
15 And what was first but fear what might be done,
Grows elder now and cares° it be not done.
And so with me: the great Antiochus,
'Gainst whom I am too little to contend,
Since he's so great can° make his will his act,
20 Will think me speaking, though I swear to silence;
Nor boots it me° to say I honor him,
If he suspect I may dishonor him.
And what may make him blush in being known°
He'll stop the course by which it might be known.
25 With hostile forces he'll o'erspread the land,
And with th' ostent° of war will look so huge,
Amazement° shall drive courage from the state,
Our men be vanquished ere they do resist,
And subjects punished that ne'er thought offense;
30 Which care of them, not pity of myself,
Who am no more but as the tops of trees
Which fence° the roots they grow by and defend
    them,
Makes both my body pine and soul to languish,
And punish that before that he would punish.

Enter [Helicanus and] all the Lords to
Pericles.

35 *First Lord.* Joy and all comfort in your sacred breast!

Second Lord. And keep your mind, till you return
    to us,
Peaceful and comfortable!°

---

13 **misdread** dread of evil   16 **cares** is anxious that   19 **can** that
he can   21 **boots it me** does it avail me   23 **in being known** if it
were known   26 **th' ostent** the display   27 **Amazement** consterna-
tion   32 **fence** protect   36–37 **And keep . . . comfortable** (these
lines must be either corrupt or misplaced, as Pericles' decision to
leave Tyre is not taken till the end of the scene)   37 **comfortable**
cheerful (a passage in which Helicanus reproves Pericles for wasting
"his body there with pining sorrow, upon whose safety depended
the lives and prosperity of a whole kingdom" [Wilkins] and is sternly
rebuked by him for his presumption, must have preceded the next
speech, but is missing from the text)

Helicanus. Peace, peace, and give experience tongue.°
  They do abuse° the King that flatter him,
  For flattery is the bellows blows up° sin;   *40*
  The thing the which is flattered but a spark
  To which that blast gives heat and stronger glowing;
  Whereas reproof, obedient and in order,
  Fits kings, as they are men, for they may err.
  When Signor Sooth° here does proclaim a peace   *45*
  He flatters you, makes war upon your life.
  Prince, pardon me, or strike me, if you please;
  I cannot be much lower than my knees.
                        [*He kneels.*]

Pericles. All leave us else!° But let your cares o'er-
  look°
  What shipping and what lading's° in our haven,   *50*
  And then return to us.   [*Exeunt Lords.*]
              Helicanus,
  Thou hast moved us. What seest thou in our looks?

Helicanus. An angry brow, dread lord.

Pericles. If there be such a dart in princes' frowns,
  How durst thy tongue move anger to our face?   *55*

Helicanus. How dares the plants look up to heaven,
  from whence
  They have their nourishment?

Pericles.   Thou knowest I have power
  To take thy life from thee.

Helicanus.   I have ground the ax myself;
  Do but you strike the blow.

Pericles.   Rise, prithee, rise.
               [*He raises him.*]
  Sit down. Thou art no flatterer.   *60*
  I thank thee for't; and heaven forbid

---

38 **give experience tongue** allow experience to speak   39 **abuse** ill-
use 40 **blows up** which fans into flame 45 **Signor Sooth** Sir Flattery 49 **All leave us else** everybody else leave us 49 **o'erlook** look
into 50 **lading** cargo

That kings should let their ears hear their faults
   hid!°
Fit counselor and servant for a prince,
Who by thy wisdom makes a prince thy servant,
What wouldst thou have me do?

65 *Helicanus.*   To bear with patience
Such griefs as you do lay upon yourself.

Pericles. Thou speak'st like a physician, Helicanus,
That ministers a potion unto me
That thou wouldst tremble to receive thyself.
70 Attend° me then: I went to Antioch,
Where, as thou know'st, against the face of death
I sought the purchase° of a glorious beauty,
From whence an issue I might propagate
Are arms° to princes and bring joys to subjects.
75 Her face was to mine eye beyond all wonder;
The rest—hark in thine ear—as black as incest;
Which by my knowledge found, the sinful father
Seemed° not to strike, but smooth;° but thou
   know'st this:
'Tis time to fear when tyrants seems to kiss.
80 Which fear so grew in me, I hither fled,
Under the covering of a careful° night,
Who seemed my good protector; and, being here,
Bethought me what was past, what might succeed.
I knew him tyrannous; and tyrants' fears
85 Decrease not, but grow faster than the years;
And should he doubt, as no doubt he doth,°
That I should open° to the list'ning air
How many worthy princes' bloods were shed
To keep his bed of blackness unlaid ope,°
90 To lop that doubt,° he'll fill this land with arms,
And make pretense of wrong that I have done him;

62 **hear their faults hid** i.e., hear the flattery which hides their faults
70 **Attend** listen to   72 **purchase** acquisition   74 **Are arms** which
are arms   78 **Seemed** pretended   78 **smooth** flatter   81 **careful**
taking good care   86 **And should . . . he doth** (the first "doubt,"
meaning "fear," is pronounced as a disyllable)   87 **open** reveal
89 **unlaid ope** undisclosed   90 **doubt** dread, fear

When all for mine, if I may call, offense
Must feel war's blow, who° spares not innocence;
Which love to all, of which thyself art one,
Who now° reprovedst me for't—

Helicanus.   Alas, sir!   95

Pericles. Drew sleep out of mine eyes, blood from my
    cheeks,
Musings into my mind, with thousand doubts
How I might stop this tempest ere it came;
And finding little comfort to relieve them,
I thought it princely charity to grieve them.°   100

Helicanus. Well, my lord, since you have given me
    leave to speak,
Freely will I speak. Antiochus you fear,
And justly, too, I think, you fear the tyrant
Who either by public war or private treason
Will take away your life.   105
Therefore, my lord, go travel for a while,
Till that his rage and anger be forgot,
Or till the Destinies do cut his thread of life.
Your rule direct° to any; if to me,
Day serves not light more faithful° than I'll be.   110

Pericles. I do not doubt thy faith.
But should he wrong my liberties° in my absence?

Helicanus. We'll mingle our bloods together in the
    earth,
From whence we had our being and our birth.

Pericles. Tyre, I now look from thee then, and to
    Tharsus   115
Intend° my travel, where I'll hear from thee,
And by whose letters I'll dispose myself.°
The care I had and have of subjects' good
On thee I lay, whose wisdom's strength can bear it.

93 **who** which   95 **now** just now   100 **grieve them** grieve for them
109 **direct** assign   110 **Day . . . faithful** day is not served by light
more faithfully   112 **liberties** prerogatives   116 **Intend** direct   117
dispose myself direct my actions

120   I'll take thy word for faith, not ask thine oath:
      Who shuns not to break one° will crack both.
      But in our orbs we'll live so round° and safe,°
      That time of both this truth shall ne'er convince:°
      Thou showed'st a subject's shine, I a true prince.°
                              Exit [with Helicanus].

                  [Scene III. *The palace at Tyre.*]

                    Enter Thaliard solus.°

Thaliard. So this is Tyre, and this the court. Here
      must I kill King Pericles; and if I do it not, I am
      sure to be hanged at home. 'Tis dangerous. Well,
      I perceive he was a wise fellow and had good dis-
5   cretion that, being bid to ask what he would of the
      King, desired he might know none of his secrets.
      Now do I see he had some reason for't: for if a
      king bid a man be a villain, he's bound by the in-
      denture° of his oath to be one. Husht, here comes
10   the lords of Tyre.

      _____

      121 one (pronounced as a disyllable)   **122 we'll live so round** (1)
      we'll live so honestly (2) we'll move in such a perfect circle
      122 safe trustworthily   **123 of both . . . convince** shall never con-
      fute this truth regarding both of us   **124 Thou . . . prince** you
      showed a subject's luster, I showed myself a true prince   I.iii.
      s.d. solus alone (Latin)   **8–9 indenture** contract binding servant to
      master

Enter Helicanus, Escanes, with other Lords.

Helicanus. You shall not need, my fellow peers of
 Tyre,
 Further to question me of your king's departure.
 His sealed commission left in trust with me
 Does speak sufficiently he's gone to travel.

Thaliard. [*Aside*] How? The King gone?   15

Helicanus. If further yet you will be satisfied
 Why, as it were, unlicensed of your loves°
 He would depart, I'll give some light unto you.
 Being at Antioch—

Thaliard.   [*Aside*] What from Antioch?

Helicanus. Royal Antiochus—on what cause I know
 not—   20
 Took some displeasure at him; at least he judged
 so;
 And doubting lest° he had erred or sinned,
 To show his sorrow, he'd correct° himself;
 So puts himself unto the shipman's toil,
 With whom each minute threatens life or death.   25

Thaliard. [*Aside*] Well, I perceive I shall not be
 hanged now
 Although I would.
 But since he's gone, the King's ears it must please
 He scaped the land, to perish at the seas.
 I'll present myself. [*Aloud*] Peace to the lords of
 Tyre!   30

Helicanus. Lord Thaliard from Antiochus is welcome.

Thaliard. From him I come
 With message unto princely Pericles.
 But since my landing I have understood
 Your lord has betook himself to unknown travels.   35
 Now message must return from whence it came.

17 **unlicensed of your loves** without your loving assent   22 **doubting
lest** fearing that ("doubting" is here trisyllabic)   23 **he'd correct** he
wanted to punish

Helicanus. We have no reason to desire it,
    Commended° to our master, not to us.
    Yet, ere you shall depart, this we desire:
40   As friends to Antioch we may feast in Tyre.

                                    Exit [with the rest].

[Scene IV. *Tharsus.*]

*Enter Cleon, the Governor of Tharsus, with
    his wife [Dionyza] and others.*

Cleon. My Dionyza, shall we rest us here,
    And by relating tales of others' griefs,
    See if 'twill teach us to forget our own?

Dionyza. That were to blow at fire in hope to quench
        it;
5   For who digs° hills because they do aspire
    Throws down one mountain to cast up a higher.
    O my distressed lord, even such our griefs are;
    Here they are but felt and seen with mischief's°
        eyes,
    But like to groves, being topped, they higher rise.

10   *Cleon.* O Dionyza,
    Who wanteth food and will not say he wants it,
    Or can conceal his hunger till he famish?
    Our tongues and sorrows cease not to sound deep

---

38 **Commended** since it is commended   **I.iv.5 digs** digs down   **8 mischief's** misfortune's

Our woes into the air, our eyes to weep,°
Till tongues fetch breath that may proclaim them
    louder,   15
That, if heaven slumber while their creatures want,
They may awake their helps to comfort them.
I'll then discourse our woes, felt several years,
And wanting breath to speak help me° with tears.

Dionyza. I'll do my best, sir.   20

Cleon. This Tharsus, o'er which I have the govern-
    ment,
A city on° whom plenty held full hand,
For riches strewed herself° even in her streets;
Whose towers bore heads so high they kissed the
    clouds,
And strangers ne'er beheld but wond'red at;   25
Whose men and dames so jetted and adorned,°
Like one another's glass to trim them by;°
Their tables were stored full, to glad the sight,
And not so much to feed on as delight;
All poverty was scorned, and pride so great,   30
The name of help grew odious to repeat.°

Dionyza. O, 'tis too true!

Cleon. But see what heaven can do by this our change:
These mouths who but of late earth, sea, and air
Were all too little to content and please,   35
Although they gave their creatures in abundance,
As houses are defiled for want of use,
They are now starved for want of exercise;
Those palates who, not yet two summers younger,
Must have inventions° to delight the taste,   40
Would now be glad of bread, and beg for it;

13–14 **Our tongues . . . to weep** let our sorrowful tongues (hendiadys)
not cease to . . ., let our eyes not cease to weep   19 **help me** do you
help me   22 **on** over   23 **riches strewed herself** ("riches" is a
feminine singular)   26 **jetted and adorned** strutted and dressed
themselves up   27 **glass to trim them by** pattern according to which
to array themselves   31 **repeat** mention   40 **inventions** ingenious
novelties

Those mothers who, to nuzzle up° their babes,
Thought nought too curious,° are ready now
To eat those little darlings whom they loved.
45 So sharp are hunger's teeth that man and wife
Draw lots who first shall die to lengthen life.
Here stands a lord, and there a lady weeping;
Here many sink, yet those which see them fall
Have scarce strength left to give them burial.
50 Is not this true?

Dionyza. Our cheeks and hollow eyes do witness it.

Cleon. O, let those cities that of plenty's cup
And her prosperities so largely taste,
With their superfluous riots,° hear these tears!
55 The misery of Tharsus may be theirs.

Enter a Lord.

Lord. Where's the Lord Governor?

Cleon. Here.
Speak out thy sorrows which thou bring'st in haste,
For comfort is too far for us to expect.

60 *Lord.* We have descried, upon our neighboring shore,
A portly sail° of ships make hitherward.

Cleon. I thought as much.
One sorrow never comes but brings an heir
That may succeed as his inheritor;
65 And so in ours: some neighboring nation,
Taking advantage of our misery,
Hath stuffed the hollow vessels with their power,°
To beat us down, the which are down already,
And make a conquest of unhappy me,
70 Whereas° no glory's got to overcome.

Lord. That's the least fear; for, by the semblance
Of their white flags displayed, they bring us peace,
And come to us as favorers, not as foes.°

42 **nuzzle up** bring up   43 **curious** exquisite   54 **superfluous riots**
inordinate revels   61 **portly sail** stately fleet   67 **power** armed force
70 **Whereas** where

Cleon. Thou speak'st like him's untutored to repeat:°
   Who makes the fairest show means most deceit.
   But bring they what they will, what need we fear?   *75*
   On ground's the lowest,° and we are halfway there.
   Go tell their general we attend° him here,
   To know for what he comes, and whence he comes,
   And what he craves.°   *80*

Lord. I go, my lord.   [*Exit.*]

Cleon. Welcome is peace, if he on peace consist;°
   If wars, we are unable to resist.

Enter Pericles, with Attendants.

Pericles. Lord Governor, for so we hear you are,
   Let not our ships and number of our men   *85*
   Be like a beacon fired t' amaze your eyes.
   We have heard your miseries as far as Tyre,
   And seen the desolation of your streets;
   Nor come we to add sorrow to your tears,
   But to relieve them of their heavy load;   *90*
   And these our ships you happily may think°
   Are like the Trojan horse was° stuffed within
   With bloody veins expecting overthrow,°
   Are stored with corn to make your needy bread,°
   And give them life whom hunger starved half dead.   *95*

All. The gods of Greece protect you!
   And we'll pray for you.   [*They kneel.*]

Pericles.   Arise, I pray you, rise;
   We do not look for reverence but for love,
   And harborage for ourself, our ships, and men.

Cleon. The which when any shall not gratify,°   *100*
   Or pay you with unthankfulness in thought,

---

74 **him's untutored to repeat** him who has never been taught to
recite   77 **On ground's the lowest** i.e., he that lies upon the ground
can fall no lower   78 **attend** await   80 **craves** desires   82 **on peace
consist** stands on peace   91 **you happily may think** you may perhaps think   92 **was** which was   93 **With . . . overthrow** i.e., with
bloodthirsty warriors waiting for the overthrow (of Troy)   94 **your
needy bread** bread for your needy citizens   100 **gratify** show gratitude for

Be it our wives, our children, or ourselves,
The curse of heaven and men succeed their evils!
Till when—the which I hope shall ne'er be seen—
105 Your Grace is welcome to our town and us.

Pericles. Which welcome we'll accept; feast here
    awhile,
Until our stars that frown lend us a smile.
                                        Exeunt.

[ACT II]

Enter Gower.

Gower. Here have you seen a mighty king
  His child iwis° to incest bring;
  A better prince and benign lord
  That will prove awful° both in deed and word.
  Be quiet, then, as men should be,   5
  Till he hath passed necessity.°
  I'll show you those in trouble's reign°
  Losing a mite, a mountain gain.
  The good in conversation,°
  To whom I give my benison,   10
  Is still at Tharsus, where each man
  Thinks all is writ he spoken can;°
  And, to remember° what he does,
  Build his statue to make him glorious.
  But tidings to the contrary   15
  Are brought your eyes; what need speak I?

II.2 **iwis** assuredly   4 **awful** commanding profound respect   6
passed necessity experienced extreme hardship   7 **those in trouble's
reign** those who under the dominion of trouble   9 **conversation**
conduct, way of life   12 **all . . . can** all his words are holy writ
13 **remember** commemorate

Dumb Show

*Enter at one door Pericles, talking with Cleon;
all the train with them. Enter at another door a
Gentleman with a letter to Pericles; Pericles
shows the letter to Cleon. Pericles gives the
Messenger a reward and knights him. Exit
Pericles at one door, and Cleon at another.*

Good Helicane, that stayed at home,
Not to eat honey like a drone
From others' labors, for he strives
20   To killen bad, keep good alive,
And to fulfill his prince' desire,
Sends word of all that haps in Tyre:
How Thaliard came full bent with° sin
And hid intent° to murder him;
25   And that in Tharsus was not best
Longer for him to make his rest.
He, doing so,° put forth to seas,
Where when men been there's seldom ease;
For now the wind begins to blow;
30   Thunder above and deeps below
Makes such unquiet that the ship
Should° house him safe is wracked and split;
And he, good prince, having all lost,
By waves from coast to coast is tossed.
35   All perishen of man, of pelf,°
Ne aught escapend° but himself;
Till fortune, tired with doing bad,
Threw him ashore, to give him glad.°
And here he comes. What shall be next,
40   Pardon old Gower—this 'longs° the text.   [*Exit.*]

---

23 **bent with** intent upon   24 **And hid intent** and with hidden intent
27 **doing so** i.e., acting as advised   32 **Should** which should   35
pelf possessions   36 **escapend** escaping   38 **glad** gladness   40 **'longs**
belongs to

[Scene I. *Pentapolis, at the seashore.*]

Enter Pericles, wet.

Pericles. Yet cease your ire, you angry stars of heaven!
  Wind, rain, and thunder, remember, earthly man
  Is but a substance that must yield to you;
  And I, as fits my nature, do obey you.
  Alas, the seas hath cast me on the rocks,   *5*
  Washed me from shore to shore, and left me breath
  Nothing to think on but ensuing death.
  Let it suffice the greatness of your powers
  To have bereft a prince of all his fortunes;
  And having thrown him from your wat'ry grave,   *10*
  Here to have death in peace is all he'll crave.

Enter three Fishermen.

First Fisherman. What ho, Pilch!°

Second Fisherman. Ha, come and bring away° the
  nets!

First Fisherman. What, Patchbreech, I say!   *15*

Third Fisherman. What say you, master?

First Fisherman. Look how thou stirr'st now!° Come
  away,° or I'll fetch thee with a wanion.°

Third Fisherman. Faith, master, I am thinking of the
  poor men that were cast away before us even now.   *20*

First Fisherman. Alas, poor souls, it grieved my heart
  to hear what pitiful cries they made to us to help

II.i.12 **Pilch** (a coarse outer garment made of leather or skin,
here used, like **Patchbreech**, jestingly as a name)   13 **bring away**
bring here without delay   17 **how thou stirr'st now!** what a stock
you are!   17–18 **Come away** come here right away   18 **with a
wanion** with a vengeance

them, when, well-a-day,° we could scarce help ourselves.

25 *Third Fisherman.* Nay, master, said not I as much
when I saw the porpoise how he bounced and
tumbled? They say they're half fish, half flesh. A
plague on them! They ne'er come but I look to be
washed. Master, I marvel how the fishes live in the
30   sea.

First Fisherman. Why, as men do a-land: the great
ones eat up the little ones. I can compare our rich
misers to nothing so fitly as to a whale; 'a° plays
and tumbles, driving the poor fry before him, and
35   at last devours them all at a mouthful: Such whales
have I heard on a' th' land,° who never leave gap-
ing till they swallowed the whole parish, church,
steeple, bells, and all.

Pericles. [*Aside*] A pretty moral.°

40 *Third Fisherman.* But, master, if I had been the sex-
ton, I would have been that day in the belfry.

Second Fisherman. Why, man?

Third Fisherman. Because he should have swallowed
me too; and when I had been in his belly, I would
45   have kept such a jangling of the beils that he should
never have left till he cast bells, steeple, church,
and parish up again. But if the good King Simonides were of my mind—

Pericles. [*Aside*] Simonides!

50 *Third Fisherman.* We would purge the land of these
drones that rob the bee of her honey.

Pericles. [*Aside*] How from the finny subject° of the
sea
These fishers tell the infirmities of men;
And from their wat'ry empire recollect°

23 **well-a-day** alas   33 **'a** he   36 **heard on a' th' land** heard of on
land   39 **moral** tale conveying a moral lesson   52 **subject** subjects,
citizens   54 **recollect** gather up

All that may men approve° or men detect!°   55
[*Aloud*] Peace be at your labor, honest fishermen!

Second Fisherman. Honest good fellow, what's that?
  If it be a day fits you, scratch it out of the calendar,
  and nobody look after it.°

Pericles. May° see the sea hath cast upon your coast——   60

Second Fisherman. What a drunken knave was the
  sea to cast° thee in our way!

Pericles. A man whom both the waters and the wind
  In that vast tennis court hath made the ball
  For them to play upon entreats you pity him.   65
  He asks of you that never used to beg.

First Fisherman. No, friend, cannot you beg? Here's
  them in our country of Greece gets more with begging than we can do with working.

Second Fisherman. Canst thou catch any fishes, then?   70

Pericles. I never practiced it.

Second Fisherman. Nay, then, thou wilt starve, sure;
  for here's nothing to be got nowadays unless thou
  canst fish for't.

Pericles. What I have been I have forgot to know;   75
  But what I am want teaches me to think on:
  A man thronged up° with cold. My veins are chill,
  And have no more of life than may suffice
  To give my tongue that heat to ask your help;
  Which if you shall refuse, when I am dead,   80
  For that° I am a man, pray you see me burièd.

First Fisherman. Die, quoth-a?° Now gods forbid't!

---

55 **approve** commend   55 **detect** expose (in wrongdoing)   57–59
Honest . . . after it (a lost line in which Pericles wishes the fishermen a good day appears to have preceded this passage. The fisherman rudely replies that if the day fitted Pericles' wretched appearance it ought to be removed from the calendar)   60 **May** you may
62 **cast** (1) cast up, vomit (2) throw   77 **thronged up** overwhelmed
81 **For that** because   82 **quoth-a** did he say

And I have a gown here! Come, put it on; keep
thee warm. Now, afore me,° a handsome fellow!
85 Come, thou shalt go home, and we'll have flesh for
holidays, fish for fasting days, and moreo'er puddings and flapjacks,° and thou shalt be welcome.

Pericles. I thank you, sir.

Second Fisherman. Hark you, my friend: you said
90 you could not beg.

Pericles. I did but crave.

Second Fisherman. But crave? Then I'll turn craver
too, and so I shall 'scape whipping.°

Pericles. Why, are your beggars whipped, then?

95 *Second Fisherman.* O, not all, my friend, not all! For
if all your beggars were whipped, I would wish no
better office than to be beadle. But, master, I'll go
draw up the net.   [*Exit with Third Fisherman.*]

Pericles. [*Aside*] How well this honest mirth becomes°
their labor!

100 *First Fisherman.* Hark you, sir, do you know where
ye are?

Pericles. Not well.

First Fisherman. Why, I'll tell you: this is called
Pentapolis, and our king the good Simonides.

105 *Pericles.* The good Simonides do you call him?

First Fisherman. Ay, sir; and he deserves so to be
called, for his peaceable reign and good government.

Pericles. He is a happy king, since he gains from his
110 subjects the name of good by his government. How
far is his court distant from this shore?

84 **afore** me upon my word 87 **flapjacks** pancakes 92–93 **Then
I'll . . . whipping** i.e., through not calling himself a beggar (whipping, administered by the beadle, was the regular punishment of
beggars in Shakespeare's day) 99 **becomes** suits with

First Fisherman. Marry,° sir, half a day's journey.
And I'll tell you, he hath a fair daughter, and tomorrow is her birthday; and there are princes and
knights come from all parts of the world to joust   *115*
and tourney for her love.

Pericles. Were my fortunes equal to my desires, I
could wish to make one there.

First Fisherman. O, sir, things must be as they may;
and what a man cannot get he may lawfully deal   *120*
for his wife's soul.°

   Enter the two Fishermen, drawing up a net.

Second Fisherman. Help, master, help! Here's a fish
hangs in the net like a poor man's right° in the
law: 'twill hardly come out. Ha, bots on't,° 'tis
come at last; and 'tis turned to a rusty armor.   *125*

Pericles. An armor, friends! I pray you, let me see it.
Thanks, Fortune, yet, that after all thy crosses
Thou givest me somewhat to repair° myself;
And though it was mine own, part of my heritage
Which my dead father did bequeath to me,   *130*
With this strict charge, even as he left his life:
"Keep it, my Pericles; it hath been a shield
'Twixt me and death"—and pointed to this
   brace°—
"For that it saved me, keep it; in like necessity—
The which the gods protect thee from!—may't de-
fend thee."   *135*
It kept where I kept, I so dearly loved it;
Till the rough seas, that spares not any man,
Took it in rage, though calmed have given't again.
I thank thee for't. My shipwreck now's no ill,
Since I have here my father gave° in his will.   *140*

---

112 **Marry** why (a mild oath, from "By the Virgin Mary")   120–21
he may . . . wife's soul (no sense can be made of the text as it stands,
nor has it been plausibly emended)   123 **right** just claim   124 **bots
on't** a plague upon it   128 **repair** renew, restore   133 **brace** armor
covering the arms   140 **my father gave** that which my father gave

First Fisherman. What mean you, sir?

Pericles. To beg of you, kind friends, this coat of
worth,
For it was sometime target° to a king;
I know it by this mark. He loved me dearly,
145 And for his sake I wish the having of it;
And that you'd guide me to your sovereign's court,
Where with it I may appear a gentleman.
And if that ever my low fortune's better,
I'll pay your bounties; till then rest your debtor.

150 *First Fisherman.* Why, wilt thou tourney for the lady?

Pericles. I'll show the virtue° I have borne in arms.

First Fisherman. Why, d' ye take it, and the gods give
thee good on't!

Second Fisherman. Ay, but hark you, my friend:
155 'twas we that made up this garment through the
rough seams of the waters. There are certain condolements,° certain vails.° I hope, sir, if you thrive,
you'll remember from whence you had them.°

Pericles. Believe't, I will!
160 By your furtherance I am clothed in steel;
And spite of all the rapture° of the sea,
This jewel holds his building° on my arm.
Unto thy value° I will mount myself
Upon a courser, whose delightful steps
165 Shall make the gazer joy to see him tread.
Only, my friend, I yet am unprovided
Of a pair of bases.°

Second Fisherman. We'll sure provide. Thou shalt

---

143 **target** literally, light shield, hence protection   151 **virtue** valor
157 **condolements** (probably a malapropism through confusion with
"dole" meaning "distribution of gifts")   157 **vails** perquisites, tips
158 **them** i.e., the armor   161 **rapture** act of plunder, seizure   162
building fixed place   163 **Unto thy value** to as high a value (as the
jewel will fetch)   167 **bases** pleated skirt, worn by knights on
horseback

have my best gown to make thee a pair; and I'll
bring thee to the court myself.   170

Pericles. Then honor be but equal to my will,
This day I'll rise, or else add ill to ill.   [*Exeunt.*]

[Scene II. *Pentapolis. The court of Simonides.
A public way leading to the lists. A pavilion
near it.*]

*Enter Simonides, with [Lords,] Attendants, and
Thaisa.*

Simonides. Are the knights ready to begin the triumph?°

First Lord. They are, my liege,
And stay your coming to present themselves.

Simonides. Return° them we are ready; and our
daughter,
In honor of whose birth these triumphs are,   5
Sits here like Beauty's child, whom Nature gat°
For men to see and seeing wonder at.
[*Exit a Lord.*]

Thaisa. It pleaseth you, my royal father, to express
My commendations great, whose merit's less.

Simonides. It's fit it should be so; for princes are   10
A model° which heaven makes like to itself:

II.ii.1 **triumph** festivity, here tournament   4 **Return** tell by way of
answer   6 **gat** begat   11 **model** likeness in little

As jewels lose their glory if neglected,
So princes their renowns if not respected.
'Tis now your honor,° daughter, to entertain°
15 The labor of each knight in his device.°

Thaisa. Which, to preserve mine honor, I'll perform.

[*Simonides and Thaisa take seats in the pavilion.*]
The first Knight passes by. [*As each Knight
passes, his page, who goes before him, presents
his shield to the Princess.*]

Simonides. Who is the first that doth prefer° himself?

Thaisa. A knight of Sparta, my renownèd father;
And the device he bears upon his shield
20 Is a black Ethiop reaching at the sun.
The word,° *Lux tua vita mihi.°*

Simonides. He loves you well that holds his life of
you.

The second Knight [*passes*].

Who is the second that presents himself?

Thaisa. A prince of Macedon, my royal father;
25 And the device he bears upon his shield
Is an armed knight that's conquered by a lady;
The motto thus, in Spanish, *Più per dolcezza che
per forza.°*

[*The*] *third Knight* [*passes*].

Simonides. And what's the third?

Thaisa.   The third of Antioch;
And his device a wreath of chivalry.°
30 The word, *Me pompae provexit apex.°*

---

14 **honor** honorable duty   14 **entertain** receive   15 **device** emble-
matic figure, accompanied by a motto, inscribed on the shield
17 **prefer** present   21 **word** motto   21 **Lux tua vita mihi** thy light is
life to me (Latin)   27 **Più . . . forza** more by gentleness than by
force (Italian)   29 **wreath of chivalry** the twisted band by which,
in heraldry, the crest is joined to the knight's helmet   30 **Me pompae
provexit apex** the crown of the triumph has led me on (Latin)

[*The*] *fourth Knight* [*passes*].

Simonides. What is the fourth?

Thaisa. A burning torch that's turnèd upside down.
  The word, *Qui me alit me extinguit.*°

Simonides. Which shows that beauty hath his° power
    and will,
  Which can as well inflame as it can kill.   33

[*The*] *fifth Knight* [*passes*].

Thaisa. The fifth, an hand environèd with clouds,
  Holding out gold that's by the touchstone tried.
  The motto thus, *Sic spectanda fides.*°

[*The*] *sixth Knight,* [*Pericles, passes, without
    page*].

Simonides. And what's the sixth and last, the which
    the knight himself
  With such a graceful courtesy delivered?°   40

Thaisa. He seems to be a stranger; but his present° is
  A withered branch, that's only green at top;
  The motto, *In hac spe vivo.*°

Simonides. A pretty moral.
  From the dejected state wherein he is,   45
  He hopes by you his fortunes yet may flourish.

First Lord. He had need mean better than his out-
    ward show
  Can any way speak in his just commend;°
  For by his rusty outside he appears
  To have practiced more the whipstock° than the
    lance.   50

---

33 **Qui . . . extinguit** who feeds me puts me out (Latin)   34 **his** its
38 **Sic spectanda fides** thus is faithfulness to be tried (Latin)   40 **delivered** presented   41 **present** object presented   43 **In hac spe vivo**
in this hope I live (Latin)   48 **commend** commendation   50 **To
have practiced more the whipstock** to have wielded more the handle
of a whip, i.e., worked as a carter

Second Lord. He well may be a stranger, for he comes
  To an honored triumph strangely furnishèd.

Third Lord. And on set purpose let his armor rust
  Until this day to scour it in the dust.

55 *Simonides.* Opinion's° but a fool that makes us scan°
  The outward habit for the inward man.
  But stay, the knights are coming!
  We will withdraw into the gallery.   [*Exeunt.*]
              Great shouts [*within*], *and all cry*
                      "The mean° Knight!"

        [Scene III. *Pentapolis. A hall of state.*]

  Enter the King, [*Thaisa, Marshal, Lords, Ladies,*]
      and Knights from tilting, [*and Attendants*].

Simonides. Knights,
  To say you're welcome were superfluous.
  To place upon the volume of your deeds,
  As in a title page, your worth in arms,°
5 Were more than you expect, or more than's fit,
  Since every worth in show commends itself.
  Prepare for mirth, for mirth becomes a feast.
  You are princes and my guests.

Thaisa. But you my knight and guest;
10   To whom this wreath of victory I give,
  And crown you king of this day's happiness.

---

55 Opinion public opinion   **55 scan** scrutinize, examine   **58 s.d.
mean** shabby   **II.iii.4 As . . . arms** (title pages of early printed
books often proclaimed the excellence of their contents)

Pericles. 'Tis more by fortune, lady, than my merit.

Simonides. Call it by what you will, the day is yours;
    And here, I hope, is none that envies it.
    In framing° an artist, art hath thus decreed: *15*
    To make some good, but others to exceed;
    And you are her labored scholar.° Come, queen
     o' th' feast—
    For, daughter, so you are—here take your place.
    Marshal, the rest as they deserve their grace.°

Knights. We are honored much by good Simonides.   *20*

Simonides. Your presence glads our days. Honor we
     love;
    For who hates honor hates the gods above.

Marshal. Sir, yonder is your place.

Pericles.   Some other is more fit.

First Knight. Contend not, sir; for we are gentlemen
    Have° neither in our hearts nor outward eyes   *25*
    Envied the great, nor shall the low despise.

Pericles. You are right courteous knights.

Simonides.   Sit, sir, sit.
    [*Aside*] By Jove I wonder, that is king of thoughts,
    These cates° resist me, he but thought upon.°

Thaisa. [*Aside*] By Juno, that is queen of marriage,   *30*
    All viands that I eat
    Do seem unsavory, wishing him my meat.
    [*To Simonides*] Sure he's a gallant gentleman.

Simonides. He's but a country gentleman;
    Has done no more than other knights have done;   *35*
    Has broken a staff or so; so let it pass.

Thaisa. [*Aside*] To me he seems like diamond to glass.

---

15 framing molding   **17 her labored scholar** the scholar over whom
art took special pains   **19 grace** favor   **25 Have** that have   **29 cates**
delicacies   **29 resist . . . upon** repel me (?) when I but think of him

Pericles. [*Aside*] Yon king's to me like to my father's
    picture,
    Which tells me in that glory once he was;
40   Had princes sit like stars about his throne,
    And he the sun for them to reverence;
    None that beheld him but, like lesser lights,
    Did vail° their crowns to his supremacy;
    Where now his son's a glowworm in the night,
45   The which hath fire in darkness, none in light.
    Whereby I see that Time's the king of men;
    He's both their parent and he is their grave,
    And gives them what he will, not what they crave.

Simonides. What, are you merry, knights?

50 *Knights.* Who can be other in this royal presence?

Simonides. Here, with a cup that's stored unto the
    brim—
    As you do love, fill to° your mistress' lips—
    We drink this health to you.

Knights.   We thank your Grace.

Simonides. Yet pause awhile.
55   Yon knight doth sit too melancholy,
    As if the entertainment in our court
    Had not a show might countervail° his worth.
    Note it not you, Thaisa?

Thaisa. What is't to me, my father?

60 *Simonides.* O, attend, my daughter:
    Princes, in this, should live like gods above,
    Who freely give to everyone that come
    To honor them.
    And princes not doing so are like to gnats,
65   Which make a sound, but killed are wond'red at.°
    Therefore, to make his entrance° more sweet,

---

43 **vail** lower   52 **to** in honor of   57 **countervail** be equal to   65 **but
killed are wond'red at** i.e., when they are found to be such small
animals, after making so great a noise   66 **entrance** (trisyllabic)

Here, say we drink this standing-bowl° of wine to
     him.

Thaisa. Alas, my father, it befits not me
     Unto a stranger knight to be so bold:
     He may my proffer take for an offense,   70
     Since men take women's gifts for impudence.

Simonides. How?
     Do as I bid you, or you'll move me else!

Thaisa. [*Aside*] Now, by the gods, he could not please
     me better.

Simonides. And furthermore tell him we desire to
     know of him   75
     Of whence he is, his name and parentage.

Thaisa. The King my father, sir, has drunk to you.

Pericles. I thank him.

Thaisa. Wishing it so much blood unto your life.

Pericles. I thank both him and you, and pledge him
     freely.   80

Thaisa. And further he desires to know of you
     Of whence you are, your name and parentage.

Pericles. A gentleman of Tyre; my name Pericles;
     My education been° in arts and arms;
     Who, looking for adventures in the world,   85
     Was by the rough seas reft of ships and men,
     And after shipwrack driven upon this shore.

Thaisa. He thanks your Grace; names himself Pericles,
     A gentleman of Tyre,
     Who only by misfortune of the seas,   90
     Bereft of ships and men, cast on this shore.

Simonides. Now, by the gods, I pity his misfortune,
     And will awake him from his melancholy.
     Come, gentlemen, we sit too long on trifles,
     And waste the time which looks for other revels.   95

67 **standing-bowl** bowl resting on a foot   84 **been** has been

Even in your armors, as you are addressed,°
Will well° become a soldier's dance.
I will not have excuse with saying this:
Loud music° is too harsh for ladies' heads,
100   Since they love men in arms° as well as beds.

They dance.°

So, this was well asked, 'twas so well performed.
Come, sir, here's a lady that wants breathing° too;
And I have heard you knights of Tyre
Are excellent in making ladies trip,°
105   And that their measures° are as excellent.

Pericles. In those that practice them they are, my lord.

Simonides. O, that's as much as you would be denied
Of your fair courtesy.°

They dance.

Unclasp, unclasp!
Thanks, gentlemen, to all; all have done well,
[*To Pericles*] But you the best. Pages and lights, to
110   conduct
These knights unto their several lodgings! Yours,
sir,
We have given order be next our own.

Pericles. I am at your Grace's pleasure.

Simonides. Princes, it is too late to talk of love,
115   And that's the mark I know you level° at.

96 addressed accoutered   **97 Will well** (two such words as "your
steps" must have originally preceded this)   **99 Loud music** i.e., the
loud noise made by the clashing of their armor (?)   **100 arms** (a
pun is presumably intended)   **100 s.d. They dance** (most editors
assume that the first dance is performed by the Knights alone, the
second by the Knights and Ladies. The text, especially line 102,
suggests rather that both dances are mixed. In the first dance Thaisa
and, perhaps, Pericles do not participate; in the second they dance
together)   **102 breathing** exercise   **104 trip** dance a light dance
(with a *double entendre*)   **105 measures** dances   **107–08 denied/Of
your fair courtesy** refused permission to show your courtesy (by
dancing with Thaisa) (?)   **115 level** aim

Therefore each one betake him to his rest;
Tomorrow all for speeding° do their best.

[*Exeunt.*]

[Scene IV. *Tyre.*]

Enter Helicanus and Escanes.

Helicanus. No, Escanes, know this of me:
  Antiochus from incest lived not free;
  For which, the most high gods not minding° longer
  To withhold the vengeance that they had in store,
  Due to this heinous capital offense,   5
  Even in the height and pride of all his glory,
  When he was seated in a chariot
  Of an inestimable value, and
  His daughter with him, a fire from heaven came,
  And shriveled up their bodies, even to loathing.   10
  For they so stunk
  That all those eyes adored° them ere their fall
  Scorn now their hand should give them burial.

Escanes. 'Twas very strange.

Helicanus. And yet but justice; for though this king
    were great,   15
  His greatness was no guard to bar heaven's shaft,
  But sin had his° reward.

Escanes.   'Tis very true.

117 speeding   success   II.iv.3 minding   being   inclined   12 adored
that adored   17 his its

Enter two or three Lords.

First Lord. See, not a man in private conference
    Or council has respect with him but he.

Second Lord. It shall no longer grieve° without
20   reproof.

Third Lord. And cursed be he that will not second it.

First Lord. Follow me then. Lord Helicane, a word.

Helicanus. With me? And welcome. Happy day, my
    lords!

First Lord. Know that our griefs° are risen to the top,
25   And now at length they overflow their banks.

Helicanus. Your griefs, for what? Wrong not your
    prince you love.

First Lord. Wrong not yourself, then, noble Helicane;
    But if the Prince do live, let us salute him,
    Or know what ground's made happy by his breath.
30   If in the world he live, we'll seek him out;
    If in his grave he rest, we'll find him there;
    And be resolved° he lives to govern us,
    Or, dead, gives cause to mourn his funeral,
    And leaves us to our free election.

Second Lord. Whose death's indeed the strongest in
35   our censure.°
    And knowing this: kingdoms without a head,
    Like goodly buildings left without a roof
    Soon fall to ruin, your noble self,
    That best know how to rule and how to reign,
40   We thus submit unto—our sovereign.

All. Live, noble Helicane!

Helicanus. For honor's cause, forbear your suffrages.
    If that you love Prince Pericles, forbear.

---

20 **grieve** be a grievance   24 **griefs** grievances   32 **resolved** satisfied
35 **the strongest in our censure** the more likely supposition in our
judgment

  Take I° your wish, I leap into the seas
  Where's hourly trouble for a minute's ease.   45
  A twelvemonth longer let me entreat you
  To forbear° the absence of your king;
  If in which time expired he not return,
  I shall with agèd patience bear your yoke.
  But if I cannot win you to this love,°   50
  Go search like nobles, like noble subjects,
  And in your search spend your adventurous worth;
  Whom if you find, and win unto return,
  You shall like diamonds sit about his crown.

First Lord. To wisdom he's a fool that will not yield; 55
  And since Lord Helicane enjoineth us,
  We with our travels will endeavor it.

Helicanus. Then you love us, we you, and we'll clasp
  hands:
  When peers thus knit, a kingdom ever stands.
                                    [Exeunt.]

[Scene V. *Pentapolis. A room in the palace.*]

*Enter the King reading of a letter at one door;
the Knights meet him.*

First Knight. Good morrow to the good Simonides.

Simonides. Knights, from my daughter this I let you
  know:

44 **Take I** if I should accept   47 **forbear** tolerate, endure   50 **love**
act of kindness

That for this twelvemonth she'll not undertake
A married life.
5 Her reason to herself is only known,
Which from her by no means° can I get.

Second Knight. May we not get access to her, my lord?

Simonides. Faith, by no means. She hath so strictly tied her
To her chamber that 'tis impossible.
One twelve moons° more she'll wear Diana's
10 livery.°
This by the eye of Cynthia° hath she vowed,
And on her virgin honor will not break it.

Third Knight. Loath° to bid farewell, we take our
leaves.   *[Exeunt Knights.]*

Simonides. So, they are well dispatched.
15 Now to my daughter's letter:
She tells me here she'll wed the stranger knight,
Or never more to view nor day nor light.
'Tis well, mistress; your choice agrees with mine.
I like that well! Nay, how absolute° she's in't,
20 Not minding whether I dislike or no!
Well, I do commend her choice,
And will no longer have it be delayed.
Soft,° here he comes! I must dissemble it.

Enter Pericles.

Pericles. All fortune to the good Simonides!

Simonides. To you as much. Sir, I am beholding° to
25 you
For your sweet music this last night. I do
Protest my ears were never better fed
With such delightful pleasing harmony.

II.v.6 means (here pronounced as a disyllable) **10 One twelve moons** one year **10 wear Diana's livery** i.e., remain a virgin **11 Cynthia** the moon **13 Loath** (here pronounced as a disyllable) **19 absolute** positive, decided **23 Soft** hold (an interjection) **25 beholding** indebted

Pericles. It is your Grace's pleasure to commend;
  Not my desert.

Simonides.   Sir, you are music's master.   *30*

Pericles. The worst of all her scholars, my good lord.

Simonides. Let me ask you one thing: What do you think of
  My daughter, sir?

Pericles.   A most virtuous princess.

Simonides. And she is fair too, is she not?

Pericles. As a fair day in summer, wondrous fair.   *35*

Simonides. Sir, my daughter thinks very well of you;
  Ay, so well that you must be her master,
  And she will be your scholar: therefore look to it.

Pericles. I am unworthy for her schoolmaster.

Simonides. She thinks not so; peruse this writing else.°   *40*

Pericles. [*Aside*] What's here?
  A letter that she loves the knight of Tyre!
  'Tis the King's subtlety to have my life.
  [*Kneels*] O, seek not to entrap me, gracious lord,
  A stranger and distressèd gentleman,   *45*
  That never aimed so high to° love your daughter,
  But bent all offices° to honor her.

Simonides. Thou hast bewitched my daughter, and thou art
  A villain!

Pericles.   By the gods, I have not.
  Never did thought of mine levy° offense;   *50*
  Nor never did my actions yet commence
  A deed might° gain her love or your displeasure.

Simonides. Traitor, thou liest!

Pericles.   Traitor?

40 else if you do not believe it   **46 to** as to   **47 bent all offices** turned all my services   **50 levy** (apparently misused for "level," i.e., aim)   **52 might** that might

Simonides.   Ay, traitor!

Pericles. Even in his throat—unless it be the King—
55   That calls me traitor I return the lie.

Simonides. [*Aside*] Now, by the gods, I do applaud
     his courage.

Pericles. My actions are as noble as my thoughts,
     That never relished of° a base descent.
     I came unto your court for honor's cause,
60   And not to be a rebel to her state;°
     And he that otherwise accounts of me,
     This sword shall prove he's honor's enemy.

Simonides. No?
     Here comes my daughter, she can witness it.

Enter Thaisa.

65   *Pericles.* Then, as you are as virtuous as fair,
     Resolve° your angry father if my tongue
     Did e'er solicit, or my hand subscribe
     To any syllable that made love to you.

Thaisa. Why, sir, say if you had,
70   Who takes offense at that would° make me glad?

Simonides. Yea, mistress, are you so peremptory?°
     (*Aside*) I am glad on't with all my heart.—
     I'll tame you; I'll bring you in subjection!
     Will you, not having my consent,
75   Bestow your love and your affections
     Upon a stranger?—(*aside*) who, for aught I know,
     May be, nor can I think the contrary,
     As great in blood as I myself—
     Therefore hear you, mistress: either frame
80   Your will to mine—and you, sir, hear you:
     Either be ruled by me, or I'll make you—
     Man and wife.
     Nay, come, your hands and lips must seal it too!
     And being joined, I'll thus your hopes destroy;

58 **relished of** had a trace of   60 **her state** honor's domain   66 **Resolve** inform   70 **would** which would   71 **peremptory** determined

And for further grief—God give you joy!   85
What, are you both pleased?

Thaisa.   Yes, if you love me, sir.

Pericles. Even as my life my blood° that fosters it.

Simonides. What, are you both agreed?

Both. Yes, if't please your Majesty.

Simonides. It pleaseth me so well that I will see you
    wed;   90
And then, with what haste you can, get you to bed.
                              Exeunt.

87 my blood i.e., loves my blood

[ACT III]

Enter Gower.

Gower. Now sleep y-slackèd° hath the rout;°
    No din but snores the house about,
    Made louder by the o'erfed breast
    Of this most pompous° marriage feast.
5   The cat, with eyne° of burning coal,
    Now couches 'fore the mouse's hole;
    And crickets sing at the oven's mouth
    All the blither for their drouth.°
    Hymen° hath brought the bride to bed,
10   Where by the loss of maidenhead
    A babe is molded. Be attent,°
    And time that is so briefly° spent
    With your fine fancies° quaintly° eche.°
    What's dumb in show I'll plain° with speech.

III.1 **y-slackèd** reduced to inactivity 1 **rout** company of revelers
4 **pompous** magnificent 5 **eyne** eyes (archaic plural) 8 **drouth** dry-
ness 9 **Hymen** the god of marriage 11 **attent** attentive 12 **briefly**
quickly 13 **fancies** imaginings 13 **quaintly** skillfully 13 **eche** aug-
ment (old spelling of "eke") 14 **plain** explain

[Dumb Show]

Enter Pericles and Simonides at one door, with At-
tendants; a Messenger meets them, kneels, and gives
Pericles a letter; Pericles shows it Simonides; the
Lords kneel to him. Then enter Thaisa with child,
with Lychorida, a nurse; the King shows her the let-
ter; she rejoices; she and Pericles take leave of her
father, and depart [with Lychorida and their Attend-
ants. Then exeunt Simonides and the rest].

By many a dern° and painful° perch°   15
Of Pericles the careful search
By the four opposing coigns°
Which the world together joins
Is made with all due diligence
That horse and sail and high expense   20
Can stead° the quest. At last from Tyre,
Fame answering the most strange inquire,°
To th' court of King Simonides
Are letters brought, the tenor these:
Antiochus and his daughter dead,   25
The men of Tyrus on the head
Of Helicanus would set on
The crown of Tyre, but he will none.
The mutiny he there hastes t' appease;
Says to 'em, if King Pericles   30
Come not home in twice six moons,
He, obedient to their dooms,°
Will take the crown. The sum° of this,
Brought hither to Pentapolis,
Y-ravishèd° the regions round,   35
And everyone with claps can° sound,°
"Our heir-apparent is a king!
Who dreamt, who thought of such a thing?"
Brief,° he must hence depart to Tyre.

15 **dern** wild, drear   15 **painful** toilsome   15 **perch** measure of land
17 **opposing coigns** opposite corners   21 **stead** be of use to   22
Fame . . . inquire Rumor having responded to inquiries in the most
distant regions (?)   32 **dooms** judgments   33 **sum** gist   35 **Y-rav-**
ishèd enraptured   36 **can** began (a Middle English variant of "gan")
36 **sound** proclaim, declare   39 **Brief** in short

40 His queen with child makes her desire—
  Which who shall cross?—along to go.
  Omit we all their dole° and woe.
  Lychorida, her nurse, she takes,
  And so to sea. Their vessel shakes
45 On Neptune's billow; half the flood
  Hath their keel cut;° but Fortune's mood
  Varies again: the grislèd° north
  Disgorges such a tempest forth
  That, as a duck for life that dives,
50 So up and down the poor ship drives.
  The lady shrieks and, well-a-near,°
  Does fall in travail with her fear;
  And what ensues in this fell storm
  Shall for itself itself perform.
55 I nill° relate, action° may
  Conveniently the rest convey;
  Which might not what by me is told.
  In your imagination hold
  This stage the ship, upon whose deck
60 The sea-tossed Pericles appears to speak.   *[Exit.*

[Scene I.]

Enter Pericles, a-shipboard.

Pericles. The god of this great vast° rebuke these
  surges,

42 **dole** grief 45–46 **half . . . cut** i.e., half the voyage has been
completed 47 **grislèd** horrible, grisly 51 **well-a-near** alas 55 **nill**
will not (Middle English) 55 **action** (here pronounced as a trisyllable) III.i.1 **vast** boundless expanse

Which wash both heaven and hell; and thou that
  hast
Upon the winds command, bind them in brass,
Having called them from the deep! O, still
Thy deaf'ning dreadful thunders; gently quench   *5*
Thy nimble° sulphurous flashes! O, how, Lychorida,
How does my queen? Thou stormest venomously;
Wilt thou spit all thyself? The seaman's whistle
Is as a whisper in the ears of death,
Unheard. Lychorida!—Lucina,° O   *10*
Divinest patroness and midwife gentle
To those that cry by night, convey thy deity
Aboard our dancing boat; make swift the pangs
Of my queen's travails! Now, Lychorida!

      Enter Lychorida [with an infant].

Lychorida. Here is a thing too young for such a place, *15*
  Who, if it had conceit,° would die, as I
  Am like to do. Take in your arms this piece
  Of your dead queen.

Pericles.   How? How, Lychorida?

Lychorida. Patience, good sir; do not assist the storm.
  Here's all that is left living of your queen— *20*
  A little daughter. For the sake of it
  Be manly, and take comfort.

Pericles.   O you gods!
  Why do you make us love your goodly gifts,
  And snatch them straight away? We here below
  Recall not what we give, and therein may *25*
  Vie honor with you.°

Lychorida.   Patience, good sir,
  Even for this charge.°

Pericles.   Now, mild may be thy life!
  For a more blusterous birth had never babe;

6 **nimble** swift 10 **Lucina** the goddess of childbirth 16 **conceit**
capacity to understand 26 **Vie honor with you** compete with you
in respect of honor 27 **Even for this charge** for the sake of the
babe left in your care

Quiet and gentle thy conditions! For
30 Thou art the rudeliest welcome to this world
That ever was prince's child. Happy what follows!
Thou hast as chiding a nativity
As fire, air, water, earth and heaven can make,
To herald thee from the womb. Even at the first
35 Thy loss is more than can thy portage quit,°
With all thou canst find here. Now the good gods
Throw their best eyes upon't!

Enter two Sailors.

First Sailor. What courage, sir? God save you!

Pericles. Courage enough. I do not fear the flaw:°
40 It hath done to me the worst. Yet, for the love
Of this poor infant, this fresh,° new seafarer,
I would it would be quiet.

First Sailor. Slack the bolins° there! Thou wilt not,
wilt thou? Blow, and split thyself!

45 *Second Sailor.* But sea-room, and° the brine and cloudy
billow kiss the moon, I care not.

First Sailor. Sir, your queen must overboard; the sea
works° high, the wind is loud, and will not lie°
till the ship be cleared of the dead.

50 *Pericles.* That's your superstition.

First Sailor. Pardon us, sir; with us at sea it hath been
still° observed; and we are strong in custom.° Therefore briefly° yield her; for she must overboard
straight.

55 *Pericles.* As you think meet. Most wretched queen!

Lychorida. Here she lies, sir.

---

35 than can thy portage quit than your cargo (i.e., all that you are
going to possess in the course of the voyage of life) can compensate
for (?) **39 flaw** gust of wind **41 fresh** raw, inexperienced **43
bolins** ropes from weather-side of square sail to bow **45 and if**
48 works rages **48 lie** subside **52 still** always **52 strong in custom** steadfast in observing customs **53 briefly** quickly

Pericles. A terrible childbed hast thou had, my dear;
　No light, no fire. Th' unfriendly elements
　Forgot thee utterly; nor have I time
　To give thee hallowed to thy grave, but straight   60
　Must cast thee, scarcely coffined, in the ooze;
　Where, for° a monument upon thy bones,
　And e'er-remaining lamps, the belching whale
　And humming water must o'erwhelm thy corpse,
　Lying with simple shells. O Lychorida,   65
　Bid Nestor bring me spices, ink and paper,
　My casket and my jewels; and bid Nicander
　Bring me the satin coffin.° Lay the babe
　Upon the pillow. Hie thee, whiles I say
　A priestly farewell to her. Suddenly,° woman!   70
　　　　　　　　　　　　　[*Exit Lychorida.*]

Second Sailor. Sir, we have a chest beneath the
　hatches,
　Caulked and bitumèd° ready.

Pericles. I thank thee. Mariner, say, what coast is this?

Second Sailor. We are near Tharsus.

Pericles.　　　　　　　　　Thither, gentle mariner,
　Alter thy course for Tyre. When canst thou reach it?   75

Second Sailor. By break of day, if the wind cease.

Pericles. O make for Tharsus!
　There will I visit Cleon, for the babe
　Cannot hold out to Tyrus. There I'll leave it
　At careful° nursing. Go thy ways,° good mariner.   80
　I'll bring the body presently.°　*Exit* [*with Sailors*].

62 for instead of   68 coffin case, box   70 Suddenly at once   72
bitumèd made watertight with bitumen   80 careful full of good
care   80 Go thy ways come along   81 presently immediately

[Scene II. *Ephesus. A room in Cerimon's house.*]

Enter Lord Cerimon with a Servant.

Cerimon. Philemon, ho!

Enter Philemon.

Philemon. Doth my lord call?

Cerimon. Get fire and meat for those poor men:
'T 'as been a turbulent and stormy night.
[*Exit Philemon.*]

5   *Servant.* I have been in many; but such a night as this
Till now I ne'er endured.

Cerimon. Your master will be dead ere you return.
There's nothing can be minist'red to nature
That can recover him. Give this to the 'pothecary,
And tell me how it works.°   [*Exit Servant.*]

Enter two Gentlemen.

10 *First Gentleman.*   Good morrow.

Second Gentleman. Good morrow to your lordship.

Cerimon.   Gentlemen,
Why do you stir so early?

First Gentleman. Sir,
Our lodgings, standing bleak upon the sea,
15   Shook as the earth did quake;
The very principals° did seem to rend
And all to topple. Pure surprise and fear
Made me to quit the house.

III.ii.9–10 **Give . . . works** (this prescription must be intended for
someone other than the servant's master)   16 **principals** chief raf-
ters of a house

Second Gentleman. That is the cause we trouble you
    so early;
  'Tis not our husbandry.°

Cerimon.   O, you say well.   20

First Gentleman. But I much marvel that your lord-
    ship, having
  Rich tire° about you, should at these early hours
  Shake off the golden slumber of repose.
  'Tis most strange,
  Nature should be so conversant with pain,°   25
  Being thereto not compelled.

Cerimon.   I held it ever
  Virtue and cunning° were endowments greater
  Than nobleness° and riches: careless heirs
  May the two latter darken and expend,
  But immortality attends° the former,   30
  Making a man a god. 'Tis known, I ever
  Have studied physic, through which secret art,
  By turning o'er authorities, I have,
  Together with my practice, made familiar
  To me and to my aid° the blest infusions   35
  That dwells in vegetives,° in metals, stones;
  And I can speak of the disturbances
  That nature works, and of her cures; which gives
    me
  A more° content in course of true delight
  Than to be thirsty after tottering honor,   40
  Or tie my treasure up in silken bags,
  To please the Fool and Death.°

Second Gentleman. Your honor has through Ephesus
    poured forth
  Your charity, and hundreds call themselves
  Your creatures, who by you have been restored;   45

20 **husbandry** zeal for work   22 **tire** belongings   25 **pain** trouble,
labor   27 **cunning** skill   28 **nobleness** nobility (i.e., social rank)
30 **attends** awaits   35 **my aid** my assistant (?)   36 **vegetives** vege-
tables, herbs   39 **more** greater   42 **the Fool and Death** (probably
an allusion to the Dance of Death, in which these two figures often
appeared as companions)

And not° your knowledge, your personal pain,° but
    even
Your purse, still° open, hath built Lord Cerimon
Such strong renown as time shall never raze.

Enter two or three [Servants] with a chest.

First Servant. So; lift there!

Cerimon.   What's that?

First Servant.   Sir, even now
50   Did the sea toss up upon our shore this chest.
'Tis of some wrack.

Cerimon.   Set't down, let's look upon't.

Second Gentleman. 'Tis like a coffin, sir.

Cerimon.   Whate'er it be,
'Tis wondrous heavy. Wrench it open straight.°
If the sea's stomach be o'ercharged with gold,
55   'Tis a good constraint of fortune
It belches upon us.°

Second Gentleman.   'Tis so, my lord.

Cerimon. How close 'tis caulked and bitumed!
    Did the sea cast it up?

First Servant. I never saw so huge a billow, sir,
    As tossed it upon shore.

60   *Cerimon.*   Wrench it open: soft! It smells
Most sweetly in my sense.

Second Gentleman.   A delicate odor.

Cerimon. As ever hit my nostril. So; up with it!
    O you most potent gods! What's here, a corse!

Second Gentleman. Most strange!

Cerimon.   Shrouded in cloth of state;°

---

46 **not** not only   46 **pain** trouble   47 **still** always   53 **straight im-**
mediately   56 **It belches upon us** that it belches this chest upon us
64 **cloth of state** magnificent fabric

Balmed,° and entreasured with full bags of spices!   65
A passport too! Apollo, perfect me°
In the characters!°   [*Reads from a scroll.*]

> Here I give to understand,
> If e'er this coffin drives a-land,
> I, King Pericles, have lost   70
> This queen, worth all our mundane cost.°
> Who finds her, give her burying;
> She was the daughter of a king.
> Besides this treasure for a fee,
> The gods requite his charity!   75

If thou livest, Pericles, thou hast a heart
That even cracks for woe! This chanced tonight.°

Second Gentleman. Most likely, sir.

Cerimon.   Nay, certainly tonight;
For look how fresh she looks! They were too rough
That threw her in the sea. Make a fire within.   80
Fetch hither all my boxes in my closet.
                        [*Exit Servant.*]
Death may usurp on nature° many hours,
And yet the fire of life kindle again
The o'erpressed spirits. [I have read
Of some Egyptians, who after four hours' death   85
Have raised impoverished° bodies, like to this,
Unto their former health.]°

    Enter one [*Servant*] *with napkins and fire.*

                        Well said,° well said;
The fire and cloths.°
The still and woeful music that we have,
Cause it to sound, beseech you. [*Music.*]   90
The viol once more! How thou stirr'st,° thou block!

55 **Balmed** anointed with fragrant oil   66 **perfect me** instruct me
fully   67 **characters** writing (the stress falls here on the second syl-
able)   71 **mundane cost** wordly riches   77 **tonight** last night   82
nature man's physical constitution   84–87 (see Introduction, p.
xxiii)   86 **impoverished** deprived of their native strength   87 **Well
said** well done   88 **cloths** napkins   91 **How thou stirr'st** how quick
you are! (used ironically)

The music there! [*Music*.] I pray you, give her air.
Gentlemen,
This queen will live: nature° awakes; a warmth
Breathes out of her. She hath not been entranced°
Above five hours. See how she 'gins to blow°
Into life's flower again!

First Gentleman.   The heavens
Through you increase our wonder, and sets up
Your fame forever.

Cerimon.   She is alive! Behold,
Her eyelids, cases to those heavenly jewels
Which Pericles hath lost, begin to part
Their fringes of bright gold; the diamonds
Of a most praisèd water° doth appear
To make the world twice rich. Live,
And make us weep to hear your fate, fair creature,
Rare as you seem to be.   *She moves.*

Thaisa.   O dear Diana,
Where am I? Where's my lord? What world is this?

Second Gentleman. Is not this strange?

First Gentleman.   Most rare!

Cerimon.   Hush, my gentle neighbors!
Lend me your hands; to the next chamber bear her.
Get linen. Now this matter must be looked to,
For her relapse is mortal.° Come, come;
And Aesculapius° guide us!
        They carry her away. Exeunt Omnes.°

---

94 nature the vital powers   **95 entranced** in a swoon   **96 blow**
bloom   **103 water** luster   **111 is mortal** would be fatal   **112 Aescu-
lapius** Greek god of medicine   **112 s.d. Omnes** all (Latin)

[Scene III. *Tharsus*.]

Enter Pericles at Tharsus with Cleon and Dionyza,
[and Lychorida with Marina in her arms].

Pericles. Most honored Cleon, I must needs be gone:
My twelve months are expired, and Tyrus stands
In a litigious° peace. You and your lady,
Take from my heart all thankfulness! The gods
Make up the rest upon you!

Cleon.   Your shafts of fortune,   *5*
Though they hurt you mortally, yet glance
Full° woundingly on us.

Dionyza.   O your sweet queen!
That the strict fates had pleased you had brought
  her hither
To have blest mine eyes with her!

Pericles.   We cannot but
Obey the powers above us. Could I rage   *10*
And roar as doth the sea she lies in, yet
The end must be as 'tis. My gentle babe,
Marina, whom, for° she was born at sea,
I have named so, here I charge
Your charity withal,° leaving her   *15*
The infant of your care; beseeching you
To give her princely training, that she may
Be mannered as she is born.

Cleon.   Fear not, my lord, but think
Your Grace, that fed my country with your corn,
For which the people's prayers still fall upon you,   *20*
Must in your child be thought on. If neglection°

III.iii.3 **litigious** productive of contention   7 **full** very   13 **for** because   15 **withal** with   21 **neglection** neglect

Should therein make me vile, the common body,°
By you relieved, would force me to my duty.
But if to that my nature need a spur,
25 The gods revenge it upon me and mine,
To the end of generation!°

Pericles.   I believe you.
Your honor and your goodness teach me to't,
Without your vows. Till she be married, madam,
By bright Diana, whom we honor all,
30 Unscissored shall this hair of mine remain,
Though I show ill in't. So I take my leave.
Good madam, make me blessèd in your care
In bringing up my child.

Dionyza.   I have one myself,
Who shall not be more dear to my respect°
Than yours, my lord.

35 *Pericles.*   Madam, my thanks and prayers.

Cleon. We'll bring your Grace e'en to the edge o' th'
      shore,
Then give you up to the masked° Neptune and
The gentlest winds of heaven.

Pericles.   I will embrace
Your offer. Come, dearest madam. O, no tears,
40 Lychorida, no tears!
Look to your little mistress, on whose grace°
You may depend hereafter. Come, my lord.

                                   [*Exeunt.*]

---

22 **common body** common people   26 **To the end of generation**
i.e., until the human race ceases to procreate (?)   34 **respect** care
37 **masked** deceptively calm (?)   41 **grace** favor

[Scene IV. *Ephesus*.]

Enter Cerimon and Thaisa.

Cerimon. Madam, this letter, and some certain jewels,
 Lay with you in your coffer; which are
 At your command. Know you the character?°

Thaisa. It is my lord's. That I was shipped at sea
 I well remember, even on my eaning time;°   *5*
 But whether there delivered, by the holy gods,
 I cannot rightly say. But since King Pericles,
 My wedded lord, I ne'er shall see again,
 A vestal livery will I take me to,°
 And never more have joy.   *10*

Cerimon. Madam, if this you purpose as ye speak,
 Diana's temple is not distant far,
 Where you may abide till your date° expire.
 Moreover, if you please, a niece of mine
 Shall there attend you.   *15*

Thaisa. My recompense is thanks, that's all;
 Yet my good will is great, though the gift small.
         Exit [*with Cerimon*].

III.iv.3 **character** handwriting 5 **eaning time** time of childbirth
9 **A vestal . . . to** i.e., I will live the life of a vestal virgin 13 **date**
term of life

[ACT IV]

Enter Gower.

Gower. Imagine Pericles arrived at Tyre,
    Welcomed and settled to his own desire.
    His woeful queen we leave at Ephesus,
    Unto Diana there's° a votaress.
5   Now to Marina bend your mind,
    Whom our fast-growing scene must find
    At Tharsus, and by Cleon trained
    In music's letters;° who hath gained
    Of education all the grace,
10   Which makes her both the heart and place°
    Of general wonder. But, alack,
    That monster, Envy, oft the wrack°
    Of earnèd praise, Marina's life
    Seeks to take off by treason's° knife.
15   And in this kind:° Our Cleon hath
    One daughter, and a full grown wench,
    Even ripe for marriage rite. This maid
    Hight° Philoten; and it is said
    For certain in our story, she
20   Would ever with Marina be.

IV.4 **there's** there as   8 **music's letters** the study of music   10 **place**
dwelling   12 **wrack** ruin   14 **treason's** treachery's   15 **in this kind**
in the following way   18 **hight** is named

Be't when she weaved the sleided° silk
With fingers long, small,° white as milk;
Or when she would with sharp needle° wound
The cambric, which she made more sound
By hurting it; or when to th' lute   25
She sung, and made the night-bird° mute,
That still records with moan;° or when
She would with rich and constant pen
Vail° to her mistress Dian; still
This Philoten contends in skill   30
With absolute° Marina: so
With dove of Paphos° might the crow
Vie° feathers white. Marina gets
All praises, which are paid as debts,
And not as given. This so darks°   35
In Philoten all graceful marks
That Cleon's wife, with envy rare,
A present° murderer does prepare°
For good Marina, that her daughter
Might stand peerless by this slaughter.   40
The sooner her vile thoughts to stead,°
Lychorida, our nurse, is dead;
And cursèd Dionyza hath
The pregnant° instrument of wrath
Prest° for this blow. The unborn event°   45
I do commend to your content;°
Only I carry wingèd time
Post° on the lame feet of my rhyme;
Which never could I so convey
Unless your thoughts went on my way.   50
Dionyza does appear,
With Leonine, a murderer.   *Exit.*

21 **sleided** (a variant of "sleaved," i.e., divided into filaments)
22 **small** slender   23 **needle** (here pronounced as a monosyllable)
26 **night-bird** nightingale   27 **still records with moan** ever sings
dolefully   29 **Vail** do homage   31 **absolute** free from imperfection
32 **dove of Paphos** Venus' dove   33 **Vie** compete in respect of
35 **darks** darkens, puts in the shade   38 **present** speedy   38 **prepare**
provide   41 **stead** aid   44 **pregnant** disposed, inclined   45 **Prest**
ready   45 **event** outcome   46 **commend to your content** commend
to you, hoping that it will please you   48 **Post** in post haste

[Scene I. *Tharsus, near the seashore.*]

Enter Dionyza with Leonine.

Dionyza. Thy oath remember; thou hast sworn to do't.
'Tis but a blow, which never shall be known.
Thou canst not do a thing in the world so soon
To yield thee so much profit. Let not conscience,
5 Which is but cold, or flaming love thy bosom
Enslave too nicely;° nor let pity, which
Even women have cast off, melt thee, but be
A soldier to° thy purpose.

Leonine. I will do't. But yet she is a goodly creature!

10 *Dionyza.* The fitter then the gods should have her.
Here she comes weeping° her old nurse's death!
Thou art resolved?

Leonine.   I am resolved.

Enter Marina with a basket of flowers.

Marina. No, I will rob Tellus° of her weed°
To strew thy green° with flowers; the yellows, blues,
15 The purple violets, and marigolds,
Shall as a carpet° hang upon thy grave,
While summer days doth last. Ay me, poor maid,
Born in a tempest, when my mother died,
This world to me is as a lasting storm,
20 Whirring° me from my friends.°

Dionyza. How now, Marina, why do you keep alone?
How chance my daughter is not with you?

IV.i.6 **nicely** scrupulously   8 **A soldier to** wholly devoted to   11
weeping lamenting   13 **Tellus** the earth   13 **weed** garment (of flowers)   14 **green** i.e., the green turf of Lychorida's grave   16 **carpet**
piece of tapestry   20 **Whirring** whirling, hurrying along   20 **friends**
relations

Do not consume your blood with sorrowing.°
Have you a nurse of me! Lord, how your favor°
Is changed with this unprofitable woe!   25
Come, give me your flowers.
On the sea margent walk with Leonine.
The air is quick° there and it pierces, and
Sharpens the stomach. Come, Leonine, take
Her by the arm, walk with her.

Marina.   No, I pray you.   30
I'll not bereave you of your servant.

Dionyza.   Come, come!
I love the King your father and yourself
With more than foreign° heart. We every day
Expect him here. When he shall come, and find
Our paragon to all reports° thus blasted,   35
He will repent the breadth° of his great voyage;
Blame both my lord and me, that we have taken
No care to your best courses.° Go, I pray you,
Walk, and be cheerful once again; reserve°
That excellent complexion, which did steal   40
The eyes of young and old. Care not for me;
I can go home alone.

Marina.   Well, I will go;
But yet I have no desire to it.

Dionyza.   Come, come,
I know 'tis good for you.
Walk half an hour, Leonine, at the least.   45
Remember what I have said.

Leonine.   I warrant° you, madam.

Dionyza. I'll leave you, my sweet lady, for a while.
Pray, walk softly,° do not heat your blood. What!
I must have care of you.

---

23 Do . . . sorrowing (alluding to the ancient notion that each sigh
takes a drop of blood from the heart) **24 favor** face, looks
28 quick sharp **33 foreign** not of one's family **35 to all reports**
according to all reports **36 breadth** extent **38 to your best courses**
to what was best for you **39 reserve** preserve, guard **46 warrant**
promise **48 softly** slowly

Marina.   My thanks, sweet madam.
                                        [*Exit Dionyza.*]
    Is this wind westerly that blows?

50 *Leonine.*   Southwest.

Marina. When I was born the wind was north.

Leonine.   Was't so?

Marina. My father, as nurse says, did never fear,
    But cried "Good seamen!" to the sailors, galling°
    His kingly hands haling ropes;
55   And, clasping° to the mast, endured a sea
    That almost burst the deck.

Leonine.   When was this?

Marina. When I was born.
    Never was waves nor wind more violent;
    And from the ladder-tackle washes off
60   A canvas-climber.° "Ha!" says one, "wolt° out?"
    And with a dropping° industry they skip
    From stem to stern; the boatswain whistles, and
    The master calls and trebles their confusion.

Leonine. Come, say your prayers!

65 *Marina.* What mean you?

Leonine. If you require a little space for prayer,
    I grant it. Pray; but be not tedious, for
    The gods are quick of ear, and I am sworn
    To do my work with haste.

Marina.   Why will you kill me?

70 *Leonine.* To satisfy my lady.

Marina. Why would she have me killed?
    Now, as° I can remember, by my troth,
    I never did her hurt in all my life.

---

53 **galling** making sore by chafing   55 **clasping** clinging   60 **canvas-climber** sailor climbing aloft to trim sails   60 **wolt** wilt   61 **dropping** dripping wet   72 **as** as far as

I never spake bad word nor did ill turn
To any living creature. Believe me, la,°   *75*
I never killed a mouse, nor hurt a fly;
I trod upon a worm against my will,
But I wept for't. How have I offended,
Wherein my death might yield her any profit,
Or my life imply her any danger?   *80*

Leonine. My commission
Is not to reason of the deed, but do't.

Marina. You will not do't for all the world, I hope.
You are well-favored,° and your looks foreshow
You have a gentle heart. I saw you lately,   *85*
When you caught hurt in parting two that fought.
Good sooth,° it showed well in you. Do so now.
Your lady seeks my life: come you between,
And save poor me, the weaker!

Leonine.   I am sworn,
And will dispatch.   [*Seizes her.*]

Enter Pirates.

First Pirate.   Hold, villain!
                             [*Leonine runs away.*]

Second Pirate.   A prize! A prize!   *90*

Third Pirate. Half-part,° mates, half-part! Come, let's
have her aboard suddenly.°
                          [*They carry off Marina.*]

Enter Leonine.

Leonine. These roguing° thieves serve the great pirate
    Valdes,
And they have seized Marina. Let her go;
There's no hope° she'll return. I'll swear she's
    dead,   *95*
And thrown into the sea. But I'll see further:

---

75 **la** (exclamation to emphasize a statement)   84 **well-favored**
good-looking   87 **good sooth** truly   91 **Half-part** go shares   92
suddenly at once   93 **roguing** vagrant   95 **hope** i.e., fear

Perhaps they will but please themselves upon her,
Not carry her aboard. If she remain,
Whom they have ravished must by me be slain.

Exit.

[Scene II. *Mytilene. In front of a brothel.*]

*Enter the three Bawds [i.e. a Pander, his servant
Boult, and a Bawd].*

Pander. Boult!

Boult. Sir?

Pander. Search the market narrowly! Mytilene is full
of gallants. We lost too much money this mart° by
being too wenchless.

Bawd. We were never so much out of creatures. We
have but poor three, and they can do no more than
they can do; and they with continual action are
even as good as rotten.

Pander. Therefore let's have fresh ones, whate'er we
pay for them. If there be not a conscience to be
used in every trade, we shall never prosper.

Bawd. Thou say'st true: 'tis not our bringing up of
poor bastards—as, I think, I have brought up some
eleven—

Boult. Ay, to eleven;° and brought them down again.°
But shall I search the market?

IV.ii.4 **mart** market-time   16 **to eleven** up to the age of eleven
16 **brought them down again** i.e., by prostituting them

Bawd. What else, man? The stuff° we have, a strong
wind will blow it to pieces, they are so pitifully
sodden.° 20

Pander. Thou sayest true; they're too unwholesome,
o' conscience.° The poor Transylvanian is dead that
lay with the little baggage.

Boult. Ay, she quickly pooped° him; she made him
roast meat for worms. But I'll go search the market. 25
Exit.

Pander. Three or four thousand chequins° were as
pretty a proportion° to live quietly, and so give
over.°

Bawd. Why to give over, I pray you? Is it a shame
to get° when we are old? 30

Pander. O, our credit° comes not in like the commodity,° nor the commodity wages not° with the
danger. Therefore, if in our youths we could pick
up some pretty estate, 'twere not amiss to keep our
door hatched.° Besides, the sore terms we stand 35
upon with the gods will be strong with us for giving o'er.

Bawd. Come, other sorts° offend as well as we.

Pander. As well as we? Ay, and better too; we offend
worse. Neither is our profession any trade;° it's no 40
calling. But here comes Boult.

Enter Boult, with the Pirates and Marina.

Boult. Come your ways,° my masters! You say she's
a virgin?

---

18 **stuff** goods for sale   20 **sodden** grown rotten by soaking (referring to the treatment of venereal disease by means of the sweating
tub)   22 **o' conscience** on my conscience   24 **pooped** foundered
(?)   26 **chequins** sequins, Italian gold coins   27 **proportion** portion,
share   28 **give over** give up, retire   30 **get** acquire money   31
credit reputation   32 **commodity** profit   32 **wages not** is not com-
mensurate   35 **hatched** with the hatch (the lower half of a divided
door) shut   38 **sorts** classes of people   40 **trade** recognized business   42 **Come your ways** come along

First Pirate. O, sir, we doubt it not.

45 *Boult.* Master, I have gone through° for this piece°
you see. If you like her, so; if not, I have lost my
earnest.°

Bawd. Boult, has she any qualities?°

Boult. She has a good face, speaks well, and has ex-
50 cellent good clothes. There's no farther necessity of
qualities can° make her be refused.

Bawd. What's her price, Boult?

Boult. It cannot be bated° one doit° of a thousand
pieces.

55 *Pander.* Well, follow me, my masters; you shall have
your money presently.° Wife, take her in. Instruct
her what she has to do, that she may not be raw°
in her entertainment.°

[*Exeunt Pander and Pirates.*]

Bawd. Boult, take you the marks of her, the color of
60 her hair, complexion, height, her age, with warrant
of her virginity; and cry "He that will give most
shall have her first!" Such a maidenhead were no
cheap thing, if men were as they have been. Get
this done as I command you.

65 *Boult.* Performance shall follow.   *Exit.*

Marina. Alack that Leonine was so slack, so slow!
He should have struck, not spoke; or that these
pirates,
Not enough barbarous, had not o'erboard
Thrown me to seek my mother!

70 *Bawd.* Why lament you, pretty one?

---

45 gone through completed the process of bargaining (?)   45 piece
girl   47 earnest money given as a deposit   48 qualities accomplishments   51 can that can   53 bated reduced   53 doit smallest coin,
worth half a farthing   56 presently immediately   57 raw inexperienced   58 entertainment manner of reception

Marina. That I am pretty.

Bawd. Come, the gods have done their part in you.

Marina. I accuse them not.

Bawd. You are light° into my hands, where you are   *73*
like to live.

Marina. The more my fault
To 'scape his hands where I was like to die.

Bawd. Ay, and you shall live in pleasure.

Marina. No.

Bawd. Yes, indeed shall you, and taste gentlemen of   *80*
all fashions. You shall fare well: you shall have the
difference° of all complexions.° What° do you stop
your ears?

Marina. Are you a woman?

Bawd. What would you have me be, and° I be not a   *85*
woman?

Marina. An honest° woman, or not a woman.

Bawd. Marry,° whip thee, gosling!° I think I shall
have something to do with you.° Come, you're a
young foolish sapling, and must be bowed as I   *90*
would have you.

Marina. The gods defend me!

Bawd. If it please the gods to defend you by men,
then men must comfort you, men must feed you,
men stir you up.° Boult's returned.   *95*

[*Enter Boult.*]

Now, sir, hast thou cried° her through the market?

---

74 **are light** have fallen   82 **difference** variety   82 **complexions** colors of skin, i.e., men of every race   82 **What** why   85 **and** if
87 **honest** chaste   88 **Marry** (interjection expressing indignation)
88 **whip thee, gosling** hang thee, greenhorn   89 **have . . . you** have
trouble with you   95 **stir you up** excite you   96 **cried** (1) advertised
by loud cries (2) extolled

Boult. I have cried her almost to the number of her
hairs;° I have drawn her picture with my voice.

Bawd. And I prithee tell me, how dost thou find the
100   inclination of the people, especially of the younger
sort?

Boult. Faith, they listened to me as they would have
hearkened to their father's testament. There was a
Spaniard's mouth wat'red and° he went to bed to
105   her very description.

Bawd. We shall have him here tomorrow with his
best ruff on.

Boult. Tonight, tonight. But, mistress, do you know
the French knight that cowers i' the hams?

110   *Bawd.* Who, Monsieur Veroles?°

Boult. Ay, he: he offered° to cut a caper at the
proclamation; but he made a groan at it, and
swore he would see her tomorrow.

Bawd. Well, well; as for him, he brought his disease
115   hither. Here he does but repair° it. I know he will
come in our shadow,° to scatter his crowns of the
sun.°

Boult. Well, if we had of every nation a traveler, we
should lodge them with this sign.°

120   *Bawd.* [*To Marina*] Pray you, come hither awhile.
You have fortunes coming upon you. Mark me:
you must seem to do that fearfully which you
commit willingly; despise profit where you have
most gain. To weep that you live as ye do makes
125   pity in your lovers: seldom but that pity begets
you a good opinion, and that opinion a mere°
profit.

97–98 **almost . . . hairs** any number of times   104 **and** as if   110
Veroles (from French *vérole*=pox)   111 **offered** attempted   115 **repair** renew   116 **shadow** shelter   116–17 **crowns of the sun** French
gold coins   119 **this sign** i.e., Marina's charms   126 **mere** downright

Marina. I understand you not.

Boult. O, take her home,° mistress, take her home!
These blushes of hers must be quenched with some   130
present° practice.

Bawd. Thou sayest true, i' faith, so they must. For
your bride goes to that with shame which is her
way to go with warrant.°

Boult. Faith, some do, and some do not. But, mistress,   135
if I have bargained for the joint—

Bawd. Thou mayest cut a morsel off the spit.

Boult. I may so?

Bawd. Who should deny it? Come, young one, I like
the manner of your garments well.   140

Boult. Ay, by my faith, they shall not be changed
yet.

Bawd. Boult, spend thou that in the town. Report
what a sojourner we have: you'll lose nothing by
custom.° When nature framed° this piece, she   145
meant thee a good turn. Therefore say what a
paragon she is, and thou hast the harvest out of
thine own report.

Boult. I warrant you, mistress, thunder shall not so
awake the beds of eels° as my giving out her   150
beauty stirs up the lewdly inclined. I'll bring home
some tonight.

Bawd. Come your ways! Follow me.

Marina. If fires be hot, knives sharp, or waters deep,
Untied I still my virgin knot will keep.   155
Diana aid my purpose!

---

129 **take her home** tell her your mind (?)   131 **present** immediate
133–34 **which . . . warrant** to which she is entitled to go   145 **by
custom** i.e., by our getting customers   145 **framed** shaped   149–50
thunder . . . eels (thunder was supposed to rouse eels from the mud)

Bawd. What have we to do with Diana? Pray you,
  will you go with us?   *Exit [with the rest].*

[Scene III. *Tharsus.*]

Enter Cleon and Dionyza.

Dionyza. Why are you foolish? Can it be undone?

Cleon. O Dionyza, such a piece of slaughter
  The sun and moon ne'er looked upon!

Dionyza. I think you'll turn a child again.

5 *Cleon.* Were I chief lord of all this spacious world,
  I'd give it to undo the deed. A lady
  Much less in blood than virtue,° yet a princess
  To equal any single crown o' th' earth
  I' th' justice of compare!° O villain Leonine!
10 Whom thou hast pois'ned too.
  If thou hadst drunk to him,° 't had been a kind-
    ness°
  Becoming° well thy fact.° What canst thou say
  When noble Pericles shall demand his child?

Dionyza. That she is dead. Nurses are not the fates°

. . . .

IV.iii.7 **Much . . . virtue** even more so in point of virtue than of
descent   9 **I' th' justice of compare** in a just comparison   11 **If . . .
him** i.e., if thou hadst poisoned thyself in pledging him   11 **a kindness** (1) a kind action (2) an appropriate action   12 **Becoming** be-
fitting   12 **fact** deed   14 **fates** (a line seems to have dropped out
here, to the effect that the nurse's power over human life is merely
"To foster it . . .")

To foster it, not ever to preserve.   15
She died at night. I'll say so. Who can cross° it?
Unless you play the pious innocent,
And for an honest attribute° cry out
"She died by foul play."

Cleon.   O, go to.° Well, well.
Of all the faults beneath the heavens the gods   20
Do like this worst.

Dionyza.   Be one of those that thinks
The petty wrens of Tharsus will fly hence
And open this to Pericles.° I do shame
To think of what a noble strain you are,
And of how coward a spirit.

Cleon.   To such proceeding   25
Whoever but his approbation added,
Though not his prime° consent, he did not flow°
From honorable sources.

Dionyza.   Be it so, then.
Yet none does know but you how she came dead,
Nor none can know, Leonine being gone.   30
She did distain° my child, and stood between
Her and her fortunes: none would look on her,
But cast their gazes on Marina's face;
Whilst ours was blurted at,° and held a malkin,°
Not worth the time of day.° It pierced me thorough; 35
And though you call my course unnatural,
You not your child well loving, yet I find
It greets° me as an enterprise of kindness°
Performed to your sole daughter.

Cleon.   Heavens forgive it!

Dionyza. And as for Pericles, what should he say?   40

16 **cross** contradict   18 **an honest attribute** the reputation of honesty   19 **go to** (an expression of disapproval)   22–23 **The petty . . . Pericles** (an allusion to the popular belief in the revelation of hidden murders by a telltale bird)   27 **prime** initial   27 **flow** issue   31 **distain** cast a slur on   34 **blurted at** treated with scorn   34 **malkin** slut   35 **the time of day** a greeting   38 **greets me** presents itself to me   38 **kindness** love

We wept after her hearse, and yet we mourn.
Her monument°
Is almost finished, and her epitaphs
In glitt'ring golden characters° express
45   A general praise to her, and care in us
At whose expense 'tis done.

Cleon.   Thou art like the harpy,
Which, to betray, dost, with thine angel's face,
Seize with thine eagle's talents.°

Dionyza. Ye're like one that superstitiously
50   Do swear to th' gods that winter kills the flies.°
But yet I know you'll do as I advise.   [*Exeunt.*]

[Scene IV. *Before Marina's monument at Tharsus.*

Enter Gower.]

Gower. Thus time we waste,° and long leagues make
       short;
Sail seas in cockles,° have and wish but for't;°
Making,° to take° our imagination,
From bourn to bourn,° region to region.
5   By you being pardoned, we commit no crime

42 **monument** (probably a few words, such as "which stands i' the market-place," have here dropped out) 44 **characters** letters 47–48 **dost . . . talents** i.e., dost, while smiling at thy victim with thine angel's face, seize it with thine eagle's talents (a common variant of talons) 49–50 **Ye're . . . flies** i.e., you are so much afraid of divine vengeance that you even swear to the gods that it is not you but winter which is guilty of the death of flies IV.iv.1 **waste** annihilate 2 **cockles** cockleshells 2 **have . . . for't** have by merely wishing for it 3 **Making** making our way 3 **take** captivate, delight 4 **bourn** frontier

To use one language in each several clime
Where our scene° seems to live. I do beseech you
To learn of me, who stand i' th' gaps to teach you
The stages of our story. Pericles
Is now again thwarting° the wayward seas,   10
Attended on by many a lord and knight,
To see his daughter, all his life's delight.
Old Helicanus goes along. Behind
Is left to govern it, you bear in mind,
Old Escanes, whom Helicanus late°   15
Advanced in Tyre to great and high estate.
Well-sailing ships and bounteous winds have
    brought
This king to Tharsus—think his pilot thought;°
So with his steerage° shall your thoughts go on—
To fetch his daughter home, who first° is gone.   20
Like motes and shadows see them move awhile.
Your ears unto your eyes I'll reconcile.

[Dumb Show]

*Enter Pericles at one door, with all his train;
Cleon and Dionyza at the other. Cleon shows
Pericles the tomb; whereat Pericles makes lamentation, puts on sackcloth, and in a mighty
passion departs. [Then Cleon, Dionyza, and the
rest go also.]*

See how belief may suffer by foul show!°
This borrowed passion° stands for true-owed° woe.
And Pericles, in sorrow all devoured,   25
With sighs shot through and biggest tears o'ershow-
    ered,
Leaves Tharsus and again embarks. He swears
Never to wash his face, nor cut his hairs.
He puts on sackcloth, and to sea. He bears

---

7 **scene** dramatic performance   10 **thwarting** crossing   15 **late** recently   18 **think his pilot thought** think that his pilot is thought
19 **with his steerage** with the course held by Pericles   20 **first** before
him   23 **suffer by foul show** be abused by hypocrisy   24 **borrowed
passion** counterfeit grief   24 **true-owed** sincerely owned

30 A tempest, which his mortal vessel° tears,
    And yet he rides it out.° Now please you wit°
    The epitaph is° for Marina writ
    By wicked Dionyza.
        [*Reads the inscription on Marina's monument.*]

    "The fairest, sweetest, and best lies here,
35   Who withered in her spring of year.
        She was of Tyrus the King's daughter,°
        On whom foul death hath made this slaughter.
        Marina was she called; and at her birth
        Thetis,° being proud, swallowed some part o' th'
            earth.
40   Therefore the earth, fearing to be o'erflowed,
        Hath Thetis' birth-child° on the heavens be-
            stowed;
        Wherefore she° does—and swears she'll never
            stint—
        Make raging battery upon shores of flint."

    No visor° does become black villainy
45 So well as soft and tender flattery.
    Let Pericles believe his daughter's dead,
    And bear his courses to be orderèd°
    By Lady Fortune; while our scene° must play
    His daughter's woe and heavy well-a-day°
50 In her unholy service. Patience, then,
    And think you now are all in Mytilen.   *Exit.*

---

30 **vessel** i.e., his body   31 **he rides it out** i.e., he survives it   31 **wit**
know   32 **is** that is   36 **of Tyrus the King's daughter** daughter of
the King of Tyrus   39 **Thetis** a sea nymph (here, as commonly in
Elizabethan literature, confused with Tethys, wife of Oceanus, hence
the sea personified)   41 **birth-child** person born in a particular
place   42 **she** i.e., the sea   44 **visor** mask, disguise   47 **bear . . .
orderèd** suffer his actions to be regulated   48 **scene** performance
49 **well-a-day** grief

[Scene V. *Mytilene. A street before the brothel.*]

Enter, [from the brothel,] two Gentlemen.

First Gentleman. Did you ever hear the like?

Second Gentleman. No, nor never shall do in such a
place as this, she being once gone.

First Gentleman. But to have divinity preached there!
Did you ever dream of such a thing?   5

Second Gentleman. No, no. Come, I am for no more
bawdy houses. Shall's go hear the vestals° sing?

First Gentleman. I'll do anything now that is virtuous; but I am out of the road of rutting° forever.
                                Exit [with the other].

[Scene VI. *Mytilene. A room in the brothel.*

Enter Pander, Bawd, and Boult.]

Pander. Well, I had rather than twice the worth of
her she had ne'er come here.

Bawd. Fie, fie upon her! She's able to freeze the god

IV.v.7 **vestals** virgin priestesses   9 **rutting** fornication

Priapus,° and undo a whole generation. We must
either get her ravished or be rid of her. When she
should do for clients her fitment° and do me the
kindness of our profession, she has me° her quirks,
her reasons, her master-reasons, her prayers, her
knees; that she would make a puritan of the devil,
if he should cheapen° a kiss of her.

Boult. Faith, I must ravish her, or she'll disfurnish°
us of all our cavalleria° and make our swearers
priests.

Pander. Now, the pox upon her green-sickness° for
me!°

Bawd. Faith, there's no way to be rid on't but by the
way to the pox.° Here comes the Lord Lysimachus
disguised.

Boult. We should have both lord and lown,° if the
peevish baggage would but give way to customers.

Enter Lysimachus.

Lysimachus. How now! How° a dozen of virginities?

Bawd. Now, the gods to-bless° your Honor!

Boult. I am glad to see your Honor in good health.

Lysimachus. You may so; 'tis the better for you that
your resorters stand upon sound legs. How now,
wholesome° iniquity, have you that° a man may
deal withal° and defy the surgeon?

Bawd. We have here one, sir, if she would—but there
never came her like in Mytilene.

IV.vi.4 **Priapus** the classical god of fertility 6 **fitment** duty 6–7 **do
me ... has me** (the "ethical dative," frequently used in narrative by
Shakespeare) 10 **cheapen** bargain for 11 **disfurnish** deprive 12
cavalleria body of gentlemen (Italian) 14 **green-sickness** squeamish-
ness 14–15 **for me** say I 17 **pox** syphilis 19 **lown** loon, lowborn
fellow 21 **to-bless** bless entirely ("to" is an
intensive prefix) 26 **wholesome** health-giving (used ironically)
26 **that** that which 27 **deal withal** have sexual relations with

Lysimachus. If she'd do the deeds of darkness, thou   30
    wouldst say.

Bawd. Your Honor knows what 'tis to say° well
    enough.

Lysimachus. Well, call forth, call forth.

Boult. For flesh and blood, sir, white and red, you   35
    shall see a rose; and she were a rose indeed, if
    she had but—

Lysimachus. What, prithee?

Boult. O, sir, I can be modest.

Lysimachus. That dignifies the renown of a bawd no   40
    less than it gives a good report to a punk to be
    chaste.°   [*Exit Boult.*]

Bawd. Here comes that which grows to° the stalk—
    never plucked yet, I can assure you.

    [*Enter Boult with Marina.*]

    Is she not a fair creature?   45

Lysimachus. Faith, she would serve after a long voy-
    age at sea. Well, there's for you. Leave us.

Bawd. I beseech your Honor, give me leave: a word,
    and I'll have done presently.°

Lysimachus. I beseech you, do.   50

Bawd. [*To Marina*] First, I would have you note, this
    is an honorable man.

Marina. I desire to find him so, that I may worthily
    note° him.

Bawd. Next, he's the governor of this country, and   55
    a man whom I am bound to.

---

32 **what 'tis to say** how to express my meaning   41–42 **it gives . . .
chaste** to be chaste gives a good reputation to a prostitute (the whole
speech is ironic)   43 **grows to** is an integral part of   49 **presently** at
once   54 **note** respect

Marina. If he govern the country, you are bound° to
  him indeed; but how honorable he is in that I
  know not.

60 *Bawd.* Pray you, without any more virginal fencing,
  will you use him kindly? He will line your apron
  with gold.

Marina. What he will do graciously, I will thankfully receive.

65 *Lysimachus.* Ha' you done?

Bawd. My lord, she's not paced° yet; you must take
  some pains to work her to your manage.° Come,
  we will leave his Honor and her together. Go thy
  ways.°   [*Exeunt Bawd, Pander, and Boult.*]

70 *Lysimachus.* Now, pretty one, how long have you
  been at this trade?

Marina. What trade, sir?

Lysimachus. Why, I cannot name't but I shall offend.

Marina. I cannot be offended with my trade. Please
75 you to name it.

Lysimachus. How long have you been of this profession?

Marina. E'er since I can remember.

Lysimachus. Did you go to't° so young? Were you a
80 gamester° at five or at seven?

Marina. Earlier too, sir, if now I be one.

Lysimachus. Why, the house you dwell in proclaims
  you to be a creature of sale.

Marina. Do you know this house to be a place of
85 such resort, and will come into't? I hear say you're

57 bound subject (another example of Marina's "quirks" of which
the bawd complained) **66 paced** taught her paces **67 manage**
action and paces to which a horse is trained **68–69 Go thy ways**
come along **79 go to't** copulate **80 gamester** one addicted to
amorous sport

of honorable parts and are the governor of this
place.

Lysimachus. Why, hath your principal° made known
    unto you who I am?

Marina. Who is my principal?   *90*

Lysimachus. Why, your herb-woman; she that sets
    seeds and roots of shame and iniquity. O, you have
    heard something of my power, and so stand aloof
    for more serious wooing. But I protest to thee,
    pretty one, my authority shall not see thee, or else   *95*
    look friendly upon thee. Come, bring me to some
    private place. Come, come.

Marina. If you were born to honor, show it now;
    If put upon you,° make the judgment good
    That thought you worthy of it.   *100*

Lysimachus. How's this? How's this? Some more;
    be sage.

Marina.   For me,
    That am a maid, though most ungentle fortune
    Have placed me in this sty, where, since I came,
    Diseases have been sold dearer than physic—
    That the gods   *105*
    Would set me free from this unhallowed place,
    Though they did change me to the meanest bird
    That flies i' th' purer air!

Lysimachus.   I did not think
    Thou couldst have spoke so well; ne'er dreamt thou
    couldst.
    Had I brought hither a corrupted mind,   *110*
    Thy speech had altered it. Hold, here's gold for
    thee:
    Persever in that clear° way thou goest,
    And the gods strengthen thee!

Marina.   The good gods preserve you!

---

88 **principal** employer   99 **If put upon you** if honor was bestowed
upon you   112 **clear** free from blame

Lysimachus. For me, be you thoughten°
115   That I came with no ill intent; for to me
    The very doors and windows savor° vilely.
    Fare thee well. Thou art a piece of virtue, and
    I doubt not but thy training hath been noble.
    Hold, here's more gold for thee.
120   A curse upon him, die he like a thief,
    That robs thee of thy goodness! If thou dost
    Hear from me, it shall be for thy good.

[Enter Boult.]

Boult. I beseech your Honor, one piece for me.

Lysimachus. Avaunt,° thou damned doorkeeper!°
125   Your house, but for this virgin that doth prop it,
    Would sink, and overwhelm you. Away!   *[Exit.]*

Boult. How's this? We must take another course with
    you. If your peevish° chastity, which is not worth
    a breakfast in the cheapest country under the
130   cope,° shall undo a whole household, let me be
    gelded like a spaniel. Come your ways.

Marina. Whither would you have me?

Boult. I must have your maidenhead taken off, or
    the common hangman shall execute it.° Come your
135   ways. We'll have no more gentlemen driven away.
    Come your ways, I say.

Enter Bawd.

Bawd. How now! What's the matter?

Boult. Worse and worse, mistress: she has here
    spoken holy words to the Lord Lysimachus.

140 *Bawd.* O abominable!

---

114 For me, be you thoughten (this line, like much else in this scene,
is undoubtedly corrupt, but the true reading seems irrecoverable;
see Introduction, pp. xxiii–vi **116 savor** smell **124 Avaunt** be off
124 doorkeeper pander **128 peevish** refractory **130 cope** sky
133–34 or the . . . execute it (with a play on the "head" of "maidenhead")

Boult. She makes our profession as it were to stink afore the face of the gods.

Bawd. Marry, hang her up forever!

Boult. The nobleman would have dealt with her like a nobleman, and she sent him away as cold as a *145* snowball; saying his prayers too.

Bawd. Boult, take her away! Use her at thy pleasure. Crack the glass of her virginity, and make the rest malleable.

Boult. And if° she were a thornier piece of ground *150* than she is, she shall be ploughed.

Marina. Hark, hark, you gods!

Bawd. She conjures!° Away with her! Would she had never come within my doors! Marry, hang you! She's born to undo us. Will you not go the *155* way of womenkind? Marry come up,° my dish of chastity with rosemary and bays!°   [*Exit.*]

Boult. Come, mistress; come your ways with me.

Marina. Whither wilt thou have me?

Boult. To take from you the jewel you hold so dear. *160*

Marina. Prithee, tell me one thing first.

Boult. Come now, your one thing.

Marina. What canst thou wish thine enemy to be?

Boult. Why, I could wish him to be my master, or, rather, my mistress.   *165*

Marina. Neither of these are so bad as thou art,
Since they do better thee in their command.°
Thou hold'st a place for which the pained'st° fiend

---

150 **And if** even if   153 **conjures** invokes supernatural aid (with the suggestion of black magic)   156 **Marry come up** (an expression of contempt akin to our "hoity-toity")   156–57 **dish . . . bays** (a gibe at Marina's ostentatious virtue; dishes at Christmas were thus garnished)   167 **do better . . . command** are superior to you through their position of authority   168 **pained'st** most tormented

Of hell would not in reputation change.
170   Thou art the damnèd doorkeeper to every
Coistrel° that comes inquiring for his Tib;°
To the choleric fisting° of every rogue
Thy ear is liable; thy food is such
As hath been belched on by infected lungs.

175 *Boult.* What would you have me do? Go to the wars,
would you? Where a man may serve seven years
for the loss of a leg, and have not money enough
in the end to buy him a wooden one?

Marina. Do any thing but this thou doest.° Empty
180   Old receptacles,° or common shores,° of filth;
Serve by indenture° to the common hangman.
Any of these ways are yet better than this.
For what thou professest° a baboon, could he
    speak,
Would own a name too dear.° That the gods
185   Would safely deliver me from this place!
Here, here's gold for thee.
If that thy master would gain by me,
Proclaim that I can sing, weave, sew, and dance,
With other virtues° which I'll keep from boast;
190   And I will undertake all these to teach.
I doubt not but this populous city will
Yield many scholars.

Boult. But can you teach all this you speak of?

Marina. Prove that I cannot, take me home again,
195   And prostitute me to the basest groom°
That doth frequent your house.

Boult. Well, I will see what I can do for thee. If I
can place thee, I will.

---

171 **Coistrel** base fellow   171 **Tib** strumpet   172 **fisting** punching
179 **doest** (pronounced as a disyllable   180 **receptacles** (the stress
here falls on the first syllable)   180 **common shores** i.e., the no-
man's-land by the sea, where filth was allowed to be deposited for
the tide to wash away   181 **by indenture** i.e., as apprentice   183
thou professest you have as an occupation   184 **Would . . . dear**
would claim to possess too high a reputation   189 **virtues** accomplishments   195 **groom** menial

Marina. But amongst honest women?

Boult. Faith, my acquaintance lies little amongst them.   200
But since my master and mistress hath bought you,
there's no going but by their consent. Therefore
I will make them acquainted with your purpose,°
and I doubt not but I shall find them tractable
enough. Come, I'll do for thee what I can; come   203
your ways.   *Exeunt.*

203 **purpose** proposition

[ACT V]

Enter Gower.

Gower. Marina thus the brothel 'scapes, and chances
Into an honest house, our story says.
She sings like one immortal, and she dances
As goddesslike to her admired lays;
Deep clerks° she dumbs, and with her neele°
⁵   composes
Nature's own shape of bud, bird, branch, or berry,
That even her art sisters° the natural roses;
Her inkle,° silk, twin with the rubied cherry;
That pupils lacks she none of noble race,
¹⁰ Who pour their bounty on her; and her gain
She gives the cursèd bawd. Here we her place;
And to her father turn our thoughts again,
Where we left him on the sea. We there him lost;
Whence, driven before the winds, he is arrived
¹⁵ Here where his daughter dwells; and on this coast
Suppose him now at anchor. The city's hived°

God Neptune's annual feast to keep; from whence
Lysimachus our Tyrian ship espies,
His banners sable, trimmed with rich expense;
And to him° in his barge with fervor hies.   20
In your supposing° once more put your sight:
Of heavy° Pericles think this his bark;
Where what is done in action, more, if might,°
Shall be discovered.° Please you, sit and hark.

                                        Exit.

[Scene I. *On board Pericles' ship, off Mytilene.
A pavilion on deck, with a curtain before it;
Pericles within, unkempt and clad in sackcloth,
reclining on a couch.*]

*Enter Helicanus, to him two Sailors, [one be-
longing to the Tyrian vessel, the other of
Mytilene.*]

Tyrian Sailor. Where is Lord Helicanus?
He can resolve° you. O, here he is.
Sir, there is a barge put off from Mytilene,
And in it is Lysimachus, the Governor,
Who craves to come aboard. What is your will?   5

Helicanus. That he have his. Call up some gentlemen.

Tyrian Sailor. Ho, gentlemen! my lord calls.

19–20 **His . . . him** its . . . it   21 **In your supposing** under the guid-
ance of your imagination   22 **heavy** sorrowful   23 **more, if might**
and more if it were possible   24 **discovered** disclosed   **V.i.2 resolve**
free from uncertainty

Enter two or three Gentlemen.

First Gentleman. Doth your lordship call?

Helicanus. Gentlemen, there is some° of worth would
   come aboard.
10   I pray, greet him fairly.°   [*Exeunt the Gentlemen.*]

      Enter Lysimachus [*and Lords, with the
                  Gentlemen*].

Mytilenian Sailor. [*To Lysimachus*] Sir,
   This is the man that can, in aught you would,
   Resolve you.

Lysimachus. Hail, reverend sir! The gods preserve
   you!

15 *Helicanus.* And you, sir, to outlive the age I am,
   And die as I would do.

Lysimachus.   You wish me well.
   Being on shore, honoring of Neptune's triumphs,°
   Seeing this goodly vessel ride before us,
   I made to it, to know of whence you are.

Helicanus. First, what is your place?°

20 *Lysimachus.*   I am the Governor of
   This place you lie before.

Helicanus. Sir,
   Our vessel is of Tyre, in it the King;
   A man who for this three months hath not spoken
25   To anyone, nor taken sustenance
   But to prorogue° his grief.

Lysimachus. Upon what ground is his distemperature?°

Helicanus. 'Twould be too tedious to repeat;
   But the main grief springs from the loss
30   Of a belovèd daughter and a wife.

---

9 some someone   **10 fairly** courteously   **17 triumphs** festivities
20 place official position   **26 prorogue** prolong   **27 distemperature**
mental disturbance

Lysimachus. May we not see him?

Helicanus. You may;
But bootless° is your sight; he will not speak
To any.

Lysimachus.   Yet let me obtain my wish.

Helicanus. [*Draws back the curtain*] Behold him. This
    was a goodly person   35
Till the disaster that, one mortal° night,
Drove him to this.

Lysimachus. Sir King, all hail! The gods preserve
    you!
Hail, royal sir!

Helicanus. It is in vain; he will not speak to you.   40

Lord. Sir,
We have a maid in Mytilene, I durst wager,
Would win some words of him.

Lysimachus.   'Tis well bethought.
She questionless, with her sweet harmony,
And other chosen° attractions, would allure,   45
And make a batt'ry through his deafened ports,°
Which now are midway stopped.
She is all happy as the fairest of all,
And with her fellow maid is now upon
The leafy shelter that abuts against   50
The island's side.

        [*He whispers to a Lord, who leaves.*]

Helicanus. Sure, all° effectless; yet nothing we'll omit
That bears recovery's name. But since your kind-
    ness
We have stretched thus far, let us beseech you
That for our gold we may provision have,   55
Wherein we are not destitute for want,
But weary for the staleness.

33 **bootless** unavailing   36 **mortal** fatal   45 **chosen** choice   46 **ports** inlets   52 **all** entirely

Lysimachus.   O sir, a courtesy
    Which if we should deny, the most just God
    For every graff° would send a caterpillar,
60   And so inflict° our province. Yet once more
    Let me entreat to know at large° the cause
    Of your king's sorrow.

Helicanus. Sit, sir, I will recount it to you.
    But see, I am prevented.°

    [*Enter Lord with Marina and another girl.*]

65 *Lysimachus.* O, here's the lady that I sent for.
    Welcome, fair one! Is't not a goodly presence?°

Helicanus. She's a gallant° lady.

Lysimachus. She's such a one that, were I well
    assured
    Came° of a gentle kind° and noble stock,
    I'd wish no better choice, and think me rarely°
70   wed.
    [*To Marina*] Fair one, all goodness that consists
    in° bounty
    Expect even here, where is a kingly patient.
    If that thy prosperous° and artificial° feat
    Can draw him but to answer thee in aught,
75   Thy sacred physic shall receive such pay
    As thy desires can wish.

Marina.   Sir, I will use
    My utmost skill in his recovery,
    Provided
    That none but I and my companion maid
    Be suffered to come near him.

80 *Lysimachus.*   Come, let us leave her;
    And the gods make her prosperous!

---

59 **graff** graft, grafted plant   60 **inflict** afflict   61 **at large** in full
64 **prevented** forestalled   66 **presence** person   67 **gallant** excellent
69 **Came** she came   69 **kind** family   70 **rarely** splendidly   71 **goodness that consists in** good things that inhere in   73 **prosperous** successful   73 **artificial** skillful

[They withdraw. Marina sings.]

Lysimachus. Marked he your music?

Marina.   No, nor looked on us.

Lysimachus. See, she will speak to him.

Marina. Hail, sir! My lord, lend ear.

Pericles. Hum, ha!   *[He pushes her back.]* 85

Marina. I am a maid,
  My lord, that ne'er before invited eyes,°
  But have been gazed on like a comet. She speaks,
  My lord, that, may be, hath endured a grief
  Might equal yours, if both were justly weighed.   90
  Though wayward fortune did malign° my state,
  My derivation was from ancestors
  Who stood equivalent with mighty kings:
  But time hath rooted out my parentage,
  And to the world and awkward casualties°   95
  Bound me in servitude. *[Aside]* I will desist.
  But there is something glows upon my cheek,
  And whispers in mine ear "Go not till he speak."

Pericles. My fortunes—parentage—good parentage—
  To equal mine—was it not thus? What say you?   100

Marina. I said, my lord, if you did know my par-
    entage,
  You would not do me violence.

Pericles.   I do think so.
  Pray you, turn your eyes upon me.
  You're like something that—what countrywoman?°
  Here of these shores?

Marina.   No, nor of any shores.   105
  Yet I was mortally° brought forth, and am
  No other than I appear.

---

87 **invited eyes** i.e., invited anyone to look at her   91 **malign** treat
malignantly   95 **awkward casualties** adverse chances   104 **what
countrywoman?** of what country?   106 **mortally** humanly

Pericles. I am great° with woe, and shall deliver°
weeping.
My dearest wife was like this maid, and such
My daughter might have been: my queen's square
110   brows;
Her stature to an inch; as wandlike straight;
As silver-voiced; her eyes as jewel-like
And cased° as richly; in pace° another Juno;
Who starves the ears she feeds, and makes them
hungry
The more she gives them speech. Where do you
115   live?

Marina. Where I am but a stranger: from the deck
You may discern the place.

Pericles.   Where were you bred?
And how achieved you these endowments, which
You make more rich to owe?°

120 *Marina.* If I
Should tell my history, it would seem like lies
Disdained in the reporting.°

Pericles.   Prithee, speak.
Falseness cannot come from thee; for thou lookest
Modest as Justice, and thou seemest a palace
For the crowned Truth to dwell in. I will believe
125   thee,
And make my senses credit thy relation
To points that seem impossible; for thou lookest
Like one I loved indeed. What were thy friends?°
Didst thou not say when I did push thee back—
Which was when I perceived thee—that thou
130   cam'st
From good descending?°

Marina.   So indeed I did.

___

108 **great** pregnant   108 **deliver** give birth to   113 **cased** encased
113 **pace** gait   119 **to owe** by owning them   122 **in the reporting**
in the very act of utterance   128 **friends** relations   131 **descending**
lineage

Pericles. Report thy parentage. I think thou said'st
    Thou hadst been tossed from wrong to injury,
    And that thou thought'st thy griefs might equal
      mine,
    If both were opened.°

Marina.   Some such thing I said,   *135*
    And said no more but what my thoughts
    Did warrant me was likely.

Pericles.   Tell thy story.
    If thine, considered, prove the thousandth part
    Of my endurance,° thou art a man, and I
    Have suffered like a girl; yet thou dost look   *140*
    Like Patience gazing on kings' graves, and smiling
    Extremity out of act.° What were thy friends?°
    How lost thou them? Thy name, my most kind
      virgin?
    Recount, I do beseech thee: come, sit by me.

Marina. My name is Marina.

Pericles.   O, I am mocked,   *145*
    And thou by some incensèd god sent hither
    To make the world to laugh at me.

Marina.   Patience, good sir,
    Or here I'll cease.

Pericles.   Nay, I'll be patient.
    Thou little know'st how thou dost startle me
    To call thyself Marina.

Marina.   The name   *150*
    Was given me by one that had some power:
    My father, and a king.

Pericles.   How, a king's daughter?
    And called Marina?

Marina.   You said you would believe me;

---

135 **opened** disclosed   139 **my endurance** what I have endured
142 **Extremity out of** act extreme calamity out of striking (?) extreme despair out of committing suicide (?)   142 **friends** relations

But, not to be a troubler of your peace,
I will end here.

155 *Pericles.*   But are you flesh and blood?
Have you a working pulse, and are no fairy?
Motion° as well? Speak on. Where were you born?
And wherefore called Marina?

Marina.   Called Marina
For I was born at sea.

Pericles.   At sea! What mother?

160 *Marina.* My mother was the daughter of a king;
Who died the minute I was born,
As my good nurse Lychorida hath oft
Delivered° weeping.

Pericles.   O, stop there a little!
This is the rarest dream that e'er dulled sleep
165 Did mock sad fools withal.° This cannot be:
My daughter's buried. Well, where were you bred?
I'll hear you more, to th' bottom of your story,
And never interrupt you.

Marina. You scorn. Believe me, 'twere best I did give
o'er.

170 *Pericles.* I will believe you by the syllable
Of what you shall deliver. Yet, give me leave:
How came you in these parts? Where were you
bred?

Marina. The King my father did in Tharsus leave me;
Till cruel Cleon, with his wicked wife,
175 Did seek to murder me;
And having wooed a villain to attempt it,
Who having drawn to do't,
A crew of pirates came and rescued me;
Brought me to Mytilene.° But, good sir,

157 **Motion** i.e., the movement of the blood and spirits through the
body   163 **Delivered** reported   165 **withal** with   179 **Mytilene** (the
final syllable is here sounded)

Whither will you have me? Why do you weep? It
  may be   *180*
You think me an impostor: no, good faith!
I am the daughter to King Pericles,
If good King Pericles be.°

Pericles.   Ho, Helicanus!

Helicanus. Calls my lord?

Pericles. Thou art a grave and noble counselor,   *185*
  Most wise in general. Tell me, if thou canst,
  What this maid is, or what is like° to be,
  That thus hath made me weep?

Helicanus.   I know not;
  But here's the regent, sir, of Mytilene
  Speaks° nobly of her.

Lysimachus.   She never would tell   *190*
  Her parentage; being demanded that,
  She would sit still° and weep.

Pericles. O Helicanus, strike me, honored sir!
  Give me a gash, put me to present pain;
  Lest this great sea of joys rushing upon me   *195*
  O'erbear° the shores of my mortality,
  And drown me with their sweetness. O, come
  hither,
  Thou that beget'st° him that did thee beget;
  Thou that wast born at sea, buried at Tharsus,
  And found at sea again! O Helicanus,   *200*
  Down on thy knees; thank the holy gods as loud
  As thunder threatens us: this is Marina!
  What was thy mother's name? Tell me but that,
  For truth can never be confirmed enough,
  Though doubts did ever sleep.

Marina.   First, sir, I pray,   *205*
  What is your title?

183 **be** i.e., be alive   187 **like** likely   190 **Speaks** that speaks
192 **still** always   196 **O'erbear** overwhelm   198 **beget'st** i.e., gives
new life to

Pericles. I am Pericles of Tyre: but tell me now
   My drowned queen's name, as in the rest you said
   Thou hast been godlike perfect, and thou art°
210   The heir of kingdoms and another life
   To Pericles, thy father.

Marina. [*Kneels*] Is it no more to be your daughter than
   To say my mother's name was Thaisa?
   Thaisa was my mother, who did end
215   The minute I began.

Pericles. Now blessing on thee! Rise; thou art my child.
   Give me fresh garments. [*To Marina*] Mine own! Helicanus,
   She is not dead at Tharsus, as she should have been°
   By° savage Cleon. She shall tell thee all;
220   When thou shalt kneel, and justify in knowledge°
   She is thy very princess. Who is this?

Helicanus. Sir, 'tis the Governor of Mytilene,
   Who, hearing of your melancholy state,
   Did come to see you.

Pericles.   I embrace you.
225   Give me my robes. I am wild in my beholding.°
   O heavens bless my girl! [*Music.*] But hark, what music?
   Tell Helicanus, my Marina, tell him
   O'er, point by point, for yet he seems to doubt,
   How sure you are my daughter. But what music?

230 *Helicanus.* My lord, I hear none.

Pericles. None?
   The music of the spheres! List, my Marina.

---

209 **and thou art** (these words are missing in the text)   218 **should have been** was said to be   219 **By** at the hands of   220 **justify in knowledge** affirm in recognition of her claim   225 **beholding** appearance, looks (?)

Lysimachus. It is not good to cross him; give him
    way.

Pericles. Rarest sounds! Do ye not hear?

Lysimachus.   Music, my lord?

Pericles. I hear most heavenly music.   *235*
    It nips me unto° list'ning, and thick slumber
    Hangs upon mine eyes. Let me rest.   [*He sleeps.*]

Lysimachus. A pillow for his head. So leave him all.
    Well, my companion friends,
    If this but answer to my just belief,   *240*
    I'll well remember you.°   [*Exeunt all but Pericles.*]

        Diana [*appears to Pericles in a vision*].

Diana. My temple stands in Ephesus. Hie thee thither,
    And do upon mine altar sacrifice.
    There, when my maiden priests are met together,
    Before the people all,   *245*
    Reveal how thou at sea didst lose thy wife.
    To mourn thy crosses,° with thy daughter's, call,
    And give them repetition to the life.°
    Perform my bidding, or thou livest in woe;
    Do't, and happy,° by my silver bow!   *250*
    Awake, and tell thy dream.   [*She vanishes.*]

Pericles. Celestial Dian, goddess argentine,°
    I will obey thee. Helicanus!

    [*Enter Helicanus, Lysimachus, and Marina.*]

Helicanus.   Sir?

Pericles. My purpose was for Tharsus, there to strike
    The inhospitable Cleon; but I am   *255*
    For other service first: toward Ephesus

---

236 **nips me unto** compels me to   240–41 **If this . . . you** i.e., if
Marina is really a princess (and therefore a fit match for me) I shall
well reward you (?) (lines 239–41 read like the reporter's addition
and ought, probably, to be omitted)   247 **crosses** misfortunes
248 **repetition to the life** lifelike recital   250 **happy** i.e., thou livest
happy   252 **argentine** silvery

Turn our blown° sails; eftsoons° I'll tell thee why.
[*To Lysimachus*] Shall we refresh us, sir, upon your
    shore,
And give you gold for such provision as
260 Our intents° will need?

Lysimachus. Sir,
With all my heart; and when you come ashore
I have another suit.

Pericles.   You shall prevail,
Were it to woo my daughter; for it seems
265 You have been noble towards her.

Lysimachus. Sir, lend me your arm.

Pericles.   Come, my Marina.
                                    Exeunt.

[Scene II. *The temple of Diana at Ephesus;
Thaisa and several maidens standing near the
altar, all appareled as priestesses; Cerimon and
other inhabitants of Ephesus attending.*

Enter Gower.]

Gower. Now our sands are almost run;
More a little, and then dumb.
This, my last boon, give me—
For such kindness must relieve me—
5   That you aptly° will suppose

257 **blown** inflated by the wind   257 **eftsoons** afterwards, shortly
260 **intents** purposes   V.ii.5 **aptly** readily

What pageantry, what feats, what shows,
What minstrelsy and pretty° din,
The regent made in Mytilin
To greet the King. So he thrived
That he is promised to be wived   10
To fair Marina; but in no wise
Till he° had done his sacrifice,
As Dian bade: whereto being bound,°
The interim, pray you, all confound.°
In feathered briefness° sails are filled,   15
And wishes fall out as they're willed.
At Ephesus the temple° see
Our king and all his company.
That he can hither come so soon
Is by your fancies' thankful doom.°   20

                                    [Exit.]

[Scene III. *The temple of Diana. Enter Pericles,
with Lysimachus, Helicanus, and Marina.*]

Pericles. Hail, Dian! To perform thy just command,
I here confess myself the King of Tyre;
Who, frighted from my country, did wed
At Pentapolis the fair Thaïsa.

---

7 **pretty** pleasing   12 **he** i.e., Pericles, whereas in lines 9–10 Lysimachus is referred to   13 **bound** on his way   14 **all confound**
entirely consume   15 **In feathered briefness** with winged speed
17 **Ephesus the temple** the temple of Ephesus   20 **your fancies'
thankful doom** the thanks-deserving verdict of your imaginations

5   At sea in childbed died she, but brought forth
    A maid-child called Marina; who, O goddess,
    Wears yet thy silver livery.° She at Tharsus
    Was nursed with Cleon;° whom at fourteen years
    He sought to murder; but her better stars
10 Brought her to Mytilene; 'gainst whose shore
    Riding,° her fortunes brought the maid aboard us,
    Where, by her own most clear remembrance, she
    Made known herself my daughter.

Thaisa.   Voice and favor!°
    You are, you are—O royal Pericles!   [*Swoons.*]

Pericles. What means the nun? She dies! Help, gen-
13 tlemen!

Cerimon. Noble sir,
    If you have told Diana's altar true,°
    This is your wife.

Pericles.   Reverend appearer,° no.
    I threw her overboard with these very arms.

Cerimon. Upon this coast, I warrant you.

20 *Pericles.*   'Tis most certain.

Cerimon. Look to the lady. O, she's but overjoyed.
    Early one blustering morn this lady
    Was thrown upon this shore. I oped the coffin,
    Found there rich jewels; recovered her,° and placed
      her
    Here in Diana's temple.

25 *Pericles.*   May we see them?

Cerimon. Great sir, they shall be brought you to my
      house,
    Whither I invite you. Look, Thaisa is
    Recoverèd.

V.iii.7 **Wears yet thy silver livery** i.e., is still a virgin   8 **with Cleon**
in Cleon's family   11 **Riding** as we rode at anchor   13 **favor** looks,
face   17 **true** the truth   18 **appearer** one who appears   24 **recovered her** restored her to consciousness

Thaisa.   O, let me look!
If he be none of mine, my sanctity
Will to my sense bend no licentious ear,°   30
But curb it, spite of seeing. O, my lord,
Are you not Pericles? Like him you spake,
Like him you are. Did you not name a tempest,
A birth and death?

Pericles.   The voice of dead Thaisa!

Thaisa. That Thaisa am I, supposèd dead and
   drowned.   35

Pericles. Immortal Dian!

Thaisa.   Now I know you better.
When we with tears parted° Pentapolis,
The King my father gave you such a ring.
                        [*Points to his ring.*]

Pericles. This, this! No more.° You gods, your pres-
   ent kindness
Makes my past miseries sports. You shall do well   40
That° on the touching of her lips I may
Melt and no more be seen. O come, be buried
A second time within these arms.

Marina.   My heart
Leaps to be gone into my mother's bosom.
                        [*Kneels to Thaisa.*]

Pericles. Look who kneels here: flesh of thy flesh,
   Thaisa;   45
Thy burden at the sea, and called Marina,
For she was yielded° there.

29–30 **If he . . . licentious ear** if he is not my husband, my holiness
will not listen licentiously to my desire   37 **parted** departed from
39 **No more** i.e., no more confirmation is needed that you are Thaisa
(alternatively one could punctuate "No more, you gods!" and interpret: give me no greater happiness, you gods!)   40–41 **You shall
do well/That** you would do well if   47 **yielded** brought forth

Thaisa.   Blest, and mine own!

Helicanus. Hail, madam, and my queen!

Thaisa.   I know you not.

Pericles. You have heard me say, when I did fly from
      Tyre
50   I left behind an ancient substitute.
      Can you remember what I called the man?
      I have named him oft.

Thaisa.   'Twas Helicanus then.

Pericles. Still confirmation.
      Embrace him, dear Thaisa; this is he.
55   Now do I long to hear how you were found;
      How possibly preserved; and who to thank,
      Besides the gods, for this great miracle.

Thaisa. Lord Cerimon, my lord: this man,
      Through whom the gods have shown their power;
         that can
      From first to last resolve you.°

60 *Pericles.*   Reverend sir,
      The gods can have no mortal officer
      More like a god than you. Will you deliver°
      How this dead queen re-lives?

Cerimon.   I will, my lord.
      Beseech you first, go with me to my house,
65   Where shall be shown you all was found with her;
      How she came placed here in the temple;
      No needful thing omitted.

Pericles.   Pure Dian,
      I bless thee for thy vision, and will offer
      Nightly oblations to thee. Thaisa,
70   This Prince, the fair betrothèd of your daughter,
      Shall marry her at Pentapolis. And now,
      This ornament

60 **resolve you** free you from doubt   62 **deliver** relate

Makes° me look dismal will I clip to form;°
And what this fourteen years no razor touched,
To grace thy marriage-day I'll beautify.   *73*

Thaisa. Lord Cerimon hath letters of good credit,°
     sir,
My father's dead.

Pericles. Heavens make a star of him! Yet there, my
     queen,
We'll celebrate their nuptials, and ourselves
Will in that kingdom spend our following days.   *80*
Our son and daughter shall in Tyrus reign.
Lord Cerimon, we do our longing stay°
To hear the rest untold.° Sir, lead's the way.
                                        [*Exeunt.*]

               [*Enter*] *Gower.*

[*Gower.*] In Antiochus and his daughter you have
     heard
Of monstrous lust the due and just reward.   *85*
In Pericles, his queen and daughter, seen,
Although assailed with fortune fierce and keen,
Virtue preserved from fell destruction's blast,°
Led on by heaven, and crowned with joy at last.
In Helicanus may you well descry   *90*
A figure of truth, of faith, of loyalty.
In reverent Cerimon there well appears
The worth that learnèd charity aye wears.
For wicked Cleon and his wife, when fame
Had spread his cursèd deed, the honored name   *95*
Of Pericles to rage the city turn,°
That him and his° they in his palace burn;
The gods for murder seemèd so content

---

73 **Makes** which makes   73 **form** proper shape   76 **credit** trust-
worthiness   82 **stay** delay   83 **untold** i.e., that is yet untold
88 **blast** blowing up (?) stroke of lightning (?) blight (?)   94 **fame**
report   94–96 **when fame . . . city turn** i.e., holding Pericles' name
in such honor, the citizens are enraged by the report of the murder
of his child   97 **his** i.e., his family

To punish them, although not done but meant.°
100 So, on your patience evermore attending,
New joy wait on you! Here our play has ending.
[*Exit.*]

FINIS.

---

99 **although not done but meant** although the murder was not carried out but merely intended

Textual Note

The booke of Pericles Prynce of Tyre (i.e., presumably, the promptbook) was entered, together with *Antony and Cleopatra,* in the Stationers' Register on May 20, 1608. Both plays were entered to Edward Blount, and, as neither of them was published by him, it has been supposed that these were "blocking entries," designed to prevent piracy. If so, this proved unsuccessful in the case of *Pericles,* for what is certainly a pirated version of the play was brought out in 1609 by another publisher, Henry Gosson. It proved so popular that a second quarto edition of the play was published by him in the same year, a third appeared in 1611, a fourth in 1619, a fifth in 1630, and a sixth in 1635 (Q2–Q6). As all of these are merely reprints of each other, they have no independent textual authority. *Pericles* was not included in the first collected edition of Shakespeare's plays, the First Folio of 1623, and was not added to any collected edition until the second impression of the Third Folio, in 1664, where it was reprinted from Q6. Varying explanations of the reason for the play's exclusion from the First Folio have been put forward: copyright difficulties; the absence of a good text available to the editors; the fact that the play is only partly Shakespeare's. The last would seem the most probable reason, and is only weakened by the inclusion in the Folio of *Henry VIII.*

The only authoritative text of *Pericles* is therefore that
of the first Quarto of 1609 (Q). It is unfortunately a
very poor text, as the list below of some hundred and
eighty corrupt readings makes immediately apparent. At
least some twenty of these would seem to be auditory
errors, due to a mishearing by the reporter of the words
spoken on the stage (apparent instances of this are found
at I.i.114; I.ii.86; II.ii.30; IV Chorus 26; IV.iv.24; V.i.
228). Most scholars are agreed that the text derives from
a report of the play as performed by Shakespeare's company. It is the degree of badness of the report about which
they are divided. Some would group it with the "bad"
Quartos, such as those of *Romeo and Juliet* and *Hamlet;*
others insist that, in spite of numerous corruptions, many
of them due to the compositors, the text is basically a
good one. My own view is that the Quarto of *Pericles*
stands somewhere between the good and the bad Quartos:
too faithful to its original to be classed as a "bad"
Quarto; too full of errors (both graphic and auditory),
of omissions, and additions, to be accounted a good one.

Next to the errors due to mishearing, the reporter seems
responsible for a variety of other deficiencies in the text:

1) In the Shakespearian part, after—for the most part
impeccably—setting out the verse of III.i, he apparently
found the task too demanding, and wrote out the remaining blank verse as prose; and that is how most of it was
set by the compositors. 2) He occasionally seems to have
added words, or even whole lines, that can scarcely have
been in the Shakespearian original (e.g. V.i.240–1). 3)
There are two scenes in the play in which an evident gap
in the report is to be found: in I.ii, where some dialogue
between Pericles and Helicanus is evidently missing (before line 38. See gloss on lines 38–48); and in IV.vi,
where some dialogue between Marina and Lysimachus
appears to have been lost (after line 109). In the first case
the reporter seems to have made little attempt to fill the
gap; in the second case he apparently tried to fill it by
reconstructing the missing lines from memory—a memory
which must have been exceedingly dim (see *Introduction*,
pp. xxiii–xxiv).

But apart from this instance, there is no indication in the text that—as in all the "bad" Quartos proper—the report was a memorial reconstruction. On the contrary—at least in the Shakespearian part—the report must have been made at the theater, probably during repeated visits to performances of the play. Long scenes such as III.i. and V.i., in which the text has every appearance of adhering faithfully to the Shakespearian original, cannot have been reported from memory.[1] In the non-Shakespearian part it is much more difficult to be sure of this, and there are some grounds for supposing that its fidelity to the original text is not as great (notably in II.i).

The majority of the corrupt readings in Q seem, in fact, to have been introduced not by the reporter but by the compositors (Philip Edwards has shown them to have been three in number), who were uniformly slovenly and careless at their task (except in II.v, which seems to be free from compositorial errors). They misread words, mis-assigned speeches, occasionally omitted speech prefixes, sometimes set prose as verse, and made only sporadic—and then quite inept—attempts to reestablish Shakespeare's blank verse division. The occasional omission of words within a line (as at I.iv.13), or of a whole line (as, apparently, after line 14 in IV.iii and probably after line 122 in I.ii), would also seem to be attributable to them rather than to the reporter.

The text of this edition diverges on a number of points from preceding ones: 1) Where the Quarto text is manifestly corrupt and we are left with nonsense, I have not hesitated to emend, even when we cannot be sure that the chosen emendation is necessarily the right one and when previous modern editors have retained the original reading. Instances of this are found at I.iv.13; III.ii.84–87; IV.i.11; and V.i.209. On the other hand, Q readings have, on a very few occasions, been retained where previous editors have emended, e.g. at III.i.67, where editors have unnecessarily emended Q's "coffin" to "coffer," since the

[1] I do not share Philip Edwards' pessimistic view that "we have in these later acts only the *disjecta membra* of once powerful verse," that "we lose sight, presumably forever, of the genuine version of the last three acts, from the opening of III.ii." (*Shakespeare Survey 5*, 1952, 38.)

two words were used interchangeably in Shakespeare's day.

2) Like other editors, I have for the most part followed Malone's relineation of Shakespeare's blank verse in the passages where it was set as prose. But occasionally, where better and more Shakespearian verse seemed to result, I have introduced line divisions not found in previous editions, e.g., at III.iii.9–15; IV.i.27–30; V.i.20–21.

3) Sometimes I have departed from the punctuation adopted by previous editors, and thereby imposed a different meaning on the text. An example of this is found at I.i.7–12:

> Bring in our daughter, clothèd like a bride,
> For the embracements even of Jove himself;
> At whose conception, till Lucina reigned,
> Nature this dowry gave to glad her presence.
> The senate house of planets all did sit,
> To knit in her their best perfections.

The last four lines are a major crux in the play, and have been much emended and discussed. Most editors put a colon in 1.10, either after "gave" or after "presence" (Q puts a semicolon after "gave" and a comma after "presence"), thus making the planetary influence itself Nature's dowry. But this does not make astrological sense, as a) beauty was considered the gift of Nature, not of the planets; b) planetary influence would be thought of as exerted at birth, not between conception and birth; c) such planetary influence would not be believed to be in the gift of Nature. By punctuating as above, I have separated Nature's gift from that of the planets, interpreting: "between conception and birth Nature gave her her beauty as dowry ('this dowry': the beauty you are about to behold); then, at her birth, the planets bestowed upon her, other, non-physical, perfections over which they have control." The change in punctuation thus restores sense to the passage, and to Nature and the stars what is the due of each.

4) Not infrequently the explanations given in the glosses

differ from those of previous editors. For example at I Chorus 42 the word "justify," instead of having its modern meaning, is, I believe, one of a series of legal metaphors, and has the archaic meaning of "acquit, absolve" (*Oxford English Dictionary* 4); while at V.i.220 I believe it has another archaic meaning, that of "affirm" (*Oxford English Dictionary* 5b).

5) I have parted company from previous editors over several stage directions, which they have taken over from Malone's edition, and which seem quite unjustified. There are two chief instances of this. At the opening of III.ii Q's direction reads, *Enter Lord Cerymon with a seruant.* Malone, followed by most subsequent editors, added to this *and some Persons who have been shipwrecked,* because of Cerimon's line, "Get fire and meat for these poor men" (line 3). But to march several characters onto the stage, only to march them off again a few lines later (line 10) without their having uttered a word, would be a most un-Shakespearian piece of dramaturgy. I have, therefore, adhered to Q's direction, and emended "these" in line 3 to "those," so that Pericles is speaking of some poor men —there is not the slightest indication that they are shipwrecked—who are never brought on stage, but are merely mentioned in order to display Cerimon in his role of benefactor. The other instance occurs at the opening of V.i. We are on board Pericles' ship, having just been told by Gower:

In your supposing once more put your sight:
Of heavy Pericles think this his bark. (V. Chorus 21–22)

Malone, with evidently little faith in the audience's capacity for supposing, has added to the required direction (*"On board Pericles' Ship"*, etc.), "A Barge lying beside the Tyrian Vessel." At line 10 he introduced the direction, *The Gentlemen and the Two Sailors descend, and go on board the Barge. Enter, from thence, Lysimachus and Lords;* at line 51, *Exit Lord, in the Barge of Lysimachus;* and at line 64, *Enter, from the Barge, Lord, Marina, and a young Lady.* And all these directions have been taken over by subsequent editors. It is not clear how Malone envisaged the staging of this, but he evidently imagined the barge—by means of some piece of stage machinery—departing, and returning a few minutes later with Marina, all in full view of the audience. There is neither need nor warrant for all this, and in the present edition Malone's barge has been silently dropped.

In the Quartos of *Pericles* the text is not divided into acts and scenes. The act division was introduced by the Third Folio, and the scene division by Malone. In the present text spelling and punctuation have been modernized, and speech prefixes expanded and regularized. All additions to Q's stage directions are indicated by square brackets. Purely typographical errors have been silently corrected. All other departures from the Quarto text are listed below, with the adopted reading, in italics, given first, followed by Q's reading, in roman.

I Chorus 39 *a* of

I.i.8 *For the embracements* For embracements   18 *razed* racte   57 *Antiochus* [Q omits]   112 *our* your   114 *cancel* counsell   121 s.d. *Exeunt . . . Pericles* Manet Pericles solus   128 *you're* you   129 *uncomely* vntimley   170 *Antiochus* [Q omits]

I.ii.s.d. *Enter Pericles* Enter Pericles with his Lords   4 *Be my* By me   21 *honor him* honour   26 *th' ostent* the stint   31 *am* once   42 *blast* sparke   45 *a peace* peace   66 *you* you yourselfe   83 *Bethought me* Bethought   84 *fears* feare   86 *doubt* doo't   100 *grieve them* griue for them   122 *we'll* will

I.iii.1 *Thaliard* [Q omits]   28 *ears it* seas   29 *seas* Sea   31 *Helicanus* [Q omits]   35 *betook* betake

I.iv.13 *sorrows cease not* sorrowes   17 *helps* helpers   36 *they* thy   39 *two summers* too sauers   58 *thou* thee   67 *Hath* That   74 *him's* himnes   76–7 *will, what need we fear?/On ground's the lowest,* will, and what they can,/What need wee leaue our grounds the lowest?

II Chorus 11 *Tharsus* Tharstill   19 *for he strives* for though he striue   22 *Sends word* Sau'd one   24 *hid intent to murder* hid in Tent to murdred [changed in some copies of Q to "had intent to murder"]

II.i.6 *me breath* my breath   12 *What ho, Pilch!* What, to pelch?
18 *fetch thee* fetch'th   35 *devours* deuowre   43 *Third Fisherman.*
I.   58 *scratch it* Search   82 *quoth-a* ke-tha   86 *holidays* all day
86 *moreo'er* more; or   94 *your* you   103 *is called Pentapolis* I cald
Pantapoles   127 *thy crosses* crosses   135 *thee from!——may't* thee,
Fame may   161 *rapture* rupture   164 *delightful* delight   171 *equal
a Goale*

II.ii.4 *daughter* daughter heere   27 *Più per dolcezza che per forza*
Pue Per doleera kee per forsa   28 *what's* with   29 *chivalry* Chiu-
ally   30 *pompae* Pompey   56 *for* by

II.iii.3 *To* I   13 *yours* your   26 *Envied* Enuies   29 *but* not   38
Yon You   39 *tells me* tels   44 *son's* sonne like   51 *stored* stur'd
52 *you do* do you   114 *Simonides* [Q omits]

II.iv.10 *their* those   33 *gives* giue's   34 *leaves* leaue   35 *death's
indeed* death in deed,   36 *this: kingdoms* this Kingdome is   42 *For*
Try   57 *endeavor it* endeauour

III Chorus 2 *the house about* about the house   6 *'fore* from   7
crickets Cricket   8 *All* Are   17 *coigns* Crignes   29 *t' appease*
t'oppresse   35 *Y-ravishèd* Iranyshed   46 *fortune's mood* fortune
mou'd   60 *sea-tossed* seas tost

III.i.7 *Thou stormest* then storme   11 *midwife* my wife   26 *Vie*
Vse   52 *custom* easterne   53–54 *for . . . straight* [In Q this is printed
after "meet" in the next line]   61 *in the ooze* in oare   63 *And* The
66 *paper* Taper

III.ii.3 *those* these   26 *held* hold   37 *And I can* and can   38 *gives*
doth giue   41 *treasure* pleasure   48 *never raze* neuer   57 *bitumed*
bottomed   77 *even* euer   84–7 *I have read/Of some Egyptians,
who after four hours' death/Have raised impoverished bodies,
like to this,/Unto their former health* I heard of an Egiptian that had 9.
howers lien dead,/Who was by good applyaunce recouered   89 *still*
rough   95 *Breathes* breath

III.iii.5 *shafts* shakes   6 *hurt* hant   7 *woundingly* wondringly   29–
30 *honor all,/Unscissored* honour,/All vnsisterd   31 *ill* will

III.iv.5 *eaning* learning

IV Chorus 10 *her* hie   10 *heart* art   14 *Seeks* Seeke   17 *ripe* right
17 *rite* sight   21 *she* they   26 *night-bird* night bed   32 *With dove
of Paphos might the crow* The Doue of Paphos might with the crow
47 *carry* carried

IV.i.5–6 *or flaming love thy bosom/Enslave* in flaming, thy loue

bosome, enflame　11 *weeping her old nurse's* weeping for her onely
Mistresse　19 *is as a* is a　24–5 *favor/Is* fauours　27 *On the sea
margent* ere the sea marre it　62 *stem* sterne　92 s.d. *They . . .
Marina* Exit.　95 *she'll* shee will

IV.ii.4 *much* much much　21 *they're too* ther's two　53 *It* I　69 *me
to* me, for to　77 *was like to* was to　109 *i' the* ethe　116 *crowns
of* crownes in　132 *Bawd.* Mari.

IV.iii.1 *are* ere　6 *A* O　12 *fact* face　17 *pious* impious　27 *prime*
prince　28 *sources* courses　31 *distain* disdaine　33 *Marina's*
Marianas

IV.iv.7 *scene* sceanes　8 *i' th' gaps* with gappes　10 *the* thy　12
life's liues　16 *Tyre* time　18 *his* this　19 *go on* grone　24 *true-
owed* true olde　29 *puts* put　48 *scene* Steare

IV.vi.s.d. *Enter . . . Boult* Enter Bawdes　3　40 *dignifies* dignities
41 *punk* number　73 *name't* name　93 *aloof* aloft　135 *ways* way
141 *She* He　158 *ways* way　190 *I* will will　199 *women* woman

V Chorus 8 *silk, twin* Silke Twine,　13 *lost* left　14 *Whence* Where
16 *city's hived* Citie striu'de

V.i.11 *Mytilenian Sailor.* Hell. [changed in some copies of Q to *I.
Say.*]　15 *you, sir, to* you to　34–36 *Lys. Yet . . . wish./Hel. Behold
. . . Till* yet . . . wish./Lys. Behold . . . person./Hell. Till　36 *night*
wight　46 *ports* parts　49 *And with her fellow maid is now* and
her fellow maides, now　66 *presence* present　70 *I'd* I do　70
rarely wed rarely to wed　71 *Fair one, all* Faire on all　71 *bounty*
beautie　73 *feat* fate　81 s.d. *They . . . sings* The Song　82 *Marked*
Marke　104 *countrywoman* Countrey women　105 *shores? . . .
shores* shewes? . . . shewes　109 *such* sucha one　126 *make my
senses* make senses　129 *say* stay　143 *thou them?* Thy　157 *Motion as well?* Motion well,　165–66 *be: My daughter's buried.*
be my daughter, buried;　183 *Pericles* Hell.　209–10 *perfect, and
thou art/The* perfit, the　210 *life* like　216 *thou art* th' art　228
doubt doat　235 *Pericles. I hear most heavenly music* Lys. I heare./
Per. Most heauenly Musicke　248–49 *life./Perform* like, or performe
263 *suit* sleight

V.iii.6 *who* whom　8 *whom* who　15 *nun* mum　22 *one* in　49
Pericles. Hell.　68 *I bless* blesse　69 *Nightly* night　83 [Q has
FINIS after this line, as well as after line 101]　88 *preserved* preferd
99 *punish them* punish

THE SOURCES OF *Pericles*

The chief literary influence discernible in *Pericles* is Sir Philip Sidney's *Arcadia*. It extends not only to structure, action, treatment of character, themes, and atmosphere (see Introduction, p. xxxiv ff.), but also to a number of verbal echoes in both parts of the play. In the non-Shakespearian part we find such echoes at I.i.11–12 ("The senate house of the planets was at no time so set, for the decreeing of perfection in a man"), and I.i.63–64 ("asking no advise of no thought, but of faithfulnes and courage"); in the Shakespearian part the echoes at III.ii. 100–04 ("Her faire liddes then hiding her fairer eyes, seemed unto him sweete boxes of mother of pearle, riche in themselves, but contaning in them farre richer Jewells") and at IV Ch. 23–5 ("the cloth loking with many eies upon her, & lovingly embracing the wounds she gave it") are less close but still manifest. The most extensive detailed parallel also belongs to Shakespeare's part: Marina's description of her father's behavior during the storm at sea in which she was born,

> My father, as nurse says, did never fear,
> But cried "Good seamen!" to the sailors, galling
> His kingly hands haling ropes   (IV.i.52–54)

was closely influenced by the great storm scene in the

Arcadia (which also seems to have left its mark on the opening scene of *The Tempest*), where we are told of the Princes that they "did in their countenances accuse no point of feare, but encouraging them [the sailors] to doo what might be done (putting their handes to everie most painefull office). . . ." While Shakespeare, as was his wont, has made the description far more vivid and dramatic, he retains the order in which the three ingredients—fearless-ness, encouragement, painful office—are mentioned in Sidney's account.

The play has two main sources: Book VIII of John Gower's *Confessio Amantis,* written towards the end of the fourteenth century and printed in 1532 and 1554; and Laurence Twine's prose narrative *The Patterne of Paine-full Aduentures,* registered in 1576, and extant in an undated edition and a reprint in 1607. Though both sources were drawn upon throughout the play, the influ-ence of Gower greatly predominates, so that his spirit is fitly chosen to act as the play's presenter. Not only does it usually follow Gower rather than Twine at points in the plot where the two diverge, but it is also much more under the verbal influence of Gower than of Twine. I have been able to find only one clear verbal echo of Twine (at I Ch. 18), while there are many such echoes of Gower; at III.ii.107 the whole line is taken over from Gower (lines 1206–07, "Ha, wher am I?/Where is my Lord, what world is this?"), and other verbal echoes are found, for instance, at I.i.156; V Ch. 14; and V.i.86.

The names, too, are mainly derived from Gower: Dionyza (*Dionise* in Gower, *Dionisiades* in Twine); Lychorida (*Lichorida* in Gower, *Ligozides* in Twine); Thaisa (derived from *Thaise,* Gower's name for Pericles' daughter, called Tharsia in Twine; Pericles' wife is there called *Lucina* and left nameless in Gower); Leonine (in Gower the name of the pander); Helicanus (from a Tyrian messenger called *Hellican* in Gower's text, but *Helicanus* in one of the Latin glosses; *Elinatus* in Twine); Philoten (*Philomacia* in Twine); Thaliard (*Taliart* in Gower, *Taliarchus* in Twine). Cerimon's name is found in both Gower and Twine. The names Pericles, Marina, Simonides, Lysimachus, Cleon, Escanes, Boult, are not found in any of the sources. They may have been Shakespeare's inventions, or may have been taken over by him from the old play.

The only exception to the predominance of Gower as a source is found in three scenes in Act IV, where Twine is principally drawn on. In IV.i. Marina's mourning for her dead nurse, and her intended visit to her grave, are entirely based on Twine, there being no mention of this in Gower; the intervention of the pirates is also much closer to Twine. Act IV, scene iii is entirely based on Twine. There is nothing in Gower to suggest that Cleon in any way disapproves of the murder. In IV.vi. the play follows Twine in making Lysimachus visit the brothel as a client, whereas in Gower he is free from any stain, never visits the brothel, and encounters Marina for the first time on board her father's ship.

Readers wishing to study Gower and Twine's share in each scene of the play should consult the headnotes in J. C. Maxwell's edition. Whether Shakespeare went directly to these sources or depended entirely on the old play which he rewrote—if this is, in fact, what happened —is a moot point. But his use of sources elsewhere suggests that he would not have shunned the labor of reading Gower, Twine, and whatever other version of the story came his way; and it seems probable that the verbal echoes of Gower were derived at first hand. The only indication that any other version of the story has been made use of is the word "bitumed" at III.i.72 and III.ii.57. This word, which is found neither in Gower nor Twine—nor anywhere else in Shakespeare—occurs in its Latin form ("cum bitumine liniri"), in the same context, in the story as told in the *Gesta Romanorum,* the Latin collection of tales, probably compiled around the turn of the thirteenth century, from which Twine's novel, by way of a French translation, is derived.

The Shakespearian part of *Pericles* follows the narrative outline of the sources with a fidelity not found elsewhere in the poet's dramatization of romance material, and this may be taken as a further indication that the scenario is not of his devising. Oddly, the non-Shakespearian part of the play adds more that is not in Gower and Twine than the Shakespearian part. No suggestion in any of the sources is provided for the figure of Helicanus, and his scene with Pericles (I.ii) and with the Tyrian Lords (II.iv); nor for the tournament scene (II.ii; see Introduction, p. xxxv, n. 3.), or for Simonides' faked anger with Pericles (II.v). As G. A. Barker has pointed out in an important article in *English Studies*, XLIV (1963), the main concern of the author of the first two acts seems to have been with political ideas—with what constitutes the good ruler. But this theme is of little importance in Shakespeare's part of the play. And neither he nor the author of the first two acts betrays much concern with what was Gower's avowed purpose in telling the Apollonius story: to make men see that unlawful love, like Antiochus', leads to disaster, whereas lawful, honorable love, like Apollonius', leads eventually to happiness (lines 1993–2019). Much closer to the heart of Shakespeare's presentation seems Twine's view of the story's events; it is well expressed by the title page of his novel, "The Patterne of painefull Aduentures: Containing the most excellent, pleasant and variable Historie of the strange accidents that befell vnto Prince Apollonius, the Lady Lucina his wife, and Tharsia his daughter. Wherein the vncertaintie of this world, and the fickle state of mans life are liuely described." To this Shakespeare adds a concern with the way in which men endure the blows of Fortune, expressed by means of the parallels and contrasts discussed in the Introduction (pp. xxxii ff.).

To provide some indication of how Shakespeare dramatized the narrative material of his sources, I have selected for reprinting the lines from Gower corresponding to Act V, and the chapters in Twine's novel corresponding to Act IV of the play (where Twine's influence is strongest). In both extracts the spelling and punctuation have been modernized, and typographical errors have been silently corrected. In the lines from Gower I have also modernized some of the word forms (e.g. "their" and "them" for "her" and "hem," "then" for "tho"), except where the demands of the rhyme made this impossible. To prevent the meter from collapsing, I have retained the letter "e" whenever it is sounded (as indicated by a dot placed above it). For the extract from Gower I have followed the text in the 1554 edition, since this is the one the playwright is most likely to have used. Words in square brackets in defective lines have been taken from the MS readings in Macaulay's edition (1901). The text used for the extract from Twine is that of the 1607 reprint.

JOHN GOWER:

from *Confessio Amantis,* Book VIII, 1554

And thus tofore° the wind they drive,
Till long° and latè they arrive
With great distress, as it was seen,
1610 Upon the town of *Mytilene,*
Which was a noble city tho.°
And happens thilkè° timè so
The lordès both and the commune°
The highè feastès of *Neptune*
1615 Upon the strand at [the] rivage,°
As it was custom and usage,
Solemnèlichè they besigh.°
When they this strangè vessel sigh°
Come in, and has his sail avaled,°
1620 The town thereof has spoke and taled.°
The lord which of the city was,
Whose name is *Athenagoras,*
Was there, and said he wouldè see

1607 **tofore** before   1608 **long** at length   1611 **tho** then   1612 **thilke** at that very   1613 **commune** common people   1615 **rivage** shore   1617 **Solemneliche they besigh** they solemnly attended to   1618 **sigh** saw   1619 **avaled** lowered   1620 **taled** talked

What ship it is, and who they be
That been therein. And after soon,   1625
When that he sigh it was to-doon,
His bargė was for him arrayed,°
And he goes forth, and has assayed.°
He found the ship of great array;°
But what thing it amountė may?°   1630
He sigh they maden heavy cheer;°
But well him thinks by the manner°
That they been° worthy men of blood,
And asketh of them how it stood.
And they him tellen all the case: 1635
How that their lord fordrivė° was,
And what a sorrow that he made,
Of which there may no man him glad.°
He prays that he their lord may see.
But they him told it may not be,   1640
For he lies in so dark a place
That there may no wight° see his face.
But for all that, though them be loath,°
He found the ladder, and down he goth,
And to him spoke, but none answer   1645
Again of him ne° might he hear,
For aught that he can do or sain:
And thus he goes him up again.
      Then was there spoke in many wise
Amongės them that weren wise   1650
Now this, now that, but at the last
The wisdom of the town thus cast:°
That young *Thaisė* was a-sent.°
For if there be amendėment
To gladė with° this woeful king,   1655

1626–27 to-doon,/His barge . . . arrayed all done—that his barge
was prepared for him   1628 assayed ventured   1629 of great array
splendidly appointed   1630 it amountė may may it mean   1631 heavy
cheer sad faces   1632 him . . . manner it seems to him by their
deportment   1633 been are   1636 fordrive driven about   1638 glad
comfort   1642 wight man   1643 them be loath they are unwilling
1645–46 none . . . ne no   1652 cast determined   1653 a-sent sent
for   1654–55 if there be amendėment/To gladė with if there were
a way to comfort

She can° so much of every thing
That she shall gladen him anon.
  A messenger for her is gone,
And she came with her harp in hand,
1660 And said them that she wouldè fond°
By all the wayès that she can
To gladè with this sorry° man.
But what he was she wistè nought,°
But all the ship her has besought
1665 That she her wit on him dispend,°
In aunter if° he might amend,
And say it shall be well acquit.°
  When she has understanden it,
She goes her down there as° he lay,
1670 Where that she harpeth many a lay,
And like an angel sang withal.
But he no morè than the wall
Took heed of anything he heard.
  And when she saw that he so fared,°
1675 She falleth with him into words,
And telleth him of sundry bords,°
And asketh him demandès° strange,
Whereof° she made his heartè change,
And to her speech his ear he laid,°
1680 And has marvel of that° she said.
For in proverb and in problem
She spoke, and bade he shouldè deem°
In many a subtle question.
But he for no suggestion
1685 Which toward him she couldè steer°
He wouldè not one word answer;
But, as a madman, at the last
His head weeping away he cast,°

1656 **can** understands   1660 **fond** endeavor   1662 **sorry** sorrowful
1663 **wiste nought** knew not at all   1665 **dispend** expend   1666 **In
aunter if** on the chance that   1669 **acquit** requited   1669 **there as**
where   1674 **fared** behaved   1676 **bords** jests   1677 **demandes**
questions   1678 **Whereof** whereby   1679 **laid** lent   1680 **has marvel
of that** marvels at what   1682 **deem** judge   1684-85 **for no suggestion . . . steer** despite any suggestion she could put to him
1688 **cast** turned

And half in wrath he bade her go.
But yet she wouldė not do so, *1690*
But in the darkė forth she goth
Till she him toucheth, and he wroth,°
And after herė with his hand
He smote.° And thus, when she him found
Diseasèd,° courteously she said: *1695*
"Avoi,° my lord, I am a maid!
And if ye wistė what I am,
And out of what lineage I came,
Ye wouldė not be so salvage."°
With that he sobers his courage° *1700*
And put away his heavy cheer.°
But of them two° a man may lere°
What is to be so sib° of blood:
None wist of other how it stood,°
And yet the father at the last *1705*
His heart upon this maidė cast,
That° he her loveth kindėly°—
And yet he wistė never why,
But all was known ere that° they went.
For God, [which] wot° their whole intent, *1710*
Their heartės both anon discloseth.
This king unto this maid opposeth,°
And asketh first what was her name,
And where she learnèd all this game,
And of what kin [that] she was come. *1715*
And she, that has his wordės nome,°
Answers and says: "My name is *Thaise*,
That was some timė° well at ease.
In *Tharse* I was forthdrawn and fed,°
There I learnèd, till I was sped,° *1720*

1692 **wroth** becomes angry   1693–94 **after . . . smote** thereupon
smote her with his hand   1695 **Diseasèd** vexed   1696 **Avoi** fie
1699 **salvage** barbarous   1700 **sobers his courage** calms down
1701 **heavy cheer** sad looks   1702 **of them two** from these two
1702 **lere** learn   1703 **sib** related   1704 **None wist . . . stood** neither
knew who the other was   1707 **That** so that   1707 **kindėly** (1)
in accordance with Nature (2) affectionately   1709 **ere that** before
1710 **wot** knows   1712 **opposeth** asks questions   1716 **his wordės
nome** taken in his words   1718 **some time** formerly   1719 **forthdrawn and fed** brought up and bred   1720 **was sped** reached the
desired end

Of that I can.° My father eke°
I not° where that I should him seek;
He was a king, men toldė me.
My mother dreint° [was] in the sea."
1725 From point to point all she him told
That she has long in heartė hold,
And never durstė make her moan
But only to this lord alone,
To whom her heartė can nought hele,°
1730 Turn it to woe, turn it to weal,
Turn it to good, turn it to harm.
    And he then took her in his arm,
But such a joy as he then made
Was never seen; thus been they glad
1735 That sorry hadden be toforn.°
From this day [forth] Fortune has sworn
To set them upward on the wheel.
So goes the world, now woe, now weal.
    This king has foundė newė grace,°
1740 So that out of his darkė place
He goes him up into the light,
And with him came that sweetė wight,°
His daughter *Thaise,* and forth anon
They both into the cabin gon
1745 Which was ordainėd° for the king.
And there he did off all his thing,°
And was arrayėd royally.
And out he came all openly,
Where *Athenagoras* he found,
1750 [The] which was lord of all the land.
He prays the king to come and see
His castle both and his city—
And thus they go forth all in fere,°
This king, this lord, this maiden dear.
1755 This lord then made them richė feast,

1721 **Of that I can** that which I know   1721 **eke** moreover   1722 **not**
know not   1724 **dreint** drowned   1729 **hele** conceal   1735 **That
sorry hadden be toforn** that had been sorrowful before   1739 **newe
grace** renewed good fortune   1742 **wight** creature   1745 **ordained**
set aside   1746 **did off all his thing** removed all his apparel   1753 **in
fere** together

With everything which was honest,°
To pleasè with this worthy king:
There lacketh him no manner thing.°
By yet, for all his noble array,°
Wifeless he was unto that day,   1760
As he that yet was° of young age.
    So fell there into his courage°
The lusty° woe, the gladè pain
Of lovè, which no man restrain
Yet never might as now tofore.°   1765
This lordè thinks all this world lore°
But if° the king will do him grace.
He waiteth time, he waiteth place,
Him thought° his heartè would to-break°
Till he may to this maidè speak   1770
And to her father eke also
For marriage. And it fell so
That all was done right as he thought.
His purpose to an end he brought.
She wedded him as for her lord—   1775
Thus been they all of one accord.
When all was done right as they would,
The king unto his sonnè told
Of *Tharsè* thilkè traitery;°
And said how in his company   1780
His daughter and himselven eke
Shall go vengeancè for to seek.
    The shippès werè ready soon,
And when they saw it was to-doon,°
Withoutè let of any went,°   1785
With sail updrawè° forth they went
Towardè *Tharse* upon the tide.
But he that wot what shall betide,

1756 **honest** honorable 1758 **no manner thing** nothing of any kind
1759 **array** state 1761 **As he that yet was** being yet 1762 **courage**
heart 1763 **lusty** pleasant 1765 **as now tofore** up to now 1766 **lore**
lost 1767 **But if** unless 1769 **Him thought** it seemed to him
1769 **to-break** break utterly 1779 **Of Tharse thilke traitery** of that
treachery at Tharsus 1784 **to-doon** completely done 1785 **With-
oute let of any went** without any hindrance in their passage
1786 **updrawe** hoist

The highė God, which would him keep,°

1790 When that this king was fast asleep
By nightės time, he has him bid
To sail into another stead:°
To *Ephesum* he bade him draw,
And, as it was that timė law,

1795 He shall do there his sacrifice.
And eke he bade in allė wise°
That in the temple, amongst all,
His fortune, as it is befall,°
Touching his daughter and his wife,

1800 He shall beknowe,° upon his life.
   The king of this avision°
Has great imagination°
What thing it signifyė may;
And natheless,° when it was day,

1805 He bade cast anchor and abode;°
And while that he on anchor rode,
The wind, that was toforė strange,°
Upon the point began to change,
And turneth thither as° it should.

1810 Then knew he well that God it would,°
And bade the master make him yare,°
Tofore the wind for he would farė°
To *Ephesum,* and so he did.
And when he came into the stead

1815 Where as he shouldė land, he landeth
With all the haste he may, and fondeth
To shapen him° in such a wise
That he may by the morrow arise
And do after the mandėment°

1820 Of him which has him thither sent.

1789 keep preserve   1792 stead place   1796 in alle wise fully
1798 is befall has happened   1800 beknowe make known   1801 avision
vision   1802 Has great imagination speculates much   1804 natheless nevertheless   1805 abode waited   1807 tofore strange before
unfriendly   1809 thither as in the direction in which   1810 it would
wanted it   1811 make him yare make himself ready   1812 Tofore
. . . fare for he wanted to sail before the wind   1816–17 fondeth/
To shapen him endeavors to dispose himself   1819 mandement
command

And, in the wise that he thought,°
Upon the morrow so he wrought.
His daughter and his son he nom,°
And forth unto the temple he com
With a great rout in company,°   1825
His giftes for to sacrify.°
   The citizens then hearden say
Of such a king that came to pray
Unto *Dianè,* the goddess,
And, left° all other business,   1830
They comen thither for to see
The king and the solemnity.
   With worthy knightes environed,
The king himself has abandoned°
To the temple in good intent.°   1835
The door is up, and in he went;
Whereas° with great devotion°
Of holy contemplation
Within his heart he made his shrift.
And after that a riche gift   1840
He offers with great reverence;
And there, in open audience°
Of them that stooden then about,
He told them, and declareth out,°
His hap,° such as him is befall;   1845
There was nothing forgot of all.
His wife, as it was God's grace,
Which was professèd° in the place,
As she that was° abessè there,
Unto his tale has laid° her ear.   1850
She knew the voice and the visage:
For pure joy as in a rage

1821 **in the wise that he thought** in the way he intended   1823 **nom** took   1825 **With a great rout in company** accompanied by a great troop   1826 **His giftes for to sacrify** in order to offer up his gifts 1830 **left** having left   1834 **himself has abandoned** has betaken himself   1835 **in good intent** for a worthy purpose   1837 **Whereas** where   1837 **devotion** devoutness, reverence   1842 **audience** hearing   1844 **out** fully   1845 **hap** fortunes   1848 **was professèd** had been received into the religious order   1849 **As she that was** being 1850 **laid** lent

She straught° [un]to him all at ones,
And fell a-swoon upon the stones
1855 Whereof the temple floor was paved.
She was anon with water laved,
Till she came to herself again,
And thennĕ she began to sain:
"Ah, blessèd be the highĕ sond°
1860 That I may see my husĕband,
Which whilom° he and I were one!"
The king with that knew her anon,
And took her in his arm and kissed;
And all the town this soon it wist.
1865 Then was there joyĕ manifold,
For every man this tale has told
As for miracle,° and were glad.
But never man such joyĕ made
As does the king, which has his wife.
1870 And when men heard how that her life
Was savèd, and by whom it was,
They wondered all of such a case:°
Through all the land arose the speech°
Of Master *Cerimon*, the leech,
1875 And of the curĕ which he did.
The king himself then has [him] bid,
And eke his queenĕ forth with him,
That he the town of *Ephesim*
Will leave and go where as they be:
1880 For never man of his degree
Has done to them so muchel° good.
And he his profit understood,
And granteth with them for to wend.°
And thus they maden there an end,
And tooken leave, and go to ship
With all the wholĕ fellowship.°

1853 **straught** went   1859 **sond** decree   1861 **whilom** once   1867 **As for miracle** as being a miracle   1872 **They wondered . . . case** they were all amazed by such a happening   1873 **speech** talk   1881 **muchel** much   1883 **with them for to wend** to go with them   1886 **fellowship** company

LAURENCE TWINE:

from *The Pattern of Painful Adventures,* 1607

CHAPTER XI.

How after the death of Ligozides, the nurse, Dionisiades, envying at the beauty of Tharsia, conspired
her death, which should have been accomplished by
a villain of the country.

Tharsia much lamented the death of Ligozides, her
nurse, and caused her body to be solemnly buried not far
off, in a field without the walls of the city, and mourned
for her a whole year following. But when the year was
expired, she put off her mourning attire, and put on her
other apparel, and frequented the schools, and the study
of liberal sciences as before. And whensoever she returned
from school, she would receive no meat before she had
visited her nurse's sepulcher, which she did daily, entering thereunto, and carrying a flagon of wine with her;
where she used to abide a space, and to call upon her
father and mother. Now on a day it fortuned that, as

she passed through the street with Dionisiades and her companion Philomacia, the people, beholding the beauty and comeliness of Tharsia, said: "Happy is that father that hath Tharsia to his daughter, but her companion that goeth with her is foul and evil favored." When Dionisiades heard Tharsia commended, and her own daughter Philomacia so dispraised, she returned home wonderful wroth, and, withdrawing herself into a solitary place, began thus secretly to discourse of the matter: "It is now fourteen years since Apollonius, this foolish girl's father, departed from hence, and he never sendeth letters for her, nor any remembrance unto her; whereby I conjecture that he is dead. Ligozides, her nurse, is departed, and there is nobody now of whom I should stand in fear. And therefore I will now slay her, and dress up mine own daughter in her apparel and jewels." When she had thus resolved herself upon this wicked purpose, in the meanwhile there came home one of their country villains, called Theophilus, whom she called, and said thus unto him: "Theophilus, my trusty friend, if ever thou look for liberty, or that I should do thee pleasure, do so much for me as to slay Tharsia." Then said Theophilus: "Alas, mistress, wherein hath that innocent maiden offended, that she should be slain?" Dionisiades answered: "She innocent? Nay, she is a wicked wretch, and therefore thou shalt not deny to fulfill my request, but do as I command thee, or else I swear, by the gods, thou shalt dearly repent it." "But how shall I best do it, mistress?" said the villain. She answered: "She hath a custom, as soon as she returneth home from school, not to eat meat before that she have gone into her nurse's sepulcher, where I would have thee stand ready, with a dagger drawn in thine hand, and when she is come in, gripe her by the hair of the head, and so slay her. Then take her body and cast it into the sea, and when thou hast so done, I will make thee free, and besides reward thee liberally." Then took the villain a dagger, and girded himself therewith, and with an heavy heart and weeping eyes went forth toward the grave, saying within himself: "Alas, poor wretch that I am, alas, poor Theophilus, that canst not deserve thy liberty but by shedding of innocent blood." And with that he went into the grave, and drew his dagger, and made him ready for the deed. Tharsia was now come from school, and made haste unto the grave with a flagon of wine, as she was wont to do, and entered within the vault. Then the villain rushed violently upon her, and caught her by the hair of the head, and threw her to the ground. And while he was now ready to stab her with the dagger, poor, silly Tharsia, all amazed casting up her eyes upon him, knew the villain, and, holding up her hands, said thus unto him: "O Theophilus, against whom have I so grievously offended that I must die therefore?" The villain answered: "Thou hast not offended, but thy father hath, which left thee behind him in Stranguilio's house with so great a treasure in money and princely ornaments." "O," said the maiden, "would God he had not done so! But I pray thee, Theophilus, since there is no hope for me to escape my life, give me licence to say my prayers before I die." "I give thee licence," said the villain. "And I take God to record that I am constrained to murder thee against my will."

CHAPTER XII

How certain pirates rescued Tharsia when she should have been slain, and carried her unto the city Machilenta, to be sold among other bondslaves.

As fortune, or rather the providence of God, served, while Tharsia was devoutly making her prayers, certain pirates, which were come aland and stood under the side of an hill, watching for some prey, beholding an armed man offering violence unto a maiden, cried unto him and said: "Thou cruel tyrant, that maiden is our prey and not thy victory, and therefore hold thine hands from her, as thou lovest thyself!" When the villain heard that, he ran away as fast as he could, and hid himself behind the sepulcher. Then came the pirates and rescued Tharsia, and carried her away to their ships, and hoist sails and departed. And the villain returned home to his mistress, and said unto her: "That which you commanded me to do is dispatched, and therefore now I think it good that you put on a mourning garment, and I also, and let us counterfeit great sorrow and heaviness in the sight of all the people, and say that she died of some grievous disease." But Stranguilio himself consented not to this treason, but so soon as he heard of the foul mischance, being as it were all amort, and mazed with heaviness and grief, he clad himself in mourning array, and lamented that woeful case, saying: "Alas, in what mischief am I wrapped, what might I do or say herein? The father of this maiden delivered this city from the peril of death; for this city's sake he suffered shipwreck, lost his goods, and endured penury. And now he is requited with evil for good. His daughter, which he committed unto me to be brought up, is now devoured by a most cruel lioness. Thus I am deprived, as it were, of mine own eyes, and forced to bewail the death of an innocent, and am utterly spoiled through the fierce biting of a most venomous serpent." Then casting his eyes up towards heaven, "O God," said he, "thou knowest that I am innocent from the blood of silly Tharsia, which thou hast to require at Dionisiades' hands." And therewithal he looked towards his wife, saying: "Thou wicked woman, tell me, how hast thou made away Prince Apollonius' daughter? Thou that livest both to the slander of God and man." Dionisiades answered in many words, evermore excusing herself, and moderating the wrath of Stranguilio, she counterfeited a feigned sorrow by attiring herself and her daughter in mourning apparel, and in dissembling tears before the people of the city, to whom she said: "Dearly beloved friends and citizens of Tharsus: for this cause we do weep and mourn in your sight, because the joy of our eyes, and staff of our old age, the maiden Tharsia is dead, leaving unto us bitter tears and sorrowful hearts. Yet have we already taken order for her funerals, and buried her according to her degree." These words were right grievous unto the people, and there was almost none that let not [fall] some tears for sorrow. And they went with one accord unto the marketplace, whereas her father's image stood, made of brass, and erected also another unto her there, with this inscription: *Unto the virgin Tharsia in lieu of her father's benefits, the citizens of Tharsus have erected this monument.*

CHAPTER XIII.

How the pirates which stole away Tharsia brought her to the city Machilenta, and sold her to a common bawd, and how she preserved her virginity.

The meantime, while these troubles were at Tharsus, the pirates, being in their course upon the sea, by benefit of a happy wind arrived at Machilenta, and came into the city. Now had they taken many more men and women besides Tharsia, whom they brought all ashore, and set them to sell as slaves for money. Then came there sundry to buy such as they lacked for their purposes, amongst whom a most vile man-bawd, beholding the beauty and tender years of Tharsia, offered money largely for her. Howbeit Athanagoras, who was prince of the same city, beholding likewise the noble countenance and regarding the great discretion of the maiden in communication, outbid the bawd, and offered for her ten sestercies of gold. But the bawd, being loath to lose so commodious a prey, offered twenty. "And I will give thirty," said Athanagoras. "Nay, I will give forty," said the bawd. "And I fifty," quoth Athanagoras. And so they continued in outbidding one another until the bawd offered an hundred sestercies of gold, to be payed ready down. "And whosoever will give more," said he, "I will yet give ten sestercies more than he." Then Prince Athanagoras thus bethought him secretly in his mind: "If I should contend with the bawd to buy her at so high a price, I must needs sell other slaves to pay for her, which were both loss and shame unto me. Wherefore I will suffer him to buy her, and when he setteth her to hire, I will be the first man that shall come unto her, and I will gather the flower of her virginity; which shall stand me in as great stead as if I had bought her." Then the bawd paid the money, and took the maiden and departed home. And when he came into his house, he brought her into a certain chapel, where stood the idol of Priapus, made of gold, and garnished with pearls and precious stones. This idol was made after the shape of a man, with a mighty member, unproportionable to the body, always erected, whom bawds and lechers do adore, making him their god, and worshipping him. Before this filthy idol he commanded Tharsia with reverence to fall down. But she answered: "God forbid, master, that I should worship such an idol. But sir," said she, "are you a Lapsatenian?" "Why askest thou?" said the bawd. "I ask," quoth she, "because the Lapsatenians do worship Priapus." This spake she of simplicity, not knowing what he was. "Ah, wretch," answered he, "knowest thou not that thou art come into the house of a covetous bawd?" When Tharsia heard that, she fell down at his feet and wept, saying: "O master, take compassion upon my virginity, and do not hire out my body for so vile a gain!" The bawd answered: "Knowest thou not that neither bawd nor hangman do regard tears or prayers?" Then called he unto him a certain villain, which was governor over his maids, and said unto him: "Let this maiden be decked in virgin's apparel, precious and costly, and write this title upon her: whosoever deflow'reth Tharsia shall pay ten pieces of gold; and afterward she shall be common unto the people for one piece at a time." The villain fulfilled his master's commandment, and the third day after that she was bought she was with great solemnity conducted through the street with music, the bawd himself with a great multitude going before, and so conveyed unto the brothel house. When she was come thither, Athanagoras, the prince, disguising his head and face because he would not be known, came first in unto her. Whom when Tharsia saw, she threw herself down at his feet and said unto him: "For the love of God, gentleman, take pity on me, and by the name of God I adjure and charge you that you do no violence unto me, but bridle your lust, and hearken unto my unhappy estate, and consider diligently from whence I am sprung. My father was poor Apollonius,

Prince of Tyrus; whom force constrained to forsake his own country. My mother was daughter to Altistrates, King of Pentapolis, who died in the birth of me, poor wretch, upon the sea. My father also is dead, as was supposed, which caused Dionisiades, wife to Stranguilio of Tharsus —to whom my father committed me, of special trust, to be brought up, being but an infant—envying mine estate, and thirsting after my wealth, to seek my death by the hands of a villain; which had been accomplished—and I would to God it had before I had seen this day—but that I was suddenly taken away by the pirates, which sold me unto this filthy bawd." With these or suchlike words declared she her heavy fortune, eftsoons sobbing and bursting out into streams of tears, that for extreme grief she could scarcely speak. When she had in this manner uttered her sorrow, the good Prince, being astonished, and moved with compassion, said unto her: "Be of good cheer, Tharsia, for surely I rue thy case; and I myself have also a daughter at home, to whom I doubt that the like chances may befall."

And when he had so said, he gave her twenty pieces of gold, saying: "Hold here a greater price or reward for thy virginity than thy master appointed. And say as much unto others that come unto thee as thou hast done unto me, and thou shalt withstand them." Then Tharsia fell on her knees, and weeping said unto him: "Sir, I give you most hearty thanks for your great compassion and courtesy, and most heartily I beseech you upon my knees not to descry unto any that which I have said unto you." "No, surely," answered Athanagoras, "unless I tell it unto my daughter, that she may take heed, when she cometh unto the like years, that she fall not into the like mishap." And when he had so said, he let fall a few tears and departed. Now as he was going, he met with another pilgrim that with like devotion came for to seek the same saint; who demanded of him how he liked of the maiden's company. "Truly," answered Athanagoras, "never better of any." Then the young man, whose name was Aportatus, entered into the chamber, and the maiden, after the manner, shut the door to, and Athanagoras listened at the window.

Then said Aportatus unto Tharsia: "How much did the Prince give unto thee?" She answered: "Forty pieces of gold." Then said he: "Receive here of me an whole pound weight of gold." The Prince, which heard this talk, thought then in his mind: "The more that you do give her, the more she will weep, as thinking that you would look for recompense, the which she meaneth not to perform."

The maiden received the money, and fell down on her knees at his feet, and declared unto him all her estate with tears, as is before showed. When Aportatus heard that, he was moved with compassion, and he took her up from the ground, saying: "Arise, Lady Tharsia, we are all men, and subject to the like chances." And therewithal he departed. And when he came forth, he found Prince Athanagoras before the door, laughing at him, to whom he said: "Is it well done, my liege, thus to delude a poor gentleman? Was there none to whom you might begin in tears but unto me only?" Then communed they further of the matter, and sware an oath between themselves that they would not bewray these words unto any. And they withdrew themselves aside into a secret place, to see the going in and coming forth of other, and they saw many which went in and gave their money, and came forth again weeping. Thus Tharsia, through the grace of God, and fair persuasions, preserved her body undefiled.

CHAPTER XIV.

How Tharsia withstood a second assault of her virginity, and by what means she was preserved.

When night was come, the master bawd used always to receive the money which his women had got by the use of their bodies the day before. And when it was demanded of Tharsia, she brought him the money, as the price and hire of her virginity. Then said the bawd unto her: "It is well done, Tharsia. Use diligence henceforth, and see that you bring me thus much money every day." When the next day was passed also, and the bawd understood that she remained a virgin still, he was offended, and called unto him the villain that had charge over the maids, and said unto him: "Sirrah, how chanceth it that Tharsia remaineth a virgin still? Take her unto thee, and spoil her of her maidenhead, or be sure thou shalt be whipped." Then said the villain unto Tharsia: "Tell me, art thou yet a virgin?" She answered: "I am, and shall be as long as God will suffer me." "How, then," said he, "hast thou gotten all this money?" She answered, with tears, falling down upon her knees: "I have declared mine estate, humbly requesting all men to take compassion on my virginity." And now likewise, falling then down at his feet also, "Take pity on me, good friend, which am a poor captive, and the daughter of a king, and do not defile me!" The villain answered: "Our master the bawd is very covetous and greedy of money, and therefore I see no means for thee to continue a virgin." Whereunto Tharsia replied: "I am skillful in the liberal sciences, and well exercised in all studies, and no man singeth or playeth on instruments better than I. Wherefore, bring me into the marketplace of the city, that men may hear my cunning. Or let the people propound any manner of questions, and I will resolve them. And I doubt not but by this practice I shall get store of money daily." When the villain heard this device, and bewailed the maiden's mishap, he willingly gave consent thereto, and brake with the bawd, his master, touching that matter, who, hearing of her skill, and hoping for the gain, was easily persuaded.

Now when she was brought into the marketplace, all the people came thronging to see and hear so learned a virgin, before whom she uttered her cunning in music, and her eloquence in speaking, and answered manifestly unto all such questions as were propounded unto her with such perspicuity that all confessed themselves fully satisfied, and she won great fame thereby, and gained great sums of money. But as for Prince Athanagoras, he had evermore a special regard in the preservation of her virginity, none otherwise than if she had been his own daughter, and rewarded the villain very liberally for his diligent care over her.

CHAPTER XV.

How Apollonius, coming to Tharsus and not finding his daughter, lamented her supposed death; and, taking ship again, was driven by a tempest to Machilenta, where Tharsia was.

Return we now again unto Prince Apollonius, who, while these things were doing at Machilenta, when the fourteenth year was expired, arrived at Tharsus, and came into the city unto the house of Stranguilio and Dionisiades, with whom he had left his young daughter Tharsia. Whom when Stranguilio beheld and knew, he ran hastily unto his wife Dionisiades and said: "Thou reportedst that Prince Apollonius was dead, and lo now, where he is come to require his daughter! What shall we now do, or say unto him?" Then cried she out: "Alas, wretched husband and wife that we are! Let us quickly put on our mourning attire, and shed forth tears, and he will believe us that his daughter died a natural death." And when they had appareled themselves, they came forth unto Apollonius, who, seeing them in mourning attire, said unto them: "My trusty friends Stranguilio and Dionisiades, why weep ye thus at my coming? And tell me, I pray you—which I rather believe—whether these tears be not rather mine than yours." "Not so, my lord Apollonius," answered the wicked woman. "And I would to God some other body and not mine husband or I were enforced to tell you these heavy tidings, that your dear daughter Tharsia is dead." When Apollonius heard that word, he was suddenly cut to the heart, and his flesh trembled that he could scarce stand on his legs. And long time he stood amazed, with his eyes intentively fixed on the ground. But at length, recovering himself and taking fresh breath, he cast up his eyes upon her and said: "O woman, if my daughter be dead, as thou sayest she is, is the money also and apparel perished with her?" She answered: "Some is, and some yet remaineth. And as for your daughter, my lord, we were always in good hope that when you came you should have found her alive and merry. But to the intent you may the better believe us concerning her death, we have a sufficient witness. For our citizens, being mindful of your benefits bestowed upon them, have erected unto her a monument of brass by yours, which you may go see if you please." And when she had so said, she brought forth such money, jewels, and apparel which it pleased her to say were remaining of Tharsia's store. And Apollonius, believing indeed that she was dead, said unto his servants: "Take up this stuff and bear it away unto the ships, and I will go walk unto my daughter's monument." And when he came there, he read the superscription in manner as above written, and he fell suddenly, as it were, into an outrageous affection, and cursed his own eyes, saying: "O, most cruel eyes, why can you not yield forth sufficient tears, and worthily bewail the death of my dear daughter?" And with that word, with grief and extreme sorrow, he fell into a swoon; from which so soon as ever he was once revived, immediately he went unto the ships unto his servants, unto whom he said: "Cast me, I beseech you, into the very bottom of the sea. For I have no joy of my life, and my desire is to yield up my ghost in the water." But his servants used great persuasions with him to assuage his sorrow, wherein presently they some deal prevailed, as they might in so woeful a case. And partly the time, which is a curer of all cares, continually mitigated some part of the grief. And he, espying the wind to serve well for their departure, hoist up sail and bid the land adieu. They had not thus sailed long in their course but the wind came about to a contrary quarter, and blew so stiffly that it troubled both sea and ships. The rain fell fiercely overhead, the sea wrought wondrously under the ship, and, to be short, the tempest was terrible for the time. It was then thought best in that extremity to strike sail and let the helm go, and to suffer the ship to drive with the tide, whither it should please God to direct it. But as joy evermore followeth heaviness, so was this sharp storm occasion of a sweet meeting of the father with the daughter, as in process hereafter it shall appear. For while Apollonius' ship runneth thus at random, it striketh upon the shore of the city Machilenta, where at that present his daughter Tharsia remained.

Commentaries

G. WILSON KNIGHT

from *The Crown of Life*

Pericles might be called a Shakespearian morality play. The epilogue asserts as much, though it does no justice to the more important scenes, which so tower above the rest and which it would be a great error to relate too sharply to any known type of drama. These, whatever we think of them, are spontaneous, new creations. And yet, in spite of their superiority, they cannot be isolated: *Pericles* is too thoroughly organic a play for that, with all its running coherences of idea, image, and event. These demand a short retrospective comment.

There are the continual references to "fortune" personified at IV.iv.48 as "Lady Fortune" (cp. *Timon of Athens,* I.i.64), variously entwined with the sequence of sad and happy adventures and used rather as in *Antony and Cleopatra* with strong suggestion of "chance." The gods are referred to as in *King Lear,* though with a greater sense of their reality, beneficence, and intervention; as in "you most potent gods" (III.ii.63); the "powers that give

From *The Crown of Life* by G. Wilson Knight. 2nd ed. London: Methuen & Co., Ltd., 1948. Reprinted by permission of Methuen & Co., Ltd., and Barnes & Noble, Inc.

heaven countless eyes to view men's acts" (I.i.73–74);
"we cannot but obey the powers above us" (III.iii.9–10).
The "most high gods" quickly punish, with "heaven's
shaft," the wicked (II.iv.3,16), but are otherwise conceived as kindly (II.iii.61). Such deities counter the
chance-like concept of "fortune." Somewhat sterner are
the Destinies, conventionally supposed as cutting the
thread of life (I.ii.108), and also the typically Shakespearian conception:

> Time's the king of men,
> He's both their parent and he is their grave.   (II.iii.46–47)

Religious reverence crystallizes into the personal deities
of Neptune and Diana; the first to be related to our voyages and tempests, the latter of high importance at the end.

To pass to the more human essences. There are a
number of variations concerning true and false value
played on riches (gold, silver and jewels) following, as we
have noted, the use of riches in *The Merchant of Venice*
and *Timon of Athens*. Now in *Timon of Athens* the gold
of the later action may be related to the aristocratic
essence, the spiritual fineness of Timon himself; and
something similar happens in *Pericles*. For our glitter of
jewels and other riches blends naturally into the play's
royalism, where again we have a divergence of directions,
with distinctions drawn between the wicked and good
princes (Antiochus, Cleon and Dionyza against Pericles
and Simonides); the former tyrannous (I.ii.103) and
regarding conscience as unworthy of noble blood (IV.iii.
23–5); the others, chivalrous and relating princely honor
to charity (I.iv.85–96; II.iii.24–6; 61–63).

Here we may approach a new subtlety creeping into
Shakespeare's royalism: his emphasis on the discovery (by
the owner or someone else) of a child's royal birth (in
Marina,[1] Perdita, Guiderius, Arviragus, Miranda). Royal
blood is felt mystically, spiritually, with Marina as a
palace "for the crowned Truth to dwell in" (V.i.125). We

[1] Professor D. G. James, in *Scepticism & Poetry,* has written interest-
ingly on the discovery of Marina's royal birth.

are reminded of Wordsworth's child forgetting "the glories he hath known and that imperial palace whence he came" (in the *Ode on Intimations of Immortality*); and of Coleridge's remarkable play *Zapolya*, specifically written on the pattern of Shakespeare's last plays, where the spiritual connotations of the discovery of royal blood are vividly felt. Where the later poets witness a "spiritual" reality, Shakespeare works from firmer basis of Tudor royalism; but he invariably develops that, as in his manipulation of Timon's innate aristocracy, into something more spiritual, chivalric, or Christian, with stress on generosity and humility (as with Theseus in *A Midsummer Night's Dream*). This development reaches its finest results in his semimystic approach to the royal children from *Pericles* to *Henry VIII;* and may delicately be referred to some yet more universal intimation concerning the royal birth and destinies of the individual human soul, widely understood; for the royal protagonist of drama is always primarily an objectification of the spectator's individual self; his "I"; and certainly in *Pericles* the greatest moments are weighted by a sense of man's universal destiny. So, whatever our political principles, we find the royalistic image radiating its lines of force; and it is precisely this princeliness that renders the rich, kindly and even humorous (III.ii.54–5) Lord Cerimon, on whom sits the aristocratic luster of Timon, more attractive than his great descendant Prospero, who, though of ducal status, is more coldly conceived. Indeed, both *Pericles* and *The Winter's Tale* hold a certain freshness that the later, more coherent, play lacks. Something is lost as miracle becomes assured.

These imaginative strands are all Shakespearian favorites; but their use is new. They are newly actualized: what was formerly imagery becomes dramatic fact. The old image of storm gives us "enter Pericles, wet"; that of bark-in-storm becomes a stage-setting, with Pericles "on shipboard"; the old association love = jewel is built into a personal sense of Thaisa's and Marina's jewel-like worth; the love-image of jewel-thrown-into-the-sea (see *The Shakespearian Tempest*, pp. 64–9; 222–3) becomes Thaisa in her jewel-stored coffin (like Portia's picture in the casket) thrown overboard. Shakespeare's continual reference to pagan deities works up to the "feast of Neptune" and actual appearance of Diana. Finally, music, for so long a dramatic accompaniment to scenes of love and reunion, becomes an active force in Cerimon's magic and explicitly mystical in Pericles' "music of the spheres" (V.i.232). A similar process develops the Friars of *Romeo and Juliet* and *Much Ado about Nothing,* both plot manipulators within their dramas with a tendency to arrange false appearances of death, into the miracle-working Cerimon taking on the plot manipulation of life itself and restoring the dead. *Pericles* is the result of no sudden vision; it is Shakespeare's total poetry on the brink of self-knowledge.

It is accordingly not strange that art, as such, should be given greater emphasis than hitherto; in stage direction, ceremonious procession (as of the tourneying knights) and ritual setting; in dumb show; in monumental inscriptions, and metaphors; in musical accomplishment (Pericles' and Marina's); in Marina's dancing and decorative needlework. The arts least emphasized in Shakespeare, the static arts of design, assume a new prominence, giving us the exquisite descriptions of Marina in monumental terms. Shakespeare's drama is aspiring towards the eternal harmony and the eternal pattern.

The new excellences are bought at a cost. Pericles himself is a passive figure, quite unlike Shakespeare's usual dynamic protagonists. He himself does nothing crucial; his fall is purely an awareness of evil, like Hamlet's, his good acts are perfunctorily set down, his repentance in sackcloth and unshaven hair a repentance for no guilt of his own but rather for the fact of mortality in a harsh universe. He is here for things to happen to and forges little or nothing for himself; his most original actions are a series of escapes or departures; he is too humble to press his suit for Thaisa. He is, indeed, less a realized person than man, almost "every man," in the morality sense, as the epilogue suggests. We can, however, improve on the epilogue by seeing the whole as a panorama of life from adolescent fantasy and a consequent fall, through good works to a sensible and fruitful marriage, and thence into tragedy, with a reemergence beyond mortal appearances into some higher recognition and rehabilitation. The medium is myth or parable, supposedly, of course, realistic: we must not expect death to be totally negated; Thaisa's father dies (V.iii.77); Cerimon cannot restore everyone (III.ii.7). But, as in parable always, it is the central person, or persons, that count; and here the deaths of Thaisa and Marina are shown, in the fiction, as false, though with an intensity surpassing fiction.

JOHN F. DANBY

from *Poets on Fortune's Hill*

Shakespeare's late verse is a poetry of feeling. For all its richness it is simpler than the verse of the middle period:

> A terrible child-bed hast thou had, my dear;
> No light, no fire; the unfriendly elements
> Forgot thee utterly; nor have I time
> To give thee hallow'd to thy grave, but straight
> Must cast thee, scarcely coffin'd, to the ooze,
> Where, for a monument upon thy bones,
> And aye-remaining lamps, the belching whale
> And humming water must o'erwhelm thy corpse,
> Lying with simple shells. (III.i.57–65)

Dr. Tillyard has referred to "that simple, yet strained, remote and magical note that sounds from time to time in the last plays." The note is sounded, though, very often, together with others—others that are strained and violent, strained in the suddenness of their contrasts. "Lying with simple shells" gives one note: the adjective

From *Poets on Fortune's Hill* by John F. Danby. London: Faber and Faber, Ltd., 1952. Reprinted by permission of Faber and Faber, Ltd.

dissolving disdain in nostalgic envy. "Belching whale"
gives another—the monstrous, indifferent, and bestial life,
and yet the mindless, contented coarseness of the creature. "Humming water" gives yet another—the dizzying
depths through which we sink to the "simple shells," the
loss of consciousness, the sound of the distant storm confused to a blind murmur, then the water itself humming
as it spins in its vortices, humming like a top, still yet
swirling: and as one consciousness is lost we adopt the
consciousness of the sea, and death is a sleep and the
sound of humming as restful as a lullaby, until we are
"lying with simple shells" in the absolute "Apathie" we
both long for and disdain.

But in addition to notes like this there is also that of
a baroque self-consciousness, the manner daring of "aye-
remaining lamps." This intrudes, too, between the intimate immediacy and naturalism of the opening lines and
the imaginative moment of the closing ones. Something
of self-consciousness has to be counted in to complete
the description of the late-Shakespearian style: a distance
to which Shakespeare projects his creation, a lack of
emotional *engagement,* and yet a rich appreciation—an
almost indulgent exaggeration—of the opportunity for
stance any moment can bring along.

Passages such as this tempt us further than Shakespeare
himself seems inclined to go. The immensely suggestive
moments can lead out beyond the frame of character and
beyond the frame of the theme: into the realm of "humming water" and "belching whale." But Shakespeare had
a frame to support him and to keep the moments co-
herently together. In the case of the last three acts of
Pericles the frame is supplied by the romance world
which had also served the writer of the first two acts.

For *Pericles* is a study of the prince in misfortune. The
first two acts show a good man embroiled, swept from
security by the tempest of another's wickedness. The misfortunes are external, the loss is the loss of a throne. The
second part begins with the more inward loss of a wife,
a loss however which brings the gain of a daughter, for
Fortune always has a "doutous or double visage." Shake-

speare is supported by what he has himself learned about the inner structure of this world as well as guided by what he knows of it from others who have also explored it.

Act III begins with the tempest and ends with Pericles making provision for his daughter, the "fresh-new seafarer," and bidding "a priestly farewell" to his wife. Scene i is a lyrical Shakespearian handling of the matter of Patience. In his opening speech Pericles addresses the "god of this great vast"—a deity higher than Fortune. In the first shock of his grief at hearing of Thaisa's death he is in danger of being overthrown. "Patience, good sir," the nurse calls to him, "do not assist the storm,"—

> Be manly and take comfort.   (III.i.22)

The force of Lychorida's last words is apt to be lost on a post-Renaissance audience. "Manly" implies the summoning up of the full fortitude manhood implies, but also assumes in this context the creaturely dependence of that manhood; virtue cannot be self-sufficient however far it exerts itself, and even though it is asserted to the full. Pericles calls out against the gods, but it is a human bewilderment rather than a passionate revolt. Again Lychorida cries, "Patience, good sir." Pericles recovers himself and turns to the child. The overflow of compassion is a good augury. Only those can take comfort who can give comfort, and there is immense tenderness in Pericles' words. By the time he is finished he has found a new balance. His reply to the sailor indicates the firm hold he now has on his reestablished manliness:

> FIRST SAILOR. *What courage, sir? God save you!*
> PERICLES. *Courage enough. I do not fear the flaw:*
>   *It hath done to me the worst.*   (III.i.38—40)

When the sailors tell him his wife must be cast overboard he submits to the necessity. In the great speech we have already analyzed he fully realizes death's final "apathie"—away from the storm, on the sea's floor, "lying

with simple shells": an apathy which is the opposite of
patience as death is the opposite of life. He bids Thaisa
"a priestly farewell."

The difference between the first and the second parts
of *Pericles* can now be more clearly seen. Instead of reporting moral precepts Shakespeare is presenting moral
occasions. The audience not only has a map to the territory, it can also see the movements of the protagonist
across the countryside. In taking over or resuming the
play Shakespeare judged rightly that what it needed was
a "voice"—the impression of a living personality, and
that personality a center of sensitive moral consciousness.
The unit of communication now is the whole scene. Inside that scene we can see the complete turn or rotation
of a person responding to a completely given moral occasion. Lyrically evocative as the scene is, the lyrical imagery would not be sufficient, however, without the clearly
mapped territory behind it—which Shakespeare shared
both with his audience and his collaborator. "Belching
whale" and "humming water," overpoweringly suggestive
as they are, are not as illuminatingly definitive as the in-
terchange between the sailor and the bereaved husband.
"Imagery" is a deceptive word to use in connection with
occasions such as this. Imagery includes more than
metaphor, more even than is usually included in the
phrase "verbal texture." Shakespeare's main controlling
image is the image of a man in certain circumstances
speaking from the midst of his situation to another man
(Shakespeare, again, gives the Sailor a "voice"). The
flow of meaning that then takes place only has significance within the moral situation that has been presented.
The emotive aura of the separable "images" (what Aristotle called "diction") is large and maybe vague. The
total moral reference of the scene, however, is specific
and precise. And the references in this case fall within the
field covered by "patience in adversity."

The two explaining systems which have been applied
recently to the interpretation of the Last Plays miss, I
think, the essentially Elizabethan—and for that matter
the more deeply human—inwardness of the romance

scheme. The first of these has been based on the *Golden Bough* and the fertility cycle and rebirth. The second has been similarly based on the Christian conception of regeneration and resurrection. Neither, I think, is as satisfactory as the contemporary and conventional scheme which Shakespeare used. Anthropology does not take us far enough. By its insidious precipitations it tends to silt over the clear and sharp contours of the Renaissance moral world. The second explaining system errs in the opposite direction. It carries us too far and too fast. It particularizes in a field of meaning beyond Shakespeare's intention—though Shakespeare, I have no doubt, would know St. Paul and the burial service, and accepted the New Testament. To theologize the last plays, however, is to distort them. Though patience as Shakespeare conceives it implies St. Paul and the New Testament, patience as Shakespeare realizes it in the Last Plays is a familiar and well-walked parish in a wider diocese. Nor is the parish presided over by the Fisher King, and in it St. Paul is taken for granted but not allegorized in every Whitsun pastoral. And this brings us to a further distortion which over-anxiety about the greatness of Shakespeare's final plays is sometimes responsible for—a distortion of their tone. Shakespeare's last plays are not conceived at the same level of seriousness as Dante's *Paradiso*. They have an *ironia* of their own. Shakespeare during the last period is comparatively relaxed. He makes a toy of thought. Drawing on the full richness of his inner life, sporadically, as they do, executed with the unanxious brilliance of the maestro who has never lost his flair for improvisation, as they are, the final plays are for all that adjusted to the level of entertainment, controlled by an intention "which was to please."

The "resurrection" scene in *Pericles,* for example, follows immediately on the storm and Thaisa's committal to the sea. The casket in which Thaisa has been placed is washed ashore near the house of Cerimon. Cerimon, as the Epilogue says, is a "reverend" example of "learned charity": as Mr. Wilson Knight has pointed out, Shakespeare's first sketch for Prospero. Cerimon prefers the

power which wisdom gives to that which the mere governor can exercise:

> I held it ever,
> Virtue and cunning were endowments greater
> Than nobleness and riches: careless heirs
> May the two latter darken and expend;
> But immortality attends the former,
> Making a man a god. 'Tis known I ever
> Have studied physic.   (III.ii.26–32)

With a kind of endearing *pietas* Shakespeare builds up
his scene along lines slightly old-fashioned. We are shown
Cerimon first in actual fact helping "some Persons who
have been shipwrecked." We then see him being greeted
by two gentlemen who announce his character:

> Your honor hath through Ephesus pour'd forth
> Your charity, and hundreds call themselves
> Your creatures, who by you have been restor'd.
>   (III.ii.43–45)

Finally Thaisa's coffin is brought in and opened, and the
moment of her resuscitation occurs. Again the lyrical note
is struck. The verse quickens and pants with wonder:

> Gentlemen,
> This queen will live: nature awakes; a warmth
> Breathes out of her . . . see how she 'gins to blow
> Into life's flower again . . .
>   . . . She is alive; behold
> Her eyelids, cases to those heavenly jewels
> Which Pericles hath lost,
> Begins to part their fringes of bright gold;
> And diamonds of a most praised water
> Do appear, to make the world twice rich. Live,
> And make us weep to hear your fate, fair creature,
> Rare as you seem to be!
> *Thaisa.*   O dear Diana!
> Where am I? Where's my lord? What world is this?
>   (III.ii.93–108)

When thinking of symbolism we must remember that one of the most important things an apple can mean is simply itself. Thaisa's reawakening feels to her like a rebirth—and also like a loss. To the spectators it is wonder enough, the more so that Thaisa is a miracle of beauty. But the moment attains its highest significance, I think, when it is brought into relation with Pericles' great speech before the committal, and into the general romance frame of "doutous fortune" and the Providence that smiles while it seems to frown. We do not need to make it more important than that—nor less. And indeed, while there is a restoration of the seeming dead to breathing warmth, it is still a world of trial and of separation to which Thaisa is brought back. Cut off from Pericles, she must retire to Diana's temple and endure her exile in patience.

KENNETH MUIR

from *Shakespeare as Collaborator*

In the restoration scene,[1] tempest imagery is again used, but now no longer expressing hatred and discord—

> Lest this great sea of joys rushing upon me
> O'erbear the shores of my mortality,
> And drown me with their sweetness.

Once again, as in *King Lear*, the restoration is accompanied by music, first by Marina's lost song, and then by the music of the spheres; it is followed by Pericles' demand for fresh garments and by the appearance of Diana in a vision—the first theophany in Shakespeare's works.[2]

The quality of the scene may be illustrated by a single image. In *Twelfth Night* Viola speaks of the love-sick maid who

> sat like Patience on a monument,
> Smiling at grief.

A similar image is used in this scene in *Pericles* with even

From *Shakespeare as Collaborator* by Kenneth Muir. London: Methuen & Co., Ltd., 1960. Reprinted by permission of Methuen & Co., Ltd., and Barnes & Noble, Inc.
[1] The reader may be referred to the chapter in Derek Traversi's *Shakespeare's Last Period* and to the masterly analysis by G. Wilson Knight in *The Crown of Life*.
[2] The appearance of Hymen in *As You Like It* is in a masque performed by human actors.

greater dramatic force. The hero, meeting his daughter after many years of suffering, sees in her face the signs of her suffering and of ordeals bravely borne. He then uses the following image:

> Yet thou dost look
> Like Patience, gazing on Kings' graves, and smiling
> Extremity out of act.

This wonderful image suggests all that Marina has undergone and all that Pericles himself has endured. It suggests that Marina is a king's daughter; it suggests her courage and patience in adversity—pursued by a murderer, captured by pirates, and sold to a brothel. Pericles is to be reborn; Thaisa is to be restored to him from the sea; and the whole family is to be reunited in an earthly resurrection. This is the situation in the play, and the image is exquisitely appropriate to it. The theme of the play is the restoration of the lost and the conquest of death by love—in so far as the theme of one of Shakespeare's plays can be expressed in abstract terms. This theme, this particular scene, its antecedents and its sequel, and the face of the girl imagined by the poet called up the inevitable image which is not merely a symbolic description of Marina but also helps to create the vision of the play.

Journeys that end in lovers' meeting, scenes in which brother and sister, husband and wife, or parents and children meet again after long separation, when each believed the other dead, were frequent episodes in Elizabethan fiction—and in the Greek Romances on which they were sometimes based—and they have always been effective on the stage, whether in Greek tragedy or Latin comedy. Two of Euripides' most effective scenes are the meeting of Iphigenia and Orestes in Tauris and the restoration of Alcestis to her husband. Even the reunion of Egeon and his wife in *The Comedy of Errors* is a moving scene in a play which is largely farcical; the silent reunion of Isabella and Claudio is a little-recognized masterstroke in *Measure for Measure;* and the meeting of Viola and Sebastian in *Twelfth Night* is a touching climax to that

play. The meeting of Pericles and Marina surpasses all
these. Its effectiveness, and the effectiveness of the whole
play, is due partly to Shakespeare's creation of a kind
of myth which he could set up against the changes and
chances of this mortal life. He is calling in a new world to
redress the balance of the old, a new world in which the
designs of evil men are frustrated and in which everything comes right in the end—the beautiful queen is not
really dead, the beautiful princess is saved from murder
and rape and the contamination of the brothel, and the
hero, after more trials and tribulations than are normally
the lot of man, is rewarded with unforeseen and un-
imagined happiness. Shakespeare is aware that his story is
too good to be true, but such fables are a criticism of life
as it is, and (as some think) a statement of faith. In a
pagan setting he creates what is virtually an immortality
myth.

The misfortunes that befall Pericles are undeserved,
and the restoration to him of his wife and child is due to
the inscrutable workings of Providence. In the plays
which followed Shakespeare set out to eliminate accident,
and to infuse the restoration theme with ethical meaning.
This could be done only by replacing the workings of an
arbitrary providence by the operations of sin and forgiveness. Leontes' jealousy causes the death of Mamillius,
and apparently of Hermione also, the loss of Perdita, and
estrangement from Polixenes. But the two kings are
reconciled through the marriage of their children; and
when Leontes by his penitence has earned forgiveness,
Hermione is restored to him. In *Pericles* Shakespeare had
dealt at length with the finding of the lost daughter and
only cursorily with the reunion of husband and wife. In
The Winter's Tale the emphasis is reversed. The father-
daughter recognition takes place off stage, and Shakespeare concentrates on the reunion of Leontes and
Hermione—because Leontes has sinned chiefly against
her and needs her forgiveness before the play can end in
reconciliation. In *Cymbeline* Imogen forgives Posthumus
for his attempted murder, and their reconciliation does
not require a marriage of children to cement it. In *The*

Tempest Shakespeare concentrates on the act of forgiveness itself. In *The Winter's Tale* and *Cymbeline* the hero is the sinner; in *The Tempest* the hero is sinned against, and the betrayal had taken place sixteen years before. By this means Shakespeare eliminated the break of sixteen years which occurs in both *Pericles* and *The Winter's Tale*. The advantages are not all on one side; and the French critic who remarked that Shakespeare finally succeeded in obeying the unity of time by eliminating action altogether was not without some justification. The looser structure of *The Winter's Tale* is necessary to the particular effects at which Shakespeare was aiming; and the yet looser structure of *Pericles* is the only way by which the story of Apollonius could be put on the stage.

In recent years there has been a revival of interest in the play, heralded by T. S. Eliot's exquisite *Marina* and by Wilson Knight's eloquent reassessment in *The Crown of Life,* and exemplified by productions at the Old Vic and Birmingham and by two at Stratford. One Stratford production omitted the first act, and the liberties taken in the other seemed to indicate a lack of confidence in the play's ability to appeal to a modern audience. But at Birmingham the audience was captivated throughout the performance; and this was yet another indication that Shakespeare knew better than his critics, and better even than modish producers, that he had hit on precisely the right form for the material he was dramatizing, and that we have no right to deplore the taste of the groundlings who were enthusiastic when the play was first performed.

M. ST. CLARE BYRNE

from *The Shakespeare Season at the Old Vic, 1957–58, and Stratford-upon-Avon, 1958*

The year's rarity was *Pericles* (8 July 1958). It surprised everybody by its stage-worthiness. This is the third time it has been produced at Stratford. The first, as might be guessed, the date being 1900 and the company Benson's, was a "purged and refined" version. In 1947, with Act I omitted, it was produced by Nugent Monck with Paul Scofield in the name part. It was given at the Old Vic in 1921, and at the Open Air Theatre in 1939. In 1854, when Phelps made it the most spectacular of all his Sadler's Wells productions, it had not been seen on the boards in London for over a hundred years. Yet it must, in its time, have been genuinely popular—witness, six quarto editions between 1609 and 1636.

Tony Richardson, now Associate Artistic Director of the English Stage Company at the Royal Court Theatre, has in the last two years made his name as the producer of John Osborne's *Look Back in Anger* and *The Entertainer*. This is his first Shakespeare production, and it is vastly to his credit that without any drastic cuts, or in-

From *Shakespeare Quarterly*, IX (1958), pp. 520–523. Reprinted by permission of the author and publisher.

deed any invention that does not spring directly from the play itself, he has contrived to make this episodic and extravagantly improbable tale hold our interest continuously and easily, not by turning it into something different but by emphasizing its inherent qualities and extracting from it the real, if mixed, values which must originally have accounted for its popularity. Even more than *Cymbeline,* it is a fairy tale, with similar folktale elements—a gorgeous mix-up of "matter of Rome," oriental fable, chivalric romance and the popular narrative ingredients that provide the medieval origins of English fiction.

The author himself explains as much, summoning the "moral Gower," as presenter or Chorus, to apologize to those "born in these latter times, when wit's more ripe," for his antique rimes, and "to sing a song that old was sung . . . at festivals, On ember-eves and holy ales." From this the producer takes his cue. Some might have been tempted to get rid of Gower; not so Mr. Richardson. His author has given him Gower; it is his problem, therefore, to turn his necessity to glorious gain. Gower is an intermediary between an ancient tale and a sophisticated age. In *Henry VIII* the author insists that all is true: the audience must "think ye see the very persons of our noble story As they were living." Here they are to see everything as images of truth, at one remove from reality. Gower is a storyteller, therefore a spellbinder, and this is where Mr. Richardson shows that his lively imagination and inventive talent are the genuine article, when with the aid of that equally imaginative and inventive stage designer, Loudon Sainthill, he combines the author's dramatic device of the chorus with a theatrical framework to give unity to the action of the play.

To a strange music—recorded, the program tells us, on "Ancient and Exotic instruments"—the play opens in complete darkness. Low down, at stage level, we become aware of flickers of light: the darkness dissolves . . . lifts . . . we have been watching the glint of the gilded blades of six great long-handled sweeps. Downstage, almost in the proscenium arch, to right and left, there are stepped and bulwarked rostrums, suggesting the beak and

stern of a rowing galley. Rowers, three a side, pull
steadily to the rhythm of a sea-shanty tune; the only
words we hear are "Roll and go!" In the background
there is a patterning of cordage and sails and spars against
open sky; and downstage, with the six rowers, is Edric
Connor, the West Indian singer and actor, who sings and
speaks Gower's linking narrative to this more intimate
audience, not to us the theatre audience. This is the translation into theatrical terms of the dramatic intention of
the chorus, which thus provides an admirable and most
adaptable permanent setting for the whole story. The continual reminder of the sea theme, which is the very thread
upon which the plot is hung, is exactly right. It anchors
the rambling yarn to an atmosphere, and enables us to
see it all through the eyes of the seamen's crude and un-
sophisticated but vivid imaginations. As the storyteller
weaves his spell, out of the background of ship and sky
his magic summons the figures of his tale; and as they
materialize he retires downstage, and when an episode
ends he steps back into the scene, sometimes before the
beings his fancy has evoked have all departed. We are not
called upon for any personal suspension of disbelief; yet
the marvels and horrors and crudities and improbabilities
need not be toned down. The "relations of Mariners"
were proverbial for a tall story long before the days of
Sir Thomas Browne. The characters have no dimensional
quality, no more depth than folktale heroes and villains.
In this world of good and evil, vice and virtue are as
flatly personified as in a morality, and visual impact is
the important thing. The gorgeous colors and opulent display of Loudon Sainthill's Graeco-Byzantine costumes
convey the melodramatic exaggeration of the sailors'
ideas of Eastern splendor and pick up these symbolic
figures, and also the moods and morals of the quickly-
changing scenes, so that Acts I and II make a real con-
tribution to the story as a whole by creating the fabulous
world in which it moves. There is nothing dull about them
when tackled in this way, with the aid of Edric Connor's
large and genial personality, his warm chuckling voice,
and the persuasive lilt of the true spellbinder.

The opening episode—incest at Antioch—catches the right note of barbaric violence and lust, all in brilliant blues, greens, purple and silver against a lurid red background. Antiochus and his men seem made of spikes and fantastic scythed spears, and there is a grim reminder of the fate that lies behind the riddle that the hero must read to win the hand of the King's daughter, when the heads of the suitors who have preceded him are borne in impaled on tall spears. Thence to Tarsus, where the starving populace, in dulled greys and greens and black, look almost incandescent with decay; and so to Pentapolis, red and gold for the triumphs and feasting, with Mark Dignam as Simonides—a delightful old codger with a twinkle in his eye—presiding over the revels as definitely a Good King. After this we shall not question either the simple characterization or the extravagances of the serious half of the drama. We know the world to which the story belongs, though I doubt if many readers have visualized it for themselves; and in comparison, what is to follow will seem the credible, sober, and human story of the loss and ultimate restoration of the wife and child of Pericles. With Act III the authentic line comes thundering in, the first wave of the Shakespearian tempest of loss and suffering: "Thou god of this great vast, rebuke these surges." When the actual storm is stilled Mr. Richardson is content to use the simplest means, as in the brief and moving scene where the learned physician, Cerimon, opens the chest in which the supposedly-dead Thaisa has been coffined and revives her from her trance. He has used his convention with the utmost theatrical boldness: he continues to use it discreetly, and it does not fail him or us.

In remaining true to the framework and fairy-tale convention in his handling of the brothel scenes Mr. Richardson probably comes nearer to an understanding of the author's intentions than some of the literary critics who have commented on them. He sets the tone for the whole episode by having the scene hailed with rich, bawdy laughter by the sailors, as the brothel itself, complete with its preposterous, bedizened inmates, comes up in scarlet splendor upon the slowly-rising stage. These scenes are not to be grim: and I think they were not meant to be. Brothels and bawds and that ilk were good Jacobean fun, and his convention enables Mr. Richardson to play it straight and simple: the sailors have again given the cue, and we know where we are with this particular brothel, whether or not we agree. Confident that virtue can "see to do what virtue would," we can settle down to enjoy the comic bewilderment of the bawdiest of bawds, Angela Baddeley, completely unrecognizable in what one might call Lush Restoration Tawdry—"How would *you* dress a Graeco-Byzantine bawd?" as I said to my companion who was captious about her costume—and of the most endearing of pimps (Patrick Wymark as Boult), who have never, in the whole course of their naughty lives, come across anything like Marina. For letting these scenes and their players play perfectly straight, but allowing himself that irresistible comment of the bead curtain over the doorway that rattled authentically at every entrance and exit, I give Mr. Richardson top marks.

What a producer should do about *sound,* when Pericles, in the recognition scene with Marina, hears the music of the spheres, is a problem as intractable as that of the breaking harpstring in *The Cherry Orchard,* and "the God Hercules now leaves him" in *Antony & Cleopatra.* The answer might be recorded sound, but it was not really satisfactory this time. One wants quivering sound "the aery region thrilling." Perhaps one day whispering microphones will breathe into the ears of audiences, but meanwhile these subtleties remain only doubtfully effective.

William Shakespeare

CYMBELINE

Edited by Richard Hosley

Contents

Introduction

In *Cymbeline* Shakespeare combines three stories which originate at three different points in space (so to speak) and gradually converge toward the end of the play. The first story is of a wife who is separated from and eventually reunited with her husband: Imogen and Posthumus. This constitutes the primary action of the play. It fills the first two acts to the exclusion of all else, and, though subordinated to a secondary and a tertiary action in Acts III and IV, it dominates the last act. Thus it is the major structural entity of the play, giving shape to the whole from beginning to end. The second story is of two sons who have been separated from their father in infancy and who eventually are reunited with him: Guiderius and Arviragus. This constitutes the secondary action of the play. It does not begin, however, in the first act and run in parallel with the primary action, as do the secondary actions of *Twelfth Night, The Merchant of Venice,* and *King Lear.* Rather, it begins in the middle of the play (III.iii), is partly joined to the primary action through the sojourn of Imogen with the sons in her assumed identity of Fidele (III.vi–IV.ii), and is fully joined to the primary action in the long last scene of the play (V.v). In this respect it bears a general resemblance to the secondary actions of *Pericles* and *The Winter's Tale* (where the subject is again the reunion of child with parent), the chief difference being that in those plays Shakespeare, having chosen to present the early story of the mother and father together with the story of the loss of the infant child, employed a mid-play lapse of many years during which the child might grow to marriageable age. The third story is of a king who successfully defends his country against invasion: Cymbeline. This, despite the emphasis given it by the play's title and by Cymbeline's presence in the primary action from the start in his role as Imogen's father, constitutes a tertiary action, beginning, like the secondary action, not in the first act but in the middle of the play, when the Roman ambassador Lucius demands tribute of Cymbeline (III.i). Gradually the tertiary action approaches the other actions of the play, joining first the primary action when Lucius accepts Fidele as his page (IV.ii), then the secondary when Guiderius and Arviragus decide to take up arms against the Romans (IV.iv). In the last scene the three actions are fused in a brilliant denouement in which no less than twenty-five plot complications are untied.

Each of the three stories of which *Cymbeline* is composed is itself a combination of various literary elements. The Imogen-Posthumus story is by all odds the most complex of the three. The basic source of this story is the ninth novella of the Second Day of Boccaccio's *Decameron* (see The Sources of *Cymbeline,* page 185). (Shakespeare also made some use of a German variant of the Boccaccio novella which had been translated into English under the title of *Frederick of Jennen* early in the sixteenth century.) In the first half of his story Shakespeare is generally faithful to the first half of Boccaccio's story. Like Boccaccio, he presents the husband's wager on the wife's chastity, the villain's stratagem of the trunk, the consequent winning of the wager, and the servant's failure to carry out the husband's order to kill the wife. A significant variation in this part of the story is that Shakespeare's villain actually attempts the seduction of the wife; Boccaccio's villain becomes by common report so convinced of the wife's chastity that he gives up all thought of winning the wager without guile and proceeds immediately to the stratagem of the trunk. Another significant variation is Shakespeare's providing a father for the heroine—and, in fact, a father who is a king. Accordingly the heroine is raised in rank from merchant's wife to princess, the initial separation on which the whole story turns being due not to the husband's casual absence on commerce but to his political exile. Thus a subsequent connection with the political story of Cymbeline is provided for.

For the first half of the Imogen-Posthumus story (and for the second as well) Shakespeare used also as source an anonymous dramatic romance entitled *The Rare Triumphs of Love and Fortune* (acted 1582). (In *Cymbeline* the two sources may be thought of as superimposed one upon the other.) In *Love and Fortune* a princess named Fidelia (compare Imogen's pseudonym Fidele) is in love with a supposed orphan who, like Posthumus, has been brought up as the King's ward. Fidelia's brother secures the banishment of the lover, who thereupon sends word to Fidelia to run away from court and meet him at a cave. (The plan miscarries and Fidelia, like Imogen, wanders about until she meets an old man who, like Belarius, had been a courtier until unjustly banished by the King and who now lives as a hermit in a cave.) To the basic situation of *Love and Fortune* Shakespeare added the folk-tale motif of the Wicked Stepmother, a significant difference from the usual situation being that Shakespeare's stepmother wishes not to substitute her own child for the father's child but to advance her son by marrying him to the father's daughter, who, in the absence of surviving male issue, is heir to the kingdom. (The Queen's motivation becomes more conventional at III.v.64.) Thus a political motive for the banishment of Posthumus is provided. The Physician is an added character required by the plot device of the potion, which Shakespeare made use of later in the play.

In the second half of the Imogen-Posthumus story Shakespeare departed more widely from Boccaccio's story, but he retained its essential framework. In Boccaccio, the wife adopts male disguise, takes service with a merchant, travels with him to Alexandria, passes into the service of the Sultan (whose especial favor she comes to enjoy), meets the villain in a shop, and succeeds in bringing him to judgment before the Sultan and her husband. The villain is forced to confess, the husband repents of his error, husband and wife are reunited, and the villain is executed. In Shakespeare, the wife adopts male disguise, travels to Wales (where she lives for a time with rustic outlaws), takes service with the general of an invading army, is captured along with the invaders by the King (whose especial favor she comes to enjoy), recognizes the villain among the captives, and succeeds in bringing him to judgment before the King and her husband. The villain repents and confesses, the husband repents of his error, husband and wife are reunited, and the villain is forgiven.

Two variations in this part of the Imogen-Posthumus story have the effect of unifying divergent strands of the triple-action plot. The disguised wife's sojourn with rustic outlaws in the mountains of Wales (apparently suggested by Fidelia's experience in *Love and Fortune* but perhaps also reflective of Erminia's pastoral sojourn in Book VII of Tasso's *Jerusalem Delivered*) connects the primary action with the secondary action involving Cymbeline's lost sons; and Imogen's acceptance of service with the Roman general Lucius (which is essentially present in Boccaccio) connects the primary action with the tertiary action of the invasion of Britain. Two further variations are of interest. The first, a structural matter, involves the point at which the author begins his story. Boccaccio begins his story at the point of the wager, Shakespeare his at a point shortly after the marriage that will make the wager possible. It is as though *Cymbeline* were the second part of an Elizabethan two-part play of which the first part, a comedy, has ended, as by convention a comedy should, with the marriage of lovers who have succeeded in overcoming all obstacles (parental opposition among them) to their union. In *Othello* Shakespeare had already used this particular starting point for a story of jealousy in marriage, beginning the action with a confrontation of angry father and successful wooer in presence of the newly married daughter. In *Cymbeline* there is the same initial confrontation, the chief difference being that the father (unlike Brabantio) does not suggest to the husband the possibility of the daughter's infidelity. Another variation from Boccaccio is the strong emphasis which Shakespeare gives to the reciprocal themes of repentance and forgiveness. Posthumus, long before he learns he has been deceived by Iachimo, sincerely repents of, and wishes to die in expiation for, the crime which he supposes he has committed against Imogen; and, as he freely repents, so Imogen freely forgives him. Again, Iachimo, when his plot is exposed, undergoes a "conversion" which may be compared with the conversion of Edmund in *King Lear* ("some good I mean to do, Despite of mine own nature") and contrasted with the defiant persistence in evil of Iago in *Othello* ("Demand me nothing. What you know, you know"). The sincerity of Iachimo's conversion is proved by his willingness to accept the punishment of death; and, as he freely repents, so Posthumus freely forgives him. Here, as in *The Winter's Tale* and *The Tempest*, Shakespeare echoes themes he had treated more fully in *The Merchant of Venice* and *Measure for Measure*.

In addition to these variations, Shakespeare made four important additions to the latter half of Boccaccio's story: the killing of Cloten, the supposed death of Imogen, Imogen's mistaking Cloten's body for that of Posthumus, and the Vision of Posthumus.

Since there is no character in Boccaccio corresponding to Cloten, his essential character may well have been suggested by Fidelia's villainous brother in *Love and Fortune*. The killing of Cloten by Guiderius is closely connected with Cloten's intention to rape Imogen. This intention makes Cloten an example of lust and villainy to be compared with the example afforded by Iachimo: the one lecherous villain is stupid and boorish, the other subtle and Italianate. The intention also "justifies" the killing of Cloten, for in effect Guiderius, even though unaware of Cloten's intention and Fidele's true identity, acts to protect his sister from rape. The manner of the killing —decapitation, with the severed head being thrown into a stream which will carry it to the sea—appears to echo a folk ritual of some sort. There is a patent allusion to the death of Orpheus, whose severed head was thrown into the river Hebrus, down which it was carried to the sea and eventually to Lesbos; and there was an analogous ritual connected with the worship of Adonis at Alexandria, where "a Head, of papyrus, representing the god, was, with every show of mourning, committed to the waves, and borne within seven days by a current . . . to Byblos . . ." (Jessie L. Weston, *From Ritual to Romance,* ed. 1957, p. 47). (These allusions, mock-epic or mock-mythic in relation to Cloten himself, may carry serious meaning in relation to Cloten as a surrogate for Posthumus.) The killing of Cloten may be compared also with the killing of Antigonus in *The Winter's Tale:* in each case a vicious or a flawed character is punished for attempted violence against the heroine, and in each case there seems to be operative a tradition of tragicomedy which goes back ultimately to what Aristotle called "tragedy with a double issue"—that is to say, a play threatening death which provides a happy ending for "good" characters but the reward of death for "bad." This tradition is involved also in the death of the Queen at the end of the play.

The general plot device of the supposed death of a beloved woman (a staple of Greek romance) was one that Shakespeare had already used in *Romeo and Juliet, Much Ado About Nothing,* and *Pericles,* and that he was to use again in *The Winter's Tale;* and the particular device of the potion that brings about the supposed death he had used in *Romeo and Juliet.* In *Cymbeline* (IV.ii) the supposed death of Imogen symbolizes the death which Posthumus had commanded, separates Imogen from the rustic outlaws, and emphasizes the operation of Providence in the accident of the malevolent Queen's having requested poison of a physician who, because of his wisdom and benevolence, supplied her instead with a harmless sleeping potion.

The killing of Cloten and the supposed death of Imogen lead to the Elizabethan-Gothic grotesquerie of Imogen's mistaking the headless body of Cloten for that of Posthumus. Through this theatrically sensational mistake (so embarrassing to modern audiences) Shakespeare makes the interesting point that Imogen, like Posthumus, can be victimized by circumstance and deceived by appearance—and in a situation outwardly suggestive of sexual compromise, for unwittingly the paragon of virtue lies beside and lovingly embraces the body of a man who is not her husband but her would-have-been rapist. (Even so she has earlier unwittingly spent the night with her would-be seducer Iachimo.) A possible source of this episode exists in an anonymous dramatic romance entitled *Clyomon and Clamydes,* dating from the 1580's. Here the heroine, Neronis, who has left the court in the disguise of a boy and taken service with a shepherd, comes upon a coffin containing the body of the King of Norway, earlier slain in combat by Neronis's lover Clyomon. Since Clyomon has left his emblazoned shield beside the coffin, Neronis mistakes the body of the King of Norway for that of Clyomon, grieves, despairs, and is on the point of committing suicide. At this moment the personification of Providence descends from heaven, gives Neronis a paper informing her that Clyomon is alive, and returns to heaven. Another possible source of this episode is afforded by the *Ethiopica* of Heliodorus, in which Theagenes embraces the body of a dead woman which he mistakes for that of his beloved, Charicleia.

The Vision of Posthumus (V.iv), in which Jupiter descends from heaven, may have been suggested by the descent of Providence in *Clyomon and Clamydes.* In any case, the Vision involves a literary tradition deriving ultimately from the appearance-of-a-god-in-a-dream of classical epic. Shakespeare had used such a dream theophany in *Pericles,* where the goddess Diana appears to the protagonist in a dream; and he had used the closely allied convention of the appearance-of-a-ghost-in-a-dream in *Richard III,* where the Ghosts of Richard's victims appear successively to the dreaming Richard and Richmond. A native stage tradition may also be influential, for the great fifteenth-century scriptural cycles frequently employ the appearance-of-an-angel-in-a-dream. An Elizabethan stage convention is certainly operative, the god who descends from stage cover to stage by means of suspension-gear: Juno in *The Tempest*, Venus in Greene's *Alphonsus King of Aragon*, Providence in the anonymous *Clyomon and Clamydes*, perhaps Diana in *Pericles*. In *Cymbeline*, as Bertrand Evans has pointed out (see Commentaries, page 226), Jupiter is not a *deus ex machina* in the sense that he resolves a complication of the plot; rather, the theophany focuses our growing awareness that God's providence is indeed at work, even though for a time (during the long and frightening absence of Iachimo, the only person who, by confessing his slander against Imogen, can resolve the major complication of the plot) we may have seen little visible evidence of it. It should be added that the authenticity of the Vision, frequently called in question by critics of the nineteenth and early twentieth centuries, is now (together with the authenticity of the rest of the play) generally accepted, perhaps largely because of the cogent demonstration by G. Wilson Knight in *The Crown of Life* (1947).

At least one other influence on the Imogen-Posthumus story can be discerned: that of Greek romance. The influence was already present in Boccaccio's story, for Greek romance characteristically involves a separation of lover from beloved (or of husband from wife), consequent wanderings over great distances and for long periods of time, and an eventual reunion of the lovers. *Apollonius of Tyre*, which Shakespeare had dramatized in *Pericles*, is a good example of the type, but an example of specific relevance to *Cymbeline* is afforded by the *Ethiopica* of Heliodorus, of which an Elizabethan translation (the first of three) appeared in 1567. From the *Ethiopica* (to which he had alluded in *Twelfth Night*, V.i.118) Shakespeare apparently took a suggestion for the striking of the disguised Imogen by Posthumus (V.v). Charicleia, who has been separated from her lover, Theagenes, comes to Memphis and recognizes him. Since she is disguised as a beggar, however, Theagenes does not recognize her.

> Frantically, as if sight of him had stung her, she ran to him, clasped him close, hung upon his neck, and caressed him with inarticulate sighs and tears. When he saw her face, begrimed and purposely discolored, and her torn and tattered garments, he took her for a shame-

less beggar. He pulled her off and thrust her away, and when she would not let go he struck her for troubling him and blocking his view of Calasiris and his sons. She said to him softly, "Pythias, have you forgotten the lamp?" The words struck Theagenes like a bolt. He remembered that the lamp was a token they had agreed upon and gazed into Charicleia's eyes, whose brilliance broke upon him like the sun's rays through a cloud. He threw his arms about her and embraced her.

(translation by Moses Hadas)

The striking of Imogen by Posthumus may also reflect a device of the romantic epics, the individual combat between two knights in which the lover, ignorant of his opponent's sex and true identity, fights with and sometimes kills his beloved in male disguise. Romantic-epic examples include the combat between Tancred and Clorinda in Book XII of Tasso's *Jerusalem Delivered* and that between Arthegal and Britomart in Book III of Spenser's *Fairy Queen;* and dramatic examples in the same tradition include the combat between the title characters of Kyd's *Soliman and Perseda* and between Amintor and Aspatia in *The Maid's Tragedy* by Beaumont and Fletcher.

The secondary action of the play—consisting of the story of Guiderius and Arviragus—begins in III.iii, although we are warned early to expect it by a reference to Cymbeline's lost sons at I.i.58. The Guiderius-Arviragus story employs that standard device of romance tradition, the "lost child." This is Shakespeare's most important innovation in the "historical" materials available to him. Usually—because of the characteristic concern of romance with love—the lost child is a girl, apparently of low degree, who is enabled to marry her lover of high degree when it is revealed that she also is of gentle birth. This is the situation of the heroine in many of the comedies of Plautus and Terence, and it is a common situation in pastoral romance. (Examples are afforded by Glycerium in the *Andria* of Terence, Pastorella in Book VI of *The Fairy Queen,* and Perdita in *The Winter's Tale.*) Sometimes the lost child is a boy, but in such cases the story does not usually involve a love situation, presumably because the mobility required of the wanderer who comes to the environment of the lost child is unsuited to the decorum of a girl. (Compare the convenience, if not the necessity, of Imogen's male disguise.) Sometimes the lost male child is involved ultimately in a situation in which he unwittingly takes or threatens the life of his father (for example, the *Oedipus* of Sophocles) or in which the father unwittingly takes or threatens the life of his son (for example, *The Captives* of Plautus). Cymbeline's threat to execute the confessed homicide Guiderius, who is actually his own son, seems to echo the oedipal situation of *The Captives,* in which the father, Hegio, threatens to execute the supposed slave, Tyndarus, who is actually his own son.

The Guiderius-Arviragus story includes the corollary story of Belarius: as they are lost children, so he is their supposed father. Belarius is primarily the "rusticated courtier" of pastoral romance: the educated and civilized gentleman or nobleman who lives in isolation or among shepherds and with whom the protagonist passes some time during his wanderings. Sometimes the rusticated courtier's exile is voluntary, the result of an unhappy love affair or some other disillusionment. An example is Philisides in Sidney's *Arcadia.* More frequently the rusticated courtier's exile is enforced, the result of banishment for political reasons. An example is the Duke Senior in *As You Like It.* Belarius, an example of the latter type, has an apparent source in Bomelio, the unjustly exiled courtier of *Love and Fortune* who lives in a cave and whom Fidelia meets after running away from court.

Belarius, however, is not only the rusticated courtier, he is also the "shepherd father" of pastoral romance. Usually the shepherd father is only a foster father and the lost child that he rears as his own is a girl. Examples are Melibee, supposed father of Pastorella in Book VI of *The Fairy Queen,* and the Shepherd, supposed father of Perdita in *The Winter's Tale.* Shakespeare makes Belarius not a shepherd but a hunter, because Guiderius and Arviragus must have had the sort of training with weapons that will fit them to fight effectively in defense of their country;

and he makes Belarius a mountaineer in order to emphasize the danger of his position as a political outlaw. (Thus Shakespeare, through discarding sheep and shepherds, emphasizes the basic primitivism which is at the core of most pastoralism.) Nevertheless, it is convenient briefly to regard Belarius as a "shepherd" father in order to understand his relation to tradition. Since the rusticated courtier is rarely a father, Shakespeare seems, in Belarius, to have combined the pastoral character-types of the courtier rusticated for political reasons and the shepherd father. He was to make the same significant combination in amplified and most original form in *The Tempest,* where the only essential departure from the combined traditions (aside from the omission of sheep and shepherds) is that Prospero is not the foster father but the true father of Miranda.

The Guiderius-Arviragus story is amplified and linked to the tertiary action of the play by Shakespeare's use of material from Holinshed's *Chronicles of England, Scotland, and Ireland* (1587): specifically the Scottish victory over Danish invaders at the Battle of Luncarty (near Perth) in 976, which was achieved through the stalwart fighting of the husbandman Hay and his two sons (see *The History of Scotland,* in The Sources of *Cymbeline,* page 205). This joining of the Guiderius-Arviragus story to the Cymbeline story (IV.iv, V.ii–iii) leads to its further joining, in the final scene of the play, to the Imogen-Posthumus story.

The tertiary action of the play—consisting of the Cymbeline story—begins in III.i with the appearance of the Roman ambassador Lucius, although we are warned to expect this action by a reference to Lucius at II.iii.55 and by another to the payment of Roman tribute at II.iv.13. The basic source is *The History of England* in Holinshed's *Chronicles* (see page 203), but particular details have been traced to other sources. Since Holinshed attributes the denial of tribute to Cymbeline's son Guiderius, Shakespeare may well have followed Spenser (*The Fairy Queen,* II.x.50) in attributing the denial to Cymbeline. Moreover, a number of Shakespearian details appear to derive from

Thomas Blenerhasset's "Guidericus" in the 1578 edition of the Second Part of *The Mirror for Magistrates* and from John Higgins's "Guiderius" in the 1587 edition of *The Mirror*. Perhaps the most interesting are the disguising of Posthumus as a British soldier and his fighting against the Romans. These details were apparently suggested by Higgins's account of the Roman captain Hamonius, who disguises himself as a British soldier and pretends to fight against the Romans in order to gain the opportunity of killing Guiderius. One other influence on the Cymbeline story is Shakespeare's own tradition of depicting the invasion of Britain or England, as in *King Lear, Richard III, 3 Henry VI,* and *King John.* In each of these cases, as in *Cymbeline,* the invasion is represented as partly or entirely beneficial to the island kingdom.

The foregoing account stresses the abundance of sources and traditions which Shakespeare characteristically blended into an organic whole in writing *Cymbeline.* The play is extremely complex in its relation to tradition. It is also complex in other respects, posing a number of problems both real and imaginary. The critics have reacted very differently to *Cymbeline.* At one extreme are the Rationalists, chief among them Dr. Johnson (1765):

> To remark the folly of the fiction, the absurdity of the conduct, the confusion of the names and manners of different times, and the impossibility of the events in any system of life, were to waste criticism upon unresisting imbecility, upon faults too evident for detection and too gross for aggravation.

At the other extreme are the Imogenolaters, of whom perhaps the best example is Swinburne (1880):

> The very crown and flower of all her father's daughters—I do not speak here of her human father but her divine—woman above all Shakespeare's women is Imogen. As in Cleopatra we found the incarnate sex, the woman everlasting, so in Imogen we find half-glorified already the immortal godhead of womanhood.

Neither critic need now be taken seriously, although it may be observed that Johnson's aversion to the violent yoking together of Roman Britain and Renaissance Rome reveals a characteristic blindness to the essence of romance.

Many other problems once posed by *Cymbeline* have been solved by recent criticism and scholarship. One such problem has already been mentioned: doubt of the authenticity of certain parts of the play, in particular the Vision of Posthumus. No one now denies that the play is entirely the work of Shakespeare. Another problem has been posed by the suggestion of a lost source-play. The theory, however, is both unnecessary and unsupported by evidence, and it seems to be at variance with what we know of Shakespeare's originality in the handling of multiple sources in such plays as *King Lear, The Merchant of Venice,* and *The Taming of the Shrew*. Another problem has been posed by A. H. Thorndike's suggestion that *Cymbeline* reveals the influence of Beaumont and Fletcher's *Philaster*. This theory has now been effectively disposed of by the late Harold S. Wilson in his English Institute lecture of 1951. Another problem has been posed by the complexity of the plot, which, entailing as it does some two dozen separate denouements, prompted Shaw, in *Cymbeline Refinished,* to rewrite the last act at half the length of the original for a production of 1937. Here Shakespeare's technical virtuosity and its relation to themes of the play have been well expounded by Bertrand Evans (see Commentaries, page 215). Still another problem has been posed by the character of Posthumus and particularly his motivation in accepting Iachimo's wager. Here W. W. Lawrence has enlightened us by setting Posthumus's action in an appropriate context of Renaissance conceptions of a wife's chastity and her husband's honor. And yet another difficulty is posed by the play's characteristic style, which is heavily metaphorical, often perverse in syntax, and sometimes so elliptical as to raise the question whether we are dealing with a metaphysical toughness of thought and angularity of expression comparable to Donne's, or simply with a corrupt text. In the large majority of cases, surely, the former interpretation is to be preferred, for the style of *Cymbeline* can be paralleled in such near-contemporary plays as *Antony and Cleopatra, Coriolanus,* and *The Winter's Tale.*

One teasing problem remains. Modern editors classify *Cymbeline* as a comedy. Why then was the play classified as a tragedy in the Shakespeare Folio of 1623? The classification could be simply an error, Heminges and Condell having forgotten that the play does not end with the death of the title character. Or, as has been suggested, the classification could be due to late receipt of copy in the printing-house, after the comedies (the first of the three genres of the Folio) had been printed off. Neither explanation is very satisfactory. On balance it seems more reasonable to assume that the classification resulted from a deliberate decision on the part of Heminges and Condell. The problem can perhaps be solved by considering two other Folio plays now classified as comedies: *The Winter's Tale* and *Troilus and Cressida.* (All three plays are tragicomedies, the first two of traditional type, the third of nontraditional.) What is the difference between, on the one hand, *The Winter's Tale* (classified as a comedy in the Folio) and, on the other, *Cymbeline* and *Troilus and Cressida* (classified as tragedies in the Folio)? Simply that the first play does not include war in its action, whereas the two latter plays do. In this respect *The Winter's Tale* is like the thirteen other "comedies" of the Folio classification, and *Cymbeline* and *Troilus and Cressida* are like the ten other "tragedies" of the Folio classification. (The distinction does not, to be sure, hold exactly in the case of *All's Well That Ends Well* and *Romeo and Juliet:* in the former play, however, war is not a political matter but a device to expose the braggart soldier Parolles; and in the latter play war is represented by the feud between the rival houses of Capulet and Montague.) Having denied themselves the convenient classification of tragicomedy, Heminges and Condell seem to have made the best of an imperfect bargain by associating *The Winter's Tale* with that Shakespearian genre (comedy) which usually excludes war from the action, *Cymbeline* and *Troilus and*

Cressida with that Shakespearian genre (tragedy) which (like history) usually includes war in the action. Some uncertainty about their decision may be reflected in the fact that in the Folio *The Winter's Tale* stands as the very last of the comedies, *Cymbeline* as the very last of the tragedies. *Troilus and Cressida,* for reasons connected with the printing of the Folio, stands by itself between the histories and the tragedies.

Cymbeline is generally dated during the theatrical season of 1609–10. It was seen by Simon Forman, presumably at the Globe, sometime before September 12, 1611, when Forman died. (Unfortunately his account of the play merely names the characters and summarizes the plot.) *Cymbeline* may have been designed for original production by the King's Men at their indoor theater, the Blackfriars, or at their outdoor theater, the Globe. The issue is relatively unimportant, however, since the same plays were frequently performed at both kinds of playhouse, public and private. On January 1, 1634, *Cymbeline* was acted "at Court by the King's Players," being "well-liked by the King." Probably the theater was the Cockpit-in-Court at Whitehall, though it may have been the Great Hall of Whitehall Palace. In original production *Cymbeline* was presumably performed on a stage generally similar to the one that appears in the well-known De Witt drawing of the Swan Playhouse—that is to say, without benefit of an "inner stage." The present text has been annotated in accordance with this assumption.

RICHARD HOSLEY
University of Arizona

Cymbeline

[Dramatis Personae

Cymbeline, King of Britain

Imogen, daughter to Cymbeline by a former wife, later disguised under the name of Fidele

Posthumus Leonatus, a gentleman, husband to Imogen

Guiderius } sons to Cymbeline, disguised under the
Arviragus } names of Polydore and Cadwal, supposed sons to Morgan

Belarius, a banished lord, disguised under the name of Morgan

The Queen, wife to Cymbeline

Cloten, son to the Queen by a former husband

Cornelius, a physician employed by the Queen

Pisanio, servant to Posthumus

Lords attending on Cymbeline

Ladies attending on the Queen

Helen, a lady attending on Imogen

Two Lords, friends to Cloten

Two Gentlemen of Cymbeline's court

Two Briton Captains

Musicians employed by Cloten

Messengers

Two Jailers

Caius Lucius, Roman ambassador, later general of the Roman forces

Two Roman Senators

Roman Tribunes

Roman Captains

A Soothsayer, named Philharmonus

Philario, an Italian friend to Posthumus

Iachimo, an Italian friend to Philario

A Frenchman, friend to Philario

Jupiter

Ghost of Sicilius Leonatus, father to Posthumus

Ghost of the Mother to Posthumus

Ghosts of the two young Brothers to Posthumus, called Leonati

Briton Soldiers, Roman Soldiers, Attendants, a Dutchman and a Spaniard (friends to Philario)

Scene: Britain, Rome, Wales]

Cymbeline

ACT I

Scene I. [*Britain.*]

Enter two Gentlemen.

First Gentleman. You do not meet a man but frowns.
    Our bloods°1
  No more obey the heavens than our courtiers
  Still seem as does the King's.°

Second Gentleman.   But what's the matter?

First Gentleman. His daughter, and the heir of's king-
    dom, whom
  He purposed to his wife's sole son—a widow   5
  That late he married—hath referred° herself
  Unto a poor but worthy gentleman. She's wedded,
  Her husband banished, she imprisoned. All
  Is outward sorrow, though I think the King
  Be touched at very heart.

---

1 The degree sign (°) indicates a footnote, which is keyed to the
text by line number. Text references are printed in **boldface** type;
the annotation follows in roman type.
I.i.1 bloods moods   **3 seem as does the King's** wear expressions like
the King's   **6 referred** given

41

10 *Second Gentleman.*   None but the King?

First Gentleman. He that hath lost her too. So is the
      Queen,
    That most desired the match. But not a courtier,
    Although they wear their faces to the bent°
    Of the King's looks, hath a heart that is not
    Glad at the thing they scowl at.

15 *Second Gentleman.*   And why so?

First Gentleman. He that hath missed the Princess is a
      thing
    Too bad for bad report, and he that hath her—
    I mean, that married her, alack good man,
    And therefore banished—is a creature such
20   As, to seek through the regions of the earth
    For one his like, there would be something failing
    In him that should compare. I do not think
    So fair an outward and such stuff within
    Endows a man but he.

Second Gentleman.   You speak him far.°

25 *First Gentleman.* I do extend him, sir, within himself,°
    Crush him together rather than unfold
    His measure duly.

Second Gentleman. What's his name and birth?

First Gentleman. I cannot delve him to the root. His
      father
    Was called Sicilius, who did join his honor°
30   Against the Romans with Cassibelan,
    But had his titles by Tenantius, whom
    He served with glory and admired° success,
    So gained the sur-addition° Leonatus;
    And had, besides this gentleman in question,
35   Two other sons, who in the wars o' th' time

13 bent inclination   **24 speak him far** praise him much   **25 do extend . . . himself** i.e., do not exaggerate his real merit   **29 honor**
reputation (as a soldier)   **32 admired** wondered at   **33 sur-addition**
additional title

Died with their swords in hand; for which their
   father,
Then old and fond of issue,° took such sorrow
That he quit being, and his gentle lady,
Big of this gentleman our theme, deceased
As he was born. The King he takes the babe   40
To his protection, calls him Posthumus Leonatus,
Breeds him and makes him of his bedchamber,°
Puts to him° all the learnings that his time°
Could make him the receiver of, which he took
As we do air, fast as 'twas minist'red,   45
And in's spring became a harvest, lived in court—
Which rare it is to do—most praised, most loved,
A sample to the youngest, to th' more mature
A glass that feated them,° and to the graver
A child that guided dotards. To his mistress,   50
For whom he now is banished—her own price°
Proclaims how she esteemed him and his virtue.
By her election° may be truly read
What kind of man he is.

Second Gentleman.   I honor him
Even out of° your report. But pray you tell me,   55
Is she sole child to th' King?

First Gentleman.   His only child.
He had two sons—if this be worth your hearing,
Mark it—the eldest of them at three years old,
I' th' swathing clothes the other, from their nursery
Were stol'n, and to this hour no guess in knowledge 60
Which way they went.

Second Gentleman.   How long is this ago?

First Gentleman. Some twenty years.

Second Gentleman. That a king's children should be
   so conveyed,°

37 **fond of issue** doting on children   42 **of his bedchamber** i.e., a
chamberlain   43 **Puts to him** sets him to work at   43 **time** age
49 **glass that feated them** mirror that reflected their features
51 **price** what she is willing to undergo for his sake   53 **election**
choice   55 **out of** beyond   63 **conveyed** stolen

So slackly guarded, and the search so slow
That could not trace them!

65 *First Gentleman.* Howsoe'er 'tis strange,
Or that the negligence may well be laughed at,
Yet is it true, sir.

Second Gentleman. I do well believe you.

First Gentleman. We must forbear.° Here comes° the gentleman,
The Queen, and Princess. *Exeun*

Enter the Queen, Posthumus, and Imogen.

70 *Queen.* No, be assured you shall not find me, daughter,
After the slander° of most stepmothers,
Evil-eyed unto you. You're my prisoner, but
Your jailer shall deliver you the keys
That lock up your restraint. For you, Posthumus,
75 So soon as I can win th' offended King,
I will be known your advocate. Marry,° yet
The fire of rage is in him, and 'twere good
You leaned unto° his sentence with what patience
Your wisdom may inform you.

Posthumus. Please your Highness,
I will from hence today.

80 *Queen.* You know the peril.
I'll fetch a turn about the garden, pitying
The pangs of barred affections, though the King
Hath charged you should not speak together. *Exit.*

Imogen. O
Dissembling courtesy! How fine this tyrant
85 Can tickle° where she wounds! My dearest husband,
I something fear my father's wrath, but nothing—

68 **forbear** withdraw 68 **Here comes** (this entrance-announcement shows that, though the stage is technically "clear" at line 69 (at which point F marks a new scene), the oncoming players enter before the offgoing ones have completed their exit) 71 **slander** ill repute 76 **Marry** indeed (by the Virgin Mary) 78 **leaned unto** deferred to 85 **tickle** (pretend to) please

Always reserved° my holy duty°—what
His rage can do on me. You must be gone,
And I shall here abide the hourly shot
Of angry eyes, not comforted to live   *90*
But that there is this jewel in the world
That I may see again.

Posthumus.   My queen, my mistress.
O lady, weep no more, lest I give cause
To be suspected of more tenderness
Than doth become a man. I will remain   *95*
The loyal'st husband that did e'er plight troth;
My residence, in Rome at one Philario's,
Who to my father was a friend, to me
Known but by letter. Thither write, my queen,
And with mine eyes I'll drink the words you send,   *100*
Though ink be made of gall.

                    Enter Queen.

Queen.   Be brief, I pray you.
If the King come, I shall incur I know not
How much of his displeasure. [*Aside*] Yet I'll move
    him
To walk this way. I never do him wrong
But he does buy° my injuries, to be friends;   *105*
Pays dear for my offenses.   [*Exit.*]

Posthumus.   Should we be taking leave
As long a term as yet we have to live,
The loathness to depart would grow. Adieu.

Imogen. Nay, stay a little.
Were you but riding forth to air yourself,   *110*
Such parting were too petty. Look here, love;
This diamond was my mother's. [*Giving a ring*]
    Take it, heart,
But° keep it till you woo another wife,
When Imogen is dead.

---

87 reserved excepting   87 duty i.e., of child to parent   105 buy i.e.,
gladly accept   113 But only

Posthumus.   How, how? Another?
115   You gentle gods, give me but this I have,
And cere up° my embracements from a next
With bonds of death! Remain, remain thou here
While sense can keep it on. And, sweetest, fairest,
As I my poor self did exchange for you
120   To your so infinite loss, so in our trifles
I still win of you. For my sake wear this.

                         [*Giving a bracelet*]

It is a manacle of love; I'll place it
Upon this fairest prisoner.

Imogen.   O the gods!
When shall we see again?

        Enter Cymbeline and Lords.

Posthumus.   Alack, the King!

Cymbeline. Thou basest thing, avoid° hence, from my
125   sight!
If after this command thou fraught° the court
With thy unworthiness, thou diest. Away!
Thou'rt poison to my blood.

Posthumus.   The gods protect you,
And bless the good remainders of° the court.
I am gone.   *Exit.*

130 *Imogen.*   There cannot be a pinch in death
More sharp than this is.

Cymbeline.   O disloyal thing
That shouldst repair° my youth, thou heap'st
A year's age on me.

Imogen.   I beseech you, sir,
Harm not yourself with your vexation.
135   I am senseless of° your wrath; a touch more rare°
Subdues all pangs, all fears.

Cymbeline.   Past grace? obedience?

---

116 **cere up** shroud   125 **avoid** go   126 **fraught** freight, burden
129 **remainders of** those who remain at   132 **repair** renew   135 **am
senseless of** do not feel   135 **touch more rare** finer anxiety

Imogen. Past hope, and in despair; that way, past
   grace.

Cymbeline. That mightst have had the sole son of my
   queen.

Imogen. O blessed that I might not! I chose an eagle
   And did avoid a puttock.°   140

Cymbeline. Thou took'st a beggar, wouldst have made
   my throne
   A seat for baseness.

Imogen.   No, I rather added
   A luster to it.

Cymbeline.   O thou vile one!

Imogen.   Sir,
   It is your fault that I have loved Posthumus.
   You bred him as my playfellow, and he is   145
   A man worth any woman; overbuys me
   Almost the sum he pays.°

Cymbeline.   What, art thou mad?

Imogen. Almost, sir. Heaven restore me! Would I were
   A neatherd's° daughter, and my Leonatus
   Our neighbor shepherd's son.

Enter Queen.

Cymbeline.   Thou foolish thing!   150
   [*To Queen*] They were again together. You have
   done
   Not after our command. Away with her
   And pen her up.

Queen.   Beseech° your patience. Peace,
   Dear lady daughter, peace! Sweet sovereign,

---

140 **puttock** kite (bird of prey)   146–47 **overbuys me . . . pays he**
exceeds me in worth by almost the price which he is now called upon
to pay, i.e., banishment (J. M. Nosworthy)   149 **neatherd's** cow-
herd's   153 **Beseech** I beseech

Leave us to ourselves, and make yourself some
155   comfort
Out of your best advice.°

Cymbeline.   Nay, let her languish
A drop of blood a day and, being aged,
Die of this folly.

                    Exeunt [Cymbeline and Lords].

                    Enter Pisanio.

Queen.   Fie, you must give way.—
Here is your servant. How now, sir? What news?

Pisanio. My lord your son drew on my master.

160 *Queen.*   Ha!
No harm, I trust, is done?

Pisanio.   There might have been
But that my master rather played than fought
And had no help of anger. They were parted
By gentlemen at hand.

Queen.   I am very glad on't.

Imogen. Your son's my father's friend; he takes his
165   part°
To draw upon an exile. O brave sir!
I would they were in Afric both together,
Myself by with a needle° that I might prick
The goer-back. Why came you from your master?

170 *Pisanio.* On his command. He would not suffer me
To bring him to the haven, left these notes
Of what commands I should be subject to
When't pleased you to employ me.

Queen.   This hath been
Your faithful servant. I dare lay° mine honor
He will remain so.

175 *Pisanio.*   I humbly thank your Highness.

155 **advice** consideration   165 **takes his part** plays his usual role
168 **needle** (pronounced "neel")   174 **lay** stake

Queen. Pray walk awhile.   [*Exit Queen.*]

Imogen. About some half-hour hence, pray you speak
     with me.
  You shall at least go see my lord aboard.
  For this time leave me.   *Exeunt* [*severally°*].

Scene II. [*Britain.*]

Enter Cloten° and two Lords.

First Lord. Sir, I would advise you to shift a shirt; the
  violence of action hath made you reek° as a sacrifice. Where air comes out, air comes in; there's none
  abroad so wholesome as that you vent.°

Cloten. If my shirt were bloody, then to shift it. Have   5
  I hurt him?

Second Lord. [*Aside*] No, faith, not so much as his
  patience.

First Lord. Hurt him? His body's a passable° carcass
  if he be not hurt. It is a throughfare for steel if it be   10
  not hurt.

Second Lord. [*Aside*] His steel was in debt. It went o'
  th' backside the town.°

Cloten. The villain would not stand° me.

Second Lord. [*Aside*] No, but he fled forward still, to-   15
  ward your face.

First Lord. Stand you? You have land enough of your

179s.d. **severally** by different tiring-house doors (Imogen follows
the Queen offstage while Pisanio exits by the other door)   I.ii.s.d.
Cloten (rhymes with "rotten"; cf. "Cloten's clotpoll," IV.ii.184)
2 **reek** give off vapors   4 **vent** give off   9 **passable** affording passage
(quibble on "tolerable")   12–13 **It went . . . the town** like a debtor
avoiding a creditor by taking a back street (i.e., his rapier missed)
14 **stand** confront

own, but he added to your having, gave you some
ground.

20   *Second Lord.* [*Aside*] As many inches as you have
oceans. Puppies!

Cloten. I would they had not come between us.

Second Lord. [*Aside*] So would I, till you had mea-
sured how long a fool you were upon the ground.

25   *Cloten.* And that she should love this fellow and refuse
me!

Second Lord. [*Aside*] If it be a sin to make a true election,° she is damned.

First Lord. Sir, as I told you always, her beauty and
30   her brain go not together. She's° a good sign,° but I
have seen small reflection of her wit.

Second Lord. [*Aside*] She shines not upon fools, lest
the reflection should hurt her.

Cloten. Come, I'll to my chamber. Would there had
35   been some hurt done!

Second Lord. [*Aside*] I wish not so—unless it had
been the fall of an ass, which is no great hurt.

Cloten. You'll go with us?

First Lord. I'll attend your lordship.

40   *Cloten.* Nay, come, let's go together.

Second Lord. Well, my lord.   *Exeunt.*

27–28 **election** choice   30 **She's** she has   30 **sign** appearance

Scene III. [*Britain.*]

Enter Imogen and Pisanio.

Imogen. I would thou grew'st unto the shores o' th'
   haven
   And questioned'st every sail. If he should write,
   And I not have it, 'twere a paper lost
   As offered mercy is.° What was the last
   That he spake to thee?

Pisanio.   It was his queen, his queen.   *5*

Imogen. Then waved his handkerchief?

Pisanio.   And kissed it, madam.

Imogen. Senseless° linen, happier therein than I!
   And that was all?

Pisanio.   No, madam. For so long
   As he could make me with this eye or ear
   Distinguish him from others, he did keep   *10*
   The deck, with glove or hat or handkerchief
   Still waving, as° the fits and stirs of's mind
   Could best express how slow his soul sailed on,
   How swift his ship.

Imogen.   Thou shouldst have made him
   As little as a crow or less, ere left   *15*
   To after-eye° him.

Pisanio.   Madam, so I did.

Imogen. I would have broke mine eyestrings, cracked
      them but

I.iii.3–4 **'twere . . . mercy** is i.e., a letter gone astray would be as
great a loss as mercy that fails to reach its object   7 **Senseless** without feeling   12 **as** as if   15–16 **ere . . . after-eye** before you stopped
looking after

To look upon him till the diminution
Of space° had pointed him sharp as my needle;
20 Nay, followed him till he had melted from
The smallness of a gnat to air, and then
Have turned mine eye and wept. But, good Pisanio,
When shall we hear from him?

Pisanio.   Be assured, madam,
With his next vantage.°

25 *Imogen.* I did not take my leave of him, but had
Most pretty things to say. Ere I could tell him
How I would think on him at certain hours
Such thoughts and such; or I could make him swear
The shes of Italy should not betray
30 Mine interest and his honor; or have charged him
At the sixth hour of morn, at noon, at midnight,
T'encounter me with orisons,° for then
I am in heaven for him; or ere I could
Give him that parting kiss which I had set
35 Betwixt two charming° words—comes in my father,
And like the tyrannous breathing of the north
Shakes all our buds from growing.

Enter a Lady.°

Lady.   The Queen, madam,
Desires your Highness' company.

Imogen. Those things I bid you do, get them dispatched.
I will attend the Queen.

40 *Pisanio.*   Madam, I shall.   *Exeunt*

19 **space** i.e., distance   24 **vantage** opportunity   32 **T'encounter**
. . . orisons join me in prayers   35 **charming** protecting from ev[il]
37s.d. (the Lady's message has the theatrical function of motivat[ing]
Imogen's exit)

Scene IV. [*Rome*.]

*Enter Philario, Iachimo,° a Frenchman, a Dutchman,
    and a Spaniard.*

Iachimo. Believe it, sir, I have seen him in Britain. He
was then of a crescent note,° expected to prove so
worthy as since he hath been allowed the name of.
But I could then have looked on him without the
help of admiration,° though the catalogue of his en-   5
dowments had been tabled° by his side and I to
peruse him by items.

Philario. You speak of him when he was less furnished
than now he is with that which makes° him both
without and within.   10

Frenchman. I have seen him in France. We had very
many there could behold the sun° with as firm eyes
as he.

Iachimo. This matter of marrying his king's daughter,
wherein he must be weighed rather by her value   15
than his own, words him, I doubt not, a great deal
from the matter.°

Frenchman. And then his banishment.

Iachimo. Ay, and the approbation of those that weep
this lamentable divorce under her colors° are won-   20
derfully to extend him,° be it but to fortify her
judgment, which else an easy battery might lay flat

I.iv.s.d. **Iachimo** (probably pronounced "Yákimo"; cf. "yellow Iachimo," II.v.14; but possibly pronounced "Jáckimo" since the name is
a variant of the Italian *Giacomo*)   2 **crescent note** growing reputation   5 **admiration** wonder   6 **tabled** tabulated   9 **makes** is the
making of   12 **behold the sun** (as the eagle—noblest of birds—
was thought to do)   16–17 **words him . . . matter** makes him out better than he truly is   20 **colors** banner   21 **extend him** enlarge his
reputation

for taking a beggar without less° quality.° But how
comes it he is to sojourn with you? How creeps
25   acquaintance?

Philario. His father and I were soldiers together, to
whom I have been often bound for no less than my
life.

Enter Posthumus.

Here comes the Briton. Let him be so entertained°
30   amongst you as suits, with gentlemen of your knowing, to a stranger° of his quality.° I beseech you all
be better known to this gentleman, whom I commend to you as a noble friend of mine. How worthy
he is I will leave to appear hereafter, rather than
35   story him in his own hearing.

Frenchman. Sir, we have known together° in Orleans.

Posthumus. Since when I have been debtor to you for
courtesies which I will be ever to pay and yet pay
still.

40 *Frenchman.* Sir, you o'errate my poor kindness. I was
glad I did atone° my countryman and you. It had
been pity you should have been put together° with
so mortal a purpose as then each bore, upon im-
portance° of so slight and trivial a nature.

45 *Posthumus.* By your pardon, sir, I was then a young
traveler; rather shunned to go even° with what I
heard than in my every action to be guided by
others' experiences. But upon my mended judgment,
if I offend not to say it is mended, my quarrel was
50   not altogether slight.

Frenchman. Faith, yes, to be put to the arbitrament of
swords, and by such two that would by all likeli-

---

23 **without less** i.e., with less (double negative)   23 **quality** inherent
worth   29 **entertained** welcomed   31 **stranger** foreigner   31 **quality** rank   36 **known together** been acquainted   41 **atone** reconcile   42 **put together** i.e., in a duel   43–44 **importance** a matter
46 **shunned . . . even** refused to agree

hood have confounded° one the other or have fall'n
both.

Iachimo. Can we with manners ask what was the dif-   55
ference?

Frenchman. Safely, I think. 'Twas a contention in
public, which may without contradiction° suffer the
report. It was much like an argument that fell out last
night, where each of us fell in praise of our coun-   60
try° mistresses; this gentleman at that time vouch-
ing—and upon warrant of bloody affirmation°—his
to be more fair, virtuous, wise, chaste, constant,
qualified,° and less attemptable than any the rarest
of our ladies in France.   65

Iachimo. That lady is not now living, or this gentleman's opinion, by this,° worn out.

Posthumus. She holds her virtue still, and I my mind.

Iachimo. You must not so far prefer her 'fore ours of
Italy.   70

Posthumus. Being so far provoked as I was in France,
I would abate° her nothing, though I profess myself
her adorer, not her friend.°

Iachimo. As fair and as good—a kind of hand-in-
hand° comparison—had been something too fair   75
and too good for any lady in Britain. If she went
before° others I have seen, as that diamond of yours
outlusters many I have beheld, I could not but believe she excelled many; but I have not seen the
most precious diamond that is, nor you the lady.   80

Posthumus. I praised her as I rated her. So do I my
stone.

53 **confounded** destroyed   58 **contradiction** objection   60–61 **country** i.e., of our own countries (with bawdy quibble)   62 **warrant
. . . affirmation** pledge to support by shedding blood (R. B. Heilman)   64 **qualified** endowed with good qualities   67 **by this** by this
time   72 **abate** depreciate   73 **friend** paramour   74–75 **hand-in-
hand** claiming equality   76–77 **went before** excelled

Iachimo. What do you esteem it at?

Posthumus. More than the world enjoys.°

85 *Iachimo.* Either your unparagoned mistress is dead, or she's outprized° by a trifle.

Posthumus. You are mistaken. The one may be sold or given, or° if there were wealth enough for the purchase or merit for the gift. The other is not a thing
90 for sale, and only the gift of the gods.

Iachimo. Which the gods have given you?

Posthumus. Which by their graces I will keep.

Iachimo. You may wear her in title yours, but you know strange fowl light upon neighboring ponds.
95 Your ring may be stol'n too. So your brace of unprizable estimations,° the one is but frail and the other casual.° A cunning thief, or a that-way-accomplished courtier, would hazard the winning both of first and last.

100 *Posthumus.* Your Italy contains none so accomplished a courtier to convince the honor° of my mistress, if, in the holding or loss of that, you term her frail. I do nothing doubt you have store of thieves; notwithstanding, I fear not my ring.

105 *Philario.* Let us leave° here, gentlemen.

Posthumus. Sir, with all my heart. This worthy signior, I thank him, makes no stranger of me; we are familiar at first.°

Iachimo. With five times so much conversation I
110 should get ground of° your fair mistress, make her go back even to the yielding, had I admittance, and opportunity to° friend.

84 **enjoys** possesses   86 **outprized** exceeded in value   88 **or** either
95–96 **unprizable estimations** inestimable values   97 **casual** liable to
accident   101 **convince the honor** conquer the chastity   105 **leave**
leave off   108 **at first** from the first   110 **get ground of** gain an
advantage over (a dueling metaphor followed by bawdy quibbles
on "go back" and "yielding")   112 **to** as a

Posthumus. No, no.

Iachimo. I dare thereupon pawn the moiety° of my
estate to your ring, which in my opinion o'ervalues   *115*
it something. But I make my wager rather against
your confidence than her reputation; and, to bar
your offense herein too, I durst attempt it against
any lady in the world.

Posthumus. You are a great deal abused° in too bold   *120*
a persuasion,° and I doubt not you sustain what
y'are worthy of by your attempt.

Iachimo. What's that?

Posthumus. A repulse—though your attempt, as you
call it, deserve more: a punishment too.   *125*

Philario. Gentlemen, enough of this. It came in too
suddenly; let it die as it was born, and I pray you
be better acquainted.

Iachimo. Would I had put my estate and my neighbor's on th' approbation° of what I have spoke!   *130*

Posthumus. What lady would you choose to assail?

Iachimo. Yours, whom in constancy you think stands
so safe. I will lay you ten thousand ducats to your
ring that, commend me to the court where your lady
is, with no more advantage than the opportunity of   *135*
a second conference, and I will bring from thence
that honor of hers which you imagine so reserved.

Posthumus. I will wage° against your gold, gold to it.
My ring I hold dear as my finger; 'tis part of it.

Iachimo. You are a friend, and therein the wiser. If   *140*
you buy ladies' flesh at a million a dram, you cannot preserve it from tainting. But I see you have
some religion in you, that° you fear.

---

114 moiety half   **120 abused** deceived   **121 persuasion** opinion
130 approbation proof   **138 wage** wager   **143 that** since

Posthumus. This° is but a custom in your tongue. You
145   bear a graver purpose, I hope.

Iachimo. I am the master of my speeches, and would
  undergo° what's spoken, I swear.

Posthumus. Will you? I shall but lend my diamond till
  your return. Let there be covenants° drawn be-
150   tween's. My mistress exceeds in goodness the huge-
  ness of your unworthy thinking. I dare you to this
  match: here's my ring.

Philario. I will have it no lay.°

Iachimo. By the gods, it is one. If I bring you no suffi-
155   cient testimony that I have enjoyed the dearest
  bodily part of your mistress, my ten thousand ducats
  are yours; so is your diamond too. If I come off and
  leave her in such honor as you have trust in, she
  your jewel, this your jewel, and my gold are yours
160   —provided I have your commendation° for my
  more free entertainment.°

Posthumus. I embrace these conditions. Let us have
  articles betwixt us. Only, thus far you shall answer:
  if you make your voyage upon her and give me di-
165   rectly° to understand you have prevailed, I am no
  further your enemy; she is not worth our debate. If
  she remain unseduced, you not making it appear
  otherwise, for your ill opinion and th' assault you
  have made to her chastity you shall answer me with
170   your sword.

Iachimo. Your hand; a covenant. We will have these
  things set down by lawful counsel, and straight
  away° for Britain, lest the bargain should catch cold
  and starve.° I will fetch my gold and have our two
175   wagers recorded.

Posthumus. Agreed. [*Exeunt Posthumus and Iachimo.*]

144 **This** i.e., what you say 147 **undergo** undertake 149 **covenants**
a legal agreement 153 **lay** wager 160 **commendation** introduction to her 161 **entertainment** welcome 164–65 **directly** plainly
172–73 **straight away** immediately I shall leave 174 **starve** die

Frenchman. Will this hold, think you?

Philario. Signior Iachimo will not from it. Pray let us
    follow 'em.   *Exeunt.*

Scene V. [*Britain.*]

Enter Queen, Ladies, and Cornelius.

Queen. Whiles yet the dew's on ground, gather those
    flowers.
  Make haste. Who has the note° of them?

Lady.   I, madam.

Queen. Dispatch.°   *Exeunt Ladies.*
  Now, Master Doctor, have you brought those drugs?

Cornelius. Pleaseth your Highness, ay. Here they are,
    madam.   [*Presenting a box*] 5
  But I beseech your Grace, without offense—
  My conscience bids me ask—wherefore you have
  Commanded of me these most poisonous com-
    pounds,°
  Which are the movers of a languishing death,
  But, though slow, deadly.

Queen.   I wonder, Doctor,   10
  Thou ask'st me such a question. Have I not been
  Thy pupil long? Hast thou not learned° me how
  To make perfumes? distil? preserve? yea, so
  That our great king himself doth woo me oft
  For my confections?° Having thus far proceeded—   15
  Unless thou think'st me devilish—is't not meet
  That I did amplify my judgment° in
  Other conclusions?° I will try the forces

I.v.2 **note** list 3 **Dispatch** make haste 8 **compounds** drugs
12 **learned** taught 15 **confections** drugs 17 **judgment** knowledge
18 **conclusions** experiments

          Of these thy compounds on such creatures as
20   We count not worth the hanging—but none human—
          To try the vigor of them and apply
          Allayments to their act,° and by them° gather
          Their° several virtues and effects.

Cornelius.   Your Highness
          Shall from this practice but make hard your heart.
25   Besides, the seeing these effects will be
          Both noisome and infectious.

Queen.   O, content thee.

                    Enter Pisanio.

          [*Aside*] Here comes a flattering rascal. Upon him
          Will I first work. He's for his master,
          And enemy to my son.—How now, Pisanio?—
30   Doctor, your service for this time is ended;
          Take your own way.

Cornelius. [*Aside*]   I do suspect you, madam,
          But you shall do no harm.

Queen. [*To Pisanio*]   Hark thee, a word.

Cornelius. [*Aside*] I do not like her. She doth think she
              has
          Strange ling'ring poisons. I do know her spirit
35   And will not trust one of her malice with
          A drug of such damned nature. Those she has
          Will stupefy and dull the sense awhile,
          Which first perchance she'll prove° on cats and
              dogs,
          Then afterward up higher; but there is
40   No danger in what show of death it makes,
          More than the locking up the spirits a time,
          To be more fresh, reviving. She is fooled
          With a most false effect, and I the truer
          So to be false with her.

22 **Allayments to their act** antidotes to their action   22 **them** i.e.,
the experiments   23 **Their** i.e., of the compounds   38 **prove** test

Queen.   No further service, Doctor,
  Until I send for thee.

Cornelius.   I humbly take my leave. *Exit.*   45

Queen. Weeps she still, say'st thou? Dost thou think in
      time
    She will not quench° and let instructions enter
    Where folly now possesses? Do thou work.
    When thou shalt bring me word she loves my son,
    I'll tell thee on the instant thou art then   50
    As great as is thy master; greater, for
    His fortunes all lie speechless and his name
    Is at last gasp. Return he cannot nor
    Continue where he is. To shift his being°
    Is to exchange one misery with another,   55
    And every day that comes comes to decay°
    A day's work in him. What shalt thou expect
    To be depender on a thing that leans,
    Who cannot be new built, nor has no friends
    So much as but to prop him?
            [*Dropping the box; Pisanio picks it up.*]
                          Thou tak'st up   60
    Thou know'st not what, but take it for thy labor.
    It is a thing I made which hath the King
    Five times redeemed from death. I do not know
    What is more cordial.° Nay, I prithee take it.
    It is an earnest° of a farther good   65
    That I mean to thee. Tell thy mistress how
    The case stands with her; do't as from thyself.
    Think what a chance thou changest on,° but think
    Thou hast thy mistress still—to boot, my son,
    Who shall take notice of thee. I'll move the King   70
    To any shape of thy preferment° such
    As thou'lt desire; and then myself, I chiefly,
    That set thee on to this desert,° am bound
    To load thy merit richly. Call my women.

47 **quench** cool down   54 **being** location   56 **decay** destroy   64 **cordial** restorative   65 **earnest** pledge   68 **chance thou changest on** i.e., opportunity you have to change service (?)   71 **preferment** advancement   73 **desert** action meriting reward

Think on my words.   *Exit Pisanio.*
75   A sly and constant knave,
Not to be shaked; the agent for his master,
And the remembrancer° of her to hold
The handfast° to her lord. I have given him that
Which, if he take, shall quite unpeople her
80 Of liegers° for her sweet,° and which she after,
Except she bend her humor,° shall be assured
To taste of too.

Enter Pisanio and Ladies.

So, so. Well done, well done.
The violets, cowslips, and the primroses
Bear to my closet.° Fare thee well, Pisanio.
Think on my words.   *Exeunt Queen and Ladies.*

85 *Pisanio.*   And shall do.
But when to my good lord I prove untrue,
I'll choke myself. There's all I'll do for you.   *Exit.*

Scene VI. [*Britain.*]

Enter Imogen alone.

Imogen. A father cruel and a stepdame false,
A foolish suitor to a wedded lady
That hath her husband banished. O, that husband,
My supreme crown of grief, and those repeated°
5 Vexations of it! Had I been thief-stol'n,
As my two brothers, happy; but most miserable
Is the desire that's glorious.° Blessed be those,

---

77 remembrancer person employed to remind someone (legal term)
78 handfast marriage contract   **80 liegers** ambassadors   **80 sweet**
lover   **81 bend her humor** change her mind   **84 closet** private room
I.vi.4 repeated (already) enumerated   **7 desire that's glorious** i.e.,
unfulfilled longing that aspires to great things (Nosworthy)

How mean° soe'er, that have their honest wills,°
Which seasons° comfort. Who may this be? Fie!

Enter Pisanio and Iachimo.

Pisanio. Madam, a noble gentleman of Rome,
Comes° from my lord with letters.   10

Iachimo.   Change you,° madam:
The worthy Leonatus is in safety
And greets your Highness dearly.
         [Presenting a letter]

Imogen.   Thanks, good sir.
You're kindly welcome.

Iachimo. [*Aside*] All of her that is out of door° most
    rich!   15
If she be furnished with a mind so rare,
She is alone th' Arabian bird,° and I
Have lost the wager. Boldness be my friend!
Arm me, audacity, from head to foot,
Or like the Parthian° I shall flying fight—   20
Rather, directly fly.

Imogen. (*Reads*) "He is one of the noblest note,° to
    whose kindnesses I am most infinitely tied. Reflect°
    upon him accordingly, as you value your trust—
                        Leonatus."   25
So far I read aloud.
But even the very middle of my heart
Is warmed by th' rest and takes it thankfully.
You are as welcome, worthy sir, as I
Have words to bid you, and shall find it so   30
In all that I can do.

Iachimo.   Thanks, fairest lady.
What, are men mad? Hath nature given them eyes

8 **mean** low-ranking   8 **honest wills** plain desires   9 **seasons** give
relish to   11 **Comes** who comes   11 **you** i.e., your expression   15 **out
of door** external, visible   17 **Arabian bird** phoenix (of which spe-
cies only one example existed at a time)   20 **Parthian** mounted
archer who shot arrows behind him while in flight (Iachimo will
resort to indirect methods)   22 **note** reputation   23 **Reflect** bestow
attention

To see this vaulted arch and the rich crop°
Of sea and land, which can distinguish 'twixt
35   The fiery orbs above and the twinnèd° stones
Upon the numbered° beach, and can we not
Partition° make with spectacles so precious°
'Twixt fair and foul?

Imogen.   What makes your admiration?°

Iachimo. It cannot be i' th' eye, for apes and monkeys,
40   'Twixt two such shes, would chatter this way° and
Contemn with mows° the other; nor i' th' judgment,
For idiots, in this case of favor,° would
Be wisely definite;° nor i' th' appetite°—
Sluttery, to such neat excellence opposed,
45   Should make desire vomit emptiness,°
Not so allured to feed.

Imogen. What is the matter, trow?°

Iachimo.   The cloyèd will°—
That satiate yet unsatisfied desire, that tub
Both filled and running—ravening first the lamb,
Longs after for the garbage.

50   *Imogen.*   What, dear sir,
Thus raps° you? Are you well?

Iachimo.   Thanks, madam, well.
[*To Pisanio*] Beseech you, sir, desire
My man's abode° where I did leave him.
He's strange and peevish.°

Pisanio.   I was going, sir,
55   To give him welcome.   *Exit.*

---

33 crop harvest   **35 twinned** exactly alike   **36 numbered** abounding
(in stones)   **37 Partition** distinction   **37 spectacles so precious** i.e.,
eyesight.   **38 admiration** wonder   **40 this way** towards Imogen
41 mows grimaces   **42 case of favor** question of beauty   **43 definite**
decisive   **43 appetite** physical desire   **45 make . . . emptiness** i.e.,
destroy desire.   **47 What . . . trow** what are you talking about,
I wonder   **47 will** sexual desire   **51 raps** transports   **52–53 desire
. . . abode** request that my servant remain   **54 strange and peevish**
a foreigner and skittish

Imogen. Continues well my lord? His health, beseech
    you?

Iachimo. Well, madam.

Imogen. Is he disposed to mirth? I hope he is.

Iachimo. Exceeding pleasant; none a stranger° there
    So merry and so gamesome. He is called   60
    The Briton reveler.

Imogen.   When he was here
    He did incline to sadness,° and ofttimes
    Not knowing why.

Iachimo.   I never saw him sad.
    There is a Frenchman his companion, one
    An eminent monsieur that, it seems, much loves   65
    A Gallian° girl at home. He furnaces°
    The thick° sighs from him, whiles the jolly Briton—
    Your lord, I mean—laughs from's free lungs, cries
        "O,
    Can my sides hold to think that man who knows
    By history, report, or his own proof°   70
    What woman is, yea, what she cannot choose
    But must be, will's free hours languish° for
    Assurèd bondage?"

Imogen.   Will my lord say so?

Iachimo. Ay, madam, with his eyes in flood with
    laughter.
    It is a recreation to be by   75
    And hear him mock the Frenchman. But heavens
    know
    Some men are much to blame.

Imogen.   Not he, I hope.

Iachimo. Not he—but yet heaven's bounty towards
    him might

---

59 **none a stranger** there is no foreigner   62 **sadness** seriousness
66 **Gallian** French   66 **furnaces** exhales like a furnace   67 **thick**
frequent   70 **proof** experience   72 **languish** pass in languishing

Be used more thankfully. In himself 'tis° much;
In you, which I account his, beyond all talents.°
Whilst I am bound to wonder, I am bound
To pity too.

Imogen.   What do you pity, sir?

Iachimo. Two creatures heartily.

Imogen.   Am I one, sir?
You look on me. What wrack° discern you in me
Deserves your pity?

Iachimo.   Lamentable! What,
To hide me from the radiant sun and solace°
I' th' dungeon by a snuff!°

Imogen.   I pray you, sir,
Deliver with more openness your answers
To my demands. Why do you pity me?

Iachimo. That others do,
I was about to say, enjoy your—but
It is an office° of the gods to venge it,
Not mine to speak on't.

Imogen.   You do seem to know
Something of me or what concerns me. Pray you,
Since doubting° things go ill often hurts more
Than to be sure they do—for certainties
Either are past remedies, or, timely knowing,°
The remedy then born—discover° to me
What° both you spur and stop.

Iachimo.   Had I this cheek
To bathe my lips upon; this hand, whose touch,
Whose every touch, would force the feeler's soul
To th' oath of loyalty; this object, which
Takes prisoner the wild motion of mine eye,
Fixing it only here; should I, damned then,

79 'tis i.e., heaven's bounty is   80 beyond all talents beyond all
natural endowments, i.e., inestimable   84 wrack disaster   86 solace
find pleasure   87 snuff candle-end   92 office duty   95 doubting
fearing   97 timely knowing if one knows in time   98 discover reveal   99 What why

Slaver with lips as common as the stairs   105
That mount the Capitol; join gripes° with hands
Made hard with hourly falsehood (falsehood, as
With labor); then bye-peeping° in an eye
Base and illustrous° as the smoky light
That's fed with stinking tallow—it were fit   110
That all the plagues of hell should at one time
Encounter° such revolt.°

Imogen.   My lord, I fear,
Has forgot Britain.

Iachimo.   And himself. Not I
Inclined to this intelligence pronounce°
The beggary° of his change, but 'tis your graces   115
That from my mutest conscience° to my tongue
Charms this report out.

Imogen.   Let me hear no more.

Iachimo. O dearest soul, your cause doth strike my
    heart
With pity that doth make me sick. A lady
So fair, and fastened to an empery°   120
Would° make the great'st king double, to be part-
    nered
With tomboys° hired with that self exhibition°
Which your own coffers yield; with diseased ven-
    tures°
That play with all infirmities for gold
Which rottenness can lend nature; such boiled stuff° 125
As well might poison poison! Be revenged,
Or she that bore you was no queen, and you
Recoil° from your great stock.

Imogen.   Revenged?

106 **gripes** grips 108 **bye-peeping** peeping sidelong 109 **illustrous** lackluster 112 **Encounter** confront 112 **revolt** inconstancy
113–14 **Not I . . . pronounce** I, though disinclined to bring this
news, report 115 **beggary** meanness 116 **conscience** knowledge
120 **empery** empire 121 **Would** which would 122 **tomboys** whores
122 **self exhibition** self-same allowance 123 **ventures** whores 125
boiled stuff i.e., women who have been "sweated" for venereal disease 128 **Recoil** decline

How should I be revenged? If this be true—
130 As I have such a heart that both mine ears
Must not in haste abuse—if it be true,
How should I be revenged?

Iachimo.   Should he make me
Live like Diana's priest betwixt cold sheets,
Whiles he is vaulting variable ramps,°
135 In your despite, upon your purse? Revenge it.
I dedicate myself to your sweet pleasure,
More noble than that runagate° to your bed,
And will continue fast to your affection,
Still close° as sure.

Imogen.   What ho, Pisanio!

140 *Iachimo.* Let me my service tender on your lips.

Imogen. Away, I do condemn mine ears that have
So long attended thee.° If thou wert honorable,
Thou wouldst have told this tale for virtue, not
For such an end thou seek'st, as base as strange.
145 Thou wrong'st a gentleman who is as far
From thy report as thou from honor, and
Solicits here a lady that disdains
Thee and the devil alike. What ho, Pisanio!
The King my father shall be made acquainted
150 Of thy assault. If he shall think it fit
A saucy stranger in his court to mart°
As in a Romish stew° and to expound
His beastly mind to us, he hath a court
He little cares for and a daughter who
155 He not respects at all. What ho, Pisanio!

Iachimo. O happy Leonatus! I may say
The credit° that thy lady hath of° thee
Deserves thy trust, and thy most perfect goodness

---

134 **variable ramps** fickle whores   137 **runagate** traitor   139 **close**
secret   142 **attended thee** listened to you (in anger Imogen shifts
from formal "you" to familiar "thee," thus treating Iachimo as an
inferior; at line 168 she reverts to "you")   151 **to mart** should do
business   152 **Romish stew** Roman bawdyhouse   157 **credit** trust
157 **of** in

    Her assured credit. Blessèd live you long,
    A lady to the worthiest sir that ever   160
    Country called his,° and you his mistress, only
    For the most worthiest fit. Give me your pardon.
    I have spoke this to know if your affiance°
    Were deeply rooted, and shall make your lord
    That which he is, new o'er; and he is one°   165
    The truest mannered,° such a holy witch°
    That he enchants societies into° him.
    Half all men's hearts are his.

Imogen.   You make amends.

Iachimo. He sits 'mongst men like a descended god.
    He hath a kind of honor sets him off   170
    More than a mortal seeming.° Be not angry,
    Most mighty Princess, that I have adventured
    To try your taking° of a false report, which hath
    Honored with confirmation your great judgment
    In the election of a sir so rare,   175
    Which° you know cannot err. The love I bear him
    Made me to fan° you thus, but the gods made you,
    Unlike all others, chaffless. Pray your pardon.

Imogen. All's well, sir. Take my pow'r i' th' court for
    yours.

Iachimo. My humble thanks. I had almost forgot   180
    T' entreat your grace but in a small request,
    And yet of moment too, for it concerns
    Your lord, myself, and other noble friends
    Are° partners in the business.

Imogen.   Pray what is't?

Iachimo. Some dozen Romans of us and your lord—   185
    The best feather of our wing—have mingled sums
    To buy a present for the Emperor;
    Which I, the factor° for the rest, have done

161 **his** its own   163 **affiance** faith   165 **one** above all   166 **truest mannered** most honestly behaved 166 **witch** charmer 167 **into** to 171 **mortal seeming** human appearance 173 **try your taking** test your reception 176 **Which** who 177 **fan** winnow 184 **Are** i.e., who are 188 **factor** agent

In France. 'Tis plate of rare device, and jewels
190 Of rich and exquisite form, their values great,
And I am something curious,° being strange,°
To have them in safe stowage. May it please you
To take them in protection?

Imogen.   Willingly;
And pawn mine honor for their safety. Since
195 My lord hath interest in them, I will keep them
In my bedchamber.

Iachimo.   They are in a trunk
Attended by my men. I will make bold
To send them to you, only for this night.
I must aboard tomorrow.

Imogen.   O, no, no.

200 _Iachimo._ Yes, I beseech, or I shall short° my word
By length'ning my return. From Gallia°
I crossed the seas on purpose and on promise
To see your grace.

Imogen.   I thank you for your pains.
But not away tomorrow!

Iachimo.   O, I must, madam.
205 Therefore I shall beseech you, if you please
To greet your lord with writing, do't tonight.
I have outstood my time, which is material
To th' tender° of our present.

Imogen.   I will write.
Send your trunk to me; it shall safe be kept
210 And truly yielded you. You're very welcome.
                              Exeunt [_severally°_].

---

191 **curious** anxious 191 **strange** a foreigner 200 **short** fall short
of 201 **Gallia** France 208 **tender** giving 210s.d. **severally** by different tiring-house doors

ACT II

Scene I. [*Britain.*]

Enter Cloten and the two Lords.

Cloten. Was there ever man had such luck? When I
kissed the jack,° upon an upcast° to be hit away! I
had a hundred pound on't. And then a whoreson
jackanapes must take me up° for swearing, as if I
borrowed mine oaths of him and might not spend   5
them at my pleasure.

First Lord. What got he by that? You have broke his
pate with your bowl.

Second Lord. [*Aside*] If his wit had been like him
that broke it, it would have run all out.   10

Cloten. When a gentleman is disposed to swear, it is
not for any standers-by to curtail his oaths. Ha?

Second Lord. No, my lord—[*Aside*] nor crop the ears
of them.

Cloten. Whoreson dog, I gave him satisfaction! Would   15
he had been one of my rank.°

Second Lord. [*Aside*] To have smelled like a fool.

_____

II.i.2 **kissed the jack** came close to the target ball (in the game of
bowls)   2 **upcast** chance   4 **take me up** rebuke me   16 **of my rank**
i.e., so I might have challenged him to a duel (the Second Lord
quibbles)

71

Cloten. I am not vexed more at anything in th' earth.
A pox on't! I had rather not be so noble as I am.
20   They dare not fight with me because of the Queen
my mother. Every jack-slave° hath his bellyful of
fighting, and I must go up and down like a cock that
nobody can match.

Second Lord. [*Aside*] You are cock and capon too,
25   and° you crow, cock, with your comb on.

Cloten. Sayest thou?

Second Lord. It is not fit your lordship should under-
take° every companion° that you give offense to.

Cloten. No, I know that, but it is fit I should commit
30   offense° to my inferiors.

Second Lord. Ay, it is fit for your lordship only.

Cloten. Why, so I say.

First Lord. Did you hear of a stranger° that's come
to court tonight?

35   *Cloten.* A stranger, and I not know on't?

Second Lord. [*Aside*] He's a strange fellow himself,
and knows it not.

First Lord. There's an Italian come, and, 'tis thought,
one of Leonatus' friends.

40   *Cloten.* Leonatus? A banished rascal, and he's another,
whatsoever he be. Who told you of this stranger?

First Lord. One of your lordship's pages.

Cloten. Is it fit I went to look upon him? Is there no
derogation° in't?

45   *Second Lord.* You cannot derogate,° my lord.

---

21 **jack-slave** lout   25 **and** if   27–28 **undertake** take on   28 **companion** low fellow   29–30 **commit offense** offer battle   33 **stranger** foreigner   44 **derogation** loss of dignity   45 **cannot derogate** do anything derogatory to your rank (with quibble on "have no dignity to lose")

Cloten. Not easily, I think.

Second Lord. [*Aside*] You are a fool, granted; there-
    fore your issues,° being foolish, do not derogate.

Cloten. Come, I'll go see this Italian. What I have lost
    today at bowls I'll win tonight of him. Come, go.   50

Second Lord. I'll attend your lordship.
                              Exeunt [*Cloten and First Lord*].
That such a crafty devil as is his mother
Should yield the world this ass! A woman that
Bears all down° with her brain, and this her son
Cannot take two from twenty, for his heart,°   55
And leave eighteen. Alas, poor princess,
Thou divine Imogen, what thou endur'st,
Betwixt a father by thy stepdame governed,
A mother hourly coining plots, a wooer
More hateful than the foul expulsion is   60
Of thy dear husband, than that horrid act
Of the divorce he'ld make. The heavens hold firm
The walls of thy dear honor, keep unshaked
That temple, thy fair mind, that thou mayst stand,
T' enjoy thy banished lord and this great land! *Exit.*   65

Scene II. [*Britain.*]

Enter Imogen in her bed,° and a Lady.

Imogen. Who's there? My woman Helen?

Lady.   Please you, madam.

Imogen. What hour is it?

48 issues deeds   54 Bears all down overcomes everything   55 for
his heart to save his life   II.ii.s.d. Enter . . . bed (in Elizabethan
open-stage production the bed is "thrust out" upon the stage by
attendants and the trunk is carried on; in modern proscenium-
arch production the bed and trunk are usually "discovered" by
raising the front curtain)

Lady.   Almost midnight, madam.

Imogen. I have read three hours then. Mine eyes are
    weak.
    Fold down the leaf where I have left. To bed.
5   Take not away the taper, leave it burning;
    And if thou canst awake by four o' th' clock,
    I prithee call me. Sleep hath seized me wholly.
                         [*Exit Lady.*]
    To your protection I commend me, gods.
    From fairies° and the tempters of the night
10   Guard me, beseech ye!
            Sleeps. Iachimo [comes] from the trunk.

Iachimo. The crickets sing, and man's o'erlabored
    sense
    Repairs itself by rest. Our Tarquin° thus
    Did softly press the rushes° ere he wakened
    The chastity he wounded. Cytherea,°
15   How bravely° thou becom'st thy bed, fresh lily,°
    And whiter than the sheets! That I might touch!
    But kiss, one kiss! Rubies unparagoned,
    How dearly they do't! 'Tis her breathing that
    Perfumes the chamber thus. The flame o' th' taper
20   Bows toward her and would underpeep her lids
    To see th' enclosèd lights, now canopied
    Under these windows,° white and azure-laced
    With blue of heaven's own tinct. But my design:
    To note the chamber. I will write all down:
25   Such and such pictures; there the window; such
    Th' adornment of her bed; the arras, figures,
    Why, such and such; and the contents o' th' story.°
    Ah, but some natural notes° about her body
    Above ten thousand meaner movables°
30   Would testify, t' enrich mine inventory.
    O sleep, thou ape° of death, lie dull° upon her.

---

9 **fairies** i.e., malignant fairies   12 **Tarquin** (who raped Lucrece)
13 **rushes** Elizabethan floor-covering   14 **Cytherea** Venus   15 **bravely** magnificently   15 **lily** emblem of chastity   22 **windows** shutters,
i.e., eyelids   27 **th' story** i.e., the story depicted on the arras (cf.
II.iv.69)   28 **notes** marks   29 **meaner movables** lesser furnishings
31 **ape** mimic   31 **dull** heavy

And be her sense but as a monument,°
Thus in a chapel lying. Come off, come off—
                         [*Removing her bracelet*]
As slippery as the Gordian knot was hard.
'Tis mine, and this will witness outwardly,   35
As strongly as the conscience° does within,
To th' madding of her lord. On her left breast
A mole cinque-spotted,° like the crimson drops
I' th' bottom of a cowslip. Here's a voucher°
Stronger than ever law could make. This secret   40
Will force him think I have picked the lock and
    ta'en
The treasure of her honor. No more. To what end?
Why should I write this down that's riveted,
Screwed to my memory? She hath been reading late
The tale of Tereus.° Here the leaf's turned down   45
Where Philomel gave up. I have enough.
To th' trunk again, and shut the spring of it.
Swift, swift, you dragons of the night, that dawning
May bare the raven's eye.° I lodge in fear.
Though this a heavenly angel, hell is here.   50
                                    Clock strikes.
One, two, three. Time, time! [*Goes into the trunk.*]
                                    Exeunt.°

2 **monument** recumbent effigy on a tomb   36 **conscience** knowl-
ige   38 **cinque-spotted** having five spots   39 **voucher** guarantee
5 **Tereus** (who raped Philomela; apparently the book is Ovid's
Metamorphoses)   49 **bare the raven's eye** (the raven supposedly
eing an early bird)   51s.d. **Exeunt** (the bed and trunk are carried
ffstage or concealed by dropping the front curtain)

Scene III. [*Britain*.]

Enter Cloten and Lords.

First Lord. Your lordship is the most patient man in
loss, the most coldest° that ever turned up ace.°

Cloten. It would make any man cold° to lose.

First Lord. But not every man patient after the noble
5   temper of your lordship. You are most hot and furi-
ous when you win.

Cloten. Winning will put any man into courage. If I
could get this foolish Imogen, I should have gold
enough. It's almost morning, is't not?

10 *First Lord.* Day, my lord.

Cloten. I would this music would come. I am advised
to give her music a-mornings; they say it will penetrate.°

Enter Musicians.

Come on, tune. If you can penetrate° her with your
15 fingering, so; we'll try with tongue too. If none will
do, let her remain, but I'll never give o'er.° First, a
very excellent good-conceited° thing; after, a wonderful sweet air with admirable rich words to it—
and then let her consider.

Song.

20   Hark, hark, the lark at heaven's gate sings,
        And Phoebus gins° arise,

II.iii.2 **coldest** calmest   2 **ace** one, the lowest throw at dice (pun on
"ass")   3 **cold** gloomy   12–13 **penetrate** affect emotionally (with
bawdy quibble)   16 **give o'er** give up   17 **good-conceited** well-
devised   21 **Phoebus gins** Apollo (the sun) begins to

His steeds to water at those springs
   On chaliced flowers that lies;
And winking Mary-buds° begin
   To ope their golden eyes.   25
With every thing that pretty is,
   My lady sweet, arise,
      Arise, arise!

Cloten. So, get you gone. If this penetrate, I will con-
sider° your music the better; if it do not, it is a   30
vice° in her ears which horsehairs° and calves'
guts,° nor the voice of unpaved° eunuch to boot,
can never amend.

                    [*Exeunt Musicians.*]

     Enter Cymbeline and Queen.

Second Lord. Here comes the King.

Cloten. I am glad I was up so late, for that's the reason   35
I was up so early. He cannot choose but take this
service I have done fatherly. Good morrow to your
Majesty and to my gracious mother.

Cymbeline. Attend you here the door of our stern
daughter? Will she not forth?   40

Cloten. I have assailed her with musics, but she vouch-
safes no notice.

Cymbeline. The exile of her minion° is too new;
She hath not yet forgot him. Some more time
Must wear the print of his remembrance out,   45
And then she's yours.

Queen.   You are most bound to th' King,
Who lets go by no vantages° that may
Prefer° you to his daughter. Frame° yourself
To orderly solicits,° and be friended

---

24 **winking Mary-buds** closed marigold buds   29–30 **consider re-**
ward 31 **vice** flaw 31 **horsehairs** bowstrings 31–32 **calves' guts**
fiddle-strings 32 **unpaved** unstoned (i.e., castrated) 43 **minion**
darling 47 **vantages** opportunities 48 **Prefer** recommend 48
Frame prepare 49 **solicits** solicitations

50   With aptness of the season. Make denials
      Increase your services. So seem as if
      You were inspired to do those duties which
      You tender to her; that you in all obey her,
      Save when command to your dismission° tends,
      And therein you are senseless.°

55 *Cloten.*   Senseless? Not so.

                    [*Enter a Messenger.*]

    Messenger. So like you,° sir, ambassadors from Rome.
      The one is Caius Lucius.

    Cymbeline.   A worthy fellow,
      Albeit he comes on angry purpose now.
      But that's no fault of his. We must receive him
60   According to the honor of his sender,
      And towards himself, his goodness forespent° on us,
      We must extend our notice. Our dear son,
      When you have given good morning to your mis-
        tress,
      Attend the Queen and us. We shall have need
      T' employ you towards this Roman. Come, our
65   queen.   *Exeunt [all but Cloten].*

    Cloten. If she be up, I'll speak with her; if not,
      Let her lie still and dream. By your leave, ho!
                                        [*Knocks.*]
      I know her women are about her. What
      If I do line° one of their hands? 'Tis gold
      Which buys admittance—oft it doth—yea, and
70   makes
      Diana's rangers° false° themselves, yield up
      Their deer to th' stand o' th' stealer;° and 'tis gold
      Which makes the true man killed and saves the
        thief,
      Nay, sometime hangs both thief and true man. What

    54 **dismission** rejection   55 **senseless** insensible   56 **So like you** if
    you please   61 **forespent** having earlier been spent   69 **line** i.e.,
    with money   71 **rangers** gamekeepers   71 **false** betray   72 **stand
    o' th' stealer** standing-place of the hunter (quibble on "erection of
    the phallus")

Can it not do and undo? I will make   75
One of her women lawyer to° me, for
I yet not understand° the case myself.
By your leave.   *Knocks.*

Enter a Lady.

Lady. Who's there that knocks?

Cloten.   A gentleman.

Lady.   No more?

Cloten. Yes, and a gentlewoman's son.

Lady.   That's more   80
Than some whose tailors are as dear as yours
Can justly boast of. What's your lordship's pleasure?

Cloten. Your lady's person. Is she ready?°

Lady.   Ay,
To keep her chamber.

Cloten.   There is gold for you.
Sell me your good report.   85

Lady. How? My good name? Or to report of you
What I shall think is good? The Princess!

Enter Imogen. [Exit Lady.]

Cloten. Good morrow, fairest sister. Your sweet hand.

Imogen. Good morrow, sir. You lay out too much
    pains
For purchasing but trouble. The thanks I give   90
Is telling you that I am poor of thanks
And scarce can spare them.

Cloten.   Still I swear I love you.

Imogen. If you but said so, 'twere as deep° with me.
If you swear still,° your recompense is still
That I regard it not.

76 **lawyer to** quibble on "lower to," i.e., lie down for   77 **understand** quibble on "stand under," i.e., penetrate   83 **ready** dressed
93 **deep** effective   94 **still** continually

95 *Cloten.*   This is no answer.

Imogen. But° that you shall not say I yield, being
     silent,
     I would not speak. I pray you spare me. Faith,
     I shall unfold° equal discourtesy°
     To your best kindness. One of your great knowing°
100   Should learn, being taught, forbearance.

Cloten. To leave you in your madness, 'twere my sin.
     I will not.

Imogen. Fools are not mad folks.

Cloten.   Do you call me fool?

Imogen. As I am mad, I do.
105   If you'll be patient, I'll no more be mad;
     That cures us both. I am much sorry, sir,
     You put me to forget a lady's manners
     By being so verbal;° and learn now for all
     That I, which know my heart, do here pronounce
110   By th' very truth of it, I care not for you,
     And am so near the lack of charity
     To accuse myself I hate° you—which I had rather
     You felt than make't my boast.

Cloten.   You sin against
     Obedience, which you owe your father. For
115   The contract you pretend° with that base wretch,
     One bred of alms and fostered with cold dishes,
     With scraps o' th' court—it is no contract, none.
     And though it be allowed in meaner° parties—
     Yet who than he more mean?—to knit their souls,
120   On whom there is no more dependency°
     But brats and beggary, in self-figured° knot;
     Yet you are curbed from that enlargement° by

---

96 **But** so   98 **unfold** display   98 **equal discourtesy** i.e., discourtesy
equal   99 **knowing** knowledge   108 **verbal** talkative   112 **To accuse . . . hate** that I accuse myself of hating   114–15 **For . . .
pretend** as for the marriage contract you claim   118 **meaner** lower-
ranking   120 **dependency** retinue   121 **self-figured** shaped by one's
self   122 **enlargement** freedom

    The consequence° o' th' crown, and must not foil°
    The precious note° of it with a base slave,
    A hilding for° a livery, a squire's cloth,   125
    A pantler°—not so eminent.

Imogen.   Profane fellow!
    Wert thou the son of Jupiter, and no more
    But what thou art besides, thou wert too base
    To be his groom. Thou wert dignified° enough,
    Even to the point of envy, if 'twere made   130
    Comparative for your virtues to be styled
    The under-hangman of his kingdom,° and hated
    For being preferred° so well.

Cloten.   The south fog° rot him!

Imogen. He never can meet more mischance than
      come
    To be but named of thee. His meanest garment   135
    That ever hath but clipped° his body is dearer
    In my respect° than all the hairs above thee,
    Were they all made such men. How now, Pisanio?

Enter Pisanio.

Cloten. "His garment"? Now the devil—

Imogen. To Dorothy my woman hie thee presently.°   140

Cloten. "His garment"?

Imogen.   I am sprited° with a fool,
    Frighted, and angered worse. Go bid my woman
    Search for a jewel that too casually
    Hath left mine arm. It was thy master's. Shrew° me
    If I would lose it for a revenue   145
    Of any king's in Europe. I do think
    I saw't this morning; confident I am

123 **consequence** importance 123 **foil** defile 124 **note** eminence,
importance 125 **hilding for** good-for-nothing fit only for 126 **pan-
tler** pantry-servant 129 **dignified** given honor 130–32 **if 'twere . . .
kingdom** if, according to the virtue of each of you, you were made
under-hangman and he king (Heilman) 133 **preferred** advanced
133 **The south fog** the damp, supposedly unhealthy, south wind
136 **clipped** embraced 137 **respect** regard 140 **presently** immediately 141 **sprited** haunted 144 **Shrew** curse

Last night 'twas on mine arm; I kissed it.
I hope it be not gone to tell my lord
That I kiss aught but he.

150 *Pisanio.*   'Twill not be lost.

Imogen. I hope so.° Go and search.   [*Exit Pisanio.*]

Cloten.   You have abused me.
"His meanest garment"?

Imogen.   Ay, I said so, sir.
If you will make't an action,° call witness to't.

Cloten. I will inform your father.

Imogen.   Your mother too.
155 She's my good lady and will conceive,° I hope,
But the worst of me. So I leave you, sir,
To th' worst of discontent.   *Exit.*

Cloten.   I'll be revenged.
"His meanest garment"? Well.   *Exit.*°

Scene IV. [*Rome.*]

Enter Posthumus and Philario.

Posthumus. Fear it not, sir. I would I were so sure
To win the King as I am bold° her honor
Will remain hers.

Philario.   What means° do you make to him?

Posthumus. Not any, but abide the change of time,
5   Quake in the present winter's state, and wish
That warmer days would come. In these feared°
hopes

151 **so** i.e., not   153 **action** lawsuit   155 **conceive** come to believe
158s.d. **Exit** (by the other door)   II.iv.2 **bold** confident   3 **means**
overtures   6 **feared** fear-laden

　I barely gratify° your love; they failing,
　I must die much your debtor.

Philario. Your very goodness and your company
　O'erpays all I can do. By this,° your king　　　　　10
　Hath heard of great Augustus; Caius Lucius
　Will do's commission throughly. And I think
　He'll grant the tribute, send th' arrearages,
　Or look upon our Romans, whose remembrance
　Is yet fresh in their grief.

Posthumus.　　　　　　　I do believe,　　　　　15
　Statist° though I am none, nor like to be,
　That this will prove a war; and you shall hear
　The legions now in Gallia sooner landed
　In our not-fearing Britain than have tidings
　Of any penny tribute paid. Our countrymen　　　　20
　Are men more ordered than when Julius Caesar
　Smiled at their lack of skill but found their courage
　Worthy his frowning at. Their discipline,
　Now mingled with their courages, will make known
　To their approvers° they are people such　　　　　25
　That mend upon° the world.

Enter Iachimo.

Philario.　　　　　　　　See, Iachimo!

Posthumus. The swiftest harts have posted° you by
　　land,
　And winds of all the corners° kissed your sails
　To make your vessel nimble.

Philario.　　　　　　　　Welcome, sir.

Posthumus. I hope the briefness of your answer° made　30
　The speediness of your return.

Iachimo.　　　　　　　　Your lady
　Is one of the fairest that I have looked upon.

---

7 **gratify** repay　10 **this** this time　16 **Statist** politician　25 **approvers** testers　26 **That mend upon** whose reputation grows with　27 **have posted** must have sped　28 **corners** i.e., of the earth　30 **your answer** the answer you received

Posthumus. And therewithal the best, or let her beauty
   Look through a casement to allure false hearts
   And be false with them.

35 *Iachimo.*   Here are letters° for you.

Posthumus. Their tenor good, I trust.

Iachimo.   'Tis very like.

Posthumus. Was Caius Lucius in the Briton court
   When you were there?

Iachimo.   He was expected then,
   But not approached.

Posthumus.   All is well yet.
40   Sparkles this stone as it was wont, or is't not
   Too dull for your good wearing?

Iachimo.   If I have lost it,
   I should have lost the worth of it in gold.
   I'll make a journey twice as far t' enjoy
   A second night of such sweet shortness which
45   Was mine in Britain—for the ring is won.

Posthumus. The stone's too hard to come by.

Iachimo.   Not a whit,
   Your lady being so easy.

Posthumus.   Make not, sir,
   Your loss your sport. I hope you know that we
   Must not continue friends.

Iachimo.   Good sir, we must,
50   If you keep covenant. Had I not brought
   The knowledge° of your mistress home, I grant
   We were to question° farther, but I now
   Profess myself the winner of her honor,
   Together with your ring, and not the wronger
55   Of her or you, having proceeded but
   By both your wills.

35 **are letters** is a letter   51 **knowledge** carnal knowledge   52 **question** dispute (as in a duel)

Posthumus.　　　　　If you can make't apparent
That you have tasted her in bed, my hand
And ring is yours. If not, the foul opinion
You had of her pure honor gains or loses
Your sword or mine, or masterless leave° both　　60
To who shall find them.

Iachimo.　　　　　　　Sir, my circumstances,°
Being so near the truth as I will make them,
Must first induce you to believe; whose strength
I will confirm with oath, which I doubt not
You'll give me leave to spare° when you shall find　65
You need it not.

Posthumus.　　　　Proceed.

Iachimo.　　　　　　　First, her bedchamber—
Where I confess I slept not, but profess
Had that was well worth watching°—it was hanged
With tapestry of silk and silver; the story
Proud Cleopatra, when she met her Roman°　　70
And Cydnus swelled above the banks, or° for
The press of boats or pride: a piece of work
So bravely° done, so rich, that it did strive
In workmanship and value;° which I wondered
Could be so rarely and exactly wrought,　　75
Since the true life on't was—

Posthumus.　　　　　　　This is true,
And this you might have heard of here, by me
Or by some other.

Iachimo.　　　　　More particulars
Must justify° my knowledge.

Posthumus.　　　　　　So they must,
Or do your honor injury.

Iachimo.　　　　　　　The chimney°　　80

---

60 **leave** let it leave　61 **circumstances** details　65 **spare** omit
68 **watching** remaining awake for　70 **Roman** Antony　71 **or** either
73 **bravely** finely　73–74 **it did strive . . . value** it was doubtful
whether the workmanship or the intrinsic value was greater
79 **justify** prove　80 **chimney** fireplace

Is south the chamber, and the chimney-piece°
Chaste Dian bathing. Never saw I figures
So likely to report° themselves. The cutter°
Was as another Nature, dumb;° outwent° her,
Motion and breath left out.

85 *Posthumus.*   This is a thing
Which you might from relation° likewise reap,
Being, as it is, much spoke of.

Iachimo.   The roof o' th' chamber
With golden cherubins is fretted.° Her andirons—
I had forgot them—were two winking° Cupids
90 Of silver, each on one foot standing, nicely
Depending on their brands.°

Posthumus.   This is her honor!
Let it be granted you have seen all this—and praise
Be given to your remembrance—the description
Of what is in her chamber nothing saves
The wager you have laid.

95 *Iachimo.*   Then, if you can
                    [*Showing the bracelet*]
Be pale,° I beg but leave to air this jewel. See!
And now 'tis up° again. It must be married
To that your diamond; I'll keep them.

Posthumus.   Jove!
Once more let me behold it. Is it that
Which I left with her?

100 *Iachimo.*   Sir, I thank her, that.
She stripped it from her arm; I see her yet.
Her pretty action did outsell° her gift,
And yet enriched it too. She gave it me and said
She prized it once.

---

81 **chimney-piece** sculpture placed over the fireplace   83 **likely to report** apt to identify   83 **cutter** sculptor   84 **as . . . dumb** like Nature in creative power although unable to make the sculpture speak   84 **outwent** surpassed   86 **relation** report   88 **fretted** carved   89 **winking** with closed eyes, i.e., blind   91 **Depending on their brands** leaning on their torches.   96 **Be pale** remain unflushed, i.e., calm   97 **up** put up, pocketed   102 **outsell** exceed in value

Posthumus.   May be she plucked it off
  To send it me.

Iachimo.   She writes so to you, doth she?   *105*

Posthumus. O, no, no, no, 'tis true. Here, take this too.
                    [*Giving the ring*]
  It is a basilisk° unto mine eye,
  Kills me to look on't. Let there be no honor
  Where there is beauty; truth, where semblance;
    love,
  Where there's another man. The vows of women   *110*
  Of no more bondage be to where they are made
  Than they are to their virtues, which is nothing.°
  O, above measure false!

Philario.   Have patience, sir,
  And take your ring again; 'tis not yet won.
  It may be probable° she lost it, or   *115*
  Who knows if one° her women, being corrupted,
  Hath stol'n it from her?

Posthumus.   Very true,
  And so I hope he came by't. Back my ring;
  Render to me some corporal sign about her
  More evident° than this, for this was stol'n.   *120*

Iachimo. By Jupiter, I had it from her arm.

Posthumus. Hark you, he swears; by Jupiter he swears.
  'Tis true—nay, keep the ring—'tis true. I am sure
  She would not lose it. Her attendants are
  All sworn° and honorable. They induced to steal it?   *125*
  And by a stranger? No, he hath enjoyed her.
  The cognizance° of her incontinency
  Is this.° She hath bought the name of whore thus
    dearly.

___

107 **basilisk** monster supposedly capable of killing by look
110–12 **The vows . . . nothing** let the vows of women be no
more binding to the recipients of them than women are bound to
their own virtues—which is not at all (Nosworthy)   115 **probable**
provable   116 **one** one of   120 **evident** conclusive   125 **sworn** i.e.,
to loyalty   127 **cognizance** badge   128 **this** the bracelet

There, take thy hire,° and all the fiends of hell
Divide themselves between you!

130 *Philario.*   Sir, be patient.
This is not strong enough to be believed
Of one persuaded° well of.

Posthumus.   Never talk on't.
She hath been colted° by him.

Iachimo.   If you seek
For further satisfying, under her breast—
135 Worthy the pressing—lies a mole, right proud
Of that most delicate lodging. By my life,
I kissed it, and it gave me present° hunger
To feed again, though full. You do remember
This stain° upon her?

Posthumus.   Ay, and it doth confirm
140 Another stain,° as big as hell can hold,
Were there no more but it.

Iachimo.   Will you hear more?

Posthumus. Spare your arithmetic; never count the
        turns.
Once, and a million!

Iachimo.   I'll be sworn.

Posthumus.   No swearing.
If you will swear you have not done't, you lie,
145 And I will kill thee if thou dost deny
Thou'st made me cuckold.

Iachimo.   I'll deny nothing.

Posthumus. O that I had her here, to tear her limb-
        meal!°
I will go there and do't i' th' court, before
Her father. I'll do something.   *Exit.*

Philario.   Quite besides

129 **hire** reward   132 **persuaded** that we are persuaded to **think**
133 **colted** possessed sexually   137 **present** immediate   139 **stain**
mark   140 **stain** corruption   147 **limb-meal** limb from limb

The government° of patience! You have won.   150
Let's follow him and pervert° the present wrath
He hath against himself.

Iachimo.   With all my heart.   *Exeunt.*

[Scene V. *Rome.*]

Enter Posthumus.

Posthumus. Is there no way for men to be,° but
    women
  Must be half-workers?° We are all bastards,
  And that most venerable man which I
  Did call my father was I know not where
  When I was stamped.° Some coiner° with his tools   5
  Made me a counterfeit; yet my mother seemed
  The Dian° of that time. So doth my wife
  The nonpareil° of this. O, vengeance, vengeance!
  Me of my lawful pleasure she restrained
  And prayed me oft forbearance—did it with   10
  A pudency° so rosy, the sweet view on't°
  Might well have warmed old Saturn°—that I
    thought her
  As chaste as unsunned snow. O, all the devils!
  This yellow° Iachimo in an hour, was't not?
  Or less? At first?° Perchance he spoke not, but,   15
  Like a full-acorned° boar, a German one,
  Cried "O!" and mounted; found no opposition
  But what he looked for should oppose and she
  Should from encounter guard. Could I find out
  The woman's part in me! For there's no motion°   20

150 **government** control   151 **pervert** divert   II.v.1 **be** exist   2 **half-workers** i.e., in begetting   5 **stamped** minted   5 **coiner** counterfeiter   7 **Dian** Diana (goddess of chastity)   8 **nonpareil** one without equal   11 **pudency** modesty   11 **on't** of it   12 **Saturn** (considered to be cold and gloomy)   14 **yellow** i.e., of complexion   15 **At first** immediately   16 **full-acorned** fed full with acorns   20 **motion** impulse

That tends to vice in man but I affirm
It is the woman's part. Be it lying, note it,
The woman's; flattering, hers; deceiving, hers;
Lust and rank° thoughts, hers, hers; revenges, hers;
25   Ambitions, covetings, change of prides,° disdain,
Nice° longing, slanders, mutability,°
All faults that have a name, nay, that hell knows,
Why, hers, in part or all, but rather all.
For even to vice
30   They are not constant, but are changing still
One vice but of a minute old for one
Not half so old as that. I'll write against them,
Detest them, curse them. Yet 'tis greater skill°
In a true hate to pray they have their will;
35   The very devils cannot plague them better.   *Exit.*

---

24 **rank** lascivious   25 **change of prides** varying extravagances
26 **Nice** wanton   26 **mutability** inconstancy   33 **skill** reason

ACT III

Scene I. [*Britain.*]

Enter in state Cymbeline, Queen, Cloten, and Lords at
one door and, at another, Caius Lucius and
Attendants.

Cymbeline. Now say, what would Augustus Caesar
    with us?

Lucius. When Julius Caesar, whose remembrance yet
    Lives in men's eyes and will to ears and tongues
    Be theme and hearing ever, was in this Britain
    And conquered it, Cassibelan thine uncle,   5
    Famous in Caesar's praises no whit less
    Than in his feats deserving it, for him
    And his succession granted Rome a tribute,
    Yearly three thousand pounds, which by thee lately
    Is left untendered.

Queen.   And, to kill the marvel,°   10
    Shall be so ever.

Cloten.   There be many Caesars
    Ere such another Julius. Britain's a world
    By itself, and we will nothing pay
    For wearing our own noses.

III.i.10 **kill the marvel** end the astonishment (caused by non-
payment)

91

Queen.   That opportunity
15 Which then they had to take from's, to resume
    We have again. Remember, sir, my liege,
    The kings your ancestors, together with
    The natural bravery of your isle, which stands
    As Neptune's park, ribbèd° and palèd° in
20 With rocks unscalable and roaring waters,
    With sands that will not bear your enemies' boats
    But suck them up to th' topmast. A kind of con-
        quest
    Caesar made here, but made not here his brag
    Of "Came and saw and overcame." With shame,
25 The first that ever touched him, he was carried
    From off our coast, twice beaten; and his shipping,
    Poor ignorant° baubles on our terrible seas,
    Like eggshells moved upon their surges, cracked
    As easily 'gainst our rocks. For joy whereof
30 The famed Cassibelan, who was once at point°—
    O giglot° Fortune!—to master° Caesar's sword,
    Made Lud's Town° with rejoicing fires bright
    And Britons strut with courage.

Cloten. Come, there's no more tribute to be paid. Our
35 kingdom is stronger than it was at that time, and, as
    I said, there is no moe such Caesars. Other of them
    may have crooked° noses, but to owe° such straight
    arms, none.

Cymbeline. Son, let your mother end.

40 *Cloten.* We have yet many among us can gripe° as
    hard as Cassibelan. I do not say I am one, but I
    have a hand. Why tribute? Why should we pay
    tribute? If Caesar can hide the sun from us with a
    blanket or put the moon in his pocket, we will pay
45 him tribute for light; else, sir, no more tribute, pray
    you now.

19 **ribbèd** enclosed   19 **palèd** fenced   27 **ignorant** inexperienced
30 **at point** at the point   31 **giglot** wanton   31 **to master** of master-
ing   32 **Lud's Town** London   37 **crooked** i.e., Roman   37 **owe** own
40 **gripe** grasp

Cymbeline. You must know,
  Till the injurious° Romans did extort
  This tribute from us, we were free. Caesar's ambi-
      tion,
  Which swelled so much that it did almost stretch   50
  The sides o' th' world, against all color° here
  Did put the yoke upon's; which to shake off
  Becomes a warlike people, whom we reckon
  Ourselves to be. We do say then to Caesar,
  Our ancestor was that Mulmutius which   55
  Ordained our laws, whose use the sword of Caesar
  Hath too much mangled, whose repair and fran-
      chise°
  Shall, by the power we hold, be our good deed,
  Though Rome be therefore angry. Mulmutius made
      our laws,
  Who was the first of Britain which did put   60
  His brows within a golden crown and called
  Himself a king.

Lucius.   I am sorry, Cymbeline,
  That I am to pronounce Augustus Caesar—
  Caesar, that hath moe kings his° servants than
  Thyself domestic officers—thine enemy.   65
  Receive it from me then: war and confusion°
  In Caesar's name pronounce I 'gainst thee. Look
  For fury not to be resisted. Thus defied,
  I thank thee for myself.

Cymbeline.   Thou art welcome, Caius.
  Thy Caesar knighted me; my youth I spent   70
  Much under him; of him I gathered honor,
  Which he to seek° of me again, perforce,
  Behooves me keep at utterance.° I am perfect°
  That the Pannonians and Dalmatians° for
  Their liberties are now in arms, a precedent   75

48 **injurious** insulting   51 **against all color** without any right
57 **franchise** free exercise   64 **his** as his   66 **confusion** destruction
72 **he to seek** his seeking   73 **keep at utterance** defend to the last
ditch   73 **perfect** well aware   74 **Pannonians and Dalmatians** inhabitants of present-day Hungary and Yugoslavia

Which not to read would show the Britons cold.°
So Caesar shall not find them.

Lucius.   Let proof° speak.

Cloten. His Majesty bids you welcome. Make pastime
with us a day or two, or longer. If you seek us after-
80 wards in other terms, you shall find us in our salt-
water girdle; if you beat us out of it, it is yours. If
you fall in the adventure, our crows shall fare the
better for you, and there's an end.

Lucius. So, sir.

Cymbeline. I know your master's pleasure, and he
85   mine.
All the remain° is, welcome.   *Exeunt.*

Scene II. [*Britain.*]

Enter Pisanio reading of a letter.

Pisanio. How? of adultery? Wherefore write you not
What monsters her accuse? Leonatus,
O master, what a strange° infection
Is fall'n into thy ear! What false Italian,
5   As poisonous-tongued as handed, hath prevailed
On thy too ready hearing? Disloyal? No.
She's punished for her truth° and undergoes,°
More goddess-like than wife-like, such assaults
As would take in° some virtue. O my master,
10   Thy mind to° her is now as low as were
Thy fortunes. How? That I should murder her,
Upon the love and truth and vows which I
Have made to thy command? I her? Her blood?
If it be so to do good service, never

---

76 cold deficient in spirit   **77 proof** experience   **86 the remain** that
remains   **III.ii.3 strange** foreign   **7 truth** fidelity   **7 undergoes** endures   **9 take in** conquer   **10 to** compared with

Let me be counted serviceable. How look I   15
That I should seem to lack humanity
So much as this fact° comes to? [*Reading*] "Do't!
   The letter
That I have sent her, by her own command
Shall give thee opportunity." O damned paper,
Black as the ink that's on thee! Senseless° bauble,   20
Art thou a fedary for° this act, and look'st
So virgin-like without? Lo, here she comes.

Enter Imogen.

I am ignorant in° what I am commanded.

Imogen. How now, Pisanio?

Pisanio. Madam, here is a letter from my lord.   25

Imogen. Who, thy lord? That is my lord Leonatus?
O, learn'd indeed were that astronomer°
That knew the stars as I his characters;°
He'ld lay the future open. You good gods,
Let what is here contained relish of love,
Of my lord's health, of his content—yet not°   30
That we two are asunder; let that grieve him.
Some griefs are med'cinable;° that is one of them,
For it doth physic love°—of his content
All but in that. Good wax, thy leave. Blest be   35
You bees that make these locks of counsel.° Lovers
And men in dangerous bonds° pray not alike;
Though forfeiters° you cast in prison, yet
You clasp young Cupid's tables.° Good news, gods!
   [*Reading*]
   "Justice and your father's wrath, should he take   40
me in his dominion, could not be so cruel to me as°
you, O the dearest of creatures, would even renew
me with your eyes. Take notice that I am in Cam-

17 fact crime   20 Senseless inanimate   21 fedary for accomplice
in   23 am ignorant in will pretend ignorance of   27 astronomer
astrologer   28 characters handwriting   31 not not content   33 med-
'cinable curative   34 physic love keep love healthy   36 locks of
counsel waxen seals   37 in dangerous bonds under contracts im-
posing penalties   38 forfeiters contract-violators   39 tables note-
books   41 as but that

bria° at Milford Haven. What your own love will
45   out of this advise you, follow. So he wishes you all
happiness, that remains loyal to his vow, and your
increasing in love.

> Leonatus Posthumus."

O, for a horse with wings! Hear'st thou, Pisanio?
50   He is at Milford Haven. Read, and tell me
How far 'tis thither. If one of mean affairs°
May plod it in a week, why may not I
Glide thither in a day? Then, true Pisanio,
Who long'st like me to see thy lord, who long'st—
55   O, let me bate°—but not like me, yet long'st,
But in a fainter kind—O, not like me!
For mine's beyond beyond: say, and speak thick°—
Love's counselor should fill the bores of hearing,°
To th' smothering of the sense—how far it is
60   To this same blessèd Milford. And by th' way°
Tell me how Wales was made so happy as
T' inherit such a haven. But first of all,
How we may steal from hence, and for the gap
That we shall make in time from our hence-going
65   And our return, to excuse. But first, how get hence?
Why should excuse be born or ere begot?°
We'll talk of that hereafter. Prithee speak,
How many score of miles may we well rid°
'Twixt hour and hour?

Pisanio.   One score 'twixt sun and sun,
70   Madam, 's enough for you, and too much too.

Imogen. Why, one that rode to's execution, man,
Could never go so slow. I have heard of riding
     wagers
Where horses have been nimbler than the sands
That run i' th' clock's behalf.° But this is fool'ry.
75   Go bid my woman feign a sickness, say

43–44 **Cambria** Wales   51 **mean affairs** ordinary business   55 **bate**
abate, modify (the statement)   57 **thick** profusely   58 **bores of
hearing** ears   60 **by th' way** on the way   66 **or ere begot** i.e., before conception (of the deed which makes excuse necessary)   68 **rid**
cover   74 **i' th' clock's behalf** in place of a clock

She'll home to her father; and provide me presently°
A riding suit, no costlier than would fit
A franklin's° housewife.°

Pisanio.   Madam, you're best consider.

Imogen. I see before me,° man. Nor here, nor here,°
Nor what ensues,° but have a fog in them   80
That I cannot look through. Away, I prithee;
Do as I bid thee. There's no more to say.
Accessible is none but Milford way.

                              Exeunt [*severally*].

Scene III. [*Wales.*]

Enter Belarius, Guiderius, and Arviragus.

Belarius. A goodly day not to keep house with such
Whose roof's as low as ours! Stoop, boys. This gate°
Instructs you how t' adore the heavens and bows
  you°
To a morning's holy office. The gates of monarchs
Are arched so high that giants may jet° through   5
And keep their impious turbans on without
Good morrow to the sun. Hail, thou fair heaven!
We house i' th' rock, yet use thee not so hardly°
As prouder livers do.

Guiderius.   Hail, heaven!

Arviragus.   Hail, heaven!

Belarius. Now for our mountain sport. Up to yond hill;   10
  Your legs are young. I'll tread these flats. Consider,

76 **presently** immediately   78 **franklin** small landowner   78 **housewife** (pronounced "huzzif")   79 **before me** i.e., what is immediately ahead   79 **Nor here, nor here** neither to this side nor that
80 **what ensues** the eventual outcome   III.iii.2 **This gate** one of the
tiring-house doors (representing the "cave")   3 **bows you** makes
you bow   5 **jet** strut   8 **hardly** badly

When you above perceive me like a crow,
That it is place° which lessens and sets off,°
And you may then revolve what tales I have told
    you
15 Of courts, of princes, of the tricks in war.
This° service is not service, so being done,
But being so allowed.° To apprehend thus
Draws us a profit from all things we see,
And often, to our comfort, shall we find
20 The sharded° beetle in a safer hold°
Than is the full-winged eagle. O, this life
Is nobler than attending for a check,°
Richer than doing nothing for a bribe,
Prouder than rustling in unpaid-for silk:
25 Such gain the cap° of him that makes him fine°
Yet keeps his book uncrossed.° No life to ours.

Guiderius. Out of your proof° you speak. We poor
    unfledged
Have never winged from view o' th' nest, nor know
    not
What air's from home. Haply this life is best
30 If quiet life be best, sweeter to you
That have a sharper known, well corresponding
With your stiff age; but unto us it is
A cell of ignorance, traveling abed,°
A prison, or a debtor that not dares
To stride a limit.°

35 *Arviragus.*   What should we speak of
When we are old as you? When we shall hear
The rain and wind beat dark December, how
In this our pinching° cave shall we discourse
The freezing hours away? We have seen nothing.

---

13 **place** position   13 **sets off** displays to advantage   16 **This** any
particular   17 **allowed** approved   20 **sharded** provided with wing-
cases   20 **hold** stronghold   22 **attending for a check** doing service
at court only to receive a rebuke   25 **gain the cap** win approval
25 **makes him fine** dresses elegantly   26 **keeps . . . uncrossed** does
not cancel the debts in his account book   27 **proof** experience
33 **abed** i.e., in imagination   35 **stride a limit** step over a boundary
38 **pinching** distressingly cold

We are beastly:° subtle as the fox for prey, 40
Like° warlike as the wolf for what we eat.
Our valor is to chase what flies. Our cage
We make a choir, as doth the prisoned bird,
And sing our bondage freely.

Belarius.   How you speak!
Did you but know the city's usuries 45
And felt them knowingly; the art o' th' court,
As hard to leave as keep,° whose top to climb
Is certain falling, or so slipp'ry that
The fear's as bad as falling; the toil o' th' war,
A pain° that only seems to seek out danger 50
I' th' name of fame and honor, which dies i' th'
    search
And hath as oft a sland'rous epitaph
As record of fair act; nay, many times
Doth ill deserve° by doing well; what's worse,
Must curtsy at the censure. O boys, this story 55
The world may read in me. My body's marked
With Roman swords, and my report° was once
First with the best of note.° Cymbeline loved me,
And when a soldier was the theme, my name
Was not far off. Then was I as a tree 60
Whose boughs did bend with fruit. But in one night
A storm or robbery, call it what you will,
Shook down my mellow hangings,° nay, my leaves,
And left me bare to weather.

Guiderius.   Uncertain favor!

Belarius. My fault being nothing, as I have told you
    oft, 65
But that two villains, whose false oaths prevailed
Before my perfect honor, swore to Cymbeline
I was confederate with the Romans. So
Followed my banishment, and this twenty years
· This rock and these demesnes have been my world, 70
Where I have lived at honest freedom, paid

40 **beastly** beast-like 41 **Like** as 47 **keep** remain at 50 **pain**
labor 54 **deserve** earn 57 **report** reputation 58 **note** reputation
63 **hangings** fruit

More pious debts to heaven than in all
The fore-end° of my time. But up to th' mountains!
This is not hunters' language. He that strikes
75 The venison first shall be the lord o' th' feast;
To him the other two shall minister,
And we will fear no poison, which attends°
In place of greater state. I'll meet you in the valleys.
                    Exeunt [Guiderius and Arviragus].
How hard it is to hide the sparks of nature!
80 These boys know little they are sons to th' King,
Nor Cymbeline dreams that they are alive.
They think they are mine, and though trained up
        thus meanly
I' th' cave wherein they bow, their thoughts do hit
The roofs of palaces, and Nature prompts them
85 In simple and low things to prince it much
Beyond the trick° of others. This Polydore,
The heir of Cymbeline and Britain, who
The King his father called Guiderius—Jove!
When on my three-foot stool I sit and tell
90 The warlike feats I have done, his spirits fly out
Into my story; say "Thus mine enemy fell,
And thus I set my foot on's neck," even then
The princely blood flows in his cheek, he sweats,
Strains his young nerves,° and puts himself in pos-
        ture
95 That acts my words. The younger brother Cadwal,
Once Arviragus, in as like a figure°
Strikes life into my speech and shows much more
                                    [Horn.]
His own conceiving.° Hark, the game is roused!
O Cymbeline, heaven and my conscience knows
100 Thou didst unjustly banish me; whereon,
At three and two years old, I stole these babes,
Thinking to bar thee of succession as
Thou refts° me of my lands. Euriphile,

73 **fore-end** early part   77 **attends** is present   86 **trick** capacity
94 **nerves** sinews   96 **in . . . figure** playing his part equally well
98 **conceiving** interpretation   103 **refts** robbed

Thou wast their nurse; they took thee for their
     mother,
And every day do honor to her grave.   105
Myself, Belarius, that am Morgan called,
They take for natural father. The game is up.°

                                             Exit.

Scene IV. [*Wales.*]

Enter Pisanio and Imogen.

Imogen. Thou told'st me, when we came from horse,
     the place
Was near at hand. Ne'er longed my mother so
To see me first as I have° now. Pisanio, man,
Where is Posthumus? What is in thy mind
That makes thee stare thus? Wherefore breaks that
     sigh   5
From th' inward of thee? One but painted thus
Would be interpreted a thing perplexed°
Beyond self-explication. Put thyself
Into a havior° of less fear, ere wildness°
Vanquish my staider senses. What's the matter?°   10
Why tender'st thou that paper to me with
A look untender? If't be summer news,
Smile to't before; if winterly, thou need'st
But keep that count'nance still. My husband's hand?
That drug-damned Italy hath outcraftied° him,   15
And he's at some hard point.° Speak, man! Thy
     tongue
May take off some extremity,° which to read
Would be even mortal to me.

107 **up** roused   III.iv.3 **have** i.e., have longing (to see Posthumus)   7 **perplexed** troubled   9 **havior** appearance   9 **wildness** panic
10 **matter** business   15 **outcraftied** outwitted   16 **at some hard
point** in some difficult situation   17 **take . . . extremity** lessen the
shock

Pisanio.   Please you read,
And you shall find me, wretched man, a thing
20 The most disdained of fortune.

Imogen. (Reads) "Thy mistress, Pisanio, hath played
the strumpet in my bed, the testimonies whereof lies
bleeding in me. I speak not out of weak surmises,
but from proof as strong as my grief and as certain
25 as I expect my revenge. That part thou, Pisanio,
must act for me, if thy faith be not tainted with the
breach of hers. Let thine own hands take away her
life. I shall give thee opportunity at Milford Haven
—she hath my letter for the purpose—where, if
30 thou fear to strike and to make me certain it is
done, thou art the pander to her dishonor and
equally to me disloyal."

Pisanio. What shall I need to draw my sword? The
paper
Hath cut her throat already. No, 'tis slander,
Whose edge is sharper than the sword, whose
35 tongue
Outvenoms all the worms° of Nile, whose breath
Rides on the posting° winds and doth belie°
All corners of the world. Kings, queens, and states,°
Maids, matrons, nay, the secrets of the grave
40 This viperous slander enters. What cheer, madam?

Imogen. False to his bed? What is it to be false?
To lie in watch° there and to think on him?
To weep 'twixt clock and clock?° If sleep charge°
nature,
To break it with a fearful° dream of him
45 And cry myself awake? That's false to's bed, is it?

Pisanio. Alas, good lady!

Imogen. I false? Thy° conscience witness! Iachimo,

36 **worms** serpents 37 **posting** speeding 37 **belie** fill with lies
38 **states** lords 42 **in watch** awake 43 **'twixt clock and clock** from
hour to hour 43 **charge** burden 44 **fearful** frightening 47 **Thy**
i.e., Posthumus'

Thou didst accuse him of incontinency.
Thou then looked'st like a villain; now, methinks,
Thy favor's° good enough. Some jay° of Italy,   *50*
Whose mother was her painting,° hath betrayed
    him.
Poor I am stale, a garment out of fashion,
And, for I am richer than to hang by th' walls,°
I must be ripped. To pieces with me! O,
Men's vows are women's traitors! All good seem-
    ing,°   *55*
By thy revolt,° O husband, shall be thought
Put on for villainy, not born where't grows,°
But worn a bait for ladies.

Pisanio.   Good madam, hear me.

Imogen. True honest men, being heard° like false
    Aeneas,°
Were in his time thought false, and Sinon's° weep-
    ing   *60*
Did scandal° many a holy tear, took pity
From most true wretchedness. So thou, Posthumus,
Wilt lay the leaven on all proper men;°
Goodly° and gallant shall be false and perjured
From thy great fail.° Come, fellow, be thou honest;   *65*
Do thou thy master's bidding. When thou seest him,
A little witness my obedience. Look,
I draw the sword myself. Take it, and hit
The innocent mansion of my love, my heart.
Fear not, 'tis empty of all things but grief.   *70*
Thy master is not there, who was indeed
The riches of it. Do his bidding, strike!
Thou mayst be valiant in a better cause,
But now thou seem'st a coward.

50 **favor** appearance   50 **jay** whore   51 **Whose . . . painting** i.e.,
dependent upon make-up   53 **for . . . walls** i.e., since I am too
valuable to be set aside   55 **seeming** appearance   56 **revolt** turning away   57 **not . . . grows** i.e., transplanted (hence assumed)
59 **heard** heard to speak   59 **Aeneas** (who jilted Dido)   60 **Sinon**
(who persuaded Troy to admit the Trojan Horse)   61 **scandal**
make disreputable   63 **lay . . . men** cause all honorable men to be
thought corrupt   64 **Goodly** handsome   65 **fail** failure

Pisanio.　　　　　　　Hence, vile instrument!
　　Thou shalt not damn my hand.

75 *Imogen.*　　　　　　　Why, I must die,
　　And if I do not by thy hand, thou art
　　No servant of thy master's. Against self-slaughter
　　There is a prohibition so divine
　　That cravens° my weak hand. Come, here's my
　　　　heart—
80　　Something's° afore't; soft,° soft, we'll no defense—
　　Obedient° as the scabbard. What is here?
　　The scriptures° of the loyal Leonatus
　　All turned to heresy? Away, away,
　　Corrupters of my faith! You shall no more
85　　Be stomachers° to my heart. Thus may poor fools
　　Believe false teachers. Though those that are be-
　　　　trayed
　　Do feel the treason sharply, yet the traitor
　　Stands in worse case of woe.
　　And thou, Posthumus, that didst set up
90　　My disobedience 'gainst the King my father
　　And make me put into contempt the suits
　　Of princely fellows, shalt hereafter find
　　It is no act of common passage, but
　　A strain of rareness;° and I grieve myself
95　　To think, when thou shalt be disedged° by her
　　That now thou tirest° on, how thy memory
　　Will then be panged° by me. Prithee dispatch,
　　The lamb entreats the butcher. Where's thy knife?
　　Thou art too slow to do thy master's bidding
　　When I desire it too.

100 *Pisanio.*　　　　　　O gracious lady,
　　Since I received command to do this business
　　I have not slept one wink.

---

79 **cravens** makes cowardly　　80 **Something** Posthumus' letter
80 **soft** wait　　81 **Obedient** i.e., as ready to receive the sword
82 **scriptures** writings　　85 **stomachers** ornamental cloth worn under
lacing of the bodice (she has been holding the letter against her
breast)　　93–94 **It . . . rareness** i.e., my choice of you was not an
everyday matter but resulted from rare qualities　　95 **be disedged**
have lost the edge (of appetite)　　96 **tirest** feedest ravenously
(hawking term)　　97 **panged** tormented

Imogen.   Do't, and to bed then.

Pisanio. I'll wake mine eyeballs out° first.

Imogen.   Wherefore then
Didst undertake it? Why hast thou abused
So many miles with a pretense? This place?   105
Mine action and thine own? Our horses' labor?
The time inviting thee? The perturbed court
For my being absent? whereunto I never
Purpose return. Why hast thou gone so far,
To be unbent° when thou hast ta'en thy stand,°   110
Th' elected° deer before thee?

Pisanio.   But to win time
To lose so bad employment, in the which
I have considered of a course. Good lady,
Hear me with patience.

Imogen.   Talk thy tongue weary, speak.
I have heard I am a strumpet, and mine ear,   115
Therein false struck, can take no greater wound,
Nor tent to bottom that.° But speak.

Pisanio.   Then, madam,
I thought you would not back° again.

Imogen.   Most like,
Bringing me here to kill me.

Pisanio.   Not so, neither.
But if I were as wise as honest, then   120
My purpose would prove well. It cannot be
But that my master is abused.° Some villain,
Ay, and singular° in his art, hath done you both
This cursèd injury.

Imogen. Some Roman courtesan.°

Pisanio.   No, on my life: 125

---

103 **wake . . . out** remain awake till my eyes drop out   110 **unbent**
with bow unbent, unprepared   110 **stand** hunting station   111
elected chosen   117 **tent . . . that** probe reaching to bottom of the
wound   118 **back** go back   122 **abused** deceived   123 **singular**
unique   125 **courtesan** courtier

I'll give but notice you are dead, and send him
Some bloody sign of it,° for 'tis commanded
I should do so. You shall be missed at court,
And that will well confirm it.

Imogen.　　　　　　　　　　　　Why, good fellow,
130　What shall I do the while? Where bide? How live?
Or in my life what comfort when I am
Dead to my husband?

Pisanio.　　　　　　　　　　If you'll back to th' court—

Imogen. No court, no father, nor no more ado
With that harsh, noble, simple nothing,
135　That Cloten, whose love suit hath been to me
As fearful as a siege.

Pisanio.　　　　　　　　If not at court,
Then not in Britain must you bide.

Imogen.　　　　　　　　　　　　Where then?
Hath Britain all the sun that shines? Day, night,
Are they not but° in Britain? I' th' world's volume
140　Our Britain seems as of it, but not in't;°
In a great pool a swan's nest. Prithee think
There's livers out of Britain.

Pisanio.　　　　　　　　　　I am most glad
You think of other place. Th' ambassador,
Lucius the Roman, comes to Milford Haven
145　Tomorrow. Now if you could wear a mind
Dark° as your fortune is, and but disguise
That° which, t' appear itself,° must not yet be
But by self-danger, you should tread a course
Pretty and full of view;° yea, haply,° near
150　The residence of Posthumus, so nigh, at least,
That though his actions were not visible, yet
Report should render° him hourly to your ear
As truly as he moves.

127 **it** your death　139 **not but** only　140 **of it . . . in't** i.e., part
of the world yet separated from it　146 **Dark** inscrutable　147 **That**
her sex　147 **itself** i.e., as itself　149 **full of view** with good pros-
pects　149 **haply** perhaps　152 **render** describe

Imogen.   O, for such means,
  Though peril to my modesty,° not death on't,
  I would adventure.

Pisanio.   Well then, here's the point: 155
  You must forget to be a woman; change
  Command° into obedience, fear and niceness°—
  The handmaids of all women, or more truly
  Woman it° pretty self—into a waggish courage;
  Ready in gibes, quick-answered,° saucy, and   160
  As quarrelous° as the weasel. Nay, you must
  Forget that rarest treasure of your cheek,
  Exposing it—but O, the harder° heart!
  Alack, no remedy—to the greedy touch
  Of common-kissing Titan,° and forget   165
  Your laborsome° and dainty trims,° wherein
  You made great Juno angry.°

Imogen.   Nay, be brief.
  I see into thy end° and am almost
  A man already.

Pisanio.   First, make yourself but like one.
  Forethinking° this, I have already fit°—   170
  'Tis in my cloak-bag—doublet, hat, hose, all
  That answer° to them. Would you, in their serving,°
  And with what imitation you can borrow
  From youth of such a season,° 'fore noble Lucius
  Present yourself, desire his service,° tell him   175
  Wherein you're happy,° which will make him
      know,°
  If that his head have ear in music; doubtless
  With joy he will embrace° you, for he's honorable,

154 **modesty** chastity   157 **Command** habit of commanding (as a
person of rank)   157 **niceness** fastidiousness   159 **it** its   160
quick-answered quick-answering   161 **quarrelous** quarrelsome   163
harder too hard   165 **common-kissing Titan** the sun which kisses
everything alike   166 **laborsome** elaborate   166 **trims** apparel
167 **angry** i.e., with jealousy   168 **end** purpose   170 **Forethinking**
planning in advance for   170 **fit** prepared   172 **answer** correspond
172 **in their serving** with their aid   174 **season** age   175 **his service**
employment as his servant   176 **happy** accomplished   176 **make
him know** satisfy him   178 **embrace** welcome

And, doubling that, most holy. Your means°
    abroad—
180 You have me, rich, and I will never fail
Beginning nor supplyment.

Imogen.   Thou art all the comfort
The gods will diet me with. Prithee away.
There's more to be considered, but we'll even°
All that good time will give us. This attempt
185 I am soldier to,° and will abide° it with
A prince's courage. Away, I prithee.

Pisanio. Well, madam, we must take a short farewell,
Lest, being missed, I be suspected of
Your carriage° from the court. My noble mistress,
190 Here is a box; I had it from the Queen.
What's in't is precious. If you are sick at sea
Or stomach-qualmed at land, a dram of this
Will drive away distemper.° To some shade,
And fit you to your manhood. May the gods
Direct you to the best.

Imogen.   Amen. I thank thee.
195   *Exeunt [severally].*

Scene V. [*Britain.*]

*Enter Cymbeline, Queen, Cloten, Lucius, [a
Messenger, Attendants,] and Lords.*

Cymbeline. Thus far, and so farewell.

Lucius.   Thanks, royal sir.
My emperor hath wrote: I must from hence,
And am right sorry that I must report ye
My master's enemy.

179 **means** i.e., of subsistence 183 **even** keep pace with 185 **soldier to** brave enough for 185 **abide** face 189 **Your carriage** removing you 193 **distemper** illness

Cymbeline.   Our subjects, sir,
Will not endure his yoke, and for ourself   5
To show less sovereignty than they, must needs
Appear unkinglike.

Lucius.   So, sir. I desire of you
A conduct° overland to Milford Haven.
Madam, all joy befall your Grace, and you.°

Cymbeline. My lords, you are appointed for that
  office;°   10
The due of honor in no point omit.
So farewell, noble Lucius.

Lucius.   Your hand, my lord.

Cloten. Receive it friendly, but from this time forth
I wear it as your enemy.

Lucius.   Sir, the event°
Is yet to name the winner. Fare you well.   15

Cymbeline. Leave not the worthy Lucius, good my
  lords,
Till he have crossed the Severn. Happiness!
          Exeunt Lucius et ceteri.°

Queen. He goes hence frowning, but it honors us
That we have given him cause.

Cloten.   'Tis all the better;
Your valiant Britons have their wishes in it.   20

Cymbeline. Lucius hath wrote already to the Emperor
How it goes here. It fits us therefore ripely°
Our chariots and our horsemen be in readiness.
The pow'rs that he already hath in Gallia
Will soon be drawn to head,° from whence he
  moves   25
His war for Britain.

III.v.8 **conduct** escort   9 **you** Cymbeline   10 **office** duty   14 **event**
outcome   17s.d. **et ceteri** and others (Attendants and Lords)   22
fits . . . ripely behooves us therefore strongly   25 **drawn to head**
gathered into an army

Queen.   'Tis not sleepy business,
   But must be looked to speedily and strongly.

Cymbeline. Our expectation that it would be thus
   Hath made us forward. But, my gentle queen,
30 Where is our daughter? She hath not appeared
   Before the Roman, nor to us hath tendered
   The duty of the day. She looks° us like
   A thing more made of malice than of duty.
   We have noted it.—Call her before us, for
   We have been too slight in sufferance.°

                  [Exit Messenger.]

35 *Queen.*   Royal sir,
   Since the exile of Posthumus, most retired
   Hath her life been; the cure whereof, my lord,
   'Tis time must do. Beseech your Majesty,
   Forbear sharp speeches to her. She's a lady
40 So tender of° rebukes that words are strokes,
   And strokes death to her.

              Enter Messenger.

Cymbeline.   Where is she, sir? How
   Can her contempt be answered?°

Messenger.   Please you, sir,
   Her chambers are all locked, and there's no answer
   That will be given to th' loud of noise we make.

45 *Queen.* My lord, when last I went to visit her,
   She prayed me to excuse her keeping close;°
   Whereto constrained by her infirmity,
   She should that duty leave unpaid to you
   Which daily she was bound to proffer. This
50 She wished me to make known, but our great court°
   Made me to blame in memory.°

Cymbeline.   Her doors locked?

---

32 looks seems to   **35 slight in sufferance** remiss in permissiveness
40 tender of sensitive to   **42 answered** accounted for   **46 close** to
herself   **50 our great court** i.e., state affairs   **51 to blame in memory** fail to remember

Not seen of late? Grant, heavens, that which I fear
Prove false!   *Exit.*

Queen.   Son, I say, follow the King.

Cloten. That man of hers, Pisanio, her old servant,
I have not seen these two days.

Queen.   Go, look after. *Exit* [*Cloten*].   55
Pisanio, thou that stand'st so for° Posthumus—
He hath a drug of mine. I pray his absence
Proceed° by swallowing that, for he believes
It is a thing most precious. But for her,
Where is she gone? Haply despair hath seized her,   60
Or, winged with fervor of her love, she's flown
To her desired Posthumus. Gone she is
To death or to dishonor, and my end
Can make good use of either. She being down,
I have the placing of the British crown.   65

Enter Cloten.

How now, my son?

Cloten.   'Tis certain she is fled.
Go in and cheer the King. He rages; none
Dare come about him.

Queen. [*Aside*]   All the better. May
This night forestall° him of the coming day!
                                        Exit Queen.

Cloten. I love and hate her, for° she's fair and royal,   70
And that° she hath all courtly parts° more exquisite
Than lady, ladies, woman. From every one
The best she hath, and she, of all compounded,
Outsells° them all. I love her therefore, but
Disdaining me and throwing favors on   75
The low Posthumus slanders° so her judgment
That what's else rare is choked; and in that point

56 **stand'st so for** so much supportest   58 **Proceed by** result from
69 **forestall** deprive   70 **for** because   71 **that** because   71 **parts**
qualities   74 **Outsells** outvalues   76 **slanders** denigrates

I will conclude to hate her, nay, indeed,
To be revenged upon her. For, when fools
Shall—

Enter Pisanio.

80   Who is here? What, are you packing,° sirrah?°
Come hither. Ah, you precious pander! Villain,
Where is thy lady? In a word, or else
Thou art straightway with the fiends.

Pisanio.   O good my lord!

Cloten. Where is thy lady? Or, by Jupiter,
85   I will not ask again. Close° villain,
I'll have this secret from thy heart or rip
Thy heart to find it. Is she with Posthumus?
From whose so many weights of baseness cannot
A dram of worth be drawn.

Pisanio.   Alas, my lord,
90   How can she be with him? When was she missed?
He is in Rome.

Cloten.   Where is she, sir? Come nearer.°
No farther halting. Satisfy me home°
What is become of her.

Pisanio. O my all-worthy lord!

Cloten.   All-worthy villain!
95   Discover° where thy mistress is at once,
At the next word. No more of "worthy lord"!
Speak, or thy silence on the instant is
Thy condemnation and thy death.

Pisanio.   Then, sir,
This paper° is the history of my knowledge
Touching her flight.   [*Presenting a letter*]

100 *Cloten.*   Let's see't. I will pursue her
Even to Augustus' throne.

---

80 **packing** plotting 80 **sirrah** (term of address to an inferior)
85 **Close** secretive 91 **nearer** to the point 92 **home** thoroughly
95 **Discover** reveal 99 **This paper** (cf. line 131 and V.v.279)

Pisanio. [*Aside*]   Or° this, or perish.
She's far enough, and what he learns by this
May prove his travel, not her danger.

Cloten.   Hum!

Pisanio. [*Aside*] I'll write to my lord she's dead. O
    Imogen,
Safe mayst thou wander, safe return again!   *105*

Cloten. Sirrah, is this letter true?

Pisanio. Sir, as I think.

Cloten. It is Posthumus' hand, I know't. Sirrah, if thou
wouldst not be a villain, but do me true service, un-
dergo° those employments wherein I should have *110*
cause to use thee with a serious industry—that is,
what villainy soe'er I bid thee do, to perform it directly and truly—I would think thee an honest man.
Thou shouldst neither want my means for thy relief
nor my voice for thy preferment.°   *115*

Pisanio. Well, my good lord.

Cloten. Wilt thou serve me? For since patiently and
constantly thou hast stuck to the bare fortune of that
beggar Posthumus, thou canst not, in the course of
gratitude, but be a diligent follower of mine. Wilt *120*
thou serve me?

Pisanio. Sir, I will.

Cloten. Give me thy hand. Here's my purse. Hast any
of thy late master's garments in thy possession?

Pisanio. I have, my lord, at my lodging the same suit *125*
he wore when he took leave of my lady and mistress.

Cloten. The first service thou dost me, fetch that suit
hither. Let it be thy first service. Go.

Pisanio. I shall, my lord.   *Exit.* *130*

101 **Or** either   109–10 **undergo** undertake   115 **preferment** advancement

Cloten. Meet thee at Milford Haven! I forgot to ask him one thing; I'll remember't anon. Even there, thou villain Posthumus, will I kill thee. I would these garments were come. She said upon a time—

135 the bitterness of it I now belch from my heart—that she held the very garment of Posthumus in more respect than my noble and natural person, together with the adornment of my qualities. With that suit upon my back will I ravish her; first kill him, and in

140 her eyes. There shall she see my valor, which will then be a torment to her contempt. He on the ground, my speech of insultment° ended on his dead body, and when my lust hath dined—which, as I say, to vex her I will execute in the clothes that she so

145 praised—to the court I'll knock her back,° foot° her home again. She hath despised me rejoicingly, and I'll be merry in my revenge.

Enter Pisanio [*with the clothes*].

Be those the garments?

Pisanio. Ay, my noble lord.

150 *Cloten.* How long is't since she went to Milford Haven?

Pisanio. She can scarce be there yet.

Cloten. Bring this apparel to my chamber; that is the second thing that I have commanded thee. The third

155 is that thou wilt be a voluntary mute to my design. Be but duteous, and true preferment shall tender itself to thee. My revenge is now at Milford. Would I had wings to follow it! Come, and be true.   *Exit.*

Pisanio. Thou bid'st me to my loss,° for true to thee

160 Were to prove false, which I will never be,
To him° that is most true. To Milford go,

---

142 **insultment** scornful triumph   145 **knock her back** beat her home   145 **foot** kick   159 **loss** i.e., of honor   161 **him** Posthumus

And find not her whom thou pursuest. Flow, flow,
You heavenly blessings, on her. This fool's speed
Be crossed° with slowness; labor be his meed.° *Exit.*

Scene VI. [*Wales.*]

Enter Imogen alone [in boy's clothes].

Imogen. I see a man's life is a tedious one.
I have tired myself, and for two nights together
Have made the ground my bed. I should be sick
But that my resolution helps me. Milford,
When from the mountain-top Pisanio showed thee,   5
Thou wast within a ken.° O Jove, I think
Foundations° fly the wretched—such, I mean,
Where they should be relieved. Two beggars told me
I could not miss my way. Will poor folks lie,
That have afflictions on them, knowing 'tis   10
A punishment or trial? Yes. No wonder,
When rich ones scarce tell true. To lapse in fulness°
Is sorer° than to lie for need, and falsehood
Is worse in kings than beggars. My dear lord,
Thou art one o' th' false ones. Now I think on thee   15
My hunger's gone, but even° before, I was
At point° to sink for° food. But what is this?
Here is a path to't. 'Tis some savage hold.°
I were best not call; I dare not call. Yet famine,
Ere clean° it o'erthrow nature, makes it valiant.   20
Plenty and peace breeds cowards; hardness° ever
Of hardiness is mother. Ho! Who's here?
If anything that's civil,° speak; if savage,
Take or lend.° Ho! No answer? Then I'll enter.

164 **crossed** thwarted   164 **meed** reward   III.vi.6 a **ken** view   7
Foundations security (quibble on "hospitals")   12 **lapse in fulness**
i.e., lie when prosperous   13 **sorer** worse   16 **even** just   17 **At
point** about   17 **for** for lack of   18 **hold** stronghold   20 **clean**
completely   21 **hardness** hardship   23 **civil** civilized   24 **Take or
lend** take (what I have) or give (what you will)

25   Best draw my sword, and if mine enemy
      But fear the sword like me, he'll scarcely look on't.
      Such a foe,° good heavens!   *Exit.*°

        Enter Belarius, Guiderius, and Arviragus.

Belarius. You, Polydore, have proved best woodman° and
      Are master of the feast. Cadwal and I
30   Will play the cook and servant; 'tis our match.°
      The sweat of industry would dry and die
      But for the end it works to. Come, our stomachs
      Will make what's homely° savory. Weariness
      Can snore upon the flint when resty° sloth
35   Finds the down pillow hard. Now peace be here,
      Poor house, that keep'st thyself.

Guiderius.   I am throughly weary.

Arviragus. I am weak with toil, yet strong in appetite.

Guiderius. There is cold meat i' th' cave. We'll browse
      on that
      Whilst what we have killed be cooked.

Belarius. [*Looking through door*]   Stay, come not in.
40   But that it eats our victuals, I should think
      Here were a fairy.

Guiderius.   What's the matter,° sir?

Belarius. By Jupiter, an angel; or, if not,
      An earthly paragon. Behold divineness
      No elder than a boy.

              Enter Imogen.

45 *Imogen.* Good masters, harm me not.
      Before I entered here, I called and thought
      To have begged or bought what I have took. Good
      troth,°

27 **Such a foe** i.e., may I have (if any) such a foe   27s.d **Exit** (at
this point, since the stage is cleared, F marks a new scene)
28 **woodman** hunter   30 **match** agreement   33 **homely** plain   34
resty lazy   41 **matter** subject (of your remark)   47 **Good troth**
in truth

I have stol'n naught, nor would not, though I had
    found
Gold strewed i' th' floor. Here's money for my meat.
I would have left it on the board so soon   50
As I had made my meal, and parted
With pray'rs for the provider.

Guiderius.   Money, youth?

Arviragus. All gold and silver rather turn to dirt,
As 'tis no better reckoned but of those
Who worship dirty gods.

Imogen.   I see you're angry.   55
Know, if you kill me for my fault, I should
Have died had I not made it.

Belarius.   Whither bound?

Imogen. To Milford Haven.

Belarius. What's your name?

Imogen. Fidele, sir. I have a kinsman who   60
Is bound for Italy; he embarked at Milford;
To whom being going, almost spent with hunger,
I am fall'n in this offense.

Belarius.   Prithee, fair youth,
Think us no churls, nor measure our good minds
By this rude place we live in. Well encountered!
'Tis almost night; you shall have better cheer°   65
Ere you depart, and thanks° to stay and eat it.
Boys, bid him welcome.

Guiderius.   Were you a woman, youth,
I should woo hard but be° your groom in honesty.
I'ld bid for you as I do buy.°

Arviragus.   I'll make't my comfort   70
He is a man. I'll love him as my brother,
And such a welcome as I'ld give to him

---

66 cheer entertainment   **67 thanks** i.e., our thanks   **69 but be** ere
I should fail to be (E. Dowden)   **70 I'ld bid . . . buy** i.e., I'd seek
your hand in earnest

    After long absence, such is yours. Most welcome.
    Be sprightly,° for you fall 'mongst friends.

Imogen.   'Mongst friends?
    —If brothers.° [*Aside*] Would it had been so that
75   they
    Had been my father's sons! Then had my prize°
    Been less,° and so more equal ballasting°
    To thee, Posthumus.

Belarius.   He wrings° at some distress.

Guiderius. Would I could free't!

Arviragus.   Or I, whate'er it be,
    What pain it cost, what danger. Gods!

80 *Belarius.*   Hark, boys. [*Whispers.*]

Imogen. Great men
    That had a court no bigger than this cave,
    That did attend themselves° and had the virtue
    Which their own conscience sealed them,° laying
      by°
85   That nothing-gift° of differing° multitudes,
    Could not outpeer° these twain. Pardon me, gods,
    I'ld change my sex to be companion with them,
    Since Leonatus false.

Belarius.   It shall be so.
    Boys, we'll go dress our hunt.° Fair youth, come in.
90   Discourse is heavy, fasting. When we have supped,
    We'll mannerly demand thee of thy story,
    So far as thou wilt speak it.

Guiderius.   Pray draw near.

---

74 sprightly in good spirits   **75 If brothers** i.e., yes, if we were indeed brothers   **76 prize** price, value (quibble on "captured ship")   **77 less** (since then she would not be heir apparent)   **77 ballasting** weight   **78 wrings** writhes   **83 attend themselves** i.e., get along without attendants   **84 sealed them** authenticated for them (as in affixing a waxen seal to a legal document)   **84 laying by** setting aside   **85 nothing-gift** worthless gift (flattery)   **85 differing** fickle   **86 outpeer** surpass   **89 hunt** quarry

Arviragus. The night to th' owl and morn to th' lark
    less welcome.

Imogen. Thanks, sir.

Arviragus. I pray draw near.   *Exeunt.*   *95*

Scene VII. *[Rome.]*

Enter two Roman Senators and Tribunes.

First Senator. This is the tenor of the Emperor's writ:°
    That since the common men are now in action
    'Gainst the Pannonians and Dalmatians,
    And that the legions now in Gallia are
    Full weak to undertake our wars against   *5*
    The fall'n-off° Britons, that we do incite
    The gentry to this business. He creates
    Lucius proconsul, and to you the tribunes,
    For this immediate levy, he commends°
    His absolute commission.° Long live Caesar!   *10*

Tribune. Is Lucius general of the forces?

Second Senator.   Ay.

Tribune. Remaining now in Gallia?

First Senator.   With those legions
    Which I have spoke of, whereunto your levy
    Must be supplyant.° The words of your commission
    Will tie you to° the numbers and the time   *15*
    Of their dispatch.

Tribune.   We will discharge our duty.
                                Exeunt.

III.vii.1 **writ** dispatch   **6 fall'n-off** revolted   **9 commends** entrusts
10 absolute commission full authority   **14 supplyant** supplementary
15 tie you to confirm for you

ACT IV

Scene I. [*Wales.*]

Enter Cloten alone.

Cloten. I am near to th' place where they should meet,
if Pisanio have mapped it truly. How fit° his garments serve me! Why should his mistress, who was
made by him that made the tailor, not be fit° too?
5 The rather, saving reverence of° the word, for° 'tis
said a woman's fitness° comes by fits. Therein I
must play the workman. I dare speak it to myself,
for it is not vainglory for a man and his glass° to
confer in his own chamber—I mean, the lines of my
10 body are as well drawn as his; no less young, more
strong, not beneath him in fortunes, beyond him in
the advantage of the time,° above him in birth, alike
conversant in general° services, and more remarkable in single oppositions.° Yet this imperceiverant°
15 thing loves him in my despite. What mortality° is!
Posthumus, thy head, which now is growing upon
thy shoulders, shall within this hour be off, thy
mistress enforced,° thy garments cut to pieces be-

IV.i.2 **fit** suitably 4 **fit** suitable 5 **saving reverence of** begging
pardon for 5 **for** since 6 **fitness** sexual inclination 8 **glass** look-
ing-glass 12 **advantage of the time** social opportunities 13 **general** i.e., military 14 **single oppositions** duels 14 **imperceiverant**
imperceptive 15 **mortality** life 18 **enforced** raped

fore her face; and all this done, spurn her home to
her father, who may haply be a little angry for my   20
so rough usage; but my mother, having power of°
his testiness, shall turn all into my commendations.
My horse is tied up safe. Out, sword, and to a sore°
purpose! Fortune put them into my hand. This is the
very description of their meeting place, and the fel-   25
low dares not deceive me.   *Exit.*

Scene II. [*Wales.*]

*Enter Belarius, Guiderius, Arviragus, and Imogen
    from the cave.*

Belarius. You are not well. Remain here in the cave;
    We'll come to you after hunting.

Arviragus.   Brother, stay here.
    Are we not brothers?

Imogen.   So man and man should be,
    But clay and clay° differs in dignity,°
    Whose dust° is both alike. I am very sick.   5

Guiderius. Go you to hunting, I'll abide with him.

Imogen. So sick I am not, yet I am not well,
    But not so citizen° a wanton° as
    To seem to die ere sick. So please you, leave me;
    Stick to your journal° course; the breach of custom   10
    Is breach of all. I am ill, but your being by me
    Cannot amend° me; society is no comfort
    To one not sociable. I am not very sick,
    Since I can reason of it. Pray you trust me here—

---

21 **power of** control over 23 **sore** causing suffering (quibble on
"wound," i.e., vagina) IV.ii.4 **clay and clay** one person and
another 4 **dignity** rank 5 **dust** remains after death 8 **citizen**
city-bred, bourgeois 8 **wanton** spoilt child 10 **journal** daily
12 **amend** cure

15   I'll rob none but myself—and let me die,
      Stealing so poorly.°

Guiderius.   I love thee—I have spoke it—
      How much° the quantity, the weight as much
      As I do love my father.

Belarius.   What? How, how?

Arviragus. If it be sin to say so, sir, I yoke me
20   In my good brother's fault. I know not why
      I love this youth, and I have heard you say
      Love's reason's without reason. The bier at door,
      And a demand who is't shall die, I'ld say
      "My father, not this youth."

Belarius. [*Aside*]   O noble strain!°
25   O worthiness of nature, breed of greatness!
      Cowards father cowards and base things sire base;
      Nature hath meal and bran, contempt and grace.
      I'm not their father; yet who this should be
      Doth miracle itself, loved before me.°—
      'Tis the ninth hour o' th' morn.

30   *Arviragus.*   Brother, farewell.

Imogen. I wish ye sport.

Arviragus.   You health.—So please you,° sir.

Imogen. [*Aside*] These are kind creatures. Gods, what
            lies I have heard!
      Our courtiers say all's savage but at court.
      Experience, O, thou disprov'st report!
35   Th' imperious° seas breeds monsters; for the dish
      Poor tributary rivers as° sweet fish.
      I am sick still, heartsick. Pisanio,
      I'll now taste of thy drug.

Guiderius.   I could not stir him.°

---

16 poorly i.e., from myself only   **17 How much** as much   **24 strain**
heredity   **28–29 who this . . . before me** that this person, whoever
he is, should be loved more than I is miraculous   **31 So please you**
at your service   **35 imperious** imperial   **36 as** just as   **38 stir him**
move him (to tell his story)

He said he was gentle,° but unfortunate;
Dishonestly afflicted, but yet honest.   40

Arviragus. Thus did he answer me, yet said hereafter
I might know more.

Belarius.   To th' field, to th' field.—
We'll leave you for this time; go in and rest.

Arviragus. We'll not be long away.

Belarius.   Pray be not sick,
For you must be our housewife.

Imogen.   Well or ill,   45
I am bound° to you.   *Exit.*

Belarius.   And shalt be ever.
This youth, howe'er distressed, appears° he hath
     had
Good ancestors.

Arviragus.   How angel-like he sings!

Guiderius. But his neat° cookery! He cut our roots in
     characters,°
And sauced our broths as Juno had been sick   50
And he her dieter.

Arviragus.   Nobly he yokes
A smiling with a sigh, as if the sigh
Was that° it was for not being such a smile;
The smile mocking the sigh that it would fly
From so divine a temple to commix   55
With winds that sailors rail at.

Guiderius.   I do note
That grief and patience, rooted in them both,
Mingle their spurs° together.

Arviragus.   Grow patience,

---

39 **gentle** well-born   46 **bound** indebted (Belarius quibbles on "tied
by affection")   47 **appears** appears as though   49 **neat** elegant
49 **characters** designs   53 **that** what   58 **spurs** chief roots

And let the stinking elder,° grief, untwine
60   His perishing° root with° the increasing vine.

Belarius. It is great morning.° Come away.—Who's
there?

Enter Cloten.

Cloten. I cannot find those runagates.° That villain
Hath mocked me. I am faint.

Belarius.   "Those runagates"?
Means he not us? I partly know him. 'Tis
65   Cloten, the son o' th' Queen. I fear some ambush.
I saw him not these many years, and yet
I know 'tis he. We are held as outlaws. Hence!

Guiderius. He is but one. You and my brother search
What companies° are near. Pray you, away.
Let me alone with him.°
[Exeunt Belarius and Arviragus.]

70   *Cloten.*   Soft,° what are you
That fly me thus? Some villain° mountaineers?
I have heard of such. What slave art thou?

Guiderius.   A thing
More slavish did I ne'er than answering
A "slave" without a knock.

Cloten.   Thou art a robber,
75   A lawbreaker, a villain. Yield thee, thief.

Guiderius. To who? To thee? What art thou? Have
not I
An arm as big as thine? A heart as big?
Thy words, I grant, are bigger, for I wear not
My dagger in my mouth. Say what thou art,
Why I should yield to thee.

---

59 **elder** elder tree   60 **perishing** destructive   60 **with** from   61
great morning broad daylight   62 **runagates** runaways   69 **com-**
panies companions   70 **Let . . . him** leave him to me   70 **Soft** wait
71 **villain** low-born

Cloten.   Thou villain base,   80
  Know'st me° not by my clothes?

Guiderius.   No, nor thy tailor, rascal,
  Who is thy grandfather. He made those clothes,
  Which, as it seems, make thee.

Cloten.   Thou precious varlet,°
  My tailor made them not.

Guiderius.   Hence then, and thank
  The man that gave them thee. Thou art some fool;   85
  I am loath to beat thee.

Cloten.   Thou injurious° thief,
  Hear but my name and tremble.

Guiderius.   What's thy name?

Cloten. Cloten, thou villain.

Guiderius. Cloten, thou double villain, be thy name,
  I cannot tremble at it. Were it Toad, or Adder,
    Spider,   90
  'Twould move me sooner.

Cloten.   To thy further fear,
  Nay, to thy mere° confusion, thou shalt know
  I am son to th' Queen.

Guiderius.   I am sorry for't; not seeming°
  So worthy as thy birth.

Cloten.   Art not afeard?

Guiderius. Those that I reverence, those I fear—the
    wise;   95
  At fools I laugh, not fear them.

Cloten.   Die the death!
  When I have slain thee with my proper° hand,
  I'll follow those that even now fled hence

81 **me** i.e., my rank   83 **precious varlet** egregious knave   86 **injurious** insulting   92 **mere** utter   93 **not seeming** since you do not seem   97 **proper** own

And on the gates of Lud's Town set your heads.
100   Yield, rustic mountaineer.   *Fight and exeunt.*

Enter Belarius and Arviragus.

Belarius. No company's abroad?°

Arviragus. None in the world. You did mistake him
     sure.

Belarius. I cannot tell. Long is it since I saw him,
     But time hath nothing blurred those lines of favor°
105   Which then he wore. The snatches° in his voice,
     And burst of speaking, were as his. I am absolute°
     'Twas very Cloten.°

Arviragus.   In this place we left them.
     I wish my brother make good time° with him,
     You say he is so fell.°

Belarius.   Being scarce made up,°
110   I mean to man, he had not apprehension
     Of roaring terrors; for defect of judgment
     Is oft the cause of fear.°

          Enter Guiderius [with Cloten's head].

                         But see, thy brother.

Guiderius. This Cloten was a fool, an empty purse;
     There was no money in't. Not Hercules
115   Could have knocked out his brains, for he had none.
     Yet I not doing this, the fool had borne
     My head as I do his.

Belarius.   What hast thou done?

Guiderius. I am perfect° what: cut off one Cloten's
     head,
     Son to the Queen, after his own report;

---

101 abroad about   **104 lines of favor** contours of his face   **105 snatches** hestitations   **106 absolute** certain   **107 very Cloten** Cloten himself   **108 make good time** have good fortune   **109 fell** fierce **109 made up** grown   **111–12 for defect . . . fear** (sense unclear and frequently emended; Belarius seems to be saying that Cloten lacked the intelligence to be frightened)   **118 perfect** well aware

Who called me traitor, mountaineer, and swore　　120
With his own single hand he'ld take us in,°
Displace our heads where—thank the gods—they
　　grow,
And set them on Lud's Town.

Belarius.　　　　　　　We are all undone.

Guiderius. Why, worthy father, what have we to lose
But that° he swore to take, our lives? The law　　125
Protects not us. Then why should we be tender
To° let an arrogant piece of flesh threat us,
Play judge and executioner all himself,
For° we do fear the law? What company
Discover you abroad?

Belarius.　　　　　No single soul　　130
Can we set eye on, but in all safe reason
He must have some attendants. Though his humor°
Was nothing but mutation—ay, and that
From one bad thing to worse—not frenzy, not
Absolute madness could so far have raved　　135
To bring him here alone. Although perhaps
It may be heard at court that such as we
Cave here, hunt here, are outlaws, and in time
May make° some stronger head;° the which he
　　hearing—
As it is like him—might break out, and swear　　140
He'ld fetch us in; yet is't not probable
To come° alone, either he so undertaking,
Or they so suffering.° Then on good ground we
　　fear,
If we do fear this body hath a tail°
More perilous than the head.

Arviragus.　　　　　　Let ordinance°　　145
Come as the gods foresay° it. Howsoe'er,
My brother hath done well.

---

121 take us in overcome us　**125 that** what　**126–27 tender/To** so
considerate as to　**129 For** because　**132 humor** chief characteristic　**139 make** make up　**139 head** force　**142 To come** for him
to come　**143 suffering** allowing　**144 tail** i.e., followers　**145 ordi-
nance** whatever is ordained　**146 foresay** foretell, determine

Belarius.   I had no mind
     To hunt this day. The boy Fidele's sickness
     Did make my way long forth.°

Guiderius.   With his own sword,
150   Which he did wave against my throat, I have ta'en
     His head from him. I'll throw't into the creek
     Behind our rock, and let it to the sea
     And tell the fishes he's the Queen's son, Cloten.
     That's all I reck.°   *Exit.*

Belarius.   I fear 'twill be revenged.
155   Would, Polydore, thou hadst not done't, though valor
     Becomes thee well enough.

Arviragus.   Would I had done't,
     So° the revenge alone pursued° me. Polydore,
     I love thee brotherly, but envy much
     Thou hast robbed me of this deed. I would revenges
     That possible° strength might meet would seek us
160   through°
     And put us to our answer.

Belarius.   Well, 'tis done.
     We'll hunt no more today, nor seek for danger
     Where there's no profit. I prithee, to our rock;
     You and Fidele play the cooks. I'll stay
165   Till hasty Polydore return, and bring him
     To dinner presently.

Arviragus.   Poor sick Fidele,
     I'll willingly to him. To gain° his color
     I'ld let a parish of such Clotens blood°
     And praise myself for charity.   *Exit.*

Belarius.   O thou goddess,
170   Thou divine Nature, thou thyself thou blazon'st°
     In these two princely boys! They are as gentle
     As zephyrs blowing below the violet,

149 **way long forth** i.e., way forth seem long   154 **reck** care   157 **So**
so that   157 **pursued** would have pursued   160 **possible** our available   160 **seek us through** search thoroughly for us   167
gain restore   168 **let . . . blood** kill a parish-full of Clotens   170
blazon'st proclaimest

Not wagging his sweet head; and yet as rough,
Their royal blood enchafed,° as the rud'st wind
That by the top doth take the mountain pine   *175*
And make him stoop to th' vale. 'Tis wonder
That an invisible instinct should frame° them
To royalty° unlearned, honor untaught,
Civility° not seen from other, valor
That wildly grows° in them but yields a crop   *180*
As if it had been sowed. Yet still it's strange
What Cloten's being here to us portends,
Or what his death will bring us.

                Enter Guiderius.

Guiderius.   Where's my brother?
I have sent Cloten's clotpoll° down the stream
In embassy to his mother; his body's hostage   *185*
For his return.   *Solemn music.*

Belarius.   My ingenious° instrument!
Hark, Polydore, it sounds. But what occasion
Hath Cadwal now to give it motion? Hark!

Guiderius. Is he at home?

Belarius.   He went hence even now.

Guiderius. What does he mean? Since death of my
     dear'st mother   *190*
It did not speak before. All solemn things
Should answer° solemn accidents.° The matter?
Triumphs° for nothing and lamenting toys°
Is jollity for apes and grief for boys.
Is Cadwal mad?

*Enter Arviragus with Imogen, dead, bearing her in his
                    arms.*

Belarius.   Look, here he comes,   *195*

---

174 **enchafed** heated   177 **frame** dispose   178 **royalty** regal conduct   179 **Civility** civilized behavior   180 **wildly grows** grows
wild   184 **clotpoll** blockhead   186 **ingenious** skillfully constructed
192 **answer** correspond to   192 **accidents** events   193 **Triumphs**
public festivities   193 **lamenting toys** lamenting over trifles

And brings the dire occasion in his arms
Of what we blame him for.

Arviragus.   The bird is dead
That we have made so much on.° I had rather
Have skipped from sixteen years of age to sixty,
200 To have turned my leaping time into a crutch,
Than have seen this.

Guiderius.   O sweetest, fairest lily!
My brother wears thee not the one half so well
As when thou grew'st thyself.

Belarius.   O Melancholy,
Who ever yet could sound thy bottom, find
205 The ooze, to show what coast thy sluggish crayer°
Might eas'liest harbor in? Thou blessèd thing,
Jove knows what man thou mightst have made; but
    I,°
Thou diedst, a most rare boy, of melancholy.
How found you him?

Arviragus.   Stark,° as you see,
210 Thus smiling, as° some fly had tickled slumber,
Not as Death's dart being laughed at;° his right
    cheek
Reposing on a cushion.

Guiderius.   Where?

Arviragus.   O' th' floor;
His arms thus leagued.° I thought he slept, and put
My clouted brogues° from off my feet, whose rude-
    ness°
Answered my steps too loud.

215 *Guiderius.*   Why, he but sleeps.
If he be gone, he'll make his grave a bed;
With female fairies will his tomb be haunted,
And worms will not come to thee.

198 **on** of   205 **crayer** small trading vessel   207 **I** i.e., what I know
is   209 **Stark** stiff (as in death)   210 **as** as if   211 **as . . . at** as if
laughing at Death's arrow   213 **leagued** folded   214 **clouted
brogues** heavy, nail-studded shoes   214 **rudeness** roughness

Arviragus.   With fairest flowers,
  Whilst summer lasts and I live here, Fidele,
  I'll sweeten thy sad grave. Thou shalt not lack   220
  The flower that's like thy face, pale primrose; nor
  The azured harebell,° like thy veins; no, nor
  The leaf of eglantine,° whom not to slander,
  Outsweet'ned not thy breath. The ruddock° would
  With charitable bill—O bill sore shaming   225
  Those rich-left heirs that let their fathers lie
  Without a monument!—bring thee all this;
  Yea, and furred moss besides, when flow'rs are
    none,
  To winter-ground° thy corse—

Guiderius.   Prithee have done,
  And do not play in wench-like words with that   230
  Which is so serious. Let us bury him,
  And not protract with admiration what
  Is now due debt. To th' grave.

Arviragus.   Say, where shall's° lay him?

Guiderius. By good Euriphile, our mother.

Arviragus.   Be't so.
  And let us, Polydore, though now our voices   235
  Have got the mannish crack, sing him to th' ground,
  As once to our mother; use like note and words,
  Save that Euriphile must be Fidele.

Guiderius. Cadwal,
  I cannot sing. I'll weep, and word° it with thee,   240
  For notes of sorrow out of tune are worse
  Than priests and fanes° that lie.

Arviragus.   We'll speak it then.

Belarius. Great griefs, I see, med'cine° the less, for
    Cloten
  Is quite forgot. He was a queen's son, boys,

---

222 **azured harebell** sky-blue wild hyacinth   223 **eglantine** sweet-
briar   224 **ruddock** robin   229 **winter-ground** protect in winter (?)
233 **shall's** shall us (we)   240 **word** speak   242 **fanes** temples
243 **med'cine** cure

245 And though he came our enemy, remember
He was paid° for that. Though mean and mighty,
      rotting
Together, have one dust, yet reverence,
That angel of the world, doth make distinction
Of place 'tween high and low. Our foe was princely,
250 And though you took his life as being° our foe,
Yet bury him as° a prince.

Guiderius.   Pray you fetch him hither.
Thersites'° body is as good as Ajax'°
When neither are alive.

Arviragus.   If you'll go fetch him,
We'll say our song the whilst. Brother, begin.

                              [*Exit Belarius.*]

Guiderius. Nay, Cadwal, we must lay his head to th'
255   east;°
My father hath a reason for't.

Arviragus.   'Tis true.

Guiderius. Come on then and remove him.

Arviragus.   So. Begin.

                    Song.

Guiderius.   Fear no more the heat o' th' sun
                  Nor the furious winter's rages;
260   Thou thy worldly task hast done,
                  Home art gone and ta'en thy wages.
              Golden lads and girls all must,
              As° chimney-sweepers, come to dust.

Arviragus.   Fear no more the frown o' th' great;
265   Thou are past the tyrant's stroke.
              Care no more to clothe and eat;
                  To thee the reed is as the oak.

---

246 **paid** punished   250 **as being** because he was   251 **as as being,**
because he was   252 **Thersites** (the vituperative Greek warrior of
the Trojan War)   252 **Ajax** (one of the Greek heroes at Troy)
255 **to th' east** (the reverse of Christian practice)   263 **As** like

               The scepter, learning, physic,° must
               All follow this and come to dust.

Guiderius.   Fear no more the lightning flash,   270

Arviragus.   Nor th' all-dreaded thunder-stone;

Guiderius.   Fear not slander, censure rash;

Arviragus.   Thou hast finished joy and moan.

Both.   All lovers young, all lovers must
               Consign to° thee and come to dust.   275

Guiderius.   No exorciser° harm thee,

Arviragus.   Nor no witchcraft charm thee.

Guiderius.   Ghost unlaid forbear thee;°

Arviragus.   Nothing ill come near thee.

Both.   Quiet consummation° have,   280
               And renownèd be thy grave.

          Enter Belarius with the body of Cloten.

Guiderius. We have done our obsequies. Come, lay
     him down.

Belarius. Here's a few flowers, but 'bout midnight,
     more.
   The herbs that have on them cold dew o' th' night
   Are strewings fitt'st for graves. Upon their faces.° 285
   You were as flow'rs, now withered; even so
   These herblets shall° which we upon you strew.
   Come on, away; apart upon our knees.
   The ground that gave them first has them again.
   Their pleasures here are past, so is their pain.   290
          Exeunt [Belarius, Guiderius, and Arviragus].

Imogen. (*Awakes*) Yes, sir, to Milford Haven. Which
     is the way?

268 **scepter, learning, physic** i.e., kings, scholars, physicians 275
Consign to co-sign with (i.e., meet the same fate) 276 **exorciser**
spirit-raiser 278 **forbear thee** let thee alone 280 **consummation**
fulfillment, end 285 **faces** fronts 287 **shall** shall be

I thank you. By yond bush? Pray, how far thither?
'Ods pittikins,° can it be six mile yet?
I have gone° all night. Faith, I'll lie down and sleep.
                                        [*Seeing Cloten*]
295   But, soft, no bedfellow! O gods and goddesses!
These flow'rs are like the pleasures of the world;
This bloody man, the care on't. I hope I dream,
For so° I thought I was a cave-keeper
And cook to honest creatures. But 'tis not so;
300   'Twas but a bolt° of nothing, shot at nothing,
Which the brain makes of fumes.° Our very eyes
Are sometimes like our judgments, blind. Good
         faith,
I tremble still with fear, but if there be
Yet left in heaven as small a drop of pity
305   As a wren's eye, feared gods, a part° of it!
The dream's here still. Even when I wake it is
Without me, as within me; not imagined, felt.
A headless man? The garments of Posthumus?
I know the shape of's leg; this is his hand,
310   His foot Mercurial,° his Martial° thigh,
The brawns° of Hercules; but his Jovial° face—
Murder in heaven? How? 'Tis gone. Pisanio,
All curses madded° Hecuba° gave the Greeks,
And mine to boot, be darted on thee! Thou,
315   Conspired° with that irregulous° devil Cloten,
Hath here cut off my lord. To write and read
Be henceforth treacherous! Damned Pisanio
Hath with his forgèd letters—damned Pisanio—
From this most bravest vessel of the world
320   Struck the maintop. O Posthumus, alas,
Where is thy head? Where's that? Ay me, where's
         that?

293 **'Ods pittikins** God's little pity, God have mercy   294 **gone**
walked   298 **so** i.e., while dreaming   300 **bolt** arrow   301 **fumes**
bodily vapors thought to rise to the brain and cause dreams   305 **a
part** i.e., grant me a part   310 **Mercurial** quick (like Mercury's)
310 **Martial** powerful (like Mars's)   311 **brawns** muscles   311
Jovial majestic (like Jove's)   313 **madded** maddened   313 **Hecuba**
(wife of Priam, king of Troy)   315 **Conspired** having conspired
315 **irregulous** lawless

Pisanio might have killed thee at the heart
And left this head on. How should this be? Pisanio?
'Tis he and Cloten. Malice and lucre° in them
Have laid this woe here. O, 'tis pregnant,° pregnant!   325
The drug he gave me, which he said was precious
And cordial° to me, have I not found it
Murd'rous to th' senses? That confirms it home.°
This is Pisanio's deed, and Cloten.° O,
Give color to my pale cheek with thy blood,   330
That we the horrider may seem to those
Which° chance to find us. O my lord, my lord!
                            [*Falling on the body.*]

Enter Lucius and Captains; a Soothsayer to them.°

Captain. The legions garrisoned in Gallia
    After° your will have crossed the sea, attending°
    You here at Milford Haven with your ships.   335
    They are in readiness.

Lucius.   But what from Rome?

Captain. The Senate hath stirred up the confiners°
    And gentlemen of Italy, most willing spirits
    That promise noble service, and they come
    Under the conduct of bold Iachimo,   340
    Siena's° brother.

Lucius.   When expect you them?

Captain. With the next benefit o' th' wind.

Lucius.   This forwardness°
    Makes our hopes fair. Command our present num-
        bers
    Be mustered; bid the captains look to't.—Now, sir,

---

324 **lucre** greed   325 **pregnant** evident   327 **cordial** restorative
328 **home** thoroughly   329 **Cloten** i.e., Cloten's   332 **Which** who
332s.d. **to them** (presumably the Soothsayer enters, a moment later,
at another door)   334 **After** according to   334 **attending** waiting
for   337 **confiners** inhabitants   341 **Siena's** i.e., the Duke of Siena's
342 **forwardness** promptness

What have you dreamed of late of this war's pur-
345   pose?

Soothsayer. Last night the very gods showed me a
    vision—
I fast° and prayed for their intelligence°—thus:
I saw Jove's bird, the Roman eagle, winged
From the spongy° south to this part of the west,
350   There vanished in the sunbeams; which portends,
Unless my sins abuse° my divination,
Success to th' Roman host.

Lucius.   Dream often so,
And never false.° Soft, ho, what trunk is here?
Without his top? The ruin speaks that sometime°
355   It was a worthy building. How, a page?
Or° dead or sleeping on him? But dead rather,
For nature doth abhor° to make his bed
With the defunct or sleep upon the dead.
Let's see the boy's face.

Captain.   He's alive, my lord.

Lucius. He'll, then, instruct us of this body. Young
360   one,
Inform us of thy fortunes, for it seems
They crave to be demanded. Who is this
Thou mak'st thy bloody pillow? Or who was he
That, otherwise than noble nature did,°
365   Hath altered that good picture? What's thy interest
In this sad wrack?° How came't? Who is't? What
    art thou?

Imogen. I am nothing, or if not,
Nothing to be were better. This was my master,
A very valiant Briton and a good,
370   That here by mountaineers lies slain. Alas,
There is no more such masters. I may wander

347 fast fasted   **347 intelligence** communication   **349 spongy** damp
351 abuse render inaccurate   **353 false** falsely   **354 sometime** once
356 Or either   **357 nature doth abhor** man naturally abhors (Heilman)   **364 did** i.e., painted (J. C. Maxwell)   **366 wrack** ruin of
a man

From east to occident, cry out for service,
Try many, all good, serve truly, never
Find such another master.

Lucius.   'Lack, good youth,
Thou mov'st no less with thy complaining than   375
Thy master in bleeding. Say his name, good friend.

Imogen. Richard du Champ. [*Aside*] If I do lie and do
No harm by it, though the gods hear, I hope
They'll pardon it.—Say you, sir?

Lucius.   Thy name?

Imogen.   Fidele, sir.

Lucius. Thou dost approve° thyself the very same;   380
Thy name well fits thy faith, thy faith thy name.
Wilt take thy chance with me? I will not say
Thou shalt be so well mastered, but be sure
No less beloved. The Roman emperor's letters
Sent by a consul to me should not sooner   385
Than thine own worth prefer° thee. Go with me.

Imogen. I'll follow, sir. But first, and't please the gods,
I'll hide my master from the flies, as deep
As these poor pickaxes° can dig; and when
With wild wood-leaves and weeds I ha' strewed his
     grave   390
And on it said a century of° prayers,
Such as I can,° twice o'er, I'll weep and sigh,
And leaving so his service, follow you,
So° please you entertain° me.

Lucius.   Ay, good youth,
And rather father thee than master thee.   395
My friends,
The boy hath taught us manly duties. Let us
Find out the prettiest daisied plot we can
And make him with our pikes and partisans°

---

380 **approve** prove   386 **prefer** recommend   389 **pickaxes** i.e., fingers   391 **century of** hundred   392 **can** know   394 **So** if it
394 **entertain** employ   399 **partisans** halberds

400 A grave. Come, arm° him. Boy, he's preferred°
     By thee to us, and he shall be interred
     As soldiers can. Be cheerful; wipe thine eyes.
     Some falls are means the happier to arise.   *Exeunt.*

Scene III. [*Britain*.]

Enter Cymbeline, Lords, and Pisanio.

Cymbeline. Again, and bring me word how 'tis with
           her.   [*Exit a Lord.*]
     A fever with° the absence of her son,
     A madness, of which her life's in danger. Heavens,
     How deeply you at once do touch° me! Imogen,
5   The great part of my comfort, gone; my queen
     Upon a desperate bed,° and in a time
     When fearful wars point at me; her son gone,
     So needful for this present. It strikes me past
     The hope of comfort.—But for thee, fellow,
10   Who needs must know of her departure and
     Dost seem so ignorant, we'll enforce it from thee
     By a sharp torture.

Pisanio.   Sir, my life is yours,
     I humbly set it at your will; but for my mistress,
     I nothing° know where she remains, why gone,
     Nor when she purposes return. Beseech your High-
15   ness,
     Hold me your loyal servant.

Lord.   Good my liege,
     The day that she was missing he was here.
     I dare be bound he's true and shall perform
     All parts of his subjection° loyally. For Cloten,

---

400 **arm** carry   400 **preferred** recommended   IV.iii.2 **with** resulting
from   4 **touch** wound   6 **Upon . . . bed** i.e., desperately ill   14
nothing not at all   19 **subjection** duty as a subject

There wants no diligence in seeking him,   20
And will° no doubt be found.

Cymbeline.   The time is troublesome.°
[*To Pisanio*] We'll slip you° for a season, but our
  jealousy°
Does yet depend.°

Lord.   So please your Majesty,
The Roman legions, all from Gallia drawn,
Are landed on your coast, with a supply   25
Of Roman gentlemen by the Senate sent.

Cymbeline. Now for° the counsel of my son and
  queen!
I am amazed with matter.°

Lord.   Good my liege,
Your preparation° can affront no less°
Than what you hear of. Come more,° for more
  you're ready.   30
The want is but° to put those pow'rs in motion
That long to move.

Cymbeline.   I thank you. Let's withdraw,
And meet the time as it seeks us. We fear not
What can from Italy annoy° us, but
We grieve at chances here. Away.   35
                    Exeunt [*all but Pisanio*].

Pisanio. I heard no letter° from my master since
I wrote him Imogen was slain. 'Tis strange.
Nor hear I from my mistress, who did promise
To yield me often tidings. Neither know I
What is betid° to Cloten, but remain   40
Perplexed in all. The heavens still must work.
Wherein I am false I am honest; not true, to be true.

---

21 **will** he will   21 **troublesome** full of troubles   22 **slip you** let
you go free   22 **jealousy** suspicion   23 **depend** remain   27 **Now
for** would I had   28 **amazed with matter** confounded by business
29 **preparation** armed forces   29 **affront no less** i.e., face larger
forces   30 **Come more** if more come   31 **The want is but** the only
thing needed is   34 **annoy** harm   36 **no letter** i.e., not at all   40 **is
betid** has happened

These present wars shall find I love my country,
Even to the note° o' th' King, or I'll fall in them.
45 All other doubts, by time let them be cleared;
Fortune brings in some boats that are not steered.

Exit.

Scene IV. [*Wales.*]

Enter Belarius, Guiderius, and Arviragus.

Guiderius. The noise is round about us.

Belarius.   Let us from it.

Arviragus. What pleasure, sir, find we in life, to lock°
it
From action and adventure?

Guiderius.   Nay, what hope
Have we in hiding us? This way° the Romans
5 Must or° for Britons slay us or receive us
For barbarous and unnatural revolts°
During their use,° and slay us after.

Belarius.   Sons,
We'll higher to the mountains, there secure us.
To the King's party there's no going. Newness
Of Cloten's death—we being not known, not mus-
10   tered
Among the bands—may drive us to a render°
Where we have lived, and so extort from's that
Which we have done, whose answer° would be
death
Drawn on° with torture.

Guiderius.   This is, sir, a doubt

44 **note** knowledge   IV.iv.2 **lock** preclude   4 **This way** i.e., if we
do so   5 **Must or** must either   6 **revolts** rebels   7 **During their use**
while they have use for us   11 **render** account   13 **answer** requital
14 **Drawn on** brought about

In such a time nothing becoming you   15
Nor satisfying us.

Arviragus.   It is not likely
That when they hear the Roman horses neigh,
Behold their quartered fires,° have both their eyes
And ears so cloyed importantly° as now,
That they will waste their time upon our note,°   20
To know from whence we are.

Belarius.   O, I am known
Of many in the army. Many years,
Though Cloten then° but young, you see, not wore
      him
From my remembrance. And besides, the King
Hath not deserved my service nor your loves,   25
Who find in my exile the want of breeding,°
The certainty° of this hard life; aye hopeless
To have the courtesy your cradle promised,
But to be still hot summer's tanlings° and
The shrinking slaves of winter.

Guiderius.   Than be so   30
Better to cease to be. Pray, sir, to th' army.
I and my brother are not known; yourself
So out of thought, and thereto so o'ergrown,°
Cannot be questioned.

Arviragus.   By this sun that shines,
I'll thither. What thing is't that I never   35
Did see man die, scarce ever looked on blood
But that of coward hares, hot° goats, and venison!
Never bestrid a horse, save one that had
A rider like myself, who ne'er wore rowel°
Nor iron on his heel! I am ashamed   40
To look upon the holy sun, to have

18 **quartered fires** camp fires   19 **cloyed importantly** burdened with
important matters   20 **upon our note** on noticing us   23 **then** i.e.,
was then   26 **Who . . . breeding** you who through sharing my exile
experience a lack of education   27 **certainty** inescapability   29
tanlings tanned persons   33 **o'ergrown** replaced in their thoughts
37 **hot** lecherous   39 **rowel** the wheel on a spur

The benefit of his blest beams, remaining
So long a poor unknown.

Guiderius.   By heavens, I'll go.
If you will bless me, sir, and give me leave,
45   I'll take the better care, but if you will not,
The hazard therefore due° fall on me by
The hands of Romans!

Arviragus.   So say I. Amen.

Belarius. No reason I, since of your lives you set
So slight a valuation, should reserve
My cracked° one to more care. Have with you,
50   boys!
If in your country° wars you chance to die,
That is my bed too, lads, and there I'll lie.
Lead, lead. [*Aside*] The time seems long; their
blood thinks scorn
Till it fly out and show them princes born.   *Exeunt.*

---

46 **hazard therefore due** risk attendant upon being unblessed   50
cracked i.e., since old   51 **country** country's

ACT V

Scene I. [*Britain.*]

Enter Posthumus alone [with a bloody handkerchief].

Posthumus. Yea, bloody cloth, I'll keep thee, for I
    wished
  Thou shouldst be colored thus. You married ones,°
  If each of you should take this course, how many
  Must murder wives much better than themselves
  For wrying° but a little! O Pisanio,   5
  Every good servant does not all commands;
  No bond but° to do just ones. Gods, if you
  Should have ta'en vengeance on my faults, I never
  Had lived to put on this;° so had you saved
  The noble Imogen to repent, and struck   10
  Me, wretch more worth your vengeance. But alack,
  You snatch some hence for little faults; that's love,
  To have them fall° no more; you some permit
  To second° ills with ills, each elder° worse,
  And make them° dread it,° to the doers' thrift.°   15
  But Imogen is your own. Do your best wills,
  And make me blest to obey. I am brought hither

V.i.2 **You married ones** (he addresses the audience)   5 **wrying** deviating, going wrong   7 **No bond but** i.e., he is bound only   9 **put on this** instigate this crime   13 **fall** i.e., from virtue   14 **second** follow up   14 **elder** i.e., later   15 **them** the doers   15 **dread it** repent the evil course   15 **thrift** profit

Among th' Italian gentry, and to fight
Against my lady's kingdom. 'Tis enough
20   That, Britain, I have killed thy mistress; peace,
I'll give no wound to thee. Therefore, good heavens,
Hear patiently my purpose. I'll disrobe me
Of these Italian weeds and suit myself
As does a Briton peasant. So I'll fight
25   Against the part° I come with; so I'll die
For thee, O Imogen, even for whom my life
Is every breath a death; and thus, unknown,
Pitied nor hated, to the face of peril
Myself I'll dedicate. Let me make men know
30   More valor in me than my habits° show.
Gods, put the strength o' th' Leonati in me.
To shame the guise° o' th' world, I will begin
The fashion, less without and more within.   *Exit.*

Scene II. [*Britain.*]

*Enter Lucius, Iachimo, and the Roman Army at one
  door, and the Briton Army at another, Leonatus
  Posthumus following like a poor soldier. They
  march over and go out.° Then enter again in skir-
  mish Iachimo and Posthumus. He vanquisheth and
  disarmeth Iachimo and then leaves him.*

Iachimo. The heaviness and guilt within my bosom
Takes off° my manhood. I have belied° a lady,
The princess of this country, and the air on't°
Revengingly enfeebles me; or° could this carl,°
5   A very drudge of nature's, have subdued me
In my profession? Knighthoods and honors, borne
As I wear mine, are titles but of scorn.

25 **part** side   30 **habits** clothes   32 **guise** custom   V.ii.s.d. **They
march . . . go out** (each group marches about the stage and exits
by the other door)   2 **Takes off** destroys   2 **belied** slandered   3
on't of it   4 **or** otherwise   4 **carl** churl

    If that thy gentry, Britain, go before°
    This lout as he exceeds our lords, the odds
    Is that we scarce are men and you are gods.   *Exit.* **10**

*The battle continues. The Britons fly; Cymbeline is
taken. Then enter to his rescue Belarius, Guiderius,
and Arviragus.*

Belarius. Stand, stand! We have th' advantage of the
    ground.
    The lane is guarded. Nothing routs us but
    The villainy of our fears.

Guiderius, Arviragus.   Stand, stand, and fight!

*Enter Posthumus and seconds the Britons. They rescue
Cymbeline and exeunt. Then enter Lucius, Iachimo,
and Imogen.*

Lucius. Away, boy, from the troops, and save thyself,
    For friends kill friends, and the disorder's such   **15**
    As War were hoodwinked.°

Iachimo.   'Tis their fresh supplies.

Lucius. It is a day turned strangely; or betimes°
    Let's reinforce or fly.   *Exeunt.*

Scene III. [*Britain.*]

Enter Posthumus and a Briton Lord.

Lord. Cam'st thou from where they made the stand?

Posthumus.   I did;
    Though you, it seems, come from the fliers.

Lord.   I did.

Posthumus. No blame be to you, sir, for all was lost,

8 go before excell 16 hoodwinked blindfolded 17 or betimes
either quickly

But that the heavens fought. The King himself
5   Of his wings destitute, the army broken,
And but the backs of Britons seen, all flying
Through a strait° lane; the enemy full-hearted,°
Lolling the tongue with slaught'ring, having work
More plentiful than tools to do't, struck down
10 Some mortally, some slightly touched,° some falling
Merely through fear, that the strait pass was dammed
With dead men hurt behind,° and cowards living
To die with lengthened shame.

Lord.   Where was this lane?

Posthumus. Close by the battle, ditched, and walled
with turf;
15 Which gave advantage to an ancient soldier,
An honest one I warrant, who deserved
So long a breeding as his white beard came to,°
In doing this for's country. Athwart the lane
He with two striplings—lads more like to run
20 The country base° than to commit such slaughter;
With faces fit for masks,° or rather fairer
Than those for preservation cased or shame°—
Made good the passage, cried to those that fled,
"Our Britain's harts die flying, not our men.
25 To darkness fleet° souls that fly backwards. Stand,
Or we are Romans° and will give you that
Like beasts which you shun beastly,° and may save
But to look back in frown.° Stand, stand!" These
three,
Three thousand confident, in act as many—
30 For three performers are the file° when all

V.iii.7 **strait** narrow   7 **full-hearted** full of courage   10 **touched**
wounded   12 **behind** i.e., while running away   17 **So long . . .
came to** i.e., to live (renowned) as long after this day as he had
lived before in growing his beard   19–20 **run/The country base**
play the game of prisoner's base   21 **masks** for protection from
sunburn (so used by ladies)   22 **for preservation . . . shame** covered for protection or modesty   25 **fleet** are wafted   26 **are Romans**
i.e., will behave like Romans   27 **beastly** i.e., like cowards   27–28
save/But to look back in frown i.e., prevent only by looking back
defiantly   30 **file** whole force

The rest do nothing—with this word "Stand, stand,"
Accommodated by the place, more charming°
With their own nobleness, which could have turned
A distaff to a lance, gilded° pale looks,
Part° shame, part spirit renewed; that some, turned
     coward   35
But by example°—O, a sin in war,
Damned in the first beginners!—gan to look
The way that they° did and to grin° like lions
Upon the pikes o' th' hunters. Then began
A stop i' th' chaser,° a retire; anon°   40
A rout, confusion thick. Forthwith they fly
Chickens, the way which they stooped° eagles;
     slaves,
The strides they victors made; and now our cow-
     ards,
Like fragments° in hard voyages, became
The life o' th' need.° Having found the back door
     open   45
Of the unguarded hearts, heavens, how they wound!
Some slain before,° some dying, some° their friends
O'erborne i' th' former wave, ten chased by one
Are now each one the slaughterman of twenty.
Those that would die or ere° resist are grown   50
The mortal bugs° o' th' field.°

Lord.   This was strange chance:
A narrow lane, an old man, and two boys.

Posthumus. Nay, do not wonder at it. You are made
Rather to wonder at the things you hear
Than to work any.° Will you rhyme upon't   55
And vent it° for a mock'ry? Here is one:

---

32 **more charming** i.e., winning over others   34 **gilded** brought color
to   35 **Part** some   36 **by example** by imitating others   38 **they** the
three men   38 **grin** bare the teeth   40 **stop . . . chaser** sudden
check (as of a horse) on the part of the pursuer   40 **anon** soon
42 **stooped** swooped (hawking term)   44 **fragments** scraps (of food)
45 **life o' th' need** a source of life in time of need   47 **slain before**
i.e., who had feigned death   47 **some** some of   50 **or ere** before
51 **mortal bugs** deadly terrors   51 **field** battle   55 **work any** perform any such deeds   56 **vent it** make it known

"Two boys, an old man twice a boy, a lane,
  Preserved the Britons, was the Romans' bane."

Lord. Nay, be not angry, sir.

Posthumus.   'Lack, to what end?
60   Who dares not stand° his foe, I'll be his friend;
For if he'll do as he is made° to do,
I know he'll quickly fly my friendship too.
You have put° me into rhyme.

Lord.   Farewell. You're angry. *Exit.*

Posthumus. Still going?° This is a lord! O noble mis-
    ery,°
65   To be i' th' field, and ask "What news?" of me!
Today how many would have given their honors
To have saved their carcasses, took heel to do't,
And yet died too! I, in mine own woe charmed,°
Could not find Death where I did hear him groan
Nor feel him where he struck. Being an ugly mon-
70   ster,
'Tis strange he hides him in fresh cups, soft beds,
Sweet words, or hath moe ministers than we
That draw his knives i' th' war. Well, I will find
    him,
For being now a favorer to° the Briton,
75   No more a Briton.° I have resumed again
The part I came in. Fight I will no more,
But yield me to the veriest hind° that shall
Once touch my shoulder.° Great the slaughter is
Here made by th' Roman; great the answer° be
80   Britons must take. For me, my ransom's death.
On either side I come to spend my breath,°
Which neither here I'll keep nor bear again,
But end it by some means for Imogen.

---

60 stand withstand   **61 made** naturally inclined   **63 put** forced
64 going running away   **64 noble misery** wretchedness of false
nobility   **68 charmed** preserved as by a charm   **74 being . . . favorer to** since he now favors   **75 No more a Briton** i.e., I will
seek Death among the Romans   **77 hind** peasant   **78 touch my
shoulder** as in a formal arrest   **79 answer** retaliation   **81 spend my
breath** give up my life

Enter two [Briton] Captains and Soldiers.

First Captain. Great Jupiter be praised, Lucius is
    taken.
  'Tis thought the old man and his sons were angels.   *85*

Second Captain. There was a fourth man, in a silly
    habit,°
  That gave th' affront° with them.

First Captain.   So 'tis reported,
  But none of 'em can be found. Stand, who's there?

Posthumus. A Roman,
  Who had not now been drooping here if seconds°   *90*
  Had answered him.°

Second Captain.   Lay hands on him. A dog,
  A leg of Rome shall not return to tell
  What crows have pecked them here. He brags his
    service
  As if he were of note.° Bring him to th' King.

*Enter Cymbeline, Belarius, Guiderius, Arviragus,
Pisanio, and Roman Captives [guarded]. The Captains present Posthumus to Cymbeline, who delivers
him over to a Jailer.*   [*Exeunt.*]

86 **a silly habit** lowly clothing   87 **affront** attack   90 **seconds** supporters   91 **answered him** acted as he did   94 **note** reputation

Scene IV. [*Britain.*]

Enter° Posthumus and [two] Jailers.

First Jailer. You shall not now be stol'n; you have
  locks upon you.
 So graze as you find pasture.

Second Jailer.   Ay, or a stomach.°
            [*Exeunt Jailers.*]

Posthumus. Most welcome, bondage, for thou art a
  way,
 I think, to liberty. Yet am I better
5 Than one that's sick o' th' gout, since he had rather
 Groan so in perpetuity than be cured
 By th' sure physician, Death, who is the key
 T' unbar these locks. My conscience, thou art fet-
  tered
 More than my shanks and wrists. You good gods,
  give me
10 The penitent instrument to pick that bolt,°
 Then free° for ever. Is't enough I am sorry?
 So children temporal fathers do appease;
 Gods are more full of mercy. Must I repent,
 I cannot do it better than in gyves,°
15 Desired more than constrained.° To satisfy,°
 If of my freedom 'tis the main part,° take
 No stricter render° of me than my all.°

V.iv.s.d. **Enter** (the action may be continuous from V.iii, Posthumus
and the Jailers remaining on stage after the exit of Cymbeline at
the end of that scene; in any case at the beginning of V.iv the locale
of the action changes from open country to a prison)   2 **stomach**
appetite (for grazing)   10 **penitent . . . bolt** tool of repentance
which will unfetter my conscience   11 **free** i.e., in death   14 **gyves**
fetters   15 **constrained** forced upon me   15 **satisfy** make atonement   16 **If . . . main part** i.e., if atonement is essential to my
freedom of conscience   17 **stricter render** sterner repayment
17 **all** i.e., life

I know you are more clement than vile men,
Who of their broken debtors take a third,
A sixth, a tenth, letting them thrive again
On their abatement.° That's not my desire.   20
For Imogen's dear life take mine; and though
'Tis not so dear,° yet 'tis a life; you coined it.
'Tween man and man they weigh not every stamp;°
Though light, take pieces for the figure's° sake;   25
You rather mine, being yours.° And so, great
    pow'rs,
If you will take this audit,° take this life
And cancel these cold bonds.° O Imogen,
I'll speak to thee in silence.   [*Sleeps.*]

Solemn music. Enter, as in an apparition, Sicilius
Leonatus, father to Posthumus, an old man attired
like a warrior; leading in his hand an ancient
Matron, his wife and mother to Posthumus with
Music° before them. Then, after other Music, fol-
lows the two young Leonati, brothers to Posthumus,
with wounds as they died in the wars. They circle
Posthumus round as he lies sleeping.

Sicilius. No more, thou Thunder-master,° show thy
    spite on mortal flies.   30
With Mars fall out, with Juno chide, that thy
    adulteries
        Rates° and revenges.
Hath my poor boy done aught but well, whose face
    I never saw?
I died whilst in the womb he stayed attending°
    Nature's law;
Whose father then, as men report thou orphans'
    father art,   35

21 **abatement** reduced amount   23 **dear** valuable   24 **stamp** coin
25 **figure** the ruler's image stamped on the "piece" (coin)   26 **You**
. . . **being yours** i.e, you should take my life the sooner since
(though light coin) it is at least stamped in your image   27 **take**
this audit accept this account   28 **cancel . . . bonds** i.e., remove
(through letting me die) these iron shackles (quibble on "void
these worthless contracts")   29s.d. **Music** musicians   30 **Thunder-**
master Jupiter   32 **Rates** scolds   34 **Attending** awaiting

Thou shouldst have been, and shielded him from
this earth-vexing smart.°

Mother. Lucina° lent not me her aid, but took me in
my throes,
That from me was Posthumus ripped, came crying
'mongst his foes,
A thing of pity.

Sicilius. Great Nature like his ancestry moulded the
40   stuff° so fair
That he deserved the praise o' th' world, as great
Sicilius' heir.

First Brother. When once he was mature for man,°
in Britain where was he
That could stand up his parallel, or fruitful° object
be
In eye of Imogen, that best could deem his dignity?°

Mother. With marriage wherefore was he mocked, to
45   be exiled and thrown
From Leonati seat and cast from her his dearest
one,
Sweet Imogen?

Sicilius. Why did you° suffer Iachimo, slight° thing of
Italy,
To taint his nobler heart and brain with needless
jealousy,
And to become the geck° and scorn o' th' other's
50   villainy?

Second Brother. For this from stiller seats° we come,
our parents and us twain,
That striking in our country's cause fell bravely
and were slain,

---

36 **earth-vexing smart** suffering which plagues the life of man
37 **Lucina** Juno Lucina (goddess of childbirth)   40 **stuff** substance
42 **mature for man** fully matured   43 **fruitful** ripe, mature   44
deem his dignity judge his worth   48 **you** Jupiter   48 **slight** worthless   50 **geck** dupe   51 **stiller seats** quieter abodes (in the Elysian
Fields)

Our fealty and Tenantius'° right with honor to
   maintain.

First Brother. Like hardiment° Posthumus hath to
   Cymbeline performed.
Then, Jupiter, thou King of gods, why hast thou
   thus adjourned°   55
The graces for his merits due, being all to dolors
   turned?

Sicilius. Thy crystal window ope; look out. No longer
   exercise
Upon a valiant race thy harsh and potent injuries.

Mother. Since, Jupiter, our son is good, take off his
   miseries.

Sicilius. Peep through thy marble mansion. Help, or
   we poor ghosts will cry   60
To th' shining synod of the rest° against thy deity.

Brothers. Help, Jupiter, or we appeal and from thy
   justice fly.

*Jupiter descends° in thunder and lightning, sitting
upon an eagle. He throws a thunderbolt. The Ghosts
fall on their knees.*

Jupiter. No more, you petty spirits of region low,°
   Offend our hearing. Hush! How dare you ghosts
Accuse the Thunderer, whose bolt, you know,   65
   Sky-planted,° batters all rebelling coasts?
Poor shadows of Elysium, hence, and rest
   Upon your never-withering banks of flow'rs.
Be not with mortal accidents° opprest.
   No care of yours it is; you know 'tis ours.   70
Whom best I love I cross;° to make my gift,
   The more delayed, delighted. Be content.
Your low-laid son our godhead will uplift;

53 Tenantius Sicilius   **54 hardiment** bold exploits   **55 adjourned**
deferred   **61 the rest** the other gods   **62 s.d. descends** (Jupiter is
lowered by suspension-gear from stage cover to stage)   **63 region
low** Hades   **66 Sky-planted** based in the sky   **69 accidents** occur-
rences   **71 cross** thwart

His comforts thrive, his trials well are spent.°
75   Our Jovial star° reigned at his birth, and in
       Our temple was he married. Rise, and fade.
He shall be lord of Lady Imogen,
       And happier much by his affliction made.
This tablet lay upon his breast, wherein
80   Our pleasure his full fortune doth confine.°
And so, away; no farther with your din
       Express impatience, lest you stir up mine.
       Mount, eagle, to my palace crystalline.   *Ascends.*

Sicilius. He came in thunder; his celestial breath
85   Was sulphurous to smell; the holy eagle
       Stooped, as to foot us.° His ascension is
       More sweet° than our blest fields;° his royal bird
       Prunes° the immortal wing and cloys° his beak,
       As when his god is pleased.

All.   Thanks, Jupiter.

90   *Sicilius.* The marble pavement closes;° he is entered
       His radiant roof. Away, and, to be blest,
       Let us with care perform his great behest.
                                   [*The Ghosts*] *vanish.*°

Posthumus. [*Waking*] Sleep, thou hast been a grandsire
       and begot
       A father to me, and thou hast created
95   A mother and two brothers; but, O scorn,°
       Gone! They went hence so soon as they were born.
       Am so I am awake. Poor wretches that depend
       On greatness' favor, dream as I have done,
       Wake, and find nothing. But, alas, I swerve.°
100 Many dream not to find, neither deserve,
       And yet are steeped in favors. So am I,
       That have this golden chance and know not why.

74 spent ended   75 Jovial star the planet Jupiter   80 confine i.e.,
state precisely   86 Stooped . . . us swooped (hawking term) as if
to seize us in his talons   87 More sweet (in contrast to his angry,
sulphurous descent)   87 our blest fields the Elysian Fields   88
Prunes preens   88 cloys claws   90 closes (apparently in allusion
to the trap door in the underside of the stage cover through which
Jupiter has ascended)   92s.d. vanish i.e., exit rapidly   95 scorn
mockery   99 swerve err

What fairies haunt this ground? A book? O rare
    one,
Be not, as is our fangled° world, a garment
Nobler than that it covers. Let thy effects   *105*
So follow to° be most unlike our courtiers,
As good as promise.   *Reads.*
    "Whenas° a lion's whelp shall, to himself un-
known, without seeking find, and be embraced by a
piece of tender air; and when from a stately cedar   *110*
shall be lopped branches which, being dead many
years, shall after revive, be jointed to the old stock,
and freshly grow; then shall Posthumus end his
miseries, Britain be fortunate and flourish in peace
and plenty."   *115*
'Tis still a dream, or else such stuff as madmen
Tongue,° and brain° not; either, both, or nothing;
Or senseless° speaking, or a speaking such
As sense° cannot untie. Be what it is,
The action of my life is like it,° which   *120*
I'll keep, if but for sympathy.°

            Enter Jailer.

Jailer. Come, sir, are you ready for death?

Posthumus. Over-roasted rather; ready long ago.

Jailer. Hanging° is the word, sir. If you be ready for
    that, you are well cooked.   *125*

Posthumus. So, if I prove a good repast to the specta-
    tors, the dish pays the shot.°

Jailer. A heavy reckoning for you, sir. But the comfort
    is, you shall be called to no more payments, fear no
    more tavern bills, which are as often the sadness of   *130*
    parting as the procuring of mirth. You come in faint

---

104 **fangled** addicted to finery 106 **to** as to 108 **Whenas** when
117 **Tongue** speak 117 **brain** understand 118 **Or senseless** either
irrational 119 **sense** the power of reason 120 **like it** i.e., without
meaning or incapable of understanding 121 **sympathy** the resemblance 124 **Hanging** (the Jailer, picking up the metaphor in "Over-
roasted," quibbles on "hanging of meat") 127 **the dish . . . shot**
i.e., the excellence of the food justifies its cost

for want of meat, depart reeling with too much
drink; sorry that you have paid too much, and sorry
that you are paid too much;° purse and brain both
135　empty; the brain the heavier for being too light, the
purse too light, being drawn° of heaviness. O, of
this contradiction you shall now be quit. O, the
charity of a penny cord! It sums up thousands in a
trice. You have no true debitor and creditor° but it;
140　of what's past, is, and to come, the discharge.° Your
neck, sir, is pen, book, and counters;° so the acquit-
tance° follows.

Posthumus. I am merrier to die than thou art to live.

Jailer. Indeed, sir, he that sleeps feels not the tooth-
145　ache; but a man that were° to sleep your sleep, and
a hangman to help him to bed, I think he would
change places with his officer;° for, look you, sir,
you know not which way you shall go.

Posthumus. Yes indeed do I, fellow.

150　*Jailer.* Your death has eyes in's head° then. I have not
seen him so pictured.° You must either be directed
by some that take upon them to know, or to take
upon yourself that which I am sure you do not
know, or jump° the after-inquiry on your own peril.
155　And how you shall speed in° your journey's end, I
think you'll never return to tell on.°

Posthumus. I tell thee, fellow, there are none want
eyes to direct them the way I am going but such as
wink° and will not use them.

160　*Jailer.* What an infinite mock is this, that a man should
have the best use of eyes to see the way of blindness! I am sure hanging's the way of winking.

134 **are paid too much** have been subdued by too much liquor
136 **drawn** emptied　139 **debitor and creditor** account book　140
discharge payment　141 **counters** (used for reckoning)　141–42 **ac-
quittance** receipt　145 **a man that were** i.e., if a man were destined
147 **officer** executioner　150 **Your death . . . head** i.e., you seem
to be informed about what will happen to you after death　151
pictured (in the traditional skull or death's head)　154 **jump** gamble
on　155 **speed in** fare at　156 **on** of　159 **wink** close

Enter a Messenger.

Messenger. Knock off his manacles; bring your prisoner to the King.

Posthumus. Thou bring'st good news; I am called to be 165
made free.°

Jailer. I'll be hanged then.

Posthumus. Thou shalt be then freer than a jailer. No
bolts for the dead.
                    [*Exeunt Posthumus and Messenger.*]

Jailer. Unless a man would marry a gallows and beget 170
young gibbets, I never saw one so prone.° Yet, on
my conscience, there are verier knaves desire to live,
for all° he be a Roman; and there be some of them°
too that die against their wills. So should I, if I were
one. I would we were all of one mind, and one mind 175
good. O, there were desolation of jailers and gal-
lowses! I speak against my present profit, but my
wish hath a preferment° in't.   *Exit.*

Scene V. [*Britain.*]

Enter Cymbeline, Belarius, Guiderius, Arviragus,
Pisanio, and Lords.

Cymbeline. Stand by my side, you whom the gods have
made
Preservers of my throne. Woe is my heart
That the poor soldier that so richly fought,
Whose rags shamed gilded arms, whose naked
breast
Stepped before targes of proof,° cannot be found.   5

166 **made free** i.e., by death   171 **prone** eager   173 **for all** even
though   173 **them** Romans   178 **preferment** promotion (for myself)   V.v.5 **targes of proof** shields of proven strength

He shall be happy that can find him, if
Our grace can make him so.

Belarius.　　　　　　　　　　I never saw
Such noble fury in so poor a thing,
Such precious deeds in one that promised naught
But beggary and poor looks.

10　*Cymbeline.*　　　　　　　　No tidings of him?

Pisanio. He hath been searched among the dead and
　　living,
But no trace of him.

Cymbeline.　　　　　　To my grief, I am
The heir of his reward, which I will add
To you, the liver, heart, and brain° of Britain,
15　By whom I grant she lives. 'Tis now the time
To ask of whence you are. Report it.

Belarius.　　　　　　　　　　　Sir,
In Cambria are we born, and gentlemen.
Further to boast were neither true nor modest,
Unless I add we are honest.

Cymbeline.　　　　　　　　Bow your knees.
20　Arise my knights o' th' battle;° I create you
Companions to our person and will fit° you
With dignities becoming your estates.°

　　　　　Enter Cornelius and Ladies.

There's business in these faces. Why so sadly
Greet you our victory? You look like Romans
And not o' th' court of Britain.

25　*Cornelius.*　　　　　　　　Hail, great King!
To sour your happiness I must report
The Queen is dead.

Cymbeline.　　　　　Who worse than a physician
Would this report become? But I consider

---

14 **liver, heart, and brain** (the vital parts—Belarius, Guiderius, and
Arviragus) 20 **knights o' th' battle** knights created on the battle-
field 21 **fit** equip 22 **estates** ranks

By med'cine life may be prolonged, yet death
Will seize the doctor too. How ended she? 30

Cornelius. With horror, madly dying, like her life,
Which, being cruel to the world, concluded
Most cruel to herself. What she confessed
I will report, so please you. These her women
Can trip me° if I err, who with wet cheeks 35
Were present when she finished.

Cymbeline.   Prithee say.

Cornelius. First, she confessed she never loved you,
 only
Affected° greatness got by you, not you;
Married your royalty, was wife to your place,
Abhorred your person.°

Cymbeline.   She alone knew this, 40
And but° she spoke it dying, I would not
Believe her lips in opening° it. Proceed.

Cornelius. Your daughter, whom she bore in hand° to
 love
With such integrity, she did confess
Was as a scorpion to her sight, whose life, 45
But that her flight prevented it, she had
Ta'en off° by poison.

Cymbeline.   O most delicate° fiend!
Who is't can read a woman? Is there more?

Cornelius. More, sir, and worse. She did confess she
 had
For you a mortal mineral,° which, being took, 50
Should by the minute° feed on life and, ling'ring,
By inches waste you. In which time she purposed,
By watching, weeping, tendance,° kissing, to
O'ercome you with her show° and, in time,

35 **trip me** expose inaccuracy 38 **Affected** loved 40 **your person**
you as a person 41 **but** except that 42 **opening** disclosing 43
bore in hand pretended 47 **Ta'en off** destroyed 47 **delicate** subtle
50 **mortal mineral** deadly poison 51 **by the minute** minute by
minute 53 **tendance** attention 54 **show** simulation (of devotion)

55 When she had fitted you° with her craft, to work
    Her son into th' adoption of the crown;
    But failing of her end by his strange absence,
    Grew shameless desperate, opened, in despite
    Of heaven and men, her purposes, repented
60 The evils she hatched were not effected, so
    Despairing died.

Cymbeline.   Heard you all this, her women?

Ladies. We did, so please your Highness.

Cymbeline.   Mine eyes
    Were not in fault, for she was beautiful;
    Mine ears, that heard her flattery; nor my heart,
    That thought her like her seeming.° It had been
65   vicious°
    To have mistrusted her. Yet, O my daughter,
    That it° was folly in me thou mayst say,
    And prove it in thy feeling.° Heaven mend all!

*Enter Lucius, Iachimo, [the Soothsayer,] and other
    Roman Prisoners, [guarded; the Messenger and
    Posthumus] Leonatus behind;° and Imogen.*

    Thou com'st not, Caius, now for tribute. That
70 The Britons have razed out,° though with the loss
    Of many a bold one; whose kinsmen have made suit
    That their° good souls may be appeased with
      slaughter
    Of you their captives, which ourself have granted.
    So think of your estate.°

75 *Lucius.* Consider, sir, the chance of war. The day
    Was yours by accident; had it gone with us,
    We should not, when the blood was cool, have
      threatened

---

55 **fitted you** shaped you to her purpose   65 **seeming** appearance
65 **had been vicious** would have been morally wrong   67 **it** trusting
her   68 **prove . . . feeling** experience the effect of my folly in your
suffering   68s.d. **behind** (Posthumus remains apart from the main
group of players till line 209)   70 **razed out** erased   72 **their** i.e.,
of those slain in battle   74 **your estate** the condition of your souls

Our prisoners with the sword. But since the gods
Will have it thus, that nothing but our lives
May be called ransom, let it come. Sufficeth   80
A Roman with a Roman's heart can suffer.
Augustus lives to think on't—and so much
For my peculiar° care. This one thing only
I will entreat: my boy, a Briton born,
Let him be ransomed. Never master had   85
A page so kind, so duteous, diligent,
So tender over his occasions,° true,
So feat,° so nurse-like. Let his virtue join
With my request, which I'll make bold your High-
    ness
Cannot deny. He hath done no Briton harm,   90
Though he have served a Roman. Save him, sir,
And spare no blood beside.

Cymbeline.   I have surely seen him;
His favor° is familiar to me. Boy,
Thou hast looked thyself into° my grace
And art mine own. I know not why, wherefore,   95
To say° "Live, boy." Ne'er thank thy master. Live,
And ask of Cymbeline what boon thou wilt,
Fitting my bounty and thy state; I'll give it,
Yea, though thou do demand a prisoner,
The noblest ta'en.

Imogen.   I humbly thank your Highness.   100

Lucius. I do not bid thee beg my life, good lad,
And yet I know thou wilt.

Imogen.   No, no, alack,
There's other work in hand. I see a thing°
Bitter to me as death; your life, good master,
Must shuffle° for itself.

Lucius.   The boy disdains me;   105

---

83 peculiar individual   **87 tender over his occasions** sensitive to his
wants   **88 feat** dexterous   **93 favor** face   **94 looked thyself into**
gained by thy looks   **96 To say** I am saying   **103 thing** the ring on
Iachimo's finger   **105 shuffle** shift

He leaves me, scorns me. Briefly° die their joys
That place them on the truth° of girls and boys.
Why stands he so perplexed?

Cymbeline.   What wouldst thou, boy?
I love thee more and more. Think more and more
What's best to ask. Know'st him thou look'st on?
110   Speak.
Wilt have him live? Is he thy kin? Thy friend?

Imogen. He is a Roman, no more kin to me
Than I to your Highness; who, being born your
    vassal,
Am something nearer.

Cymbeline.   Wherefore ey'st him so?

115 *Imogen.* I'll tell you, sir, in private, if you please
To give me hearing.

Cymbeline.   Ay, with all my heart,
And lend my best attention. What's thy name?

Imogen. Fidele, sir.

Cymbeline.   Thou'rt my good youth, my page;
I'll be thy master. Walk with me; speak freely.

Belarius. Is not this boy revived from death?

120 *Arviragus.*   One sand another
Not more resembles that sweet rosy lad
Who died, and was Fidele. What think you?

Guiderius. The same dead thing alive.

Belarius. Peace, peace, see further. He eyes us not;
    forbear.
125   Creatures may be alike. Were't he, I am sure
He would have spoke to us.

Guiderius.   But we saw him dead.

Belarius. Be silent, let's see further.

Pisanio. [*Aside*]   It is my mistress.

106 Briefly quickly   **107 truth** loyalty

Since she is living, let the time run on
To good or bad.

Cymbeline.   Come, stand thou by our side;
Make thy demand aloud.—Sir, step you forth,   *130*
Give answer to this boy, and do it freely;
Or, by our greatness and the grace of it,
Which is our honor, bitter torture shall
Winnow the truth from falsehood.—On, speak to
    him.

Imogen. My boon is that this gentleman may render°   *135*
Of whom he had this ring.

Posthumus. [*Aside*]   What's that to him?

Cymbeline. That diamond upon your finger, say
How came it yours.

Iachimo. Thou'lt torture me to leave° unspoken that
Which to be spoke would torture thee.

Cymbeline.   How? Me?   *140*

Iachimo. I am glad to be constrained to utter that
Which torments me to conceal. By villainy
I got this ring. 'Twas Leonatus' jewel,
Whom thou didst banish, and—which more may
    grieve thee,
As it doth me—a nobler sir ne'er lived   *145*
'Twixt sky and ground. Wilt thou hear more, my
    lord?

Cymbeline. All that belongs to this.

Iachimo.   That paragon, thy daughter,
For whom my heart drops blood and° my false
    spirits
Quail to remember—Give me leave, I faint.

Cymbeline. My daughter? What of her? Renew thy
    strength.   *150*

---

135 render state   **139 to leave** for leaving   **148 and** and
whom

I had rather thou shouldst live while nature will°
Than die ere I hear more. Strive, man, and speak.

Iachimo. Upon a time—unhappy was the clock
That struck the hour!—it was in Rome—accursed
155 The mansion where!—'twas at a feast—O, would
Our viands had been poisoned, or at least
Those which I heaved to head!°—the good Posthu-
mus—
What should I say? He was too good to be
Where ill men were, and was the best of all
160 Amongst the rar'st of good ones—sitting sadly,
Hearing us praise our loves of Italy
For beauty that made barren the swelled boast
Of him that best could speak; for feature,° laming
The shrine° of Venus or straight-pight° Minerva,
165 Postures° beyond brief nature;° for condition,°
A shop° of all the qualities that man
Loves woman for; besides that hook° of wiving,
Fairness which strikes the eye—

Cymbeline.   I stand on fire.
Come to the matter.°

Iachimo.   All too soon I shall,
Unless thou wouldst grieve quickly. This Posthu-
170 mus,
Most like a noble lord in love and one
That had a royal lover, took his hint,°
And not dispraising whom we praised—therein
He was as calm as virtue—he began
His mistress' picture; which by his tongue being
175 made,
And then a mind put in't,° either our brags

151 **while nature will** i.e., the rest of your natural life   157 **heaved
to head** lifted to mouth   163 **feature** shapeliness   163 **laming/The
shrine** making deformed (by comparison) the image   164 **straight-
pight** tall, erect   165 **Postures** forms   165 **beyond brief nature** i.e.,
more richly endowed than mortal beings   165 **condition** character   166 **shop** repository   167 **hook** fishhook   169 **matter** point
172 **hint** opportunity   176 **And then . . . in't** i.e., added to which was
a good mind

   Were cracked° of kitchen trulls, or his description
   Proved us unspeaking sots.°

Cymbeline.   Nay, nay, to th' purpose.

Iachimo. Your daughter's chastity—there it begins.
   He spake of her as° Dian had hot dreams   *180*
   And she alone were cold;° whereat I, wretch,
   Made scruple of° his praise and wagered with him
   Pieces of gold 'gainst this which then he wore
   Upon his honored finger, to attain
   In suit° the place of's bed and win this ring   *185*
   By hers and mine adultery. He, true knight,
   No lesser of her honor confident
   Than I did truly find her, stakes this ring;
   And would so, had it been a carbuncle°
   Of Phoebus' wheel,° and might so safely had it   *190*
   Been all the worth of's car. Away to Britain
   Post I in this design. Well may you, sir,
   Remember me at court, where I was taught
   Of° your chaste daughter the wide difference
   'Twixt amorous° and villainous. Being thus
       quenched   *195*
   Of hope, not longing,° mine Italian brain
   Gan in your duller Britain operate
   Most vilely; for my vantage,° excellent.
   And, to be brief, my practice° so prevailed
   That I returned with simular° proof enough   *200*
   To make the noble Leonatus mad
   By wounding his belief in her renown°
   With tokens thus and thus; averring° notes
   Of chamber hanging, pictures, this her bracelet—
   O cunning, how I got it!—nay, some marks   *205*
   Of secret on her person, that he could not

177 **cracked** boasted   178 **unspeaking sots** inarticulate fools   180 **as**
as if   181 **cold** chaste   182 **Made scruple of** expressed doubt about,
disputed   185 **suit** amorous solicitation (Maxwell)   189 **carbuncle**
red precious stone   190 **Of Phoebus' wheel** (decorating the sun-
god's chariot)   194 **Of** by   195 **amorous** i.e., faithful   195–96 **Being thus . . . longing** the fire of hope (though not of desire) being
thus put out   198 **vantage** profit   199 **practice** plot   200 **simu-
lar** simulated, specious   202 **renown** good name   203 **averring**
avouching

But think her bond of chastity quite cracked,
I having ta'en the forfeit.° Whereupon—
Methinks I see him now—

Posthumus. [*Advancing*]   Ay, so thou dost,
210   Italian fiend! Ay me, most credulous fool,
Egregious murderer, thief, anything
That's due° to all the villains past, in being,
To come! O, give me cord or knife or poison,
Some upright justicer!° Thou, King, send out
215   For torturers ingenious. It is I
That all th' abhorrèd things o' th' earth amend°
By being worse than they. I am Posthumus,
That killed thy daughter—villain-like, I lie—
That caused a lesser villain than myself,
220   A sacrilegious thief, to do't. The temple
Of Virtue was she; yea, and she herself.°
Spit, and throw stones, cast mire upon me, set
The dogs o' th' street to bay me; every villain
Be called Posthumus Leonatus, and
225   Be villainy less° than 'twas! O Imogen!
My queen, my life, my wife! O Imogen,
Imogen, Imogen!

Imogen.   Peace, my lord. Hear, hear—

Posthumus. Shall's° have a play of this? Thou scornful page,
There lie thy part.°   [*Striking her; she falls.*]

Pisanio.   O gentlemen, help!
230   Mine and your mistress! O my lord Posthumus,
You ne'er killed Imogen till now. Help, help!
Mine honored lady!

Cymbeline.   Does the world go round?

Posthumus. How comes these staggers° on me?

---

208 **forfeit** that which was forfeited for breach of contract
211–12 **anything/That's** due i.e., any word that's appropriate
214 **justicer** judge   216 **amend** make better (by contrast)   221 **she
herself** Virtue herself   225 **less** i.e., by comparison with my villainy
228 **Shall's** shall us (we)   229 **There lie thy part** play your role lying
there   233 **staggers** dizziness

Pisanio.   Wake, my mistress!

Cymbeline. If this be so, the gods do mean to strike me
  To death with mortal° joy.

Pisanio.   How fares my mistress?   235

Imogen. O, get thee from my sight;
  Thou gav'st me poison. Dangerous fellow, hence;
  Breathe not where princes are.

Cymbeline.   The tune° of Imogen!

Pisanio. Lady,
  The gods throw stones of sulphur° on me if   240
  That box I gave you was not thought by me
  A precious° thing; I had it from the Queen.

Cymbeline. New matter still.

Imogen.   It poisoned me.

Cornelius.   O gods!
  I left out one thing which the Queen confessed,
  Which must approve° thee honest. "If Pisanio   245
  Have," said she, "given his mistress that confection°
  Which I gave him for cordial, she is served
  As I would serve a rat."

Cymbeline.   What's this, Cornelius?

Cornelius. The Queen, sir, very oft importuned me
  To temper° poisons for her, still pretending°   250
  The satisfaction of her knowledge only
  In killing creatures vile, as cats and dogs
  Of no esteem.° I, dreading that her purpose
  Was of more danger, did compound for her
  A certain stuff which, being ta'en, would cease°   255
  The present pow'r of life, but in short time
  All offices of nature° should again
  Do their due functions. Have you ta'en of it?

235 **mortal** deadly, fatal   238 **tune** voice   240 **stones of sulphur**
thunderbolts   242 **precious** i.e., beneficial   245 **approve** prove
246 **confection** drug   250 **temper** mix   250 **still pretending** always
alleging   as   her   purpose   253 **esteem** value   255 **cease** suspend
257 **offices of nature** bodily parts

Imogen. Most like° I did, for I was dead.°

Belarius.   My boys,
There was our error.

260 *Guiderius.*   This is sure Fidele.

Imogen. Why did you throw your wedded lady from
    you?
Think that you are upon a rock,° and now
Throw me again.   [*Embracing him*]

Posthumus.   Hang there like fruit, my soul,
Till the tree die!

Cymbeline.   How now, my flesh, my child?
265 What, mak'st thou me a dullard° in this act?°
Wilt thou not speak to me?

Imogen. [*Kneeling*]   Your blessing, sir.

Belarius. Though you did love this youth, I blame ye
    not;
You had a motive° for't.

Cymbeline.   My tears that fall
Prove holy water on thee. Imogen,
270 Thy mother's° dead.

Imogen.   I am sorry for't, my lord.

Cymbeline. O, she was naught,° and long of° her it
    was
That we meet here so strangely; but her son
Is gone, we know not how nor where.

Pisanio.   My lord,
Now fear is from me, I'll speak troth.° Lord Cloten,
275 Upon my lady's missing, came to me
With his sword drawn, foamed at the mouth, and
    swore,

---

259 **like** probably   259 **dead** as if dead   262 **upon a rock** (sense unclear; "rock" is sometimes emended to "lock," a hold in wrestling)
265 **mak'st . . . dullard** treat me like a fool (by ignoring me)
265 **act** action, scene   268 **motive** cause   270 **mother** step-mother
271 **naught** wicked   271 **long of** because of   274 **troth** truth

If I discovered° not which way she was gone,
It was my instant death. By accident
I had a feignèd letter of my master's
Then in my pocket, which directed him   280
To seek her on the mountains near to Milford;
Where, in a frenzy, in my master's garments,
Which he enforced from me, away he posts
With unchaste purpose and with oath to violate
My lady's honor. What became of him   285
I further know not.

Guiderius.   Let me end the story:
I slew him there.

Cymbeline.   Marry,° the gods forfend!°
I would not thy good deeds° should from my lips
Pluck a hard sentence. Prithee, valiant youth,
Deny't again.°

Guiderius.   I have spoke it, and I did it.   290

Cymbeline. He was a prince.

Guiderius. A most incivil° one. The wrongs he did me
Were nothing princelike, for he did provoke me
With language that would make me spurn the sea
If it could so roar to me. I cut off's head,   295
And am right glad he is not standing here
To tell this tale of mine.

Cymbeline.   I am sorry for thee.
By thine own tongue thou art condemned and must
Endure our law. Thou'rt dead.

Imogen.   That headless man
I thought had been my lord.

Cymbeline.   Bind the offender   300
And take him from our presence.

Belarius.   Stay, sir King.

---

277 **discovered** revealed   287 **Marry** indeed (by the Virgin Mary)
287 **forfend** forbid   288 **thy good deeds** i.e., in view of thy good
deeds (in battle) that thou   290 **Deny't again** speak again and
deny what you have said (Nosworthy)   292 **incivil** unmannerly

This man is better than the man he slew,
As well descended as thyself, and hath
More of thee merited than a band of Clotens
305 Had ever scar for.°——Let his arms alone;
They were not born for bondage.

Cymbeline.   Why, old soldier:
Wilt thou undo the worth thou art unpaid for°
By tasting of our wrath? How of descent
As good as we?

Arviragus.   In that he spake too far.

Cymbeline. And thou° shalt die for't.

310 *Belarius.*   We will die all three
But I will prove° that two on's° are as good
As I have given out him. My sons, I must
For mine own part unfold a dangerous speech,
Though haply well for you.

Arviragus.   Your danger's ours.

Guiderius. And our good his.

315 *Belarius.*   Have at it then. By leave,°
Thou hadst, great King, a subject who
Was called Belarius.

Cymbeline.   What of him? He is
A banished traitor.

Belarius.   He it is that hath
Assumed° this age; indeed a banished man,
I know not how a traitor.

320 *Cymbeline.*   Take him hence.
The whole world shall not save him.

Belarius.   Not too hot.°

---

305 **Had ever scar for** ever earned by wounds   307 **the worth . . .
for** thy not yet rewarded esteem (?)   310 **thou** Belarius   311 **But I
will prove** if I do not prove (Maxwell)   311 **on's** of us   315 **By
leave** by your permission   319 **Assumed** attained to   321 **hot** fast

First pay me for the nursing of thy sons,
And let it° be confiscate all, so soon
As I have received it.

Cymbeline.   Nursing of my sons?

Belarius. I am too blunt and saucy; here's my knee.   325
   Ere I arise I will prefer° my sons;
   Then spare not the old father. Mighty sir,
   These two young gentlemen that call me father
   And think they are my sons are none of mine;
   They are the issue of your loins, my liege,   330
   And blood of your begetting.

Cymbeline.   How? My issue?

Belarius. So sure as you your father's. I, old Morgan,
   Am that Belarius whom you sometime° banished.
   Your pleasure was my mere° offense, my punishment
   Itself, and all my treason; that I suffered   335
   Was all the harm I did. These gentle princes—
   For such and so they are—these twenty years
   Have I trained up; those arts° they have as I
   Could put into them. My breeding was, sir, as
   Your Highness knows. Their nurse, Euriphile,   340
   Whom for the theft I wedded, stole these children
   Upon my banishment. I moved° her to't,
   Having received the punishment before
   For that which I did then. Beaten° for loyalty
   Excited me to treason. Their dear loss,   345
   The more of° you 'twas felt, the more it shaped
   Unto° my end of stealing them. But, gracious sir,
   Here are your sons again, and I must lose
   Two of the sweet'st companions in the world.
   The benediction of these covering heavens   350

---

323 **it** the payment   326 **prefer** promote (in rank)   333 **sometime** once
334 **mere** entire   338 **arts** accomplishments   342 **moved** incited
344 **Beaten** my having been beaten   346 **of** by   346–47 **shaped/
Unto** served

Fall on their heads like dew, for they are worthy
To inlay heaven with stars.

Cymbeline.   Thou weep'st and speak'st.
The service° that you three have done is more
Unlike° than this thou tell'st. I lost my children;
355   If these be they, I know not how to wish
A pair of worthier sons.

Belarius.   Be pleased awhile.
This gentleman whom I call Polydore,
Most worthy prince, as yours, is true Guiderius;
This gentleman, my Cadwal, Arviragus,
360   Your younger princely son. He, sir, was lapped°
In a most curious° mantle, wrought by th' hand
Of his queen mother, which for more probation°
I can with ease produce.

Cymbeline.   Guiderius had
Upon his neck a mole, a sanguine° star;
It was a mark of wonder.

365 *Belarius.*   This is he,
Who hath upon him still that natural stamp.
It was wise Nature's end° in the donation
To be his evidence now.

Cymbeline.   O, what am I?
A mother to the birth of three? Ne'er mother
370   Rejoiced deliverance more. Blest pray you be,
That, after this strange starting from your orbs,°
You may reign in them now! O Imogen,
Thou hast lost by this a kingdom.

Imogen.   No, my lord,
I have got two worlds by't. O my gentle brothers,
375   Have we thus met? O, never say hereafter
But I am truest speaker. You called me brother

---

353 **service** i.e., in battle   354 **Unlike** improbable   360 **lapped**
wrapped   361 **curious** elaborately wrought   362 **probation** proof
364 **sanguine** blood-red   367 **end** purpose   371 **orbs** spheres, orbits
(of planets)

When I was but your sister, I you brothers
When ye were so indeed.

Cymbeline.   Did you e'er meet?

Arviragus. Ay, my good lord.

Guiderius.   And at first meeting loved,
Continued so until we thought he died.   380

Cornelius. By the Queen's dram she swallowed.

Cymbeline.   O rare instinct!
When shall I hear all through? This fierce° abridgment
Hath to it circumstantial° branches, which
Distinction should be rich in.° Where, how lived
you?
And when came you to serve our Roman captive?   385
How parted with your brothers? How first met
them?
Why fled you from the court? And whither? These,
And your three motives° to the battle, with
I know not how much more, should be demanded,
And all the other bye-dependences°   390
From chance° to chance; but nor° the time nor
place
Will serve our long inter'gatories. See,
Posthumus anchors upon Imogen,
And she like harmless lightning throws her eye
On him, her brothers, me, her master, hitting   395
Each object with a joy; the counterchange°
Is severally in all.° Let's quit this ground
And smoke° the temple with our sacrifices.
Thou° art my brother; so we'll hold thee ever.

382 **fierce** drastic   383 **circumstantial** detailed   383–84 **which . . .
rich in** which deserves to be elaborately discriminated (Maxwell)
388 **your three motives** the motives of you three   390 **bye-depen-
dences** connected circumstances   391 **chance** event   391 **but nor**
but neither   396 **counterchange** exchange   397 **severally in all** in
each and in all   398 **smoke** fill with smoke   399 **Thou** Belarius

400 *Imogen.* You° are my father too, and did relieve° me
    To see this gracious season.°

Cymbeline.   All o'erjoyed
    Save these in bonds; let them be joyful too,
    For they shall taste our comfort.°

Imogen.   My good master,
    I will yet do you service.

Lucius.   Happy be you!

405 *Cymbeline.* The forlorn° soldier, that so nobly fought,
    He would have well becomed this place and graced
    The thankings of a king.

Posthumus.   I am, sir,
    The soldier that did company these three
    In poor beseeming;° 'twas a fitment° for
410 The purpose I then followed. That I was he,
    Speak, Iachimo. I had you down and might
    Have made you finish.°

Iachimo. [*Kneeling*]   I am down again,
    But now my heavy conscience sinks° my knee,
    As then your force did. Take that life, beseech you,
415 Which I so often° owe; but your ring first,
    And here the bracelet of the truest princess
    That ever swore her faith.

Posthumus.   Kneel not to me.
    The pow'r that I have on you is to spare you;
    The malice towards you to forgive you. Live,
    And deal with others better.

420 *Cymbeline.*   Nobly doomed!°
    We'll learn our freeness° of a son-in-law:
    Pardon's the word to all.

---

400 **You** Belarius   400 **relieve** aid   401 **gracious season** joyful occasion   403 **taste our comfort** share in our joy   405 **forlorn** lost, missing   409 **beseeming** appearance, clothing   409 **fitment** suitable device   412 **finish** die   413 **sinks** lowers   415 **often** many times over   420 **doomed** judged   421 **freeness** generosity

Arviragus.   You holp us, sir,
As° you did mean indeed to be our brother.
Joyed are we that you are.

Posthumus. Your servant, princes. Good my lord of
     Rome,   425
Call forth your soothsayer. As I slept, methought
Great Jupiter, upon his eagle backed,°
Appeared to me, with other spritely° shows
Of mine own kindred. When I waked, I found
This label° on my bosom, whose containing°   430
Is so from° sense in hardness that I can
Make no collection of° it. Let him show
His skill in the construction.°

Lucius.   Philharmonus!

Soothsayer. Here, my good lord.

Lucius.   Read, and declare the meaning.

Soothsayer. (*Reads*) "Whenas a lion's whelp shall, to   435
himself unknown, without seeking find, and be embraced by a piece of tender air; and when from a
stately cedar shall be lopped branches which, being
dead many years, shall after revive, be jointed to the
old stock, and freshly grow; then shall Posthumus   440
end his miseries, Britain be fortunate and flourish
in peace and plenty."
Thou, Leonatus, art the lion's whelp;
The fit and apt construction of thy name,
Being *Leo-natus*,° doth import so much.—   445
The piece of tender air, thy virtuous daughter,
Which we call *mollis aer*,° and *mollis aer*
We term it *mulier*.°—Which *mulier* I divine
Is thy most constant wife, who° even now

---

423 **As** as if   427 **upon his eagle backed** upon the back of his eagle
428 **spritely** ghostly   430 **label** piece of paper   430 **containing** contents   431 **from** remote from   432 **collection of** conclusion about
433 **construction** interpretation   445 **Leo-natus** lion-born   447 **mollis aer** tender air   448 **mulier** woman (thought to derive from
mollis, soft)   449 **who** thou who (Posthumus)

450   Answering the letter of the oracle,
    Unknown to you, unsought, were clipped° about
    With this most tender air.

Cymbeline.   This hath some seeming.°

Soothsayer. The lofty cedar, royal Cymbeline,
    Personates° thee, and thy lopped branches point
455   Thy two sons forth; who, by Belarius stol'n,
    For many years thought dead, are now revived,
    To the majestic cedar joined, whose issue
    Promises Britain peace and plenty.

Cymbeline.   Well,
    My peace we will begin. And, Caius Lucius,
460   Although the victor, we submit to Caesar
    And to the Roman empire, promising
    To pay our wonted tribute, from the which
    We were dissuaded by our wicked queen,
    Whom° heavens in justice, both on her and hers,°
465   Have laid most heavy hand.

Soothsayer. The fingers of the pow'rs above do tune
    The harmony of this peace. The vision
    Which I made known to Lucius ere the stroke
    Of this yet scarce-cold battle, at this instant
470   Is full accomplished; for the Roman eagle,
    From south to west on wing soaring aloft,
    Lessened herself and in the beams o' th' sun
    So vanished; which foreshowed our princely eagle,
    Th' imperial Caesar, should again unite
475   His favor with the radiant Cymbeline,
    Which shines here in the west.

Cymbeline.   Laud we the gods,
    And let our crooked° smokes climb to their nostrils
    From our blest altars. Publish we this peace
    To all our subjects. Set we forward;° let
480   A Roman and a British ensign wave

---

451 **clipped** embraced   452 **seeming** plausibility   454 **Personates** represents   464 **Whom** on whom   464 **hers** i.e., Cloten   477 **crooked** curling   479 **Set we forward** let us march

Friendly together. So through Lud's Town march,
And in the temple of great Jupiter
Our peace we'll ratify, seal it with feasts.
Set on there!° Never was a war did cease,
Ere bloody hands were washed, with such a peace.　485
　　　　　　　　　　　　　　　Exeunt.

F I N I S

484 **Set on there** begin marching

Textual Note

There is only one "substantive" edition of *Cymbeline,* the Shakespeare Folio of 1623. Because of incomplete notation of properties and music in the stage directions of F, it seems clear that the printer's copy for F was not a promptbook or the faithful transcript of one; and several directions are phrased in the "fictive" language characteristic of an author writing his own stage directions. Probably therefore the copy for F consisted of an authorial manuscript or the faithful transcript of one: either (1) "foul papers" (the author's last working draft of the play before preparation of a promptbook) in unusually clean condition (like the copy for *Antony and Cleopatra*); (2) authorial "fair copy" (the author's faithful transcript of his own foul papers); or (3) a faithful scribal transcript of foul papers or authorial fair copy. The type for F was set by a single compositor, Jaggard's Compositor B. (See Charlton Hinman, *The Printing and Proof-Reading of the First Folio of Shakespeare,* 1963.) F provides, in general, a good text, correctly lined and with relatively few corruptions. In the present edition "accidental" errors in F have been emended silently; "substantive" errors requiring emendation are listed at the end of this note.

F is divided into acts and scenes. Division into acts presumably derives from original production of the play with four intervals for nondramatic music. (Cf. Wilfred T. Jewkes, *Act Division in Elizabethan and Jacobean Plays,* 1958.) Division into scenes presumably derives from annotation of the printer's copy by a Folio editor wishing to give the text a semblance of neoclassical style. The present edition follows the act divisions of F and, for convenience of reference, the scene divisions of the Globe edition, although at three points these vary (both correctly and incorrectly) from those of F. Globe I.i combines F I.i and ii, incorrectly since the stage (despite notice by players going off of those coming on) is technically clear at I.i.69 (the "overlap" of players is paralleled at I.ii.118 of *Measure for Measure*). Globe II.iv and v divide F II.iv, correctly since the stage is clear at II.iv.152. And Globe III.vi combines F III.vi and vii, incorrectly since the stage is clear at III.vi.27. Both Globe and F fail to mark a new scene at IV.ii.100, incorrectly since the stage is clear at that point.

F contains no place headings, for the reason that the play was originally produced without changeable scenery. (Cf. Richard Southern, *Changeable Scenery: Its Origin and Development in the British Theatre,* 1952.) Place headings have been added to the present edition in accordance with a general requirement of the Signet Classic Shakespeare Series, but such headings designate only the three general locales of the action, Britain, Rome, and Wales. A more specific designation is impossible in at least three instances (I.ii, II.i, II.v); and in any case specific designations are misleading since they suggest a change of scenery for each scene with a particular locale different from that of the preceding scene.

In the following list of substantive emendations the reading of the present edition is given in italic type, that of F in roman type.

I.i.4 *First Gentleman* 1 [so throughout balance of scene]　10 *Second Gentleman* 2 [so throughout balance of scene]　158 *Exeunt* Exit

I.ii.1 *First Lord* 1 [so throughout balance of scene and in II.i and II.iii]　7 *Second Lord* 2 [so throughout balance of scene and in II.i and II.iii]

I.iii.9 *this* his

I.iv.49 *not* [not in F]　76 *Britain* Britanie　78–79 *but believe* beleeue　88–89 *purchase* purchases　133 *thousand* thousands

I.v.3s.d. *Exeunt* Exit   75s.d. [occurs after 1.74 in F]   85s.d. *Exeunt* Exit

I.vi.7 *desire* desires   28 *takes* take   104 *Fixing* Fiering   109 *illustrous* illustrious   168 *men's* men   169 *descended* defended

II.i.27 *your* you   34 *tonight* night   51s.d. *Exeunt* Exit   61 *husband, than* Husband. Then   62 *make. The* make the   65s.d. *Exit* Exeunt

II.ii.49 *bare* beare   51s.d. *Exeunt* Exit

II.iii.7 *Cloten* [not in F]   29 *Cloten* [not in F]   31 *vice* voyce   45 *out* on't   49 *solicits* solicity   139 *garment* Garments   156 *you* your

II.iv.6 *hopes* hope   18 *legions* Legion   24 *mingled* wing-led   47 *not* note   100–01 *that. She* that She   135 *the* her

II.v.16 *German* Iarmen   27 *have a* [not in F]

III.i.19 *ribbèd . . . palèd* ribb'd . . . pal'd   20 *rocks* Oakes   54 *be. We do say* be, we do. Say

III.ii.68 *score* store   79 *here, nor* heere, not

III.iii.2 *Stoop* Sleepe   23 *bribe* Babe   28 *know* knowes   83 *wherein they* whereon the

III.iv.80 *afore't* a-foot   91 *make* makes   103 *out* [not in F]   125 *courtesan.* Curtezan?   149 *haply* happily

III.v.17s.d. *Exeunt* Exit   32 *looks* looke   40 *strokes* stroke   41s.d. *Messenger* a Messenger   55s.d. [occurs after "days" in F]   142 *insultment* insulment

III.vi.70 *I'ld* I

III.vii.9 *commends* commands

IV.i.19 *her* thy   20 *haply* happily

IV.ii.49 [speech heading Arui. precedes "He" in F]   58 *patience* patient   122 *thank* thanks   132 *humor* Honor   186 *ingenious* ingenuous   205 *crayer* care   206 *Might* Might'st   290 *is* are   332s.d.–333 *Enter Lucius and Captains; a Soothsayer to them.*

Captain. The legions Enter Lucius, Captaines, and a Soothsayer.
Cap. To them, the Legions   336 *are in* are heere in

IV.iv.2 *find we* we finde.   8 *us* v.   17 *the* their   27 *hard* heard

V.i.1 *wished* am wisht

V.iii.24 *harts* hearts   42 *stooped* stopt   43 *they* the   84 *First Captain* 1 [so throughout balance of scene]   86 *Second Captain* 2 [so throughout balance of scene]

V.iv.s.d. *Jailers* Gaoler   1 *First Jailer* Gao   51 *come* came   57 *look* looke, looke   130 *are as often* are often   141 *sir* Sis   156 *on* one   178s.d. *Exit* Exeunt

V.v.62 *Ladies* La   64 *heard* heare   126 *saw* see   134 *On* One   205 *it* [not in F]   297 *sorry* sorrow   334 *mere* neere   378 *ye* we   386 *brothers* Brother   392 *inter'gatories* Interrogatories   405 *so* no   435 *Soothsayer* [not in F]   445 *Leo-natus* Leonatus   449 *thy* this   469 *this yet* yet this

The Sources of Cymbeline

The sources of *Cymbeline* are discussed in the Introduction. The ninth novella of the Second Day of Boccaccio's *Decameron* is reprinted here in the anonymous translation of 1620. *Frederick of Jennen* is reprinted in an appendix to the New Arden edition of *Cymbeline* (1955). *The Rare Triumphs of Love and Fortune* is edited by W. W. Greg in the Malone Society Reprints (1931), *Clyomon and Clamydes* by Betty Littleton (1968). The *Ethiopica* of Heliodorus has been translated by Moses Hadas: *Heliodorus: An Ethiopian Romance* (1957). Relevant parts of the *History of England* and the *History of Scotland* in Holinshed's *Chronicles* (1587) are reprinted here. Blenerhasset's "Guidericus" and Higgins's "Guiderius" have been edited by Lily B. Campbell, in *Parts Added to the Mirror for Magistrates* (1946).

GIOVANNI BOCCACCIO

from *The Decameron*

The Second Day . . . ,

The Ninth Novel.

Wherein is declared that by over-liberal commending
the chastity of women it falleth out (oftentimes) to be
very dangerous, especially by the means of treacherers,[1]
who yet (in the end) are justly punished for their treachery. . . .

There was a fair and good inn in Paris much frequented
by many great Italian merchants according to such variety
of occasions and business as urged their often resorting
thither. One night among many other, having had a merry
supper together, they began to discourse on divers mat-
tres, and, falling from one relation to another, they com-
moned[2] in very friendly manner concerning their wives
left at home in their houses. Quoth the first: "I cannot
well imagine what my wife is now doing, but I am able to

---

1 deceivers.   2 talked.

From *The Decameron, Containing an Hundred Pleasant Novels,* trans-
lator unknown, vol. I, fols. 68–73v. London: Isaac Jaggard, 1620. In the
present edition the traditional forms *Bernabò* (from *Bernardobuono*),
Ambrogiuolo (English *Ambrose*), and *Zinevra* are substituted for the
variant forms of 1620: *Bernardo, Ambroginolo* (a textual error), and
Genevra (a linguistic variant). Spelling and punctuation are modernized,
and a few necessary emendations are indicated in footnotes.

say for myself that if a pretty female should fall into my company, I could easily forget my love to my wife and make use of such an advantage offered."

A second replied: "And, trust me, I should do no less, because I am persuaded that if my wife be willing to wander, the law is in her own hand and I am far enough from home. Dumb walls blab no tales and offenses unknown are seldom or never called in question." A third man was apt[3] in censure[4] with his former fellows of the jury; and it plainly appeared that all the rest were of the same opinion, condemning their wives overrashly and alleging that, when husbands strayed so far from home, their wives had wit enough to make use of their time.

Only one man among them all, named Bernabò Lomellino and dwelling in Genoa, maintained the contrary, boldly avouching that by the especial favor of Fortune he had a wife so perfectly complete in all graces and virtues as any lady in the world possibly could be and that Italy scarcely contained her equal. For she was goodly of person and yet very young, quick, quaint,[5] mild, and courteous, and not anything appertaining to the office of a wife either for domestic affairs or any other employment whatsoever but in womanhood she went beyond all other. No lord, knight, esquire, or gentleman could be better served at his table than himself daily was with more wisdom, modesty, and discretion. After all this, he praised her for riding, hawking, hunting, fishing, fowling, reading, writing, enditing,[6] and most absolute keeping his books of accounts that neither himself or any other merchant could therein excel her. After infinite other commendations he came to the former point of their argument concerning the easy falling of women into wantonness, maintaining with a solemn oath that no woman possibly could be more chaste and honest[7] than she. In which respect he was verily persuaded that if he stayed from her ten years' space, yea, all his lifetime out of his house, yet never would she falsify her faith to him or be lewdly allured by any other man.

Among these merchants thus commoning together, there

---

[3] For "was apt" 1620 has "unapt."   [4] opinion.   [5] clever.   [6] composing.   [7] chaste.

was a young proper man named Ambrogiuolo[8] of Piacenza who began to laugh at the last praises which Bernabò had used of his wife and, seeming to make a mockery thereat, demanded if the Emperor had given him this privilege above all other married men. Bernabò, being somewhat offended, answered: "No emperor hath done it but the especial blessing of heaven, exceeding all the emperors on the earth in grace, and thereby have [I] received this favor." Whereto Ambrogiuolo presently[9] thus replied: "Bernabò, without all question to the contrary I believe that what thou hast said is true, but for aught I can perceive thou hast slender judgment in the nature of things, because if thou didst observe them well thou couldst not be of so gross understanding. For, by comprehending matters in their true kind and nature, thou wouldst speak of them more correctly than thou dost. And, to the end thou mayst not imagine that we who have spoken of our wives do think any otherwise of them than as well and honestly as thou canst of thine, nor that anything else did urge these speeches of them or falling into this kind of discourse but only by a natural instinct and admonition, I will proceed familiarly a little further with thee upon the matter already propounded.

"I have evermore understood that man was the most noble creature formed by God to live in this world, and woman in the next degree to him. But man, as generally is believed and as is discerned by apparent effects, is the most perfect of both. Having then the most perfection in him, without all doubt he must be so much the more firm and constant. So in like manner it hath been and is universally granted that woman is more various and mutable, and the reason thereof may be approved[10] by many natural circumstances which were needless now to make any mention of. If a man then be possessed of the greater stability and yet cannot contain himself from condescending[11]—I say not to one that entreats him—but to desire any other that may please him and, beside, to covet the enjoying of his own pleasing contentment (a thing not

8 pronounced *Ambroj-wolo*.   9 immediately.   10 proven.   11 restrain himself from falling.

chancing to him once in a month but infinite times in a
day's space), what can you then conceive of a frail woman,
subject by nature to entreaties, flatteries, gifts, persuasions,
and a thousand other enticing means which a man that is
affected to[12] her can use? Dost thou think then that she
hath any power to contain?[13] Assuredly, though thou
shouldst rest so resolved, yet cannot I be of the same
opinion. For I am sure thou believest and must needs
confess it that thy wife is a woman, made of flesh and
blood as other women are. If it be so, she cannot be
without the same desires and the weakness or strength
as other women have to resist such natural appetites as
her own are. In regard whereof it is merely[14] impossible,
although she be most honest, but she must needs do that
which other women do, for there is nothing else possible
either to be denied or affirmed to the contrary as thou
most unadvisedly hast done."

Bernabò answered in this manner: "I am a merchant
and no philosopher, and like a merchant I mean to answer
thee. I am not to learn that these accidents by thee related
may happen to fools who are void of understanding or
shame, but such as are wise and endued with virtue have
always such a precious esteem of their honor that they
will contain those principles of constancy which men are
merely careless of, and I justify[15] my wife to be one of
them." "Believe me, Bernabò," replied Ambrogiuolo, "if,
so often as thy wife's mind is addicted to wanton folly, a
badge of scorn should arise on thy forehead to render
testimony of her female frailty, I believe the number of
them would be more than willingly you would wish them
to be. And among all married men in every degree the
notes are so secret of their wives' imperfections that the
sharpest sight is not able to discern them, and the wiser
sort of men are willing not to know them because shame
and loss of honor is never imposed but in cases evident
and apparent.

"Persuade thyself then, Bernabò, that what women may
accomplish in secret they will rarely fail to do, or if
they abstain, it is through fear and folly. Wherefore hold

12 in love with.   13 be continent.   14 absolutely.   15 affirm.

it for a certain rule that that woman is only chaste that never was solicited personally, or if she endured any such suit, either she answered yea or no. And, albeit I know this to be true by many infallible and natural reasons, yet could I not speak so exactly as I do if I had not tried experimentally the humors and affections of divers women. Yea, and let me tell thee more, Bernabò, were I in private company with thy wife, howsoever pure and precise[16] thou presumest her to be, I should account it a matter of no impossibility to find in her the selfsame frailty."

Bernabò's blood began now to boil and, patience being a little put down by choler,[17] thus he replied: "A combat of words requires overlong continuance, for I maintain the matter which thou deniest and all this sorts to nothing in the end. But seeing thou presumest that all women are so apt and tractable and thyself so confident of thine own power, I willingly yield for the better assurance of my wife's constant loyalty to have my head smitten off if thou canst win her to any such dishonest act by any means whatsoever thou canst use unto her; which if thou canst not do thou shalt only lose a thousand ducats of gold." Now began Ambrogiuolo to be heated with these words, answering thus: "Bernabò, if I had won the wager, I know not what I should do with thy head; but, if thou be willing to stand upon the proof,[18] pawn down five thousand ducats of gold, a matter of much less value than thy head, against a thousand ducats of mine, granting me a lawful limited time which I require to be no more than the space of three months after the day of my departing hence. I will stand bound[19] to go for Genoa and there win such kind consent of thy wife as shall be to mine own content.[20] In witness whereof, I will bring back with me such private and especial tokens as thou thyself shalt confess that I have not failed, provided that thou do first promise upon thy faith to absent thyself thence during my limited time and be no hindrance to me by thy letters concerning the attempt by me undertaken."

Bernabò said: "Be it a bargain. I am the man that will

16 strict.   17 anger.   18 put the matter to a test.   19 ready.   20 1620 has "consent."

make good my five thousand ducats." And albeit the
other merchants then present earnestly labored to break
the wager, knowing great harm must needs ensue thereon,
yet both the parties were so hot and fiery as all the other
men spoke to no effect but writings were made, sealed,[21]
and delivered under either of their hands, Bernabò remaining at Paris and Ambrogiuolo departing for Genoa. There
he remained some few days to learn the street's name
where Bernabò dwelt as also the conditions and qualities
of his wife; which scarcely pleased him when he heard
them because they were far beyond her husband's relation
and she reputed to be the only wonder of women, whereby
he plainly perceived that he had undertaken a very idle
enterprise. Yet would he not give it over so but proceeded
therein a little further.

He wrought such means that he came acquainted with a
poor woman who often frequented Bernabò's house and
was greatly in favor with his wife; upon whose poverty he
so prevailed by earnest persuasions but much more by
large gifts of money that he won her to further him in this
manner following. A fair and artificial[22] chest he caused
to be purposely made wherein himself might be aptly contained and so conveyed into the house of Bernabò's wife
under color[23] of a formal excuse that the poor woman
should be absent from the city two or three days and she
must keep it safe till she[24] return. The gentlewoman, sus-
pecting no guile but that the chest was the receptacle of
all the woman's wealth, would trust it in no other room
than her own bedchamber, which was the place where
Ambrogiuolo most desired to be.

Being thus conveyed into the chamber, the night going
on apace and the gentlewoman fast asleep in her bed, a
lighted taper stood burning on the table by her as in her
husband's absence she ever used to have. Ambrogiuolo
softly opened the chest according as cunningly he had contrived it and, stepping forth in his socks made of cloth,
observed the situation of the chamber, the paintings, pic-

21 confirmed by the attaching of waxen seals.   22 skillfully designed.
23 pretense.   24 1620 has "he."

tures, and beautiful hangings, with all things else that were
remarkable; which perfectly he committed to his memory.
Going near to the bed, he saw her lie there sweetly sleeping and her young daughter in like manner by her, she
seeming then as complete and pleasing a creature as when
she was attired in her best bravery.[25] No especial note or
mark could he descry whereof he might make credible
report but only a small wart upon her left pap with some
few hairs growing thereon appearing to be as yellow as
gold.

Sufficient had he seen and durst presume no further, but,
taking one of her rings which lay upon the table, a purse
of hers hanging by on the wall, a light-wearing robe of silk,
and her girdle,[26] all which he put into the chest and, being
in himself, closed it fast as it was before; so continuing
there in the chamber two several nights, the gentlewoman
neither mistrusting or missing anything. The third day
being come, the poor woman according as formerly was
concluded came to have home her chest again and brought
it safely into her own house, where Ambrogiuolo, coming
forth of it, satisfied the poor woman to her own liking,
returning with all the forenamed things so fast as conveniently he could to Paris.

Being arrived there long before his limited time, he
called the merchants together who were present at the
passed words and wager, avouching before Bernabò that
he had won his five thousand ducats and performed the
task he undertook. To make good his protestation, first he
described the form of the chamber, the curious pictures
hanging about it, in what manner the bed stood, and every
circumstance else beside. Next he showed the several
things which he brought away thence with him, affirming
that he had received them of herself. Bernabò confessed
that his description of the chamber was true and acknowledged moreover that these other things did belong to his
wife. "But," quoth he, "this may be gotten by corrupting
some servant of mine, both for intelligence of the chamber
as also of the ring, purse, and what else is beside, all

25 finery. 26 sash.

which suffice not to win the wager without some other more apparent and pregnant token." "In troth," answered Ambrogiuolo, "methinks these should serve for sufficient proofs, but seeing thou art so desirous to know more, I plainly tell thee that fair Zinevra thy wife hath a small round wart upon her left pap and some few little golden hairs growing thereon."

When Bernabò heard these words, they were as so many stabs to his heart, yea, beyond all compass of patient sufferance, and by the changing of his color it was noted manifestly (being unable to utter one word) that Ambrogiuolo had spoken nothing but the truth. Within a while after, he said: "Gentlemen, that which Ambrogiuolo hath said is very true. Wherefore let him come when he will and he shall be paid." Which accordingly he performed on the very next day, even to the utmost penny, departing then from Paris towards Genoa with a most malicious intention to his wife. Being come near to the city, he would not enter it but rode to a country house of his standing about ten miles distant thence. Being there arrived, he called a servant in whom he reposed especial trust, sending him to Genoa with two horses, writing to his wife that he was returned and she should come thither to see him. But secretly he charged his servant that, so soon as he had brought her to a convenient place, he should there kill her without any pity or compassion and then return to him again.

When the servant was come to Genoa and had delivered his letter and message, Zinevra gave him most joyful welcome and, on the morrow morning, mounting on horseback, with the servant rode merrily towards the country house. Divers things she discoursed on by the way, till they descended into a deep solitary valley, very thickly beset with high and huge spreading trees, which the servant supposed to be a meet place for the execution of his master's command. Suddenly drawing forth his sword and holding Zinevra fast by the arm, he said: "Mistress, quickly commend your soul to God, for you must die before you pass any further." Zinevra, seeing the naked sword and hearing the words so peremptorily delivered, fearfully answered: "Alas, dear friend, mercy for God's sake, and before thou kill me tell me wherein I have offended thee and why thou must kill me." "Alas, good mistress," replied the servant, "you have not any way offended me, but in what occasion you have displeased your husband, it is utterly unknown to me, for he hath strictly commanded me, without respect of pity or compassion, to kill you by the way as I bring you, and if I do it not, he hath sworn to hang me by the neck. You know, good mistress, how much I stand obliged to him and how impossible it is for me to contradict anything that he commandeth. God is my witness that I am truly compassionate of you, and yet by no means may I let you live."

Zinevra, kneeling before him weeping, wringing her hands, thus replied: "Wilt thou turn monster and be a murderer of her that never wronged thee, to please another man and on a bare command? God, who truly knoweth all things, is my faithful witness that I never committed any offense whereby to deserve the dislike of my husband, much less so harsh a recompense as this is. But, flying from mine own justification and appealing to thy manly[27] mercy, thou mayst (wert thou but so well pleased) in a moment satisfy both thy master and me in such manner as I will make plain and apparent to thee. Take thou my garments; spare me only thy doublet and such a bonnet as is fitting for a man. So return with my habit to thy master, assuring him that the deed is done. And here I swear to thee by that life which I enjoy but by thy mercy, I will so strangely[28] disguise myself and wander so far off from these countries as neither he or thou nor any person belonging to these parts shall ever hear any tidings of me."

The servant, who had no great good will to kill her, very easily grew pitiful, took off her upper[29] garments, and gave her a poor ragged doublet, a silly chaperon,[30] and such small store of money as he had, desiring her to for-

27 human.   28 i.e., completely.   29 outer.   30 simple hood.

sake that country, and so left her to walk on foot out of
the valley. When he came to his master and had delivered
him her garments, he assured him that he had not only
accomplished his command but also was most secure from
any discovery because he had no sooner done the deed
but four or five very ravenous wolves came presently running to the dead body and gave it burial in their bellies.
Bernabò, soon after returning to Genoa, was much blamed
for such unkind[31] cruelty to his wife. But his constant
avouching of her treason to him, according then to the
country's custom, did clear him from all pursuit of law.

Poor Zinevra was left thus alone and disconsolate, and,
night stealing fast upon her, she went to a silly[32] village
near adjoining where, by the means of a good old woman,
she got such provision as the place afforded, making the
doublet fit to her body and converting her petticoat to a
pair of breeches according to the mariners' fashion. Then,
cutting her hair and quaintly[33] disguised like to a sailor,
she went to the seacoast. By good fortune she met there
with a gentleman of Catalonia whose name was Signior
Encararch who came on land from his ship, which lay
hulling there about Alba[34] to refresh himself at a pleasant
spring. Encararch taking her to be a man, as she appeared
no otherwise by her habit, upon some conference passing
between them, she was entertained[35] into his service, and,
being brought aboard the ship, she went under the name
of Sicurano da Finale. There she had better apparel bestown
on her by the gentleman, and her service proved so pleasing and acceptable to him that he liked her care and
diligence beyond all comparison.

It came to pass within a short while after that this
gentleman of Catalonia sailed with some charge[36] of his
into Alexandria, carrying thither certain peregrine falcons
which he presented to the Sultan, who oftentimes welcomed this gentleman to his table, where he observed the
behavior of Sicurano attending on his master's trencher
and therewith was so highly pleased that he requested to

---

31 unnatural.   32 humble.   33 cleverly.   34 1620 has "Albagia."   35
hired.   36 cargo, merchandise.

have him from the gentleman, who for his more advancement willingly parted with his so lately entertained servant. Sicurano was so ready and discreet in his daily services that he grew in as great grace with the Sultan as before he had done with Encararch.

At a certain season in the year, as customary order (there observed) had formerly been in the city of Acre, which was under the Sultan's subjection, there yearly met a great assembly of merchants, as Christians, Moors, Jews, Saracens, and many other nations beside, as at a common mart or fair. And to the end that the merchants, for the better sale of their goods, might be there in the safer assurance, the Sultan used to send thither some of his ordinary[37] officers, and a strong guard of soldiers beside, to defend them from all injuries and molestation; because he reaped thereby no mean[38] benefit. And who should be now sent about this business but his new-elected favorite, Sicurano, because she was skillful and perfect in the languages.

Sicurano, being come to Acre as lord and captain of the guard for the merchants and for the safety of their merchandises, she discharged her office most commendably, walking with her train through every part of the fair where she observed a worthy company of merchants, Sicilians, Pisans, Genoese, Venetians, and other Italians, whom the more willingly she noted in remembrance of her native country. At one especial time among other, chancing into a shop or booth belonging to the Venetians, she espied hanging up with other costly wares a purse and a girdle which suddenly she remembered to be sometime[39] her own; whereat she was not a little abashed in her mind. But, without making any such outward show, courteously she requested to know whose they were and whether they should be sold or no.

Ambrogiuolo of Piacenza was likewise come thither, and great store of merchandises he had brought with him in a carrack appertaining to the Venetians, and he, hearing the Captain of the Guard demand whose they were, stepped

37 regular.   38 inconsiderable.   39 once.

forth before him and, smiling, answered that they were his, but not to be sold, yet if he liked them, gladly he would bestow them on him. Sicurano, seeing him smile, suspected lest himself had by some unfitting behavior been the occasion thereof, and therefore, with a more settled countenance, he said: "Perhaps thou smilest because I that am a man, professing arms, should question after such womanish toys?" Ambrogiuolo replied: "My lord, pardon me; I smile not at you or your demand but at the manner how I came by these things."

Sicurano upon this answer was ten times more desirous than before and said: "If Fortune favored thee in friendly manner by the obtaining of these things, if it may be spoken, tell me how thou hadst them." "My lord," answered Ambrogiuolo, "these things, with many more beside, were given me by a gentlewoman of Genoa named Madam Zinevra, the wife to one Bernabò Lomellino, in recompense of one night's lodging with her, and she desired me to keep them for her sake. Now, the main reason of my smiling was the remembrance of her husband's folly in waging five thousand ducats of gold against one thousand of mine that I should not obtain my will of his wife, which I did and thereby won the wager. But he, who better deserved to be punished for his folly than she who was but sick of all women's disease, returning from Paris to Genoa, caused her to be slain, as afterward it was reported by himself."

When Sicurano heard this horrible lie, immediately she conceived[40] that this was the occasion of her husband's hatred to her and all the hard haps which she had since suffered. Whereupon she reputed it for more than a mortal sin if such a villain should pass without due punishment. Sicurano seemed to like well this report and grew into such familiarity with Ambrogiuolo that, by her persuasions, when the fair was ended, she took him higher[41] with her into Alexandria and all his wares along with him, furnishing him with a fit and convenient shop where he made great benefit of his merchandises, trusting all his moneys

40 understood. 41 farther inland.

in the Captain's custody because it was the safest course
for him; and so he continued there with no mean contentment.

Much did she pity her husband's perplexity, devising
by what good and warrantable means she might make
known her innocency to him, wherein her place and
authority did greatly stead her; and she wrought with
divers gallant merchants of Genoa that then remained in
Alexandria, and by virtue of the Sultan's friendly letters
beside, to bring him thither upon an especial occasion.
Come he did, albeit in poor and mean order, which soon
was better altered by her appointment and he very honor-
ably though in private entertained[42] by divers of her
worthy friends till time did favor what she further intended.

In the expectation of Bernabò's arrival, she had so
prevailed with Ambrogiuolo that the same tale which he
formerly told to her he delivered again in presence of the
Sultan, who seemed to be well pleased with it. But after
she had once seen her husband, she thought upon her
more serious business, providing herself of an apt opportunity when she entreated such favor of the Sultan that
both the men might be brought before him where, if
Ambrogiuolo would not confess without constraint that
which he had made his vaunt of concerning Bernabò's
wife, he might be compelled thereto perforce.

Sicurano's word was a law with the Sultan, so that,
Ambrogiuolo and Bernabò being brought face to face, the
Sultan with a stern and angry countenance, in the presence
of a most princely assembly, commanded Ambrogiuolo
to declare the truth, yea, upon peril of his life, by what
means he won the wager of the five thousand golden ducats
he received of Bernabò. Ambrogiuolo, seeing Sicurano
there present, upon whose favor he wholly relied, yet perceiving her looks likewise to be as dreadful as the Sultan's
and hearing her threaten him with most grievous torments
except he revealed the truth indeed, you may easily guess,
fair company, in what condition he stood at that instant.

[42] welcomed.

Frowns and fury he beheld on either side, and Bernabò
standing before him (with a world of famous witnesses)
to hear his lie confounded by his own confession and his
tongue to deny what it had before so constantly avouched.
Yet, dreaming on no other pain or penalty but restoring
back the five thousand ducats of gold and the other things
by him purloined, truly he revealed the whole form of his
falsehood. Then Sicurano, according as the Sultan had
formerly commanded him, turning to Bernabò, said: "And
thou, upon the suggestion of this foul lie, what didst thou
to thy wife?" "Being," quoth Bernabò, "overcome with
rage for the loss of my money and the dishonor I supposed
to receive by my wife, I caused a servant of mine to kill
her, and, as he credibly avouched, her body was devoured
by ravenous wolves in a moment after."

These things being thus spoken and heard in the
presence of the Sultan, and no reason as yet made known
why the case was so seriously urged and to what end it
would succeed, Sicurano spoke in this manner to the
Sultan. "My gracious lord, you may plainly perceive in
what degree that poor gentlewoman might make her
vaunt, being so well provided both of a loving friend and
a husband. Such was the friend's love that in an instant
and by a wicked lie he robbed her both of her renown
and honor and bereft her also of her husband. And her
husband, rather crediting another's falsehood than the
invincible truth whereof he had faithful knowledge by
long and very honorable experience, caused her to be
slain and made food for devouring wolves. Beside all this,
such was the good will and affection borne to that woman
both by friend and husband that the longest continuer of
them in her company makes them alike in knowledge of
her. But, because your great wisdom knoweth perfectly
what each of them have worthily deserved, if you please,
in your ever-known gracious benignity, to permit the
punishment of the deceiver and pardon the party so
deceived, I will procure such means that she shall appear
here in your presence and theirs."

The Sultan, being desirous to give Sicurano all manner

of satisfaction, having followed the course so industriously, bade him to produce the woman and he was well contented. Whereat Bernabò stood much amazed because he verily believed that she was dead. And Ambrogiuolo, foreseeing already a preparation for punishment, feared that the repayment of the money would not now serve his turn, not knowing also what he should further hope or suspect if the woman herself did personally appear, which he imagined would be a miracle. Sicurano, having thus obtained the Sultan's permission, in tears humbling herself at his feet, in a moment she lost her manly voice and demeanor as knowing that she was now no longer to use them but must truly witness what she was indeed; and therefore thus spoke:

"Great Sultan, I am the miserable and unfortunate Zinevra, that for the space of six whole years have wandered through the world in the habit of a man, falsely and most maliciously slandered by this villainous traitor Ambrogiuolo, and by this unkind, cruel husband betrayed to his servant to be slain and left to be devoured by savage beasts." Afterward, desiring such garments as better fitted for her and showing her breasts, she made it apparent before the Sultan and his assistants that she was the very same woman indeed. Then, turning herself to Ambrogiuolo with more than manly courage, she demanded of him when and where it was that he lay with her, as villainously he was not ashamed to make his vaunt. But he, having already acknowledged the contrary, being stricken dumb with shameful disgrace, was not able to utter one word.

The Sultan, who had always reputed Sicurano to be a man, having heard and seen so admirable an accident,[43] was so amazed in his mind that many times he was very doubtful whether this was a dream or an absolute relation of truth. But, after he had more seriously considered thereon and found it to be real and infallible, with extraordinary gracious praises he commended the life, constancy, conditions, and virtues of Zinevra, whom till that time he had always called Sicurano. So, committing

[43] so wondrous an event.

her to the company of honorable ladies to be changed from her manly habit, he pardoned Bernabò her husband according to her request formerly made, although he had more justly deserved death; which likewise himself confessed and, falling at the feet of Zinevra, desired her in tears to forgive his rash transgression; which most lovingly she did, kissing and embracing him a thousand times.

Then the Sultan strictly commanded that on some high and eminent place of the city Ambrogiuolo should be bound and impaled on a stake, having his naked body anointed all over with honey and never to be taken off until of itself it fell in pieces, which according to the sentence was presently[44] performed. Next, he gave express charge that all his money and goods should be given to Zinevra; which valued above ten thousand double ducats. Forthwith[45] a solemn feast was prepared wherein much honor was done to Bernabò, being the husband of Zinevra; and to her, as to a most worthy woman and matchless wife, he gave in costly jewels as also vessels of gold and silver plate so much as amounted to above ten thousand double ducats more.

When the feasting was finished, he caused a ship to be furnished for them, granting them license to depart for Genoa when they pleased, whither they returned most rich and joyfully, being welcomed home with great honor; especially Madam Zinevra, whom everyone supposed to be dead. And always after, so long as she lived, she was most famous for her manifold virtues. But as for Ambrogiuolo, the very same day that he was impaled on the stake, anointed with honey, and fixed in the place appointed to his no mean[46] torment, he not only died but likewise was devoured to the bare bones by flies, wasps, and hornets, whereof the country notoriously aboundeth. And his bones in full form and fashion remained strangely black for a long while after, knit together by the sinews; as a witness, to many thousands of people which afterward beheld the[47] carcass, of his wickedness against so good and virtuous a woman that had not so much as a thought of any evil towards him. And thus was the proverb truly verified that shame succeedeth after ugly sin and the deceiver is trampled and trod by such as himself hath deceived.

RAPHAEL HOLINSHED

from *The Chronicles of England, Scotland, and Ireland* (1587)

[32][1] "Kymbeline" or "Cymbeline," the son of Theomantius, was of the Britons made king after the decease of his father in the year of the world 3944, after the building of Rome 728, and before the birth of our Saviour 33. This man (as some write) was brought up at Rome and there made knight by Augustus Caesar, under whom he served in the wars, and was in such favor with him that he was at liberty to pay his tribute or not. Little other mention is made of his doings, except that during his reign the Saviour of the world, our Lord Jesus Christ the only son of God, was borne of a virgin about the twenty-third year of the reign of this Cymbeline. . . . Touching the continuance of the years of Cymbeline's reign, some writers do vary, but the best approved affirm that he reigned thirty-five years and then died, and was buried at London, leaving behind him two sons Guiderius and Arviragus.

But here is to be noted that, although our histories do affirm that as well this Cymbeline as also his father Theomantius lived in quiet with the Romans, and continually to them paid the tributes which the Britons had covenanted

---

1 Vol. 1, *History of England*. [References at heads of paragraphs are to pages of the appropriate volume of Holinshed (editor's note).]

From *Shakespeare's Holinshed*, edited by Richard Hosley. New York: G. P. Putnam's Sons, 1968, pp. 4–8. Copyright © 1968 by Richard Hosley. Reprinted by permission of the publisher.

with Julius Caesar to pay, yet we find in the Roman writers that after Julius Caesar's death, when Augustus had taken upon him the rule of the empire, the Britons refused to pay that tribute. Whereat, as Cornelius Tacitus reporteth, Augustus (being otherwise occupied) was contented to wink. Howbeit, through earnest calling upon to recover his right by such as were desirous to see the uttermost of the British kingdom, at length, to wit in the tenth year after the death of Julius Caesar, which was about the thirteenth year of the said Theomantius, Augustus made provision to pass with an army over into Britain, and was come forward upon his journey into Gallia Celtica or, as we may say, into these hither parts of France.

But here receiving advertisements that the Pannonians, which inhabited the country now called Hungary, and the Dalmatians, whom now we call Slavonians, had rebelled, he thought it best first to subdue those rebels near home rather than to seek new countries and leave such in hazard whereof he had present possession. And so, turning his power against the Pannonians and Dalmatians, he left off for a time the wars of Britain. . . . But whether this controversy, which appeareth to fall forth betwixt the Britons and Augustus, was occasioned by Cymbeline or some other prince of the Britons, I have not to avouch. For that by our writers it is reported that Cymbeline, being brought up in Rome and knighted in the court of Augustus, ever showed himself a friend to the Romans, and chiefly was loath to break with them because[2] the youth of the Briton nation should not be deprived of the benefit to be trained and brought up among the Romans; whereby they might learn both to behave themselves like civil[3] men and to attain to the knowledge of feats of war.

[33] But whether for this respect or for that it pleased the almighty God so to dispose the minds of men at that present, not only the Britons but in manner all other nations were contented to be obedient to the Roman Empire. That this was true in the Britons, it is evident enough by Strabo's words, which are in effect as followeth.

2 So that. 3 Educated.

At this present (saith he) certain princes of Britain, procuring by ambassadors and dutiful demeanors the amity of the Emperor Augustus, have offered in the Capitol unto the gods presents or gifts, and have ordained the whole isle in a manner to be appertinent, proper, and familiar to the Romans. They are burdened with sore customs which they pay for wares, either to be sent forth into Gallia or brought from thence, which are commonly ivory vessels, shears, ouches[4] or earrings, and other conceits[5] made of amber and glasses, and suchlike manner of merchandise. So that now there is no need of any army or garrison of men-of-war to keep the isle, for there needeth not past one legion of footmen, or some wing of horsemen, to gather up and receive the tribute. . . .

Guiderius, the first son of Cymbeline (of whom Harrison saith nothing), began his reign in the seventeenth year after the incarnation of Christ. This Guiderius, being a man of stout courage,[6] gave occasion of breach of peace betwixt the Britons and Romans, denying to pay them tribute and procuring the people to new insurrections, which by one mean or other made open rebellion, as Gyldas saith.

* * *

[154][7] From thence the army of the Danes passed through Angus unto the river of Tay, all the people of the countries by which they marched fleeing afore them. King Kenneth [of Scotland] at the same time lay at Stirling, where, hearing of these grievous news, he determined forthwith to raise his people and to go against his enemies. . . .

[155] The Danes, being backed with the mountain, were constrained to leave the same and with all speed to come forward upon their enemies, that by joining, they might avoid the danger of the Scottishmen's arrows and darts. By this means therefore they came to hand strokes, in manner before the sign was given on either part to the battle. The fight was cruel on both sides; and nothing hindered the Scots so much as going about to cut off the heads of the Danes, ever as they might overcome them.

4 Brooches. 5 Fancy articles. 6 Brave spirit. 7 Vol. 2, *History of Scotland*.

Which manner being noted of the Danes, and perceiving that there was no hope of life but in victory, they rushed forth with such violence upon their adversaries that first the right and then after the left wing of the Scots was constrained to retire and flee back, the middleward[8] stoutly yet keeping their ground; but the same stood in such danger, being now left naked on the sides, that the victory must needs have remained with the Danes had not a renewer of the battle come in time by the appointment (as is to be thought) of almighty God.

For as it chanced, there was in the next field at the same time an husbandman, with two of his sons busy about his work, named Hay; a man strong and stiff in making and shape of body but endued with a valiant courage [5.3.15]. This Hay, beholding the King with the most part of the nobles fighting with great valiancy in the middleward, now destitute of the wings and in great danger to be oppressed by the great violence of his enemies, caught a ploughbeam in his hand and, with the same exhorting his sons to do the like, hasted toward the battle, there to die rather amongst other in defense of his country than to remain alive after the discomfiture, in miserable thralldom and bondage, of the cruel and most unmerciful enemies. There was near to the place of the battle a long lane fenced on the sides with ditches and walls made of turf, through the which the Scots which fled were beaten down by the enemies on heaps.

Here Hay with his sons supposing they might best stay the flight, placed themselves overthwart the lane, beat them back whom they met fleeing, and spared neither friend nor foe; but down they went, all such as came within their reach, wherewith divers hardy personages cried unto their fellows to return back unto the battle, for there was a new power of Scottishmen come to their succors by whose aid the victory might be easily obtained of their most cruel adversaries the Danes. Therefore might they choose whether they would be slain of their own fellows coming to their aid, or to return again to fight with the enemies. The Danes, being here stayed in the lane by the great

8 Main body of soldiers.

valiancy of the father and the sons, thought verily there had been some great succors of Scots come to the aid of their King and, thereupon, ceasing from further pursuit, fled back in great disorder unto the other of their fellows fighting with the middleward of the Scots.

The Scots also that before was chased, being encouraged herewith, pursued the Danes unto the place of the battle right fiercely. Whereupon Kenneth, perceiving his people to be thus recomforted, and his enemies partly abashed,[9] called upon his men to remember their duties; and now, sith their adversaries' hearts began (as they might perceive) to faint, he willed them to follow upon them manfully, which if they did he assured them that the victory undoubtedly should be theirs. The Scots, encouraged with the King's words, laid about them so earnestly that in the end the Danes were constrained to forsake the field, and the Scots, eagerly pursuing in the chase, made great slaughter of them as they fled. This victory turned highly to the praise of the Scottish nobility, the which, fighting in the middleward, bore still the brunt of the battle, continuing manfully therein even to the end. But Hay, who in such wise (as is before mentioned) stayed them that fled, causing them to return again to the field, deserved immortal fame and commendation, for by his means chiefly was the victory achieved. And therefore, on the morrow after, when the spoil of the field and of the enemies' camp (which they had left void) should be divided, the chiefest part was bestowed on him and his two sons, by consent of all the multitude; the residue being divided amongst the soldiers and men-of-war, according to the ancient custom used amongst this nation.

9 Put to confusion.

Commentaries

NORTHROP FRYE

from *A Natural Perspective*

Cymbeline, a play that might have been subtitled "Much Ado About Everything," is the apotheosis of the problem comedies: it combines the *Much Ado* theme of the slandered heroine, the *All's Well* theme of the expulsion of the hero's false friend, the *Measure for Measure* theme of the confusion and clarifying of government, and many others. There are even some curious echoes of names from *Much Ado:* in *Cymbeline* we have Sicilius Leonatus betrothed to Imogen, whose name is Innogen in Shakespeare's sources; in *Much Ado* we have Leonato, Governor of Messina in Sicily, whose wife's name, though she has no speaking part, is Innogen. The former name goes on echoing in *The Winter's Tale* as Leontes, King of Sicilia. The repetition may mean very little in itself, but we notice in the romances a technique of what might be called spatial

From *A Natural Perspective: The Development of Shakespearean Comedy and Romance,* by Northrop Frye. New York: Columbia University Press, 1965, pp. 65–70. Reprinted by permission of the publisher.

anachronism, in which Mediterranean and Atlantic settings
seem to be superposed on top of each other, as Bermudan
imagery is superposed on the island in *The Tempest*. In
particular, there is a convention, referred to in the Prologue to Jonson's *Sad Shepherd* and prominent in *Comus*
and *Lycidas,* of mixing British with Sicilian and Arcadian
imagery in the pastoral.

The same technique of superposition is used temporally
as well, binding together primitive Wales, Roman Britain,
and Italian Rome. *Cymbeline* has at least a token connection with the history plays of some significance. History
is a prominent genre in Shakespeare until *Henry V,* when
it seems to disappear and revive only in the much suspected *Henry VIII* at the end of the canon. Yet the history
of Britain to Shakespeare's audience began with the Trojan
War, the setting of *Troilus and Cressida,* and included the
story of Lear as well as the story of Macbeth. Even *Hamlet* is dimly linked with the period of Danish ascendancy
over England. Alternating with these plays of a Britain
older than King John are the Roman or Plutarchan plays,
dealing with what, again, to Shakespeare's audience was
the history of a cousin nation, another descendant of Troy.
In *Cymbeline* the theme of reconciliation between the two
Trojan nations is central, as though it were intended to
conclude the double series started by *Troilus and Cressida.*

The reason for the choice of the theme may be partly
that Cymbeline was king of Britain at the time of Christ.
The sense of a large change in human fortunes taking
place off-stage has to be read into *Cymbeline,* and as a
rule reading things into Shakespeare in the light of some
external information is a dubious practice. Still, we notice
the curiously oracular jailer, who speaks for a world that
knows of no other world, and yet can say: "I would we
were all of one mind, and one mind good." We notice,
too, the word "peace" at the end of the play, and the
way that the promise to pay tribute to Augustus fits into
that emperor's decree that all the world should be taxed,
the decree that begins the story of the birth of Christ. But
Cymbeline is not, to put it mildly, a historical play: it is
pure folk tale, featuring a cruel stepmother with her loutish

son, a calumniated maiden, lost princes brought up in a cave by a foster father, a ring of recognition that works in reverse, villains displaying false trophies of adultery and faithful servants displaying equally false trophies of murder, along with a great firework display of dreams, prophecies, signs, portents, and wonders.

What strikes one at once about the play is the extraordinary blindness of the characters in it. Imogen begins her journey to Milford Haven by saying:

> I see before me, man: nor here, nor here,
> Nor what ensues, but have a fog in them,
> That I cannot look through.

Lucius, after the battle he was so confident of winning has gone so awry, says:

> For friends kill friends, and the disorder's such
> As war were hoodwinked

and the jailer tells Posthumus how little he knows of where he is going. Posthumus replies that "none want eyes to direct them the way I am going, but such as wink and will not use them." Yet Posthumus himself has believed an even sillier story than Claudio does in *Much Ado*. The crafty Queen wastes her energies trying to teach Cloten the subtleties of courtship; Belarius tries to persuade his adopted sons to be disillusioned about a world they have never seen. The word "election," implying free choice, is used several times, but no one's choice seems very well considered; the word "note," meaning distinction or prestige, also echoes, but distinctions are difficult to establish when "Reverence,/ The angel of the world" is compelled to focus on the idiot Cloten, stepson of the weak and deluded Cymbeline. In *Cymbeline,* as in all the romances, there is a scaling down of the human perspective. Posthumus is peevishly and querulously jealous, he is no Othello; the Queen is squalidly unscrupulous, and is no Lady Macbeth.

Imogen is by long odds the most intelligent character in the play, and Imogen throughout is surrounded by a kind of atmospheric pressure of unconsciousness. The emotional climaxes of the play are the two great songs of the awakening and the laying to rest of Imogen, and in neither of them has she any notion of the context. The aubade is sung to her indifferent ear by the agency of Cloten after she has unknowingly spent a night with Iachimo; the obsequy is sung to her unconscious body by two boys whom she does not know to be her brothers while the headless Cloten is being laid beside her in the clothes of Posthumus. We feel in *Pericles* that Marina's magical chastity will get her safely through the peril of the brothel, but at least she knows it is a peril: in other words, there is much less dramatic irony in *Pericles* than in *Cymbeline*. The ironic complications of *Cymbeline* are in themselves, of course, the customary conventions of pastoral romance, where the simple childlike pleasure of knowing more than the characters do is constantly appealed to by the author. But there also seems to be a strong emphasis on the misdirection of human will, which culminates in the prison scene.

In this scene a number of characters appear who are new to us but are older than the action of the play. They speak in a naïve doggerel verse not unlike in its dramatic effect to the verse of Gower in *Pericles,* and like it they are a sign that we are being confronted with something traditional and archaic. They are ghosts from the world of the dead, who have been invisible spectators of the action and now come to speak for us as spectators, impeaching the wisdom of Jupiter for allowing things to get in such a muddle. Jupiter tells them what, in fact, we have been seeing all along, that a skillful and quite benevolent design is being woven of the action despite all the efforts of human folly to destroy it. This scene is soon followed by the great contrapuntal tour de force of the recognition scene, when the truth is torn out of a score of mysteries, disguisings, and misunderstandings; when out of all the confusion of action a very simple conclusion is reached, and one which sounds very like peace on earth, good will toward men. The difference between *Cymbeline* and the earlier problem comedies, then, is that the counter-problem force, so to speak, which brings a festive conclusion out of all the mistakes of the characters, is explicitly associated with the working of a divine providence, here called Jupiter. Jupiter is as much a projection of the author's craftsmanship as the Duke in *Measure for Measure:* that is, the difference between *Cymbeline* and the problem comedies is not that *Cymbeline* is adding a religious allegory to the dramatic action. What it is adding to the dramatic action is the primitive mythical dimension which is only implicit in the problem comedies. *Cymbeline* is not a more religious play than *Much Ado:* it is a more academic play, with a greater technical interest in dramatic structure.

BERTRAND EVANS

from *Shakespeare's Comedies*

Though winds and waves, tempests and seas are absent from it, the world of *Cymbeline,* too, presents a lasting storm; what is more, it offers even less assurance than was ours during *Pericles* that the storm will ever blow to a happy ending. Whereas in *Pericles,* through such signs as the billow that saves Thaisa, we sensed a force, blurred but benign, protecting the royal family, and knew during the latter half of the action that Thaisa and Marina were merely lost, not dead—in *Cymbeline* we must scrutinize the face of the universe intently in order to discern the slightest sign of comfort. In the wisdom of the physician Cornelius and the loyalty of the servant Pisanio we have signs that goodness and truth at least have allies; but these are mainly bystanders to the torrent that sweeps Posthumus and Imogen along, and though they mean well we cannot suppose that their utmost will prevail against the great odds. Moreover, even as late as IV. iii, when Pisanio hopefully ventures that "Fortune brings in some boats that are not steer'd," we lack evidence that any "outside" intelligence, for good or ill, watches over man; and Pisanio's comment, besides coming later in the action, is not even so reassuring as the giant billow of *Pericles*. We do not learn until Posthumus's vision in v. iv, when Jupiter

From *Shakespeare's Comedies*, by Bertrand Evans. Oxford: The Clarendon Press, 1960, pp. 247-8, 252-8, 277-8, 283-9. Reprinted by permission of the publisher.

claims the credit for the conduct and control of everything—

> Be not with mortal accidents opprest;
> No care of yours it is; you know 'tis ours.
> Whom best I love I cross; to make my gift,
> The more delay'd, delighted. (v. iv. 99–102.)

—that any hand holds the rudder of man's ship. In this respect, then, *Cymbeline* resembles *Pericles* but goes much farther in the same direction—away from the old, insistent reassurance, toward fear that all can never be well.

But though the worlds represented are thus alike, the workmanship of representation differs as ineptness from virtuosity. On the evidence of *Pericles* and *Troilus and Cressida* alone, it would be necessary to conclude that when Shakespeare attempted to depict a world lacking design and purpose, uncontrolled by either man's will or external force, his own art caught the disorder of the world represented. *Cymbeline* is the contradiction of this evidence: as an exhibition of technical skill in the management of the dramatic devices he had favored from the first, it has no equal. *The Merry Wives of Windsor,* which put on an earlier dazzling display, is only a finger exercise beside *Cymbeline*.

To master the representation of his new world, Shakespeare called on all the old devices—but especially on those most useful in creating and exploiting discrepant awarenesses.[1] Whereas in *Pericles* the high proportion of scenes in which we hold advantage resulted mainly from use of extra-dramatic features, in *Cymbeline* it results entirely from dramatic devising. In managing the discrepant awarenesses of this one play, Shakespeare calls upon all the means he had found useful from *The Comedy of Errors* through *Measure for Measure*. As a result we hold advantage over some or all participants in twenty-three of twenty-seven scenes; advantage at some time over every

---

1 That is, dramatic ironies; compare Evans, p. vii: "Between the awareness that packs our minds and the ignorance that afflicts the participants lies a crucial—and highly exploitable—discrepancy" [editor's note].

named person; and simultaneous, multiple advantages over all persons in many scenes.

These facts would not alone make *Cymbeline* exceptional: even in *The Comedy of Errors* we held advantage in all scenes except the first and over all persons except Aemilia, and in all of the mature romantic comedies multiplicity of discrepancies created by multiple dramatic devices, and multiplicity of effects resulting from exploitation of these discrepancies are the rule rather than the exception. What does make *Cymbeline* extraordinary is at once the fantastic complexity of its uses of discrepant awarenesses and the consummate skill with which its intricacies are managed: with greater finality than does any other play, it evinces Shakespeare's mastery of infinitely complex art. From the first his methods made heavy demands on our minds in requiring them to accept, hold, and actively use the advantages provided; but the tasks imposed by our advantages in *Cymbeline* are unprecedented. Here the uses of awareness are fairly gymnastic; our awareness is compelled through a harder course of exercises than ever. From the point of view of the creation, maintenance, and exploitation of discrepant awarenesses —considered both quantitatively and artistically—*Cymbeline* is Shakespeare's greatest achievement.

* * *

. . . Iachimo is unique outside of tragedy—a villain whose vantage-point is above that of other participants, and over whom we ourselves have no advantage. In earlier plays some benevolent force has stood guard over villainy, eyeing its passes, ready to check it at need. The highest awareness has always belonged to good people. Don John of *Much Ado,* Shylock of *The Merchant of Venice,* Angelo of *Measure for Measure* are prevented not only from doing harm but even from appearing really dangerous; at last, because of Prospero, the monsters of *The Tempest* are pitiful even in their most swaggering moments. But no force—*to our knowledge while action continues*—watches Iachimo as Vincentio and Prospero watch Angelo and Caliban.

The scene (I. iv) of Posthumus and Iachimo's wager on Imogen's virtue gives us advantage over the heroine when she next appears; henceforth she is never again mistress of her situation and partner in our awareness. No heroine in the comedies is cast in such a role—kept unaware so long, ignorant of so many secrets, abused by so many practices, endangered from so many quarters. Only Isabella of *Measure for Measure* spends nearly as long in ignorance—but the cases are not comparable, for the fact unknown to Isabella is the most comforting in her world, the fact that her friendly "friar" is the all-powerful Duke. Beside Imogen's, the unknowing moments of earlier heroines seem blessed, brief, trivial: those of Viola, unaware that Sebastian lives, and that the fierce duellist confronting her is a great booby who wants only to make peace or run away; of Hero, unaware that cruel denunciation waits at the altar—but unaware also that her name is already in process of being cleared; even of Marina—after she has escaped the assassin's blow—unaware that forces of her "lasting storm" are converging on general reunion. If much that Imogen does not know is better than she supposes, yet much also is worse—and, worst of all, uncertain. "I see before me, man," she says ecstatically to Pisanio, setting off for Milford-Haven to meet her banished husband; "nor here, nor here,/Nor what ensues, but have a fog in them/That I cannot look through." But in truth she cannot see even straight ahead: not only will Posthumus not be at Milford-Haven, but he has ordered her to be murdered on the road.

But Imogen is a deeply unaware heroine only because she is cast into an uncertain universe, too large for its puny inhabitants, where a lasting storm whirs friend from friend and all events "have a fog in them/That I cannot look through." Her unawareness is itself a sign of the fearsome world; for Imogen is anything but naïve, anything but naturally incompetent. She has no trace of that congenital affliction of persons who need no deceiving to be deceived —Bottom, Dogberry, Aguecheek, Malvolio: yet not even one of these remains so long ignorant of so much. The fact is that she is keen and capable. She looks through and through the Queen and Cloten, and her analysis of the situation in which we first find her and Posthumus is brilliant; so is her analysis of her circumstances after Posthumus has gone:

> A father cruel, and a step-dame false;
> A foolish suitor to a wedded lady
> That hath her husband banish'd. . . .
>   (i. vi. 1–3.)

If she lacks the aggressive self-sufficiency of Rosalind, yet she would have had no difficulty managing Rosalind's world. She would have managed Viola's tangled affairs with far less than Viola's distress. She would have failed at Helena's task—but, then, she would never have wished to succeed at it! She is approximately as able as Marina, who talks brothel-keepers into giving her more congenial work, converts brothel habitués to church-goers, and so far transforms one of these as to make him a proper husband. Neither Imogen nor Marina shows a decline in heroinely competence; *they are lost in their worlds only because their worlds are as they are.* Isabella of *Measure for Measure,* whose perspective is less true than Imogen's and whose capability of dealing with life is inferior, is never so lost and abused as Imogen; but her wicked world has Vincentio, without whom she would have either to escape to the nunnery or be destroyed. Imogen strives alone in a world which has at least as dire a need for a Vincentio, and in which there seems to be none.

It is certainly not a sign of incompetence that Imogen falls victim to Iachimo's practice. She is quick to recognize and denounce his first attempt, when he makes a false report of Posthumus's behavior in Rome and urges her to reciprocate:

> I dedicate myself to your sweet pleasure,
> More noble than that runagate to your bed,
> And will continue fast to your affection,
> Still close as sure.
>   (i. vi. 136–9.)

"Away!" replies Imogen; "I do condemn mine ears that have/So long attended thee." Both her virtue and her rare acumen speak here. There was every cause for her to be taken in by Iachimo's report: she knows nothing of the wager; she has perfect faith in Iachimo, who comes introduced by Posthumus himself as "one of the noblest note, to•whose kindnesses I am most infinitely tied"; she has heard of such Italian temptations as might have overcome her own or any husband, as she shows later in referring to "Some jay of Italy/Whose mother was her painting."

But more than all is the reason of Iachimo himself, with his subtle persuasiveness, the representation of which excels the best of the kind that Shakespeare had achieved or would achieve again. Iachimo works like Iago, seeming preoccupied with his own musings while, as though unintentionally, he teases on the mind of the victim; thus, with an apparent disregard of Imogen, as though she should not hear, he debates with himself how Posthumus could ever have been induced to change mistresses:

> It cannot be i' th' eye, for apes and monkeys
> 'Twixt two such shes would chatter this way and
> Condemn with mows the other; nor i' th' judgement,
> For idiots in this case of favour would
> Be wisely definite; nor i' th' appetite;
> Sluttery to such neat excellence oppos'd
> Should make desire vomit emptiness,
> Not so allur'd to feed.
>
> (i. vi. 39–46.)

Not at all the meanest, Iachimo is the smoothest of Shakespeare's villains. Iago's front of a plain, blunt man is adequate to deceive Othello and everyone else in Venice and Cyprus; Iachimo's front is silken smooth, his persuasive charm irresistible. By all odds his is the finest language in the play. Shakespeare gives him the poet's tongue and the artist's eye: "On her left breast,/A mole cinque-spotted, like the crimson drops/I' th' bottom of a cowslip." The fifty lines he speaks while Imogen lies asleep, "her sense but as a monument,/Thus in a chapel lying," have a hypnotic fascination beyond any other passage in Shakespeare. It does not at all diminish Imogen that she is briefly spellbound by this villain's tongue; she is the more remarkable for having the strength to break the spell: "Away! I do condemn mine ears that have/So long attended thee."

Shakespeare does not with Iachimo, as with Iago, cause him to expose to us in advance the devices of his cunning mind—and there is reason. Imogen's intellectual prestige is thus further protected: when she consents to receive the trunk in her own chamber "And pawn mine honour" for the safety of its contents, we, too, are ignorant that the contents will be Iachimo himself. Perhaps we may guess; but the dramatist gives us no help in guessing. When his first attempt has failed, we have no way of knowing that Iachimo will try again. Never shrewder in all his shrewd management of our awareness than now, the dramatist gives him no private word with us, but allows us to hear exactly what Imogen hears:

> *Iach.* I have spoke this to know if your affiance
>   Were deeply rooted, and shall make your lord,
>   That which he is, new o'er; and he is one
>   The truest manner'd, such a holy witch
>   That he enchants societies into him;
>   Half all men's hearts are his.
> *Imo.*   You make amends.
> *Iach.* He sits 'mongst men like a descended god;
>   He hath a kind of honour sets him off,
>   More than a mortal seeming. Be not angry,
>   Most mighty princess, that I have adventur'd
>   To try your taking of a false report; which hath
>   Honour'd with confirmation your great judgement
>   In the election of a sir so rare,
>   Which you know cannot err.
>   (i. vi. 163–75.)

Iachimo is cunning past men's thought: though we know of the wager, whereas Imogen does not, we have no cause to doubt that he has forfeited. When he turns as with an afterthought—"I had almost forgot"—to the next piece of business, it is made to appear *to us as to Imogen* that his new request has no possible connection with what has just passed. He does not immediately mention a trunk, but describes with fine circumstantial detail—not neglecting, as if incidentally, to lavish more praise on Posthumus—the occasion of his journey and the character of his purchase:

> 'Tis plate of rare device, and jewels
> Of rich and exquisite form, their values great;
> And I am something curious, being strange,
> To have them in safe stowage. May it please you
> To take them in protection?

(i. vi. 189–93.)

"I will keep them/In my bedchamber," says Imogen, and then Iachimo: "They are in a trunk,/Attended by my men." There is no more discussion of the matter, the subject being suddenly changed to the question of Iachimo's return to Rome. Only at the tag end of the scene is the trunk mentioned again—and now without reference to the bedchamber. Thus, the last idea left in our minds is of no possible trick of Iachimo's, but of Imogen's responsibility to guard the plate and jewels: ". . . it shall safe be kept,/And truly yielded you." If we have any anxious thought, it is only that she may somehow fail in this responsibility.

Since we are not to see Iachimo again until he emerges from the trunk beside Imogen's bed, we should ordinarily expect him to linger at the end of this scene in order to explain his intention. But he leaves with Imogen, without so much as a smirk for our advisement. The omission contradicts Shakespeare's method in every play until now. Usually we would have been advised explicitly even earlier —when Iachimo seemed to give up his hope of winning the wager—that he would shift from an honest test of Imogen's virtue to some treacherous device; next, as he continued to talk with Imogen about the plate and the jewels, the outline of his device would have taken definite shape in our minds; next, at the conclusion of the scene with Imogen, he would have remained for a moment to tell us plainly that he would enter the bedchamber in the trunk. There would have been even more: the bedchamber scene would not open as it now does—Imogen reading in bed, attended by her maid, the trunk resting to one side —but with the trunk being brought in, the bearers leaving, Iachimo then lifting the lid to glance around and speak a word to us: all this before Imogen should enter and go to bed. There would have followed Imogen's conversation with the maid—probably with some ironic allusions to the trunk and its precious contents—and then sleep, and only thereafter the emergence of Iachimo.

As the scenes are actually devised, however, not only is the usual care to make assurance double sure omitted, but the least suggestion that Iachimo will enter in the trunk is avoided. We may have guessed the truth, of course, or even have worked it out by reasoning that Iachimo's story of his mission to France to buy a present for the Emperor must be false, since Posthumus, whom he mentions as one of the contributors, would not have joined a group with Iachimo as "the factor for the rest." Yet so finely detailed is Iachimo's account of the mission, the jewels, and the "plate of rare device" that even after the incident is past we may wonder, at one level of consciousness, just where Iachimo temporarily hid these jewels and plate while he occupied their place in the trunk during the night!

The point, in any event, is that Shakespeare has not told us what to expect. He has not even told us that Iachimo is a villain; we cannot know that he is dishonorable until he emerges from the trunk. Though the wager he proposed to Posthumus was insulting, yet Posthumus accepted it— and Posthumus is a paragon. His first test of Imogen, though deceitful, is quite within the terms of the wager, hence no proof of villainy. When his first attempt fails, we have been given no reason to doubt that, finding Imogen's virtue so far incorruptible as to make further trial absurd, he simply abandons his attempt to win Posthumus's ring. We have been given no reason to know, therefore, while Imogen lies reading, attended by her maid, that the trunk beside the bed contains other than jewels and plate. We have been given no reason to suppose but that Iachimo lies in his own room, sleeping or contemplating his return to Rome and his admission of failure.

By denying us the usual advance notice, Shakespeare prevents our gaining advantage over his heroine during the part of the action which is most vital for what follows. We are less likely to think her naïve in being deceived by the trunk when we ourselves have been deceived. It is the perfection of Shakespeare's management of the awarenesses during this central incident that he has at once made it convincing that Iachimo's trick should succeed, and avoided dimming Imogen's heroinely lustre. Once Iachimo has gained access to the chamber, the problem of protecting Imogen from seeming too easily "taken in" vanishes—for she is now asleep, "her sense but as a monument,/Thus in a chapel lying," while Iachimo greedily—yet somehow worshipfully, with an aesthete's relish—stores his mind with the evidence of precise detail. In short, Imogen is a truly great person, as brilliant as Rosalind and Portia, even more than worthy of the paragon Posthumus, and Shakespeare has taken pains to keep us in that opinion of her. We gain advantage over her only when and because she is asleep.

* * *

For where is Iachimo? From nothing that Shakespeare has told, shown, or hinted since II. iv can we think other than that the partner in our black secret has vanished from the earth, leaving no means by which truth can be exposed.
. . .

And yet none of it is so: our facts contradict her beliefs at every point. Moreover—again as in *Pericles*—it is in this darkest moment just at the ending of Imogen's soliloquy—

> O!
> Give colour to my pale cheek with thy blood,
> That we the horrider may seem to those
> Which chance to find us. O, my lord, my lord!
> (*Falls on the body.*)
> (IV. ii. 329–32.)

that we catch our first glimpse of dawn through a sudden
sign of a kind that has been denied until now. Says the
First Captain to Lucius, as they approach the spot where
Imogen lies with headless Cloten:

> . . . gentlemen of Italy, most willing spirits
> That promise noble service; and they come
> Under the conduct of bold Iachimo. . . .
>
> (IV. ii. 338–40.)

"Bold Iachimo": the bare mention is nearly worth actual
sight. While Iachimo was lost in silence an element indispensable to the clearing of multiple errors was missing;
notification of his return from oblivion is notification that
all can yet be well. This hint of hope comes just after
Imogen, in a gesture marking total defeat, has fallen
upon the headless body and daubed her face with its
blood.

* * *

. . . It is a fact that until v. iv Shakespeare has exhibited
only an uncontrolled universe the character of which is
summed up by Pisanio's statement in the last line of IV. iii:
"Fortune brings in some boats that are not steer'd." By
the time of this summation we have been shown some
inconclusive signs that the drift of events may be toward
a happy ending: the death of Cloten; the mention of the
imminent arrival in Britain of Iachimo; the report of the
Queen's illness. Finally, the summation is itself reassuring,
for surely, no matter what force or lack of force brings
them in, it is better that boats come in than that they be
lost.

But though these signs are reassuring, *they are only
signs of favorable chance*. There has been no hint of existence of any directing force: indeed, Pisanio's summation argues that there is none. So far as our awareness was
advised, the world of *Pericles,* too, until Act III, lacked a
controlling force; then the dramatist—plainly dissatisfied
with Gower's whim-directed universe—introduced the extraordinary billow that brought Thaisa's body to Cerimon,
and from that point on, by various means, implied the

existence of a benevolent intelligence behind the erstwhile
seemingly unruled winds and waves. Gower's world of the
first two acts of *Pericles* is extended through the first four
and a half acts of *Cymbeline*—with nothing even so inconclusive as an extraordinary billow to suggest that any
force is in control. Though we finally perceive an aus-
picious drift, yet we do so with the sense that things might
as easily go ill as well. Nevertheless, v. iii makes it plain
that *Cymbeline* could now end happily without the services
of a controlling force, for all the persons needed to dis-
entangle truth are assembled. The denouement of v. v, that
is to say, could follow immediately after v. iii, without
v. iv.

But a chance ending, for artistic if not philosophical
reasons, was manifestly intolerable to Shakespeare: always, everywhere, he must have a divinity—either within
or without man—that shapes the ends of action. Hence in
v. iv Jupiter advises us of what we could not have guessed
during the first four and a half acts—that the world of
Cymbeline has been under control all the while; says
Jupiter to the spirits of the four Leonati, Posthumus's kin:

> Be not with mortal accidents opprest;
> No care of yours it is; you know 'tis ours.
> Whom best I love I cross; to make my gift,
> The more delay'd, delighted. Be content;
> Your low-laid son our godhead will uplift.
> (v. iv. 99–103.)

This is more than a promise that all will be well: *it is an
assertion that all has been well all the while.* During those
four and a half acts when we feared that nobody knew the
troubles we saw, the action lay in fact in Jupiter's palm—
as that of *Measure for Measure* in Vincentio's and that of
The Tempest in Prospero's.

But the difference is vast: we knew at once about Vincentio and Prospero, and we were left ignorant of Jupiter.
So far as the dramatic effect during the first four and a half
acts is concerned, Jupiter had as well not have been, since
he was not in our awareness. Yet on the evidence of
Shakespeare's usual method, the reason for his introduc-

tion of Jupiter is apparent: he would not tolerate action that stumbles to one ending but could have stumbled to another. His means of avoiding an accidental ending is always some controlling force, mortal or immortal: a fairy king, a brilliant heroine in disguise, an all-powerful duke— or a Jupiter. The great question, then, is not why he introduced Jupiter, but why he left us unaware of him until the denouement.

A possible answer is that both *Pericles* and *Cymbeline* are deliberate experiments with the dramatic effects of uncertainty. This answer would make it appear that the dramatist toys with us during the first four and a half acts just as Jupiter toyed with Imogen and Posthumus, and for the same reason: "Whom best I love I cross; to make my gift,/The more delay'd, delighted." One formula, at least, is common to *Pericles* and *Cymbeline:* it is to make good people—Pericles, Thaisa, Marina; Cymbeline, Imogen, Posthumus—believe at first that they have suffered irreparable loss in an indifferent universe, and then to restore all. Applied to our own awareness, the formula is not quite so severe in these plays: though we are long denied the comforting knowledge that the world is benevolently controlled and are therefore subjected to the anxiety that comes of uncertainty, we are not made to believe that anyone has suffered irrecoverable loss. We know that death has not claimed Pericles' Thaisa and Marina, Imogen's Posthumus, or Posthumus's Imogen. But in the third romance, *The Winter's Tale,* as will be seen, the dramatist, *progressively deepening our anxiety* in the plays of the lasting storm, applies the same formula to our awareness as to that of Leontes: we, too, are made to believe that Hermione is dead. After reaching this extremity, Shakespeare returns to his old, habitual way: we are advised of Prospero immediately after the opening scene of *The Tempest,* and thereafter misgivings are impossible. If, therefore, the withholding of reassurance was a deliberate experiment, it was followed by quick, absolute repudiation. There are some objections to regarding it so, however, and there are other possible answers; but these must wait on the evidence of *The Winter's Tale* and *The Tempest.*

In any event, the introduction of Jupiter, however belated, serves unqualified notice that all now not only will
but must be, and in fact always has been, well. It thus
prevents the appearance of adventitious action running to
adventitious ending. It enables us to watch the tortuous
denouement with minds free from anxiety. From this point
of view it is an artistic masterstroke.

But it is also an artistic fraud. The fact is that at the
end of v. iii all lines of action have converged and all
elements needed for a happy ending have been assembled;
but more, it is a fact that to the denouement of v. v the
eagle-borne Jupiter of v. iv actually contributes nothing
but a riddling prophecy for the Soothsayer to interpret—
and even this comes late, after all the secrets have been
opened, and serves only to seem to prove Jupiter's earlier
claim that he knew and controlled all, all the while. It is
not Jupiter—nor is it Posthumus, to whom Jupiter appeared and on whose breast the prophetic tablet was laid
—*but the bright-eyed heroine herself* who, having glimpsed
a ring on the captive Iachimo's finger, finds her way up
through mountains of error to the truth. So Jupiter is an
artistic fraud—but perhaps the shrewdest in the plays.
For while he gives the look of intention to what would
otherwise seem accident, he actually does nothing, but
leaves the participants to find their own way. As *deus ex
machina* he is thus at once indispensable and superfluous.

The denouement, then, runs from v. iii to the end, with
Jupiter serving only as a reassuring illusion. This is Shakespeare's longest final scene, and all but the very first and
very last lines bustle with the exposure of secrets—for
the preceding acts have buried more truths more deeply
than in any other play. The opening of no other final
scene finds our awareness so laden with secrets; no other
finds the vision of so many participants so limited to small
corners and pockets. The *King* is ignorant (1) that the
Queen contrived the separation of Imogen and Posthumus
for her own and Cloten's gain; (2) that Imogen lives and
is present as the Roman page; (3) that the heroes who
rescued him are his sons and his old servant; (4) that
the prisoner he has handed over to the jailer is Posthumus;

(5) that this same prisoner was the fourth hero of the narrow lane. *Imogen* is ignorant (1) that both she and Posthumus were abused by Iachimo; (2) that Posthumus lives and is present; (3) that Pisanio was and is loyal; (4) that the rustics are her brothers; (5) that the drug given her by Pisanio was intended by the Queen to be fatal; (6) that she escaped death only by virtue of the physician's counter-practice. *Posthumus* is ignorant (1) that he and Imogen were abused by Iachimo; (2) that Pisanio deceived him with a false token of Imogen's death; (3) that Imogen is present as the Roman page; (4) that the mountaineers with whom he saved the kingdom are his brothers-in-law. *Arviragus* and *Guiderius* are ignorant (1) that they are princes; (2) that "Fidele" was their sister; (3) that she yet lives and is present as the Roman page; (4) that their heroic assistant in the battle of the narrow lane was their brother-in-law and that he is present now in Roman dress. *Belarius* is ignorant (1) that "Fidele" was sister to the King's sons; (2) that she is alive and present as the Roman page. *Iachimo* is ignorant that both his victims are present. *Lucius* is ignorant that his page is Cymbeline's daughter—and of all that led to her final masquerade. *Pisanio* is ignorant (1) that the drug given him by the Queen was meant to kill him; (2) that both his master and his mistress are present.

At the same time that each is ignorant of others' secrets, most participants are also either proprietors of current practices or secret-sharers of past practices that contributed to the present condition. Only Cymbeline and Lucius are denied the privilege of holding any secrets. *Cornelius* alone knows that the Queen—whose death and true character are quickly reported—intended murder, and that the drug with which he provided her was capable of producing only the appearance of death. *Iachimo* alone bears the secret of the "proofs" of Imogen's infidelity. *Pisanio* alone holds the secret of his deception of Posthumus in Imogen's "death," and of Cloten's practice in dressing himself as Posthumus. *Imogen* holds the secret of her own identity and of her former role as "Fidele." *Posthumus* holds the secret of his double masquerade—as the heroic Briton, and, just now, as the Roman prisoner. *Belarius* alone holds the secret of the rustic youths' identities. *Arviragus* and *Guiderius*, with Belarius, hold the secret of Cloten's disappearance. Such is the general disposition of awarenesses at the opening of the most elaborate final scene in Shakespeare. What is most remarkable is that, though the strands are many and marvellously intertwined, nothing snarls, and no loose end remains at last.

Jupiter being absent, no participant knows all that we know, but each fact of ours is known to some participant. Our vantage-point is perfect; as usual the denouement has nothing to expose to us. For us, then, the experience of the closing scene is that of witnessing the revelation of secrets that have been locked in our minds, and of observing the effects of their revelation upon the persons who have been ignorant of them and to whom they are of most concern; of being at hand when Imogen learns that Posthumus lives, when Posthumus learns that Imogen lives and is chaste, when Cymbeline learns that the heroes who saved his kingdom are his own sons and his son-in-law. The process of making everything known is extended and exploited as nowhere else in Shakespeare. The release of each secret accomplishes a welcome reduction, degree by degree, of the pressure that has been mounting in our minds since error first began to pile on error; one effect of the scene, thus, is the relief of overmuch understanding, painful because it has been unsharable.

From the first comedies Shakespeare has concentrated exploitative efforts upon two great moments: *that in which ignorance has achieved greatest depth and universality, and that in which persons who have acted in ignorance learn of their errors.* *Cymbeline* surpasses all other plays in the celebration of these contrasting moments—the first, already examined, "Fidele's" funeral and Imogen's soliloquy over "Posthumus's" body; and the second, now, the explosion of secrets in the closing scene. Never one to surrender a secret until he has exhausted its potentiality, Shakespeare relieves pressures on our awareness only after a last intensification which raises them to the bursting-point. Thus when Iachimo has told how he destroyed

Posthumus's faith in Imogen, the hero advances, identifies himself, curses Iachimo, and falls to berating himself for the Imogen he supposes dead. There is wilful cruelty to us in this last-minute exploitation of the space between Posthumus's ignorance and our awareness that Imogen stands within arm's length! Posthumus's speech raises the pressure to where the pain of the unsharable becomes excruciating. But Shakespeare is not yet through with us. Since the pressure can be raised no further by verbal exploitation, he raises it by physical action to the level of bursting:

> *Post.*   Imogen,
>   Imogen, Imogen!
> *Imo.*   Peace, my lord; hear, hear—
> *Post.* Shall's have a play of this? Thou scornful page,
>   There lie thy part.   (*Striking her; she falls.*)
>   (v. v. 226–9.)

This is a final turn of the screw. The physical blow, the ultimate expression of Posthumus's unawareness, is followed instantly by relief, with Pisanio's "O, my Lord Posthumus!/You ne'er kill'd Imogen till now."

This effective, if cruel, formula the dramatist repeats in yielding the last great secret. Guiderius grandly announces that it was he who slew Cloten: "I have spoke it, and I did it." Cymbeline, who earlier had knighted Belarius and the unknown youths for their heroic stand that saved his kingdom, now condemns Guiderius: "Thou'rt dead." Through forty lines, from Guiderius's confession until Belarius makes known the youths' royalty, Shakespeare sustains the painful pressure of our awareness by exploiting the King's unawareness that he has condemned his own son. Though no blow like that which felled Imogen is struck, yet physical action again pushes pressure to the bursting-point when Guiderius is roughly seized by guards. This time it is Belarius whose word releases the pressure: "Let his arms alone;/They were not born for bondage."

William Shakespeare
and
John Fletcher

THE TWO
NOBLE KINSMEN

Edited by Clifford Leech

Contents

Introduction

The Two Noble Kinsmen was first published in a quarto edition of 1634, with statements on its title page that it had been "Presented at the Blackfriers by the Kings Maiesties servants, with great applause" and that it was "Written by the memorable Worthies of their time; Mr. *John Fletcher,* and Mr. *William Shakespeare,* Gent." The publisher was John Waterson, a reputable figure who brought out other plays belonging to the King's Men, the company with which Shakespeare and Fletcher had been intimately associated. Although in 1646, when Waterson assigned to Humphrey Moseley his rights in the play, it was included with two others as simply the work of "Mr. Flesher," there is an immediately strong case for accepting the title page's statement of authorship. If Waterson were looking for a way of attracting custom, it would have been at least as effective in 1634 to attribute the play to Beaumont and Fletcher. Moreover, it appears that the manuscript from which he printed had been used in the theater itself[1] and that Waterson had bought it from the players in the normal way of business. And we shall see that the probable date of composition and first performance was 1613, when we have other evidence that Shakespeare and Fletcher were working in close association.

It is true, on the other hand, that Heminges and Condell did not include *The Two Noble Kinsmen* in the Shakespeare Folio of 1623, where in the preliminary address *"To the great Variety of Readers"* there is an implication that all of Shakespeare's plays were being published in the collection. But it appears that *Timon of Athens* was not origi-

1 See Textual Note, pp. 177–80.

nally included in their plans for the volume, and we know that *Troilus and Cressida,* probably through difficulties over copyright, was almost left out. And they did omit *Pericles.* That *The Two Noble Kinsmen* was included in the 1679 Folio of "Beaumont and Fletcher" plays is also not substantial evidence against Shakespeare's part-authorship, for that volume brought together many plays in which Fletcher collaborated with various dramatists of his time, the linking of his name with Beaumont's on the title page (as in the earlier Beaumont and Fletcher Folio of 1647) being merely a tribute to the brief association of the two men which laid the basis for Fletcher's fame and established a mode of dramatic writing which was long influential in the English theater.

Nevertheless, the publishing history of the play belongs far more with Beaumont and Fletcher than with Shakespeare. It has been regularly included in collected editions of Beaumont and Fletcher since their Folio of 1679, from Tonson's edition of 1711 to the Cambridge edition of Arnold Glover and A. R. Waller of 1905–12. It did not appear in a collected Shakespeare until 1841, when Charles Knight (who believed that Fletcher's collaborator here was George Chapman) yielded to the extent of including it in a volume of "Doubtful Plays" appended to his Pictorial Shakespeare. By then, though dissentient voices were not infrequently raised, the case for Shakespeare's part-authorship had become more than formidable. Pope, in his Shakespeare of 1725, thought the play contained "more of our author than some of those which have been received as genuine," and Lamb and Coleridge and De Quincey were all convinced of Shakespeare's presence, though Hazlitt and Shelley could find nothing of it. William Spalding, however, in his *Letter on Shakspere's Authorship of The Two Noble Kinsmen* (Edinburgh, 1833; reprinted in the *Transactions of the New Shakspere Society,* 1874), Samuel Hickson in his article "The Shares of Shakspere and Fletcher in The Two Noble Kinsmen'" (*Westminster Review,* 1847; reprinted in the *Transactions of the New Shakspere Society,* 1874), and above all Harold Littledale in the introduction to his edition of the play for the New Shakspere Society (1876–85) brought the techniques of nineteenth-century scholarship to bear on the problem and, though they differed to some extent in assigning to the two dramatists their respective shares, they left little doubt in most readers' minds that here we have a collaboration between the leading dramatist of the King's Men and the writer who succeeded him in that role in 1613.

Yet it is still exceptional to find *The Two Noble Kinsmen* in a collected edition of Shakespeare's plays. Most of its readers during this century have come to know it through its inclusion in C. F. Tucker Brooke's *The Shakespeare Apocrypha* (Oxford, 1908). G. L. Kittredge has it in his *Complete Works of Shakespeare* (Boston, 1936); it is planned for inclusion in the "New Cambridge" edition; and it is now presented as part of the Signet Shakespeare.

The elder dramatist's authorship is commonly recognized most surely in the first and fifth acts, particularly in the first three scenes of Act I and the first, third, and fourth scenes of Act V: that is, the solemn approach of the three Queens to Theseus on his wedding day, the conversation of Palamon and Arcite while they are still in Thebes, the scene where Emilia and Hippolyta talk of friendship, the invocations addressed to Mars and Venus and Diana, and the conclusion of the whole story in Arcite's victory and death. In addition, Shakespeare has been generally found in the opening lines of II.i, where the Jailer's Daughter makes her first appearance, and in III.i, where the escaped Palamon meets the disguised Arcite. In the rest of the play there are frequent echoes of other plays by Shakespeare: the madness of the Jailer's Daughter has obvious associations with Ophelia's, and in the later pages of this Introduction it will be suggested that Fletcher for special purposes was drawing upon his intimate knowledge of his collaborator's work. If we accept the commonly held view of the two writers' shares (and there is little reason to be skeptical about it), it was Shakespeare who wrote the beginning and the ending and introduced all the major characters and strands of action.

But by the time this play was composed he may have been less regularly in attendance at the playhouse than formerly, and it seems likely enough that the final putting together of the manuscript was left to Fletcher. Indeed, more than one scholar has come to the conclusion that he made some insertions in the Shakespeare scenes.

It will be convenient to set out the probable authorship of the play's various scenes thus:

Prologue .... Fletcher?

Act I, sc. i–iii .... Shakespeare
     sc. iv–v .... Shakespeare?

Act II, sc. i (lines 1–59) .... Shakespeare
     sc. i (remainder), ii–v .... Fletcher

Act III, sc. i .... Shakespeare
     sc. ii–vi .... Fletcher

Act IV, sc. i–iii .... Fletcher

Act V, sc. i .... Shakespeare
     sc. ii .... Fletcher
     sc. iii–iv .... Shakespeare

Epilogue .... Fletcher?

The dividing of the play between Shakespeare and Fletcher has been worked out by scholars primarily on the basis of the stylistic differences between their writing. Certainly even a casual reading of the play will show that certain scenes have a complex, "knotted" verse that is close to Shakespeare's in his later years, while others belong clearly with the open-textured, casual style that Beaumont and Fletcher developed in manifest reaction against the involutions of the earliest Jacobeans. The difference has been brought home forcibly to the present editor through the process of annotation. If one compares the scenes where Palamon and Arcite talk together, putting I.ii and III.i on one side and II.i (from the exit of the Jailer, his Daughter, and her Wooer), III.iii, and III.vi on the other, one sees immediately that the first group requires continuous attention from the reader, and probably frequent recourse to the annotations, while the second group has nearly the familiarity of the English now current. When the editor was preparing the annotations, it was with no thought of giving fuller comment on Shakespeare's portion than on Fletcher's, but in the event it proved that in Shakespeare's the proportion of notes to lines was 51% in the scenes just indicated while in Fletcher's the proportion of notes to lines was 25%. Elsewhere in Fletcher's part of the play the figure is higher, as the terms used in connection with the morris dance of III.v needed comment, and Fletcher can use a more elaborate vocabulary for special purposes (as in the description of the knights in IV.ii and in the account of madness in IV.iii). Nevertheless, the presence of the two hands is obvious almost throughout, and evident at a glance in scenes where the basic material (Palamon and Arcite talking together) is similar.

The time of composition is hardly in dispute. The entertainment which the country Schoolmaster presents to Theseus and his court in III.v is taken over from an antimasque in Francis Beaumont's *Masque of the Inner Temple and Gray's Inn,* presented at Whitehall on 20 February 1613. In the published book of the masque we learn that this part of the entertainment was so well liked by the King that he asked to have it danced again at the end of the whole performance. Such antimasques at court were commonly entrusted to professional players, and it would be an easy matter for Fletcher, with his friend and former collaborator Beaumont's permission, to make further use of what had already proved successful. But clearly this would not be likely except soon after the original performance. The date 1613 for *The Two Noble Kinsmen* is confirmed by the reference in Jonson's *Bartholomew Fair* (1614) to "Palamon" as a character in a play (IV.iii): this is not certain evidence, for the name also occurs in Samuel Daniel's *The Queen's Arcadia* (1605), but Daniel's work was a university play and was already some years old in 1614; Jonson is far more likely to have had a recent and better-known play in mind. Moreover,

1613 was the year in which a lost play called *Cardenio*[2] (which in 1653 was attributed to Fletcher and Shakespeare by the publisher Humphrey Moseley) was twice acted at court, and it was the year too in which *Henry VIII* was almost certainly acted for the first time. Although by no means all Shakespeare scholars are agreed on the double authorship of *Henry VIII,* there is strong cumulative evidence that in 1613, after Shakespeare had come to the end of his series of "romances" and was about to retire from the stage, and when Beaumont on his marriage had broken with the theater and thus terminated the short but highly profitable collaboration that he and Fletcher had known for some five years, a new and brief association was established between Fletcher and Shakespeare, and that *The Two Noble Kinsmen* was one of its fruits.

In these circumstances, and with the assumption that the main planning of the play was, as it has seemed likely, Shakespeare's, we should expect to find a clear enough relationship to the "romances" which Shakespeare had been writing since *Pericles* (c. 1609) and which he had brought to a conclusion in *The Tempest* (1611). And resemblances are hardly to be missed. In *Pericles* he had gone to Gower's *Confessio Amantis* for his story: here he goes to Gower's contemporary, Chaucer. *Pericles* and *The Winter's Tale* have Hellenistic settings: *The Two Noble Kinsmen* takes us to Athens and briefly to Thebes. The "romances" present a world where the gods are freely invoked and where they play a direct part in the action— Diana appearing to Pericles in a dream and sending him to Ephesus so that he may find his lost wife Thaisa, Jupiter appearing to Posthumus Leonatus in prison and offering a riddling promise of good fortune to him and of a happy ending to the strife between Rome and Britain, Apollo being consulted on the question of Hermione's guilt and striking dead Mamillius when his father Leontes rejects the message from the oracle. In *The Tempest* there are, it is true, no gods—they would be out of place in a drama where a human character has unlimited control over events

---

2 It may exist in an altered form in Lewis Theobald's version of the story, called *Double Falsehood* and published in 1728.

(though not over the human will)—but there are spirits
who represent Juno and Ceres and Iris and who offer
divine blessings and admonitions. *The Two Noble Kinsmen*
keeps the gods off the stage too, but their altars are there,
they are solemnly invoked, and tokens of their favor are
given. At the play's end Theseus marvels how the apparently contradictory promises of Mars and Venus have both
been fulfilled. More obviously, more disturbingly indeed,
than in the previous plays the human characters of *The
Two Noble Kinsmen* are subject to divine power. Theseus
can devise a plan for finding out Emilia's husband and for
ending the strife between the knights, but it is the gods who
circuitously determine things, to the wonder and embar-
rassment of those concerned.

In some striking features this play has a special relationship with *Pericles*. That had a detachable first act
(which was omitted at a Stratford-on-Avon revival in
1947), with formal speechmaking in a context of love
and death: so has *The Two Noble Kinsmen,* which could
easily have been adjusted to begin with Palamon and
Arcite already in prison. Then Arcite's encounter in II.ii
with the countrymen who will take part in the games for
Emilia's birthday resembles Pericles' encounter with the
fishermen in II.i, where he learns there are games to be
held in Thaisa's honor: both Pericles and Arcite are victors
and are received into the lady's favor. But in *Pericles* the
games are a formal tournament, which takes place in an
atmosphere of high ceremonial, while in *The Two Noble
Kinsmen* it is a matter of simple running and wrestling.
The tournament, however, is not forgotten and occurs off-
stage in the final encounter between Palamon and Arcite,
each aided by his three knights. The cry of "The mean
knight!" which indicates at the end of II.ii that Pericles
has been victorious anticipates the cries of "Palamon!"
and "Arcite!" and "Victory!" that Emilia hears in V.iii.
Here the influence of one of Shakespeare's romances is
seen operative on a Fletcher portion of the later play.

But there is a more subtle echo of *The Winter's Tale*.
Commentators have sometimes seen there a suggestion
that Leontes, believing his wife is being unfaithful to him

with his best friend, is unconsciously more deeply outraged
by the breach in friendship than by the breach in marriage.
Certainly the nostalgic reminiscences of Leontes and
Polixenes in I.ii, their sense that an Eden was lost when
they grew up and took wives, is to be linked with the passage in *The Two Noble Kinsmen*, I.iii, where Emilia and
Hippolyta talk of the friendship between Theseus and
Pirithous and the friendship between Emilia and the dead
girl Flavina: Hippolyta is not sure that even now she has
the first place in Theseus' heart, Emilia has no thought
that a husband can be as near to her as Flavina was. In
the center of the later play, moreover, there is the friendship of Palamon and Arcite: it is broken when they both
love Emilia, but even as they plan to fight to the death (in
III.iii) they look back with some longing on their earlier
and lighter loves which did not harm their friendship. That
is a brief respite, for Palamon is soon asserting his claim
again, but the scene where they help to arm each other
(III.vi) is strong in its suggestion of enduring affection.
They embrace solemnly before the invocation of their
respective divine patrons (V.i), and Arcite's words to
Emilia when he appears to have won her are heavily
charged with a sense of the price he has paid:

> Emily,
> To buy you I have lost what's dearest to me
> Save what is bought, and yet I purchase cheaply
> As I do rate your value.
>
> (V.iii.111–14)

Shakespeare's "romances" are, among other things, love
stories, but they are not simple exaltations of the bond
which ties most men to women.

This indeed suggests a connection with his earliest plays.
The Two Gentlemen of Verona was also a play about
friendship, and it is difficult not to believe that its very
title was echoed in that of *The Two Noble Kinsmen*.
There Valentine and Proteus were firm friends until
Proteus fell in love with the girl his friend loved. The right
and wrong of the matter were simple: Proteus is thor-

oughly treacherous and gets to the point of attempting rape. When he repents, Valentine has so high a sense of what friendship demands that he is willing to let Proteus have the girl, not thinking even of consulting her. At that time Shakespeare could make discreet fun of the friendship-idea and could quickly make all things come right. Moreover, it was Proteus' villainy and Valentine's simple faith that caused the trouble, while in *The Two Noble Kinsmen* Palamon and Arcite love Emilia because they have to, and Arcite dies because the gods have determined so. That Shakespeare thought back to *The Two Gentlemen* is, I think, indubitable, just as he thought back to *The Comedy of Errors* in the final turn of events in *Pericles,* just as he remembered the rambling romantic plays of the popular theater he first knew when he wrote *Pericles* and *Cymbeline* and *The Winter's Tale.* In going back to beginnings, *The Two Noble Kinsmen* is of a piece with the "romances," though it has a formality of structure, as we shall see, that links it with *The Tempest* more than with the plays that immediately preceded that.

It is, however, another early play that is here most prominently in his mind, and again the resemblance goes along with contrast and deliberate reconsideration. Like *The Two Noble Kinsmen, A Midsummer Night's Dream* begins with preparations for the wedding of Theseus and Hippolyta, it is partly concerned with an amateur performance given before the Duke by his subjects, and it shows the court during a May-morning ceremony coming upon two men who have fallen out through rivalry in love. In the earlier play the wedding is not interrupted, there being merely a planned delay before it takes place; the play-within-the-play occurs at the end, not the middle; the rivals in love have had their quarrel already sorted out by Puck and Oberon before Theseus arrives. And it is not quite the same Theseus in the two plays. The earlier Duke has the authority of the later one, but he is ever sanguine and relaxed: he will not believe the "story of the night," he is patronizing toward play-acting and somewhat ill-mannered during the performance. The Duke of *The Two Noble Kinsmen* may finally attempt to console himself by marveling at the divine legerdemain, but there is an un-relaxed seriousness in him and a continuing puzzlement. The man who at first decrees perpetual imprisonment for Palamon and Arcite, and later death for them both, and after that death for the loser (and his supporters) in the tournament, is a shrewd realist very different from the man who told Hermia he could not bend the law for her sake— her father's authority being supreme—and finally acqui-esced in her marriage with Lysander and told Egeus he must accept the situation. We can see a similar change, along with a resemblance, in the later play's echoing of Helena's account of her girlhood friendship with Hermia (III.ii): when Emilia speaks of the relationship between herself and Flavina, Shakespeare is no longer offering a merely gentle picture of two girls together.

Shakespeare, then, using a well-known story that had been prominently in his mind when he wrote *A Midsum-mer Night's Dream* (c. 1595–96), helped to compose a play that had strong links both with the late "romances" and with early comedies that he had already shown a disposition to recall and to look upon with a changed vision. The reunions at the ends of *The Comedy of Errors* and *Pericles* are as different as we can imagine; the span-ning of the years in *Pericles* and *The Winter's Tale* does not make those plays similar in spirit to the romances of the 1570's (and the following decade or so) that Sidney made fun of in *An Apology for Poetry;* magic has a dif-ferent look in *The Tempest* when we compare that play with *A Midsummer Night's Dream*. There is a certain casualness of manner in *The Two Noble Kinsmen,* such indeed as Lytton Strachey saw in the late "romances" as a whole, but it goes along with a reserving of judgment about human beings and the conditions under which they live.

And in this situation Fletcher was no longer with Beau-mont but with an elder dramatist whose plays were always strongly in his mind, to the point where he would deliber-ately modify an initial Shakespeare-situation and then work out the pattern of event that would result. He and Beau-mont had done that with *Philaster* (c. 1609), taking the

Hamlet-situation without the ghost, as later—on his own —he was to write a sequel to *The Taming of the Shrew* in *The Woman's Prize, or The Tamer Tamed* (c. 1611) and, probably along with Massinger, to invert the *Lear*-situation in *Thierry and Theodoret* (c. 1617). With Beaumont he had shared a lodging and had developed a dramatic mode in which their two minds functioned, it seemed, as one: though we may perhaps be able to differentiate his verse from Beaumont's, we do not get the feeling in their joint plays that two diverse attitudes are alternating as each in his turn pushes his pen. Fletcher's later collaboration with Massinger resembles his collaboration with Shakespeare in *The Two Noble Kinsmen* to the extent that we feel the characterization and the march of event are seen through different eyes in different parts of the play. If we are correct, as many people have thought, in assuming that Shakespeare put his scenes into Fletcher's hands and let him do the job of conflating the two shares, this was a situation new to this dramatist. That the story would have attracted him is understandable: the clash between love and friendship in Palamon and Arcite has some similarity to that between friendship and honor in Melantius and Amintor in *The Maid's Tragedy* (c. 1610) and would similarly lend itself to the patterned alternations of conduct that Fletcher delighted in; and there must have been a piquancy in working in association with Shakespeare, to whom he owed much, whose work, however, must have seemed old-fashioned, imperfectly sophisticated. He and Beaumont had pulled Hamlet down to the comic level of Philaster; now Shakespeare's Palamon and Arcite could be irreverently handled in the same play as Shakespeare was presenting them.

It is not that Fletcher makes the kinsmen directly absurd (though coming near it in their exchange of sentiments, followed at once by their quarrel, in II.i), and he clearly has some partiality for Arcite; but he does take a feline pleasure in the way love holds them, in the way they try to live up to the friendship code at the same time as they are protesting their separate devotions to Emilia. And this goes along with a special fluency in his writing (seen, for example, in the prison-and-garden sequence of II.i), and a fondness for setting the story in brakes and flowers. Nature is never ominous for Fletcher, but its presence as a framework for strife is always ironic.

In one place the work of Fletcher's deflating hand reminds us of an effect found in Shakespeare's own *The Winter's Tale,* V.ii, and in scenes frequently ascribed to Fletcher in *Henry VIII* (II.i, IV.i). The Messenger in *The Two Noble Kinsmen,* IV.ii, seems to the present editor's ear to be intentionally comic, with his ecstatic praise of the attendant knights, his overreadiness to speak at line 72, his general extravagance of imagery, and in particular the doting on one knight's freckles and the ludicrous comparison of his sinews to the bodily shape of a pregnant woman (lines 128–29). Here I believe we have Fletcher taking up what he found in *The Winter's Tale,* and pushing it much further both in *Henry VIII* and in *The Two Noble Kinsmen.*

If general opinion is right in assigning the opening of II.i to Shakespeare, it was he who introduced the Jailer's Daughter. But the use made of her is characteristically Fletcher's. First we should note his boldness in giving her so many scenes alone (II.iii, II.v, III.ii, III.iv): the contrast with Emilia's safe establishment in Theseus' court is striking; and while Emilia is always herself, never in love, protesting yet acquiescent, grieved rather than disturbed, the Jailer's Daughter moves from light-hearted romance:

> Out upon't,
> What pushes are we wenches driven to
> When fifteen once has found us!
>   (II.iii.5–7)

to fear and hunger, and thence to a sense of exposure:

> I am very cold, and all the stars are out too,
> The little stars and all, that look like aglets.
> The sun has seen my folly.
>
>   (III.iv.1–3)

and thence to madness. The descent is not merely pathetic:

it is comic, as we see in her taking part in the morris dance of III.v, and it is powerfully suggestive of the casual destructiveness of the love-impulse. Aspatia in *The Maid's Tragedy* is too often seen as a merely pathetic figure: there is destructiveness there too, for herself and for Amintor. Fletcher had a strong sense of how disintegration worked, most brilliantly realized in his Maximus in *Valentinian* (c. 1614). And we may, I think, assume that it was Fletcher's idea to have the girl in *The Two Noble Kinsmen* "cured" by making her take her humble Wooer for Palamon, and thus in imagination lie with the man she loved. At the end of the play Emilia is almost on the point of marrying Arcite: the gods intervene, and she is in Palamon's arms. Neither girl has choice, neither girl has, ultimately it seems, the power to differentiate. Moreover, they are linked in that the Jailer's Daughter has to play her part in the morris dance, her madness making her, in the opinion of the Countrymen, the more apt for the grotesque gambols required, while Emilia, trying to preserve neutrality and sobriety, is nevertheless shuttled from one knight's arms to the other's. This gives to the country entertainment of III.v a function in the play: it is a comic counterpart to, and an anticipation of, the final tournament, and their respective roles in the two spectacles bring together the girl who loves Palamon and the girl who weds him. In his development of the subplot, Fletcher seems thus to have continued his work of deflation.

Here, however, it is necessary to distinguish with some care. Shakespeare's handling of Palamon and Arcite and Theseus and Emilia is no simple romancing, as we have seen. They are powerless human beings manipulated by the gods, and in a measure comic in their subjection. But the comedy is wry and serious, nowhere more so than in Palamon's invocation of Venus in V.i.[3] Fletcher's comedy is much more self-conscious, more obviously grotesque, and though it too is wry there is laughter in it.

Not only deflation of the elder dramatist can be seen, but a measure of parody too. The Jailer's Daughter echoes Ophelia; Emilia brooding over the pictures of Palamon

[3] See "A Note on the Source," pp. 188–89.

and Arcite in IV.ii echoes the Gertrude who was made to look on pictures of Claudius and the elder Hamlet; even the Doctor's bed-trick in V.ii (for it is substantially that) may echo Shakespeare's elaborate employments of the device. And again and again there are tricks of wording—e.g., the Doctor's "I think she has a perturbed mind, which I cannot minister to" (IV.iii.60–61)—which take up phrases which Fletcher knew from Shakespeare. The parodying is not hostile or unadmiring. We can remember that in 1613 Shakespeare was forty-nine and Fletcher thirty-four, that we have strong evidence that they worked together on two, perhaps on three, plays: the relationship must have been a complex one. Through the remaining twelve years of Fletcher's career his predecessor's work was never far from his mind, but he enjoyed it without a total reverence. That in writing his share of *The Two Noble Kinsmen* he made the play something of a medley would not deeply disturb him. He did not bring to the writing of any play a sense of full commitment.

A court record suggests that Shakespeare's and Fletcher's play was given there in 1619,[4] and the occurrence in the text of two actors' names[5] enables us to deduce that the play was revived about 1625–26. The title page of 1634 is perhaps deliberately ambiguous in its "Presented at the Blackfriers": this could imply, but need not, that the play was still in the repertory. But after 1642 for a very long time the stage had almost no use for the play.[6]

4 E. K. Chambers, *William Shakespeare: A Study of Facts and Problems*, Oxford, 1930, II, 346.

5 See Textual Note, p. 178.

6 The almost complete disregard of our play in the late seventeenth century is indicated by Dryden's failure to mention it in his Preface to his volume of *Fables* (1700) or to give in his *Palamon and Arcite* included in that volume any clear indication that he had read it. He does, when writing of Emilia at Book I, line 175, use the phrase "To do the observance due to sprightly May," which is a little nearer to "to do observance/To flow'ry May" (*The Two Noble Kinsmen*, II.iv.50–51) than to Chaucer's "to have remembrance/To don honour to May" (*The Knight's Tale*, lines 188–89), but Chaucer in another context has "to doon his observaunce to May" (line 642). Dryden also makes a little more of the freckled face of one of the kinsmen's supporters (Book III, lines 76, 475) than Chaucer does (lines 1311–12), which could be due to the stress on this feature in *The Two Noble Kinsmen*, IV.ii.120–23. Neither of these points can make us firmly deduce that Dryden gave the play a thought as he adapted Chaucer.

In 1664 Pepys saw at Lincoln's Inn Fields Theatre *The Rivals* (not a new play then), which is a free adaptation of *The Two Noble Kinsmen* and, though it was published anonymously in 1668, can be safely attributed to Sir William Davenant. He was a dramatist of experience and some note in Charles I's reign, he was largely responsible for the restarting of theater performances in London during the Interregnum (his operatic *The Siege of Rhodes* being acted in 1656), and he was one of the two London theater managers in the earliest Restoration years. He made free use of pre-1642 drama, adapting *Macbeth* and (with Dryden) *The Tempest* for current taste. In *The Rivals* he contrived a version of the story he found in Shakespeare and Fletcher, with no Theseus, no petitioning Queens, no invocation of the gods, no tournament, and a happy ending. Though he occasionally keeps to the words he found, he uses none of the old names and changes the place of action to Arcadia. Heraclea, corresponding to Emilia, cannot make up her mind between Theocles and Philander, but finds that Philander is loved by Celania, the daughter of the Provost (no mere jailer): therefore she decides to take Theocles, and Philander consents to love Celania. Davenant wanted to make a refined comedy, and to do it he had to remove most of the action and all the grossness. Celania does go distracted for a while, but only in a polite way. The play is of no importance, but so far as is known it provided the occasion for the only contact with the stage that *The Two Noble Kinsmen* had between the early seventeenth century and the early twentieth century. Not even William Poel is on record as having thought of a revival.

Then in March 1928 the Old Vic staged it, with Ernest Milton as Palamon, Eric Portman as Arcite, Jean Forbes-Robertson as the Jailer's Daughter, and Barbara Everest as Emilia. Writing in *The London Mercury* for April 1928, A. G. MacDonell praised Jean Forbes-Robertson, and noted that Palamon was done comically, in a red wig. This reviewer was much taken with the realistic playing of the mad scenes, and grateful that he did not have to endure simple nobility in two kinsmen. The only other production

I have been able to trace is that at the Antioch Area Theatre, Antioch College, Ohio, which was given eight times in August and September 1955 under the direction of Arthur Lithgow. I am most grateful to Mr. Lithgow, now of the McCarter Theatre at Princeton, and to Miss Marcia Overstreet and Miss Ernestine C. Brecht of Antioch College, for writing to me about this production. Mr. Lithgow reports that the play proved "very stage-worthy," particularly the scenes involving the Jailer's Daughter, and that Mr. Ellis Rabb was "very grand" as Palamon. Some cutting had to be done of "repetitive passages," but Shakespeare's hand was felt in the "high imagery."

This is a relatively inglorious stage history for a play in which Shakespeare was concerned, and we must honor the Old Vic and Antioch College for going against the current. Despite the coldness of the London reviewers (MacDonell was typical), it is evident that something happened to the Jailer's Daughter scenes when they got on the stage, and this was confirmed at Antioch College, where indeed the play as a whole seems to have found itself at home. It is more than time that a further attempt was made to see it in action. It does, after all, contain the invocations to the gods in V.i, passages of dramatic verse outstanding even in 1613, a good time for dramatic verse; it contains some of Fletcher's most skillful and characteristic writing; it will one day, perhaps, come to be recognized as throwing a new kind of light on Shakespeare's concluding work in the theater. It needs a large and flexible stage: there is a most suitable one at Stratford, Ontario, another at Chichester in England, and others—both indoor and outdoor—easily found in the United States. One of these might well meet the challenge of what was perhaps Shakespeare's (though only partly Shakespeare's) last play.

It has some good verse and a fairly realistic picture of the onset of madness, but the director contemplating a revival will want to be assured of more than that. It is true that he must face difficulties. The play has the appearance of a romantic story, as Beaumont and Fletcher's *Philaster* has, but in neither instance does the romantic effect prop-

erly work. With *Philaster* that was because Beaumont and
Fletcher were determined on a sophisticated undercutting
of the romantic gesture; with *The Two Noble Kinsmen*
there is the complication that two men of widely differing
temperaments shared the writing. Shakespeare had used
"romance" with high authority in *The Winter's Tale* and
The Tempest, involving his audience in a love story in a
setting that was both natural and strange, and at the same
time making them feel that they were in the presence of
stern and unknowable powers. But now he was working
with Fletcher, whose sights were lower, essentially those
that had characterized *Philaster*. For Shakespeare, we can
assume it was the sense of the inscrutable that made the
story attractive to him; for Fletcher, it was its essential,
often painful, but never overwhelming, absurdity. Because
it seems likely that Fletcher had the task of putting together his and Shakespeare's work on the play, the over-
riding effect is Fletcherian: we are taken to high realms
of thought, and deliberately let down, as we are so often,
but less extravagantly, in the other plays in which Fletcher
had a main hand. It is a paradox that Shakespeare seems
to have planned *The Two Noble Kinsmen* and that
Fletcher gave it its dominant tone. But that tone is dominant, not exclusive: from Shakespeare we get the solemn
pageant of the Queens' mission in I.i, the sage talk of
Emilia and Hippolyta in I.iii, the sharp magniloquence of
the prayers in V.i; and Fletcher's deflations do not take
them from our memory.

But what has probably put off most readers and poten-
tial directors has been the nature of the characterization.
Shakespeare's handling of character from *Pericles* onwards
was lacking in the complexity and verisimilitude that had
marked the comedies and frequently the tragedies of his
middle and mature years. But audiences have been ready
to accept Leontes in place of Othello, Miranda in place
of Rosalind, Prospero in place of Hamlet, because in these
plays they are led consistently toward the idea of "great
creating Nature," toward a sense of epiphany, toward an
austere assertion that to accept what is remains the best
hope, the highest wisdom, we have. But Fletcher has been

little more successful on the stage from the eighteenth to the twentieth century, either alone or in collaboration with Beaumont, than he has been in association with Shakespeare. Reviewing the Old Vic performance of *The Two Noble Kinsmen* in 1928, James Agate asked how any actress could make anything of Emilia, passed from hero to hero as from pillar to post.[7] A. G. MacDonell, we have seen, found even one manifestly noble kinsman enough to bear. Fletcher offers nothing in the way of obvious compensation for his stereotyping of human characters: these are, he suggests, the types that men fall into, or imagine they fall into, or try to live up to the idea of falling into. The Fletcherian drama is a drama about men's refusal to live as individuals. In his plays, men avoid nakedness by doing what they feel the codes and traditions of society demand from them. We may differentiate Palamon from Arcite: one is more rough, the other ready to see himself as sinning because he devoted himself to Emilia a few seconds after his friend did. But each keeps within a stereotype, a notion that belongs to the playhouse of the mind that men are always imagining for themselves: they are alike victims and worshipers of Bacon's Idols of the Theater. It is a kind of characterization that in recent years Brecht has familiarized us with, and we should now therefore be the more fitted to respond to the mode and to see what the play as a whole is saying.

It is indeed a well-arranged play, despite the duality of authorship and the dichotomy of attitude that in this instance is thus imposed. Instead of the loose story-telling we might expect, we have a fairly tight structure, and in "A Note on the Source" (p. 187) we shall see that this has been achieved partly through the changes made in adapting Chaucer. The action involves three interwoven strands: (1) the prologue-action, as we may call it, concerning the conflict between Athens and Thebes; (2) the story of the rivalry for Emilia; (3) the story of the Jailer's Daughter. The first makes the play begin in a manner of high seriousness and formal rhetoric, and it is in manifest contrast with the slighter, more personal stories of the

7 *Brief Chronicles,* London, 1943, pp. 53–56.

knights and the girls. The subplot, as we have seen, reflects ironically on the plot of the knights.

The act division throughout is firm, and is related to the play's changes of locality. Act I concerns itself with the conflict between Athens (chivalrous) and Thebes (ignoble), ending with the imprisonment of the nearly dead Palamon and Arcite (noble on the wrong side). Act II gives us their falling in love and release from prison, and introduces the subplot. Act III is wholly outside the town: it shows how Palamon and Arcite meet again, how the Jailer's Daughter loses Palamon, how Theseus and his court are entertained by a group of rustics including the Daughter, and finally how the Duke comes upon the kinsmen and decrees their final trial. Act IV, which is briefly and quietly indeterminate, makes toward the cure of the Daughter and emphasizes the perplexity of Emilia: it is, as often with a fourth act, a halting place before the catastrophe. Act V gives us the tournament and its curious consequences, with both girls in some sense pledged to Palamon. Athens and Thebes are the localities of Act I, Athens and the country nearby those of Act II; the country consistently is the place of action in Act III, the city of Athens (but alternating between palace and prison) in Acts IV and V. As the play progresses its range of locality shrinks, so that what begins as an opposition of Thebes and Athens ends as an opposition of palace and prison within a single city. The point of rest toward which we move is marked by death and bereavement and acquiescence: the Jailer who freed Arcite in Act II, and put Palamon under further restraint, is prominently in the stage picture when Palamon is prepared for execution and then, at the news of Arcite's death, for marriage.

The play's recurrent irony is supported by other details of the planning. Theseus is ceremoniously petitioned by the Queens in I.i and by Hippolyta, Emilia, and Pirithous in III.vi: he yields in both instances, though with eloquence in the earlier, Shakespearian passage and with the cleverness of compromise in Fletcher's III.vi. The talk between Palamon and Arcite in I.ii, where they show their wish to leave a corrupt Thebes, becomes ironic when in fighting for Thebes they come near death and are sentenced to life imprisonment. The discussion of friendship by Hippolyta and Emilia in I.iii not only anticipates the dominant friendship motif in the play as a whole, but casts an ironic light on the knights' subsequent devotion to Emilia. And just as the subplot as a whole reflects on Emilia and her ultimate disposal, so the entertainment devised by the Schoolmaster, which brings Theseus and the Jailer's Daughter together on the stage for the only time, is not only a contrast to and an anticipation of the wryly presented tournament of Act V: it also gives a distorted image of the entertainment that the kinsmen and the Duke and his ladies offer to the audience in the theater.

Of course, this is a Blackfriars play. The King's Men had taken over that "private" theater (previously used by the child actors) around 1610 and had begun by using it as their winter house, keeping the Globe for the summer. The title page of 1634 mentions only the Blackfriars, and we may assume that at least by the 1620's this play had found its right home there. It is a sophisticated—even, we have seen, a dislocated—play, not firm, ultimately, in its implications but surely fascinating, if disturbing and at times irritating, to watch. Its epilogue calls it "the tale we have told—/For 'tis no other." That was what Shakespeare had insistently, in the text as well as in the title, called *The Winter's Tale. The Two Noble Kinsmen,* like that earlier "romance," is a strange story with many reversals of fortune, but like that too it has its unromantic aftertaste and is more carefully structured than a casual glance suggests. The Blackfriars audience was at times most gullible, ready to lose itself in a merely romanticized wonderland, but it could rise to the appreciation of something complex: it welcomed Fletcher's masterpiece in comedy, *The Humorous Lieutenant* (c. 1619–20), and, though we cannot be sure that it much liked the experience, it saw Ford's *The Broken Heart* some dozen years after that. There were doubtless moments of puzzlement with *The Two Noble Kinsmen* in 1613 and the following years, but some at least of the spectators must have noticed that the

supreme dramatist and his more than clever successor
were not failing them.

Nor would they, I think, fail us now if we put their
joint play again on the stage.[8]

CLIFFORD LEECH
University of Toronto

---

[8] Since this Introduction was written, Paul Bertram has published a
substantial book with the title *Shakespeare and The Two Noble Kinsmen*
(New Brunswick, 1965), arguing that Shakespeare was the sole author
of the play. It is a piece of well-informed writing, and Bertram has scored
some good points in showing how the nineteenth-century scholars seized
on the idea of dual authorship because of a reluctance to imagine Shakespeare writing the franker sections of the play. He argues, moreover, that
the play has unity in its plotting (as indeed it has) and that throughout
there is the same full use of Chaucer. Less successfully, he disposes of the
evidence of verse tests by insisting that some of the scenes treated by the
editors as verse are really in prose (as they are presented in the quarto):
this is, I think, to disregard the strong blank-verse character of much of
the writing. The reader of the present edition will be able to decide
whether the scenes involving the Countrymen and the Jailer and his
Daughter (apart from the beginning of II.i and the whole of IV.iii) are
legitimately printed as verse. Moreover, Bertram is one of the, alas, many
who have a low regard for Fletcher: he insists on Shakespeare's sole
authorship of *Henry VIII* and *The Two Noble Kinsmen*, but will let
Fletcher have *Cardenio*, which seems to him of minor weight. And he does
not successfully meet the evidence of the 1634 title page. It is possible to
quote, as he does, the statement of Leonard Digges, in the 1640 edition
of Shakespeare's *Poems*, that Shakespeare did not beg "from each witty
friend a Scene/To peece his Acts with," but that is another matter than
the frank and equal sharing of a play with his obvious successor in 1613.
It used to be necessary to argue for Shakespeare's participation in *The
Two Noble Kinsmen*: now we have to safeguard Fletcher's right to a part
of it. And the argument of this Introduction is that there are, despite close
cooperation, a difference of view and a difference of style which indicate
two authors, one of them supreme and the other at least major in his time.

The Two Noble Kinsmen

PROLOGUE

Flourish.°[1]

New plays and maidenheads are near akin:
Much followed° both, for both much money gi'en,
If they stand sound and well. And a good play—
Whose modest scenes blush on his marriage day,
And shake to lose his honor—is like her   *5*
That after holy tie and first night's stir
Yet still is modesty, and still retains
More of the maid to sight than husband's pains.°
We pray our play may be so, for I am sure
It has a noble breeder, and a pure,   *10*
A learnèd, and a poet never went
More famous yet 'twixt Po and silver Trent.
Chaucer, of all admired, the story gives:
There constant to eternity it lives.
If we let fall° the nobleness of this,°   *15*
And the first sound this child hear be a hiss,
How will it shake the bones of that good man,
And make him cry from under ground, "O fan
From me the witless chaff of such a writer°
That blasts my bays, and my famed works makes
    lighter   *20*

---

[1] The degree sign (°) indicates a footnote, which is keyed to the
text by line number. Text references are printed in **boldface type**;
the annotation follows in roman type.
Prologue s.d. **Flourish** i.e., of trumpets   2 **followed** pursued, culti-
vated   8 **pains** endeavors   15 **let fall** fail to maintain   15 **this** i.e.,
Chaucer's poem   19 **such a writer** (the singular is notable, but by
no means decisive on the question of authorship)

Than Robin Hood!" This is the fear we bring;
For, to say truth, it were an endless° thing,
And too ambitious, to aspire to him.
Weak as we are, and almost breathless swim
25   In this deep water, do but you hold out
Your helping hands, and we shall tack about,°
And something do to save us. You shall hear
Scenes, though below his art, may yet appear
Worth two hours' travail.° To his bones sweet
    sleep;
30   Content to you. If this play do not keep
A little dull time from us, we perceive
Our losses fall so thick we must needs leave.°

                                  Flourish.

---

22 **endless** purposeless, vain   26 **tack about** change direction   29 **travail** labor (with a suggestion of "travel," as the play's action moves from place to place)   32 **leave** give up acting

ACT I

[Scene I. *Athens. Before a temple.*]

Enter Hymen° with a torch burning; a boy in a white
robe before, singing and strewing flowers; after
Hymen, a nymph, encompassed in her tresses,°
bearing a wheaten garland;° then Theseus between
two other nymphs with wheaten chaplets° on their
heads; then Hippolyta the bride, led by Pirithous,
and another holding a garland over her head, her
tresses likewise hanging; after her, Emilia holding
up her train; [Artesius and Attendants].   Music.

The Song

Roses, their sharp spines being gone,
Not royal in their smells alone,
But in their hue;
Maiden pinks, of odor faint,
Daisies smell-less, yet most quaint,°   5
And sweet thyme true;

Primrose, first-born child of Ver,°
Merry spring-time's harbinger,
With harebells dim;
Oxlips, in their cradles growing,   10
Marigolds, on death-beds blowing,°
Lark's-heels trim;°

I.i. s.d. **Hymen** god of marriage   **encompassed in her tresses** with
hair loose, in token of virginity   **wheaten garland** a symbol of fertility and peace   **chaplets** wreaths   **5 quaint** pretty   **7 Ver** spring
11 on death-beds blowing blooming on graves   **12 trim** neat

47

All dear Nature's children sweet
Lie 'fore bride and bridegroom's feet,   *Strew flowers.*
15 Blessing their sense;
Not an angel° of the air,
Bird melodious, or bird fair,
Is° absent hence;

The crow, the sland'rous cuckoo, nor
20 The boding raven, nor chough hoar,
Nor chatt'ring pie,
May on our bridehouse° perch or sing,
Or with them any discord bring,
But from it fly.

*Enter three Queens in black, with veils stained, with
imperial crowns. The first Queen falls down at the
foot of Theseus; the second falls down at the foot of
Hippolyta; the third before Emilia.*

25 *First Queen.* For pity's sake and true gentility's,°
Hear and respect° me.

Second Queen.   For your mother's sake,
And as you wish your womb may thrive with fair
ones,
Hear and respect me.

Third Queen. Now for the love of him whom Jove
hath marked
30 The honor of your bed,° and for the sake
Of clear° virginity, be advocate
For us, and our distresses. This good deed
Shall raze you° out o' th' Book of Trespasses°
All you are set down there.

Theseus. Sad lady, rise.

Hippolyta.   Stand up.

16 angel here a synonym for "bird"   18 Is (often emended to "Be,"
but the indicative seems acceptable)   22 bridehouse house where a
wedding is celebrated   25 gentility nobleness   26 respect give attention to   29–30 whom . . . bed for whom Jove has destined the
honor of wedding you   31 clear pure   33 raze you delete for you
33 Book of Trespasses recording angel's register of sins

Emilia.   No knees to me.   35
What woman I may stead° that is distressed
Does bind me to her.

Theseus. What's your request? Deliver you for all.

First Queen. We are three queens, whose sovereigns
      fell before
The wrath of cruel Creon;° who endured°   40
The beaks of ravens, talons of the kites,
And pecks of crows, in the foul fields of Thebes.
He will not suffer us to burn their bones,
To urn their ashes, nor to take th' offense
Of mortal loathsomeness from the blest eye   45
Of holy Phoebus,° but infects the winds
With stench of our slain lords. O pity, duke,
Thou purger of the earth, draw thy feared sword
That does good turns to th' world; give us the bones
Of our dead kings, that we may chapel° them;   50
And of thy boundless goodness take some note
That for our crownèd heads we have no roof,
Save this which is the lion's and the bear's,
And vault° to everything.

Theseus.   Pray you kneel not.
I was transported with your speech, and suffered   55
Your knees to wrong themselves. I have heard the
      fortunes
Of your dead lords, which gives me such lamenting
As wakes my vengeance and revenge for 'em.
King Capaneus° was your lord. The day
That he should° marry you, at such a season   60
As now it is with me, I met your groom.
By Mars's altar, you were that time fair:
Not Juno's mantle° fairer than your tresses,

---

36 **stead** help   40 **Creon** king of Thebes after Oedipus   40 **endured**
have endured   45–46 **blest eye/Of holy Phoebus** i.e., the sun   50
chapel bury in a chapel   54 **vault** arched roof (here the sky)   59
Capaneus (here four syllables, though classically three)   60 **should**
was to   63 **Juno's mantle** (Juno was goddess of marriage and her
mantle is described in *Iliad*, XIV; but the peacock was sacred to
Juno, and "mantle" also suggests the bird's spread tail)

Nor in more bounty spread her; your wheaten
 wreath
Was then nor threshed° nor blasted;° Fortune at
65 you
Dimpled her cheek with smiles. Hercules our kins-
 man,°
Then weaker than your eyes, laid by his club:
He tumbled down upon his Nemean hide°
And swore his sinews thawed. O grief and time,
70 Fearful consumers, you will all devour.

First Queen. O I hope some god,
Some god hath put his mercy in your manhood,
Whereto he'll infuse pow'r, and press you forth
Our undertaker.°

Theseus.   O no knees, none, widow,
75 Unto the helmeted Bellona° use them,
And pray for me your soldier.
Troubled I am.   *Turns away.*
      [The Queens rise.]

Second Queen. Honored Hippolyta,
Most dreaded Amazonian, that hast slain
The scythe-tusked boar, that with thy arm as strong
80 As it is white, wast near to make the male
To thy sex captive, but that this thy lord,
Born to uphold creation in that honor
First Nature 'stilled it in,° shrunk thee into
The bound° thou wast o'erflowing, at once subduing
85 Thy force and thy affection; soldieress,
That equally canst poise° sternness with pity,

65 threshed beaten so as to separate grain from husks (here an image for fertilizing: cf. I.i opening s.d.) **65 blasted** i.e., by widowhood **66 kinsman** (according to Plutarch's "Life of Theseus," both he and Hercules were descended on their mothers' side from Pelops; moreover, Theseus as alleged son of Poseidon could claim kinship with Hercules, son of Zeus) **68 Nemean hide** (Hercules customarily wore the hide of the lion of Nemea, which he had slain) 73–74 **press you forth/Our undertaker** impel you to champion our cause **75 Bellona** goddess of war 83 **'stilled it in** instilled in it 84 **bound** limit, as bank of a river 86 **equally canst poise** canst justly balance

Whom° now I know hast much more power on him
Than ever he had on thee, who ow'st° his strength
And his love too, who is a servant for
The tenor of thy speech;° dear glass of° ladies,   90
Bid him that we whom flaming war doth scorch
Under the shadow of his sword may cool us;
Require him he advance it o'er our heads;
Speak't in a woman's key, like such a woman
As any of us three; weep ere you fail;   95
Lend us a knee;
But° touch the ground for us no longer time
Than a dove's motion when the head's plucked off;
Tell him if he i' th' blood-sized° field lay swoll'n,
Showing the sun his teeth, grinning at the moon,   100
What you would do.

Hippolyta.   Poor lady, say no more.
I had as lief trace° this good action with you
As that whereto I am going, and never yet
Went I so willing way.° My lord is taken
Heart-deep with your distress. Let him consider.   105
I'll speak anon.

Third Queen. (*Kneel*[*s*] *to Emilia*) O my petition was
Set down in ice, which by hot grief uncandied°
Melts into drops, so sorrow wanting form
Is pressed with deeper matter.°

Emilia.   Pray stand up,
Your grief is written in your cheek.

Third Queen.   O woe,   110
You cannot read it there; there through my tears,°
Like wrinkled pebbles in a glassy stream

---

87 **Whom** (usual in seventeenth century before a parenthetic clause)
88 **ow'st** possessest   89–90 **who . . . speech** who is obedient to everything you say   90 **glass of** mirror for (as in "mirror for magistrates," etc.)   97 **But** only   99 **blood-sized** spread with blood   102
trace pursue   104 **so willing way** any way so willingly   106–09 **O
my . . . deeper matter** i.e., the formality of her previous speech (lines
29–34) now melts into tears, but grief in its formlessness can receive
the imprint of a "deeper matter" (in this instance the desire for
funeral rites and vengeance)   107 **uncandied** dissolved   111 **there
through my tears** i.e., in her eyes

You may behold 'em.° Lady, lady, alack!
He that will all the treasure know o' th' earth
115 Must know the center° too; he that will fish
For my least minnow, let him lead his line°
To catch one at my heart. O pardon me,
Extremity that sharpens sundry wits
Makes me a fool.   [*She rises.*]

Emilia.   Pray you say nothing, pray you.
120 Who cannot feel nor see the rain, being in't,
Knows neither wet nor dry. If that you were
The ground-piece° of some painter, I would buy
        you
T' instruct me 'gainst a capital grief indeed
Such heart-pierced° demonstration.° But alas,
125 Being a natural sister of our sex,°
Your sorrow beats so ardently upon me
That it shall make a counter-reflect° 'gainst
My brother's heart, and warm it to some pity
Though it were made of stone. Pray have good
        comfort.

130 *Theseus.* Forward to th' temple, leave not out a jot
O' th' sacred ceremony.

First Queen.   O this celebration
Will long last, and be more costly than
Your suppliants' war. Remember that your fame
Knolls in the ear o' th' world; what you do quickly
135 Is not done rashly; your first thought is more
Than others' labored meditance,° your premedi-
        tating
More than their actions. But O Jove, your actions,
Soon as they move, as ospreys do the fish,°

---

113 **'em** i.e., her eyes, where her grief is imaged   115 **center** i.e., of
the earth   116 **lead his line** weight it with lead   122 **ground-piece**
flat representation (?)   124 **heart-pierced** heart-piercing   124 **demonstration** i.e., your demonstration of grief would instruct me how to
bear any great grief   125 **Being . . . sex** since you are a woman like
me (but "sifter" may be the right reading: see Textual Note)   127
counter-reflect reflection   136 **meditance** meditation, planning   138
ospreys do the fish (the osprey was believed to fascinate the fish
before catching it)

Subdue before they touch. Think, dear duke, think
What beds our slain kings have.

Second Queen.   What griefs our beds   *140*
That our dear lords have none.

Third Queen.   None fit for th' dead.
Those that with cords, knives, drams' precipitance,°
Weary of this world's light, have to themselves
Been death's most horrid agents, human grace°
Affords them dust and shadow.°

First Queen.   But our lords   *145*
Lie blist'ring 'fore the visiting° sun,
And were good kings when living.

Theseus.   It is true,
And I will give you comfort, to give° your dead
   lords graves.
The which to do, must make some work with
   Creon.

First Queen. And that work presents itself to th'
   doing.°   *150*
Now 'twill take form,° the heats are gone to-
   morrow.
Then bootless toil must recompense itself
With its own sweat. Now he's secure,°
Not dreams we stand before your puissance,
Rinsing our holy begging in our eyes   *155*
To make petition clear.

Second Queen.   Now you may take him,
Drunk with his victory.

Third Queen.   And his army full
Of bread° and sloth.

Theseus.   Artesius, that best knowest

---

142 **drams' precipitance** suicide by taking poison   144 **grace** mercy
145 **shadow** shelter   146 **visiting** inflicting harm (?)   148 **to give**
by giving   150 **presents itself to th' doing** offers itself to be done at
once   151 **form** shape   153 **secure** confident   158 **bread** food,
feasting

How to draw out° fit to this enterprise
160 The prim'st for this proceeding, and the number
To carry° such a business, forth and levy
Our worthiest instruments, whilst we dispatch
This grand act of our life, this daring deed
Of fate° in wedlock.

First Queen.   Dowagers, take hands,
165 Let us be widows to our woes,° delay
Commends us to a famishing hope.

All [*Queens*].   Farewell.

Second Queen. We come unseasonably, but when
        could grief
Cull forth,° as unpanged° judgment can, fitt'st time
For best solicitation?

Theseus.   Why, good ladies,
170 This is a service whereto I am going
Greater than any was; it more imports me
Than all the actions that I have foregone°
Or futurely° can cope.

First Queen.   The more proclaiming
Our suit shall be neglected. When her arms,
175 Able to lock Jove from a synod,° shall
By warranting° moonlight corslet thee, O when
Her twining cherries shall their sweetness fall°
Upon thy tasteful° lips, what wilt thou think
Of rotten kings or blubbered queens, what care
For what thou feel'st not, what thou feel'st being
180   able
To make Mars spurn his drum? O if thou couch
But one night with her, every hour in't will
Take hostage of thee for a hundred,° and

---

159 **draw out** select   161 **carry** carry out   163–64 **daring deed/Of
fate** deed challenging fate   165 **be widows to our woes** live with our
woes like widows (as we are)   168 **Cull forth** choose   168 **un-
panged** untormented   172 **foregone** previously experienced   173
futurely in the future   175 **synod** council   176 **warranting** au-
thorizing   177 **fall** let fall   178 **tasteful** tasting   183 **Take . . . hundred** i.e., you will feel committed to spend a hundred more with her

Thou shalt remember nothing more than what
That banquet bids thee to.

Hippolyta. [*Kneels*]   Though much unlike   185
You should be so transported, as much sorry
I should be such a suitor;° yet I think,
Did I not by th' abstaining of my joy,
Which breeds a deeper longing, cure their surfeit
That craves a present med'cine, I should pluck   190
All ladies' scandal° on me. Therefore, sir,
As I shall here make trial of my pray'rs,
Either presuming them to have some force
Or sentencing for aye their vigor dumb,°
Prorogue° this business we are going about, and
          hang   195
Your shield afore your heart, about that neck
Which is my fee,° and which I freely lend
To do these poor queens service.

All Queens. [*To Emilia*]   O help now,
Our cause cries for your knee.

Emilia. [*Kneels*]   If you grant not
My sister her petition in that force,°   200
With that celerity and nature which
She makes it in,° from henceforth I'll not dare
To ask you anything, nor be so hardy°
Ever to take a husband.

Theseus.   Pray stand up.
          [*Hippolyta and Emilia rise.*]
I am entreating of myself to do   205
That which you kneel to have me. Pirithous,
Lead on the bride; get you and pray the gods
For success, and return; omit not anything
In the pretended° celebration. Queens,

185–87 **Though . . . suitor** i.e., my reluctance to ask this is as great
as my doubt that you would be so moved by our lovemaking   191
scandal disgrace   194 **sentencing . . . dumb** declaring that they shall
never be uttered again   195 **Prorogue** postpone   197 **fee** property
200 **in that force** with that vigor   201–02 **nature which/She makes
it in** condition of mind in which she makes it   203 **hardy** bold   209
pretended intended

Follow your soldier, as before.° [*To Artesius*]
210   Hence you,
And at the banks of Aulis° meet us with
The forces you can raise, where we shall find
The moiety of a number for a business
More bigger-looked.°   [*Exit Artesius.*]
                         Since that our theme is haste,
215   I stamp this kiss upon thy current° lip.
Sweet, keep it as my token. [*Kisses Hippolyta.*]
    Set you forward,
For I will see you gone.

[*Hippolyta, Emilia, Pirithous and Attendants begin to
         move*] *towards the temple.*

Farewell, my beauteous sister. Pirithous,
Keep the feast full,° bate not an hour on't.

Pirithous.   Sir,
220   I'll follow you at heels. The feast's solemnity
Shall want° till your return.

Theseus.   Cousin, I charge you
Budge not from Athens. We shall be returning
Ere you can end this feast, of which I pray you
Make no abatement. Once more, farewell all.
                    [*The procession enters the temple.*]

First Queen. Thus dost thou still make good the
225   tongue o' th' world.°

Second Queen. And earn'st a deity equal with Mars.

Third Queen. If not above him, for
    Thou being but mortal makest affections bend

---

210 **as before** as I have already declared myself 211 **banks of
Aulis** (see Textual Note: Aulis was a seaport, but "banks" could
refer to the shore; however, this was an odd way to proceed from
Athens to Thebes) 212–14 **where . . . bigger-looked** while I shall
gather the other half of a force that would serve for a larger undertaking than this 215 **current** fleeting (transferred from Theseus,
who is in haste), with a suggestion also of putting his royal stamp
on her lip as on a coin 219 **full** fully 221 **want** be incomplete
225 **make good the tongue o' th' world** justify what the world says
of you

　　To godlike honors.° They themselves,° some say,
　　Groan under such a mast'ry.°

Theseus.　　　　　　　　　　　　As we are men,　　230
　　Thus should we do. Being sensually subdued,
　　We lose our human title.° Good cheer, ladies.
　　Now turn we towards your comforts.

　　　　　　　　　　　　　　Flourish. Exeunt.

Scene II. [*Thebes.*]

Enter Palamon and Arcite.

Arcite. Dear Palamon, dearer in love than blood°
　　And our prime° cousin, yet° unhardened in
　　The crimes of nature, let us leave the city
　　Thebes, and the temptings in't, before we further
　　Sully our gloss of youth;　　　　　　　　　　5
　　And here to keep in abstinence we shame
　　As in incontinence:° for not to swim
　　I' th' aid o'° th' current were almost to sink,
　　At least to frustrate striving;° and to follow
　　The common stream, 'twould bring us to an eddy　　10
　　Where we should turn° or drown; if labor through,
　　Our gain but life and weakness.

Palamon.　　　　　　　　　　　　Your advice
　　Is cried up° with example: what strange ruins
　　Since first we went to school may we perceive
　　Walking in Thebes? Scars and bare weeds　　15

228–29 **makest . . . honors** turn your natural inclinations toward the
winning of divine honors　229 **They themselves** i.e., the gods　230
mast'ry i.e., as yours　231–32 **Being . . . title** by yielding to our
senses we lose our claim to be considered men　I.ii.1 **blood** kinship
2 **prime** closest　2 **yet** as yet　6–7 **here . . . incontinence** here it is as
shameful to abstain from vice as (elsewhere) to indulge in it　8 **I' th'
aid o'** i.e., with　9 **frustrate striving** make our efforts useless　11
turn i.e., turn and begin to swim with the current　13 **cried up** supported

The gain o' th' Martialist,° who did propound
To his bold ends honor and golden ingots,
Which though he won he had not, and now flirted°
By peace for whom he fought: who then shall offer
20   To Mars's so scorned altar? I do bleed
When such I meet, and wish great Juno would
Resume her ancient fit of jealousy°
To get the soldier work, that peace might purge
For her repletion,° and retain° anew
25   Her charitable heart, now hard and harsher
Than strife or war could be.

Arcite.   Are you not out?°
Meet you no ruin but the soldier in
The cranks and turns° of Thebes? You did begin
As if you met decays of many kinds.
30   Perceive you none that do arouse your pity
But th' unconsidered° soldier?

Palamon.   Yes, I pity
Decays where'er I find them, but such most
That sweating in an honorable toil
Are paid with ice° to cool 'em.

Arcite.   'Tis not this
35   I did begin to speak of: this is virtue
Of no respect in Thebes. I spake of Thebes,
How dangerous if we will keep our honors
It is for our residing, where every evil
Hath a good color,° where every seeming good's
40   A certain evil, where not to be ev'n jump°
As they° are, here were to be° strangers, and

---

16 **Martialist** follower of Mars (i.e., soldier)   18 **flirted** mocked
21–22 **Juno . . . jealousy** (Juno's jealousy was a contributing factor
to the Trojan War)   23–24 **peace might purge/For her repletion**
(a common image: war was seen as a recurrent necessity so that
society might "purge" itself of the results of too self-indulgent living:
"for" here means "as a remedy for")   24 **retain** take into service
26 **Are you not out?** are you not mistaking the matter?   28 **cranks
and turns** winding streets and passages   31 **unconsidered** neglected
34 **Are paid with ice** i.e., are treated coolly (ironically appropriate,
because they have been sweating)   39 **color** appearance   40 **jump**
exactly   41 **they** i.e., the Thebans   41 **were to be** would be

Such things to be,° mere° monsters.

Palamon.   'Tis in our power
      (Unless we fear that apes can tutor's) to
      Be masters of our manners. What need I
      Affect° another's gait, which is not catching   45
      Where there is faith, or to be fond upon
      Another's way of speech, when by mine own
      I may be reasonably conceived°—saved too,
      Speaking it truly?° Why am I bound
      By any generous bond° to follow him   50
      Follows his tailor,° haply so long until
      The followed make pursuit?° Or let me know
      Why mine own barber is unblest, with him
      My poor chin too, for° 'tis not scissored just
      To such a favorite's glass.° What canon° is there   55
      That does command my rapier from my hip
      To dangle't in my hand, or to go tiptoe
      Before the street be foul?° Either I am
      The fore-horse in the team, or I am none
      That draw i' th' sequent trace.° These poor slight
            sores   60
      Need not a plantain.° That which rips my bosom
      Almost to th' heart's—

Arcite.   Our uncle Creon.

Palamon.   He,

42 **Such things to be** to be such things as they (the Thebans) are   42
mere absolute   45 **Affect** imitate   48 **conceived** understood   49
Speaking it truly i.e., if I speak the truth   50 **generous bond** nobleman's obligation   50–51 **follow him/Follows his tailor** imitate a
man who takes instruction about conduct from his tailor   51–52
until/The followed make pursuit until the tailor, not having been
paid, pursues his client to dun him   54 **for** because   54–55 **just/To
such a favorite's glass** exactly in the fashion affected by such-and-
such a favored person   55 **canon** law (particularly divine or eccle-
siastical law)   57–58 **go tip-toe/Before the street be foul** (suggestive either of a mincing gait or of a way of walking so as to avoid
noise, for purposes of surprise attack)   58–60 **Either . . . trace**
either I shall lead or I shall refuse to be one that merely follows
(the image being from a team of horses)   61 **plantain** (the leaves
of the plantain herb were much used for treating wounds, stanching
blood, etc.)

A most unbounded tyrant, whose successes
Makes heaven unfeared, and villainy assured
65   Beyond its power there's nothing; almost puts
Faith in a fever, and deifies alone
Voluble° chance; who° only attributes
The faculties of other instruments
To his own nerves and act;° commands men service,
70   And what they win in't, boot° and glory; one
That fears not to do harm; good, dares not.° Let
The blood of mine that's sib° to him be sucked
From me with leeches, let them break and fall
Off me with that corruption.

Arcite.   Clear-spirited° cousin,
75   Let's leave his court, that we may nothing share
Of his loud infamy; for our milk
Will relish of the pasture,° and we must
Be vile or disobedient, not his kinsmen
In blood unless in quality.°

Palamon.   Nothing truer.
80   I think the echoes of his shames have deafed
The ears of heav'nly justice: widows' cries
Descend again into their throats, and have not
Due audience of° the gods.

Enter Valerius.

Valerius!

Valerius. The king calls for you; yet be leaden-footed°
85   Till his great rage be off him. Phoebus, when
He broke his whipstock° and exclaimed against

---

67 **Voluble** inconstant   67 **who** i.e., the "tyrant" of line 63   67–69 **who . . . act** i.e., who takes what his subjects do as his own achievement   70 **boot** profit, booty   71 **good, dares not** dares not do good   72 **sib** related   74 **Clear-spirited** noble-spirited   76–77 **our milk/ Will relish of the pasture** i.e., what we produce will be affected by our environment   78–79 **not his kinsmen . . . quality** i.e., we must not hold the position of members of his family unless we are like him in character   83 **Due audience of** fitting attention from   84 **be leaden-footed** do not hasten   86 **whipstock** (here) whip

The horses of the sun, but whispered to°
The loudness of his fury.

Palamon.   Small winds shake him,
But what's the matter?°

Valerius. Theseus, who where he threats appalls, hath
    sent   90
Deadly defiance to him and pronounces
Ruin to Thebes, who is at hand to seal
The promise of his wrath.°

Arcite.   Let him approach.
But that we fear the gods in him,° he brings not
A jot of terror to us. Yet what° man   95
Thirds° his own worth (the case is each of ours)
When that his action's dregged,° with mind assured
'Tis bad he goes about.

Palamon.   Leave that unreasoned.°
Our services stand now for Thebes, not Creon.
Yet to be neutral to him were dishonor,   100
Rebellious to oppose: therefore we must
With him stand to the mercy of our Fate,
Who hath bounded our last minute.°

Arcite.   So we must.
Is't said this war's afoot, or it shall be
On fail of some condition?°

Valerius.   'Tis in motion: 105
The intelligence of state came in the instant
With the defier.°

---

87 **to** in comparison with   89 **the matter** the cause of disturbance
92–93 **seal/The promise of his wrath** confirm what his angry words
have spoken   94 **fear the gods in him** fear him as an emissary of the
gods   95 **what** here equivalent to "every"   96 **Thirds** reduces to a
third of its former strength   97 **dregged** accompanied by dross
matter   98 **unreasoned** unspoken, not argued about   103 **Who
hath bounded our last minute** who has already settled the time when
our lives end   105 **On fail of some condition** if stated terms of peace
are not agreed to   106–07 **The intelligence . . . defier** i.e., the news
that the war had started came at the same time as the declaration

Palamon.   Let's to the king, who were he
          A quarter carrier of that honor which
          His enemy come in, the blood we venture
110   Should be as for our health, which were not spent,
          Rather laid out for purchase.° But alas,
          Our hands advanced before our hearts,° what will
          The fall o' th' stroke do damage?

Arcite.   Let th' event,°
          That never erring arbitrator, tell us
115   When we know all ourselves, and let us follow
          The becking of our chance.   *Exeunt.*

Scene III. [*Athens.*]

Enter Pirithous, Hippolyta, Emilia.

Pirithous. No further.

Hippolyta.   Sir, farewell. Repeat my wishes
          To our great lord, of whose success I dare not
          Make any timorous question, yet I wish him
          Excess and overflow of power, and't might be
5   To dure° ill-dealing Fortune. Speed° to him:
          Store never hurts good governors.°

Pirithous.   Though I know
          His ocean needs not my poor drops, yet they
          Must yield their tribute there. [*To Emilia*] My pre-
              cious maid,
          Those best affections° that the heavens infuse

---

111 **laid out for purchase** invested for profit   112 **Our hands advanced before our hearts** i.e., our hands being engaged rather than
our desires   113 **event** result   I.iii.4–5 **and't might be/To dure** in
case it were necessary to undergo   5 **Speed** hasten   6 **Store never
hurts good governors** plenty is never a handicap to good leaders   9
affections inclinations

In their best-tempered pieces,° keep enthroned   10
In your dear heart.

Emilia.   Thanks, sir. Remember me
To our all-royal brother, for whose speed°
The great Bellona I'll solicit; and
Since in our terrene° state petitions are not
Without gifts understood, I'll offer to her   15
What I shall be advised° she likes: our hearts
Are in his army, in his tent.

Hippolyta.   In's bosom.
We have been soldiers, and we cannot weep
When our friends don their helms, or put to sea,
Or tell of babes broached on the lance, or women   20
That have sod° their infants in—and after eat
    them—
The brine they wept at killing 'em.° Then if
You stay to see of us such spinsters,° we
Should hold you here forever.

Pirithous.   Peace be to you
As I pursue this war, which shall be then   25
Beyond further requiring.°   *Exit Pirithous.*

Emilia.   How his longing
Follows his friend! Since his depart,° his sports,
Though craving seriousness and skill, passed slightly
His careless execution,° where nor gain
Made him regard, or loss consider, but   30
Playing one business in his hand, another
Directing in his head—his mind nurse equal
To these so diff'ring twins.° Have you observed
    him,

---

10 **best-tempered pieces** most harmoniously wrought creatures   12
speed success   14 **terrene** earthly   16 **shall be advised** am told
21 **sod** boiled   22 **brine they wept at killing 'em** tears they shed as
they killed them   23 **spinsters** i.e., weak women   25–26 **which . . .
requiring** i.e., peace will be ensured   27 **depart** departure   28–29
passed slightly/His careless execution i.e., were given only slight and
careless attention   32–33 **his mind . . . twins** i.e., his mind was
equally concerned with what he was doing and with what he was
imagining (fighting with Theseus)

Since our great lord departed?

Hippolyta.   With much labor;°
35   And I did love him for't. They two have cabined°
In many as dangerous as poor a corner,
Peril and want contending.° They have skiffed
Torrents whose roaring tyranny and power
I' th' least of these° was dreadful; and they have
40   Fought out together where Death's self was lodged,
Yet Fate hath brought them off.° Their knot of
love,
Tied, weaved, entangled, with so true, so long,
And with a finger of so deep a cunning,
May be outworn, never undone.° I think
45   Theseus cannot be umpire to himself,
Cleaving his conscience° into twain and doing
Each side like° justice, which he loves best.°

Emilia.   Doubtless
There is a best, and Reason has no manners
To say it is not you.° I was acquainted
50   Once with a time when I enjoyed a playfellow.
You were at wars, when she the grave enriched
Who made too proud the bed, took leave o' th'
moon
(Which then looked pale at parting) when our
count°
Was each eleven.

Hippolyta.   'Twas Flavina.

Emilia.   Yes.

34 labor attention   35 cabined lodged together   37 contending i.e.,
being comparable in degree   39 I' th' least of these (referring either
to "Peril and want," line 37, or to "tyranny and power," line 38)
41 brought them off brought them to safety   44 May be outworn,
never undone i.e., may be worn out by death, not unknotted before
45–47 Theseus . . . best i.e., even Theseus cannot judge whether he
loves best himself or Pirithous   46 conscience consciousness   47
like equal   49 To say it is not you (Emilia, taking Hippolyta's remark in a different way from that intended, suggests that Theseus
must love Hippolyta best of all; lines 95–96 make it less likely that
"you" is indefinite, meaning that Theseus must in reason love himself better than his friend)   53 our count the number of our years

You talk of Pirithous' and Theseus' love.   55
Theirs has more ground,° is more maturely sea-
    soned,
More buckled° with strong judgment, and their
    needs
The one of th' other may be said to water
Their intertangled roots of love. But I
And she I sigh and spoke of were things innocent,   60
Loved for we did,° and like the elements
That know not what, nor why, yet do effect
Rare issues by their operance,° our souls
Did so to one another: what she liked
Was then of me approved, what not condemned—   65
No more arraignment;° the flow'r that I would
    pluck
And put between my breasts, O then but beginning
To swell about the blossom, she would long
Till she had such another, and commit it
To the like innocent cradle, where phoenix-like   70
They died in perfume;° on my head no toy°
But was her pattern;° her affections°—pretty
Though happily her careless were°—I followed
For my most serious decking;° had mine ear
Stol'n some new air, or at adventure hummed on   75
From musical coinage,° why, it was a note
Whereon her spirits would sojourn, rather dwell on,
And sing it in her slumbers. This rehearsal,°
Which—every innocent° wots well—comes in
Like old importment's bastard,° has this end   80

56 **ground** foundation   57 **buckled** supported   61 **for we did**
merely because we did   62–63 **effect/Rare issues by their operance**
produce strange happenings through their operation   65–66 **what
not condemned—/No more arraignment** what she did not like was
condemned by me, without further consideration of the case   70–
71 **phoenix-like/They died in perfume** (referring to the legendary
phoenix, from whose fragrant funeral pyre the next phoenix was
born)   71 **toy** trifling ornament   72 **pattern** i.e., for imitation   72
affections inclinations, preferences   73 **Though happily her careless
were** though her preferences might be carelessly made   74 **decking**
adornment   75–76 **hummed on/From musical coinage** i.e., impro-
vised   78 **rehearsal** recital   79 **innocent** child   80 **Like old importment's bastard** like a feeble imitation of the experience itself

That the true love 'tween maid and maid may be
More than in sex dividual.°

Hippolyta.   Y' are out of breath,
And this high-speeded pace is but to say
That you shall never, like the maid Flavina,
Love any that's called man.

85   *Emilia.*   I am sure I shall not.

Hippolyta. Now alack, weak sister,
I must no more believe thee in this point,
Though in't I know thou dost believe thyself,
Than I will trust a sickly appetite
90   That loathes even as it longs. But sure, my sister,
If I were ripe for your persuasion, you
Have said enough to shake me from the arm
Of the all-noble Theseus, for whose fortunes
I will now in and kneel, with great assurance
95   That we, more than his Pirithous, possess
The high throne in his heart.

Emilia.   I am not against
Your faith, yet I continue mine.   *Exeunt.*

81–82 **That . . . dividual** i.e., that their love may be greater than the
love of those different in sex

Scene IV. [*Thebes.*]

*Cornets. A battle struck° within. Then a retreat.
Flourish. Then enter Theseus (victor) [with a
Herald, Lords and Attendants and with Palamon
and Arcite carried on hearses].° The three Queens
meet him, and fall on their faces before him.*

First Queen. To thee no star be dark!°

Second Queen.   Both heaven and earth
Friend° thee forever!

Third Queen.   All the good that may
Be wished upon thy head, I cry "amen" to't!

Theseus. Th' impartial gods, who from the mounted°
    heavens
View us their mortal herd, behold who err   5
And in their time chastise. Go and find out
The bones of your dead lords, and honor them
With treble ceremony; rather than a gap
Should be in their dear° rites, we would supply't.
But those we will depute which shall invest   10
You in your dignities, and even° each thing
Our haste does leave imperfect. So adieu,
And heaven's good eyes look on you.
                              Exeunt Queens.
                              What are those?

Herald. Men of great quality, as may be judged
By their appointment.° Some of Thebes have told's   15
They are sisters' children, nephews to the king.

I.iv. s.d. **struck** sounded **hearses** carriages   1 **To thee no star be
dark** let all stars be favorable to you   2 **Friend** befriend   4 **mounted**
high (with a suggestion of the gods on horseback looking down on
men as beasts under their control)   9 **dear** valued   11 **even** make
right   15 **appointment** accouterment

Theseus. By th' helm of Mars, I saw them in the war,
Like to a pair of lions smeared with prey,
Make lanes in troops aghast. I fixed my note°
20 Constantly on them, for they were a mark
Worth a god's view. What prisoner was't that told
     me°
When I enquired their names?

Herald.   We 'lieve° they're called
Arcite and Palamon.

Theseus.   'Tis right: those, those;
They are not dead?

23 *Herald.* Nor in a state of life: had they been taken
When their last hurts were given, 'twas possible
They might have been recovered. Yet they breathe
And have the name of men.°

Theseus.   Then like men use 'em.
The very lees of such—millions of rates°—
30 Exceed the wine of others. All our surgeons
Convent° in their behoof, our richest balms,
Rather than niggard, waste. Their lives concern us
Much more than Thebes is worth. Rather than have
     'em
Freed of this plight and in their morning state,°
33 Sound and at liberty, I would 'em dead,°
But forty-thousandfold we had rather have 'em
Prisoners to us than Death.° Bear 'em speedily
From our kind air, to them unkind,° and minister
What man to man may do—for our sake more,
40 Since I have known frights, fury, friends' behests,
Love's provocations, zeal, a mistress' task,
Desire of liberty, a fever, madness,
Hath set a mark which Nature could not reach to

---

19 **fixed my note** directed my attention   21 **What . . . me** i.e., what
was it that a prisoner told me   22 **'lieve** believe   28 **have the name
of men** can still be called men   29 **millions of rates** millions of
times   31 **Convent** summon   34 **in their morning state** as they were
this morning   35 **would 'em dead** would rather they were dead   37
Death i.e., prisoners to Death   38 **kind air, to them unkind** i.e., the
open air is healthy to us but not to them

Without some imposition—sickness in will
O'er-wrestling strength in reason.° For our love   45
And great Apollo's° mercy, all our best
Their best skill tender.° Lead into the city,
Where, having bound things scattered, we will post
To Athens 'fore our army.   *Flourish. Exeunt.*

Scene V. [*Thebes.*]

*Music. Enter the Queens with the hearses of their
knights, in a funeral solemnity, &c.*

[*Song*]

Urns and odors bring away,°
Vapors, sighs, darken the day;
Our dole more deadly looks than dying:
Balms and gums° and heavy cheers,°
Sacred vials filled with tears,   5
And clamors through the wild air flying.

Come, all sad and solemn shows
That are quick-eyed Pleasure's foes:
We convent° nought else but woes,
We convent, &c.   10

Third Queen. [*To Second Queen*] This funeral path
     brings° to your household's grave.
Joy seize on you again. Peace sleep with him.

Second Queen. [*To First Queen*] And this to yours.°

40–45 Since . . . reason i.e., since I have known cases where unusual
physical or emotional disturbance has produced results that Nature
could not produce without some special stimulus ("imposition"), this
disturbance being able to overcome what could be reasonably expected   46 Apollo as god of healing   47 tender minister I.v.1
bring away accompany us   4 gums (used for perfume at the funeral
rites)   4 heavy cheers sad faces   9 convent summon, bring together
11 brings leads   13 this to yours (the Queens now take their different
paths home)

First Queen. [*To Third Queen*] Yours this way. Heavens lend°
　A thousand differing ways to one sure end.

Third Queen. This world's a city full of straying° streets,
　And death's the market place where each one meets.　　　　*Exeunt severally.*

13 **lend** provide　15 **straying** winding

ACT II

Scene I. [*Athens. A garden with a room in a prison
above.*]

Enter Jailer and Wooer.

Jailer. I may depart with° little while I live: something I may cast to you, not much. Alas, the prison
I keep, though it be for great ones, yet they seldom
come. Before one salmon you shall take a number
of minnows. I am given out to be better lined than   5
it can appear to me report is a true speaker.° I
would I were really that I am delivered° to be.
Marry,° what I have, be it what it will, I will as-
sure° upon my daughter at the day of my death.

Wooer. Sir, I demand no more than your own offer,   10
and I will estate° your daughter in what I have
promised.

Jailer. Well, we will talk more of this when the solem-
nity° is passed. But have you a full promise of her?

Enter Daughter.

When that shall be seen, I tender my consent.   15

Wooer. I have, sir. Here she comes.

II.i.1 **depart with** give   5–6 **I am . . . speaker** I am generally believed
to be better off than there seems to me cause for rumor to assert
7 **delivered** said   8 **Marry** indeed   8–9 **assure** i.e., bestow   11 **estate**
endow   13–14 **solemnity** i.e., wedding

71

Jailer. Your friend and I have chanced to name you
here, upon the old business; but no more of that
now. So soon as the court-hurry° is over, we will
20 have an end of it. I' th' meantime look tenderly to
the two prisoners. I can tell you they are princes.

Daughter. These strewings° are for their chamber.
'Tis pity they are in prison, and 'twere pity they
should be out. I do think they have patience to
25 make any adversity ashamed: the prison itself is
proud of 'em, and they have all the world in their
chamber.°

Jailer. They are famed to be a pair of absolute° men.

Daughter. By my troth, I think Fame but stammers
30 'em:° they stand a grize° above the reach of report.

Jailer. I heard them reported in the battle to be the
only doers.°

Daughter. Nay, most likely, for they are noble suff'-
rers. I marvel how they would have looked had
35 they been victors, that with such a constant nobility enforce a freedom out of bondage, making
misery their mirth, and affliction a toy to jest at.

Jailer. Do they so?

Daughter. It seems to me they have no more sense of
40 their captivity than I of ruling Athens. They eat
well, look merrily, discourse of many things, but
nothing of their own restraint° and disasters. Yet
sometime a divided° sigh, martyred as 'twere i' th'
deliverance, will break from one of them—when
45 the other presently° gives it so sweet a rebuke that
I could wish myself a sigh to be so chid, or at least
a sigher to be comforted.

19 court-hurry celebrations at court (?) 22 strewings rushes 26–
27 they . . . chamber their nobility makes their chamber into a whole
world (?), everyone visits them (?) 28 absolute complete 29–30
Fame but stammers 'em i.e., their reputation falls short of their
worth 30 grize step 32 only doers unique performers 42 restraint imprisonment 43 divided broken off 45 presently at once

Wooer. I never saw 'em.

Jailer. The duke himself came privately in the night, and so did they:° what the reason of it is I know 50 not.

   Enter Palamon and Arcite above.

Look, yonder they are. That's Arcite looks out.

Daughter. No, sir, no! That's Palamon! Arcite is the lower° of the twain. You may perceive a part of him.   55

Jailer. Go to, leave your pointing. They would not make us their object.° Out of their sight!

Daughter. It is a holiday to look on them. Lord, the diff'rence of men!
     Exeunt [*Jailer, Wooer, Daughter*].

Palamon. How do you, noble cousin?

Arcite.   How do you, sir? 60

Palamon. Why, strong enough to laugh at misery,
And bear the chance of war. Yet we are prisoners
I fear forever, cousin.

Arcite.   I believe it,
And to that destiny have patiently
Laid up my hour to come.°

Palamon.   O cousin Arcite, 65
Where is Thebes now? Where is our noble country?
Where are our friends, and kindreds?° Never more
Must we behold those comforts, never see
The hardy youths strive for the games of honor,
Hung with the painted favors of their ladies, 70

49–50 **The duke . . . they** i.e., Theseus brought the princes secretly to the prison   54 **lower** shorter   56–57 **They would not make us their object** they would not point at us   65 **Laid up my hour to come** i.e., resolved myself   66–67 **Where is Thebes . . . kindreds** (these references to Thebes are very different from those in the princes' conversation of I.ii)

Like tall ships under sail; then start amongst 'em
And as an east wind leave 'em all behind us,
Like lazy clouds, whilst Palamon and Arcite,
Even in the wagging of a wanton leg,°
75　Outstripped the people's praises, won the garlands
Ere they have time to wish 'em ours. O never
Shall we two exercise, like twins of Honor,
Our arms again, and feel our fiery horses
Like proud seas under us! Our good swords now—
80　Better the red-eyed god of war ne'er wore!—
Ravished our sides, like age must run to rust
And deck the temples of those gods that hate us.
These hands shall never draw 'em out like lightning
To blast whole armies more.

Arcite.　　　　　　　　　　　No, Palamon,
85　Those hopes are prisoners with us: here we are
And here the graces of our youths must wither
Like a too timely° spring; here age must find us,
And which is heaviest, Palamon, unmarried;
The sweet embraces of a loving wife,
90　Loaden with kisses, armed with thousand Cupids,
Shall never clasp our necks, no issue° know us,
No figures of ourselves shall we e'er see,
To glad our age, and like young eagles teach 'em
Boldly to gaze against bright arms,° and say:
95　"Remember what your fathers were, and conquer."
The fair-eyed maids shall weep our banishments,
And in their songs curse ever-blinded Fortune
Till she for shame see what a wrong she has done
To youth and nature. This is all our world:
100　We shall know nothing here but one another,
Hear nothing but the clock that tells° our woes.
The vine shall grow, but we shall never see it;
Summer shall come, and with her all delights;
But dead-cold winter must inhabit here still.

---

74 Even . . . leg as quickly as a leg might be wantonly or idly moved
87 too timely too early　**91 issue** children　**94 arms** weapons and
armor (with an allusion to the eagle's ability to look directly at the
sun)　**101 tells** counts

Palamon. 'Tis too true, Arcite. To our Theban hounds, 105
    That shook the agèd forest with their echoes
    No more now must we halloo, no more shake
    Our pointed javelins, whilst the angry swine°
    Flies like a Parthian quiver° from our rages,
    Struck with our well-steeled darts. All valiant uses,° 110
    The food and nourishment of noble minds,
    In us two here shall perish. We shall die—
    Which is the curse of honor—lastly,°
    Children of grief and ignorance.

Arcite.   Yet, cousin,
    Even from the bottom of these miseries, 115
    From all that Fortune can inflict upon us,
    I see two comforts rising, two mere° blessings,
    If the gods please: to hold here a brave patience,
    And the enjoying of our griefs together.
    Whilst Palamon is with me, let me perish 120
    If I think this our prison.

Palamon.   Certainly,
    'Tis a main° goodness, cousin, that our fortunes
    Were twined together. 'Tis most true, two souls
    Put in two noble bodies, let 'em suffer
    The gall of hazard,° so° they grow together, 125
    Will never sink; they must not, say° they could.
    A willing man dies sleeping, and all's done.°

Arcite. Shall we make worthy uses of this place
    That all men hate so much?

Palamon.   How, gentle cousin?

Arcite. Let's think this prison holy sanctuary, 130
    To keep us from corruption of worse men.
    We are young and yet desire the ways of honor

108 **angry swine** wild boar   109 **Parthian quiver** (the Parthian bow-man was famed for shooting his arrows while retreating: here the fleeing boar, with the arrows stuck in it, is seen as the Parthian's quiver)   110 **uses** customs, practices   113 **lastly** (three syllables)   117 **mere** pure   122 **main** principal   125 **The gall of hazard** the bitterness of misadventure   125 **so** provided that   126 **say** even if   127 **A willing . . . done** a man resigned to his fate dies as gently as falling asleep (but the tone of this line is not resigned)

That liberty and common conversation,
The poison of pure spirits, might like women
135 Woo us to wander from. What worthy blessing
Can be but our imaginations
May make it ours? And here being thus together,
We are an endless mine° to one another;
We are one another's wife, ever begetting
New births of love; we are father, friends, acquain-
140   tance;
We are in one another families;
I am your heir, and you are mine. This place
Is our inheritance; no hard oppressor
Dare take this from us; here with a little patience
145 We shall live long, and loving; no surfeits seek us;
The hand of war hurts none here, nor the seas
Swallow their youth. Were we at liberty,
A wife might part us lawfully, or business,
Quarrels consume us, envy of ill men
150 Crave our acquaintance.° I might sicken, cousin,
Where you should never know it, and so perish
Without your noble hand to close mine eyes,
Or prayers to the gods. A thousand chances,
Were we from hence, would sever us.

Palamon.   You have made me—
155 I thank you, cousin Arcite—almost wanton°
With my captivity. What a misery
It is to live abroad, and everywhere!
'Tis like a beast, methinks. I find the court here,
I am sure a more content,° and all those pleasures
160 That woo the wills of men to vanity
I see through now, and am sufficient°
To tell the world 'tis but a gaudy shadow
That old Time, as he passes by, takes with him.
What had we been old° in the court of Creon,

---

138 **mine** source of wealth   150 **Crave our acquaintance** i.e., con-
taminate by impact on us (editors have variously emended, e.g. to
"Grave" = bury, "Cleave" = separate)   155 **wanton** i.e., delighted
159 **a more content** i.e., a court more contented than the real one
161 **sufficient** able   164 **What had we been old** what if we had
been old (editors have emended to "What had we been, old . . .")

Where sin is justice, lust and ignorance   165
The virtues of the great ones! Cousin Arcite,
Had not the loving gods found this place for us,
We had died as they do, ill old men, unwept,
And had their epitaphs, the people's curses.
Shall I say more?

Arcite.   I would hear you still.

Palamon.   Ye shall. 170
Is there record of any two that loved
Better than we do, Arcite?

Arcite.   Sure there cannot.

Palamon. I do not think it possible our friendship
Should ever leave us.

Arcite.   Till our deaths it cannot,

          Enter Emilia and her Woman [below].

And after death our spirits shall be led   175
To those that love eternally.° Speak on, sir.
                    [*Palamon sees Emilia.*]

Emilia. This garden has a world of pleasures in't.
What flow'r is this?

Woman.   'Tis called Narcissus, madam.

Emilia. That was a fair boy certain, but a fool
To love himself:° were there not maids enough?   180

Arcite. Pray, forward.°

Palamon.   Yes.

Emilia.   Or were they all hard-hearted?

Woman. They could not be to one so fair.

Emilia.   Thou wouldst not.

175–76 **our . . . eternally** our souls shall be with famous lovers in
Elysium   178–80 **Narcissus . . . himself** (Narcissus fell in love with
his own reflection in water, and drowned in trying to embrace it)
181 **forward** i.e., continue

Woman. I think I should not, madam.

Emilia.   That's a good wench;
But take heed to your kindness, though.

Woman.   Why, madam?

Emilia. Men are mad things.

185 *Arcite.*   Will ye go forward, cousin?

Emilia. Canst not thou work such flowers in silk,
wench?

Woman.   Yes.

Emilia. I'll have a gown full of 'em and of these.
This is a pretty color, will't not do
Rarely upon a skirt, wench?

Woman.   Dainty, madam.

Arcite. Cousin, cousin, how do you, sir? Why, Pala-
190   mon!

Palamon. Never till now I was in prison, Arcite.

Arcite. Why, what's the matter, man?

Palamon.   Behold, and wonder.
By heaven, she is a goddess.

Arcite. [*Seeing Emilia*]   Ha!

Palamon.   Do reverence.
She is a goddess, Arcite.

Emilia.   Of all flow'rs
Methinks a rose is best.

195 *Woman.*   Why, gentle madam?

Emilia. It is the very emblem of a maid.
For when the west wind courts her gently°
How modestly she blows,° and paints° the sun

---

197 gently (three syllables)   **198 blows** opens into flower   **198 paints**
gives an image of

With her chaste blushes! When the north comes
   near her,
Rude and impatient, then like chastity   *200*
She locks her beauties in her bud again,
And leaves him to base briers.°

Woman.   Yet, good madam,
Sometimes her modesty will blow so far
She falls for't:° a maid,
If she have any honor, would be loath   *205*
To take example by her.

Emilia.   Thou art wanton.

Arcite. She is wondrous fair.

Palamon.   She is all the beauty extant.°

Emilia. The sun grows high, let's walk in. Keep these
   flowers:
We'll see how mere art can come near their colors.
I am wondrous merry-hearted, I could laugh now. *210*

Woman. I could lie down,° I am sure.

Emilia.   And take one with you?°

Woman. That's as we bargain,° madam.

Emilia.   Well, agree° then.
                    Exeunt Emilia and Woman.

Palamon. What think you of this beauty?

Arcite.   'Tis a rare one.

Palamon. Is't but a rare one?

Arcite.   Yes, a matchless beauty.

Palamon. Might not a man well lose himself and love
   her?   *215*

202 **leaves him to base briers** leaves only base briers for him   204
for't as a result of it   207 **extant** in existence   210–11 **laugh . . .
lie down** (the waiting-woman turns Emilia's merriment into an allusion to the proverb "laugh and lie down")   211 **And take one
with you** i.e., lie down with a (male) companion   212 **bargain, agree**
come to terms

Arcite. I cannot tell what you have done. I have.
  Beshrew mine eyes for't, now I feel my shackles.

Palamon. You love her, then?

Arcite.   Who would not?

Palamon.   And desire her?

Arcite. Before my liberty.

Palamon.   I saw her first.

Arcite. That's nothing.

Palamon.   But it shall be.

220 *Arcite.*   I saw her too.

Palamon. Yes, but you must not love her.

Arcite. I will not as you do, to worship her,
  As she is heavenly and a blessèd goddess:
  I love her as a woman, to enjoy her.
225 So both may love.

Palamon. You shall not love at all.

Arcite.   Not love at all?
  Who shall deny me?

Palamon. I that first saw her, I that took possession
  First with mine eye of all those beauties
230 In her revealed to mankind. If thou lov'st her,
  Or entertain'st a hope to blast my wishes,
  Thou art a traitor, Arcite, and a fellow°
  False as thy title to her. Friendship, blood°
  And all the ties between us I disclaim
  If thou once think upon her.

235 *Arcite.*   Yes, I love her,
  And if the lives of all my name° lay on it,
  I must do so, I love her with my soul.
  If that will lose ye,° farewell, Palamon:
  I say again, I love, and in loving her maintain

232 **fellow** (often used contemptuously at this time)   233 **blood** kinship   236 **name** family   238 **lose ye** make me lose you

I am as worthy and as free a lover   240
And have as just a title to her beauty
As any Palamon or any living
That is a man's son.

Palamon.   Have I called thee friend?

Arcite. Yes, and have found me so; why are you
  moved thus?
Let me deal coldly° with you: am not I   245
Part of your blood, part of your soul? You have
  told me
That I was Palamon and you were Arcite.

Palamon. Yes.

Arcite.   Am not I liable to those affections,°
Those joys, griefs, angers, fears, my friend shall
  suffer?

Palamon. Ye may be.

Arcite.   Why then would you deal so cunningly,   250
So strangely, so unlike a noble kinsman,
To love alone? Speak truly, do you think me
Unworthy of her sight?

Palamon.   No, but unjust,
If thou pursue that sight.

Arcite.   Because another
First sees the enemy, shall I stand still   255
And let mine honor down, and never charge?

Palamon. Yes, if he be but one.

Arcite.   But say that one
Had rather combat me?

Palamon.   Let that one say so,
And use thy freedom; else if thou pursuest her,
Be as that cursèd man that hates his country,   260
A branded villain.

245 **coldly** rationally   248 **affections** emotions

Arcite.   You are mad.

Palamon.   I must be,
Till thou art worthy, Arcite: it concerns me.°
And in this madness if I hazard thee°
And take thy life, I deal but truly.

Arcite.   Fie, sir.
265 You play the child extremely. I will love her,
I must, I ought to do so, and I dare,
And all this justly.

Palamon.   O that now, that now
Thy false self and thy friend had but this fortune
To be one hour at liberty, and grasp
Our good swords in our hands, I would quickly
270   teach thee
What 'twere to filch affection from another.
Thou art baser in it than a cutpurse.
Put but thy head out of this window more,
And as I have a soul, I'll nail thy life to't.

Arcite. Thou dar'st not, fool, thou canst not, thou art
275   feeble.
Put my head out? I'll throw my body out,
And leap° the garden, when I see her next

Enter Jailer [*above*].

And pitch° between her arms to anger thee.

Palamon. No more; the keeper's coming; I shall live
To knock thy brains out with my shackles.

280 *Arcite*.   Do.

Jailer. By your leave, gentlemen.

Palamon.   Now, honest keeper?

Jailer. Lord Arcite, you must presently° to th' duke;
The cause I know not yet.

262 **it concerns me** it is of importance to me   263 **hazard thee** put
your life in danger (?), risk losing your friendship (?)   277 **leap**
leap down into   278 **pitch** plant myself   282 **presently** immediately

Arcite.   I am ready, keeper.

Jailer. Prince Palamon, I must awhile bereave you
  Of your fair cousin's company.
                              Exeunt Arcite and Jailer.

Palamon.   And me too,   285
  Even when you please, of life. Why is he sent for?
  It may be he shall marry her, he's goodly,°
  And like enough the duke hath taken notice
  Both of his blood and body. But his falsehood—
  Why should a friend be treacherous? If that   290
  Get him a wife so noble and so fair,
  Let honest men ne'er love again. Once more
  I would but see this fair one. Blessed garden,
  And fruit, and flowers more blessed that still°
    blossom
  As her bright eyes shine on ye! Would I were   295
  For° all the fortune of my life hereafter
  Yon little tree, yon blooming apricock!
  How I would spread, and fling my wanton arms
  In at her window! I would bring her fruit
  Fit for the gods to feed on; youth and pleasure   300
  Still as she tasted should be doubled on her,
  And if she be not heavenly I would make her
  So near the gods in nature, they should fear her.

              Enter Jailer [above].

  And then I am sure she would love me. How now,
    keeper,
  Where's Arcite?

Jailer.   Banished. Prince Pirithous   305
  Obtained his liberty; but never more
  Upon his oath and life must he set foot
  Upon this kingdom.

Palamon. [*Aside*]   He's a blessed man,
  He shall see Thebes again, and call to arms
  The bold young men, that when he bids 'em charge   310

287 **goodly** handsome   294 **still** ever   296 **For** in exchange for

Fall on like fire. Arcite shall have a fortune,°
If he dare make himself a worthy lover,
Yet in the field to strike a battle° for her,
And if he lose her then, he's a cold coward.
313 How bravely may he bear himself to win her
If he be noble Arcite! Thousand ways.°
Were I at liberty, I would do things
Of such a virtuous greatness that this lady,
This blushing virgin, should take manhood to her
And seek to ravish me.

320 *Jailer.*   My lord, for you
I have this charge too.

Palamon.   To discharge my life?

Jailer. No, but from this place to remove your lord-
    ship:
The windows are too open.°

Palamon.   Devils take 'em
That are so envious° to me! Prithee kill me.

Jailer. And hang for't afterward.

325 *Palamon.*   By this good light,
Had I a sword I would kill thee.

Jailer. -   Why, my lord?

Palamon. Thou bring'st such pelting° scurvy news
    continually
Thou art not worthy life. I will not go.

Jailer. Indeed you must, my lord.

Palamon.   May I see the garden?

Jailer. No.

330 *Palamon.* Then I am resolved, I will not go.

---

311 **a fortune** a chance   313 **strike a battle** sound a call to battle
316 **Thousand ways** i.e., there are a thousand ways in which he may
show himself brave   323 **open** easy to escape from   324 **envious**
malicious   327 **pelting** paltry, contemptible

Jailer. I must constrain you then; and for you are
    dangerous,
  I'll clap more irons on you.

Palamon.   Do, good keeper.
  I'll shake 'em so, ye shall not sleep,
  I'll make ye a new morris.° Must I go?

Jailer. There is no remedy.

Palamon.   Farewell, kind window.   335
  May rude wind never hurt thee. O my lady,
  If ever thou hast felt what sorrow was,
  Dream how I suffer. Come; now bury me.
                          Exeunt Palamon and Jailer.

Scene II. [*The open country.*]

Enter Arcite.

Arcite. Banished the kingdom! 'Tis a benefit,
  A mercy I must thank 'em for; but banished
  The free enjoying of that face I die for,
  O 'twas a studied punishment, a death
  Beyond imagination! Such a vengeance   5
  That, were I old and wicked, all my sins
  Could never pluck upon me. Palamon,
  Thou has the start now, thou shalt stay and see
  Her bright eyes break each morning 'gainst thy
    window,
  And let in life into thee; thou shalt feed   10
  Upon the sweetness of a noble beauty
  That Nature ne'er exceeded, nor ne'er shall.
  Good gods! What happiness has Palamon!
  Twenty to one, he'll come to speak to her,
  And if she be as gentle as she's fair,   15

334 make ye a new morris dance a new morris dance for you (in
which bells would jingle on the dancer's coat)

I know she's his: he has a tongue will tame
Tempests, and make the wild rocks wanton. Come
    what can come,
The worst is death. I will not leave the kingdom.
I know mine own° is but a heap of ruins,
20 And no redress there. If I go, he has her.
I am resolved another shape° shall make me,°
Or end my fortunes. Either way I am happy:
I'll see her and be near her, or no more.

*Enter four country people, and one with a garland
before them.*

First Countryman. My masters, I'll be there, that's
    certain.

25 *Second Countryman.* And I'll be there.

Third Countryman. And I.

Fourth Countryman. Why, then, have with ye,° boys.
    'Tis but a chiding.°
Let the plough play today; I'll tickle't out
Of the jades'° tails tomorrow.

First Countryman.   I am sure
30 To have my wife as jealous as a turkey,
But that's all one.° I'll go through,° let her mumble.

Second Countryman. Clap her aboard° tomorrow
    night, and stow° her,
And all's made up again.

Third Countryman.   Aye, do but put
A fescue in her fist,° and you shall see her

II.ii.19 **mine own** i.e., Thebes   21 **another shape** a disguise 21
make me bring good fortune to me   27 **have with ye** i.e., I'll be there ·
too   27 **'Tis but a chiding** the worst that can happen is a chiding
29 **jades'** nags'   31 **that's all one** that's a matter of indifference   31
go through i.e., go through with it   32 **Clap her aboard** board her
(as a conquered ship)   32 **stow** fill the hold with cargo (continuing
the metaphor)   33–34 **put/A fescue in her fist** (a "fescue" was a
small stick, etc., which a teacher used as a pointer: here it indicates
a penis, the idea being "give *her* something to point with")

Take a new lesson out° and be a good wench.   35
Do we all hold,° against° the Maying?

Fourth Countryman.   Hold?
What should ail us?°

Third Countryman.   Arcas will be there.

Second Countryman.   And Sennois
And Rycas, and three better lads ne'er danced
Under green tree; and ye know what wenches, ha?
But will the dainty dominie,° the schoolmaster,   40
Keep touch,° do you think? For he does all,° ye
know.

Third Countryman. He'll eat a hornbook° ere he fail.
Go to,
The matter's too far driven between
Him and the tanner's daughter to let slip now,°
And she must see the duke, and she must dance too.   45

Fourth Countryman. Shall we be lusty!°

Second Countryman. [*Dances*] All the boys in Athens
Blow wind i' th' breech on's,° and here I'll be
And there I'll be, for our town, and here again
And there again! Ha, boys, hey for the weavers!°

First Countryman. This must be done i' th' woods.

Fourth Countryman.   O pardon me.°   50

Second Countryman. By any means.° Our thing of
learning° says so,

35 **Take a new lesson out** learn a new lesson (continuing the meta-phor)   36 **hold** hold to our purposes   36 **against** in regard to   37 **ail us** make us incapable   40 **dainty dominie** fine schoolmaster   41 **Keep touch** hold to his word   41 **does all** i.e., is indispensable   42 **hornbook** sheet of paper protected by a sheet of transparent horn, used in teaching the alphabet, etc.   43–44 **The matter's . . . slip now** i.e., their love affair cannot fail to lead to marriage   46 **lusty** vigor-ous   46–47 **All . . . breech on's** i.e., all the boys in Athens are sup-porting us (literally, are helping us to dance by blowing us from the ground)   49 **hey for the weavers** (the Second Countryman, like Bottom, is a weaver and will dance in honor of his craft)   50 **pardon me** (indicating dissent)   51 **By any means** in any case   51 **Our thing of learning** i.e., the schoolmaster

Where he himself will edify the duke
Most parlously° in our behalfs. He's excellent i' th'
    woods;
Bring him to th' plains,° his learning makes no
    cry.°

Third Countryman. We'll see the sports, then every
55   man to's tackle.°
And, sweet companions, let's rehearse by any
    means
Before the ladies see us, and do sweetly,°
And God knows what may come on't.

Fourth Countryman.   Content;
The sports once ended, we'll perform. Away, boys,
    and hold!°

Arcite. [*Comes forward*] By your leaves, honest
60   friends. Pray you, whither go you?

Fourth Countryman. Whither? Why, what a ques-
    tion's that!

Arcite. Yes, 'tis a question to me that know not.

Third Countryman. To the games, my friend.

Second Countryman. Where were you bred you know
    it not?

Arcite.   Not far, sir.
Are there such games today?

65 *First Countryman.*   Yes, marry are there,
And such as you never saw. The duke himself
Will be in person there.

Arcite.   What pastimes are they?

---

53 parlously amazingly   **53–54 He's excellent . . . plains** (a *double-
entendre* is fairly obvious, implying that the schoolmaster is better in
the earlier than in the later stages of sexual activity)   **54 makes no
cry** wins no applause (and, continuing the metaphor, he will not
make a girl cry out)   **55 every man to's tackle** let every man keep
his engagement   **57 sweetly** delectably   **59 hold** hold to your purposes

Second Countryman. Wrestling and running. [*Aside*]
　'Tis a pretty fellow.

Third Countryman. Thou wilt not go along?

Arcite.　　　　　　　　　　Not yet, sir.

Fourth Countryman.　　　　　　　　　Well, sir,
　Take your own time. Come, boys.

First Countryman.　　　　　　My mind misgives me.　70
　This fellow has a vengeance° trick o' th' hip:
　Mark how his body's made for't.°

Second Countryman.　　　　　I'll be hanged, though,
　If he dare venture. Hang him! Plum porridge,°
　He wrestle? He roast eggs!° Come, let's be gone,
　lads.　　　　　　*Exeunt* [*the*] *four* [*Countrymen*].

Arcite. This is an offered opportunity　　　75
　I durst not wish for. Well, I could have wrestled,°
　The best men called it excellent, and run
　Swifter than wind upon a field of corn,
　Curling the wealthy ears, never flew.° I'll venture,
　And in some poor disguise be there. Who knows　80
　Whether my brows may not be girt with garlands,
　And happiness° prefer me to a place
　Where I may ever dwell in sight of her?

　　　　　　　　　　　　　　Exit Arcite.

---

71 **vengeance** confounded　72 **for't** i.e., for wrestling　73 **Plum porridge** dish made of plums thickened with barley, etc. (here used as a term of contempt for one not likely to excel in wrestling)　74 **He roast eggs** i.e., he would be more capable of cooking an egg　76 **could have wrestled** used to be able to wrestle　78–79 **Swifter . . . flew** swifter than wind . . . ever flew (the illogical negative "never" is idiomatic in the seventeenth century, but editors have frequently emended)　82 **happiness** good fortune

Scene III. [*The prison.*]

Enter Jailer's Daughter alone.

Daughter. Why should I love this gentleman? 'Tis odds
    He never will affect° me; I am base,°
    My father the mean keeper of his prison,
    And he a prince; to marry him is hopeless,
5   To be his whore is witless. Out upon't,
    What pushes° are we wenches driven to
    When fifteen once has found us!° First I saw him:
    I, seeing, thought he was a goodly man:
    He has as much to please a woman in him,
10   If he please to bestow it so, as ever
    These eyes yet looked on. Next, I pitied him,
    And so would any young wench o' my conscience
    That ever dreamed, or vowed her maidenhead
    To a young handsome man. Then I loved him,
15   Extremely loved him, infinitely loved him.
    And yet he had a cousin, fair as he too.
    But in my heart was Palamon, and there,
    Lord, what a coil he keeps!° To hear him
    Sing in an evening, what a heaven it is!
20   And yet his songs are sad ones. Fairer spoken
    Was never gentleman. When I come in
    To bring him water in a morning, first
    He bows his noble body, then salutes me thus:
    "Fair, gentle maid, good-morrow, may thy good-
       ness
25   Get thee a happy husband." Once he kissed me.
    I loved my lips the better ten days after—
    Would he would do so ev'ry day! He grieves much,

II.iii.2 **affect** love **2 base** of low birth **6 pushes** shifts **7 When
fifteen once has found us** when we have reached the age of fifteen
18 coil he keeps disturbance he makes

And me as much to see his misery.
What should I do to make him know I love him,
For I would fain enjoy him? Say I ventured   30
To set him free? What says the law then? Thus much
For law, or kindred!° I will do it,
And this night, or tomorrow, he shall love me.

Exit.

Scene IV. [*At the games.*]

*Short flourish of cornets,° and shouts within. Enter
Theseus, Hippolyta, Pirithous, Emilia, Arcite [disguised] with a garland, &c.*

Theseus. You have done worthily. I have not seen,
Since Hercules, a man of tougher sinews.
Whate'er you are, you run the best and wrestle
That these times can allow.°

Arcite.   I am proud to please you.

Theseus. What country bred you?

Arcite.   This; but far off, prince.   5

Theseus. Are you a gentleman?

Arcite.   My father said so,
And to those gentle uses gave me life.°

Theseus. Are you his heir?

Arcite.   His youngest, sir.

Theseus.   Your father

31–32 **Thus much/For law, or kindred** (we can imagine her clicking
her fingers, thus filling out line 32)   II.iv.s.d. **cornets** hunting horns
4 **allow** acknowledge, praise   7 **to those gentle uses gave me life**
brought me up to practice such noble customs

Sure is a happy sire, then. What proves you?°

10 *Arcite.* A little of all noble qualities:°
I could have kept° a hawk, and well have halloo'd
To a deep cry° of dogs; I dare not praise
My feat in horsemanship, yet they that knew me
Would say it was my best piece;° last, and greatest,
I would be thought a soldier.

15 *Theseus.*   You are perfect.

Pirithous. Upon my soul, a proper man.

Emilia.   He is so.

Pirithous. How do you like him, lady?

Hippolyta.   I admire° him:
I have not seen so young a man so noble,
If he say true, of his sort.

Emilia.   I believe
20 His mother was a wondrous handsome woman:
His face methinks goes that way.°

Hippolyta.   But his body
And fiery mind illustrate° a brave father.

Pirithous. Mark how his virtue,° like a hidden sun,
Breaks through his baser garments.

Hippolyta.   He's well got,° sure.

Theseus. What made you seek this place, sir?

25 *Arcite.*   Noble Theseus,
To purchase name,° and do my ablest service
To such a well-found° wonder as thy worth,
For only in thy court, of all the world,
Dwells fair-eyed Honor.

---

9 **What proves you** what can you show for yourself   10 **qualities**
abilities   11 **could have kept** was able to keep   12 **deep cry** loud
pack   14 **piece** feature, accomplishment   17 **admire** wonder at
21 **goes that way** suggests that   22 **illustrate** confer honor on
(stressed on second syllable)   23 **virtue** nobility   24 **well got** nobly
descended   26 **purchase name** win reputation   27 **well-found** well-
reputed

Pirithous.　　　　　　　All his words are worthy.

Theseus. Sir, we are much indebted to your travel,°　　30
　　Nor shall you lose your wish. Pirithous,
　　Dispose of° this fair gentleman.

Pirithous.　　　　　　　Thanks, Theseus.
　　[*To Arcite*] Whate'er you are y' are mine, and I
　　　　shall give you
　　To a most noble service, to this lady,
　　This bright young virgin; pray observe her good-
　　　　ness;　　　　　　　　　　　　　　　　　　35
　　You have honored her fair birthday with your
　　　　virtues,
　　And as your due y' are hers. Kiss her fair hand, sir.

Arcite. Sir, y' are a noble giver. Dearest beauty,
　　Thus let me seal my vowed faith. [*Kisses her hand.*]
　　　　When your servant,
　　Your most unworthy creature, but offends you,　　40
　　Command him die: he shall.

Emilia.　　　　　　　That were too cruel.
　　If you deserve well, sir, I shall soon see't.
　　Y' are mine, and somewhat better than your rank
　　I'll use you.

Pirithous. I'll see you furnished,° and because you say
　　You are a horseman, I must needs entreat you　　45
　　This afternoon to ride, but 'tis a rough one.°

Arcite. I like him better, prince: I shall not then
　　Freeze in my saddle.

Theseus.　　　　　　　Sweet, you must be ready,
　　And you, Emilia, and you, friend, and all,
　　Tomorrow by the sun° to do observance　　　　　50
　　To flow'ry May in Dian's wood. Wait well, sir,
　　Upon your mistress. Emily, I hope
　　He shall not go afoot.

30 **travel** journey (or, perhaps, labor)　32 **Dispose of** take charge of
44 **furnished** provided (with what you need)　46 **a rough one** i.e., an
untrained or unruly horse　50 **by the sun** by sunrise

Emilia.   That were a shame, sir,
    While I have horses. [*To Arcite*] Take your choice,
        and what
55 You want at any time, let me but know it.
    If you serve faithfully, I dare assure you
    You'll find a loving mistress.

Arcite.   If I do not,
    Let me find that my father ever hated,
    Disgrace and blows.

Theseus.   Go, lead the way: you have
        won it.°
60 It shall be so; you shall receive all dues
    Fit for the honor you have won; 'twere wrong else.
    Sister, beshrew my heart, you have a servant
    That, if I were a woman, would be master.
    But you are wise.

Emilia.   I hope too wise for that,° sir.
                          Flourish. Exeunt omnes.

Scene V. [*The prison.*]

Enter Jailer's Daughter alone.

Daughter. Let all the dukes, and all the devils, roar:
    He is at liberty. I have ventured for him,
    And out I have brought him to a little wood
    A mile hence. I have sent him where a cedar,
5   Higher than all the rest, spreads like a plane
    Fast by a brook, and there he shall keep close°
    Till I provide him files and food, for yet
    His iron bracelets are not off. O Love,
    What a stout-hearted child thou art! My father

59 **you have won it** i.e., your success in the games makes you deserve
to lead the way   64 **I hope too wise for that** (Emilia rejects Theseus'
suggestion of marriage)   II.v.6 **keep close** stay in hiding

Durst better have endured cold iron° than done it. 10
I love him, beyond love and beyond reason,
Or wit,° or safety: I have made him know it.
I care not, I am desperate. If the law
Find me,° and then condemn me for't, some wenches,
Some honest-hearted maids, will sing my dirge, 15
And tell to memory my death was noble,
Dying almost a martyr. That way he takes
I purpose is my way too. Sure he cannot
Be so unmanly as to leave me here.
If he do, maids will not so easily 20
Trust men again. And yet he has not thanked me
For what I have done—no, not so much as kissed me,
And that methinks is not so well. Nor scarcely
Could I persuade him to become a freeman,
He made such scruples of the wrong he did 25
To me, and to my father. Yet I hope,
When he considers more, this love of mine
Will take more root within him. Let him do
What he will with me, so he use me kindly,
For use me so he shall, or I'll proclaim him, 30
And to his face, no man.° I'll presently°
Provide him necessaries, and pack my clothes up,
And where there is a path of ground° I'll venture,
So° he be with me. By him, like a shadow,
I'll ever dwell. Within this hour the hubbub 35
Will be all o'er the prison: I am then
Kissing the man they look for. Farewell, father;
Get many more such prisoners, and such daughters,
And shortly you may keep yourself.° Now to him.
                                        [*Exit.*]

---

10 **endured cold iron** suffered death with sword or ax   12 **wit** good sense   14 **Find me** bring me to judgment   31 **no man** impotent   31 **presently** at once   33 **path of ground** way through woods, etc. (some editors emend to "patch of ground")   34 **So** provided that   39 **shortly you may keep yourself** i.e., you will lose all of them and will have only yourself to look after

ACT III

Scene I. [*The open country.*]

Cornets in sundry places. Noise and hallooing° as people a-Maying. Enter Arcite alone.

Arcite. The duke has lost Hippolyta; each took
 A several° laund.° This is a solemn rite
 They owe bloomed May, and the Athenians pay it
 To th' heart of ceremony.° O Queen Emilia,
5 Fresher than May, sweeter
 Than her gold buttons° on the boughs or all
 Th' enameled knacks° o' th' mead or garden—yea,
 We challenge too the bank of any nymph
 That makes the stream seem flowers!° Thou, O jewel
10 O' th' wood, o' th' world, hast likewise° blest a place
 With thy sole presence, in thy rumination,°
 That I, poor man, might eftsoons° come between
 And chop on some cold thought.° Thrice blessed chance

III.i. s.d. **hallooing** cries of people calling to each other from a distance, or urging dogs in the chase   2 **several** different   2 **laund** open space among woods (obsolete form of "lawn")   4 **To th' heart of ceremony** most ceremoniously   6 **buttons** buds   7 **enameled knacks** trifles of various colors   8–9 **the bank ... flowers** i.e., by the stream reflecting the flowers on its bank   10 **likewise** like the "nymph" of line 8   11 **in thy rumination** as you meditate there   12 **eftsoons** quickly   12–13 **come ... thought** ("chop" was a hunting term meaning to seize prey before it was away from cover: here the idea is apparently that Arcite hopes merely to come into Emilia's chaste ["cold"] thoughts)

96

To drop on° such a mistress, expectation
Most guiltless on't!° Tell me, O lady Fortune,   15
Next after Emily my sovereign, how far
I may be proud. She takes strong note of° me,
Hath made me near her;° and this beauteous morn,
The prim'st° of all the year, presents me with
A brace of horses: two such steeds might well   20
Be by a pair of kings backed, in a field
That their crowns' titles tried.° Alas, alas,
Poor cousin Palamon, poor prisoner, thou
So little dream'st upon my fortune that
Thou think'st thyself the happier thing, to be   25
So near Emilia! Me thou deem'st at Thebes,
And therein wretched, although free. But if
Thou knew'st my mistress breathed on me, and that
I eared° her language, lived in her eye°—O coz,
What passion would enclose thee!°

Enter Palamon as out of a bush, with his shackles.
[He] bends his fist at Arcite.

Palamon.   Traitor kinsman,   30
Thou shouldst perceive my passion, if these signs
Of prisonment were off me, and this hand
But owner of a sword. By all oaths in one,
I and the justice of my love would make thee
A confessed traitor, O thou most perfidious   35
That ever gently° looked, the void'st of honor
That e'er bore gentle token!° Falsest cousin
That ever blood made kin, call'st thou her thine?
I'll prove it in my shackles, with these hands

14 **drop on** come upon   14–15 **expectation/Most guiltless on't** i.e., without at all expecting it   17 **takes strong note of** observes closely   18 **made me near her** made me attend on her   19 **prim'st** supreme   22 **That their crowns' titles tried** where their claims to the crowns were being decided   29 **eared** listened to, with also a suggestion of "ear" = to plow   29 **in her eye** where she can see me, but with the suggestion of being so close as to see his reflection in her eye   30 **enclose thee** i.e., imprison you (doubly ironic in that Arcite thinks Palamon physically in prison while he is actually free but is "enclosed" by the passion indicated)   36 **gently** nobly   37 **bore gentle token** showed outward sign of nobility

40   Void of appointment,° that thou liest, and art
        A very thief in love, a chaffy° lord,
        Nor worth the name of villain—had I a sword,
        And these house-clogs° away.

Arcite.   Dear cousin Palamon—

Palamon. Cozener Arcite, give me language such
        As thou hast showed me feat.°

45   *Arcite.*   Not finding in
        The circuit of my breast any gross stuff
        To form me like your blazon,° holds me to
        This gentleness of answer: 'tis your passion
        That thus mistakes, the which to you being enemy
50   Cannot to me be kind;° honor and honesty
        I cherish, and depend on, howsoe'er
        You skip° them in me, and with them, fair coz,
        I'll maintain my proceedings. Pray be pleased
        To show in generous° terms your griefs,° since that
55   Your question's° with your equal, who professes
        To clear his own way,° with the mind and sword
        Of a true gentleman.

Palamon.   That thou durst, Arcite!

Arcite. My coz, my coz, you have been well adver-
            tised°
        How much I dare. Y' have seen me use my sword
60   Against th' advice° of fear. Sure° of another
        You would not hear me doubted, but your silence
        Should break out, though i' th' sanctuary.°

Palamon.   Sir,

40 **Void of appointment** without weapons to fight with   41 **chaffy**
worthless   43 **house-clogs** i.e., his shackles   44–45 **give . . . feat** i.e.,
let your language correspond with your actions   47 **your blazon**
your description of me   49–50 **the which . . . kind** as your passion
is your enemy, it cannot be kind to me, your friend and other self
52 **skip** overlook   54 **generous** noble   54 **griefs** grievances   55
question's quarrel's   55–56 **professes/To clear his own way** claims
to justify his conduct   58 **advertised** informed (stressed on second
syllable)   60 **advice** warning   60 **Sure** surely   62 **i' th' sanctuary**
in a church, but also with the suggestion of breaking out of "sanctuary" (a place of safety) for the sake of righting his friend

I have seen you move in such a place° which well
Might justify your manhood: you were called
A good knight and a bold. But the whole week's not
 fair   65
If any day it rain. Their valiant temper°
Men lose when they incline° to treachery,
And then they fight like compelled° bears, would
 fly
Were they not tied.

Arcite.   Kinsman, you might as well
Speak this and act it in your glass, as to   70
His ear which now disdains you.

Palamon.   Come up to me,
Quit me of these cold gyves,° give me a sword,
Though it be rusty, and the charity
Of one meal lend me. Come before me then,
A good sword in thy hand, and do but say 75
That Emily is thine, I will forgive
The trespass thou hast done me, yea my life
If then thou carry't;° and brave souls in shades
That have died manly, which will seek of me
Some news from earth, they shall get none but this, 80
That thou art brave and noble.

Arcite.   Be content.
Again betake you to your hawthorn house.°
With counsel of the night,° I will be here
With wholesome viands. These impediments°
Will I file off. You shall have garments, and 85
Perfumes to kill the smell o' th' prison. After,
When you shall stretch yourself and say but "Arcite,
I am in plight,"° there shall be at your choice
Both sword and armor.

---

63 **in such a place** i.e., in battle or tournament 66 **temper** character
67 **incline** yield 68 **compelled** i.e., in bear-baiting (stressed on first
syllable here) 72 **gyves** fetters 78 **If then thou carry't** i.e., if you
then kill me 82 **hawthorn house** shelter in the hawthorn bush 83
With counsel of the night with only night as my confidant 84 **These
impediments** Palamon's shackles 88 **in plight** in good condition,
ready

Palamon.   O you heavens, dares any
90   So noble bear° a guilty business? None
       But only Arcite. Therefore none but Arcite
       In this kind is so bold.

Arcite.   Sweet Palamon!

Palamon. I do embrace you and your offer. For
       Your offer do't I only, sir. Your person
95   Without hypocrisy I may not wish
                                   Wind horns off.
       More than my sword's edge on't.

Arcite.   You hear the horns.
       Enter your musit° lest this match between's
       Be crossed ere met.° Give me your hand. Farewell.
       I'll bring you every needful thing. I pray you
       Take comfort and be strong.

100 *Palamon.*   Pray hold your promise,
       And do the deed with a bent brow°—most certain
       You love me not; be rough with me, and pour
       This oil° out of your language. By this air,
       I could for each word give a cuff,° my stomach°
       Not reconciled by reason.

105 *Arcite.*   Plainly spoken,
       Yet pardon me hard language.° When I spur
                                   Wind horns.
       My horse, I chide him not. Content and anger
       In me have but one face.° Hark, sir, they call
       The scattered to the banquet:° you must guess
       I have an office° there.

110 *Palamon.*   Sir, your attendance
       Cannot please heaven, and I know your office
       Unjustly is achieved.°

90 **bear** carry out   97 **musit** gap in a hedge through which a hare,
etc., might pass when hunted   98 **crossed ere met** i.e., prevented before begun   101 **with a bent brow** sternly   103 **oil** courtesy, gentleness   104 **cuff** blow   104 **stomach** anger   106 **pardon me hard
language** allow me not to use hostile language   108 **one face** the
same outward manifestation   109 **banquet** light repast, as for a
hunting party   110 **office** duty to perform   112 **Unjustly is achieved**
has been unfairly won

Arcite.   If a good title°—
  I am persuaded this question, sick between's,
  By bleeding must be cured.° I am a suitor
  That to your sword you will bequeath this plea,°   115
  And talk of it no more.

Palamon.   But this one word:
  You are going now to gaze upon my mistress,
  For, note you, mine she is.

Arcite.   Nay, then.

Palamon.   Nay, pray you,
  You talk of feeding me to breed me strength.
  You are going now to look upon a sun   120
  That strengthens what it looks on: there you have
  A vantage o'er me, but enjoy't till
  I may enforce my remedy. Farewell.
                              Exeunt [severally].

Scene II. [*The open country.*]

Enter Jailer's Daughter alone.

Daughter. He has mistook the brake° I meant, is gone
  After his fancy.° 'Tis now well nigh morning.
  No matter, would it were perpetual night,
  And darkness lord o' th' world. Hark! 'Tis a wolf!
  In me hath grief slain fear, and but for one thing   5
  I care for nothing, and that's Palamon.
  I reck not if the wolves would jaw me, so
  He had this file. What if I halloo'd for him?
  I cannot halloo. If I whooped, what then?

112 **If a good title** (either Arcite interrupts himself or, as some editors have done, we should emend "If" to "I've")   113–14 **this question . . . cured** (Arcite sees the quarrel as a sick person standing
between them: they must cure the sickness by letting blood from it)
115 **plea** lawsuit   III.ii.1 **brake** thicket   2 **After his fancy** where his
fancy has led him

10 If he not answered, I should call a wolf
And do him but that service.° I have heard
Strange howls this live-long night: why may't not be
They have made prey of him? He has no weapons,
He cannot run, the jingling of his gyves
15 Might call fell° things to listen, who have in them
A sense to know a man unarmed, and can
Smell where resistance° is. I'll set it down°
He's torn to pieces: they howled many together
And then they fed on him. So much for that;
20 Be bold to ring the bell.° How stand I then?
All's chared° when he is gone. No, no, I lie.
My father's to be hanged for his escape,
Myself to beg, if I prized life so much
As to deny my act, but that I would not,
25 Should I try death by dozens.° I am moped:°
Food took I none these two days,
Sipped some water. I have not closed mine eyes
Save when my lids scoured off their brine.° Alas,
Dissolve my life, let not my sense unsettle,
30 Lest I should drown, or stab, or hang myself.
O state of nature,° fail together° in me,
Since thy best props are warped! So which way
   now?
The best way is the next° way to a grave:
Each errant step beside° is torment. Lo,
The moon is down, the crickets chirp, the screech-
   owl
35 Calls in° the dawn. All offices° are done
Save what I fail in. But the point is this:
An end, and that is all.°   *Exit.*

11 **do him but that service** i.e., (ironically) bring a wolf to him   15 **fell** savage   17 **resistance** the power to resist   17 **set it down** take it as settled   20 **ring the bell** i.e., toll the bell for his death   21 **All's chared** all tasks are ended   25 **Should I try death by dozens** should I have to die many times or in many ways   25 **moped** bewildered, numbed   28 **when my lids scoured off their brine** when I closed them to get rid of my tears   31 **state of nature** condition of being alive   31 **together** altogether   33 **next** nearest   34 **Each errant step beside** i.e., each step that does not lead directly to my grave   36 **Calls in** summons (the owl, doing duty for the cock, indicates the upside-downness of her world)   36 **offices** tasks   38 **An end, and that is all** i.e., only death is to come

Scene III. [*The open country.*]

Enter Arcite, with meat, wine, and files.

Arcite. I should be near the place. Ho, cousin
   Palamon!

Enter Palamon.

Palamon. Arcite?

Arcite.   The same. I have brought you food
   and files.
   Come forth and fear not; here's no Theseus.

Palamon. Nor none so honest, Arcite.

Arcite.   That's no matter,
   We'll argue that hereafter. Come, take courage,   5
   You shall not die thus beastly;° here, sir, drink,
   I know you are faint; then I'll talk further with you.

Palamon. Arcite, thou mightst now poison me.

Arcite.   I might;
   But I must° fear you first. Sit down, and good
   now,°
   No more of these vain parleys: let us not,   10
   Having our ancient reputation with us,
   Make talk for fools and cowards.° To your health,
   &c.   [*He drinks.*]

Palamon. Do.°

III.iii.6 **thus beastly** in your present beastlike condition   9 **must**
should have to   9 **good now** please   12 **Make talk for fools and
cowards** give matter for fools and cowards to talk about   13 **Do**
i.e., do drink

Arcite.   Pray sit down then, and let me entreat you,
By all the honesty and honor in you,
15   No mention of this woman, 'twill disturb us;
We shall have time enough.

Palamon.   Well, sir, I'll pledge you.
                        [*He drinks.*]

Arcite. Drink a good hearty draught, it breeds good blood, man.
Do not you feel it thaw you?

Palamon.   Stay, I'll tell you
After a draught or two more.

Arcite.   Spare it not,
The duke has more, coz. Eat now.

Palamon.   Yes. [*He eats.*]

20   *Arcite.*   I am glad
You have so good a stomach.°

Palamon.   I am gladder
I have so good meat to't.

Arcite.   Is't not mad° lodging
Here in the wild woods, cousin?

Palamon.   Yes, for them
That have wild° consciences.

Arcite.   How tastes your victuals?
Your hunger needs no sauce, I see.

25   *Palamon.*   Not much.
But if it did, yours° is too tart. Sweet cousin,
What is this?

Arcite.   Venison.

Palamon.   'Tis a lusty° meat.

21 **stomach** appetite   22 **mad** fantastic   24 **wild** disordered   26
yours i.e., the sauce you bring in your words and presence   27 **lusty**
hearty, invigorating

Give me more wine. [*Arcite gives him the wine.*]
    Here, Arcite, to the wenches
We have known in our days. The Lord Steward's
    daughter,
Do you remember her?
                    [*He offers the wine to Arcite.*]

Arcite.   After you, coz.   30

Palamon. She loved a black-haired man.

Arcite.   She did so. Well, sir?

Palamon. And I have heard some call him Arcite,
    and—

Arcite. Out with't, 'faith.

Palamon.   She met him in an arbor:
    What did she there, coz? Play o' th' virginals?°

Arcite. Something she did, sir.

Palamon.   Made her groan a month for't;   35
    Or two, or three, or ten.°

Arcite.   The Marshal's sister
    Had her share too, as I remember, cousin,
    Else there be tales° abroad. You'll pledge her?

Palamon.   Yes.
                    [*He drinks.*]

Arcite. A pretty brown wench 'tis. There was a time
    When young men went a-hunting—and a wood,   40
    And a broad beech, and thereby hangs a tale.
    Heigh ho!

Palamon.   For Emily, upon my life! Fool,
    Away with this strained mirth! I say again
    That sigh was breathed for Emily. Base cousin,

---

34 **Play o' th' virginals** ("virginals" was the name of a small instrument like a spinet: here punningly used with reference to sexual in-
tercourse)   35–36 **groan . . . ten** (Palamon leads archly to the idea
of gestation)   38 **tales** false reports

Dar'st thou break° first?

Arcite.   You are wide.°

45 *Palamon.*   By heaven and earth,
There's nothing in thee honest.

Arcite.   Then I'll leave you:
You are a beast° now.

Palamon.   As thou mak'st me, traitor.

Arcite. There's all things needful: files and shirts and
     perfumes.
I'll come again some two hours hence, and bring
That that shall quiet all.

50 *Palamon.*   A sword and armor?

Arcite. Fear me not; you are now too foul;° farewell.
Get off your trinkets,° you shall want nought.

Palamon.   Sirrah°—

Arcite. I'll hear no more.   *Exit.*

Palamon.   If he keep touch,° he dies for't.
                                        Exit.

Scene IV. [*The open country.*]

Enter Jailer's Daughter.

Daughter. I am very cold, and all the stars are out too,
The little stars and all, that look like aglets.°
The sun has seen my folly. Palamon!

45 **break** break our agreement not to refer to Emilia (but also with a
suggestion of emotion breaking out)   45 **wide** wide of the mark   47
beast i.e., not fit for conversation   51 **foul** unwashed, etc.   52
trinkets i.e., shackles   52 **Sirrah** (contemptuous form of address)
53 **keep touch** keep his promise   III.iv.2 **aglets** jewels used as hair
ornaments and for tags to laces

Alas, no, he's in heaven. Where am I now?
Yonder's the sea, and there's a ship: how't tumbles,   5
And there's a rock lies watching under water;
Now, now, it beats upon it;° now, now, now!
There's a leak sprung, a sound° one; how they cry!
Spoon° her before the wind, you'll lose all else!
Up with a course° or two, and tack about,° boys!   10
Good night, good night, y' are gone. I am very
    hungry.
Would I could find a fine frog; he would tell me
News from all parts o' th' world; then would I
    make
A carack° of a cockleshell, and sail
By east and north-east to the King of Pigmies,   15
For he tells fortunes rarely. Now my father
Twenty to one is trussed up in a trice°
Tomorrow morning. I'll say never a word.

(*Sing[s]*) For I'll cut my green coat, a foot above my
        knee,
        And I'll clip my yellow locks, an inch below
        mine eye.   20
                Hey, nonny, nonny, nonny!
        He's° buy me a white cut,° forth for to ride,
        And I'll go seek him, through the world that
        is so wide.
                Hey, nonny, nonny, nonny!

O for a prick now like a nightingale,   25
To put my breast against!° I shall sleep like a top
    else.   *Exit.*

---

7 **it beats upon it** i.e., the ship strikes the rock   8 **sound** great   9
Spoon scud   10 **course** sail attached to the lower yards of a ship
10 **tack about** change direction   14 **carack** ship of large burden   17
trussed up in a trice hanged immediately   22 **He's** (vulgar form of
"He'll")   22 **cut** laboring horse, so called because either with docked
tail or gelded   25–26 **prick . . . against** (alluding to the common belief that the nightingale presses against a thorn in order to stay awake
and sing)

Scene V. [*The open country.*]

*Enter a Schoolmaster, four Countrymen and Bavian,°
five wenches, with a Taborer.°*

Schoolmaster. Fie, fie,
    What tediosity and disensanity°
    Is here among ye? Have my rudiments
    Been labored so long with ye, milked unto ye,
5   And, by a figure,° even the very plumbroth°
    And marrow of my understanding laid upon ye?
    And do you still cry "where" and "how" and
        "wherefore"?
    You most coarse frieze° capacities, ye jean° judg-
        ments,
    Have I said "thus let be," and "there let be,"
10   And "then let be," and no man understand me?
    Proh deum, medius fidius,° ye are all dunces!
    For why, here stand I. Here the duke comes; there
       are you
    Close° in the thicket; the duke appears; I meet him
    And unto him I utter learnèd things,
15   And many figures; he hears, and nods, and hums,
    And then cries "Rare!", and I go forward; at length
    I fling my cap up—mark there—then do you,
    As once did Meleager and the boar,°
    Break comely° out before him—like true lovers,°

III.v. s.d. **Bavian** the fool in the morris dance (the word signifying
either "driveler" or "baboon") **Taborer** one who plays a small
drum 2 **disensanity** insanity ("dis-" here being intensive) 5 **figure**
i.e., of speech 5 **plumbroth** (as "plum porridge," II.ii.73) 8 **frieze**
rough woollen cloth 8 **jean** a kind of fustian (also spelt "jane")
11 **Proh deum, medius fidius** O God, most certainly 13 **Close** secretly 18 **Meleager and the boar** (alluding to Meleager's killing the
Calydonian boar, and his bringing the boar's head to Atalanta) 19
comely fittingly 19 **lovers** i.e., of Theseus

Cast yourselves in a body° decently,   20
And sweetly, by a figure, trace and turn,° boys.

First Countryman. And sweetly we will do it, Master
Gerald.

Second Countryman. Draw up the company. Where's
the taborer?

Third Countryman. Why, Timothy!

Taborer.   Here, my mad boys, have at ye!°

Schoolmaster. But, I say, where's their women?

Fourth Countryman.   Here's Friz and Maudlin.   25

Second Countryman. And little Luce with the white
legs, and bouncing° Barbary.

First Countryman. And freckled Nell, that never failed
her master.°

Schoolmaster. Where be your ribands, maids? Swim°
with your bodies,
And carry it° sweetly and deliverly,°
And now and then a favor,° and a frisk.°   30

Nell. Let us alone,° sir.

Schoolmaster.   Where's the rest o' th' music?°

Third Countryman. Dispersed° as you commanded.

Schoolmaster.   Couple° then,
And see what's wanting. Where's the Bavian?
My friend, carry your tail without offense
Or scandal to the ladies; and be sure   35
You tumble with audacity, and manhood,
And when you bark do it with judgment.

---

20 **Cast yourselves in a body** arrange yourselves in a group for the
dance   21 **trace and turn** dance and revolve   24 **have at ye** i.e., I
am ready for you   26 **bouncing** large of body   27 **that never failed
her master** i.e., did whatever he wanted of her   28 **Swim** move flow-
ingly   29 **carry it** i.e., perform the dance   29 **deliverly** nimbly   30
favor (presumably a kiss)   30 **frisk** caper   31 **Let us alone** leave it
to us   31 **music** musicians   32 **Dispersed** i.e., scattered in arranged
places   32 **Couple** take your partners

Bavian.   Yes, sir.

Schoolmaster. Quo usque tandem?° Here is a woman
    wanting.°

Fourth Countryman. We may go whistle.° All the fat's
    i' th' fire.

40 *Schoolmaster.* We have,
    As learnèd authors utter, washed a tile,°
    We have been *fatuus,*° and labored vainly.

Second Countryman. This is that scornful piece,° that
    scurvy hilding,°
    That gave her promise faithfully she would be here,
45   Cicely the sempster's° daughter.
    The next gloves that I give her shall be dogskin.
    Nay, and° she fail me once! You can tell, Arcas,°
    She swore by wine and bread she would not break.°

Schoolmaster. An eel and woman,
50   A learnèd poet says,° unless by th' tail
    And with thy teeth thou hold, will either° fail.
    In manners this was false position.°

First Countryman. A fire ill° take her! Does she flinch
    now?

Third Countryman.   What
    Shall we determine,° sir?

Schoolmaster.   Nothing.
55   Our business is become a nullity,
    Yea, and a woeful, and a piteous nullity.

---

38 **Quo usque tandem** how long now   38 **wanting** missing   39 **We
may go whistle** we have occupied ourselves to no purpose   41
washed a tile labored in vain (Latin "*laterem lavare*")   42 **fatuus**
foolish   43 **piece** creature   43 **hilding** good-for-nothing   45 **sempster's** probably here = sempstress's   47 **and if** if   47 **Arcas** (the name
of one of the Countrymen: cf. II.ii.37)   48 **break** break her word
50 **A learnèd poet says** (no one has identified the "poet," if he existed;
but Fletcher used the proverb in other plays)   51 **either** both   52
position statement of a proposition, affirmation (the Schoolmaster
means that Cicely's breaking her word was the equivalent in manners to the stating of a false proposition in logic)   53 **fire ill** (perhaps equivalent to "pox," or "ill" may be adverbial)   54 **determine**
decide to do

Fourth Countryman. Now when the credit of our town
    lay on it,
  Now to be frampel,° now to piss o' th' nettle!°
  Go thy ways, I'll remember thee, I'll fit thee!°

Enter Jailer's Daughter.

Daughter.

    [*Sings*] The George Alow° came from the south,   60
        From the coast of Barbary-a,
    And there he met with brave gallants of war,
        By one, by two, by three-a.
    Well hailed, well hailed, you jolly gallants,
        And whither now are you bound-a?   65
    O let me have your company
        Till we come to the sound-a.

There was three fools fell out about an owlet.

    The one said it was an owl;
    The other he said nay;   70
    The third he said it was a hawk,
    And her bells° were cut away.

Third Countryman. There's a dainty° mad woman,
    master,
  Comes i' th' nick,° as mad as a march hare.
  If we can get her dance, we are made again:°   75
  I warrant her, she'll do the rarest° gambols.

First Countryman. A mad woman? We are made,
    boys.

Schoolmaster. And are you mad, good woman?

---

58 **frampel** peevish, froward   58 **piss o' th' nettle** give herself occasion to show bad temper   59 **fit thee** punish you as you deserve   60
George Alow (this was the name of a ship in a ballad published in
1611)   72 **bells** (used on a hawk for ease in tracing it)   73 **dainty**
fine   74 **i' th' nick** i.e., just when we need her   75 **we are made**
again our fortune is once more secure   76 **rarest** finest

Daughter.   I would be sorry else.
Give me your hand.

Schoolmaster.   Why?

Daughter.   I can tell your fortune.
80   You are a fool. Tell ten. I have posed him.° Buzz.°
Friend, you must eat no white bread; if you do,
Your teeth will bleed extremely. Shall we dance,
   ho?
I know you, y' are a tinker: sirrah tinker,
Stop no more holes but what you should.°

Schoolmaster.   *Dii boni!*°
A tinker, damsel?

85 *Daughter.*   Or a conjuror.
Raise me a devil now, and let him play
Qui passa,° o' th' bells and bones.°

Schoolmaster.   Go take her,
And fluently° persuade her to a peace.
Et opus exegi, quod nec Iovis ira, nec ignis.°
Strike up,° and lead her in.°

90 *Second Countryman.*   Come, lass, let's trip it.

Daughter. I'll lead.

Third Countryman. Do, do.

Schoolmaster.   Persuasively, and cunningly!°
                              Wind horns.

---

80 **Tell ten. I have posed him** (counting on one's fingers was a common method of testing idiocy: the Jailer's Daughter decides the Schoolmaster cannot pass the test)   80 **Buzz** (exclamation commanding silence)   84 **Stop . . . should** (alluding to the proverb "A tinker stops one hole and makes others"; but with an obvious double meaning here)   84 **Dii boni** good gods   87 **Qui passa** (the song "Chi passa per questa strada")   87 **bells and bones** (similar to Bottom's "the tongs and the bones," *A Midsummer Night's Dream,* IV.i.32: "bones" were bone clappers held between the fingers)   88 **fluently** quickly   89 **Et . . . ignis** I have achieved something which neither Jove's anger nor fire . . . (from Ovid's *Metamorphoses,* xv. 871, where it reads "*Jamque opus . . . nec ignes*")   90 **Strike up** begin the music   90 **in** offstage, into the thicket where the dancers will wait   91 **cunningly** skillfully

Away, boys! I hear the horns.
Give me some meditation,° and mark your cue.
                    Exeunt all but Schoolmaster.

Pallas° inspire me!

*Enter Theseus, Pirithous, Hippolyta, Emilia, Arcite,
    and train. [A chair and stools are brought out.]°*

Theseus.   This way the stag took.

Schoolmaster. Stay, and edify!°

Theseus.   What have we here?   95

Pirithous. Some country sport, upon my life, sir.

Theseus. Well, sir, go forward, we will edify.
    Ladies, sit down; we'll stay it.°   [*They sit.*]

Schoolmaster. Thou doughty duke, all hail! All hail,
    sweet ladies!

Theseus. This is a cold beginning.°   100

Schoolmaster. If you but favor, our country pastime
        made is.
    We are a few of those collected here
    That ruder tongues distinguish° villager.
    And to say verity, and not to fable,
    We are a merry rout, or else a rabble   105
    Or company, or by a figure *Chorus*,°
    That 'fore thy dignity will dance a morris.
    And I that am the rectifier° of all,
    By title Pedagogus, that let fall
    The birch upon the breeches of the small ones, 110
    And humble with a ferula° the tall ones,

93 **meditation** time for meditation (?), attention (?)   94 **Pallas as**
goddess of learning   94 s.d. **A chair and stools are brought out** (see
Textual Note for lines 65–67)   95 **edify** (the Schoolmaster's English
for "profit mentally," "be edified")   98 **stay it** wait here for it   100
cold beginning (deliberately taking "hail" for a reference to the
weather)   103 **distinguish** classify   106 **by a figure Chorus** (the
Schoolmaster's "figure" allows him to compare the morris dancers
with the chorus of a classical play)   108 **rectifier** (pedant's word for
"director")   111 **ferula** cane

Do here present this machine,° or this frame;°
And dainty duke, whose doughty dismal fame
From Dis to Daedalus,° from post to pillar°
115 Is blown abroad, help me, thy poor well-willer,
And with thy twinkling eyes look right and straight
Upon this mighty "Morr," of mickle weight;
"Is" now comes in—which being glued together
Makes "Morris,"° and the cause that we came
     hither,
120 The body of our sport of no small study.
I first appear, though rude, and raw, and muddy,
To speak before thy noble grace this tenor,°
At whose great feet I offer up my penner;°
The next° the Lord of May, and Lady bright,
125 The Chambermaid and Servingman by night
That seek out silent hanging;° then mine Host
And his fat Spouse, that welcomes to their° cost
The gallèd° Traveler, and with a beck'ning
Informs the Tapster to inflame the reck'ning;
130 Then the beest-eating° Clown, and next the Fool,
The Bavian with long tail, and eke long tool,°
Cum multis aliis° that make a dance.
Say "Aye," and all shall presently advance.

Theseus. Aye, aye, by any means, dear dominie.

Pirithous.   Produce.°

---

112 machine structure, device (stressed on first syllable)   **112 frame**
contrivance   **114 Dis to Daedalus** (Dis was the Greek god of the
underworld, Daedalus the maker of the Labyrinth in Crete: the
Schoolmaster's use of learning is indiscriminate)   **114 from post to
pillar** from one resource to another (the Schoolmaster is desperate
for a rhyme)   **117–19 Morr ... Morris** (perhaps the Schoolmaster
holds up two boards in turn, with the syllables "Morr" and "is" on
them, and then puts them together; but the first board could show a
picture of a Moor)   **122 tenor** properly, the wording of a document;
drift   **123 penner** pen case (offered as a token of his services to
Theseus)   **124 next** i.e., next to appear   **126 seek out silent hanging**
i.e., seek out a curtain or tapestry behind which they can make love
127 their (perhaps plural because "Traveler" is so understood)   **128
gallèd** distressed   **130 beest-eating** (probably indicates the Clown's
partiality for "beest," the milk of a cow soon after calving, used in
making puddings)   **131 tool** sexual organ   **132 Cum multis aliis**
with many others   **134 Produce** bring forth

Schoolmaster. Intrate, filii!° Come forth and foot it.   *135*

    Knock.°   *Enter the Dance.   Music.   [They] dance.*

Ladies, if we have been merry
And have pleased ye with a derry,
And a derry, and a down,
Say the Schoolmaster's no Clown.
Duke, if we have pleased thee too   *140*
And have done as good boys should do,
Give us but a tree or twain
For a maypole, and again,
Ere another year run out,
We'll make thee laugh and all this rout.°   *145*

Theseus. Take twenty, dominie. [*To Hippolyta*] How
    does my sweetheart?

Hippolyta. Never so pleased, sir.

Emilia.   'Twas an excellent dance,
    And for a preface I never heard a better.

Theseus. Schoolmaster, I thank you. One see 'em all
    rewarded.

Pirithous. [*Gives money.*] And here's something to
    paint your pole withal.   *150*

Theseus. Now to our sports again.

Schoolmaster. May the stag thou hunt'st stand° long,
And thy dogs be swift and strong,
May they kill him without lets,°
And the ladies eat his dowsets!°   *Wind horns.*   *155*
[*To the dancers*] Come, we are all made. *Dii deaeque
    omnes!*°
Ye have danced rarely, wenches.   *Exeunt.*

---

135 **Intrate, filii** enter, my sons   135 s.d. **Knock** (the Schoolmaster
gives a signal for the entry: but see Textual Note, p. 179)   145 **rout**
company   152 **stand** endure   154 **lets** hindrances   155 **dowsets** tes-
ticles   156 **Dii deaeque omnes** all gods and goddesses

Scene VI. [*The open country.*]

Enter Palamon from the bush.

Palamon. About this hour my cousin gave his faith
   To visit me again, and with him bring
   Two swords and two good armors: if he fail,
   He's neither man nor soldier. When he left me,
5   I did not think a week could have restored
   My lost strength to me, I was grown so low
   And crestfall'n with my wants. I thank thee, Arcite,
   Thou art yet a fair foe, and I feel myself,
   With this refreshing, able once again
10   To outdure° danger. To delay it longer
   Would make the world think when it comes to
      hearing
   That I lay fatting like a swine to fight,°
   And not a soldier. Therefore this blest morning
   Shall be the last; and that sword he refuses,°
15   If it but hold,° I kill him with: 'tis justice.
   So love and Fortune for me!

Enter Arcite with armors and swords.

                    O good-morrow!

Arcite. Good-morrow, noble kinsman.

Palamon.   I have put you
   To too much pains, sir.

Arcite.   That too much, fair cousin,
   Is but a debt to honor, and my duty.

III.vi.10 **outdure** survive 12 **fatting like a swine to fight** being fattened to fight as a swine is fattened to be eaten 14 **that sword he refuses** (Palamon will give Arcite his choice) 15 **If it but hold** if it does not break

Palamon. Would you were so in all, sir! I could wish
ye   20
    As kind a kinsman as you force me find
    A beneficial foe, that my embraces
    Might thank ye, not my blows.

Arcite.   I shall think either,
    Well done, a noble recompense.

Palamon.   Then I shall quit° you.

Arcite. Defy me in these fair terms, and you show°   25
    More than a mistress to me. No more anger,
    As you love anything that's honorable!
    We were not bred° to talk, man. When we are
        armed
    And both upon our guards, then let our fury,
    Like meeting of two tides, fly strongly from us,   30
    And then to whom the birthright° of this beauty
    Truly pertains—without upbraidings, scorns,
    Despisings of our persons, and such poutings
    Fitter for girls and schoolboys—will be seen,
    And quickly, yours or mine. Will't please you arm,
        sir?   35
    Or if you feel yourself not fitting yet
    And furnished with your old strength, I'll stay,°
        cousin,
    And ev'ry day discourse you into health,
    As I am spared.° Your person I am friends with,
    And I could wish I had not said I loved her,   40
    Though I had died.° But loving such a lady
    And justifying° my love, I must not fly from't.

Palamon. Arcite, thou art so brave an enemy
    That no man but thy cousin's fit to kill thee.

---

24 **quit** requite   25 **show** appear   28 **bred** brought up   31 **birth-
right** the right to possess her, given to one of us at birth   37 **stay**
wait   39 **As I am spared** as long as I am alive   41 **Though I had
died** i.e., as a result of my silence   42 **justifying** affirming, defending

I am well and lusty.° Choose your arms.

45 *Arcite.*   Choose you, sir.

Palamon. Wilt thou exceed in all, or dost thou do it
    To make me spare thee?

Arcite.   If you think so, cousin,
    You are deceived, for as I am a soldier
    I will not spare you.

Palamon.   That's well said.

Arcite.   You'll find it.°

50 *Palamon.* Then as I am an honest man and love,
    With all the justice of affection°
    I'll pay thee soundly.° This I'll take.

                          [*Chooses an armor.*]

Arcite.   That's mine then.
                               [*Takes the other.*]
    I'll arm you first.

Palamon.   Do. [*Arcite arms him.*] Pray thee
    tell me, cousin,
    Where gott'st thou this good armor?

Arcite.   'Tis the duke's,
55 And to say true, I stole it. Do I pinch you?

Palamon. No.

Arcite.   Is't not too heavy?

Palamon.   I have worn a lighter,
    But I shall make it serve.

Arcite.   I'll buckle't close.

Palamon. By any means.°

Arcite.   You care not for a grand guard?°

45 **lusty** vigorous   49 **find it** i.e., find it so   51 **justice of affection**
justice administered by one who loves the offender   52 **soundly**
fully, strongly   58 **By any means** i.e., please do   58 **grand guard**
part of armor worn by knight on horseback

Palamon. No, no, we'll use no horses. I perceive
   You would fain be at that fight.°

Arcite.   I am indifferent.°   *60*

Palamon. 'Faith, so am I. Good cousin, thrust the
   buckle
   Through far enough.

Arcite.   I warrant you.

Palamon.   My casque° now.

Arcite. Will you fight bare-armed?

Palamon.   We shall be the nimbler.

Arcite. But use your gauntlets, though. Those are o'
   th' least:°
   Prithee take mine, good cousin.

Palamon.   Thank you, Arcite.   *65*
   How do I look, am I fall'n much away?°

Arcite. 'Faith, very little: love has used you kindly.

Palamon. I warrant thee, I'll strike home.

Arcite.   Do, and spare not;
   I'll give you cause, sweet cousin.

Palamon.   Now to you, sir.
                [*He arms Arcite.*]
   Methinks this armor's very like that, Arcite,   *70*
   Thou wor'st that day the three kings fell, but
   lighter.

Arcite. That was a very good one, and that day
   I well remember you outdid me, cousin.
   I never saw such valor: when you charged
   Upon the left wing of the enemy,   *75*
   I spurred hard to come up, and under me

---

60 **at that fight** i.e., fight on horseback   60 **indifferent** i.e., as to how
we fight   62 **casque** helmet   64 **Those are o' th' least** i.e., those you
have are the smallest possible   66 **am I fall'n much away** have I got
much thinner

I had a right good horse.

Palamon.   You had indeed:
A bright bay, I remember.

Arcite.   Yes, but all
Was vainly labored in me: you outwent me,
80   Nor could my wishes reach you.° Yet a little
I did by imitation.

Palamon.   More by virtue;°
You are modest, cousin.

Arcite.   When I saw you charge first,
Methought I heard a dreadful clap of thunder
Break from the troop.

Palamon.   But still before that flew
85   The lightning of your valor. Stay a little,
Is not this piece too strait?°

Arcite.   No, no, 'tis well.

Palamon. I would have nothing hurt thee but my
     sword,
A bruise would be dishonor.

Arcite.   Now I am perfect.°

Palamon. Stand off° then.

Arcite.   Take my sword, I hold° it better.

90 *Palamon.* I thank ye. No, keep it, your life lies° on it.
Here's one: if it but hold, I ask no more
For all my hopes. My cause and honor guard me!

Arcite. And me my love!

They bow several ways;° then advance and stand.

                    Is there ought else to say?

---

80 **Nor could my wishes reach you** i.e., my wish to be by your side
could not put me there   81 **virtue** natural talent   86 **strait** tight
88 **perfect** ready   89 **Stand off** stand away   89 **hold** think   90 **lies**
depends   93 s.d. **bow several ways** bow formally in different directions, as in the lists

Palamon. This only, and no more. Thou art mine
    aunt's son,
And that blood we desire to shed is mutual,   *95*
In me thine, and in thee mine. My sword
Is in my hand, and if thou kill'st me
The gods and I forgive thee. If there be
A place prepared for those that sleep in honor,
I wish his weary soul that falls may win it.   *100*
Fight bravely, cousin. Give me thy noble hand.

Arcite. Here, Palamon. [*They take hands.*] This hand
    shall never more
Come near thee with such friendship.

Palamon.   I commend° thee.

Arcite. If I fall, curse me, and say I was a coward,
For none but such dare die in these just trials.   *105*
Once more farewell, my cousin.

Palamon.   Farewell, Arcite.
                        [*They*] *fight.*
              Horns within; they stand.

Arcite. Lo, cousin, lo, our folly has undone us.

Palamon. Why?

Arcite. This is the duke, a-hunting as I told you:
If we be found, we are wretched. O retire   *110*
For honor's sake, and safety, presently°
Into your bush again. Sir, we shall find
Too many hours to die in, gentle cousin.
If you be seen, you perish instantly
For breaking prison, and I, if you reveal me,   *115*
For my contempt;° then all the world will scorn us,
And say we had a noble difference,°
But base disposers° of it.

Palamon.   No, no, cousin,
I will no more be hidden, nor put off

103 **commend** praise, honor   111 **presently** at once   116 **contempt**
i.e., of Theseus' banishment of him   117 **difference** quarrel   118
disposers controllers

120   This great adventure to a second trial.
       I know your cunning, and I know your cause.°
       He that faints° now, shame take him: put thyself
       Upon thy present guard.°

Arcite.   You are not mad?

Palamon. Or I will make th' advantage of this hour
125   Mine own, and what to come shall threaten me
       I fear less than my fortune.° Know, weak cousin,
       I love Emilia, and in that I'll bury
       Thee, and all crosses° else.

Arcite.   Then come what can come,
       Thou shalt know, Palamon, I dare as well
130   Die as discourse or sleep. Only this fears me:°
       The law will have the honor of our ends.
       Have at thy life!

Palamon.   Look to thine own well, Arcite.
                    [*They*] *fight again. Horns.*

Enter Theseus, Hippolyta, Emilia, Pirithous and train.

Theseus. What ignorant and mad malicious° traitors
       Are you, that 'gainst the tenor° of my laws
135   Are making battle, thus like knights appointed,
       Without my leave, and officers of arms?°
       By Castor,° both shall die.

Palamon.   Hold° thy word, Theseus.
       We are certainly both traitors, both despisers
       Of thee, and of thy goodness. I am Palamon
140   That cannot love thee, he that broke thy prison:
       Think well what that deserves; and this is Arcite:
       A bolder traitor never trod thy ground,

---

121 your cause i.e., why you wish to postpone the fight   **122 faints**
draws back   **123 Upon thy present guard** on guard at once   **126 my
fortune** i.e., my fortune in this fight   **128 crosses** obstacles   **130
fears me** makes me fear   **133 malicious** evilly disposed   **134 tenor**
purport   **136 officers of arms** officials formally appointed to super-
vise a fight   **137 Castor** (son of Zeus by Leda, twin brother to Pol-
lux)   **137 Hold** keep

A falser ne'er seemed friend. This is the man
Was begged° and banished, this is he contemns thee
And what thou dar'st do; and in this disguise   *145*
Against thy own edict follows thy sister,
That fortunate bright star,° the fair Emilia,
Whose servant—if there be a right in seeing,
And first bequeathing of the soul to—justly
I am, and which is more, dares think her his.   *150*
This treachery, like a most trusty lover,
I called him now to answer. If thou be'st
As thou art spoken, great and virtuous,
The true decider of all injuries,
Say "Fight again," and thou shalt see me, Theseus.   *155*
Do such a justice thou thyself wilt envy.
Then take my life, I'll woo thee to't.

Pirithous.   O heaven,
What more than man is this!

Theseus.   I have sworn.

Arcite.   We seek not
Thy breath of mercy, Theseus: 'tis to me
A thing as soon to die as thee to say it,   *160*
And no more moved. Where° this man calls me
    traitor,
Let me say thus much: if in love be treason
In service of so excellent a beauty,
As I love most, and in that faith will perish,
As I have brought my life here to confirm it,   *165*
As I have served her truest, worthiest,
As I dare kill this cousin that denies it,
So let me be most traitor, and ye please me.
For° scorning thy edict, duke, ask that lady
Why she is fair, and why her eyes command me   *170*
Stay here to love her; and if she say "traitor,"
I am a villain fit to lie unburied.

Palamon. Thou shalt have pity of us both, O Theseus,
If unto neither thou show mercy. Stop,

144 **begged** petitioned for   147 **fortunate bright star** star bringing
good fortune   161 **Where** whereas   169 **For** as for

175 As thou art just, thy noble ear against us;
      As thou art valiant, for thy cousin's soul
      Whose twelve strong labors crown his memory,°
      Let's die together, at one instant, duke:
      Only a little let him fall before me,
180 That I may tell my soul he shall not have her.

Theseus. I grant your wish, for to say true your cousin
      Has ten times more offended, for I gave him
      More mercy than you found, sir, your offenses
      Being no more than his. None here speak for 'em,
185 For ere the sun set both shall sleep forever.

Hippolyta. Alas the pity! Now or never, sister,
      Speak not to be denied: that face of yours
      Will bear the curses else of after ages
      For these lost cousins.

Emilia.   In my face, dear sister,
190 I find no anger to 'em, nor no ruin:
      The misadventure of their own eyes kill° 'em.
      Yet that I will be woman, and have pity,
      My knees shall grow to th' ground but° I'll get
        mercy.
      Help me, dear sister; in a deed so virtuous
195 The powers of all women will be with us.
                              [*They kneel.*]
      Most royal brother!

Hippolyta.   Sir, by our tie of marriage!

Emilia. By your own spotless honor!

Hippolyta.   By that faith,
      That fair hand, and that honest heart you gave me!

Emilia. By that you would have pity° in another,
      By your own virtues infinite!

176–77 **thy cousin's . . . memory** i.e., the soul of Hercules, who leg-
endarily performed twelve great labors   191 **kill** (plural verb
through association with "eyes," despite the singular subject)   193
but unless (or until)   199 **By that you would have pity** by whatever
you would have pity on

Hippolyta.   By valor,   200
  By all the chaste nights I have ever pleased you!

Theseus. These are strange conjurings.°

Pirithous.   Nay, then I'll in too:
                                      [*He kneels.*]
  By all our friendship, sir, by all our dangers,
  By all you love most—wars, and this sweet lady!

Emilia. By that you would have trembled to deny   205
  A blushing maid!°

Hippolyta.   By your own eyes; by strength,
  In which you swore I went beyond all women,
  Almost all men, and yet I yielded, Theseus.

Pirithous. To crown all this: by your most noble soul,
  Which cannot want° due mercy! I beg first.   210

Hippolyta. Next hear my prayers.

Emilia.   Last let me entreat, sir.

Pirithous. For mercy!

Hippolyta.   Mercy!

Emilia.   Mercy on these princes!

Theseus. Ye make my faith° reel. [*They rise.*] Say I
  felt
  Compassion to 'em both, how would you place it?°

Emilia. Upon their lives—but with their banishments.   215

Theseus. You are a right° woman, sister. You have
  pity,
  But want the understanding where to use it.
  If you desire their lives, invent a way
  Safer than banishment. Can these two live
  And have the agony of love about 'em,   220

202 **conjurings** conjurations   205–06 **By that . . . maid** presumably,
the love the maid asked for   210 **want** fail to get (?), lack the power
to feel (?)   213 **faith** i.e., in his own judgment   214 **how would you
place it** i.e., in what way would you have it bestowed   216 **right** true,
typical

And not kill one another? Every day
They'd fight about you, hourly bring your honor
In public question with their swords. Be wise then,
And here forget 'em. It concerns your credit,
225 And my oath equally. I have said they die:
Better they fall by th' law than one another.
Bow° not my honor.

Emilia.   O my noble brother,
That oath was rashly made, and in your anger;
Your reason will not hold° it. If such vows
230 Stand for express will,° all the world must perish.
Beside, I have another oath, 'gainst yours,
Of more authority, I am sure more love,
Not made in passion neither, but good heed.

Theseus. What is it, sister?

Pirithous.   Urge it home, brave lady.

235 *Emilia.* That you would ne'er deny me anything
Fit for my modest suit, and your free granting.
I tie you to your word now: if ye fall in't,°
Think how you maim your honor—
For now I am set a-begging, sir, I am deaf
240 To all but your compassion—how their lives
Might breed the ruin of my name, opinion.°
Shall anything that loves me perish for me?
That were a cruel wisdom. Do men prune
The straight young boughs that blush with thousand
      blossoms
245 Because they may be rotten?° O duke Theseus,
The goodly mothers that have groaned for these,
And all the longing maids that ever loved,
If your vow stand, shall curse me and my beauty,
And in their funeral songs for these two cousins

227 **Bow** humiliate, bring disgrace on   229 **hold** hold to   230 **express will** unshakable resolve   237 **fall in't** renege on it   240–41 **how . . . opinion** i.e., how the taking away of their lives might lead to the ruin of my name and reputation (some editors emend to "name's opinion"; some take "opinion" as an exclamation of contempt)   245 **Because they may be rotten** because they may later become rotten

Despise my cruelty, and cry woe worth° me,   250
Till I am nothing but the scorn of women.
For heaven's sake save their lives, and banish 'em.

Theseus. On what conditions?

Emilia.   Swear 'em never more
To make me their contention, or to know me,°
To tread upon thy dukedom, and to be,   255
Wherever they shall travel, ever strangers
To one another.

Palamon.   I'll be cut a-pieces
Before I take this oath: forget I love her?
O all ye gods despise me then! Thy banishment
I not mislike, so° we may fairly carry   260
Our swords and cause along. Else never trifle,
But take our lives, duke: I must love and will,
And for that love must and dare kill this cousin
On any piece° the earth has.

Theseus.   Will you, Arcite,
Take these conditions?

Palamon.   He's a villain then.   265

Pirithous. These are men.°

Arcite. No, never, duke. 'Tis worse to me than beg-
      ging
To take my life so basely. Though I think
I never shall enjoy her, yet I'll preserve
The honor of affection, and die for her,   270
Make° death a devil.

Theseus. What may be done? For now I feel compas-
      sion.

Pirithous. Let it not fall° again, sir.

Theseus.   Say, Emilia,
If one of them were dead, as one must, are you

---

250 **woe worth** woe befall   254 **know me** hold me in their minds
260 **so** provided that   264 **piece** i.e., of ground   266 **men** i.e., complete men   271 **Make** though you make   273 **fall** weaken

275 Content to take th' other to your husband?
They cannot both enjoy you. They are princes
As goodly as your own eyes, and as noble
As ever Fame yet spoke of. Look upon 'em,
And if you can love, end this difference.
280 I give consent; are you content too, princes?

Both [*Cousins*]. With all our souls.

Theseus. He that she refuses
Must die then.

Both [*Cousins*]. Any death thou canst invent, duke.

Palamon. If I fall from that mouth,° I fall with favor,
And lovers yet unborn shall bless my ashes.

285 *Arcite.* If she refuse me, yet my grave will wed me,
And soldiers sing my epitaph.

Theseus. Make choice, then.

Emilia. I cannot, sir, they are both too excellent:
For me, a hair shall never fall of these men.°

Hippolyta. What will become of 'em?

Theseus. Thus I ordain it,
290 And by mine honor, once again, it stands,
Or both shall die. You shall both to your country,
And each within this month, accompanied
With three fair knights, appear again in this place,
In which I'll plant a pyramid;° and whether,°
295 Before us that are here, can force his cousin
By fair and knightly strength to touch the pillar,
He shall enjoy her; the other lose his head,
And all his friends.° Nor shall he grudge to fall,
Nor think he dies with interest in this lady.
Will this content ye?

283 **from that mouth** i.e., the sentence being spoken by her 288
For . . . men it will not be from me that a hair of either shall perish
294 **pyramid** obelisk 294 **whether** which of the two 298 **And all
his friends** i.e., they shall lose their heads too

Palamon.   Yes. Here, cousin Arcite,   *300*
I am friends again, till that hour.

Arcite.   I embrace ye.

Theseus. Are you content, sister?

Emilia.   Yes, I must, sir,
Else both miscarry.

Theseus.   Come, shake hands again, then,
And take heed, as you are gentlemen, this quarrel
Sleep till the hour prefixed,° and hold your course.°   *305*

Palamon. We dare not fail thee, Theseus.

Theseus.   Come, I'll give ye
Now usage like to princes, and to friends.
When ye return, who wins I'll settle here,°
Who loses°—yet I'll weep upon his bier.   *Exeunt.*

---

305 **prefixed** arranged   305 **hold your course** keep to your resolve
308 **settle here** give him a home in Athens   309 **Who loses**— (Theseus, by changing the construction, shows his realization that the second half of the antithesis must be anticlimactic)

ACT IV

Scene I. [*The prison.*]

Enter Jailer and his friend.

Jailer. Hear you no more, was nothing said of me
  Concerning the escape of Palamon?
  Good sir, remember.

First Friend.   Nothing that I heard,
  For I came home before the business°
5 Was fully ended. Yet I might perceive,
  Ere I departed, a great likelihood
  Of both their pardons. For Hippolyta
  And fair-eyed Emily upon their knees
  Begged with such handsome pity that the duke
  Methought stood staggering, whether he should
10   follow
  His rash oath or the sweet compassion
  Of those two ladies; and to second them
  That truly noble prince Pirithous,
  Half his own heart,° set in too,° that° I hope
15 All shall be well. Neither heard I one question
  Of your name, or his 'scape.

Enter Second Friend.

Jailer.   Pray heaven it hold so.

IV.i.4 **business** (three syllables) 14 **Half his own heart** i.e., the pos-
sessor of half of Theseus' heart 14 **set in too** joined in as well 14
that so that

Second Friend. Be of good comfort, man; I bring you
   news,
  Good news.

Jailer.   They are welcome.

Second Friend.   Palamon has cleared you,
  And got your pardon, and discovered° how
  And by whose means he escaped, which was your
   daughter's,   20
  Whose pardon is procured too, and the prisoner,
  Not to be held ungrateful to her goodness,
  Has given a sum of money to her marriage,
  A large one I'll assure you.

Jailer.   Ye are a good man
  And ever bring good news.

First Friend.   How was it ended?   25

Second Friend. Why, as it should be: they that never
   begged
  But they prevailed had their suits fairly granted.
  The prisoners have their lives.

First Friend.   I knew 'twould be so.

Second Friend. But there be new conditions, which
   you'll hear of
  At better time.

Jailer.   I hope they are good.

Second Friend.   They are honorable; 30
  How good they'll prove I know not.

Enter Wooer.

First Friend.   'Twill be known.

Wooer. Alas, sir, where's your daughter?

Jailer.   Why do you ask?

Wooer. O sir, when did you see her?

19 discovered revealed

Second Friend.   How he looks!

Jailer. This morning.

Wooer.   Was she well? Was she in health?
  Sir, when did she sleep?

35 *First Friend.*   These are strange questions.

Jailer. I do not think she was very well, for now
  You make me mind her,° but° this very day
  I asked her questions, and she answered me
  So far from what she was, so childishly,
40 So sillily, as if she were a fool,
  An innocent,° and I was very angry.
  But what of her, sir?

Wooer.   Nothing but my pity;°
  But you must know it, and as good by me
  As by another that less loves her.

Jailer.   Well, sir?

First Friend. Not right?°

Second Friend.   Not well?

45 *Wooer.*   No, sir, not well.
  'Tis too true, she is mad.

First Friend.   It cannot be.

Wooer. Believe you'll find it so.

Jailer.   I half suspected
  What you have told me: the gods comfort her!
  Either this was her love to Palamon,
50 Or fear of my miscarrying° on his 'scape,
  Or both.

Wooer.   'Tis likely.

Jailer.   But why all this haste,° sir?

---

37 mind her call her to mind   **37 but** only   **41 innocent** idiot   **42
Nothing but my pity** it is only pity that makes me speak   **45 Not
right** i.e., in the head   **50 miscarrying** dying   **51 haste** (the Wooer's
haste in coming to tell the Jailer)

Wooer. I'll tell you quickly. As I late was angling
　In the great lake that lies behind the palace,
　From the far shore, thick set with reeds and sedges,
　As patiently I was attending sport,   55
　I heard a voice, a shrill one, and attentive
　I gave my ear, when I might well perceive
　'Twas one that sung, and by the smallness of it
　A boy or woman. I then left my angle
　To his own skill, came near, but yet perceived not   60
　Who made the sound, the rushes and the reeds
　Had so encompassed it.° I laid me down
　And listened to the words she sung, for then,
　Through a small glade cut by the fishermen,
　I saw it was your daughter.

Jailer.   Pray go on, sir.   65

Wooer. She sung much, but no sense. Only I heard
　　her
　Repeat this often: "Palamon is gone,
　Is gone to th' wood to gather mulberries;
　I'll find him out tomorrow."

First Friend.   Pretty soul!

Wooer. "His shackles will betray him, he'll be taken,   70
　And what shall I do then? I'll bring a bevy,
　A hundred black-eyed maids, that love as I do,
　With chaplets° on their heads of daffadillies,
　With cherry lips, and cheeks of damask roses,
　And all we'll dance an antic° 'fore the duke,   75
　And beg his° pardon." Then she talked of you, sir,
　That you must lose your head tomorrow morning,
　And she must gather flowers to bury you,
　And see the house made handsome. Then she sung
　Nothing but "Willow, willow, willow,"° and be-
　　tween   80
　Ever was "Palamon, fair Palamon,"

62 **it** i.e., the place   73 **chaplets** wreaths   75 **antic** grotesque dance,
as in an antimasque   76 **his** i.e., Palamon's   80 **Willow, willow,
willow** (Desdemona's song in *Othello*, IV.iii)

And "Palamon was a tall young man."° The place
Was knee-deep where she sat; her careless tresses
A wreath of bullrush rounded; about her stuck
85 Thousand fresh water flowers of several colors—
That methought she appeared like the fair nymph
That feeds the lake with waters, or as Iris°
Newly dropped down from heaven. Rings she made
Of rushes that grew by, and to 'em spoke
90 The prettiest posies:° "Thus our true love's tied,"
"This you may loose,° not me," and many a one.
And then she wept, and sung again, and sighed,
And with the same breath smiled, and kissed her
hand.

Second Friend. Alas, what pity it is!

Wooer.   I made in to her.°
She saw me, and straight sought the flood; I saved
95 her,
And set her safe to land—when presently°
She slipped away, and to the city made,
With such a cry, and swiftness, that believe me
She left me far behind her. Three or four
100 I saw from far off cross° her: one of 'em
I knew to be your brother; where she stayed,°
And fell, scarce to be got away. I left them with
her,

Enter Brother, Daughter, and others.

And hither came to tell you. Here they are.

Daughter.

[*Sings*] May you never more enjoy the light, &c.

---

82 **Palamon was a tall young man** (a variant of the song "When Samson was a tall young man," possibly referred to in *Love's Labor's Lost*, I.ii.171)   87 **Iris** goddess of the rainbow   90 **posies** mottoes engraved on rings   91 **loose** (may have the meaning "lose," the two words being commonly spelled "loose")   94 **made in to her** i.e., forced my way through the rushes to her   96 **presently** at once   100 **cross** intercept   101 **stayed** stopped

Is not this a fine song?

Brother.   O, a very fine one.   105

Daughter. I can sing twenty more.

Brother.   I think you can.

Daughter. Yes, truly can I. I can sing "The Broom"°
    And "Bonny Robin."° Are not you a tailor?

Brother. Yes.

Daughter.   Where's my wedding gown?

Brother.   I'll bring it tomorrow.

Daughter. Do, very rearly,° I must be abroad else°   110
    To call the maids, and pay the minstrels,
    For I must lose my maidenhead by cocklight:°
    'Twill never thrive else.°

    (*Sings*) O fair, O sweet,° &c.

Brother. You must e'en take it patiently.

Jailer.   'Tis true.   115

Daughter. Good e'en, good men, pray did you ever
    hear
    Of one young Palamon?

Jailer.   Yes, wench, we know him.

Daughter. Is't not a fine young gentleman?

Jailer.   'Tis, love.

Brother. By no mean cross her, she is then distem-
    pered

107 **The Broom** (a popular song quoted in W. Wager's play *The Longer thou livest the more Fool thou art* [*c.* 1559] and elsewhere: "broom" here is the shrub of that name)   108 **Bonny Robin** (a song preserved in Queen Elizabeth's Virginal Book and in William Ballet's Lute Book: Ophelia sings a line of it in *Hamlet,* IV.v, where, as here, it may imply a sexual meaning for "Robin")   110 **rearly** early   110 **I must be abroad else** otherwise I shall be away from home   112 **by cocklight** before dawn   113 **'Twill never thrive else** otherwise things will never prosper with me   114 **O fair, O sweet** (a song included among "Certaine Sonets" in Sidney's 1598 Folio)

Far worse than now she shows.

120 *First Friend.*   Yes, he's a fine man.

Daughter. O, is he so? You have a sister?

First Friend.   Yes.

Daughter. But she shall never have him, tell her so,
For a trick that I know.° Y' had best look to her,
For if she see him once, she's gone, she's done,
125 And undone in an hour. All the young maids
Of our town are in love with him, but I laugh at 'em
And let 'em all alone.° Is't not a wise course?

First Friend.   Yes.

Daughter. There is at least two hundred now with
    child by him,
There must be four; yet I keep close° for all this,
130 Close as a cockle;° and all these must be boys—
He has the trick° on't—and at ten years old
They must be all gelt for musicians,
And sing the wars of Theseus.

Second Friend.   This is strange.

Daughter. As ever you heard, but say nothing.

First Friend.   No.

Daughter. They come from all parts of the dukedom
135   to him.
I'll warrant ye, he had not so few last night
As twenty to dispatch: he'll tickle 't up°
In two hours, if his hand be in.°

Jailer.   She's lost
Past all cure.

123 **For a trick that I know** because of a stratagem that I know   127
let 'em all alone pay no attention to them   129 **keep close** maintain
secrecy   130 **Close as a cockle** (the proverb occurs also in Shirley's
The School of Compliment [1625]: "cockle" here indicates "cockleshell," formerly used for the shells of mollusks generally)   131 **trick**
method   137 **tickle 't up** i.e., finish the task (with a strong suggestion of sexual pleasure)   138 **if his hand be in** if he is in good form

Brother.   Heaven forbid, man.

Daughter. Come hither, you are a wise man.

First Friend.   Does she know him? 140

Second Friend. No, would she did.

Daughter.   You are master of a ship?°

Jailer. Yes.

Daughter. Where's your compass?

Jailer.   Here.

Daughter.   Set it to th' north.
    And now direct your course to th' wood, where
        Palamon
    Lies longing for me. For the tackling let me alone.
    Come° weigh, my hearts, cheerly all! O, O, O, 'tis
        up!°   145
    The wind's fair: top the bowling!° Out with the
        mainsail!
    Where's your whistle, master?

Brother.   Let's get her in.

Jailer. Up to the top, boy!

Brother.   Where's the pilot?

First Friend.   Here.

Daughter. What ken'st° thou?

---

141 master of a ship (the Daughter has taken the Schoolmaster for a
tinker, III.v.83, and the Brother for a tailor, IV.i.108: Palamon is
always a soldier, and she completes the proverbial four occupations
by taking her father for a sailor)   **145 Come** (lines 145–49 are
hardly verse, and the 1634 quarto prints mainly as prose; but a faint
sense of line breaks seems to lie behind the Daughter's staccato
phrases)   **145 'tis up** (i.e., the tackling: the "O, O, O" indicating
the Daughter's imaginary exertions)   **146 top the bowling** slant
the bowline (rope run from the middle of the perpendicular of the
weather side of a sail to the larboard or starboard bow, for the purpose of keeping the sail steady in a wind)   **149 ken'st** seest

Second Friend.   A fair wood.

Daughter.   Bear for° it, master! Tack about!

150   (*Sings*) When Cynthia with her borrowed light, &c.

                                        Exeunt.

Scene II. [*The palace of Theseus.*]

Enter Emilia alone, with two pictures.

Emilia. Yet I may bind those wounds up,° that must open
        And bleed to death for my sake else: I'll choose,
        And end their strife. Two such young handsome men
        Shall never fall for me; their weeping mothers,
5   Following the dead cold ashes of their sons,
        Shall never curse my cruelty. Good heaven,
        What a sweet face has Arcite! If wise Nature
        With all her best endowments, all those beauties
        She sows into the births of noble bodies,
10   Were here a mortal woman, and had in her
        The coy denials of young maids, yet doubtless
        She would run mad for this man. What an eye,
        Of what a fiery sparkle, and quick° sweetness,
        Has this young prince! Here° Love himself sits smiling:
15   Just such another° wanton Ganymede
        Set Jove a-fire with and enforced the god
        Snatch up the goodly boy° and set him by him,
        A shining constellation. What a brow
        Of what a spacious majesty he carries—

---

149 **Bear for** sail toward   IV.ii.1 **bind those wounds up** (proleptic for "prevent those wounds from being given")   13 **quick** vital   14 **Here** i.e., in his eye   15 **another** i.e., another smile (or eye?)   17 **the goodly boy** i.e., Ganymede

Arched like the great-eyed Juno's, but far sweeter,   20
Smoother than Pelops' shoulder!° Fame and Honor
Methinks from hence,° as from a promontory
Pointed° in heaven, should clap their wings and
    sing
To all the under-world° the loves and fights
Of gods and such men near 'em.° Palamon   25
Is but his foil, to him a mere dull shadow:
He's swarth,° and meager, of an eye as heavy
As if he had lost his mother; a still temper,°
No stirring in him, no alacrity,
Of all this spritely sharpness not a smile.°   30
Yet these that we count errors may become him:
Narcissus° was a sad boy, but a heavenly.
O who can find the bent of woman's fancy?
I am a fool, my reason is lost in me,
I have no choice,° and I have lied so lewdly°   35
That women ought to beat me. On my knees
I ask thy pardon, Palamon: thou art alone,°
And only beautiful, and these the eyes,
These the bright lamps of beauty, that command
And threaten Love, and what young maid dare
    cross° 'em?   40
What a bold gravity, and yet inviting,
Has this brown manly face! O Love, this only
From this hour is complexion.° Lie there, Arcite,
Thou art a changeling° to him, a mere gipsy,
And this the noble body. I am sotted,°   45
Utterly lost, my virgin's faith has fled me!
For if my brother but even now had asked me

21 **Pelops' shoulder** (Pelops was son of Tantalus and father of
Atreus: Marlowe, *Hero and Leander*, i.65, mentions his shoulder as
a standard of whiteness)   22 **from hence** i.e., from Arcite's brow
23 **Pointed** coming to its point   24 **the under-world** the earth   25
such men near 'em demigods, etc.   27 **swarth** dark-complexioned
28 **still temper** placid disposition   30 **smile** trace (with an echo of
Arcite's smiling mentioned in lines 14–15)   32 **Narcissus** (cf. II.i.
178–80)   35 **choice** ability to choose   35 **lewdly** grossly   37 **alone**
unique, supreme   40 **cross** gainsay   42–43 **this only/From this hour
is complexion** i.e., only this complexion is acceptable   44 **changeling**
child left by the fairies in place of another   45 **sotted** reduced to
stupidity

Whether° I loved, I had run mad for Arcite;
Now if my sister, more for Palamon.
50   Stand both together:° now come ask me, brother.
Alas, I know not. Ask me now, sweet sister.
I may go look.° What a mere child is Fancy,
That having two fair gawds° of equal sweetness
Cannot distinguish, but must cry for both!

Enter [a] Gentleman.

How now, sir?

53   *Gentleman.*   From the noble duke your brother,
Madam, I bring you news: the knights are come.

Emilia. To end the quarrel?

Gentleman.   Yes.

Emilia.   Would I might end first!
What sins have I committed, chaste Diana,°
That my unspotted youth must now be soiled
60   With blood of princes, and my chastity
Be made the altar where the lives of lovers,
Two greater and two better never yet
Made mothers joy, must be the sacrifice
To my unhappy beauty?

Enter Theseus, Hippolyta, Pirithous and Attendants.

Theseus.   Bring 'em in
65   Quickly: by any means,° I long to see 'em.
Your two contending lovers are returned,
And with them their fair knights. Now, my fair
        sister,
You must love one of them.

---

48 **Whether** which of the two   50 **Stand both together** (she puts the
two pictures side by side)   52 **I may go look** i.e., I may go seek (for
I do not yet know)   53 **gawds** toys, trifles   58 **Diana** (appropriately
invoked by Emilia, as in V.i, as Diana was the patron of Amazons)
65 **by any means** indeed

Emilia.   I had rather both,
  So° neither for my sake should fall untimely.

Enter [a] Messenger.

Theseus. Who saw 'em?

Pirithous.   I a while.°

Gentleman.   And I.   70

Theseus. From whence come you, sir?

Messenger.   From the knights.

Theseus.   Pray speak,
  You that have seen them, what they are.

Mesenger.   I will, sir,
  And truly what I think. Six braver spirits
  Than these they have brought, if we judge by the
    outside,
  I never saw nor read of. He that stands   73
  In the first place with Arcite, by his seeming
  Should be a stout° man, by his face a prince.
  His very looks so say him: his complexion
  Nearer a brown than black; stern, and yet noble,
  Which shows him hardy, fearless, proud of dangers;   80
  The circles of his eyes show fire within him,
  And as a heated° lion so he looks;
  His hair hangs long behind him, black and shining
  Like ravens' wings; his shoulders broad and strong,
  Armed long and round,° and on his thigh a sword   85
  Hung by a curious baldric,° when he frowns
  To seal his will with:° better o' my conscience
  Was never soldier's friend.°

Theseus. Thou hast well described him.

---

69 **So** provided that   70 **a while** briefly   77 **stout** bold, strong   82
heated enraged (with perhaps a suggestion of "in heat")   85 **Armed
long and round** with long, round arms   86 **baldric** belt   86–87
when he frowns/To seal his will with to effect his desire with when
he is angry   87–88 **better . . . friend** i.e., no soldier has had a better,
more trustworthy sword

Pirithous.   Yet a great deal short,
90   Methinks, of him that's first with Palamon.

Theseus. Pray speak him, friend.

Pirithous.   I guess he is a prince too,
      And if it may be, greater;° for his show°
      Has all the ornament of honor in't.
      He's somewhat bigger than the knight he° spoke of,
95   But of a face far sweeter. His complexion
      Is, as a ripe grape, ruddy. He has felt
      Without doubt what he fights for,° and so apter
      To make this cause his own. In's face appears
      All the fair hopes of what he undertakes,°
100   And when he's angry, then a settled° valor,
      Not tainted with extremes, runs through his body
      And guides his arm to brave things. Fear he cannot,
      He shows no such soft temper. His head's yellow,
      Hard-haired, and curled, thick twined like ivy
            tods,°
105   Not to undo° with thunder. In his face
      The livery of the warlike maid° appears,
      Pure red and white, for yet no beard has blest him;
      And in his rolling eyes sits Victory,
      As if she ever meant to court his valor.°
110   His nose stands high, a character° of honor;
      His red lips, after fights,° are fit for ladies.

Emilia. Must these men die too?

Pirithous.   When he speaks, his tongue
      Sounds like a trumpet. All his lineaments
      Are as a man would wish 'em, strong and clean.
115   He wears a well-steeled ax, the staff of gold.
      His age some five and twenty.

92 **greater** i.e., more than a prince   92 **show** appearance   94 **he** i.e.,
the Messenger   97 **what he fights for** i.e., love   98–99 **In's face . . .
undertakes** i.e., he shows great hope of success   100 **settled** steady
104 **ivy tods** ivy bushes   105 **Not to undo** not to be undone, not dis-
heveled   106 **the warlike maid** (the goddess of war, Bellona)   109
court his valor (if "court" is right—see Textual Note—the image is
strained: the look in his eyes seems in love with his own valor)   110
character token   111 **after fights** when fighting is over

Messenger.   There's another,
  A little man, but of a tough soul, seeming
  As great as any: fairer promises
  In such a body yet I never looked on.

Pirithous. O, he that's freckle-faced?

Messenger.   The same, my lord. *120*
  Are they° not sweet ones?

Pirithous.   Yes, they are well.

Messenger.   Methinks,
  Being so few and well disposed,° they show
  Great and fine art in nature. He's white-haired,°
  Not wanton white, but such a manly color
  Next to an auburn;° tough, and nimble set, *125*
  Which shows an active soul. His arms are brawny,
  Lined with strong sinews: to the shoulder-piece
  Gently they swell, like women new-conceived,°
  Which speaks him prone to labor,° never fainting
  Under the weight of arms; stout-hearted, still,° *130*
  But when he stirs, a tiger. He's gray-eyed,
  Which yields compassion where he conquers;°
    sharp
  To spy advantages, and where he finds 'em
  He's swift to make 'em his. He does no wrongs,
  Nor takes none.° He's round-faced, and when he
    smiles *135*
  He shows° a lover, when he frowns a soldier.
  About his head he wears the winner's oak,°
  And in it stuck the favor of his lady.
  His age some six and thirty. In his hand
  He bears a charging staff,° embossed with silver. *140*

121 **they** i.e., the freckles 122 **disposed** arranged 123 **white-haired** blond 125 **auburn** yellowish white 128 **new-conceived** recently made pregnant 129 **labor** toil (but continuing the image of "new-conceived") 130 **still** quiet 131–32 **gray-eyed . . . conquers** (apparently gray eyes were considered a sign of mercy) 134–35 **He does no wrongs/Nor takes none** he neither inflicts nor submits to an unfair attack 136 **shows** appears 137 **winner's oak** wreath of oak leaves bestowed for valor 140 **charging staff** spear used in charging an enemy

Theseus. Are they all thus?

Pirithous.   They are all the sons of Honor.

Theseus. Now as I have a soul I long to see 'em!
Lady, you shall see men fight now.°

Hippolyta.   I wish it,
But not the cause, my lord. They would show
145   Bravely about the titles of two kingdoms;°
'Tis pity Love should be so tyrannous.
O my soft-hearted sister, what think you?
Weep not till they weep blood. Wench, it must be.

Theseus. You have steeled 'em with your beauty.
    Honored friend,
150   To you I give the field:° pray order it
Fitting the persons that must use it.

Pirithous.   Yes, sir.

Theseus. Come, I'll go visit 'em: I cannot stay,°
Their fame has fired me so. Till they appear,
Good friend, be royal.°

Pirithous.   There shall want no bravery.°

155 *Emilia.* Poor wench, go weep, for whosoever wins
Loses a noble cousin, for thy sins.   *Exeunt.*

---

143 **you shall see men fight now** (Hippolyta, as an Amazon, would
have a prejudice in favor of women as fighters: Theseus assures her
she will now see fighting on a higher level than she has known)
144–45 **would ... kingdoms** i.e., would be good to watch if they
were fighting to win each other's kingdoms   150 **give the field** assign the task of arranging the tournament   152 **stay** wait   154 **be
royal** make the arrangements with magnificence   154 **bravery** splendor

Scene III. [*The prison.*]

Enter Jailer, Wooer, Doctor.

Doctor. Her distraction is more at some time of the
    moon than at other some, is it not?

Jailer. She is continually in a harmless distemper,
    sleeps little, altogether without appetite, save often
    drinking, dreaming of another world, and a better;   5
    and what broken° piece of matter soe'er she's
    about, the name Palamon lards it,° that she farces°
    ev'ry business withal, fits it to every question.

Enter Daughter.

Look where she comes, you shall perceive her be-
    havior.   10

Daughter. I have forgot it quite. The burden° on't was
    "Down-a down-a," and penned by no worse man
    than Geraldo, Emilia's schoolmaster.° He's as fan-
    tastical° too, as ever he may go upon's legs,° for
    in the next world will Dido see Palamon, and then   15
    will she be out of love with Aeneas.°

Doctor. What stuff's here? Poor soul!

Jailer. E'en thus all day long.

Daughter. Now for this charm that I told you of, you
    must bring a piece of silver on the tip of your   20

IV.iii.6 **broken** disconnected   7 **lards it** fills it (is rubbed into it like
lard)   7 **farces** stuffs   11 **burden** refrain   13 **Emilia's schoolmaster**
(the Daughter is of course mistaken)   13–14 **fantastical** fanciful
14 **as ever he may go upon's legs** i.e., as he could possibly be   14–16
for . . . Aeneas (she imagines that the Schoolmaster has taught her a
song about Dido after death loving Palamon, now dead too, instead
of Aeneas)

tongue, or no ferry.° Then if it be your chance to
come where the blessed spirits—as there's a sight
now°—we maids that have our livers perished,°
cracked to pieces with love, we shall come there,
25   and do nothing all day long but pick flowers with
Proserpine.° Then will I make Palamon a nosegay,
then let him mark me°—then!

Doctor. How prettily she's amiss! Note her a little
further.

30   *Daughter.* 'Faith, I'll tell you, sometime we go to
barley-break,° we of the blessed. Alas, 'tis a sore
life they have i' th' other place, such burning, fry-
ing, boiling, hissing, howling, chatt'ring, cursing—O
they have shrewd measure;° take heed! If one be
35   mad, or hang or drown themselves, thither they go,
Jupiter bless us, and there shall we be put in a
cauldron of lead and usurers' grease,° amongst
a whole million of cutpurses, and there boil like a
gammon of bacon that will never be enough.°
Exit.

40   *Doctor.* How her brain coins!°

[*Enter Daughter.*]

Daughter. Lords and courtiers, that have got maids
with child, they are in this place, they shall stand
in fire up to the navel, and in ice up to th' heart,
and there th' offending part burns, and the deceiv-
45   ing part freezes: in troth a very grievous punish-

21 no ferry (Charon, the ferryman of the underworld, will not take
you across the Styx)   **22–23 as there's a sight now** i.e., as I can see
them now ("as" may be merely exclamatory, and possibly "sight"
here means "great number")   **23 perished** shriveled up (the liver was
believed to be the seat of the affections)   **25–26 pick flowers with
Proserpine** (Proserpine was picking flowers when Pluto carried her
off to be queen of the underworld)   **27 mark me** pay attention to
me   **31 barley-break** (a game played by six persons in couples, in
which one couple occupies a marked space called "hell")   **34 shrewd
measure** harsh punishment   **37 usurers' grease** fat sweated by usurers   **39 enough** done, cooked   **40 coins** spins fancies

ment, as one would think, for such a trifle. Believe
me, one would marry a leprous witch to be rid on't,
I'll assure you.

Doctor. How she continues this fancy! 'Tis not an
engraffed° madness, but a most thick and profound   50
melancholy.°

Daughter. To hear there a proud lady, and a proud
city wife, howl together! I were a beast and° I'd
call it good sport. One cries "O this smoke!",
another "This fire!" One cries "O that ever I did it   55
behind the arras!" and then howls; th' other curses
a suing fellow° and her garden house.°

(*Sings*) I will be true, my stars, my fate, &c.
                                        Exit Daughter.

Jailer. What think you of her, sir?

Doctor. I think she has a perturbed mind, which I   60
cannot minister to.

   Jailer. Alas, what then?

Doctor. Understand you she ever affected any man ere
she beheld Palamon?

Jailer. I was once, sir, in great hope she had fixed her   65
liking on this gentleman my friend.

Wooer. I did think so too, and would account I had a
great penn'orth° on't, to give half my 'state° that
both she and I at this present stood unfeignedly on
the same terms.   70

Doctor. That intemperate surfeit of her eye° hath dis-
tempered the other senses: they may return and
settle again to execute their preordained faculties,
but they are now in a most extravagant vagary.

---

50 **engraffed** implanted, firmly planted   50–51 **thick and profound
melancholy** (morbid condition known as "melancholy," to be distinguished from the normal "melancholy" humor)   53 **and if**   57
suing fellow persistent wooer   57 **garden house** (notoriously used
for assignations)   68 **penn'orth** bargain   68 **'state** property   71 **intemperate surfeit of her eye** i.e., by seeing Palamon

75 This you must do: confine her to a place where the
light may rather seem to steal in than be permitted;
take upon you, young sir her friend, the name of
Palamon; say you come to eat with her, and to
commune of love. This will catch her attention, for
80 this her mind beats upon:° other objects that are
inserted 'tween her mind and eye become the
pranks and friskins° of her madness. Sing to her
such green° songs of love as she says Palamon hath
sung in prison. Come to her, stuck in° as sweet
85 flowers as the season is mistress of, and thereto make
an addition of some other compounded° odors,
which are grateful° to the sense. All this shall be-
come° Palamon, for Palamon can sing, and Palamon is sweet and ev'ry good thing. Desire to eat
90 with her, carve her,° drink to her, and, still among,°
intermingle your petition of grace and acceptance
into her favor. Learn what maids have been her
companions and play-feres,° and let them repair
to her with "Palamon" in their mouths, and appear
95 with tokens, as if they suggested° for him. It is a
falsehood she is in, which is with falsehoods to be
combated. This may bring her to eat, to sleep, and
reduce° what's now out of square° in her into their
former law and regiment.° I have seen it ap-
100 proved,° how many times I know not, but to make
the number more I have great hope in this. I will
between the passages° of this project come in with
my appliance.° Let us put it in execution and
hasten the success,° which doubt not will bring
105 forth comfort.   *Exeunt.*

---

80 **beats upon** is preoccupied with   82 **friskins** vagaries   83 **green**
youthful   84 **stuck in** adorned with   86 **compounded** mixed   87
grateful pleasing   87–88 **become** be suitable for   90 **carve her** carve
for her   90 **still among** ever betweenwhiles   93 **play-feres** playfel-
lows   95 **suggested** interceded   98 **reduce** bring back   98 **out of
square** irregular   99 **regiment** government, order   99–100 **approved**
confirmed   102 **passages** separate stages   103 **appliance** device,
stratagem (presumably his device of making the disguised Wooer
sleep with her)   104 **success** result

ACT V

Scene I. [*Before the altars of Mars, Venus and Diana.*]

*Flourish. Enter Theseus, Pirithous, Hippolyta,
Attendants.*

Theseus. Now let 'em enter, and before the gods
  Tender their holy prayers. Let the temples
  Burn bright with sacred fires, and the altars
  In hallowed clouds commend their swelling in-
  cense°
  To those above us. Let no due be wanting: 5
  They have a noble work in hand, will honor°
  The very powers that love 'em.

*Flourish of cornets. Enter Palamon and Arcite and
  their Knights.*

Pirithous.   Sir, they enter.

Theseus. You valiant and strong-hearted enemies,
  You royal german-foes,° that this day come
  To blow that nearness° out that flames between ye,   10
  Lay by your anger for an hour, and dove-like
  Before the holy altars of your helpers,
  The all-feared gods, bow down your stubborn
  bodies.
  Your ire is more than mortal: so your help be;

V.i.4 **swelling incense** incense that swells into clouds   6 **will honor**
i.e., which will honor   9 **german-foes** foes who are of the same family   10 **nearness** kinship and friendship (editors have suggested "furnace" and "fierceness" as emendations)

149

15   And as the gods regard ye,° fight with justice.
      I'll leave you to your prayers, and betwixt ye
      I part° my wishes.

Pirithous.   Honor crown the worthiest!
                               Exit Theseus and his train.

Palamon. The glass° is running now that cannot finish
      Till one of us expire. Think you but thus,
20   That were there ought in me which strove to show°
      Mine enemy in this business, were't one eye
      Against another, arm oppressed by arm,°
      I would destroy th' offender, coz, I would
      Though parcel° of myself. Then from this gather
      How I should tender° you.

25 *Arcite.*   I am in labor°
      To push your name, your ancient love, our kindred
      Out of my memory, and i' th' self same place
      To seat something I would confound.° So hoist
         we°
      The sails that must these vessels° port° even where
      The heavenly limiter° pleases.

30 *Palamon.*   You speak well.
      Before I turn,° let me embrace thee, cousin.
                               [*They embrace.*]
      This I shall never do again.

    Arcite.   One farewell.

    Palamon. Why, let it be so: farewell, coz.
                               Exeunt Palamon and his Knights.

    Arcite.   Farewell, sir.

---

15 **as the gods regard ye** i.e., as they are just to you   17 **part** divide
18 **glass** hourglass   20 **show** i.e., show itself   22 **arm oppressed by
arm** if one of my arms were tyrannized over by the other   24 **parcel**
part   25 **tender** treat (with an ironical suggestion of the adjectival
sense)   25 **in labor** endeavoring (as a woman in childbed endeavors
to give birth)   28 **confound** destroy   28 **hoist** we let us hoist   29
these vessels our fortunes and persons   29 **port** bring to port   30
limiter (the god who sets limits to things)   31 **turn** turn away

Knights, kinsmen, lovers, yea my sacrifices,
True worshippers of Mars—whose spirit in you   35
Expels the seeds of fear, and th' apprehension,
Which still is farther off it°—go with me
Before the god of our profession. There
Require of him the hearts of lions, and
The breath of tigers, yea the fierceness too,   40
Yea the speed also—to go on,° I mean,
Else wish we to be snails. You know my prize
Must be dragged out of blood, force and great feat
Must put my garland on, where she sticks
The queen of flowers:° our intercession then   45
Must be to him that makes the camp a cistern
Brimmed with the blood of men. Give me your aid
And bend your spirits towards him.

*They [prostrate themselves and then] kneel [before
Mars's altar].*

Thou mighty one, that with thy power hast turned
Green Neptune° into purple, [whose approach]   50
Comets prewarn,° whose havoc in vast field
Unearthèd skulls proclaim, whose breath blows
   down
The teeming Ceres' foison,° who dost pluck
With hand armipotent from forth blue clouds°
The masoned turrets, that both mak'st and break'st   55
The stony girths° of cities! Me thy pupil,
Youngest follower of thy drum, instruct this day
With military skill, that to thy laud
I may advance my streamer,° and by thee
Be styled the lord o' th' day! Give me, great Mars,   60
Some token of thy pleasure.

---

37 farther off it (the idea of fear is farther from fear itself than its
"seeds," or first beginnings, are)   **41 go on** advance   **44–45 where
she sticks/The queen of flowers** where Emilia places her favor (the
queen of flowers because it is hers)   **50 Green Neptune** i.e., the sea
(as the Textual Note explains, the bracketed words at the end of this
line are not in the quarto, but some such words seem necessary)   **51
prewarn** give warning of   **53 The teeming Ceres' foison** the harvest
(whose goddess Ceres was)   **54 from forth blue clouds** from their
height in the sky   **56 stony girths** walls   **59 streamer** banner, pen-
non

*Here they fall on their faces as formerly,° and there is
heard clanging of armor, with a short thunder as
the burst of a battle, whereupon they all rise and
bow to the altar.*

O great corrector of enormous° times,
Shaker of o'er-rank° states, thou grand decider
Of dusty and old titles, that heal'st with blood
65 The earth when it is sick, and cur'st the world
O' th' plurisy° of people! I do take
Thy signs auspiciously and, in thy name,
To my design° march boldly. Let us go. *Exeunt.*

*Enter Palamon and his Knights, with the former
observance.°*

Palamon. Our stars must glister with new fire, or be
70 Today extinct. Our argument is love,
Which if the goddess of it grant, she gives
Victory too: then blend your spirits with mine,
You whose free nobleness do make my cause
Your personal hazard; to the goddess Venus
75 Commend we our proceeding, and implore
Her power unto our party.

Here they kneel as formerly° [to Venus's altar].

Hail sovereign queen of secrets, who hast power
To call the fiercest tyrant from his rage
And weep unto a girl;° that hast the might
80 Even with an eye-glance to choke Mars's drum
And turn th' alarm to whispers; that canst make
A cripple flourish with° his crutch, and cure him
Before Apollo;° that may'st force the king

61 s.d. as formerly (suggesting they had done so at line 48)   **62 enormous** monstrous, degenerate   **63 o'er-rank** overripe   **66 plurisy**
plethora   **68 design** goal   **68 s.d. former observance** (the prostra-
tion and kneeling used by Arcite and his Knights, but paid now to
Venus's altar, at line 76)   **76 s.d. as formerly** (again referring to
Arcite and his Knights)   **79 weep unto a girl** i.e., make him weep
like a girl   **82 flourish with** brandish   **83 Before Apollo** sooner than
Apollo (the god of healing)

To be his subject's vassal, and induce
Stale Gravity to dance: the pollèd° bachelor   85
Whose youth like wanton boys through bonfires
Have° skipped thy flame, at seventy thou canst
    catch
And make him, to the scorn of his hoarse throat,°
Abuse° young lays of love; what godlike power
Hast thou not power upon? To Phoebus° thou   90
Add'st flames, hotter than his; the heavenly fires
Did scorch his mortal son,° thine him;° the hunt-
    ress,°
All moist and cold, some say began to throw
Her bow away, and sigh. Take to thy grace
Me thy vowed soldier, who do bear thy yoke   95
As 'twere a wreath of roses, yet is heavier
Than lead itself, stings more than nettles.
I have never been foul-mouthed against thy law,
Ne'er revealed secret, for I knew none; would not,
Had I kenned all that were;° I never practiced°   100
Upon man's wife, nor would the libels read
Of liberal wits;° I never at great feasts
Sought to betray a beauty,° but have blushed
At simp'ring sirs that did. I have been harsh
To large confessors,° and have hotly asked them   105
If they had mothers: I had one, a woman,
And women 'twere they wronged. I knew a man
Of eighty winters, this I told them, who
A lass of fourteen brided. 'Twas thy power
To put life into dust: the aged cramp   110

85 pollèd bald   87 Have (plural through the influence of "boys")
88 to the scorn of his hoarse throat so that his hoarseness is mocked
89 Abuse employ in a ludicrous fashion   90 Phoebus (as sun god)
92 his mortal son Phäethon, who was destroyed when Phoebus allowed him to drive the sun chariot   92 thine him (Phoebus was made
to feel the heat of love)   92 huntress (Diana, who loved Endymion)
100 all that were all secrets in existence   100 practiced entered into
designs   101–02 the libels read/Of liberal wits read the abusive writings of licentious wits   103 betray a beauty i.e., reveal her frailty
105 large confessors those who boasted much of their love conquests

Had screwed his square foot round,°
The gout had knit his fingers into knots,
Torturing convulsions from his globy eyes
Had almost drawn their spheres,° that what was life
115 In him seemed torture. This anatomy°
Had by his young fair fere° a boy, and I
Believed it was his, for she swore it was,
And who would not believe her? Brief,° I am
To those that prate and have done no companion;
120 To those that boast and have not a defier;
To those that would and cannot a rejoicer.
Yea him I do not love, that tells close offices°
The foulest way, nor names concealments° in
The boldest language. Such a one I am,
125 And vow that lover never yet made sigh
Truer than I. O then most soft sweet goddess,
Give me the victory of this question, which
Is true love's merit,° and bless me with a sign
Of thy great pleasure.

*Here music is heard, doves° are seen to flutter; they
fall again upon their faces, then on their knees.*

130 O thou that from eleven to ninety reign'st
In mortal bosoms, whose chase° is this world
And we in herds thy game,° I give thee thanks
For this fair token, which being laid unto
Mine innocent true heart, arms in assurance
135 My body to this business. Let us rise
And bow before the goddess.   *They bow.*
                    Time comes on.   *Exeunt.*

---

111 **screwed his square foot round** (the play on "square" and "round"
makes the image more grotesque)   113–14 **globy . . . spheres**
("globy" suggests "swollen," and here "spheres" must be the eyes
themselves, drawn from their sockets; but there is a suggestion of the
spheres of the Ptolemaic universe being distorted through pain)   115
anatomy skeleton   116 **fere** mate   118 **Brief** in brief   122 **close
offices** secret actions   123 **concealments** things that should be concealed   128 **merit** reward   129 s.d. **doves** (birds sacred to Venus)
131 **chase** place of hunting   132 **in herds thy game** (cf. the similar
image at I.iv.5)

*Still° music of records.° Enter Emilia in white, her
hair about her shoulders, a wheaten wreath;° one in
white holding up her train, her hair stuck° with
flowers; one before her carrying a silver hind,° in
which is conveyed incense and sweet odors, which
being set upon the altar [of Diana], her maids standing aloof, she sets fire to it; then they curtsy and
kneel.*

Emilia. O sacred, shadowy, cold and constant queen,
　Abandoner of revels, mute contemplative,
　Sweet, solitary, white as chaste, and pure
　As wind-fanned snow, who to thy female knights   *140*
　Allow'st no more blood than will make a blush,
　Which is their order's robe! I here thy priest
　Am humbled 'fore thine altar. O vouchsafe
　With that thy rare green eye, which never yet
　Beheld thing maculate, look on thy virgin;   *145*
　And sacred silver mistress, lend thine ear—
　Which ne'er heard scurrile term, into whose port°
　Ne'er entered wanton sound—to my petition
　Seasoned with holy fear. This is my last
　Of vestal office: I am bride-habited,   *150*
　But maiden-hearted; a husband I have 'pointed,°
　But do not know him; out of two I should
　Choose one, and pray for his success, but I
　Am guiltless of election.° Of mine eyes
　Were I to lose one, they are equal precious,   *155*
　I could doom neither: that which perished should
　Go to't unsentenced. Therefore, most modest
　　　queen,
　He of the two pretenders° that best loves me
　And has the truest title° in't, let him
　Take off my wheaten garland, or else grant   *153*

136 s.d. **still** soft　**records** recorders　**her hair about her shoulders,
a wheaten wreath** (cf. I.i s.d.)　**stuck** adorned　**hind** female red
deer, emblem of virginity, sacred to Diana　147 **port** portal　151
'pointed had appointed for me　154 **Am guiltless of election** have
made no choice (with the suggestion that she would betray Diana if
she made a choice)　158 **pretenders** claimants　159 **truest title** best
claim

The file and quality° I hold I may
Continue° in thy band.

*Here the hind vanishes under the altar, and in the
place ascends a rose tree, having one rose upon it.*

See what our general of ebbs and flows°
Out from the bowels of her holy altar
165 With sacred act advances: but one rose.
If well inspired,° this battle shall confound°
Both these brave knights, and I a virgin flow'r
Must grow alone, unplucked.

*Here is heard a sudden twang of instruments, and the
rose falls from the tree.*

The flow'r is fall'n, the tree descends. O mistress,
170 Thou here dischargest me, I shall be gathered.
I think so, but I know not thine own will:
Unclasp thy mystery.
I hope she's pleased, her signs were gracious.
        They curtsy and exeunt.

Scene II. [*The prison.*]

*Enter Doctor, Jailer, and Wooer (in habit of Pala-
mon).*

Doctor. Has this advice I told you done any good
   upon her?

Wooer. O very much. The maids that kept her com-
   pany
Have half-persuaded her that I am Palamon.
Within this half-hour she came smiling to me,

---

161 **file and quality** station and character   162 **Continue** continue
to have   163 **general of ebbs and flows** (Diana as goddess of the
moon)   166 **well inspired** prompted by the goddess   166 **confound**
destroy

And asked me what I would eat, and when I would
    kiss her.   5
I told her presently,° and kissed her twice.

Doctor. 'Twas well done. Twenty times had been far
    better,
For there the cure lies mainly.

Wooer.   Then she told me
She would watch° with me tonight, for well she
    knew
What hour my fit would take me.

Doctor.   Let her do so,   10
And when your fit comes, fit her home,° and
    presently.

Wooer. She would have me sing.

Doctor. You did so?

Wooer.   No.

Doctor.   'Twas very ill done, then:
You should observe° her ev'ry way.

Wooer.   Alas,
I have no voice, sir, to confirm° her that way.   15

Doctor. That's all one,° if ye make a noise.
If she entreat again, do anything:
Lie with her if she ask you.

Jailer.   Ho° there, doctor!

Doctor. Yes, in the way of cure.

Jailer.   But first, by your leave,
I' th' way of honesty.°

Doctor.   That's but a niceness:°   20
Ne'er cast your child away for honesty;

V.ii.6 **presently** at once   9 **watch** stay awake   11 **fit her home** give
her the right treatment (lie with her)   14 **observe** humor   15 **confirm** convince   16 **That's all one** that is a matter of indifference   18
Ho hold, stop   20 **honesty** chastity (i.e., in marriage)   20 **niceness**
overscrupulousness

    Cure her first this way, then if she will be honest,
    She has the path before her.°

Jailer.   Thank ye, doctor.

Doctor. Pray bring her in and let's see how she is.

23 *Jailer.* I will, and tell her her Palamon stays for her.
    But, doctor, methinks you are i' th' wrong still.
                                Exit Jailer.

Doctor.   Go, go.
    You fathers are fine fools! Her honesty?
    And° we should give her physic till we find that—

Wooer. Why, do you think she is not honest, sir?

Doctor. How old is she?

Wooer.   She's eighteen.

30 *Doctor.*   She may be,
    But that's all one, 'tis nothing to our purpose.
    Whate'er her father says, if you perceive
    Her mood inclining that way that I spoke of,
    Videlicet,° the way of flesh—you have me?°

Wooer. Yet very well, sir.

35 *Doctor.*   Please her appetite
    And do it home:° it cures her° *ipso facto*°
    The melancholy humor that infects her.

Wooer. I am of your mind, doctor.

        Enter Jailer, Daughter, Maid.

Doctor. You'll find it so. She comes: pray humor her.

40 *Jailer.* Come, your love Palamon stays° for you, child,
    And has done this long hour, to visit you.

Daughter. I thank him for his gentle patience.

---

23 **has the path before her** i.e., can marry afterwards 28 **And** if
34 **Videlicet** namely 34 **have me** understand me 36 **do it home**
do it thoroughly 36 **her** (an "ethic" dative) 36 **ipso facto** in itself, through its own power 40 **stays** waits

He's a kind gentleman, and I am much bound to
    him.
Did you ne'er see the horse he gave me?

Jailer.   Yes.

Daughter. How do you like him?

Jailer.   He's a very fair° one.   45

Daughter. You never saw him dance?

Jailer.   No.

Daughter.   I have often.
He dances very finely, very comely,
And for a jig°—come cut and long tail to him°—
He turns ye like a top.

Jailer.   That's fine indeed.

Daughter. He'll dance the morris twenty mile an hour,   50
And that will founder the best hobby-horse,
If I have any skill,° in all the parish;
And gallops to the tune of "Light o' Love."°
What think you of this horse?

Jailer.   Having these virtues,
I think he might be brought to play at tennis.   55

Daughter. Alas, that's nothing.

Jailer.   Can he write and read too?

Daughter. A very fair hand, and casts° himself th'
    accounts
Of all his hay and provender: that ostler
Must rise betime that cozens him. You know
The chestnut mare the duke has?

Jailer.   Very well.   60

45 **fair** fine   48 **jig** (a boisterous dance, often accompanied by song
and used after a play)   48 **come cut and long tail to him** i.e., whatever the competition ("cut and long tail," derived from the practice
of docking horses' and dogs' tails, means "all kinds," "everybody")
52 **have any skill** know anything about it   53 **Light o' Love** (a well-
known song, referred to in *The Two Gentlemen of Verona*, I.ii.83)
57 **casts** makes up

Daughter. She is horribly in love with him, poor beast,
 But he is like his master, coy and scornful.

Jailer. What dowry has she?

Daughter.   Some two hundred bottles,°
 And twenty strike° of oats; but he'll ne'er have her.
65 He lisps in's neighing able to entice
 A miller's mare:° he'll be the death of her.°

Doctor. What stuff she utters!

Jailer. Make curtsy, here your love comes.

Wooer. [*Comes forward.*]   Pretty soul,
 How do ye? That's a fine maid! There's a curtsy!

70 *Daughter.* Yours to command i' th' way of honesty.
 How far is't now to th' end o' th' world, my
  masters?

Doctor. Why, a day's journey, wench.

Daughter. [*To Wooer*]   Will you go with me?

Wooer. What shall we do there, wench?

Daughter.   Why, play at stool-ball.°
 What is there else to do?

Wooer.   I am content,
 If we shall keep our wedding there.

75 *Daughter.*   'Tis true,
 For there, I will assure you, we shall find
 Some blind° priest for the purpose, that will venture
 To marry us, for here they are nice° and foolish.

---

63 **bottles** bundles 64 **strike** (measure usually equivalent to the
bushel) 66 **miller's mare** (a mare used for turning a mill wheel
would be the least likely to behave wantonly) 66 **he'll be the death
of her** (this passage on a wonderful horse, lines 44–66, looks back to
the famous horse of John Banks, whose tricks and apparent intelligence are frequently referred to in Elizabethan literature: it performed at least between 1588 and 1600, and was remembered) 73
stool-ball (ball game played most often by women, and requiring a
stool or stools) 77 **blind** (so that he should not recognize them) 78
nice overscrupulous

Besides, my father must be hanged tomorrow,
And that would be a blot i' th' business.   80
Are not you Palamon?

Wooer.   Do not you know me?

Daughter. Yes, but you care not for me. I have
    nothing
But this poor petticoat and two coarse smocks.°

Wooer. That's all one, I will have you.

Daughter.   Will you surely?

Wooer. Yes, by this fair hand will I.

                    [*Takes her hand.*]

Daughter.   We'll to bed, then.   85

Wooer. E'en when you will.   [*Kisses her.*]

Daughter.   O sir, you would fain be nibbling.

Wooer. Why do you rub my kiss off?

Daughter.   'Tis a sweet one,
And will perfume me finely against the wedding.
Is not this your cousin Arcite?

Doctor.   Yes, sweetheart,
And I am glad my cousin Palamon   90
Has made so fair a choice.

Daughter.   Do you think he'll have me?

Doctor. Yes, without doubt.

Daughter.   Do you think so too?

Jailer.   Yes.

Daughter. We shall have many children. [*To the Doc-
    tor*] Lord, how y' are grown!°
My Palamon I hope will grow, too, finely
Now he's at liberty. Alas, poor chicken,°   95

83 **smocks** undergarments, shifts   93 **how y' are grown** (she noted
that Arcite was shorter than Palamon at II.i.53–54   95 **chicken**
child

He was kept down with hard meat° and ill lodging,
But I'll kiss him up again.°

Enter a Messenger.

Messenger. What do you here? You'll lose the noblest
 sight
That e'er was seen.

Jailer.   Are they i' th' field?

Messenger.   They are.
 You bear a charge° there, too.

100 *Jailer.*   I'll away straight.
 I must e'en leave you here.

Doctor.   Nay, we'll go with you:
 I will not lose the fight.°

Jailer.   How did you like her?°

Doctor. I'll warrant you within these three or four
 days
I'll make her right again. [*To Wooer*] You must not
 from her,
But still preserve her in this way.

105 *Wooer.*   I will.

Doctor. Let's get her in.

Wooer.   Come, sweet, we'll go to dinner,
 And then we'll play at cards.

Daughter.   And shall we kiss too?

Wooer. A hundred times.

Daughter.   And twenty?

---

96 **hard meat** coarse food   97 **kiss him up again** make him grow
with kissing (with a phallic suggestion)   100 **bear a charge** have a
duty   102 **fight** (the emendation "sight" has been suggested and
may be right: cf. line 98 and V.iii.1)   102 **How did you like her**
what did you think of her condition

Wooer.   Aye, and twenty.

Daughter. And then we'll sleep together?

Doctor.   Take her offer.

Wooer. Yes, marry will we.

Daughter.   But you shall not hurt me.   110

Wooer. I will not, sweet.

Daughter.   If you do, love, I'll cry.   *Exeunt.*

Scene III. [*Near the place of the tournament.*]

*Flourish. Enter Theseus, Hippolyta, Emilia, Pirithous,
    and some Attendants.*

Emilia. I'll no step further.

Pirithous.   Will you lose this sight?

Emilia. I had rather see a wren hawk at a fly
    Than this decision: ev'ry blow that falls
    Threats a brave life, each stroke laments the place
    Whereon it falls, and sounds more like a bell°   5
    Than blade. I will stay here. It is enough
    My hearing shall be punishèd with what
    Shall happen, 'gainst the which there is
    No deafing°—but to hear, not taint mine eye
    With dread sights it may shun.

Pirithous.   Sir, my good lord,   10
    Your sister will no further.

Theseus.   O she must.
    She shall see deeds of honor in their kind,°
    Which sometime show well, penciled.° Nature now

V.iii.5 **bell** i.e., a bell that tolls for the dead   9 **deafing** i.e., closing
the ear   12 **in their kind** in their true shape   13 **penciled** when por-
trayed in art

Shall make and act the story, the belief
Both sealed with eye and ear.° [*To Emilia*] You
15   must be present.
You are the victor's meed,° the price,° and garland
To crown the question's title.°

Emilia.   Pardon me.
If I were there, I'd wink.°

Theseus.   You must be there:
This trial is as 'twere i' th' night, and you
The only star to shine.

20 *Emilia.*   I am extinct.°
There is but envy° in that light which shows
The one the other: Darkness, which ever was
The dam° of Horror, who does stand accursed
Of many mortal millions, may even now,
25 By casting her black mantle over both,
That° neither could find other, get herself
Some part of a good name,° and many a murder
Set off° whereto she's guilty.

Hippolyta.   You must go.

Emilia. In faith, I will not.

Theseus.   Why, the knights must kindle
30 Their valor at your eye. Know of this war
You are the treasure, and must needs be by
To give the service pay.°

Emilia.   Sir, pardon me,
The title of a kingdom may be tried
Out of itself.°

14–15 the belief/Both sealed with eye and ear (i.e., so that we both
see and hear the action, while a painting merely gives us the dumb
sight) **16 meed** reward **16 price** prize **17 crown the question's
title** bestow the title which is in question **18 wink** close my eyes
20 extinct no longer shining (continuing the image of the star) **21
envy** malice **23 dam** mother **26 That** so that **27 Some part of a
good name** a partly good reputation **28 Set off** atone for **32 give
the service pay** reward the service **33–34 The title . . . itself** a claim
to a kingdom may be settled in a battle fought outside the kingdom

Theseus.   Well, well, then, at your pleasure.
Those that remain with you could wish their office   35
To any of their enemies.

Hippolyta.   Farewell, sister.
I am like to know your husband 'fore yourself
By some small start of time. He whom the gods
Do of the two know best,° I pray them he
Be made your lot.   40
          Exeunt Theseus, Hippolyta, Pirithous, &c.

Emilia. Arcite is gently visaged; yet his eye
Is like an engine° bent, or a sharp weapon
In a soft sheath: mercy and manly courage
Are bedfellows in his visage. Palamon
Has a most menacing aspect,° his brow   45
Is graved,° and seems to bury what it frowns on;
Yet sometime 'tis not so, but alters to
The quality of his thoughts:° long time his eye
Will dwell upon his object; melancholy
Becomes him nobly. So does Arcite's mirth,   50
But Palamon's sadness is a kind of mirth,
So mingled° as if mirth did make him sad,
And sadness merry. Those darker humors that
Stick misbecomingly on others, on him
Live in fair dwelling.   55
          Cornets. Trumpets sound as to a charge.
Hark how yon spurs to spirit do incite
The princes to their proof!° Arcite may win me,
And yet may Palamon wound Arcite to
The spoiling of his figure.° O what pity
Enough for such a chance?° If I were by,   60
I might do hurt, for they would glance their eyes
Toward my seat, and in that motion might

38–39 He . . . best the one known by the gods to be best   42 engine
instrument (here suggesting "bow")   45 aspect (stressed on second
syllable)   46 graved engraved, furrowed (with the play on "grave,"
suggesting that he kills)   47–48 alters to/The quality of his thoughts
changes according to the character of his thoughts   52 mingled
complex   57 proof test   59 figure body   59–60 O what . . . chance
i.e., how much pity would be sufficient for such a happening

Omit a ward,° or forfeit an offense°
Which craved that very time. It is much better
65 I am not there. O better never born
Than minister to such harm!

Cornets. A great cry and noise within, crying "A Palamon!" Enter [a] Servant.

What is the chance?

Servant. The cry's "A Palamon!"

Emilia. Then he has won: 'twas ever likely.
He looked all grace° and success, and he is
70 Doubtless the prim'st of men. I prithee run
And tell me how it goes.

Shout, and cornets. Crying "A Palamon!"

Servant.   Still "Palamon!"

Emilia. Run and inquire. [*Exit Servant.*] Poor serv-
ant,° thou hast lost!
Upon my right side still° I wore thy picture,
Palamon's on the left. Why so I know not,
75 I had no end in't else:° chance would have it so.
On the sinister° side the heart lies: Palamon
Had the best boding chance.°

Another cry, and shout within, and cornets.
                              This burst of clamor
Is sure th' end o' th' combat.

Enter Servant.

Servant. They said that Palamon had Arcite's body
80 Within an inch o' th' pyramid, that the cry
Was general "A Palamon!" But anon
Th' assistants° made a brave redemption,° and

63 **ward** pass of defense   63 **forfeit an offense** lose the opportunity
of making an attack   69 **grace** favor   72 **Poor servant** i.e., Arcite
73 **still** always   75 **no end in't else** no purpose at all in it   76 **sinister**
left   77 **the best boding chance** i.e., the most favorable omen   82
assistants i.e., Arcite's knights   82 **redemption** rescue

The two bold titlers° at this instant are
Hand-to-hand at it.

Emilia.   Were° they metamorphosed
  Both into one! O why? There were no woman   **85**
  Worth so composed a man:° their single share,°
  Their nobleness peculiar to them, gives
  The prejudice of disparity, value's shortness,°
  To any lady breathing.
                    Cornets. Cry within: "Arcite! Arcite!"
                         More exulting?
  "Palamon" still?

Servant.   Nay, now the sound is "Arcite!" **90**

Emilia. I prithee lay attention to the cry.
  Set both thine ears to th' business.

Cornets. A great shout and cry: "Arcite! Victory!"

Servant.   The cry is
  "Arcite!" and "Victory!" Hark! "Arcite! Victory!"
  The combat's consummation is proclaimed
  By the wind instruments.

Emilia.   Half-sights° saw   **95**
  That Arcite was no babe. God's lid,° his richness
  And costliness° of spirit looked through him:° it
    could
  No more be hid in him than fire in flax,
  Than humble banks can go to law° with waters
  That drift° winds force to raging. I did think   **100**
  Good Palamon would miscarry, yet I knew not
  Why I did think so: our reasons are not prophets
  When oft our fancies are. They are coming off.°
  Alas, poor Palamon!

---

83 **titlers** claimants to the title   84 **Were** O that they were   86 **so
composed a man** a man so compounded   86 **their single share** the
share of virtue that each has singly   88 **The prejudice . . . shortness**
i.e., the disadvantage of inequality, the state of inferiority   95 **Half-
sights** glimpses   96 **lid** eyelid   97 **costliness** rareness   97 **looked
through him** was apparent in him   99 **go to law** engage in conflict
100 **drift** driving   103 **coming off** leaving the place of tournament

*Cornets. Enter Theseus, Hippolyta, Pirithous, Arcite
as victor, and Attendants, &c.*

105 *Theseus.* Lo, where our sister is in expectation,
Yet quaking and unsettled!° Fairest Emily,
The gods by their divine arbitrament
Have given you this knight: he is a good one
As ever struck at head. Give me your hands.
110 Receive you her, you him; be plighted with
A love that grows as you decay.

Arcite.   Emily,
To buy you I have lost what's dearest to me
Save what is bought, and yet I purchase cheaply
As I do rate your value.

Theseus.   O loved sister,
115 He speaks now of as brave a knight as e'er
Did spur a noble steed. Surely the gods
Would have him die a bachelor, lest his race
Should show i' th' world too godlike! His behavior
So charmed me that methought Alcides° was
120 To him a sow° of lead. If I could praise
Each part of him to th' all I have spoke,° your
    Arcite
Did° not lose by't, for he that was thus good
Encount'red yet his better. I have heard
Two emulous Philomels° beat the ear o' th' night
125 With their contentious throats, now one the higher,
Anon the other, then again the first,
And by and by outbreasted,° that the sense°
Could not be judge between 'em: so it fared
Good space between these kinsmen, till heavens did
130 Make hardly° one the winner. Wear the garland
With joy that you have won. For the subdued,

106 **unsettled** uncertain, still disturbed   119 **Alcides** Hercules   120
sow mass of solidified metal taken from a furnace   120–21 **If . . .
spoke** if I were to praise his every quality in the same way as I have
praised him in general terms   122 **Did** would   124 **Philomels** night-
ingales   127 **outbreasted** outsung   127 **that the sense** so that the
hearing   130 **hardly** with difficulty

Give them our present justice,° since I know
Their lives but pinch° 'em. Let it here be done.
The scene's not for our seeing: go we hence
Right joyful, with some sorrow. [*To Arcite*] Arm
    your prize:°   135
I know you will not loose her. Hippolyta,
I see one eye of yours conceives a tear
The which it will deliver.   *Flourish.*

Emilia.   Is this winning?
O all you heavenly powers, where is your mercy?
But that your wills have said it must be so,   140
And charge me live to comfort this unfriended,
This miserable prince, that cuts away
A life more worthy from him than all women,
I should, and would, die too.

Hippolyta.   Infinite pity
That four such eyes should be so fixed on one   145
That two must needs be blind for't!°

Theseus.   So it is.   *Exeunt.*

Scene IV. [*The same.*]

*Enter Palamon and his Knights pinioned, Jailer, Exe-
cutioner, &c., Guard.*

Palamon. There's many a man alive that hath outlived
The love o' th' people, yea i' th' self same state°
Stands many a father with his child: some comfort
We have by so considering. We expire,
And not without men's pity; to live still   5
Have their good wishes;° we prevent

132 **present justice** i.e., immediate execution   133 **pinch** irk   135
Arm your prize i.e., take Emilia to your arms   146 **That two must
needs be blind for't** i.e., that one of the men must die   V.iv.2 **state**
condition   5–6 **to live still/Have their good wishes** have their good
wishes that we should still live

The loathsome misery of age, beguile
The gout and rheum that in lag° hours attend
For gray approachers.° We come towards the gods
Young and unwappered,° not halting under crimes
Many and stale:° that sure shall please the gods
Sooner than such,° to give° us nectar with 'em,
For we are more clear° spirits. My dear kinsmen,
Whose lives for this poor comfort° are laid down,
You have sold 'em too too cheap.

First Knight.   What ending could be
Of more content? O'er us the victors have
Fortune, whose title° is as momentary
As to us death is certain. A grain of honor
They not o'er-weigh us.

Second Knight.   Let us bid farewell,
And with our patience anger tott'ring Fortune,
Who at her certain'st° reels.

Third Knight.   Come, who begins?

Palamon. E'en he that led you to this banquet shall
Taste to you all.° [*To Jailer*] Ah, ha, my friend, my
    friend,
Your gentle daughter gave me freedom once:
You'll see't done now forever.° Pray, how does she?
I heard she was not well. Her kind of ill°
Gave me some sorrow.

Jailer.   Sir, she's well restored,
And to be married shortly.

Palamon.   By my short life,
I am most glad on't: 'tis the latest thing
I shall be glad of, prithee tell her so.

8 lag last   9 gray approachers gray-haired men approaching death
10 unwappered unwearied (perhaps with a suggestion of sexual excess)   11 stale of long standing   12 such i.e., men such as described
12 to give so that they will give   13 clear noble, unstained   14 this
poor comfort (Palamon admits the puniness of his own consolation)
17 title i.e., favor   21 at her certain'st when she seems most stable
23 Taste to you all act as taster at a banquet for you   25 You'll see't
done now forever i.e., you will see me win a final freedom   26 kind
of ill i.e., madness

Commend me to her, and to piece° her portion
Tender her this.   [*Gives him a purse.*]

First Knight.   Nay, let's be offerers all.

Second Knight. Is it a maid?

Palamon.   Verily I think so,
A right good creature, more to me° deserving
Than I can 'quite° or speak of.

All Knights.   Commend us to her.   35
                  They give their purses.

Jailer. The gods requite you all, and make her thankful.

Palamon. Adieu; and let my life be now as short
As my leave-taking.   *Lies on the block.*

First Knight.   Lead, courageous cousin.

Second and Third Knights. We'll follow cheerfully.

A great noise within, crying "Run! Save! Hold!"
Enter in haste a Messenger.

Messenger.   Hold, hold, O hold, hold, hold!

Enter Pirithous in haste.

Pirithous. Hold, ho! It is a cursèd haste you made   40
If you have done° so quickly. Noble Palamon,
The gods will show their glory in a life°
That thou art yet to lead.

Palamon.   Can that be,
When Venus I have said° is false? How do things
fare?°

Pirithous. Arise, great sir, and give the tidings ear   45
That are most dearly° sweet and bitter.

31 **piece** contribute to   34 **to me** i.e., from me   35 **'quite** requite
41 **done** finished   42 **show their glory in a life** i.e., through your life
(as their creature) their glory will be manifested   44 **I have said** i.e.,
as I have said   44 **How do things fare** what has happened   46
dearly intensely

Palamon.   What
  Hath waked us from our dream?°

Pirithous.   List then. Your cousin,
  Mounted upon a steed that Emily
  Did first bestow on him, a black one, owing°
50 Not a hair-worth of white, which some will say
  Weakens his price, and many will not buy
  His goodness with this note°—which superstition
  Here finds allowance°—on this horse is Arcite
  Trotting the stones of Athens, which the calkins°
55 Did rather tell° than trample, for the horse
  Would make his length a mile,° if't pleased his
      rider
  To put pride in him. As he thus went counting
  The flinty pavement, dancing as 'twere to th' music
  His own hoofs made—for as they say from iron
60 Came music's origin—what envious flint,
  Cold as old Saturn, and like him possessed
  With fire malevolent, darted a spark,
  Or what fierce sulphur else to this end made,
  I comment not: the hot horse, hot as fire,
65 Took toy° at this, and fell to what disorder
  His power could give his will, bounds, comes on
      end,
  Forgets school-doing,° being therein trained
  And of kind manage;° pig-like he whines
  At the sharp rowel, which he frets at rather
70 Than any jot obeys; seeks all foul means
  Of boist'rous and rough jadery to dis-seat
  His lord, that kept it° bravely. When nought served,
  When neither curb would crack, girth break, nor
      diff'ring° plunges
  Dis-root his rider whence he grew, but that

---

47 **dream** i.e., of death   49 **owing** possessing   52 **with this note** because of this peculiarity   53 **Here finds allowance** is here confirmed
54 **calkins** (parts of a horseshoe turned down to prevent slipping)
55 **tell** count   56 **make his length a mile** take mile-long paces   65
toy fright, exception   67 **school-doing** training   68 **of kind manage**
well disciplined   72 **it** i.e., his seat   73 **diff'ring** varying

He kept him 'tween his legs, on his hind hoofs   75
On end he stands,
That Arcite's legs being higher than his head
Seemed with strange art to hang; his victor's wreath
Even then fell off his head; and presently°
Backward the jade comes o'er, and his full poise°   80
Becomes the rider's load. Yet is he living,
But such a vessel 'tis that floats but for
The surge that next approaches. He much desires
To have some speech with you. Lo, he appears.

Enter Theseus, Hippolyta, Emilia, Arcite in a chair.

Palamon. O miserable end of our alliance!   85
   The gods are mighty! Arcite, if thy heart,
   Thy worthy, manly heart be yet unbroken,
   Give me thy last words: I am Palamon,
   One that yet loves thee dying.

Arcite.   Take Emilia,
   And with her all the world's joy. Reach° thy hand. 90
   Farewell. I have told° my last hour. I was false,
   Yet never treacherous.° Forgive me, cousin.
   One kiss from fair Emilia. [*She kisses him.*] 'Tis
      done.
   Take her. I die.   [*Dies.*]

Palamon.   Thy brave soul seek Elysium!

Emilia. I'll close thine eyes, prince. Blessed souls be
   with thee!°   95
   Thou art a right good man, and while I live
   This day° I give to tears.

Palamon.   And I to honor.°

79 **presently** at once   80 **poise** weight   90 **Reach** i.e., give me   91
told counted, lived through   91–92 **false,/Yet never treacherous**
(Arcite admits Palamon's greater right to Emilia in seeing her first,
but declares he took no unfair advantage)   95 **Blessed souls be with
thee** i.e., may you be with the blessed souls   97 **This day** i.e., the
anniversaries of this day   97 **to honor** i.e., to honoring Arcite's
memory

Theseus. In this place first you fought: e'en very here
　　I sund'red you. Acknowledge to the gods
100　Our thanks that you are living.°
　　His part is played, and though it were too short
　　He did it well. Your day is lengthened, and
　　The blissful dew of heaven does arrouse° you.
　　The powerful Venus well hath graced her altar,
105　And given you your love. Our master Mars
　　Hath vouched his oracle, and to Arcite gave
　　The grace of the contention.° So the deities
　　Have showed due justice. Bear this° hence.

Palamon.　　　　　　　　　　　　　　O cousin,
　　That we should things desire which do cost us
110　The loss of our desire!° That nought could buy
　　Dear love but loss of dear love!°

Theseus.　　　　　　　　　　Never Fortune
　　Did play a subtler game. The conquered triumphs,
　　The victor has the loss; yet in the passage°
　　The gods have been most equal.° Palamon,
115　Your kinsman hath confessed the right o' th' lady
　　Did lie in you, for you first saw her, and
　　Even then proclaimed your fancy. He restored her
　　As your stol'n jewel, and desired your spirit
　　To send him hence forgiven. The gods my justice
120　Take from my hand,° and they themselves become
　　The executioners. Lead your lady off,
　　And call your lovers° from the stage of death,°
　　Whom I adopt my friends. A day or two
　　Let us look sadly, and give grace unto
125　The funeral of Arcite, in whose end°

99–100 **Acknowledge . . . living** declare to the gods that we rejoice
in your being alive (the emendation of "Our" to "Your" has been
suggested)　103 **arrouse** sprinkle　107 **grace of the contention** i.e.,
good fortune in the contest　108 **this** i.e., Arcite's body　109–10
That we . . . desire i.e., alas that the winning of what we want takes
away our desire for it　110–11 **That nought . . . dear love** i.e., that
one love (Emilia) could be won only by losing another (Arcite)　113
passage course of events　114 **equal** just　120 **Take from my hand**
i.e., take away from me　122 **lovers** i.e., his Knights　122 **stage of
death** scaffold　125 **in whose end** at the conclusion of which

The visages of bridegrooms we'll put on
And smile with Palamon; for whom an hour,
But one hour since, I was as dearly sorry
As glad of Arcite; and am now as glad
As for him sorry. O you heavenly charmers,°   130
What things you make of us! For what we lack,
We laugh;° for what we have, are sorry;° still
Are children in some kind. Let us be thankful
For that which is, and with you leave° dispute
That are above our question. Let's go off,   135
And bear us like the time.°   *Flourish. Exeunt.*

EPILOGUE

I would now ask ye how ye like the play,
But, as it is with schoolboys, cannot say.°
I am cruel° fearful. Pray yet stay a while,
And let me look upon ye. No man smile?

⁵ Then it goes hard, I see. He that has
Loved a young handsome wench, then, show his
        face—
'Tis strange if none be here—and if he will
Against his conscience, let him hiss, and kill
Our market. 'Tis in vain, I see, to stay° ye.
Have at the worst can come,° then! Now what say

¹⁰   ye?
And yet mistake me not: I am not bold;
We have no such cause. If the tale° we have told—
For 'tis no other—any way content ye,
For to that honest purpose it was meant ye,°

¹³ We have our end; and ye shall have ere long
I dare say many a better, to prolong
Your old loves to us. We, and all our might,
Rest at your service. Gentlemen, good night.

                                        Flourish.

FINIS

Epilogue   2 say speak   3 cruel dreadfully   9 stay i.e., try to prevent   10 Have at the worst can come let us face the worst event
possible   12 tale (alluding to the title of the source)   14 meant ye
intended for you

Textual Note

There is no doubt that the text used by the printer of the quarto of 1634 had been in the hands of a prompter (presumably of the Blackfriars Theatre). The most obvious evidence of this is the appearance in the margin of three "warnings"—i.e., reminders that preparation must be made for an ensuing entry. These are noted below in the list of places where the present edition varies from the quarto, but it will be useful to bring them together here:

(1) On C3ᵛ of the quarto, in the left margin opposite I.iii.58–64:

> 2. Hearses rea-/dy with Pala-/mon: and Arci-/ te: the 3./ Queenes./ Theseus: and/ his Lordes/ ready.

At this point the scene has more than thirty lines to run: the "warning" is of what will be required at the beginning of I.iv, which comes on C4ʳ.

(2) On C4ᵛ, in the left margin opposite I.iv.26–27:

> 3. Hearses rea-/dy.

These hearses are for the bodies of the three kings slain at Thebes and will be brought on at the beginning of I.v twenty lines later, on the same page of the quarto.

(3) On G2ᵛ, in the left margin opposite III.v.65–66:

> Chaire and/ stooles out.

These properties are required for Theseus and his company to sit on to watch the Schoolmaster's entertainment: the dialogue indicates that they sit some thirty lines later, at III.v.98.

Further evidence of theater use of the copy behind the quarto is in the appearance of actors' names in the entries. At IV.ii.69 the quarto stage direction reads *"Enter Messengers. Curtis."* (*"Messengers"* being clearly an error for *"Messenger"*), and the entry which opens V.iii reads ". . . *and/ some Attendants, T. Tucke: Curtis."* The actors referred to can be identified as Curtis Greville, who was a hired man in the King's Company in 1626, probably having joined them the preceding year, and Thomas Tuckfield, whose name appears in a list of "Musitions and other necessary attendantes" of the King's Company in 1624.[1] From these dates it is clear that the actors' names were inserted on the occasion of a revival in the 1620's, not for the original performance of 1613.

Actors' names appearing in a text may be due to an author who has a particular member of the company in mind for a part, but this could not be the case with the two names in *The Two Noble Kinsmen*. For one thing, Greville and Tuckfield were not with the company when Shakespeare and Fletcher were writing the play; for another, the messenger of IV.ii and the attendants of V.iii are characterless parts: an author would have no views on who should play them, but a prompter might wish to remind himself of the actors' identities.

The quarto contains further indications of playhouse use. Act IV ends with the stage direction *"Florish. Exeunt."*, the *"Florish"* obviously being wrongly placed: it is needed for the entry of Theseus and the rest at the beginning of Act V. The same thing occurs at the end of V.ii. In these instances we can deduce that "Florish" was added in the margin between IV.iii and V.i and between V.ii and V.iii respectively, and the printer took it as going with the exits and not with the following entries. Then we have several marginal stage directions printed, like the "warnings" noted above, in roman type—one at the beginning of II.iv:

This short flo-/rish of Cor-/nets and/ Showtes with-/in.

[1] Gerald Eades Bentley, *The Jacobean and Caroline Stage*, II (Oxford, 1941), 451–52, 606–07.

and another opposite the heading *"Actus Tertius."*:

> Cornets in/ sundry places./ Noise and/ hallowing as/
> people a May-/ing:

The marginal placing, the use of roman type, and the curious phrasing "This short florish" all suggest that here we have prompter's additions to the manuscript. A third instance of this is at III.v.134–37, where the text in the quarto is as follows:

	Per. Produce.	*Musicke Dance.*
Knocke for	*Intrate filij,* Come forth, and foot it,	
Schoole. Enter	*Ladies, if we have been merry*	
The Dance.	*And have pleased thee with a derry,*	

The italic stage direction can be taken as authorial. In the original manuscript we can assume there was a space after the one-word speech of Pirithous, and this could explain the omission of a speech heading before the next line, which is clearly the beginning of a speech by the Schoolmaster after the dance. But a prompter would see no clearly marked entry and would want one. Moreover, he might feel it necessary to indicate a signal to be given by the Schoolmaster, and therefore insert "Knocke for Schoole[master]"—i.e., the Schoolmaster should strike the floor of the stage with a staff. But at III.v.17 the agreed signal was to be his flinging up his cap: the author of the scene would not be likely to forget this so quickly, but a prompter might at first reading. Like the two previously noted stage directions, this one is in roman.

One other stage direction is marginal and in roman. This occurs at III.vi.93:

> They bow se-/verall wayes:/ then advance/ and stand.

An asterisk is inserted in III.vi.93 after Arcite has said "And me my love:" and before he continues "Is there ought else to say?" This is, I think, likely to be an authorial addition: it is literary in character, and the placing of the asterisk looks like an author's wish to indicate that the action must come between the two halves of Arcite's speech. But for the printer it would appear in the margin along with the prompter's additional stage directions and warnings, so he has used roman type for this as for those.

Even so, the evidence for the presence of the prompter's hand is fairly plentiful, and he may also have been responsible for all the indications of sound effects (horns, cornets, flourishes), not merely for those noted above. Yet it does not seem very likely that in 1634 the printer had in front of him a promptbook actually used in performance. Sir Walter Greg drew attention to the possibility that even "warnings" could appear in a manuscript which was merely annotated by a prompter before the promptbook itself was made.[2] And it is evident that the "warnings" here given are not complete: an executioner's block would be needed for V.iv, and a chair for Arcite at V.iv.86. Also, some of the entries are incomplete: Artesius and Attendants must be added at I.i.1 (though we can assume that the printer is responsible for the apparent omission of Pirithous); a Herald, Lords, Attendants, Palamon and Arcite must be added at I.iv.1; at III.v.1 the entry includes "2. *or* 3 *wenches*", but five are needed for the dance; at IV.i.102 the vague "*and others*", though possible in a prompt copy, may be an additional sign of authorial inexactitude.

Our text also contains certain things that might well have been eliminated in a prompt copy. At I.i.217 there is the stage direction "*Exeunt towards the Temple.*" This indicates that Hippolyta, Emilia, Pirithous and the Attendants begin to move toward the stage door that here represents the temple entrance, but Theseus has still an exchange with Pirithous (lines 219–24) before the procession has left the stage. This is clear enough to a reader, but a prompter would be likely to tidy it up. Then at II.i.51 there is the direction "*Enter Palamon and Arcite, above.*" The Jailer and his Daughter comment from below and then leave the stage. The quarto marks a general "*Exeunt.*" and then gives a new scene heading:

2 *The Shakespeare First Folio* (Oxford, 1955), p. 141.

Scæna 2. *Enter Palamon, and Arcite in prison.*

The action is surely continuous, and in the present edition
a new scene is not started at this point. The kinsmen
need to remain above, as the later part of the scene will
be more effective if they look down to the garden to see
Emilia, as they do in Chaucer: moreover, the "leap the
garden . . . and pitch between her arms" of II.i.277–78
strongly suggests that Arcite is above. The explanation
of the condition of the text here is probably that II.i.1–59
are by Shakespeare and the rest of the scene by Fletcher:
they had worked out in advance that Shakespeare would
introduce the new characters (Jailer, Daughter, Wooer)
and Fletcher would do the kinsmen's first encounter with
Emilia. So the two sections of the scene would be separate: II.i.60 would start a new sheet of paper. In other
words, this suggests that the printer in 1634 had in front
of him either the holograph manuscript of Shakespeare
and Fletcher or a transcript faithful to it. It should also
be noted that the quarto is unusual in its indications of
locality: in addition to the *"Temple"* and *"prison"* already noted, we have *"Enter Palamon as out of a Bush"*
at III.i.30 and *"Enter Palamon from the Bush"* at III.vi.1.
Such indications of locality are of course rare in seven-
teenth-century play texts: those in our play are similar to
"Enter Timon in the woods" and *"Enter Timon from his
Caue"* in the Folio text *Timon of Athens,* IV.iii.1 and
V.i.30. *Timon* was almost certainly printed either from
Shakespeare's own manuscript or from a faithful tran-
script of it.

Now it must be remembered that we know of performances of *The Two Noble Kinsmen* in 1613, probably in
1619, and around 1625.[3] The printer's copy in 1634 has
some relation to the last of these (from the evidence of
the two actors' names), but it is puzzling to think of the
prompter on that occasion annotating the authors' original
manuscript if a prompt copy for 1613 (and 1619) were
available. It could of course have been lost or not immediately available. And we cannot be sure that all the

[3] See Introduction, p. xxxiv.

prompter's additions were made at the same time: the "warnings" and additional stage directions could have been inserted in 1613 and the actors' names in 1625. Nevertheless, there is a good case for believing that the quarto is directly based on the author's manuscript (or a faithful transcript of it) which the prompter had annotated before the making of a promptbook. When the play came to be printed, the company would be more likely to give such a manuscript to the publisher rather than the promptbook itself, which would be needed at the theater if the play were to be acted again.[4]

When the play was reprinted in the Beaumont and Fletcher Folio of 1679, the text was based on that of the quarto. This is firmly established not only by the statement in the Folio itself but by the frequent agreement between the texts in accidentals. Although the 1679 printing shows a considerable number of variants, they have no independent authority and are mainly corrections of misprints, new misprints, and casual changes in accidentals. For the present edition, therefore, the Folio readings have been treated in the same way as those of all subsequent texts: that is, they have been regarded as editorial emendations or errors, to be taken into account in emending the quarto text but not recorded where they have not been accepted by the present editor.

All substantive departures from the quarto are recorded below, with the reading of the present edition in italic followed by the quarto reading in roman. It will be seen that the prompter's "warnings" have been transposed into stage directions and inserted in square brackets at the appropriate places. The stage directions which have been noted above as almost certainly the prompter's are, however, printed in this edition in the same way as

---

4 F. O. Waller in his article "Printer's Copy for *The Two Noble Kinsmen*," *Studies in Bibliography*, XI (1958), 61–84, has argued along these lines. This article incorporates material in Waller's unpublished Chicago dissertation of 1958, *A Critical, Old-spelling Edition of "The Two Noble Kinsmen*": the fullest textual studies so far made of the play are to be found in this thesis and in Paul Bertram's *Shakespeare and The Two Noble Kinsmen* (New Brunswick, 1965). Bertram, however, takes the view that the printer in 1634 had before him a holograph Shakespeare manuscript which had been used as a prompt book.

other stage directions (which may of course be either author's or prompter's).

It may be noted that, unlike most of his predecessors, the present editor accepts Skeat's emendation "harebells" at I.i.9, and that he is the first to take the quarto speech heading *"All"* at IV.i.146 as part of the Jailer's Daughter's speech.

In this edition italic type is used for speech headings and stage directions, as generally in the quarto, and roman type is used for all dialogue and songs (in place of the quarto's italic for proper names in the dialogue and for the songs). Punctuation and spelling have been modernized, obvious typographical errors have been silently corrected, and the quarto's Latin headings for acts and scenes are given in English. The quarto's "nev'r," "ev'r," "ev'n" spellings are here rendered as "ne'er," "e'er," "e'en," whenever the meter seems to require a monosyllable; elsewhere the full spellings of these words are used. When a quarto reading exists in two states, corrected and uncorrected, the list below indicates the uncorrected state by a raised "a" after the reading given, the corrected state by a raised "b."

In a number of places the quarto prints lines as prose which there seems to be good reason to take as blank verse. Decisions in such cases are always difficult, but the present edition follows several of its predecessors in printing as verse where a blank verse rhythm seems to underlie, and sometimes clearly to emerge from, the fairly free dialogue pattern.

In conformity with the practice of this series, localities have been inserted in scene headings, but these and all other editorial additions to the quarto are given in square brackets.

Prologue 19 *writer* wrighter   25 *water, do* water. Do   26 *tack*
take   29 *travail* travell

I.i. s.d. *Pirithous* Theseus   9 *harebells* her bels   16 *angel* angle
20 *chough hoar* Clough hee   59 *lord. The day* Lord the day
61 *groom.* Groome,   68 *Nemean* Nenuan   83 *'stilled* stilde (Folio
"stil'd")   90 *thy* the   99 *blood-sized* blood cizd   112 *glassy* glasse
125 *sister* sifter   138 *move* mooves   155 *Rinsing* Wrinching
210 *soldier, as before.* Soldier (as before)   211 *Aulis* Anly
217 s.d. *Hippolyta . . . towards* Exeunt towards

I.ii.65 *power there's nothing; almost puts* power: there's nothing,
almost puts   70 *glory; one* glory on;[b] glory on[a]

I.iii.22 *brine* brine,   31 *one* ore   54 *eleven* a eleven   54 *Flavina*
Flauia 58–64 (note in quarto margin: "2. Hearses rea-/dy with
Palamon: and Arci-/te: the 3./ Queenes./ Theseus: and/ his
Lordes/ ready.")   79 *every innocent* fury-innocent   82 *dividual*
individuall

I.iv.18 *smeared* smeard[b] succard[a]   22 *We 'lieve* We leave   26–27
(note in quarto margin: "3. Hearses rea-/dy.")   40 *friends' behests* friends, beheastes   41 *Love's provocations* Loves, provocations   45 *O'er-wrestling* Or wrastling   49 *'fore* for

II.i.1 *little . . . live:* little, . . . live,   18–19 *that now. So* that.
Now, so   51 s.d. (in quarto, after "night" in line 49)   59 (in
quarto, new scene heading: "Scæna 2. Enter Palamon, and Arcite
in prison.")   62 *war. Yet* warre yet   80 *wore* were   81 *Ravished*
Bravishd   126 *could.* could,   177 (quarto makes this the last line
of Arcite's speech)   209 *mere* neere   216 *have.* have,   261 *be,*
be.   262 *Arcite:* Arcite,   277 s.d. (and throughout rest of scene)
Jailer Keeper   321 *life?* life.

II.ii (quarto marks as "Scæna 3.")   39 *ye* yet   51 *means.* meanes
51 *says* sees   73 *him!* him

II.iii (quarto marks as "Scæna 4.")

II.iv s.d. *Short . . . within.* This short . . . within (in margin)
19 *I believe* Beleeve,

II.v (quarto marks as "Scæna 6.")

III.i s.d. *Cornets . . . a-Maying* (in quarto, in margin)   2 *laund*
land   2 *rite* Right   10 *place* pace   36 *looked, the void'st* lookd
the voydes   94 *only, sir. Your* onely, Sir your   95 *Wind horns
off* Winde hornes of Cornets   97 *musit* Musicke   107 *not.* nor;

III.ii.1 *brake* Beake   7 *reck* wreake   19 *fed* feed   28 *brine* bine

III.iii.23 *them* then   50 *armor?* Armour.

III.iv.9 *Spoon* Vpon   10 *tack* take

III.v (quarto marks as "Scæna 6.") s.d. *Bavian* Baum five [italic]
2. or 3. 8 *jean* jave 47 *once*l *You can tell, Arcas*, once, you can
tell Arcas 65–67 (note in quarto margin: "Chaire and/stooles
out.") 67 *till we* till 91 *Wind horns* (in quarto after "I'll lead")
93 *Exeunt . . . Schoolmaster* (in quarto, after "boys," line 92)
97 *Theseus* Per. 135 s.d. *Knock* Knocke for Schoole (in margin)
135 (quarto omits speech heading) 137 *ye* thee 140 *thee* three
155 *Wind horns* (in quarto, after "made," line 156)

III.vi (quarto marks as "Scæna 7.") 28 *man. When* man, when
39 *spared. Your* spard, your 68 *I warrant* Ile warrant 86 *strait*
streight 111 *safety*, safely 146 *thy* this 175 *us*; us, 176 *valiant*, valiant; 243 *prune* proyne 290 *again, it* againe it

IV.i.45–46 *Wooer. No, sir . . . 'Tis*— Wooer, [italic] No Sir not
well. / Woo. [speech heading] Tis 48 *have told* told 84 *wreath*
wreake 110 *rearly* rarely 120 *Far* For 141 *Second Friend* 1.
Fr. 145 *cheerly all*l *O, O, O* cheerely./ All. [speech heading]
Owgh, owgh, owgh 149 *Tack* take

IV.ii.16 *Jove* Love 37 *pardon, Palamon:* pardon: Palamon, 54
s.d. *Enter a Gentleman* Enter Emil. and Gent. 69 s.d. *Enter a
Messenger* Enter Messengers. Curtis 76 *first* fitst 81 *fire* faire
86–87 *baldric, . . . with:* Bauldricke; . . . with, 104 *tods* tops
109 *court* corect

IV.iii.8 s.d. (in quarto, after "business," line 8) 32 *i' th' other*
i'th/Thother 90 *carve* crave

V.i.s.d. *Flourish* (in quarto, precedes "*Exeunt.*" of IV.iii) 7 s.d.
Flourish of cornets (in quarto, at line 5) 50 *whose approach*
(first added by Seward in 1750: the words, or something like
them, seem necessary) 54 *armipotent* armenypotent 68 *design
march boldly.* designe; march boldly, 91 *his*; his 118–21 *Brief,
I . . . done no companion;/ To . . . not a defier;/ To . . . rejoicer.*
briefe I . . . done; no Companion/ To . . . not; a defyer/ To . . .
cannot; a Rejoycer, 130 (quarto inserts speech heading "Pal.")
136 *They bow* (in quarto, after line 134) 151 *'pointed* pointed
152 *him; out of two* him out of two, 154 *election. Of mine eyes*
election of mine eyes,

V.ii.34 *Videlicet, the way of flesh* (quarto has "Videlicet" in roman
and "way of flesh" in italic, doubtless through a casual error)
39 *humor* honour 53 *tune* turne

V.iii s.d. *Flourish* (in quarto, precedes "*Exeunt*" of V.ii) *Attendants* (quarto adds: "T. Tucke: Curtis.") 13 *well, penciled* well
pencild 54 *him* them 66 s.d. *Cornets . . . "A Palamon!"* (in
quarto, at line 64) *Enter a Servant* (may be erroneous, as there
were attendants on stage, and the servant brings no news) 75 *in't
else:* in't; else 77 s.d. (in quarto, at line 75) 92 s.d. (in quarto,
at line 91) 121 *to th' all I* to'th all; I

V.iv.1 (quarto omits speech heading)   5–6 *pity; to live still . . . wishes;* pitty. To live still, . . . wishes,   39 *Second and Third Knights* 1. 2. K   46 *dearly* early   76 *On end he stands* (in quarto, printed at the end of the line, perhaps indicating that it was preceded by some illegible words in the manuscript   78 *victor's* victoros   86–87 *mighty! . . . unbroken,* mightie . . . unbroken: 106 *Hath* Hast   132 *sorry; still* sorry still,

A Note on the Source of
The Two Noble Kinsmen

The play's source, we have seen, is *The Knight's Tale,* which was most easily available to the collaborators in Speght's edition of Chaucer published in 1598 (reprinted three times by 1602). In the dramatization a considerable number of changes were made. We may notice them under several heads:

(1) The action throughout is compressed. In Chaucer there is a time lapse between the first seeing of Emilia by the kinsmen and the release of Arcite. Then Arcite spends some years in Thebes before returning to Athens to see Emilia again. Meanwhile Palamon has seven years in prison. When Theseus has arranged the tournament, the kinsmen are to return to Athens in a year's time. Arcite takes some time to die after the horse has thrown him, and it is a matter of years before Emilia brings herself to marry Palamon. In the play we are not told how long Palamon and Arcite are in prison, but there is no suggestion that it is a great while. Clearly Palamon escapes soon after Arcite has entered Emilia's service. The time lapse before the tournament is a single month. Arcite dies almost immediately, and Emilia is to marry Palamon, it appears, the next day.

These changes are partly to give an effect of tighter structure to what is in Chaucer a diffuse narrative, but they also increase the sense of divine manipulation. The kinsmen in II.i look forward to a slow lifetime in prison: instead, they are whirled through a series of events, and at the end of the play Emilia is passed from arm to arm in a manner that suggests no cosmic concern for her dignity.

(2) There are also changes for the sake of obvious dramatic effectiveness. In the poem Theseus' wedding is not interrupted by the mission of the Queens. There are not three Queens but a crowd of queens and duchesses. Emilia has no attendant in the garden with whom she can talk informally and lightly. Palamon is not removed from the garden-room after Arcite's departure. At the tournament each of the kinsmen is to be accompanied by a hundred knights. The invocations to the gods are in the order Venus, Diana, Mars, which has not the climactic effect secured in the play by Emilia's prayer coming last. The falling of the single rose from the tree brings the whole scene to a striking (and disturbing) conclusion.

(3) Other changes increase this sense of disturbance. Most obvious among these is the decree of Theseus that the knights defeated in the tournament shall die. Of course, this allows the theatrically effective saving of Palamon from the block, and it puts more at stake than the disposal of Emilia's person. Shakespeare may have thought of this change because in *Pericles* the unsuccessful suitors of Antiochus' daughter were similarly vowed to death. In any event, it is an element in the play that links it with the dangers and actual deaths that are found in the preceding "romances." Moreover, there is nothing in the invocation of Venus in *The Knight's Tale* that resembles the words on the goddess' power that Palamon speaks. He hails her as

> sovereign queen of secrets, . . .
> that canst make
> A cripple flourish with his crutch, and cure him
> Before Apollo; that may'st force the king
> To be his subject's vassal, and induce
> Stale Gravity to dance: the pollèd bachelor
> Whose youth like wanton boys through bonfires
> Have skipped thy flame, at seventy thou canst catch
> And make him, to the scorn of his hoarse throat,
> Abuse young lays of love.
>
> (V.i.77, 81–9)

The images of the cripple grotesquely cured, of authority
submissive and dancing, of old age straining its throat
with a love song, contribute powerfully to that harsh
strain in Shakespeare's section of the play that has been
noted in the Introduction. And then we find Palamon
seeking favor by boasting of his own credulity, and doing
it in terms that, for an audience, are surely meant to be
repellent:

> I knew a man
> Of eighty winters, this I told them, who
> A lass of fourteen brided. 'Twas thy power
> To put life into dust: the aged cramp
> Had screwed his square foot round,
> The gout had knit his fingers into knots,
> Torturing convulsions from his globy eyes
> Had almost drawn their spheres, that what was life
> In him seemed torture. This anatomy
> Had by his young fair fere a boy, and I
> Believed it was his, for she swore it was,
> And who would not believe her?
>
> (V.i.107–18)

We may think back to Antony's concern with his gray
hairs, to Leontes' finding wrinkles in what he thinks is
Hermione's statue, but the degree of frankness is new.
Palamon, the servant of Venus, puts himself side by side
with the other victims he describes.*

(4) Nothing in Chaucer corresponds to the Jailer's
Daughter plot. We are simply told that Palamon escaped
with the help of a friend. In the Introduction (pp. xxxii–
xxxiii) we have seen how Shakespeare and Fletcher use the
subplot to affect the audience's response to the story of
the knights and their love.

(5) In Chaucer the gods are at odds with each other,
and the quarrel is settled by the ingenuity of Saturn, so

---

* In his introduction to the Signet edition of Shakespeare's *Sonnets*
(1964), W. H. Auden has commented on this passage's choice of "humili-
ating or horrid" examples of the power of Venus and on "the intensity of
the disgust at masculine sexual vanity."

that all promises can be kept. In the play we are rather
made to feel that a single power speaks through the
gods, that the matter is predetermined, that all that the
gods do is to give hints of a future which neither prayer
nor divine intervention can modify.

In a few places the play includes some quite incidental
echoes of Chaucer. Thus Arcas, one of the Countrymen
named at II.ii.37 and III.v.47, is the name of the son
of Callisto, who, as "Calystope," is referred to in *The
Knight's Tale*, line 1198. The Schoolmaster mentions the
story of Meleager and Atalanta at III.v.18: Chaucer
mentions it at *The Knight's Tale*, lines 1212–13. In the
play the tournament is held in the place where Theseus
found the knights fighting (III.vi.293): in *The Knight's
Tale*, lines 1999–2006, we learn that it is Arcite's funeral pyre that is to be erected in that place. The consolation that Palamon offers to his friends as they are
about to submit themselves to the block (V.iv.1–13),
although altogether sharper in its comments on the nature
of life, bears an obvious relation to the arguments that
Theseus uses in *The Knight's Tale*, lines 2189–98, in
order to persuade Palamon and Emilia to give up their
mourning for Arcite and enter into marriage. Such points
of casual resemblance between play and poem, with the
dramatists freely manipulating the words and images they
found in Chaucer, show the intimacy of their acquaintance
with the source.

The Knight's Tale had been twice dramatized before
1613. In 1566 Richard Edwardes' *Palamon and Arcite*
was acted at Christ Church, Oxford, before Elizabeth,
and Henslowe's *Diary* registers a *Palamon and Arcite*
acted in 1594, probably as a new play. Neither of these
is extant, but there is no reason to believe that they had
any connection with *The Two Noble Kinsmen*.

In the Introduction (pp. xxviii–xxxii) we have seen that
Shakespeare and Fletcher were dependent also on their
memories of several earlier Shakespeare plays, ranging
from *The Two Gentlemen of Verona* to the late "ro-

mances," and that this has helped to make the play into something very different from a straightforward dramatization of Chaucer.

Commentaries

GERALD EADES BENTLEY

Shakespeare and the Blackfriars Theatre

It is necessary at the outset in a discussion of this sort to place Shakespeare in what seems to me his proper context—a context which none but the Baconians and Oxfordians deny, but which most scholars and critics tend to ignore. That context is the London commercial theatre and the organized professional acting troupe.

Shakespeare was more completely and continuously involved with theatres and acting companies than any other Elizabethan dramatist whose life we know. Most Elizabethan dramatists had only their writing connection with the theatres, but Shakespeare belonged to the small group which both wrote and acted. In this small group of actor-dramatists, the best-known names are those of Heywood, Rowley, Field and Shakespeare. Of this thoroughly professionalized band, Shakespeare is the one most closely bound to his company and his theatre, for he is the only one of the four who did not shift about from company to company but maintained his close association with a single acting troupe for more than twenty years. Besides this, he was bound to theatres and actors

From *Shakespeare Survey I* (1948), pp. 38–50. Reprinted by permission of the author and the editor.

in still another fashion which makes him unique among all Elizabethan dramatists: he is the only dramatist we know who owned stock in theatre buildings over an extended period. His income was derived from acting, from writing plays, from shares in dramatic enterprises, and from theatre rents. From the beginning to the end of his writing career we must see him in a theatrical context if we are not to do violence to the recorded facts. At the beginning is our first reference to him in Greene's allusion to the "Tygers hart wrapt in a Players hyde"; at the end are his own last words, so far as we know them, in his will. This will is mostly concerned with Stratford affairs, but when he does turn to the years of his London life and his many London associates, he singles out only three for a last remembrance. These men are John Heminges, Henry Condell, and Richard Burbage—all three actors, all three fellow-sharers in the acting company of the King's men, all three fellow-stockholders in the Globe and the Blackfriars. If Shakespeare's proper context is not the London commercial theatres and the professional troupes, then evidence has no meaning, and one man's irresponsible fancies are as good as another's.

Now in spite of all the evidence that Shakespeare's dominant preoccupation throughout his creative life was the theatre, most scholars and critics of the last 150 years have written of him as the professional poet and not as the professional playwright. For the most part he has been studied as Spenser and Milton and Keats are studied. For a century and a half the great majority of studies of Shakespeare's genius and development have been concerned with literary influences and biographical influences and not with theatrical influences.[1] We have studied his

1 *The Cambridge Bibliography of English Literature* will serve as an example. The bibliography of Shakespeare fills 136 columns, of which one half-column is devoted to "The Influence of Theatrical Conditions." This is not to say, of course, that there have been no proper studies of the theatres and acting companies of Shakespeare's time. There are many. But there are comparatively few books and articles devoted to the examination of Shakespeare's work in the light of this knowledge or to a consideration of the specific influence such matters had on his methods and development.

sources and his text, his indebtedness to Ovid and Holinshed and Montaigne and Plutarch. Even in biographical studies the preference has always been for the nontheatrical aspects of Shakespeare's life—his boyhood in the woods and fields about Stratford, his marriage and his wife, the death of his son Hamnet, his relations with Southampton and Essex, his supposed breakdown, his retirement to Stratford. Now any or all of these facts, or alleged facts, no doubt had an influence on the great creations of Shakespeare. I do not suggest that our study of them should be discontinued. But given the verified documentary evidence which we have, is it not dubious practice to devote a large part of our investigations to the more or less problematical influences in Shakespeare's career and to devote a very small part of our efforts to that enormously significant influence which dominated the majority of his waking hours for the twenty-odd years of his creative maturity? A dozen or more unquestioned documents show that Shakespeare's daily concern was the enterprise of the Lord Chamberlain-King's company. Shakespeare had obviously read Ovid and Holinshed and Lord North's *Plutarch;* surely he must have mourned for the untimely death of his only son; but none of these can have occupied his mind for so long as his daily association with the enterprise of the Lord Chamberlain-King's men. Of the factors in his life and development which we can now identify, this was surely the most important.

Now what are the events in his long and absorbing association with this troupe which we can expect to have influenced his work? One of the first must have been the protracted plague closings of 1593 and 1594, for out of this disaster to all London players the Lord Chamberlain's company apparently rose.[2] Another must have been the assembling of the players and the drawing up of the agreement for the formal organization of the Lord Chamberlain's company. The record suggests that Shakespeare was one of the leaders in this organization, for when

2 E. K. Chambers, *The Elizabethan Stage,* II, 192–93 and IV, 348–49; *William Shakespeare,* I, 27–56.

the new company performed before the court in the Christmas season of 1594–95, payment was made to Richard Burbage, the principal actor, Will Kemp, the principal comedian, and William Shakespeare.[3] How did the great possibilities offered by this new troupe, destined to become the most famous and most successful in the history of the English theatre, affect the writing of its chief dramatist?

In the winter of 1598–99 occurred another event which must have been of absorbing interest for all members of the company. This was of course the building of the Globe on the Bankside. Here was a theatre built for the occupancy of a particular company, and six of the seven owners were actors in the company. Assuredly it was built, so far as available funds would allow, to the specific requirements of the productions of the Lord Chamberlain's men. What facilities did Shakespeare get which he had not had before? How did he alter his composition to take advantage of the new possibilities? Can there be any doubt that as a successful man of the theatre he did so? Yet I know of no study which attempts to assess this vital new factor in relation to Shakespeare's development.

The next event which must have been of great importance for Shakespeare's company was its involvement in the Essex rebellion. This exceptional case has received the full attention of critics and scholars because of its supposed relation to a performance of Shakespeare's *Richard II*. Actually, however, the Essex rebellion, much though it must have excited the company for a few months, was the least influential of all these factors affecting the company's activities and Shakespeare's development. Apparently the company's innocence was established without much difficulty.[4] There is no indication that their later performances or Shakespeare's later writing were affected by the experience. Though the events were sensational, and though they must have caused great anxiety for a time, they cannot be thought of as events of long-term significance in the history of this group of men

3 *The Elizabethan Stage*, IV, 164.
4 *William Shakespeare*, I, 353–55; *The Elizabethan Stage*, II, 204–07.

who were so important and influential in Shakespeare's career and development.

Of much more importance in the affairs of the company was their attainment of the patronage of James I less than two months after the death of Elizabeth.[5] This patronage and the King's livery certainly became one of the important factors in creating the great prestige of the company. In the ten years before they became the King's company, their known performances at court average about three a year; in the ten years after they attained their new service their known performances at court average about thirteen a year, more than those of all other London companies combined.[6] They were officially the premier company in London; a good part of their time must have been devoted to the preparation of command performances. Surely this new status of the troupe must have been a steady and pervasive influence in the development of its principal dramatist, William Shakespeare.

The final event which I wish to mention in the affairs of the King's company was perhaps the most important of all. There is no doubt that it made a great change in the activities of the company, and I do not see how it can have failed to be a principal influence in Shakespeare's development as a dramatist. This event was the acquisition of the famous private theatre in Blackfriars. No adult company in London had ever before performed regularly in a private theatre. For thirty years the private theatres with their superior audiences, their concerts, their comfortable accommodations, their traffic in sophisticated drama and the latest literary fads, had been the exclusive homes of the boy companies, the pets of Society. Now for the first time a troupe of those rogues and vagabonds, the common players, had the temerity to present themselves to the sophisticates of London in a repertory at the town's most exclusive theatre. I suspect that this was one of the turning points in Tudor and Stuart dramatic history. Beaumont and Jonson and Fletcher had

5 *The Elizabethan Stage*, II, 208–09.
6 *Ibid.*, IV, 108–30.

begun to make the craft of the playwright more socially respectable. The increasing patronage of the drama by the royal family, and the growing splendor and frequency of the court masques which were written by ordinary playwrights and performed in part by common players, were raising the prestige of the drama and the theatre from its Elizabethan to its Caroline state. The acquisition of the Blackfriars in 1608 by the King's company and the full exploitation of the new playhouse must have been the most conspicuous evidence to Londoners of the changing state of affairs. Surely it is impossible that the King's men and their principal dramatist, William Shakespeare, could have been unaware of this situation. Surely they must have bent all their efforts in the selection and performance of old plays and in the commissioning and writing of new ones to the full exploitation of this unprecedented opportunity. The new state of affairs must have been apparent in much that they did, and it must have influenced decidedly the dramatic compositions of Shakespeare.

So far, it has been my contention that all we know of William Shakespeare has shown him to be above all else a man of the theatre, that during the twenty years of his creative maturity most of his time was spent in closest association with members of the Lord Chamberlain-King's company and in thought about their needs and their interests, and that therefore in the affairs of this company we should seek one of the principal influences in his creative life. I have mentioned six events which (so far as we can tell through the mists of 350 years) seem to have been important in the affairs of that theatrical organization. These events are not all of equal importance, but each of them, except possibly the Essex rebellion, must have had a marked effect on the activities of Shakespeare's company and therefore on the dramatic creations of Shakespeare himself. Each one, it seems to me, deserves more study that it has received in its relation to the development of Shakespeare's work.

Let me invite your attention now to a fuller consideration of one of the most important of these events in the history of the Lord Chamberlain-King's company, namely the acquisition of the Blackfriars Theatre. What did this event mean in the history of the company, and how did it affect the writing of William Shakespeare?

Probably we should note first the time at which the Blackfriars would have begun to influence the company and the writing of Shakespeare. All the dramatic histories say that the King's men took over the Blackfriars Theatre in 1608, and this is true in a legal sense, for on 9 August 1608 leases were executed conveying the Blackfriars Playhouse to seven lessees: Cuthbert Burbage, Thomas Evans, and five members of the King's company—John Heminges, William Sly, Henry Condell, Richard Burbage, and William Shakespeare.[7] The few scholars who have examined in detail the history of the King's company have noted, however, that Shakespeare and his fellows probably did not begin to act at the Blackfriars in August of 1608. The plague was rife in London at that time; fifty plague deaths had been recorded for the week ending 28 July, and for a year and a half, or until December 1609, the bills of mortality show an abnormally high rate from the plague.[8] Though specific records about the closing of the theatres are not extant, we have definite statements that they were closed for part of this period, and comparison with other years suggests that there must have been very little if any public acting allowed in London between the first of August 1608 and the middle of December 1609. Therefore, it has occasionally been said, the Blackfriars was not used by the King's men much before 1610, and no influence on their plays and their productions can be sought before that year.

This conclusion of little or no influence before 1610 is, I think, a false one. It is based on the erroneous assumption that the actors and playwrights of the King's company would have known nothing about the peculiarities of the Blackfriars and that they would have had no plays

---

[7] *The Elizabethan Stage*, II, 509–10. Technically Richard Burbage leased one-seventh of the theatre to each of the other six.

[8] *Ibid.*, IV, 351.

prepared especially for that theatre until after they had begun performing in it. Actors are never so stupid or so insular as this in any time. The King's men, we may be sure, were well aware of the Blackfriars and the type of performance it required, or specialized in, long before they came to lease the theatre. There must be many evidences of this, but three in particular come readily to mind.

Seven years before, in 1601, the King's men had been involved in the War of the Theatres, which was in part a row between the public theatres and the private theatres. The chief attack on the public theatres and adult actors was made in Jonson's *Poetaster,* performed at the Blackfriars. Certain actors of the Lord Chamberlain's company, and possibly Shakespeare himself, were ridiculed in this Blackfriars play. The reply, *Satiromastix,* was written by Thomas Dekker and performed by Shakespeare's company at the Globe.[9] Certainly in 1601 at least, the company was well aware of the goings on at Blackfriars.

A second piece of evidence pointing to their knowledge of the peculiar requirements of the Blackfriars is the case of Marston's *Malcontent.* Marston wrote this play for the boys at the Blackfriars, who performed it in that theatre in 1604. The King's men stole the play, as they admitted, and performed it at the Globe; the third edition, also 1604, shows the alterations they commissioned John Webster to make in order to adapt a Blackfriars script to a Globe performance, and in the induction to the play Richard Burbage, speaking in his own person, points out one or two of the differences between Blackfriars requirements and Globe requirements.[10]

Finally, and most familiar of all evidence that the King's men were quite alive to what went on at Blackfriars, is the "little eyases" passage in *Hamlet* and Shakespeare's rueful admission that, for a time at any rate, the competition of the Blackfriars was too much for the company at the Globe.

9 See J. H. Penniman, *The War of the Theatres,* and R. A. Small, *The Stage Quarrel.*

10 F. L. Lucas, *The Works of John Webster,* III, 294–309.

Clearly the King's men did not have to wait until their performances of 1610 at the Blackfriars to know how their plays needed to be changed to fit them to that theatre and its select audience. They had known for several years what the general characteristics of Blackfriars performances were. Indeed, the leading member of the company, Richard Burbage, had a double reason for being familiar with all the peculiarities of the Blackfriars, for since his father's death in 1597 he had been the owner of the theatre and the landlord of the boy company that made it famous.[11] We can be perfectly sure, then, that from the day of the first proposal that the King's men take over the Blackfriars they had talked among themselves about what they would do with it and had discussed what kinds of plays they would have to have written to exploit it. It is all too often forgotten that in all such discussions among the members of the King's company William Shakespeare would have had an important part. He had more kinds of connections with the company than any other man: he was actor, shareholder, patented member, principal playwright, and one of the housekeepers of the Globe; even Burbage did not serve so many functions in the company. Few men in theatrical history have been so completely and inextricably bound up with the affairs of an acting troupe.

When would the King's men have begun planning for their performances at the Blackfriars? We cannot, of course, set the exact date, but we can approximate it. There is one faint suggestion that consideration of the project may have started very early indeed. Richard Burbage said that Henry Evans, who had leased the theatre from him for the Children of the Queen's Revels, began talking to him about the surrender of his lease in 1603 or 1604.[12] These early discussions evidently came to nothing, for we know that the boys continued in the theatre for three or four years longer. Burbage's statement

---

[11] J. Q. Adams, *Shakespearean Playhouses*, pp. 199–223.
[12] "The Answers of Heminges and Burbage to Edward Kirkham," 1612, printed by F. G. Fleay, *A Chronicle History of the London Stage*, p. 235.

about Evans does suggest the interesting possibility that the King's men may have dallied with the project of leasing the Blackfriars Theatre as early as 1603 or 1604. This, however, is only the faintest of possibilities. The Blackfriars was tentatively in the market then, but all we know is that Burbage had to consider for a short time the possibility of getting other tenants for his theatre. Whether the King's men came to his mind and theirs as possible tenants, we do not know.

We can be sure that active planning for performances at the Blackfriars did get under way when Burbage, who was both the leading actor of the King's men and owner of the Blackfriars Theatre, knew for certain that the boy actors would give up their lease and that arrangements for a syndicate of King's men to take over the theatre could be made. Conferences among these men—the Burbages, Heminges, Condell, Shakespeare, and Sly—and probably preliminary financial arrangements would have been going on before a scrivener was called in to draw up a rough draft of the lease. Such preliminaries, which must come before a lease can be formally signed, often consume months. We know that the leases were formally executed on 9 August 1608;[13] therefore discussions in June and July or even in April and May are likely enough. We know that the Blackfriars Theatre was available as early as March 1608, for in a letter dated 11 March 1608 Sir Thomas Lake officially notified Lord Salisbury that the company of the Children of Blackfriars must be suppressed and that the King had vowed that they should never act again even if they had to beg their bread. General confirmation of this fact is found in a letter written two weeks later by the French ambassador.[14] Thus it is evident that in March of 1608 Richard Burbage knew his theatre was without a tenant. March to July 1608, then, are the months for discussions among the King's men of prospective performances at the Blackfriars.

What did this little group of Shakespeare and his

13 *William Shakespeare*, II, 62–63.
14 *The Elizabethan Stage*, II, 53–54.

intimate associates of the last fourteen years work out during their discussions in the months of March to July 1608?

One of the things they must have considered was alterations of their style of acting. As Granville-Barker has pointed out,[15] the acting in the new Blackfriars before a sophisticated audience would have to be more quiet than in the large open-air Globe before the groundlings. It would be easier to emphasize points in the quiet candlelit surroundings, and "sentiment would become as telling as passion." There must also have been extended discussions of what to do about the repertory: which of the company's plays would be suitable for the elegant new theatre and which should be kept for the old audience at the Globe? Some of their decisions are fairly obvious. *Mucedorus,* which Rafe in *The Knight of the Burning Pestle* says he had played before the Wardens of his company and which went through fifteen editions before the Restoration, was clearly one of the Globe plays which might be laughed at by a Blackfriars audience. Similarly, *The Merry Devil of Edmonton* was not a good Blackfriars prospect. Certain other plays in the repertory might be expected to please at the Blackfriars; Marston's *Malcontent,* for instance, could easily be changed back to its original Blackfriars form, and Jonson's *Every Man in His Humour* and *Every Man out of His Humour*, though nine and ten years old, had been played by the company at court in the last three years and ought to be suitable for the Blackfriars.

These discussions of the old repertory, though no doubt important to the company then, are fruitless for us now. I know of no evidence as to their decisions. More important are the proposals for new plays for the Blackfriars, and I think we do have some evidence as to what these decisions were. The experienced members of the King's company were familiar with the fact so commonly recorded in the annals of the Jacobean theatre that new plays were in constant demand. With the acquisition of the new theatre they had an opportunity to claim for their

15 *Prefaces to Shakespeare*, 2nd ser., pp. 249–50.

own the most profitable audience in London. We know from the later Jacobean and Caroline records that this is just what they did.[16] It seems likely that one of the foundations of their later unquestioned dominance of the audiences of the gentry was their decision about plays and playwrights made in their discussions of March to July 1608.

One of their decisions, I suggest, was to get Jonson to write Blackfriars plays for them. He was a likely choice for three reasons. First, because he was developing a following among the courtly audience (always prominent at the Blackfriars) by his great court masques. At this time he had already written his six early entertainments for King James—those at the Coronation, at the Opening of Parliament, at Althorp, at Highgate, and the two at Theobalds. He had written for performance at Whitehall *The Masque of Blackness, The Masque of Beauty, Hymenaei,* and the famous *Lord Haddington's Masque.* The sensational success of these courtly entertainments made Jonson a most promising choice to write plays for the courtly audience which the King's men did succeed in attracting to Blackfriars.

A second reason which would have led the King's men to Jonson as a writer for their new theatre was his great reputation among the literati and critics. In this decade from 1601 to 1610 the literary allusions to him are numerous, more numerous than to Shakespeare himself. The poems to Jonson and the long prose passages about him in this time are far more frequent than to Shakespeare; quotations from his work occur oftener, and I find three times as many literary and social references to performances of his plays and masques as to Shakespeare's. Poems about him or references to his work are written in these years by John Donne, Sir John Roe, Sir Dudley Carleton, the Venetian ambassador, John Chamberlain, Sir Thomas Lake, Sir George Buc, Sir Thomas Salusbury.[17] This is just the kind of audience which

16 See Bentley, *The Jacobean and Caroline Stage,* Vol. I, chap. I *passim*; II, 673–81.

17 See Bentley, *Shakespeare and Jonson,* I, 38–41, 65–67, 73–79, 87–90, and Bradley and Adams, *The Jonson Allusion-Book, passim.*

might be attracted to the Blackfriars, and which, eventually, the King's men did attract there.

There was a third reason which would have made Jonson seem to the King's men a very likely bet for their new theatre: he had already had experience in writing plays for this theatre when it was occupied by boys. Before the conferences of the King's men about their new project he had already had performed at Blackfriars *Cynthia's Revels, The Poetaster, The Case Is Altered,* and *Eastward Ho.* Possibly just before the time of the conferences of the King's men he had been writing for the Blackfriars another play, *Epicoene,* for he says in the Folio of 1616 that the play was performed by the Children of Blackfriars, but the date he gives for performance comes after their expulsion from the Blackfriars Theatre. Not only had Jonson had the valuable experience of writing four or five plays for the Blackfriars, but the Induction to *Cynthia's Revels* and his personal statements about boys of the company, like Nathan Field and Salathiel, or Solomon, Pavy,[18] strongly suggest that he had directed them in their rehearsals. What valuable experience for the King's men planning their first performance in this new theatre!

Now all these qualifications of Jonson as a prospect for the King's men are, in sober fact, only speculations. Perhaps they simply show that if *I* had been participating in the conferences about the Blackfriars I should have argued long and lustily for Ben Jonson. Alas, I was not there! What evidence is there that they really did agree to secure his services for the company? The evidence is that before these conferences he had written only four plays for the Lord Chamberlain's or King's company—three, nine, and ten years before—nothing for the company in the years 1605–08. After these conferences, he wrote all his remaining plays for the company, with the exception of *Bartholomew Fair* six years later, a play which he gave to his good friend and protégé Nathan Field for the Lady Elizabeth's company at the Hope, and *A Tale of a Tub,* twenty-five years later, which he gave to Queen Henri-

---

18 See "A Good Name Lost," *Times Literary Supplement* (30 May 1942), p. 276.

etta's men. Jonson's first play after the reopening of Black-friars was *The Alchemist;* it was written for the King's men, and numerous allusions show clearly that it was written for Blackfriars. So were *Catiline, The Devil Is an Ass, The Staple of News, The New Inn,* and *The Magnetic Lady.* Of course we lack the final proof of recorded reference to a definite agreement, but the evidence is such as to suggest that one of the decisions reached by the King's men in the reorganization of their enterprise was to exploit the great advantages of their new theatre was to secure the services of Ben Jonson to write plays for the literate and courtly audience at Blackfriars.

Another decision, which I suggest the King's men made at these conferences, was to secure for their new theatre the services of the rising young collaborators, Francis Beaumont and John Fletcher. These gentlemen were younger than Jonson by about ten years, and as yet their reputations were distinctly inferior to his, but they had already displayed those talents which were to make their plays the stage favorites at Blackfriars for the next thirty-four years,[19] and were to cause Dryden to say sixty years later that "their plays are now the most pleasant and frequent entertainments of the stage."

One of the great assets of Beaumont and Fletcher was social. In the years immediately before and after 1608, the London theatre audience was developing the social cleavage which is such a marked characteristic of the Jacobean and Caroline drama and stage. In Elizabeth's time the London theatre was a universal one, in which a single audience at the Globe could embrace Lord Monteagle, Sir Charles Percy, city merchants, lawyers, Inns of Court students, apprentices, servants, beggars, pickpockets, and prostitutes. The later Jacobean and Caroline audience was a dual one. The gentry, the court, the professional classes, and the Inns of Court men went to the Blackfriars, the Phoenix, and later to the Salisbury Court; the London masses went to the larger and noisier Red Bull and Fortune and Globe. This new state of affairs was just developing when the King's men had their confer-

19 *The Jacobean and Caroline Stage,* 1, 29 and 109–14.

ences about the Blackfriars in 1608. They evidently saw what was coming, however, for in the next few years they understood and exploited the situation more effectively than any other troupe in London. Indeed, the very acquisition of the Blackfriars and its operation in conjunction with the Globe was a device which had never been tried before in London and which is the clearest evidence that the King's men knew just what was happening.

Under these circumstances, then, the social status of Beaumont and Fletcher was an asset for the company in their new house. Francis Beaumont came of an ancient and distinguished Leicestershire family, with many connections among the nobility. John Fletcher was the son of a Lord Bishop of London and one-time favorite of Elizabeth. To a Blackfriars audience the social standing of these two young men would have been more acceptable than that of any other dramatist writing in London in 1608.

Another asset which made Beaumont and Fletcher valuable for the new enterprise of the King's men was their private theatre experience. So far as we can make out now, all their plays before this time had been written for private theatres and most of them for the Blackfriars. *The Woman Hater* had been prepared for the private theatre in St. Paul's, but *The Knight of the Burning Pestle, The Scornful Lady,* and *The Faithful Shepherdess* were Blackfriars plays. I think we can add to this list *Cupid's Revenge.* This play has been variously dated, but two forthcoming articles by James Savage[20] seem to me to offer convincing evidence that the play was prepared for Blackfriars about 1607 and that it displays a crude preliminary working out of much of the material which made *Philaster* one of the great hits of its time and one of the most influential plays of the seventeenth century. In any event, Beaumont and Fletcher were among the most experienced Blackfriars playwrights available in 1608. It is true that in 1608 none of their plays had been a great success; indeed the two best, *The Knight of the*

20 "The Date of Beaumont and Fletcher's *Cupid's Revenge*" and "Beaumont and Fletcher's *Philaster* and Sidney's *Arcadia*."

Burning Pestle and *The Faithful Shepherdess,* are known to have been unsuccessful at first. The King's men, however, were experienced in the ways of the theatre; it does not seem rash to assume that at least one of them knew enough about audiences and about dramatic talents to see that these young men were writers of brilliant promise—especially since that one was William Shakespeare.

Beaumont and Fletcher, then, because of their experience and social standing were very desirable dramatists for the King's men to acquire in 1608 for their new private theatre. What is the evidence that they did acquire them? The evidence is that all the Beaumont and Fletcher plays of the next few years are King's men's plays, several of them famous hits—*Philaster, The Maid's Tragedy, A King and No King, The Captain, The Two Noble Kinsmen, Bonduca, Monsieur Thomas, Valentinian.* The dating of many of the Beaumont and Fletcher plays is very uncertain because of their late publication, and it may be that two or three of the later plays were written for other companies, but at least forty-five plays by Beaumont and Fletcher were the property of the Jacobean and Caroline King's men.[21] None of their plays before 1608, when Blackfriars was acquired, was, so far as we can find, written for the King's men. It seems a reasonable assumption, therefore, that another of the policies agreed upon at the conferences of 1608 was to secure the services of Beaumont and Fletcher for the company in its new enterprise at the Blackfriars.

The third of these three important changes in policy which I think the King's men agreed upon at their conferences about the new Blackfriars enterprise in 1608, is the most interesting of all to us, but it was the easiest and most obvious for them. Indeed, it may well have been assumed almost without discussion. It was, of course, that William Shakespeare should write henceforth with the Blackfriars in mind and not the Globe.

Why was this decision an easy and obvious one? The company could assume, of course, that he would continue to write for them, since he was a shareholder and a

21 *The Jacobean and Caroline Stage,* I, 109–15.

patented member of the company and a housekeeper in both their theatres. Since the formation of the company, fourteen years before, all his plays had been written for performance by them, always, in the last ten years, for performance at the Globe. All his professional associations as well as his financial ones were with this company, and probably no one in the group even considered his defection. Burbage, Shakespeare, Heminges, and Condell were the real nucleus of the organization.

This new enterprise at the Blackfriars was a very risky business. As we have noted, no adult company had ever tried to run a private theatre before. The King's men not only proposed to make a heavy investment in this new departure, but they intended to continue running their old public theatre at the same time. Every possible precaution against failure needed to be taken. One such precaution would be the devotion of Shakespeare's full-time energies to the Blackfriars instead of the Globe. They could trust Shakespeare; he knew their potentialities and their shortcomings as no other dramatist did—indeed, few dramatists in the history of the English theatre have ever had such a long and intimate association with an acting company as William Shakespeare had had with these men. If anybody knew what Burbage and Heminges and Condell and Robert Armyn and Richard Cowley could do on the stage and what they should not be asked to do, that man was William Shakespeare. He could make them a success at the Blackfriars as they had been at the Globe if any one could.

Another reason for the transfer of Shakespeare's efforts was the fact that the Globe could be left to take care of itself with an old repertory as the Blackfriars could not. For one thing, there was no old repertory for the Blackfriars, since the departing boys appear to have held on to their old plays. For another thing, it was the Blackfriars audience which showed the greater avidity for new plays; the public theatre audiences were much more faithful to old favorites. They were still playing *Friar Bacon and Friar Bungay* at the Fortune in 1630 and Marlowe's *Edward II* at the Red Bull in 1620 and *Dr. Faustus* at the Fortune in 1621 and *Richard II* and *Pericles* at the Globe in 1631.[22] In the archives of the Globe at this time there must have been a repertory of more than a hundred plays, including at least twenty-five of Shakespeare's. Moreover, certain plays written for the Globe in the last few years, like Wilkins's *Miseries of Enforced Marriage* and the anonymous *Yorkshire Tragedy* and *The Fair Maid of Bristol* and *The London Prodigal,* had provided playwrights who might be expected to entertain a Globe audience with more of the same fare, but who could scarcely come up to the requirements of sophistication at Blackfriars. Altogether, then, the Globe repertory had much less need of Shakespeare's efforts in 1608 than did the Blackfriars repertory.

Why should Shakespeare have wanted to write for the Blackfriars, or at least have agreed to do so? The most compelling of the apparent reasons is that he had money invested in the project and stood to lose by its failure and gain by its success. He was one of the seven lessees of the new theatre; he had paid down an unknown sum and had agreed to pay £5. 14s. 4d. per year in rent.[23] He had at least a financial reason for doing everything he could to establish the success of the Blackfriars venture, and what Shakespeare could do most effectively was to write plays which would insure the company's popularity with the audience in its new private theatre.

A third reason for this postulated decision of the King's men in 1608 to have Shakespeare devote his entire attention to the Blackfriars and abandon the Globe was that the King's men saw that the real future of the theatrical profession in London lay with the court and the court party in the private theatres. Their receipts for performances at court showed them this very clearly. In the last nine years of Elizabeth, 1594–1602, they had received from court performances an average of £35 a year; in the first five years of the reign of the new king, 1603–07, they had averaged £131 per year in addition to their new

22 *Ibid.,* I, 156, 174, 157, 24, 129.
23 *Shakespearean Playhouses,* pp. 224–25.

allowances for liveries as servants of the King.[24] The Blackfriars and not the Globe was the theatre where they could entertain this courtly audience with commercial performances. There is no doubt that in the next few years after 1608 the Blackfriars did become the principal theatre of the company. In 1612 Edward Kirkham said they took £1,000 a winter more at the Blackfriars than they had formerly taken at the Globe.[25] When Sir Henry Herbert listed receipts from the two theatres early in the reign of King Charles, the receipts for single performances at the Globe averaged £6. 13*s*. 8*d*.; those for single performances at the Blackfriars averaged £15. 15*s*., or about two and one-half times as much.[26] In 1634 an Oxford don who wrote up the company simply called them the company of the Blackfriars and did not mention the Globe at all;[27] when the plays of the company were published in the Jacobean and Caroline period, the Blackfriars was mentioned as their theatre more than four times as often as the Globe was.[28] Such evidence proves that the Blackfriars certainly did become the principal theatre of the King's men. I am suggesting that in the conferences of 1608 the King's men had some intimation that it would, and accordingly they persuaded William Shakespeare to devote his attention to that theatre in the future instead of to the Globe.

So much for the reasons that Shakespeare might be expected to change the planning of his plays in 1608. What is the evidence that he did? The evidence, it seems to me, is to be seen in *Cymbeline, The Winter's Tale, The Tempest,* and *The Two Noble Kinsmen,* and probably it was to be seen also in the lost play, *Cardenio.* The variations which these plays show from the Shakespearian norm have long been a subject for critical comment. The first three of them in particular, since they are the only ones which have been universally accepted as part of the

24 *The Elizabethan Stage,* IV, 164–75.
25 C. W. Wallace, *University of Nebraska Studies,* VIII (1908), 36–37, n. 6.
26 *The Jacobean and Caroline Stage,* I, 23–24.
27 *Ibid.,* I, 26, n. 5.
28 *Ibid.,* I, 30, n. 1.

Shakespeare canon, have commonly been discussed as a distinct genre. Widely as critics and scholars have disagreed over the reasons for their peculiar characteristics, those peculiarities have generally been recognized, whether the plays are called Shakespeare's Romances, or Shakespeare's Tragi-Comedies, or his Romantic Tragi-Comedies, or simply the plays of the fourth period. No competent critic who has read carefully through the Shakespeare canon has failed to notice that there is something different about *Cymbeline, The Winter's Tale, The Tempest,* and *The Two Noble Kinsmen.*

When critics and scholars have tried to explain this difference between the plays of the last period and Shakespeare's earlier work, they have set up a variety of hypotheses. Most of these hypotheses have in common only the trait which I noted at the beginning of this paper —namely, they agree in considering Shakespeare as the professional poet and not the professional playwright. They turn to Shakespeare's sources, or to his inspiration, or to his personal affairs, or to the bucolic environment of his Stratford retirement, but not to the theatre which was his daily preoccupation for more than twenty years. Dowden called this late group in the Shakespeare canon "On the Heights," because he thought the plays reflected Shakespeare's new-found serenity. Such a fine optimism had, perhaps, something to recommend it to the imaginations of the Victorians, but to modern scholars it seems to throw more light on Dowden's mind than on Shakespeare's development. Dowden's explanation seemed utterly fatuous to Lytton Strachey, who thought that the plays of "Shakespeare's Final Period" were written by a Shakespeare far from serene, who was really "half enchanted by visions of beauty and loveliness and half bored to death." Violently as Dowden and Strachey differ, they agree in seeking subjective interpretations.

Best known of the old explanations of the peculiarities of the plays of this last period is probably Thorndike's:[29] the contention that the great success of *Philaster* caused

29 Ashley H. Thorndike, *The Influence of Beaumont and Fletcher on Shakespeare.*

Shakespeare to imitate it in *Cymbeline* and to a lesser extent in *The Winter's Tale* and *The Tempest*. In spite of the great horror of the Shakespeare idolaters at the thought of the master imitating superficial young whipper-snappers like Beaumont and Fletcher, no one can read the two plays together without noting the striking similarities between them. The difficulty is that although the approximate dates of the two plays are clear enough, their *precise* dates are so close together and so uncertain that neither Thorndike nor any subsequent scholar has been able to prove that *Philaster* came before *Cymbeline*, and the Shakespeare idolaters have been equally unable to prove that *Cymbeline* came before *Philaster*.

I suggest that the really important point is not the priority of either play. The significant and revealing facts are that both were written for the King's company; both were written, or at least completed, after the important decision made by the leaders of the troupe in the spring of 1608 to commission new plays for Blackfriars, and both were prepared to be acted in the private theatre in Blackfriars before the sophisticated audience attracted to that house. It is their common purpose and environment, not imitation of one by the other, which makes them similar. Both *Philaster* and *Cymbeline* are somewhat like Beaumont and Fletcher's earlier plays, especially *Cupid's Revenge,* because Beaumont and Fletcher's earlier plays had all been written for private theatres and all but one for Blackfriars. Both *Philaster* and *Cymbeline* are unlike Shakespeare's earlier plays because none of those plays had been written for private theatres. The subsequent plays of both Beaumont and Fletcher and Shakespeare resemble *Philaster* and *Cymbeline* because they too were written to be performed by the King's men before the sophisticated and courtly audience in the private theatre at Blackfriars.

So much I think we can say with some assurance. This explanation of the character of Shakespeare's last plays is in accord with the known facts of theatrical history; it accords with the biographical evidence of Shakespeare's long and close association with all the enterprises of the

Lord Chamberlain's-King's men for twenty years; it is in accord with his fabulously acute sense of the theatre and the problems of the actor; and it does no violence to his artistic integrity or to his poetic genius.

May I add one further point much more in the realm of speculation? Since John Fletcher became a playwright for the King's men at this time and continued so for the remaining seventeen years of his life, and since the activities of the King's men had been one of Shakespeare's chief preoccupations for many years, is it not likely that the association between Fletcher and Shakespeare from 1608 to 1614 was closer than has usually been thought? Shakespeare was nearing retirement; after 1608 he wrote plays less frequently than before; Fletcher became his successor as chief dramatist for the King's company. In these years they collaborated in *The Two Noble Kinsmen, Henry VIII,* and probably in *Cardenio.* Is it too fantastic to suppose that Shakespeare was at least an adviser in the preparation of *Philaster, A King and No King,* and *The Maid's Tragedy* for his fellows? Is it even more fantastic to think that Shakespeare, the old public theatre playwright, preparing his first and crucial play for a private theatre, might have asked advice—or even taken it—from the two young dramatists who had written plays for this theatre and audience four or five times before?

Perhaps this is going too far. I do not wish to close on a note of speculation. My basic contention is that Shakespeare was, before all else, a man of the theatre and a devoted member of the King's company. One of the most important events in the history of that company was its acquisition of the Blackfriars Playhouse in 1608 and its subsequent brilliantly successful exploitation of its stage and audience. The company was experienced and theatre-wise; the most elementary theatrical foresight demanded that in 1608 they prepare new and different plays for a new and different theatre and audience. Shakespeare was their loved and trusted fellow. How could they fail to ask him for new Blackfriars plays, and how could he fail them? All the facts at our command seem to me to demonstrate that he did not fail them. He turned from his old and tested methods and produced a new kind of play for the new theatre and audience. Somewhat unsurely at first he wrote *Cymbeline* for them, then, with greater dexterity in his new medium, *The Winter's Tale*, and finally, triumphant in his old mastery, *The Tempest*.

THEODORE SPENCER

The Two Noble Kinsmen

For about a hundred years critical opinion has been divided as to whether Shakespeare did or did not write a large part of *The Two Noble Kinsmen*. The play was entered on the Stationers' Register in 1634 as "by John Fletcher and William Shakespeare," and the quarto was printed in the same year with their names on the title page. But the play does not occur in any of the Shakespeare folios, and though Fletcher's style is unmistakably present, in the so-called Shakespearean scenes there are characteristics which to many readers have seemed un-Shakespearean. Professor Tucker Brooke sums up the negative case: "When we consider individually the parts of *The Two Noble Kinsmen* which have been ascribed to Shakespeare, we find invariably that each act, scene or verse falls just short of what it should be. Always there is the strong Shakespearean reminiscence, but nowhere the full and perfect reality that we could swear to."[1] Consequently other authors, especially Massinger, have been suggested for these scenes, and the play is ordinarily omitted from Shakespeare's collected works.[2]

From *Modern Philology*, XXXVI (1939), 255–76. Reprinted by permission of The University of Chicago Press.

[1] The *Shakespeare Apocrypha* (Oxford, 1908), p. xliii.
[2] There is a good summary of the history of the criticism of *The Two Noble Kinsmen* by Henry D. Gray. "Beaumont and *The Two Noble Kinsmen*," *PQ*, II (1923), 112–31. Mr. Gray's own theory is, however, one of the most fantastic of the lot. He suggests that Fletcher timorously began the play alone, then got stuck and asked for Beaumont's help. Beaumont saw a chance of giving wider publicity to his recent *Masque of the Temple and Gray's Inn*, and started to assist Fletcher by inserting some of the characters from it in the third act; he also wrote a first draft of most of the other scenes. Before he finished, however, he got married and went to live in Kent, out of reach. Fletcher, in despair, and feeling quite unable to write the play alone, turned to Shakespeare. Shakespeare agreed to help, rewrote most of Act III, scene i, and brightened up the characters of Palamon and Arcite. But he too left town before he finished, going home to Stratford for good, and the play remained largely as Beaumont had drafted it.

But there is opinion of equal weight on the other side, and it is, I believe, now generally agreed that Shakespeare wrote Act I, scenes i–iii; Act III, scene i; Act V, except scene ii, and possibly more, and that he was equally responsible with Fletcher for the characterization and the plotting. To my mind the matter is clinched by a remarkably able and interesting article by Mr. Alfred Hart,[3] which analyzes the language of the Shakespearean scenes in the play in great detail, and by showing how closely it resembles that of Shakespeare's other plays, makes Shakespeare's authorship entirely convincing.

That the play was written in 1613 there can also be little doubt: the inclusion of the characters from Beaumont's masque of that date is strong evidence. As Professor Kittredge says, it "may be put immediately after *Henry VIII*."[4] Shakespeare's share in it, therefore, is the last thing he wrote, and it may be of considerable interest to study the play in the light of that fact. We may be able, as a result, to understand more clearly Shakespeare's latest style; we may be able to reach some conclusions as to why he ended his dramatic career when he did; and we may get a clearer picture not only of Jacobean drama at the end of Shakespeare's career, but of the different ways human experience can be represented on the stage.

II

The story of Palamon and Arcite, whether told by Boccaccio, Chaucer, or Shakespeare and Fletcher, is intrinsically feeble, superficial, and undramatic. For there is no real difference between Palamon and Arcite; they are both noble individuals, and the only reasons Palamon, rather than Arcite, wins the lady whom they both love are (*a*) that he saw her first and (*b*) that he had the sense to pray for success to Venus rather than to Mars. These reasons, to be sure, may have been more forceful in Chaucer's day, when the courtly ideal of love still had

---

[3] "Shakespeare and the Vocabulary of *The Two Noble Kinsmen*," *RES*, X (1934), 274–87.
[4] *Complete Works of William Shakespeare* (Boston, 1936), p. 1409.

some literary vitality, than they were in Shakespeare's, but even in Chaucer they are entirely external; they have nothing to do with character; when Palamon finally wins the lady, he does so by the help of a supernatural trick, not because he is the better man. Granted the outline of the story, anyone who tells it is forced to make the two heroes colorless and indistinguishable: should he do anything else, the story disappears. The same albinism extends to Emily, the heroine. She has no will of her own; if she should express a preference for either Arcite or Palamon, it would ruin the plot, which is based entirely on external motivation, and as a result she can be only a passive, if beautiful, doll, a shop-window dummy, forced to take whichever husband the gods decide. The whole thing is two-dimensional and unreal, a piece of tapestry, not, like the story of Troilus and Cressida, an active conflict.

Chaucer, however, makes it very appealing, and after reading *The Knight's Tale,* subdued by its grace and charm, we can see why an Elizabethan dramatist might think the story suitable for the stage. The opportunity, of which Chaucer takes such admirable advantage, for set speeches; the apparent, though superficial, conflict between the two heroes; the extension of their personal quarrel into a quarrel that involves the gods—all these things look like good dramatic material. Actually, of course, they are not, and I imagine that both Shakespeare and Fletcher, once they got started on their dramatization, realized that they were faced with a tough problem. They solved it very differently, and—as far as the immediate result was concerned, i.e., the writing of an effective play—Fletcher succeeded, and Shakespeare failed. The failure, to us, is more interesting than the success, but we must not be fooled by our idolatry of Shakespeare into taking credit away from Fletcher. The artificiality and spurious dramatic validity of the story offered a good opportunity for his accomplished and unscrupulous talent, and within his usual limits he made an expert job of it. The Fletcherian parts of the play are first-rate theater; their contrasts and conflicts make an immediate and successful impression. The Shakespearean parts, on the other hand, are static and, though with splendor, stiff. They are slow, and dense, compared with Fletcher's easy liquescence. They have a deliberate yet vague grandeur, a remote and half-exhausted exaltation; they are expressed through a clotted rhetoric that is the poetry of a man who has finished with action. Their style is the style of old age, and the imagery is an old man's imagery. Nevertheless, there is underneath a nobility, a control, a mastery of words, however fatigued, which make Fletcher's cleverness look cheap.[5] That mastery, and its peculiarity, its poetic success and its dramatic failure, its relation to Shakespeare's work as a whole, are worth careful study.

The play begins with an uninteresting prologue of a very conventional variety, a piece of hack writing (whoever wrote it) without significance. But the first scene of the first act, a scene which is unquestionably by Shakespeare, starts in a fashion as characteristic of Shakespeare's part in this play as it is uncharacteristic of nearly all his previous writing. It starts with a pageant: Hymen and a nymph symbolically attend the majestic entrance of Theseus, Hippolyta, and Emilia. It is processional, static, dignified, in the manner of a masque: the exact opposite to the opening of *The Tempest,* where all is action and excitement. It is the kind of thing that in an earlier play Shakespeare would have saved for a later scene, after the interest of the audience had been aroused by a personality or a conflict. And the entrance of these three chief characters is followed not by speech, but by a song:

> Roses, their sharp spines being gone,
> Not royal in their smells alone,
>   But in their hue;
> Maiden pinks, of odor faint,
> Daisies smell-less, yet most quaint
>   And sweet thyme true—

[5] De Quincey (*Works,* ed. Black [1862], X, 49), in his essay on rhetoric, wrote of Shakespeare's part of the play as follows: "The first and the last acts of *The Two Noble Kinsmen,* which in point of composition, is perhaps the most superb work in the language . . . had been the most gorgeous rhetoric, had they not happened to be something far better."

It is a song about flowers, echoing the subject matter of
Perdita's flower speeches in the fourth act of *The Winter's
Tale,* and with a reminiscence, it seems, of the tone of
The Phoenix and the Turtle:

> The crow, the sland'rous cuckoo, nor
> The boding raven, nor chough hoar,
>   Nor chatt'ring pie
> May on our bridehouse perch or sing,
> Or with them any discord bring,
>   But from it fly!

Even when the song is over, and the semiritualistic, removed, pageant-like tone is established, the action does
not begin vigorously: it still moves slowly, in a kind of
dramatic pavane: "Enter three *Queens,* in black, with
veils stain'd, with imperial crowns. The first *Queen* falls
down at the foot of *Theseus;* the second falls down at the
foot of *Hippolyta;* the third before *Emilia.*" And the three
queens, thus disposed about the stage in a formal design,
begin the dialogue rhythmically, almost in a chant:

1. *Queen:* For pity's sake and true gentility's,
          Hear and respect me!
2. *Queen:*   For your mother's sake,
          And as you wish your womb may thrive with
               fair ones,
          Hear and respect me!
3. *Queen:* Now for the love of him whom Jove hath
               mark'd
          The honor of your bed, and for the sake
          Of clear virginity, be advocate
          For us and our distresses!

Theseus, Hippolyta, and Emilia reply in turn, with the
same formal grace, in slow rhythms, the courtly echoes of
dramatic action.

The queens request Theseus to do justice to their dead
lords, and Theseus, interrupted in his wedding ceremony,
is "transported" by their words, being carried out of the
action back into the past. His speech to the first queen

(ll. 54 ff.) illustrates one of the kinds of rhythm which seems to be natural to Shakespeare at the close of his career. The thought almost invariably stops, not at the end, but in the middle of the line, there is a striking reliance on strong verbs for descriptive effect, and the slow lines move like figures in heavy garments:

> King Capaneus was your lord. The day
> That he should marry you, at such a season
> As now it is with me, I met your groom
> By Mars's altar. You were that time fair;
> Not Juno's mantle fairer than your tresses,
> Nor in more bounty spread. Your wheaten wreath
> Was then nor thresh'd nor blasted; Fortune at you
> Dimpled her cheek with smiles. Hercules our kinsman
> (Then weaker than your eyes) laid by his club;
> He tumbled down upon his Nemean hide,
> And swore his sinews thaw'd. O grief and time,
> Fearful consumers, you will all devour!

As usual with Shakespeare, the situation is generalized at the end. But the speech does not advance the action in any way: it is more like the comment of a chorus than the speech of a protagonist, it is melancholy and dreamlike. Theseus' reflections about the ravages made by grief and time on the queen's once beautiful face disturb him, and he turns aside—"Troubled I am"—abstracted by his thoughts of evanescence and decay.

The ritualistic movement proceeds, and the second queen appeals for help to Hippolyta. Her speech, too, has a tone which is characteristic of Shakespeare's final style. It is not, like the tone of Theseus' speech, the tone of remembrance, or of reverie, though it is related to that, being also "nonactive"; it is rather the tone of invocation, of apostrophe, of worship. It is again "removed," the tone of a looker-on, not a participant: appropriate as it is to the particular situation, it is also, one feels, appropriate to Shakespeare's own feeling about human experience at this last period in his life. Everyone who has written poetry knows that there are times when the tension of the immediate practical problem of composition is half-consciously resolved by a relapse or release into a semihypnotic incantation. The immature poet will fall into an incantation borrowed from someone else; the poet who is ripe and rich in technical experience discovers in words the beat of his own emotional vibration, and will produce, when set in his maturity at a particular job, the incantation, the tone, and the order which belong only to him. These may be different at different periods of his career, but to a sensitive reader they are unmistakable. And there are, in the Shakespearean parts of *The Two Noble Kinsmen,* an unmistakable incantation, tone, and order: the incantation which accepts illusion, the tone which has forgotten tragedy, and an order melted at the edges into a larger unity of acceptance and wonder. They appear again, in a tired fashion, in the long speech which Palamon makes to Venus in the first scene of the fifth act; in that speech, as in the speech of the second queen to Hippolyta, there is something trancelike and remote. In both speeches we feel a continuation of the mood of Miranda's "O brave, new world," and the rhythm of the queen's words is an adagio rhythm, haunting, invocatory, spoken, as it were, behind a veil.

As rhetoric, the speech is superb. It consists of a twenty-three-line sentence, the first nine lines invariably running over, to break in the middle, leading in the tenth line to a variation, with the pause at the end of the line for once, which alters the flow and hence commands attention. And yet, in spite of its excellence, the writing is tired, the muscles behind it seem slack and old, and, like the speech of Theseus I have already quoted, it ends unconvincingly.

> Honored Hippolyta,
> Most dreaded Amazonian, that hast slain
> The scythe-tusk'd boar; that with thy arm, as strong
> As it is white, was near to make the male
> To thy sex captive, but that this thy lord—
> Born to uphold creation in that honor
> First Nature styl'd it in—shrunk thee into
> The bound thou wast o'erflowing, at once subduing

> Thy force and thy affection; soldieress
> That equally canst poise sternness with pity:
> Who now, I know, hast much more power on him
> Than ever he had on thee; who ow'st his strength,
> And his love too, who is a servant for
> The tenor of thy speech; dear glass of ladies,
> Bid him that we, whom flaming War doth scorch,
> Under the shadow of his sword may cool us;
> Require him he advance it o'er our heads;
> Speak't in a woman's key, like such a woman
> As any of us three; weep ere you fail;
> Lend us a knee;
> But touch the ground for us no longer time
> Than a dove's motion when the head's plucked off;
> Tell him, if he i' th' blood-siz'd field lay swol'n,
> Showing the sun his teeth, grinning at the moon,
> What you would do.

To this prayer Hippolyta offers a consoling answer, and then the third queen turns to Emilia, with the same studied, elaborate, and removed kind of expression used by the other queens. Emilia replies at some length; her speeches are deliberately longer than those of Theseus and Hippolyta so that, being the heroine of the play, she may appear more prominent at the opening. When she has finished, Theseus starts abruptly out of his trance, and in a peremptory tone orders the wedding procession to proceed:

> Forward to th' temple! Leave not out a jot
> O' th' sacred ceremony.

But the queens delay him still further, in their eloquent speeches begging him to bury their slain husbands. At first Theseus continues to hold out against them:

> Why, good ladies,
> This is a service, whereto I am going,
> Greater than any war. It more imports me
> Than all the actions that I have foregone
> Or futurely can cope.

But they persuade him still. The rhythm of the first queen's speech on this occasion is again the rhythm of invocation, although she speaks in a different tone, and from a different angle than before. She still, however, describes experience contemplated from a distance; as, in a sense, the writing of Fletcher describes experience contemplated from a distance. But, as we shall see, the distance from which Fletcher contemplates is very different in altitude, and in direction, from Shakespeare's:

1. *Queen:*   The more proclaiming
        Our suit shall be neglected. When her arms,
        Able to lock Jove from a synod, shall
        By warranting moonlight corslet thee—O, when
        Her twinning cherries shall their sweetness fall
        Upon thy tasteful lips, what wilt thou think
        Of rotten kings or blubber'd queens? What care
        For what thou feel'st not? What thou feel'st
            being able
        To make Mars spurn his drum. O, if thou couch
        But one night with her, every hour in't will
        Take hostage of thee for a hundred, and
        Thou shalt remember nothing more than what
        That banquet bids thee to![6]

Finally, Theseus succumbs; he will postpone his marriage and revenge the queens, and he ends by saying—it is the third example in this scene of an un-electrified platitude:

                        As we are men,
        Thus should we do. Being sensually subdu'd,
        We lose our human title. Good cheer, ladies!
        Now turn we towards your comforts.

[6] This speech illustrates a peculiarity of the Shakespearean parts of the play: the number of invocatory "O's." In this first scene, of 234 lines, there are 12 of such "O's"—a minor reflection of the general tone. In a typical Fletcher scene, II, ii, of 277 lines, there are only 4 invocatory "O's."

III

I have discussed the opening scene of this play at length
because it has several striking characteristics. In the first
place, it represents a great elaboration, on Shakespeare's
part, of his source. Chaucer describes the supplication of
the queens and Theseus' determination to help them in
about eighty lines; there is no suggestion that they are
appealing to Theseus on his marriage day, and there is no
suggestion of the conflict in his mind between love and
war. Chaucer is too anxious to get started on the story
of Palamon and Arcite to waste time on any but the most
necessary of preliminaries. Yet Shakespeare makes a great
deal of the preliminaries: each of the queens speaks, each
of the main characters responds, and there is an obvious,
if incomplete, expression of a conflict in values. The value
of war and the value of love, the standard of action and
the standard of emotion, which, as Mr. Wilson Knight
has observed, play so large a part in Shakespeare's work,
are here, in the mind of Theseus, deliberately presented,
and yet, dramatically speaking, they are the ghosts of
themselves. For Theseus' queerly abstracted conflict between the joys of marriage and his responsibility to the
queens has no real bearing on the course of the main
events in the play, and the decisions he comes to are
abrupt, apart from the action—if we can call it "action."
It is as if Shakespeare had written the scene half automatically, recalling the kind of conflict which he had
described earlier with passion and penetration, but which
he was now using as merely the most convenient means
for dramatic exposition; a remembered technique, with
the emotional content forgotten. Technically, as I have
tried to suggest, the scene is admirable. The first queen
is set against Theseus, the second queen is set against
Hippolyta, the third queen is set against Emilia: each
responds to each, in a mounting rhythm, in a verbal
counterpoint, like voices in a chorale; it is planned, deliberate and controlled. But it is not the technique of
Julius Caesar or of *Lear*. If we imagine the scene on the
stage, we see gesture rather than action. Drama has re-

turned to its womb, and has once more become ritual. It is the dramatic writing of a man to whom action has lost importance, but who is trying to recapture, for the immediate necessity of writing a money-making play, the devices and the lost enthusiasm of a forgotten intensity. It is the writing of a man who has come out on the other side of human experience, and who, looking back, can no longer be interested in what he has once seen so vividly and so passionately felt. The figures still struggling in the *selva oscura* are the figures of a pageant or a dream.

IV

Fletcher's share in the play is very different. The emotional tone is not that of a man who has been *through* experience: it is the tone of a man who has never got there. His rhythms are the rhythms, not of remote or incandescent contemplation, but of the easy lullaby of sentiment. We are not abstracted or lifted up; there is no incantation. Instead we are soothed, smoothed, softened. And yet, theatrically speaking, it is a great success; and only when we reflect do we realize that we are in so much smaller a dimension. Act II, scene ii, is a good example of Fletcher's ability.

Arcite and Palamon are in prison, having been captured by Theseus in his avenging war against Creon. They enter on the upper stage and begin discussing their situation. They are in prison for life, and all activity is over. "Here we are," says Arcite,

> And here the graces of our youth must wither
> Like a too timely spring. Here age must find us,
> And, which is heaviest, Palamon, unmarried.
> The sweet embraces of a loving wife,
> Loaden with kisses, arm'd with thousand Cupids,
> Shall never clasp our necks; no issue know us;
> No figures of ourselves shall we ev'r see
> To glad our age, and like young eagles teach 'em
> Boldly to gaze against bright arms, and say
> "Remember what your fathers were, and conquer!"

The technique and the tone are typically Fletcherian: the great majority of the lines end with an extra syllable; there are few of those heavy pauses in the middle of the lines which produce in Shakespeare's latest style so rich and full an effect; all is languorous and gentle. The tone, like Shakespeare's tone, might be called remote. Yet it is remote in a very different sense. If we compare what Arcite says about "The sweet embraces of a loving wife" with what Theseus has said earlier to the first queen (I, i, 59 ff.), we realize that what weakens Fletcher's writing is that he is describing something that has never happened. It is one of his favorite emotional tricks to project us into a fanciful future, and then to melt us by telling us what may go on there in relation to the character who is speaking. For example, in *Henry VIII* (III, i, 431 ff.) Wolsey speaks to Cromwell:

> And when I am forgotten, as I shall be,
> And sleep in dull cold marble, where no mention
> Of me more must be heard of, say I taught thee—
> Say Wolsey, that once trod the ways of glory
> And sounded all the depths and shoals of honor,
> Found thee a way (out of his wrack) to rise in—

There are a thousand examples of this kind of writing in Fletcher's plays; this emotional tone is perhaps the surest mark of his style, and the falling lines, with their lingering feminine endings, fit it very appropriately. But, as far as I am aware, it never occurs in Shakespeare; Shakespeare has too strong a sense of reality. To tease our feelings by summoning up melancholy pictures of how people are going to behave when a character is dead, or to lament the loss of imaginary blessings, are not devices which occur to his more robust and unsentimental temperament. Fletcher, on the other hand, could not write an emotional scene without using them. They make an immediate effect on the audience, and we are moved by a vague feeling of rather complacent pity as we listen. Such scenes seem to have caught the Elizabethan ear at once, and to have held the affection of audiences for nearly a

century. The emotion is so much easier than Shakespeare's;
it is no trouble to understand because there is no mental
toughness or gristle combined with it. Fletcher's share in
The Two Noble Kinsmen is, as I have said, much better
theater than Shakespeare's.[7]

The rest of this particular scene is very cleverly written.
Palamon and Arcite console themselves for the prospect
of their long imprisonment by thinking that they will at
least have each other, and they work themselves up to
vows of mutual affection:

> *Palamon:* Is there record of any two that lov'd
>   Better than we do, Arcite?
> *Arcite:*   Sure, there cannot.
> *Palamon:* I do not think it possible our friendship
>   Should ever leave us.
> *Arcite:*   Till our deaths, it cannot.

[7] Once we become aware of this emotional habit of Fletcher's we can
detect his hand where we might otherwise be uncertain. For example, the
beginning of Act III, scene i, is unquestionably Shakespeare's; style, meter,
tone, and vocabulary are firmly his. Yet all these begin to weaken as the
scene progresses. We move from incantation to action, and Fletcher's
hand becomes unmistakable. Palamon (ll. 72 ff.) asks Arcite to fight with
him for Emily, and the first thing he does is to project himself into an
imaginary future, producing in the rhythm of the lines and in the minds of
the audience that sentimental, unreal, and melting sensation which I have
just tried to describe.

> Give me a sword . . .
> and do but say
>   That Emily is thine, I will forgive
>   That trespass thou hast done me, yea, my life,
>   If then thou carry't; and brave souls in shades,
>   That have died manly, which will seek of me
>   Some news from earth, they shall get none but this—
>   That thou art brave and noble.

Another sure sign of Fletcher's hand in the end of this scene is the way
Palamon and Arcite use each other's names when they address each other:

> *Palamon:*   O you heavens, dares any
> So noble bear a guilty business? None
> But only Arcite; therefore none but Arcite
> In this kind is so bold.
> *Arcite:*   Sweet Palamon

There is something soft about this; it is the equivalent, in poetry, of the
action of a man who, having mortally offended his wife, thinks that he
can make up to her by stroking her cheek.

But then Emilia, who is to be the cause of their dissension, appears below with the waiting woman, talking about flowers. Palamon sees her first and stands transfixed. Arcite tries to urge him on to further protestations of friendship, but he can get nothing out of him, so he too looks down at the garden, is hopelessly smitten, and a very deftly managed series of interwoven short speeches follows, in which Arcite and Palamon comment on the beauty of Emilia while she and her woman go on talking about flowers. When Emilia leaves it is all over with the friendship between Palamon and Arcite; they are both in love up to the ears, they can think of nothing but Emilia, and the scene comes to an end with their mutual recriminations, an ironic and successful contrast to their feelings toward each other at the beginning.

This smooth and accomplished action is almost the reverse of Shakespeare's static pageantry. And the way Fletcher describes his two heroes is very different from the way Shakespeare had described them earlier, the first time we see them, in Act I, scene ii. The words Shakespeare puts into their mouths are not the words of sentiment; Palamon and Arcite are not like two graceful saplings, swaying in unison in a sentimental moonlight. They are a pair of moralists, with a strong sense of evil and a strong sense of indignation at the corruption engendered in Thebes by their wicked uncle, Creon. What Fletcher tells us about them bears only on the immediate dramatic situation; they say no more than is necessary to put the particular scene across. But Shakespeare reveals their characters by their attitude to a general situation, and we are in a different, a wider world of perception. His Arcite and Palamon talk as follows:

Arcite: Dear Palamon, dearer in love than blood,
And our prime cousin, yet unhard'ned in
The crimes of nature—let us leave the city
Thebes and the temptings in't before we further
Sully our gloss of youth.
And here to keep in abstinence we shame
As in incontinence; for not to swim

I' th' aid o' th' current were almost to sink,
At least to frustrate striving; and to follow
The common stream, 'twould bring us to an eddy
Where we should turn or drown; if labor through,
Our gain but life and weakness.

Palamon: Your advice
Is cried up with example. What strange ruins,
Since first we went to school, may we perceive
Walking in Thebes!

He goes on to describe how the soldier, dedicated to Mars, receives nothing but scars and rags for his reward. Arcite widens the application: in Thebes there is nothing good; it is a place

where every evil
Hath a good color; where ev'ry seeming good's
A certain evil; where not to be ev'n jump
As they are here, were to be strangers, and
Such things to be mere monsters.

They talk in this style for some eighty lines, and it is only when they are told that they must fight for Thebes against Theseus that their sense of duty makes them cast off their bitter mood and find a solution in action.

Now this is a very extraordinary way of presenting a pair of romantic lovers to an audience. To be sure, it shows them as highly idealistic, but we have only to think of Romeo to realize that what they are being idealistic about has nothing to do with what is to be their predominant emotion in the action that follows. Romeo, when he is first presented to us, is an idealist; but he is a positive idealist in the sense that he is in a dream of illusion, and that his waking is the fulfillment of his dream. Palamon and Arcite are *dis*-illusioned; their view of the world they live in may be said to begin where the view of Shakespeare's tragic heroes leaves off: in an awareness of the evil which conditions their existence. Their speeches are haunted by the ghost of Timon. But Timon looks back at Athens and curses its vileness as a result of a disillusionment which has been led up to by the previous action.

Palamon and Arcite look back in disgust at Thebes before
we have been given any satisfactory reason for their disgust. One cannot help wondering why Shakespeare should
have presented them in so remarkable a fashion. Was he
relying, in a fatigued or bored state of mind, on a means
of arousing interest which he had found useful in the past,
and was here repeating half automatically because he
could not think of anything else? This explanation is
borne out by the fact that Palamon and Arcite use, in
their disgusted speeches, a rather stock set of images and
comparisons. The hard lot of the unrewarded soldier is
an Elizabethan commonplace; so is the foolishness,
described by Palamon, of contemporary fashions in dress;
and the shocking difference between what seems and what
is, which Palamon emphasizes in the speech I have just
quoted, is one of the main themes in all of Shakespeare's
mature work. In other words, just as we find, in the first
scene of the play, the almost ritualistic manipulation of
the ghosts of dramatic action, so we find here the ghosts
of familiar themes, used as convenient means for exposition, but lacking, in the long run, the reality of conviction. Shakespeare, we feel, is looking back on what once
mattered, but which matters no longer, and his description of the emotions of Palamon and Arcite about the
world they live in does not quite convince us because it
no longer seems necessary to Shakespeare to have those
emotions explained: they can, undramatically, be taken
for granted.

V

Yet the composition of Shakespeare's opening scenes
consists by no means merely of repetitions or echoes of his
earlier emotional grooves and dramatic triumphs; these
scenes emphasize a positive value of their own—the value
of loyalty. The queens are passionately loyal to their dead
husbands; Palamon and Arcite, "dearer in love than
blood," share a common view of their debased country;
the intimate friendship of Theseus and Pirithous is richly
described (I, iii, 41):

> Their knot of love
> Tied, weav'd, entangled, with so true, so long,
> And with a finger of so deep a cunning,
> May be outworn, never undone—

and the first (if only) human, individualizing fact we learn
about Emilia is that she once had an intimate friendship
of a similar kind with a girl named Flavina who died at
the age of eleven.[8] "You talk," says Emilia (I, iii, 55 ff.):

> You talk of Pirithous' and Theseus' love.
> Theirs has more ground, is more maturely season'd,
> More buckled with strong judgment, and their needs
> The one of th' other may be said to water
> Their intertangled roots of love, but I
> And she I sigh and spoke of, were things innocent,
> Lov'd for we did, and like the elements
> That know not what nor why, yet do effect
> Rare issues by their operance, our souls
> Did so to one another. What she lik'd
> Was then of me approv'd; what not, condemn'd,
> No more arraignment. The flow'r that I would pluck
> And put between my breasts (then but beginning
> To swell about the blossom) she would long
> Till she had such another, and commit
> To the like innocent cradle, where, phoenix-like,
> They died in perfume. On my head no toy
> But was her pattern; her affections (pretty,
> Though happily her careless wear) I followed
> For my most serious decking. Had mine ear
> Stol'n some new air, or at adventure humm'd one
> From musical coinage, why, it was a note
> Whereon her spirits would sojourn (rather dwell on)
> And sing it in her slumbers.

This charming, this delicious speech crowns the theme
of friendship, already so clearly illustrated by Theseus and
Pirithous and by Palamon and Arcite. But the theme is to
be disrupted by the subsequent behavior of Palamon and
Arcite; that is one reason why it is so strongly emphasized
at the start. One of Shakespeare's favorite dramatic de-

8 There is no hint of this in Chaucer.

vices in his mature work is to establish a set of values and then to show how it is violated by the individual action which follows. He does this in *Troilus and Cressida* through the speeches of Ulysses; he does it more indirectly in *Hamlet, Othello,* and *King Lear;* he clearly had it in mind when planning *The Two Noble Kinsmen.* But Fletcher, tied by temperament to the immediate and the obviously practical, was not concerned with such matters, and, when he took charge of the situation after the first act, the wider implication, the fundamental and general contrast which the story, in Shakespeare's eyes, could be seen to illustrate, disappeared. It was not appropriate to Fletcher's romantic and myopic vision.

That Shakespeare should have so strongly emphasized the theme of union through friendship is as characteristic of the tone of his final period as his habit of breaking the thought in the middle of a line is characteristic of his final metrical technique. It is not, to be sure, quite the same as the theme of reconciliation, which we find in all the plays from *Pericles* on. But it is the state of mind which occurs *after* reconciliation. And as the vile picture of Thebes given by Palamon and Arcite is different, not being the result of previous action, from the picture of Athens given by Timon, so Emilia's account of her friendship with Flavina is different from the reunion of Pericles with Marina or of Leontes with Hermione. The union of Emilia and Flavina did not come about as the result of a dramatic process. It just was. Such writing, as I have already observed, is the writing of a man who has been *through* experience, for whom process and movement are over, who does not care about how or why things happen, as long as they are. In such a state of mind one may plan dramatic action, in a routine, habitual way, but one cannot put one's heart into making it exciting. Another desire is much more important; the desire to contemplate—not turmoil, or contrast, or fraction—which are dreams—but the beauty of the individual life itself, in a garland of flowers.

O queen Emilia,

Fresher than May, sweeter
Than her gold buttons on the boughs or all
Th' enamel'd knacks o' th' mead or garden! Yea,
We challenge too the bank of any nymph,
That makes the stream seem flowers! Thou, O jewel
O' th' wood, o' the world, hast likewise bless'd a place
With thy sole presence.[9]

There is some uncertainty in the phrasing of Arcite's
speech; it has not the perfection of Perdita's flower
speeches in *The Winter's Tale;* but the caught breath,
the broken wonder; the magical invocation are still here,
trembling through a shattered rhythm into words.

VI

There is one episode in the story of Arcite and Palamon
which, unlike the previous parts, definitely demands the
tone of invocation; it is the episode where the two lovers
pray respectively to Mars and Venus for success in their
combat. The scene, as was to be expected, is obviously
by Shakespeare; it was his meat exactly, and he does it
handsomely, in a manner that repays close attention. The
first speech (V, i, 49 ff.), that of Arcite before the altar
of Mars, is a dignified and exalted piece of writing, and
the familiar invocatory rhythms of Shakespeare's latest
style are obvious throughout:

O great corrector of enormous times,
Shaker of o'er-rank states, thou grand decider
Of dusty and old titles, that heal'st with blood
The earth when it is sick, and cur'st the world
O' th' plurisy of people! I do take
Thy signs auspiciously, and in thy name
To my design march boldly.

This is more or less what we would expect in an address
to Mars, and it is not unlike what we find in Chaucer.
But when Arcite leaves the stage, and Palamon takes his
place to pray to Venus, we have a very remarkable speech

9 III,i,4ff

indeed, so remarkable that it is odd that no one seems to
have noticed its peculiarity. It is not in the least like the
speech made by Chaucer's Palamon, who praises the goddess, and swears to serve her forever if she will give him
Emily. Chaucer's Palamon is devoted and charming, his
words are tender and youthful, full of graceful pleading.
Shakespeare's Palamon addresses Venus in a different
manner—I give the long speech entire:

Hail, sovereign queen of secrets, who hast power
To call the fiercest tyrant from his rage,
And weep unto a girl; that hast the might,
Even with an eye-glance, to choke Mars's drum
And turn th' alarm to whispers; that canst make
A cripple flourish with his crutch, and cure him
Before Apollo; that mayst force the king
To be his subject's vassal, and induce
Stale gravity to dance; the polled bachelor—
Whose youth, like wanton boys through bonfires,
Have skipp'd thy flame—at seventy thou canst catch,
And make him, to the scorn of his hoarse throat,
Abuse young lays of love. What godlike power
Hast thou not power upon? To Phoebus thou
Add'st flames, hotter than his: the heavenly fires
Did scorch his mortal son, thine him. The huntress
All moist and cold, some say, began to throw
Her bow away, and sigh. Take to thy grace
Me thy vowed soldier, who do bear thy yoke
As 'twere a wreath of roses, yet is heavier
Than lead itself, stings more than nettles. I
Have never been foul-mouth'd against thy law;
Nev'r reveal'd secret, for I knew none—would not,
Had I learn'd all that were. I never practic'd
Upon man's wife, nor would the libels read
Of liberal wits. I never at great feasts
Sought to betray a beauty, but have blush'd
At simp'ring sirs that did. I have been harsh
To large confessors, and have hotly ask'd them
If they had mothers. I had one, a woman,
And women 'twere they wrong'd. I knew a man
Of eighty winters—this I told them—who

A lass of fourteen brided. 'Twas thy power
To put life into dust. The aged cramp
Had screw'd his square foot round,
The gout had knit his fingers into knots,
Torturing convulsions from his globy eyes
Had almost drawn their spheres, that what was life
In him seem'd torture. This anatomy
Had by his young fair fere a boy, and I
Believ'd it was his, for she swore it was,
And who would not believe her? Brief, I am
To those that prate and have done, no companion;
To those that boast and have not, a defier;
To those that would and cannot, a rejoicer.
Yea, him I do not love that tells close offices
The foulest way, nor names concealments in
The boldest language. Such a one I am,
And vow that lover never yet made sigh
Truer than I. O, then, most soft-sweet goddess,
Give me the victory of this question, which
Is true love's merit, and bless me with a sign
Of thy great pleasure.

Here music is heard and doves are seen to
flutter. They fall again upon their faces,
then on their knees.

O thou that from eleven to ninety reign'st
In mortal bosoms, whose chase is this world,
And we in herds thy game, I give thee thanks
For this fair token; which being laid unto
Mine innocent true heart, arms in assurance
My body to this business.

I have quoted the whole of this speech because its
peculiarity can only be fully seen if all of it is taken into
account. It is divided into three main parts: the first
describes the effects of Venus, the second describes the
purity of Palamon, the third is a final invocation in (as
usual) generalized terms, which unites the other two. But
what extraordinary images, for a prayer to Venus, the
speech contains! We are first told that love affects a man
of seventy, then that it affects a man of eighty, and finally
that it affects a man of ninety. The emphasis is, through-

out, on old age, and the result is that what impresses us, after reading or hearing the speech, is not the power of love, but a series of images of decay. The speech accomplishes the reverse of what is intended; the negatives dominate the positives; it is, as it were, poetry inside out. The cripple and his crutch, the "polled bachelor" of seventy, his hoarse throat abusing "young lays of love," the gouty old man of eighty with his foot screwed around and his eyes convulsed—such are the vivid pictures that remain in the mind. And even if we think of these ancient wrecks as being rejuvenated by love, the process is not an agreeable one. The flames of love scorch more than the sun; the yoke of love, while it seems like a wreath of roses, is actually heavier than lead and stings more than nettles. And as Palamon goes on to describe his own purity, and his avoidance of the way society in general treats love, we notice, not his avoidance, but rather the things he avoids —the liberal wits, the simp'ring sirs, and the large confessors. So that when, toward the end of the speech, Palamon calls Venus a "soft-sweet goddess," we are surprised; hardly anything he has previously told us about her has prepared us for such a description.

This speech is interesting in yet another fashion. For it is a mixture, not quite fused, of the two moods which we have already seen as predominant in Shakespeare's part of the play: the invocatory mood of Arcite's speech in Act III to the imagined Emilia, and the satirical mood of Arcite's and Palamon's speeches about Thebes in Act I. As it begins we are once more caught by the echo of that indescribable slow magic, that rich exalted wonder of the final style:

> who hast power
> To call the fiercest tyrant from his rage,
> And weep unto a girl.

But it is not sustained, and Shakespeare calls back, with a good deal of inappropriateness, the ghost of his almost forgotten mood of disillusionment to fill out the remaining lines. He does not seem, in other words, to be interested

in writing for Palamon the kind of speech which Palamon
—eager and ardent with young love—should speak. Writing rapidly, as it is likely he did, to get a job finished, he
relied on habitual tones and habitual rhythms, using the
artifice of long practice without the intensity of the appropriately dramatic emotion.

But Emilia's speech to Diana, which follows Palamon's
to Venus, is eminently appropriate, and it is significant
that Emilia must pray "bride-habited, but maiden-
hearted," and without passion to her "sacred, silver mistress." Hers is a prayer with which reality has nothing to
do, for it cannot, under the circumstances, be granted.
And here Shakespeare's words fit their occasion admir-
ably:

> O sacred, shadowy, cold, and constant queen,
> Abandoner of revels, mute, contemplative,
> Sweet, solitary, white as chaste, and pure
> As wind-fann'd snow . . . .
>   I here, thy priest,
> Am humbled fore thine altar.

VII

The rest of the play—the subplot of the jailer's daughter who goes mad for love of Palamon, the meeting of
Palamon and Arcite in the forest, the entertainment given
to Theseus by the yokels, and the denouement—all this
moves competently and swiftly; situation rather than character is emphasized, the style is clear and easily understood, and it was doubtless entirely successful on the stage.
Now and then we recognize Shakespeare's hand, as in the
extremely vivid account, in the last scene, of the rearing
horse that killed Arcite, but most of it is Fletcher's, and,
for our present purposes, not worth careful analysis.

The Shakespearean parts of the play, however—as I
hope I have shown—*are* worth careful analysis, for they
illustrate what was happening to Shakespeare at the end
of his career more clearly than anything in *The Tempest*
or *Henry VIII*. The most striking fact that stands out is

that Shakespeare seems no longer to be interested in process or in change and hence is no longer interested in the development of character. Whether he wrote the lines or not, what is apparently his state of mind is summed up in Theseus' address to the gods in the last speech of the play:

> Let us be thankful
> For that which is, and with you leave dispute
> That are above our question.

And in this acceptance of "that which is," there is a mingling—it is of course inevitable—of an awareness of good and an awareness of evil, the one felt almost ecstatically, though never, as in *The Winter's Tale,* entirely so; the other felt as being continually in the background, though never pressing into the immediate situation. The speeches of Theseus, of the queens, of Palamon and Arcite are contemplative, not active, and what change occurs in the main characters is very superficial. The story itself, to be sure, demands remoteness, a pageant-like treatment, and a slighting of differences in character, but though Shakespeare must obviously have seen this, his seeing it does not satisfactorily account for the almost unnecessary *stasis* of his presentation. Nor does it account for the incompleteness of much of the actual writing. Professor Tucker Brooke is right when he speaks of each act, scene, or verse falling "just short of what it should be." Professor Brooke thinks that this means that Shakespeare could not have written those acts or scenes, but that is not a necessary conclusion. It means more probably that he was no longer fully interested in what he was doing. The style of the Shakespearean parts of *The Two Noble Kinsmen,* as Palamon's address to Venus so clearly shows, is the style of an old man, a style that reveals, to be sure, an expert technique in handling words, and a mastery of incantation, but which has little concern for the tricks that would please an audience, and which is, in a sense, dramatically stagnant. After studying Shakespeare's part of the play, we feel that his return to Stratford and his abandonment of writing were almost inevitable. In fact, it is possible to wonder whether his retirement was entirely voluntary. The shareholders in the Globe knew what the public wanted; the differences between Shakespeare's slow pageantry—its faded, difficult magnificence, its elaborate remoteness—and Fletcher's easy, accomplished manipulation, were clear enough to anyone with an eye on the box office: Fletcher's style was obviously much better adapted to the increasing superficiality of the popular taste. One can even imagine a deputation calling on Shakespeare—it is not an agreeable thought—to suggest that, all things considered, it would be wise to go home and write no more.

PHILIP EDWARDS

On the Design of
"The Two Noble Kinsmen"

I suspect that most readers of *The Two Noble Kinsmen* have at some time felt reluctant to acknowledge that Shakespeare had much to do with the play. No doubt they are put off because the work is so undramatic: the action, particularly in the "Shakespearian" first and last acts, is sluggish, and the whole plot, twice boiled down from Boccaccio's epic, remains essentially narrative; the characters lack the interest of real individuality, and, though a great deal happens to them, they do not grow, or alter, in a Shakespearian way. Yet we are prepared to accept much that is similarly "undramatic" as Shakespeare's, in the work of the five years or so between the time he engaged himself with *Pericles* and the writing of *The Two Noble Kinsmen,* probably in 1613. Again, the quality of the verse perplexes readers in search of Shakespeare; there is something wordy in those long speeches which fail to advance the action, something elaborate and self-conscious in the weighing of the rhythms, in the complex network of syntax, in the bold images; there seems a tendency to "write it up":

> O, when
> Her twining cherries shall their sweetness fall
> Upon thy tasteful lips, what wilt thou think
> Of rotten kings or blubber'd queens?
>
> (I.i.177–80)

From *A Review of English Literature*, V (1964), 89–105. Reprinted by permission of the author and the editor.

When we come across a passage like that, we may feel some sympathy with Tucker Brooke: "Always there is the strong Shakespearian reminiscence, but nowhere quite the full and perfect reality that we could swear to."[1] But it is not really debatable that the verse of part of *The Two Noble Kinsmen* is Shakespeare's, the rest being Fletcher's. Theodore Spencer, Marco Mincoff and Kenneth Muir have all written excellent essays, approaching the verse along different paths, which strongly back up the old evidence of the metrical tests.[2] The arguments for Shakespeare do not need rehearsing here.

The reluctance to believe that *The Two Noble Kinsmen*, even in part, is a product of Shakespeare's mind and art really comes, not from the feeling that the play is undramatic or that the verse cannot be his, but from a conviction that the play is inane. It is worth quoting Tucker Brooke again: "It contains no spark of psychological insight or philosophy of life which can in sober moments be thought either worthy of the mature Shakespeare or even suggestive of him."[3] I am sure that it is the seeming want of "idea" in the play that makes readers find fault with verse and dramaturgy which they would be content to accept as Shakespeare's if the play were, to them, more intellectually respectable. That rich fund of suggestion which sets us on to our theories of what Shakespeare *meant* by the Romances certainly seems absent from the play. Even Spencer, acknowledging Shakespeare's hand, and admiring so much in the verse, saw the Shakespeare of this play as an old man who had been *through* experience, no longer interested in process or in change, not caring how or why things happen, but speaking of "that which is"; and, working rapidly to get a job finished, giving us tired writing, the muscles behind it slack and old. So re-

---

1 *The Shakespeare Apocrypha* (1908), p. xliii.
2 *Modern Philology*, xxxvi (1938–9), pp. 255–76; *English Studies*, xxxiii (1952), pp. 97–115; *Shakespeare as Collaborator* (1960), pp. 98–147. See also A. Hart, *Shakespeare and the Homilies* (1934), pp. 242–256. Putting aside some scenes about which there *could* be debate, the Shakespearian portions are I.i–iii, III.i, V.i, iii, iv.
3 *op. cit.*, p. xliii.

mote and so dramatically stagnant is the result, in Spencer's view, that he imagines a deputation calling on Shakespeare to suggest that "it would be wise to go home and write no more."

It seems to me that there is much more purposeful thought in the play than Brooke and Spencer saw; we really need not be ashamed of it. It is strange that the pensiveness of the play, in the first and last acts, has not aroused more interest: a pensiveness which, through those slow-moving scenes, hatches an "idea" bewildering enough but subtle (however unsubtle it seems in the simplifications of one's commentary). So far as I know, Clifford Leech has been the only critic to remark on the curious division of view which belittles the love in the play, and on the insistence that "mature" love means abandoning something more worthwhile.[4] Though Leech finds a contradiction where I find consistency, and though the "totality of its effect" speaks to him of Fletcher and to me of Shakespeare, it was from his remarks that this small exploration began.

Spencer noted the strangeness of Palamon's address to Venus (V.i.77–136) in the ceremonial scene of prayer to the gods for divine aid before the great tournament. As seen by Palamon, the power of Venus is a power that changes her victims' natures, overturns them rather, that grips them the more the older they get, making them more and more ludicrous and grotesque. As the apparently sincere tribute to the might of Venus continues, the operations of almighty love seem more and more disgusting. The invocation is fairly harmless:

> Hail, sovereign queen of secrets, who hast power
> To call the fiercest tyrant from his rage,
> And weep unto a girl . . .

But before we reach the parallel invocation, "that may'st force the king/To be his subject's vassal," we hear the words, "that canst make/A cripple flourish with his crutch"; it is in this manner the address goes on:

4 *The John Fletcher Plays* (1962), pp. 147–50.

                         the poll'd bachelor—
Whose youth, like wanton boys through bonfires,
Have skipt thy flame—at seventy thou canst catch,
And make him, to the scorn of his hoarse throat,
Abuse young lays of love.

The "tributes" grow more satirical as the man of eighty
takes the place of the man of seventy:

                         I knew a man
Of eighty winters—this I told them—who
A lass of fourteen brided: 'twas thy power
To put life into dust; the aged cramp
Had screw'd his square foot round,
The gout had knit his fingers into knots,
Torturing convulsions from his globy eyes
Had almost drawn their spheres, that what was life
In him seem'd torture: this anatomy
Had by his young fair fere a boy, and I
Believ'd it was his, for she swore it was,
And who would not believe her?

This emblem of the power of love is used in the address
as a defense of the chastity of wives! Eighty does not see
the end of Venus' power:

O thou that from eleven to ninety reign'st
In mortal bosoms, whose chase is this world,
And we in herds thy game . . .

The long speech emphasizes not only the power of love
to transform and to make the deformed more deformed,
but also the surreptitious and clandestine. It is the close
chamber work that is described, even if Palamon professes to reject it. As Muir mildly sums up, "The pleas-
anter side of love is not represented." Palamon, one of the
victims of Venus, describes himself as:

Thy vow'd soldier, who do bear thy yoke
As 'twere a wreath of roses, yet is heavier
Than lead itself, stings more than nettles.

Of this strange speech, Muir says it is absurd to think that Shakespeare "was putting his own personal sentiments into Palamon's mouth," and remarks that "Shakespeare was in danger of shattering the conventions in which the play was written." Muir makes a good justification of the speech in terms of Palamon's disillusioned temperament, the suffering and loss he has undergone through his love for Emilia, and the pains he has still to undergo—either to win the tournament and so cause the death of his blood-brother, Arcite, or else to lose, and so be executed. But perhaps Palamon is not meant to recognize the drift of his own speech; the cynicism *may* be not his, but Shakespeare's; I think we must consider what the conventions of this play are, before we say that this speech risks shattering them.

Both Spencer and Muir say that this address to Venus does not at all resemble the corresponding speech in Chaucer's *The Knight's Tale* (the source of the play). True, but in Chaucer's poem the walls of Venus' temple are painted with all the miseries of love:

> First in the temple of Venus maystow se,
> Wroght on the wal, ful pitous to biholde,
> The broken slepes, and the sikes colde,
> The sacred teeris, and the waymentynge,
> The firy strokes of the desirynge
> That loves servantz in this lyf enduren . . .
> (1918–23)[5]

The famous victims of love are also there, Solomon, Hercules, Medea and so on:

> Thus may ye seen that wysdom ne richesse,
> Beautee ne sleighte, strengthe ne hardyesse,
> Ne may with Venus holde champartie,
> For as hir list the world than may she gye.
> Lo, alle thise folk so caught were in hir las,
> Til they for wo ful ofte seyde 'allas!'

[5] Quotations from *The Knight's Tale* are taken from *The Works of Geoffrey Chaucer*, ed. F. N. Robinson, Cambridge, Mass. (1957).

> Suffiseth heere ensamples oon or two,
> And though I koude rekene a thousand mo.
>   (1947-54)

Chaucer's lines are an effective shortening of Boccaccio, and are central to his story. There is a corresponding mood in Theseus' derisive words as he finds the cousins, Arcite and Palamon, fighting to the death over a woman they have never spoken to, who knows nothing of their desire:

> Se how they blede! be they noght wel arrayed?
> Thus hath thir lord, the god of love, ypayed
> Hir wages and hir fees for hir servyse!   (1801-03)

The Knight's Tale is a magnificent study of human helplessness, of men and women floundering after happiness, but, being entirely at the mercy of love, of the mighty of this world, and of the gods—or destiny—or fortune, moving steadily into wretchedness. The image which comes out on top is the Boethian image of the drunken man: every step he takes toward his house is a step away from it.

> Infinite harmes been in this mateere.
> We witen nat what thing we preyen heere.
> We faren as he that dronke is as a mouse.
> A dronke man woot wel he hath an hous,
> But he noot which the righte wey is thider;
> And to a dronke man the wey is slider.
> And certes, in this world so faren we;
> We seken faste after felicitee,
> But we goon wrong ful often, trewely.   (1259-67)

In the Prologue to *The Two Noble Kinsmen* is a tribute to Chaucer, the seriousness of which is perhaps obscured by the facetious tone of the opening lines and the conventional humility of the plea for sympathy. Twenty of the thirty-two lines keep Chaucer in mind:

Chaucer, of all admir'd, the story gives;
There constant to eternity it lives . . .
. . . to say truth, it were an endless thing,
And too ambitious, to aspire to him,
Weak as we are, and almost breathless swim
In this deep water.

It seems to me that Shakespeare was fired by the dark
Chaucerian vision of what happened to two men pursuing
their desires, or being pursued by their desires. Emulation
would be the wrong word—the Prologue discounts it—
but he had his own dark vision to present of men moving
into their future as through a thick fog, and so slight a
play as The Two Noble Kinsmen is made much less slight
when we understand this vision, and realize that Palamon's address to Venus is the center of the play. And
what of Fletcher? According to Spencer, Fletcher was
congenitally incapable of appreciating the significance of
the Shakespearian scenes. Certainly, Shakespeare's grand
design sags when Fletcher takes over; but that he knew
the design and tried to fill it out is inescapable.

To take simple matters first, the address to Venus is at
all times relevant to the subplot of the jailer's daughter.
She falls in love with Palamon, who is quite unaware of
her passion during the whole of its wretched course. She
acts to bind him to her, secretly letting him out of prison,
but her action has no effect. She goes mad, her mind filled
with images of sexual pleasure, and in the end she is
brought towards a cure by her former wooer's pretending
to be Palamon and going to bed with her. "For all the
genuineness of her love," says Leech, "it is not proof
against substitution," and he notices here an important
link with Emilia's acquiescence in either of the two cousins
as a husband. This we must look at later: at the moment,
it is enough to say that the story of the jailer's daughter
gives a particularly unpleasant picture of what happens
when sexual desire gets hold of one:

What pushes are we wenches driven to
When fifteen once has found us!   (II.iv.6–7)

The idea of the play is very carefully worked into those first three slow-moving scenes which are unquestionably Shakespeare's. In the first scene, the solemn wedding of Theseus and Hippolyta is interrupted by the three widowed queens, who beseech Theseus to break off the wedding and go to war against Creon at Thebes; in the end he consents.

It is clear that Shakespeare is taking trouble to show us the marriage as a momentous change in Theseus' life. Before a word is spoken, there is the solemn ritual of the wedding procession, described in an elaborate stage direction. As the queens plead that he should turn aside, he insists on the magnitude of his resolution:

> This is a service, whereto I am going,
> Greater than any war;[6] it more imports me
> Than all the actions that I have foregone
> Or futurely can cope.   (I.i.171–74)

More portentously, he calls his marriage

> This grand act of our life, this daring deed
> Of fate in wedlock.   (I.i.164–65)

"This daring deed of fate" means, I think, "this deed which dares fate." Theseus sees himself as consciously bringing about, by marriage, an elemental change in his life. The sense of new life in marriage, of metempsychosis, almost, is seen more clearly in the appeal of one of the queens to Hippolyta:

> Honor'd Hippolyta,
> Most dreaded Amazonian, that hast slain
> The scythe-tusk'd boar; that, with thy arm as strong
> As it is white, wast near to make the male
> To thy sex captive, but that this thy lord—
> Born to uphold creation in that honor
> First Nature styl'd it in—shrunk thee into
> The bound thou wast o'erflowing, at once subduing
> Thy force and thy affection . . .   (I.i.77–85)

---

6 'was' in the Quarto.

Here, marriage is more than a change in a manner of life, it is the shaping of a new identity for Hippolyta. The images for this change of personality are startling. In making the Amazonian warrior a bride, Theseus is confirming the order of nature, but it is constriction and not release: "*shrunk* thee into/The bound thou wast o'erflowing"; "*subduing*/Thy force and thy affection." There is no sense here, of course, of crude subjugation; Hippolyta is more than acquiescent in her "shrinking": "never yet," she says, "went I so willing way" (I.i.103–04). Like Theseus, she moves by resolve into a new continent of her life; she moves also into a state which nature demands; but she moves also out of freedom into restriction.

By itself, this passing reference to Hippolyta's past life is nothing, and the images of containment might point only to the commonplace idea of there being truer fulfillment and freedom in the service and subordination of self in marriage. But the reference looks forward to the third scene, which elaborates, disconcertingly, the comparison between the two stages of life, youth and the riper days of marriage. Hippolyta and Emilia mention the former life of Theseus as they discuss the depth of his friendship with Pirithous; Hippolyta appears to excuse herself from the charge of supplanting Pirithous:

> Their knot of love
> Tied, weav'd, entangled, with so true, so long,
> And with a finger of so deep a cunning,
> May be out-worn, never undone. I think
> Theseus cannot be umpire to himself,
> Cleaving his conscience into twain, and doing
> Each side like justice, which he loves best. (I.iii.41–47)

To this, Emilia, all politeness, replies

> Doubtless
> There is a best, and reason has no manners
> To say it is not you.

But her real reply follows at once in her very beautiful

story of her childhood love for Flavina, who died when
she was—eleven ("O thou that from eleven to ninety
reign'st"). Theirs was a love of absolute spontaneity and
absolute Innocence:

> But I,
> And she I sigh and spoke of, were things innocent.
> Lov'd for we did, and like the elements
> That know not what nor why, yet do effect
> Rare issues by their operance, our souls
> Did so to one another: what she lik'd
> Was then of me approv'd; what not, condemn'd,
> No more arraignment; the flower that I would pluck
> And put between my breasts, O—then but beginning
> To swell about the blossom—she would long
> Till she had such another, and commit it
> To the like innocent cradle . . .   (I.iii.59–70)

The evocation of a state of happiness and innocent impulse is wonderful, but Emilia calls it

> this rehearsal
> Which, every innocent wots well, comes in
> Like old importment's bastard.

This must mean (as Herford glimpsed) that words can
give only the feeblest picture of what was once all-important. Finally, Emilia says she has told her story with this
purpose, to show

> That the true love 'tween maid and maid may be
> More than in sex dividual.[7]   (I.iii.81–82)

That Hippolyta is shaken by this firm belief that the second stage of life can yield nothing to compare with the
spontaneous love of youth is clear from some asperity
and assertiveness in her reply, which ends:

> But sure, my sister,

7 "Individual" in the Quarto.

If I were ripe for your persuasion, you
Have said enough to shake me from the arm
Of the all-noble Theseus; for whose fortunes
I will now in and kneel, with great assurance
That we, more than his Pirithous, possess
The high throne in his heart.

Emilia.   I am not
Against your faith; yet I continue mine.

(I.iii.90–97)

In these two scenes, there is the clearest presentation
of three people conscious of the two major "ways of life"
it is necessary to tread, innocence and experience, the
impulsive life of youth with its friendship, and the more
contained life of marriage. The first stage of each of the
three characters has been shown to us: Hippolyta the
"o'erflowing" Amazon, Theseus the warrior in firm bands
of mutually supporting friendship with Pirithous, and,
most fully, Emilia in childish love with Flavina. Theseus
and Hippolyta have willingly moved to the second stage
which Emilia refuses; she is sure she will not "love any
that's call'd man" (I.iii.85). The two ways of life have
already been compared in value; the poetic weight is obviously with innocence and Flavina.

The second scene of the play, introducing us to the
noble kinsmen and having nothing to do with marriage,
can now be seen to interlock. Palamon and Arcite, disgusted by the corruption of Thebes, dedicated to each
other and to honor, resolve to break with their past and
begin a new life elsewhere; they are prevented by the
interruption of the news that Theseus is moving against
Thebes; they decide that they must fight for their city in
spite of their contempt for Creon. The course of this scene
is parallel with the course of the first scene. In that first
scene, Theseus, resolved to enter a new life, has to alter
his resolution when the queens burst in on his wedding.
Both Theseus and the cousins must put a good face on
their being diverted from their intentions, justifying themselves as following the only honorable course, but the fact
of diversion is underlined very strongly: the *action* of each
scene is basically the action of change of cherished pur-

pose under the pressure of unexpected events. It is, I
think, a Chaucerian view of the frailty of our determinations which comes across, accompanied by the Chaucerian irony that the protagonists, accepting the change
of purpose as being the only honorable choice, usher in
the misery which follows. By supporting the queens,
Theseus brings war to Thebes; by staying to fight in that
war, Palamon and Arcite are captured and so brought to
their fatal sight of Emily.

Palamon is troubled by the exigence of things pulling
us aside from what we purpose; he knows it is his duty to
fight under a man he despises, but will it not damage his
soul? he asks:

> Our hands advanc'd before our hearts, what will
> The fall o' the stroke do damage?

Arcite's dour reply is deeper than it looks:

> Let th' event,
> That never-erring arbitrator, tell us
> When we know all ourselves; and let us follow
> The becking of our chance.   (I.ii.112–16)

In other words, we shall know enough to comment on the
morality of actions only when we see what the actions
have led to; from that point of view, Palamon's question
is idle, for we cannot judge beforehand the advisability of
an action. That his question is idle from a second point
of view is implied by Arcite's closing words; which suggest that we have little choice but to follow where chance
beckons us. Perhaps I overinterpret, but I set these remarks, comments on the ignorance and ineffectiveness of
man, by Theseus' famous remarks at the end of the play:

> O you heavenly charmers,
> What things you make of us! For what we lack
> We laugh, for what we have are sorry; still
> Are children in some kind. Let us be thankful

For that which is, and with you leave dispute
That are above our question.   (V.iv.131–36)

The first two scenes show the breaking of resolutions;
the third scene stops short with a resolution—Emilia's,
not to marry. Even if we did not know the story, we might
guess the play would go on to tell us how she was proved
wrong.

There is one more touch in these first three scenes
which must be noted, Hippolyta's disbelief that Emilia
will never "love any that's call'd man":

I must no more believe thee in this point—
Though in't I know thou dost believe thyself—
Than I will trust a sickly appetite,
That loathes even as it longs.   (I.iii.87–90)

We are here introduced to that division of the self, one
of Venus' tortures, which has been seen in Palamon's invocation, when he spoke of himself bearing Venus' yoke
as though it were a wreath of roses, "yet is heavier than
lead itself." We seek what we know destroys. When a
resolution means resisting a stage of life on which nature
insists, the life of sexual relations, there will be more than
unexpected happenings to fight against it, there will be
one's own desires. In essence, Emilia's resolve is to live
in the past, in the age before puberty; if the rest of the
play is to show how vain such a resolve is, it is also going
to show good grounds for that nostalgia for innocence.

We move from the first act with the themes of the play
set out in full: a simplified division of life into the two
stages of innocence and experience, the uncertainty of
feeling with which one moves from one to another, a
sense of how fragile our determinations are. We may well
wish that Shakespeare had gone on to develop the themes
and not left so much to Fletcher. But obviously Fletcher
was working to Shakespeare's design (I hardly suppose
it was Fletcher's in the first place).

In Act II, scene ii, the imprisoned Palamon and Arcite

talk about their predicament. The pleasures of their youth are ended, the pleasures of the future are closed to them:

> Here the graces of our youth must wither,
> Like a too timely spring; here age must find us,
> And which is heaviest, Palamon, unmarried.
> (II.ii.27–29)

Arcite expatiates (it is too feeble to quote) on the pleasures of marriage and having children. He is thinking conventionally of the two stages of life, one kind of happiness following another in due season. But as the kinsmen try to rouse themselves from their dejection, they realize that the one thing which they can keep while they are in prison, their friendship and brotherhood, is in fact something finer than what marriage would bring:

> Here being thus together
> We are an endless mine to one another;
> We're one another's wife, ever begetting
> New births of love . . .
> Were we at liberty,
> A wife might part us lawfully, or business.
> (II.ii.78–81; 88–89)

But almost at once they catch sight of Emilia, and, in wrangling over their "rights" to her love, their vaunted friendship and their vaunted superiority to the claims of women are alike shattered; the long and bitter rivalry begins.

Before Emilia walks in the garden, Arcite shows both a longing for marriage and an intenser clinging to a friendship which is above marriage. He is both the Theseus and the Emilia of the first act. But what are his divided sentiments worth? "Let us follow the becking of our chance"—even in prison. Once Emilia has walked beneath the window of their cell, there is no more basking in youthful friendship. They must take their future in the way in which chance and Venus insist upon it. It is a horrible enough future, because the Venus who debases them as they struggle with each other for Emilia is of course their own sexual nature.

It is interesting that Shakespeare and Fletcher, in handling the story, from the duel in the wood onwards, insist as Chaucer does not that whichever of the two cousins does *not* get Emily shall die. An extra incident is brought in (III.vi.273–82) in which Emilia is given her choice of the two lovers, and the one not chosen is to die. In the deciding tournament, the dramatists leave out the ban on slaughter which Chaucer's Theseus pronounces. Not only do they leave it out, but they put in an extra scene of preparation for the execution of the loser, Palamon. One reason for this emphasis is, no doubt, to increase the painfulness of Emilia's position. But it is also a very strong way of indicating that to gain the new love is to destroy the old; it is the development of the theme played quietly in the first act, on the "rivalry" between Pirithous and Hippolyta for Theseus' affection. When Arcite is the victor in the lists, he says:

> Emily,
> To buy you I have lost what's dearest to me,
> Save what is bought.　　　　　　　(V.iii.111–13)

When Arcite has met with his fatal accident and Palamon is in turn received as husband, Palamon speaks to the dying man:

> O cousin,
> That we should things desire, which do cost us
> The loss of our desire! That naught could buy
> Dear love but loss of dear love.　　　　(V.iv.109–12)

Emilia's role in both the old tale and in the play is central to the author's exhibition of the pains of love. In Chaucer, it is managed mainly by silence: Emily's passiveness and aloofness add much to the sense of the absurdity of the strife of the two cousins, and to the whole comment on human helplessness. Her prayer to Diana is that she be left alone:

> Chaste goddesse, wel wostow that I
> Desire to been a maiden al my lif,
> Ne nevere wol I be no love ne wif.   (2304–06)

There is too little in this figure of silence and withdrawal
to make a character in a play; but up to the time of the
tournament, her role is amplified rather than changed. Her
reasons for wishing to remain a maiden are magnificently
filled out in the Flavina scene and though she plays a
more active part in the scene in which the cousins are
discovered fighting in the wood, her answers are strictly
neutral; she is moved by pity that these young men should
miscarry, not by affection or any desire for a husband.
But, from Act IV onwards, Chaucer's Emily is completely
altered and, in Fletcher's hands, immensely cheapened.
There is something missing in the play; we do not see her
moving towards accepting her role as a wife; she is suddenly there, trying to make up her mind which one of the
cousins she likes best. The design of the play has only
temporarily disappeared. When Shakespeare resumes with
Emilia in Act V, we can see what was meant to happen;
to romance a little, that Emilia should move, listlessly and
as in a dream, to abandon her old resolution and accept
"the becking of her chance":

> This is my last
> Of vestal office: I'm bride-habited,
> But maiden-hearted: a husband I have 'pointed
> But do not know him; out of two I should
> Choose one, and pray for his success, but I
> Am guiltless of election.   (V.i.149–54)

With the phrase, "I am guiltless of election," Emilia's indecision over the merits of Palamon and Arcite, of which
so much is made, falls into place as a contrast with her
relations with Flavina— "Lov'd for we did." If we take
Clifford Leech's hint, and link her indecision with the
willingness of the jailer's daughter to accept a pseudo-
Palamon as a lover, we can see more sharply the distinction between the two stages of love: the first all impulse

and spontaneity, the second a forced movement into a love so half-hearted that the object might be either of two cousins, a love so uncentered that a substitute will do as well as the real thing. The absurdity of the ending of the story—that Emilia should accept Arcite because he wins a fight, and then, when Arcite is killed, accept with equal readiness his cousin—is not "got round" by Shakespeare; it is the clinching of the case against Venus and the poverty of the relationships which she provides.

In this play, shared between two authors, the central idea is again and again approached from a different point; the idea is built up cumulatively by a series of comments and speeches which lie about the hub of the plot; the plot gets its true meaning by the reflected light of the surrounding meditations. We are given, clearly enough, a life in two stages: youth, in which the passion of spontaneous friendship is dominant, and the riper age in which there is a dominant sexual passion, leading to marriage where it can. The movement from one stage to the next, the unavoidable process of growth, is a movement away from innocence, away from joy. Theseus and Hippolyta apparently succeed in avoiding misery (are we meant to recall any of the tragic stories of love associated with the Theseus legend?), but the backward look to a fuller, richer youth is there for both; indeed, the lack of misery in Theseus and Hippolyta gives strength to a thesis of the loss of innocence which otherwise becomes too lurid.

The growth into experience I described as walking into the future as through a fog. Theseus goes forward boldly enough, but the postponement of the wedding by the three queens is an omen of the weakness of our powers. It is not our contriving that sends us steadily forward; we have to do what chance and circumstance and our own sexuality drives us to. The ingredients will differ. But, in the range between Emilia, with hardly any sexuality, and the jailer's daughter, all sexuality, there is not much free choice evident; the example of Palamon and Arcite is obviously meant to be the most striking. The irony of the way in which their course is shaped by chance and coincidence is harped on more by Chaucer than by Shakespeare, but it is in *The Two Noble Kinsmen*; what is most impressive is that every step, whether forced or free, in the course of that love which is the strongest thing in their lives, further disrupts the friendship which they know to be the finest thing in their lives. They are like men enchanted, gladly accepting what they are forced to do, yet knowing it to be ruin. The only arbitrator is "th' event."

If I see Shakespeare looking dim-eyed at innocence and seeing salvation disappear with puberty, I have to ask what relevance this "attack" on maturer life and love has to the portrayal of innocence in the earlier romances. There, sexual love may seem the natural and beautiful fulfillment of an otherwise immature innocence, particularly in Perdita and Miranda. But the idea of the deforming power of sexuality does exist in the romances; it is there in *Pericles,* when the youthful Pericles meets Antiochus' daughter and when Marina is in the brothel. It is there in *The Winter's Tale*; Clifford Leech most aptly cites (*op. cit.,* p. 149) Polixenes' recollection of his idyllic youth in friendship with Leontes:

> We were as twinn'd lambs that did frisk i' the sun,
> And bleat the one at the other: what we changed
> Was innocence for innocence; we knew not
> The doctrine of ill-doing, nor dream'd
> That any did. Had we pursued that life,
> And our weak spirits ne'er been higher rear'd
> With stronger blood, we should have answer'd heaven
> Boldly "not guilty"; the imposition clear'd,
> Hereditary ours.　　　　　　　　　　　　(I.ii.67–75)

There is no holding Shakespeare to one set of ideas; always, a new play releases a new evaluation; if we sense inconsistency it is generally because our vision is too myopic; we cannot hold such a range of focus as Shakespeare could. *The Two Noble Kinsmen* seems to me to give the most cynical assessment of the progress of life since the writing of *Troilus and Cressida*. It is a pity that Shakespeare did not write the whole of the play, but there is real intellectual substance in the work even as it is. Perhaps the flavor is unpalatable, still not the sort of thing one wants to associate Shakespeare with. Certainly, the vision is rather sweeping and careless of detail, but I believe it is Shakespearian.

Suggested References

The number of possible references is vast and grows alarmingly. (The *Shakespeare Quarterly* devotes one issue each year to a list of the previous year's work, and *Shakespeare Survey* —an annual publication—includes a substantial review of recent scholarship, as well as an occasional essay surveying a few decades of scholarship on a chosen topic.) Though no works are indispensable, those listed below have been found helpful.

1. Shakespeare's Times

Byrne, M. St. Clare. *Elizabethan Life in Town and Country.* Rev. ed. New York: Barnes & Noble, 1961. Chapters on manners, beliefs, education, etc., with illustrations.

Joseph, B. L. *Shakespeare's Eden: The Commonwealth of England 1558–1629.* New York: Barnes & Noble, 1971. An account of the social, political, economic, and cultural life of England.

Schoenbaum, S. *Shakespeare: The Globe and the World.* New York: Oxford University Press, 1979. A readable, handsomely illustrated book on the world of the Elizabethans.

Shakespeare's England. 2 vols. London: The Oxford University Press, 1916. A large collection of scholarly essays on a wide variety of topics (e.g., astrology, costume, gardening, horsemanship), with special attention to Shakespeare's references to these topics.

Stone, Laurence. *The Crisis of the Aristocracy, 1558–1641,* abridged edition. London: Oxford University Press, 1967.

2. Shakespeare

Barnet, Sylvan. *A Short Guide to Shakespeare.* New York: Harcourt Brace Jovanovich, 1974. An introduction to all of the works and to the dramatic traditions behind them.

Bentley, Gerald E. *Shakespeare: A Biographical Handbook.* New Haven, Conn.: Yale University Press, 1961. The facts about Shakespeare, with virtually no conjecture intermingled.

Bush, Geoffrey. *Shakespeare and the Natural Condition.* Cambridge, Mass.: Harvard University Press, 1956. A short, sensitive account of Shakespeare's view of "Nature," touching most of the works.

Chambers, E. K. *William Shakespeare: A Study of Facts and Problems.* 2 vols. London: Oxford University Press, 1930. An invaluable, detailed reference work; not for the casual reader.

Chute, Marchette. *Shakespeare of London.* New York: Dutton, 1949. A readable biography fused with portraits of Stratford and London life.

Clemen, Wolfgang H. *The Development of Shakespeare's Imagery.* Cambridge, Mass.: Harvard University Press, 1951. (Originally published in German, 1936.) A temperate account of a subject often abused.

Granville-Barker, Harley. *Prefaces to Shakespeare.* 2 vols. Princeton, N. J.: Princeton University Press, 1946–47. Essays on ten plays by a scholarly man of the theater.

Harbage, Alfred. *As They Liked It.* New York: Macmillan, 1947. A sensitive, long essay on Shakespeare, morality, and the audience's expectations.

Kernan, Alvin B., ed. *Modern Shakespearean Criticism: Essays on Style, Dramaturgy, and the Major Plays.* New York: Harcourt Brace Jovanovich, 1970. A collection of major formalist criticism.

————. "The Plays and the Playwrights." In *The Revels History of Drama in English*, general editors Clifford Leech and T. W. Craik. Vol. III. London: Methuen, 1975. A book-length essay surveying Elizabethan drama with substantial discussions of Shakespeare's plays.

Schoenbaum, S. *Shakespeare's Lives.* Oxford: Clarendon Press, 1970. A review of the evidence, and an examination of many biographies, including those by Baconians and other heretics.

————. *William Shakespeare: A Compact Documentary Life.* New York: Oxford University Press, 1977. A readable presentation of all that the documents tell us about Shakespeare.

Traversi, D. A. *An Approach to Shakespeare*. 3rd rev. ed. New York: Doubleday, 1968–69. An analysis of the plays, beginning with words, images, and themes, rather than with characters.

Van Doren, Mark. *Shakespeare*. New York: Holt, 1939. Brief, perceptive readings of all the plays.

3. Shakespeare's Theater

Beckerman, Bernard. *Shakespeare at the Globe, 1599–1609*. New York: Macmillan, 1962. On the playhouse and on Elizabethan dramaturgy, acting, and staging.

Chambers, E. K. *The Elizabethan Stage*. 4 vols. New York: Oxford University Press, 1945. A major reference work on theaters, theatrical companies, and staging at court.

Cook, Ann Jennalie. *The Privileged Playgoers of Shakespeare's London, 1576–1642*. Princeton, N.J.: Princeton University Press, 1981. Sees Shakespeare's audience as more middle-class and more intellectual than Harbage (below) does.

Gurr, Andrew. *The Shakespearean Stage 1579–1642*. 2nd edition. Cambridge: Cambridge University Press, 1980. On the acting companies, the actors, the playhouses, the stages, and the audiences.

Harbage, Alfred. *Shakespeare's Audience*. New York: Columbia University Press, 1941. A study of the size and nature of the theatrical public, emphasizing its representativeness.

Hodges, C. Walter. *The Globe Restored*. London: Ernest Benn, 1953; New York: Coward-McCann, Inc., 1954. A well-illustrated and readable attempt to reconstruct the Globe Theatre.

Hosley, Richard. "The Playhouses." In *The Revels History of Drama in English*, general editors Clifford Leech and T. W. Craik. Vol. III. London: Methuen, 1975. An essay of one hundred pages on the physical aspects of the playhouses.

Kernodle, George R. *From Art to Theatre: Form and Convention in the Renaissance*. Chicago: University of Chicago Press, 1944. Pioneering and stimulating work on the symbolic and cultural meanings of theater construction.

Nagler, A. M. *Shakespeare's Stage*. Tr. by Ralph Manheim. New Haven, Conn.: Yale University Press, 1958. An excellent brief introduction to the physical aspect of the playhouse.

Slater, Ann Pasternak. *Shakespeare the Director*. Totowa, N.J.: Barnes & Noble, 1982. An analysis of theatrical effects (e.g., kissing, kneeling) in stage directions and dialogue.

Thomson, Peter. *Shakespeare's Theatre*. London: Routledge and Kegan Paul, 1983. A discussion of how plays were staged in Shakespeare's time.

4. Miscellaneous Reference Works

Abbott, E. A. *A Shakespearean Grammar*. New edition. New York: Macmillan, 1877. An examination of differences between Elizabethan and modern grammar.

Bevington, David. *Shakespeare*. Arlington Heights, Ill.: A. H. M. Publishing, 1978. A short guide to hundreds of important writings on the works.

Bullough, Geoffrey. *Narrative and Dramatic Sources of Shakespeare*. 8 vols. New York: Columbia University Press, 1957–1975. A collection of many of the books Shakespeare drew upon with judicious comments.

Campbell, Oscar James, and Edward G. Quinn. *The Reader's Encyclopedia of Shakespeare*. New York: Crowell, 1966. More than 2,600 entries, from a few sentences to a few pages on everything related to Shakespeare.

Greg, W. W. *The Shakespeare First Folio*. New York: Oxford University Press, 1955. A detailed yet readable history of the first collection (1623) of Shakespeare's plays.

Kökeritz, Helge. *Shakespeare's Names*. New Haven, Conn.: Yale University Press, 1959. A guide to the pronunciation of some 1,800 names appearing in Shakespeare.

————. *Shakespeare's Pronunciation*. New Haven, Conn.: Yale University Press, 1953. Contains much information about puns and rhymes.

Muir, Kenneth. *The Sources of Shakespeare's Plays*. New Haven, Conn.: Yale University Press, 1978. An account of Shakespeare's use of his reading.

The Norton Facsimile: The First Folio of Shakespeare. Prepared by Charlton Hinman. New York: Norton, 1968. A handsome and accurate facsimile of the first collection (1623) of Shakespeare's plays.

Onions, C. T. *A Shakespeare Glossary*. 2d ed., rev., with enlarged addenda. London: Oxford University Press, 1953. Definitions of words (or senses of words) now obsolete.

Partridge, Eric. *Shakespeare's Bawdy*. Rev. ed. New York: Dutton; London: Routledge & Kegan Paul, 1955. A glossary of bawdy words and phrases.

Shakespeare Quarterly. See headnote to Suggested References.

Shakespeare Survey. See headnote to Suggested References.

Shakespeare's Plays in Quarto. A Facsimile Edition. Ed. Michael J. B. Allen and Kenneth Muir. Berkeley, Calif.: University of California Press, 1981. A book of nine hundred pages, containing facsimiles of twenty-two of the quarto editions of Shakespeare's plays. An invaluable complement to *The Norton Facsimile. The First Folio of Shakespeare* (see above).

Smith, Gordon Ross. *A Classified Shakespeare Bibliography 1936–1958*. University Park, Pa.: Pennsylvania State University Press, 1963. A list of some 20,000 items on Shakespeare.

Spevack, Marvin. *The Harvard Concordance to Shakespeare*. Cambridge, Mass.: Harvard University Press, 1973. An index to Shakespeare's words.

Wells, Stanley, ed. *Shakespeare: Select Bibliographies*. London: Oxford University Press, 1973. Seventeen essays surveying scholarship and criticism of Shakespeare's life, work, and theater.

5. Pericles

Arthos, John. "*Pericles, Prince of Tyre:* A Study in the Dramatic Use of Romantic Narrative," *Shakespeare Quarterly*, IV (1953), 257–70.

Barker, G. A. "Themes and Variations in Shakespeare's *Pericles*," *English Studies*, 44 (1963), 401–14.

Brockbank, J. P., "*Pericles* and the Dream of Immortality," *Shakespeare Survey 24*, ed. Kenneth Muir. Cambridge: Cambridge University Press, 1971.

Brownlow, F. W. *Two Shakespearean Sequences*. Pittsburgh: University of Pittsburgh, 1977.

Danby, John F. "Sidney and the Late-Shakespearian Romance," in *Poets on Fortune's Hill*. London: Faber and Faber, 1952. Part of this chapter is reprinted above, pp. 186–92.

Edwards, Philip. "An Approach to the Problem of *Pericles*," *Shakespeare Survey*, 5 (1952), 25–49.

————. "Shakespeare's Romances: 1900–1957," *Shakespeare Survey, 11*, ed. Allardyce Nicoll. Cambridge: Cambridge University Press, 1958.

Felperin, Howard. *Shakespearean Romance*. Princeton: Princeton University Press, 1972.

Frye, Northrop. *A Natural Perspective*. New York: Columbia University Press, 1965.

Hoeniger, F. D. (ed.). *The Arden Edition of the Works of William Shakespeare: Pericles*. Cambridge, Mass.: Harvard University Press; London: Methuen, 1963.

James, D. G. "The Failure of the Ballad-Makers," in *Skepticism and Poetry*. New York: Barnes & Noble, 1960; London: George Allen & Unwin, 1937.

Knight, G. Wilson. *The Crown of Life*. London: Methuen, 1948. Part of the chapter on *Pericles* is reprinted above, pp. 181–85.

Maxwell, J. C. (ed.). The New Shakespeare Edition of *The Works of Shakespeare: Pericles*. New York and London: Cambridge University Press, 1956.

Muir, Kenneth. *Shakespeare as Collaborator*. New York: Barnes & Noble; London: Methuen, 1960. Part of the section on *Pericles* is reprinted above, pp. 193–96.

Musgrove, S. "The First Quarto of *Pericles* Reconsidered," *Shakespeare* Quarterly, 29 (1978), 201–15.

Tillyard, E. M. W. *Shakespeare's Last Plays*. London: Chatto & Windus, 1938.

Tompkins, J. M. S. "Why Pericles?" *Review of English Studies*, 3 (1952), 315–24.

Traversi, D. A. *Shakespeare: The Last Phase*. New York: Harcourt, Brace, 1955; London: Hollis & Carter, 1954.

6. *Cymbeline*

Brockbank, J. P. "History and Histrionics in *Cymbeline*," *Shakespeare Survey 11* (1958), pp. 42–49.

Edwards, Philip. "Shakespeare's Romances: 1900–1957," *Shakespeare Survey 11* (1958), pp. 1–18.

Evans, Bertrand. *"Cymbeline,"* in *Shakespeare's Comedies*. Oxford: The Clarendon Press, 1960, pp. 245–89. Reprinted in part on pp. 215–31 of this edition.

Foakes, R. A. *Shakespeare: The Dark Comedies to the Last Plays.* Charlottesville: University of Virginia Press, 1971.

Frye, Northrop. *A Natural Perspective: The Development of Shakespearean Comedy and Romance.* New York: Columbia University Press, 1965, pp. 65–70. Reprinted in part on pp. 209–13 of this edition.

Gesner, Carol. "*Cymbeline* and the Greek Romance: A Study in Genre," in *Studies in English Renaissance Literature,* ed. W. F. McNeir, Baton Rouge, La.: Louisiana State University Press, 1962, pp. 105–31.

Greenlaw, Edwin. "Shakespeare's Pastorals," *Studies in Philology,* 13 (1916), 122–54.

Hoeniger, F. D. "Irony and Romance in *Cymbeline,*" *Studies in English Literature,* II (1962), 219–28.

Jones, Emrys. "Stuart Cymbeline," *Essays in Criticism,* 11 (1961), 84–99.

Knight, G. Wilson. "*Cymbeline,*" in *The Crown of Life.* London: Oxford University Press, 1948, pp. 129–202.

Lawrence, William Witherle. "The Wager in *Cymbeline,*" in *Shakespeare's Problem Comedies.* New York: Macmillan, 1931, pp. 174–205.

Nosworthy, J. M. "The Sources of the Wager Plot in *Cymbeline,*" *Notes and Queries,* 197 (1952), 93–6.

Ribner, Irving. "Shakespeare and Legendary History: *Lear* and *Cymbeline,*" *Shakespeare Quarterly,* 7 (1956), 47–52.

Richmond, Hugh M. "Shakespeare's Roman Trilogy: The Climax in *Cymbeline,*" *Studies in the Literary Imagination,* 5 (April 1972), 129–39.

Salingar, Leo. *Shakespeare and the Traditions of Comedy.* Cambridge: Cambridge University Press, 1974.

Shakespeare, William. *Cymbeline,* ed. J. C. Maxwell, The New Cambridge Shakespeare. London: Cambridge University Press, 1960.

Shakespeare, William. *Cymbeline,* ed., J. M. Nosworthy, The Arden Shakespeare, London: Methuen; Cambridge, Mass.: Harvard University Press, 1955. Reprints *Frederick of Jennen* in an appendix.

Stauffer, Donald A. "*Cymbeline,*" in *Shakespeare's World of Images: The Development of His Moral Ideas.* New York: Norton, 1949, pp. 278–91.

Stephenson, A. A. "The Significance of *Cymbeline*," *Scrutiny*, 10 (1942), 329–38. On imagery.

Thrall, William F. "*Cymbeline*, Boccaccio, and the Wager Story in England," *Studies in Philology*, 28 (1931), 639–51.

Warren, Roger, "Theatrical Virtuosity and Poetic Complexity in 'Cymbeline,' " in *Shakespeare Survey 29*, ed. Kenneth Muir. Cambridge: Cambridge University Press, 1976, pp. 41–49.

Wilson, Harold S. "*Philaster* and *Cymbeline*," in *English Institute Essays 1951*, ed. Alan S. Downer (1952), pp. 146–67. Demonstrates the independence of the two plays and thus that there is no reason to suppose the influence of Beaumont and Fletcher on Shakespeare.

7. *The Two Noble Kinsmen*

Agate, James. *Brief Chronicles, a Survey of the Plays of Shakespeare and the Elizabethans in Actual Performance.* London: Jonathan Cape, 1943. [Contains a review of the 1928 Old Vic performance, pp. 153–56.]

Bertram, Paul. *Shakespeare and The Two Noble Kinsman.* New Brunswick: Rutgers University Press, 1965.

Brownlow, F. W. *Two Shakespearean Sequences.* Pittsburgh: University of Pittsburgh Press, 1977.

Hart, Alfred. "Shakespeare and the Vocabulary of *The Two Noble Kinsmen*," *The Review of English Studies*, 10 (July 1934), 274–87. [Reprinted in Alfred Hart, *Shakespeare and the Homilies*. Melbourne: Melbourne University Press, 1935.]

Kermode, Frank. *William Shakespeare: The Final Plays.* (Writers and their Work, No. 155.) London: Longmans Green, 1963. [Reprinted in Bonamy Dobrée (ed.), *Shakespeare: The Writer and His Work*. London: Longmans, 1964.]

Leech, Clifford. *The John Fletcher Plays.* London: Chatto & Windus; Cambridge, Mass.: Harvard University Press, 1962. [Contains a chapter on "Fletcher and Shakespeare."]

Mincoff, Marco. "The Authorship of *The Two Noble Kinsmen*," *English Studies*, 33 (1952), 97–115.

Muir, Kenneth. *Shakespeare as Collaborator*. London: Methuen, 1960. [Contains two chapters on *The Two Noble Kinsmen*.]

Proudfoot, Richard, "Shakespeare and the New Dramatists of the King's Men," *Stratford-upon-Avon Studies 8: Later Shakespeare*, ed. John Russell Brown and Bernard Harris. London: Edward Arnold, 1966.

Thompson, Ann. *Shakespeare's Chaucer: A Study in Literary Origins*. New York: Barnes and Noble, 1978.

Waller, Frederick O. "Printer's Copy for *The Two Noble Kinsmen*," *Studies in Bibliography*, 11 (1958), 61–84.

27 million Americans can't read a bedtime story to a child.

It's because 27 million adults in this country simply can't read.

Functional illiteracy has reached one out of five Americans. It robs them of even the simplest of human pleasures, like reading a fairy tale to a child.

You can change all this by joining the fight against illiteracy.

Call the Coalition for Literacy at toll-free **1-800-228-8813** and volunteer.

Volunteer Against Illiteracy. The only degree you need is a degree of caring.